The Street Sweeper

Elliot Perlman

THE street sweeper

A NOVEL

(signature)

ff

faber and faber

First published in Australia by Vintage in 2011
Random House Australia Pty Ltd
Level 3, 100 Pacific Highway, North Sydney NSW 2060

First published in the UK by Faber and Faber Ltd in 2012
Bloomsbury House
74–77 Great Russell Street
London WC1B 3DA

Printed and bound by CPI Group (UK) Ltd, Croydon, CR0 4YY

A CIP record for this book
is available from the British Library

ISBN 978–0–571–23684–8

FSC
www.fsc.org
MIX
Paper from
responsible sources
FSC® C101712

10 9 8 7 6 5 4 3 2 1

In memory of
Rosa Robota, Estusia Wajcblum, Ala Gertner, Regina Safirztain
and
Denise McNair, Carole Robertson, Cynthia Wesley, Addie Mae Collins,
who all died from different manifestations of the same disease

Mountains bow down to this grief . . .
But hope keeps singing from afar.

Anna Akhmatova

part one

Seneca,
the first frozen apple juice,
enriched with vitamin C.
Rich, delicious Seneca . . .

Memory is a wilful dog. It won't be summoned or dismissed but it cannot survive without you. It can sustain you or feed on you. It visits when it is hungry, not when you are. It has a schedule all its own that you can never know. It can capture you, corner you or liberate you. It can leave you howling and it can make you smile.

Rich, delicious Seneca,
sweetened naturally.

'The trick is not to hate yourself.' That's what he'd been told inside. 'If you can manage not to hate yourself, then it won't hurt to remember almost anything: your childhood, your parents, what you've done or what's been done to you,' he was told. But even at the time, it struck Lamont that a lot of the people who had been locked up with him did not 'hate themselves' quite enough. He remembers a lot of the people being fairly forgiving towards themselves. Some, positively brimming with forgiveness for themselves, could not understand it when others

1

were not so forgiving of them. This dissociation from who you were, where you were, could even be funny.

One night alone at lockdown, he found himself smiling about it, and implicit in the smile was a sense of being different from all the other men in all the other cells. It was not simply innocence Lamont felt that night but something additional that made him feel as though he was only visiting his present circumstances, as though he was only a guest there. He thought of himself then as being like a man who had mistakenly got on the wrong train or the wrong bus and for the moment was unable to get off. He had to live with it for a while, a temporary inconvenience. It could have happened to anybody. He went to sleep with this feeling, comforted by it. But in the morning the smile had gone and so had the sense of being different from all the other men. By the time he too was shuffling in a long hot line of incarcerated men waiting for breakfast, the grievances of the other men didn't seem funny at all and it was impossible for him to understand how they ever had been. He remembers wanting that feeling back. He still wants it back, even now. Sometimes the memory of the feeling is almost enough. It's funny what you remember. There's no controlling it.

There was one prisoner in there – they called him Numbers – a little guy. He would make you smile. Numbers would say anything that occurred to him, anything that found its way into his head, and try to sell it as though it were a fact, a fact that God himself had just sweetly whispered in his ear. Numbers once told Lamont that seventy-two months was the national average of time served for robbery. Numbers was sure of it. Even as Lamont heard it, he knew Numbers was making it up. Even if he was *right*, Numbers was making it up. What did it mean? Did this cover all states? What about federal cases? Did it include *armed* robbery? What about cases with more than one charge, where only one of the charges was robbery? What if you had no prior convictions? Lamont had had no prior convictions. He had been charged a couple of times, but just as a juvenile and nothing had stuck. One hot night a friend of his had asked him if he would drive the friend and some other much younger man from the neighbourhood to the liquor store on their way to get some pizza before a night of videos and television. Lamont stayed double-parked in the van, listening to the radio while the other two went into the liquor store. The first time Lamont knew what they had really had in mind was when they ran out of the store screaming for him to drive away as fast as he could. The much younger man, still a teenager really, the one Lamont barely knew, had had a gun. Lamont Williams had not met this man more than three times in his life. The other, the older one, had been Lamont's friend since they were in grade school.

Seventy-two months was the national average for armed robbery, Numbers had said. First it had been the average for robbery, then it was the average for *armed* robbery. He was making it up as he went along, just as he always did. But what if you hadn't known anything about it beforehand? What if some kid had taken you for a ride and let you do the driving? Well, these were all factors, Numbers agreed. What if you never wanted any trouble? What if you lived alone with your grandmother? What if the prettiest girl in the neighbourhood was your cousin, your best friend and your confidante? What if she was smart and said she saw something in *you*? What if she had trusted you not to get into trouble any more? Michelle was never in any trouble. She was going places. She said Lamont could come with her. What is the average number of years you would serve if you were someone like that? What if the other two testified on oath that you hadn't known anything about it? 'That could be a factor,' Numbers conceded. Numbers was an idiot. He hadn't always been an idiot, but by the time Lamont met him, the combined effects of drugs and the beatings he had received in prison had left him overly fond of statistics. But when asked what the chances were that the defence of a black man from the Bronx would be believed, when the two co-accused black men were pleading guilty to armed robbery, Numbers' eyes seemed suddenly to brim with sentience. They welled up with a momentary understanding. 'You in trouble, Lamont.'

Now out of prison, Lamont was in his thirties and back living with his grandmother again in Co-op City, the Bronx. Standing in the elevator going down, he smiled to himself. 'The trick is not to hate yourself,' they had told him in one of the counselling sessions. No it wasn't. He had never hated himself and that was not the trick. The trick was to stay calm, and to avoid or outlast the problem. That was how he had survived prison. It was how he had finally found a job and how he would keep that job. It was how he would save for an apartment of his own and it was how he would become some kind of father for his daughter again. 'Good morning, Mrs Martinez.' She'd been a neighbour for as long as he could remember.

The express bus to Manhattan was scheduled to come twice an hour, once on the half-hour and then again on the hour. Lamont was there at twenty past, and so was ten minutes early. He stood near Dreiser Loop opposite the shopping centre in Section 1. It was the first stop for people going to Manhattan and the last stop for those coming home. An empty bus with only the driver in it was already on the street a hundred yards behind the bus stop. Its doors were closed while it waited to leave on time. A few women – most, but not all of them, older than Lamont – waited there too. One Hispanic man in a suit paced up and down as he waited. He seemed to be about Lamont's age. Lamont wondered if he knew him, but was careful not to stare. The man had his back towards Lamont and, anyway, wasn't keeping still long enough for Lamont to see properly. Lamont looked around the street. On the other side, a group of teenagers were making a noise. There was a paint store there and a ninety-nine cent store where there used to be an Amalgamated Bank. Lamont's grandmother said that it had moved to Section 4, but she couldn't remember exactly when. There was no particular reason she should remember that but then, Lamont wondered, what does reason have to do with memory?

Seneca,
the first frozen apple juice . . .

Eight minutes before the half-hour the bus driver inched the bus the hundred yards to the bus stop and turned off the engine. The Hispanic man in the suit was the first to get on. It looked as though the bus driver was prepared to leave a little early. Lamont was pleased. He had been ready early and now he might even get to work early. He let the women get on before boarding himself. He passed the Hispanic man who, although first on, remained standing at the front of the bus, as

4

though poised to engage the driver. Lamont sat about halfway down on the driver's side with the women scattered around him. 'You're sitting back there for over twenty minutes!' Lamont heard the Hispanic man in the suit say to the bus driver. 'Why have you been sitting here for over twenty minutes? Some of us have a job, you know! Some of us have to get to work *on time*!'

The waiting bus was a replacement for one scheduled to depart on the half-hour that had broken down. The bus driver, an old black man in a blue MTA uniform, sat motionless and silent, looking out the window in front of him. The door was still open. The Hispanic man pointed to the machine that read the magnetic strip on the Metrocards and continued, 'Now I gotta have one of those fucking cards for this on top of everything else.'

The bus driver continued to stare straight ahead and out the window but it seemed only to anger the man in the suit even more. 'You gonna answer me? Twenty minutes! You sit back there with the door shut; don't let no one on for twenty minutes. Twenty minutes! Twenty fucking minutes! You gonna say something? I gotta right to know. What's your ID number?' The bus driver, still looking straight ahead and saying nothing, closed the door and started the engine. If he thought that this was going to placate the man in the suit he was wrong. The man appeared to have no intention of sitting down. He continued standing menacingly close to the driver and shouting at him. 'Why would you just fucking sit there for twenty fucking minutes doing nothing?' The passengers froze in their seats. A few of the women eventually looked at each other furtively. Nobody wanted any trouble. Nobody needed another anecdote. Nobody wanted to be late. The engine was running, but the bus wasn't moving and their day had just been hijacked.

'You think we have to put up with this? This is bullshit. *You're* bullshit! Do you think we're stupid? What were you doing – sleeping? Can the MTA do *anything* right? You don't have anything to say, do you, mother-fucker? That's right, just shut up. Don't say anything. I'm gonna report you, you know that? Then see if you have something to say. You people . . . Then you expect us to support your union when you don't show us no respect?'

The driver could feel the man's breath on his skin. Lamont imagined how that must have felt. He knew exactly how it felt. He too had been in positions in which the heated breeze from another man's mouth had fanned his own sense of powerlessness. It was bad enough just to be in this position but so much worse when other people saw it. You lived it in three ways when other people saw it: once through your skin, a second time through the eyes of the witnesses and thirdly, at a slight remove, when you remembered it in a cold sweat in bed at night or at any other time you found yourself suddenly again prey to an almost unconscious and visceral terror. Sometimes the sweat came first to tell you what you were about to remember.

There was only one remedy for this. The man who felt the breath on him had to strike back, no matter how futile the effort, no matter how much of a beating he was going to take when his resistance had been overcome. It was a chance to save your dignity even if at a violent price. Perhaps, after it was all over, you would still consider it had been worth it. But how can you know in advance? Wherever you end up afterwards, there will always be a face in the mirror. Would it be the face of the man who fought back or the face of the man who felt the stinking hot breath of another man and took it, swallowed it? So you sit there with the exhalation of another man gusting on to you. You're sizing up the options, trying to decide. No doubt you're discounting the pain you'll feel and its duration. So just when you need all your resources, a second front opens – your body against your mind. You can't save them both. You'll need all your anger, clarity of purpose and perfect resolve to get up and do something quickly, but there's always a part of you begging to be heard, telling you it's not worth it. Lamont sat half the bus away from the bus driver and the man in the suit, but he too could feel the man's breath on his skin.

'You gonna give me your number?' the Hispanic man shouted. Lamont was the only other man on the bus. Could he take this angry man in a suit? He wondered whether he was capable of overpowering him. There'd be no surprising him. Lamont winced at even the thought of trying. The old driver might not even be capable of assisting in his own rescue. Why did the man in the suit have to choose *this* time to snap? Why couldn't there be any other male passengers on the bus?

'I want his number,' the suited man continued, now addressing the frightened passengers. 'You gonna give me your number, motherfucker? . . . I'm talking to you! *Maricón*. I want your number and I want to know why the fuck . . . why the *fuck* you were just sitting there for twenty fucking minutes. I have a job. I gotta go to work. Some people work, you know.' He continued, turning intermittently to address the other passengers, 'I gotta go to work'; he offered it in his own defence.

'We *all* gotta go to work,' an older black woman suddenly spoke up. Lamont slumped down in his chair. No good could come of this.

'That's what I'm saying,' the Hispanic man in the suit continued, as though the older woman had merely bolstered his argument. '*We* people, some people have *real* jobs, but . . . you know it's been this way ever since the MTA took over. Since they took over this route –'

'Let him drive,' the older black woman called out bravely. The bus had still not begun to move. The bus driver continued to stare straight ahead. 'Now *you're* making us late,' a younger black woman added. Lamont was feeling the pressure of being the only other male passenger on the bus. Did they know he was the only other male passenger? Of course they knew. If he'd registered the shape of the young woman's earrings, the scent of her perfume, if he knew what colour bra this young woman was wearing, then she knew and all the other women knew he was the only other man on the bus. But still he hoped he wasn't going to be called upon to do something. What kind of man sits there and lets this happen? A man on parole. But what kind of man lets innocent women sit in fear on a public bus without doing a thing? 'The trick is not to hate yourself,' they'd told him in prison. No, the trick was to be born the person that gets to tell you this. Lamont had a daughter. How would he teach his daughter to regard a man who would sit on this bus and do nothing? The trick was to stay calm and to avoid or outlast the problem, to survive long enough to have the luxury of hating yourself.

'He can drive,' the Hispanic man called out from the front of the bus. 'I just want him . . . I'm just *asking* him to give me . . . I gotta right to have his fucking number. Your number, *pendejo*!' There was no sound between his various shouted demands other than the hum of the engine as though promising progress. Lamont felt tiny beads of moisture forming on his forehead.

'Sit down!' another woman called all of a sudden.

'You know it's been this way ever since the MTA took over. You gotta fucking cushy union job and you don't give a shit about people who really gotta work. *They* don't gotta work. They strike. Anything they like.' The Hispanic man was alternating between addressing the bus driver and the passengers. 'Do we have to take this outside? You *have* to give me your number. I have witnesses. You have to give me your number or are we going to have to take it outside?' The bus driver, still silent, checked the rear-view mirror and the side mirror and began to pull out, but this didn't placate the Hispanic man. 'You chicken or deaf? . . . Not man enough to take it outside. *Pendejo!*' he screamed at the bus driver.

The bus began to move. Lamont sneaked a look at the back of the bus driver's head. Any normal person would respond to this man's abuse sooner or later. He thought he could see the bus driver shaking slightly. If he had to shake, he ought to try to disguise it by doing it in time with the bus. Lamont thought the bus driver was finished if he let the man in the suit see any hint of a tremor. He had to concentrate on not looking afraid. He had to focus. He also had to drive the bus. It didn't have to end badly. Lamont closed his eyes, just for a moment. The younger black woman whispered loudly to him, 'You gonna do something?' It was loud enough for the others to hear. Lamont didn't answer. The Hispanic man in the suit wasn't sitting down.

'I said I want your number, motherfucker! If I'm gonna lose *my* job, you gonna lose *yours* too . . .'

Addressing Lamont again in a furious whisper, the younger black woman said, 'You gonna just sit there?'

'Well, I don't –' Lamont began. What did she want him to do?

'He'll just make it worse,' the older woman interrupted quietly.

Surely the bus driver was going to break. Sooner or later he had to respond in some way. Lamont noticed a large truck gaining on the bus on the left side. Should he do something? What should he do? He had a whole plan for getting back on his feet. He had a job. He had a daughter.

That idiot might have a gun. The man was crazy. Lamont understood his own crazy, but this was Puerto Rican crazy. He'd seen Puerto Rican crazy in prison. It had to be respected. The bus driver might have a gun. 'Call the company,' the older woman said in an attempt to placate the man.

'It's the MTA. I need his ID number,' he said in reply and then turning back to the driver, 'Just give me your fucking number, bitch.'

'Will you sit down, please? You're causing a danger to my passengers.' Finally the bus driver spoke. His voice was quiet, his accent Jamaican.

'*You* the fucking danger, pal! I want your number, *maricón*!'

'Will you please sit down, sir?' the old bus driver repeated calmly.

'You gonna make me? I want your fucking number before I sit down.'

'*Oye, el número está allá*,' an older Hispanic woman called out.

'Where?' the angry man asked her. The Hispanic woman pointed to the panel above where the man was standing.

'*Cálmate. Basta ya. Coge el número*, and sit down, OK?'

The man looked up and saw the identification number. It was there above him as she had said. He was running out of reasons not to sit down. He was thinking. All the passengers watched him thinking and he watched them knowing that whatever they were pretending to do, they were watching him. Why did they have to stare like that? The bus was moving and he now had the driver's number. But he didn't want to sit down yet. Not yet. That would let the driver off the hook much too easily. This bus driver had kept him waiting twenty minutes and was going to be the cause of his unemployment. *He* was going to lose his job while the bus driver got to sit down for union pay, driving only when he felt like it. What in hell was he going to do with the driver's number? Everybody knows they all stick together. But he'd made such a show of asking for it and now he had it. The man looked at the number and pulled out a pen from his breast pocket before frisking himself with one hand. 'Anyone got some paper?' The bus driver handed him his copy of the *New York Post*. He took it, wrote the number on the bottom of the front page, tore off the scrap and handed the newspaper back to the bus driver, who accepted it without taking his eyes off the road. The man put the scrap of paper and the pen in his breast pocket and walked with embarrassment down the aisle of the bus. For the first time, he imagined

9

the way he must have looked to the other passengers on the bus. He sat down in the seat in front of Lamont. 'I don't usually curse at my elders,' he said quietly to both the older and the younger black women.

'It's okay. I'm sure you don't,' the older woman said to him.

'It's not the way I was brought up, but . . . twenty minutes he just sat there, and *now* . . . I mean, I could lose my job.'

'I'm sure it will turn out fine,' the older woman said, giving a small wink to the younger woman who turned away from the Hispanic man to face the front of the bus again. Lamont noticed the younger woman roll her eyes at him as she was turning to the front. What did that mean? Why had she done that? There was no trick in making her think well of him. He didn't need her to think anything in particular. Fools thought that was the trick, fools and younger men. There was a woman like her on every bus and in every subway car. He had only one daughter. He had a job. This could all have been much worse. *He* wasn't late for work. Not yet. It didn't matter what this woman thought. Lamont watched the bus driver and saw him rub the back of one hand over his forehead.

'Since the MTA . . . they . . . put the fare up to five dollars. I wouldn't . . . I wasn't brought up to curse at my elders . . . It's just that it's my *job*,' the Hispanic man said quietly to anyone who could hear him.

What did it mean, the way she had looked at him, Lamont wondered. The trick is not to hate yourself. It's funny what you remember. He looked out the window and still couldn't get the song out of his head.

Seneca,
the first frozen apple juice,
enriched with vitamin C.

He had drunk that apple juice as a child. His grandmother had bought it for him then, and she was buying it for him again now. What good did vitamin C actually do? Does anyone really know, Lamont wondered. The Hispanic man was sitting quietly. The bus had almost reached midtown. Perhaps the worst was over. Lamont's grandmother swore by vitamin C – vitamin C and Jesus. Do people still talk as much as they used to about vitamin C? Lamont didn't think so. Jesus was still good, though. With all the work they're doing on cancer and stuff, you would think they would have finally found something vitamin C could cure. Probably not, judging by how quiet vitamin C had gone, compared to when he was a kid. His grandmother had left a glass of apple juice for him. This was how the song got fixed in his head. He had forgotten to drink it, forgotten all about it until he saw it on the kitchen table as he ran out the door not to be late for the bus. The traffic was crawling.

'Oh Jesus,' Lamont said under his breath when he saw the Hispanic man getting up at 59th Street, just as he was. As he headed for the door, Lamont waited for a moment. He couldn't help himself, and turned in the direction of the young black woman who had been sitting near him. Was she aware he was getting off? Had she seen his eyes? Did she have a grandmother who poured her apple juice? She was younger but they probably grew up eating the same food, catching the same childhood diseases, seeing the same local doctor. Growing up in the neighbourhood, they'd been warmed and cooled by the same winter and summer. Had she really rolled her eyes? Lamont stood up slowly. If she'd grown up where he had, she had to understand. Did she understand *anything*? He took one small step. The bus was slowing. This was as long as he could wait without missing his stop. She wouldn't look at him. He saw the Hispanic man disappear in the crowd on 59th Street as he started to walk to 57th Street to catch the 31 all the way east to York Avenue. She wouldn't look at him.

Lamont was the first candidate in a new outreach program deemed suitable for hiring by Memorial Sloan-Kettering Cancer Center. The hospital had agreed to participate in a pilot scheme that would see non-violent offenders with exemplary prison records given an employment opportunity in an area that entailed a chance to, in the words of the program, 'give something back to the community'. It was only by luck that Lamont had heard about it. On learning that Lamont was eligible for early release, a friend in prison had told him to go to a place in east Harlem where they might be able to help him find a job. That place turned out to be the Exodus Transitional Community. Lamont hadn't remembered the name, but somehow he had remembered the address – 104th Street and Lexington. Cobbling together private donations, a trickle of intermittent government funding and as much goodwill as it could find, Exodus Transitional Community had managed to secure the participation of Memorial Sloan-Kettering. But the agreement had not amounted to much because Exodus had not found any ex-prisoners who satisfied the hospital's strict requirements. The successful ex-prisoner was required to have no history of violence or substance abuse, and a permanent domestic address. None of Exodus' clients until Lamont Williams had been able to satisfy all of these conditions. The importance of his participation in the 'trial' was impressed upon him by both parties to the agreement.

Once he had been screened, approved and accepted, Lamont had been treated like any other new employee at Memorial Sloan-Kettering and placed on six months' probation. The first three days had gone well enough and now, notwithstanding his humiliating paralysis in the face of the bus driver's ordeal, Lamont had arrived on time for day four. He liked the fact that he was working in a hospital. It pleased him. He liked being able to ask someone from another department a question by simply picking up the internal phone, dialling the other person's extension and beginning with, 'This is Lamont Williams from Building Services . . .'

He entered from First Avenue and signed in, but was told that as soon as he was in his uniform he should go immediately to the York Avenue entrance. He was needed for something and he would be told what it was when he got there. When he arrived at the York Avenue entrance, he couldn't see anyone from Building Services, and certainly not anyone senior to him. He looked around and decided to wait a little while. Maybe the supervisor was just about to arrive? Although he was wearing a watch, he had forgotten to take notice of the time he'd got to the York Avenue entrance. He had not expected to be interested in what time it was precisely that he had got there – it couldn't have been long after the shift had started – but now it seemed to him as though he had been waiting ages. Surely it had been only minutes? Maybe he was meant to be waiting outside, on the street side of the entrance. Maybe that's where the supervisor was already. He quickly stuck his head through the doors to the street side of the York Avenue entrance, but he couldn't see the supervisor there either. Should he find an internal phone and call someone? Maybe he had misheard the instruction in the first place. This was only day four. This was a good job. He had to get past probation. It was only six months. They told him that after twelve months, you were eligible to have the company pay for your college tuition if you were able to get into a college. How good would that sound – a hospital employee for twelve months and going to college? How good would that sound to a judge? If he had to apply to a court to see his daughter, how good would that sound? He asked one of the others if he had understood the policy correctly. It sounded too good. 'Yeah, when you get into Harvard, they'll pay.'

Probation lasts six months. This was the first hour of day four, and the supervisor wasn't to be found outside either. Maybe Lamont was meant to *see* the job at hand, to identify the problem himself and show some initiative. He looked outside to see if there was anything that looked like an obvious job for someone in Building Services. Everyone outside was smoking under the hospital awning – paramedics, anxious family members, even patients themselves. It didn't make any sense. Maybe they were all just about to quit. Maybe the patients among the smokers had a cancer *other* than lung cancer, and needed the comfort of cigarettes to get them through it. Whatever the explanation, there was no doubting the pile of cigarette butts scattered on the sidewalk near the entrance. Could that be what he was meant to do, get rid of the cigarette butts from the sidewalk at the York Avenue entrance? It didn't look like anyone from the previous shift had done it, but it didn't look so urgent, either.

There was a storeroom not far away. Lamont was aware of it. He could get a broom and pan and be sweeping up the sidewalk when the supervisor arrived. Maybe the supervisor had been delayed. Wouldn't that look good – Lamont sweeping up the cigarette butts off the sidewalk when the supervisor arrived? Lamont was turning to go back inside to the storeroom for the broom and pan when a man entering from the street stopped him. 'Do you know Yale Bronfman? He's in Regulatory.'

'Sorry, sir, I'm in Building Services.'

'You don't know Yale Bronfman?'

'No, sir, I'm –'

'Is this the right entrance for Regulatory Affairs?'

'I don't know, sir. I'm in Building Services.'

'But . . . You don't know the building?'

'Maybe you want to ask the man at the information desk there, sir . . . ? I'm sure he can help you.'

'Jesus Christ!' the man said, heading inside towards the information desk.

Was Lamont meant to know everybody who worked there? Was he meant to know where Regulatory Affairs was or even *what* Regulatory Affairs was? Had he been told? Had he already forgotten? He went to the storeroom as quickly as he could. It would be best if the supervisor arrived at the York Avenue entrance and saw Lamont working while he waited for further instructions. At the end of every twelve months of employment, the supervisor awarded you a score between zero and five. That score represented your pay increase, and it was a percentage of your salary. No one in the history of the hospital had ever got a score of five. You could get three, or three-point-seven, or four-point-two, but no one had ever got five because a score of five represents perfection, and, as everybody knows, nobody's perfect. The supervisor had a lot of power. He determined how close you got to perfection.

Lamont was sweeping outside the York Avenue entrance, and still there was no sign of his supervisor. Clouds of smoke blew across his face and through his hair. He sneezed. It was probably hay fever. The trees across the street at Rockefeller University could traumatise a sensitive nose. Lamont had already been told to blame a sneeze on the trees at Rockefeller University, or else on the smokers' cigarettes at the entrances, because you were not permitted to come to work sick. You were permitted a certain number of hours off sick a year, but only a fool would take them because the supervisor would see it on your record and hold it against you. If you sneezed, you'd better blame it on the trees at Rockefeller. If you were really sick, it was best to come in anyway, and then after a little while you could report that you felt sick. They would send you home immediately, but it wouldn't show up on your record. It would look good. You made the effort to come in. Remember the trees at Rockefeller. They can help you. Lamont knew this already. He had been told this unofficially by the man who had shown him around on his first day. No one had said anything about Regulatory Affairs. If they had, he didn't remember it. It's funny what you remember. It's not up to you.

It felt good to be sweeping up. At least for a moment, he knew he was doing the right thing, and was doing it well. It wouldn't take long, and he had decided that if the supervisor hadn't appeared by the time he was finished sweeping, he would go back to where he had signed in on the First Avenue side of the building.

'Excuse me.' Lamont heard a voice, but assumed it asked for someone else's attention. But when it persisted, he turned around. 'Excuse me,' an elderly patient in a wheelchair asked. 'I was brought down from my room for some air, but there's too much . . . It's too smoky, so I should go inside. Can you take me back to my room?' The old man – he spoke with some kind of accent – was attached to an IV drip.

'You wanna go inside, sir?'

'Yes, it's too smoky here. I can't believe they all smoke.'

Lamont looked around. Another thing he remembered being told was that the customer was always right. This sick old white man with a foreign accent was a patient, so he was a customer. 'Well, see, sir, I'm in Building Services . . .'

'What are you?'

'Building Services.'

'Yes, in the building . . . on the ninth floor.'

Lamont looked around. 'Wasn't there someone who brought you down?'

'Yes, from the ninth floor but it's too smoky.'

There were rules about the transportation of patients. Only certain members of staff were permitted to move patients from one place to another. Special warnings needed to be given about steps and elevators. Training was essential for this. The hospital's insurance policies made it all very clear.

'Sir, wasn't there someone from Patient Escort Services who brought you down?'

'Yes, of course. Someone brought me down. He said he'd be back and now . . . Now he's not back. Can you take me back up . . . on the ninth floor?'

'I'm not supposed to.'

'What?'

'I'm not allowed to . . .'

'It's too smoky . . . with all of them.'

'Let me see if I can get you someone from PES. I'll be right back.' Lamont clutched his broom and pan in one hand and went inside to the concierge. 'I got a patient out here who wants to go back to his room. Isn't there supposed to be someone from PES with him?' The concierge rolled his eyes. 'Fucking Jamal! He left the patient on the street! And his probation ends next week. I hope he's cramming for his test. He's got the HIPAA test.'

'Well, he left the patient out on the street. What's the HIPAA test? Will I have to –'

'Shit! Okay, you go back and stay with the patient. I'll try to get hold of someone from PES. Fucking Jamal!'

Lamont went back to the old man in the wheelchair. He was sitting there, holding his robe closed with one hand, among the smokers on York Avenue. A breeze blew through his wisps of hair. He looked alone. 'I'm sorry. The man, the *other* man, he shouldn't have left you.'

'I agree with you,' the old man said.

'Someone should be here soon.'

''Cause it's not a *smoking* jacket, you know.'

'What?'

'It's not a *smoking* jacket,' the old man said with a smile, pointing to the bathrobe.

'No, no, it's not.'

When the man asked again for Lamont to take him back to his room on the ninth floor, Lamont explained again that he was not permitted to do it. He explained that it was against the rules. He repeated what he had been told about the hospital's insurance. The supervisor was never coming. Or maybe he had been and gone while Lamont was with the concierge. Jamal had almost made it to the end of his six months' probation. 'It's the rules.'

'You know something? I bet you would be very careful.'

'I can't do it.'

'But if you *could*, you would watch out for the steps.'

'I'm sorry, sir. I can't.'

'Because of the rules?'

'Yes, sir.'

'Otherwise you would?'

'I would if I could.'

'I'm an old man . . .'

'I'm sorry, sir.'

'You know why I'm here?'

'Cancer?'

'You could take me up in the service elevator. The only people who would see us would *also* be in Building Services, so you wouldn't get into trouble.'

'Sorry, sir.'

'Then you could just drop me off in my room and I could ring the buzzer for a nurse.'

'I can't do it.'

'You'd be gone, and then the nurse would be the one to help me back into bed.'

'I know what you're sayin', sir, but I really can't do it.'

'Because of the rules, right?'

'That's right.'

The old man beckoned Lamont with his finger to lean close to him. Closer, closer, the finger kept beckoning, moving with surprising vigour until Lamont was kneeling beside the old man, enabling the patient to whisper into Lamont's ear above the noise of the traffic on York Avenue. 'To hell with the rules.' Lamont had to smile.

The service elevator was empty, and they made it to the ninth floor without anyone looking twice. On the way up, neither of them spoke. Lamont kept looking at the floor, watching out for all the steps. He would go looking for the supervisor when this was over. What were the chances anyone would ever know about this? What were the chances he'd make it to the end of probation and have to learn the HIPAA rules like Jamal? Where was Numbers when you needed him? He was still inside, if he was anywhere. What were the HIPAA rules, anyway? Did you actually have to know them by heart?

The old man directed Lamont to his room on the ninth floor, over-looking York Avenue. How long was it going to take him before he got that Seneca song out of his head? He had no control over it. There were worse things to remember. Now he had to worry about memorising the HIPAA rules. He had six months to worry about that, if he could survive that long. He worried about surviving all the time. When they got to the window of the room, the old man put one hand up to ask him to stop. The old man looked out the window. 'Is that the East River?'

'Uh-huh.'

'So that's . . . New Jersey?'

'No, New Jersey's on the west side, over the Hudson. That's Queens.'

'And that . . . that land there?'

'That's Roosevelt Island.'

'Roosevelt?'

'Uh-huh. I'm gonna have to go, sir.'

'What are *they*?'

'What . . . the chimneys?'

'Yes . . . three chimneys . . . Where are they, Roosevelt?'

'I don't think so . . . probably Queens. You're not from here, are you? I should go.'

The trick is not to hate yourself. No matter what you remember.

'I need to go now. You okay to call the nurse? I have to go. You happy by the window? They'll help you to get back to . . . Sir? Sir?' The old man was staring out the window.

'There were six death camps.'

'What?'

'There were six death camps.'

'Six what?'

'Death camps.'

'What do you mean, "death camp"?'

'There were exactly six death camps but you could die more than once in any of them.'

part two

Shortly before 4.30 am one Monday morning, Adam Zignelik, almost forty, was to awake momentarily uncertain of where he was and experience a shortness of breath sometimes associated with a heart attack or at least with the tart panic of a nightmare. Though the blinds were drawn, the bedroom of the Morningside Heights apartment he rented from Columbia University where he worked was bathed with a faint grey-bluish glow familiar to anyone who had ever been awake at that hour in the nearby cross streets. In other parts of Manhattan the light was variously somehow different, something no one ever seemed to talk about. When he awoke shortly before 4.30 am that Monday morning the character of the light would only add to the surreal quality his unconscious was spraying in a fine mist over his perception of the new and already fugitive day.

In the minutes before he woke a montage of images in his mind, mostly in monochrome, had induced a series of increasingly violent bodily tremors ultimately almost indistinguishable from a convulsion. The images, mainly of black people, were from another time, his father's time. There was Emmett Till, seated, forever fourteen, his mother's hand resting on his shoulder. In August 1955, Emmett left his home on the south side of Chicago to visit relatives in Money, Mississippi. Armed only with a speech impediment bequeathed to him by a bout of polio contracted when he was three, the fourteen-year-old black boy went into Bryant's Grocery and Meat Market to buy some gum. As he was leaving he said, perhaps shyly, perhaps not, 'Bye, Baby' to the older white town beauty, Carolyn Bryant. When Emmett's body was found three days later in the Tallahatchie River, he was recognisable to his southern relative only by his initialled ring. Barbed wire had been used to hold a cotton-gin fan around his neck, one eye had been gouged out, a bullet had been lodged in his skull and one side of his forehead had been crushed. Adam Zignelik's sleep took in the image of Emmett Till with his mother's hand resting on Emmett's shoulder as well as the later one, the last one, of Emmett's bashed, bloated, river-soaked head, the one that his mother, Mamie Till Bradley Mobley, allowed to be published in *Jet* magazine so it could be seen as widely as possible. Adam saw these images flicker by and falter before him and then for a moment he saw his own father, also in black and white. Then his father too disappeared.

He saw the images of Carole Robertson, Cynthia Wesley, Addie Mae Collins – three fourteen-year-old girls, and eleven-year-old Denise McNair, her braided hair tied tight with ribbons, smiling – four little black girls who, one Sunday in September 1963, had, as they had every Sunday, gone to Bible class at the 16th Street Baptist Church in Birmingham, Alabama. But on the 15th of September these little girls attained national prominence when the church was bombed by segregationists. Fifteen people were injured. All four of the girls were killed. It was estimated that in Birmingham, Alabama, at the time of their murder one-third of all police officers were either Klansmen or had a Klan affiliation. Though the girls were killed before he was born, Adam Zignelik knew them and saw them in the minutes before waking in a sweat around 4.30 am that Monday morning. He saw his father briefly then too, a white man, in black and white.

He saw fifteen-year-old Elizabeth Eckford alone on 4 September 1957 at the centre of a crowd outside Central High School in Little Rock, Arkansas. Elizabeth was one of nine black students attempting to become the first students of their race to attend the school. All nine students were meant to be arriving together. They were to have met at 8.30 am on the corner of 12th Street and Park Avenue where two police cars were to take them to school. That had been the plan. Elizabeth's father, Oscar, worked as a dining car maintenance worker and her mother, Birdee, taught blind and deaf children how to wash and iron their own clothes at a segregated school. But in September 1957 the Eckfords didn't yet own a telephone. No one had told Elizabeth the plan.

Elizabeth got up that morning to go to her new school. She put on a new black-and-white dress that she and her mother had made for the occasion. It was perfectly pressed. Adam Zignelik could see the pleats that flowed down from Elizabeth's waist where the dress tapered in. The television news was on in the Eckford house. Before Birdee Eckford could switch it off, she and her husband, Oscar, who was walking the floorboards of the hallway to a rhythm in his chest, an unlit cigar in one hand and an unlit pipe in the other, both heard the newscaster speculate, between the weather report and a series of advertisements, about whether the nine coloured children would be going to school that day, the day after Governor Orval Eugene Faubus had warned that – if they did – 'blood will run in the streets'. Elizabeth had heard it too. 'Don't let her go!' Adam Zignelik called out but no articulate sound, nothing resembling language, came out of him. And, anyway, he was in an apartment in New York, asleep beside his girlfriend, Diana, some fifty years later. 'Don't let her go, for Christ's sake. Don't let her go!'

But neither Elizabeth nor her parents, Birdee and Oscar Eckford, heard Adam Zignelik nor, as they knelt down to pray together, did they feel the force of him thrashing in his bed, pleading with his father to intervene and stop Elizabeth from trying to go to Central High that day. Adam's father, Jake Zignelik, ignored him too. She *had* to go. Far from stopping her, Jake Zignelik *wanted* her to go. That was the whole idea. Adam had to understand that.

Elizabeth put on her black sunglasses. She said goodbye to her parents, kissed them and walked to the public bus stop where she waited quietly for the bus that would take her to her new school. But when she got off at the bus stop closest to Central High she didn't see any of the other eight black children who were meant to be starting at the school with her that day.

'For Christ's sake, please don't let her go!'

She didn't see any black people at all. She saw a sea of white people, thousands of them from all over the state and, judging from the out-of-state licence plates, from other states as well. She saw hundreds of soldiers in full battledress: boots, helmets. The soldiers were armed. She saw bayonets, too many to count.

'She has to go, Adam. Don't be a child.'

She looked at the guards lined up along the road leading to the school building and she looked at the white crowd. The day before, she had been told to go to the school's main entrance. It was a block away from where she was standing. It occurred to her that when walking the block to the front of the school she might be safer if she walked it from behind the guards so that for the length of the block there would be a line of guards between her and the crowd. It was at the corner of the block that she chose to try to pass through the line of guards in order to stand on the other side of them. She was wearing sunglasses and the black-and-white pleated dress she had made with her mother. It was her first day at a new school. She was fifteen and she chose a soldier at random. The soldier didn't speak but pointed across the street in the direction of the crowd. She tried not to look frightened and walked as the random soldier had directed her. What might another soldier have done? Elizabeth had always achieved high grades, always been an excellent student.

'Dad, she's fifteen!'

'Don't bother me, Adam.'

Elizabeth Eckford walked towards the crowd and, at least at first, that section of it closest to her moved back, away from her, almost as though afraid of her, as though afraid they might catch something from her. If you stood too near her perhaps you could *become* her. People would look at you. You would stand out simply by being in that part of the crowd nearest to her. You hadn't gone there expecting to stand out. That wasn't why you were there. But now you might stand out through no fault of your own. So you had better make sure that everybody around knows where you really stand. You hate her. You hate her as much as anyone else in the crowd hates her. You might even hate her more. By standing near you, she's making you especially uncomfortable, more uncomfortable than she makes everybody else feel, and how *they* feel is only how you felt moments ago before she chose you to make especially uncomfortable. Why did she have to choose you? She brings trouble with her wherever she goes. You can see it. You've been told this all your life, known it all your life, but now you can actually feel it. She's making you sweat. She's making your heart race. Everybody's looking as she stands near you. Oh Christ, you hate her. Why did she have to make you feel like this? You hate her so much.

'Dad!'

Then the crowd began to move in towards her. Mouths opened wide to let the anger and the hate pour out. All the toxic putrefaction that lived in the dark foetid recesses of the bowels of their minds was directed at a fifteen-year-old girl trying to go to school. Her legs began to shake and she wondered if it was discernible to the crowd. She had the whole block to negotiate before reaching the main entrance. She needn't be afraid, she told herself. She needn't be afraid no matter what the crowd was calling out because there were guards. There was a whole line of guards to protect her. The crowd was moving in.

'Here she comes. Get ready!' someone shouted.

Elizabeth moved away from the crowd and closer to the guards. She walked briskly but she didn't run. The noise of the crowd was everywhere. All she had to do, she told herself, was make it to the main entrance at the end of the block.

'Dad!' Adam Zignelik tried to call out fifty years later.

Elizabeth managed to reach the front of the school. She approached another guard. This one wouldn't meet her eyes. He stared out beyond her, over her head like she wasn't there. The noise was all around her as though attached to the air. The guard wouldn't let her pass. She saw that there was a path which led directly to the front entrance a little further on. She turned and took it. She hadn't realised the school was so big. White students were walking up to the guards at the front door and were being let through. Still with the feeling that her legs could give way at any moment, she walked towards the guard who was letting the white students through. He didn't move. Again it was like she wasn't there. She tried to get in between him and the guard next to him. He raised his bayonet to block her. Then the other guards moved in. They raised their bayonets too. As though sensing something, some change or new phase, a quiet descended on the crowd for a moment. Elizabeth didn't know what to do. She turned away from the guards and just stood there, between them and the crowd. Now the crowd moved towards her, closer, and she heard, 'Lynch her! Lynch her!'

Where was Jake Zignelik now? Was there anyone who would help her, anyone who was actually there? What happens to human kindness in the belly of a mob? Can it exist there at all or is it utterly extinguished? Elizabeth's eyes fell on an older white woman with a face whose features had a cut not inconsistent with kindness. It was just a glance at first but from behind her sunglasses Elizabeth saw something she needed then more than anything else. She turned and walked towards this old white woman but when she got closer the woman spat in her face. The spit stayed there. She didn't want to touch it. The crowd moved in closer and she heard someone shout, 'No nigger bitch is going to get into our school. Get her out of here!'

She turned around to face the guards again but they remained impassive and impassable. The noise of those thousands of angry white people was like nothing she had ever heard before. She had always got good grades. She had always been very polite, always been a good girl, been no trouble to her teachers, always paid attention. These people didn't know her. Where in her fifteen years of life was the thing she had done that was so bad they should hate her this much? There were so many of them and they all hated her. They appeared to feel this so strongly even though none of them knew her. It was hard to think but she found and clutched at the thought that somehow it might be better for her if she could make it back to the bus stop from where she'd arrived. It was a new plan, to make it back to the bench at the bus stop. She turned around and started the journey back, flanked by the crowd on each side. Still she didn't run but her legs felt as though they might buckle at any time. She carried an old white woman's spit on her. When she finally got to the bench at the bus stop her legs did buckle slightly but she propped herself up on the back of the bench.

Despite everything she saw and everything she heard and despite the fear she felt like shocks of electricity coming in surges through her viscera to her sinews to the nerve endings in her skin, she reached within herself for a dignity that seemed to belong to a foreign code of conduct, foreign to the world she was then experiencing. It was a dignity that somehow her parents had planted in her. For fifteen years they had nurtured it. Elizabeth sat down on the bench at the bus stop and went digging for it deep inside herself. The crowd moved in closer to her and she heard someone shout, 'Drag her over to this tree! Let's take care of that nigger.'

'Dad!'

Adam Zignelik hadn't been born when this happened, when some young men in the crowd who had followed her back to the bus stop and were now behind Elizabeth Eckford started calling, 'Lynch her! No nigger bitch is going to get into our school. We gotta lynch her! Lynch her! Lynch her!' Jake Zignelik had been born but he wasn't there. Who was there for Elizabeth Eckford at the bench at the bus stop near the tree in Little Rock, Arkansas, on the morning of 4 September 1957? Thousands of people were there. Was there anyone else there for her?

Television news cameras were there. Radio journalists were there. Daisy Bates was the president of the Arkansas state branch of the National Association for the Advancement of Colored People (the NAACP) and editor-in-chief of the black newspaper, the *Arkansas State Press*, and her husband, L. C. Bates, was the newspaper's publisher They hadn't been able to sleep the night before because of the cars tearing up and down past their home with the horns honking and the passengers calling out, 'Daisy, Daisy, did you hear the news? The Coons won't be going to Central!' Daisy and L. C. Bates were in the car that morning on their way, expecting to be meeting nine black children, when they heard the radio announcer on the car radio.

'A Negro girl is being mobbed at Central High . . .'

Daisy Bates realised the girl had to be Elizabeth, the girl who lived with her parents and her little brother in a house without a telephone. Elizabeth hadn't known the plan. No one had told her. They stopped the car suddenly and L. C. Bates jumped out and started running to find her. Daisy would drive there. But they were only two people, they were black and they were blocks away.

Thousands of people were already near the bench at the bus stop by the tree before L. C. Bates could get there. Jake Zignelik wasn't there. Adam Zignelik, who saw it all shortly before 4.30 am that Monday morning, hadn't been born yet. Was there anybody else there?

Benjamin Fine was an education writer for *The New York Times* and he was there. He manoeuvred himself behind Elizabeth, behind the bench at the bus stop. Then he pushed a little further forward. He managed to get beside Elizabeth and to sit next to her. He put his arm around her. He raised her chin just slightly and said, 'Don't let them see you cry.' Grace Lorch was there, a white woman married to a white man who taught at a local black college. She made her way to Elizabeth and spoke kindly to her but in Elizabeth's terror the kindness did not register. Grace Lorch took Elizabeth through the jeering crowd to a nearby drugstore in an attempt to call a cab. But the door of the drugstore was slammed shut in their faces. Grace Lorch took her to the bus and the two of them rode the bus to the segregated school where Birdee Eckford taught blind and deaf children how to wash and iron their own clothes.

After this, crowds were always mobs for Elizabeth Eckford and when she would see the mob in her room at night she would scream. When they heard this scream her brother would wake and her parents would come to her. But sometimes when she screamed no sound came out, just as it didn't for Adam Zignelik shortly before 4.30 am one Monday morning some fifty years later in the Morningside Heights apartment rented from Columbia University, where he – the son of Jake Zignelik – taught history.

It all had to be seen in context, Jake Zignelik explained to his son. The 'Little Rock Nine', as the students became known, was the name given to the first black students to try to enrol in public schools in Arkansas but it was already three years after the Supreme Court had handed down its decision in *Brown versus Board of Education*. 'Is three years a long time?' Jake Zignelik had asked his eight-year-old son over chicken salad sandwiches and soda in Bryant Park. Adam thought for a moment before answering tentatively.

'That depends,' Adam said. At this his father hugged him.

'That's right! That's exactly right. Perfect answer. It depends. Three years is a long time to hold your breath, right? Is it a long time to change the mentality of more than half the nation? Is it a long time to shift vested interests? Is it a long time to break down generations of fear?'

It seemed to young Adam that his father was leading him towards an answer of 'no', but surely 'no' was the *wrong* answer so he waited before replying. But his father kept talking, as he knew he would, and he didn't have to answer.

'When was the Civil War?'

'1861 to 1865,' young Adam answered.

'Right. And what was it about?'

'Emancipation of the slaves,' the eight-year-old shot back with a mouth full of sandwich.

'Among other things, yes. Right. Right. And when did Lincoln issue the Emancipation Proclamation?'

'1863.'

'Well, Lincoln announced it in September 1862 but it didn't come into effect until 1 January 1863. And when was the Supreme Court decision in *Brown versus Board of Education*?'

'Nineteen fifty-four.'

'And what did that decision do, what was its intended effect?'

At this Adam spoke as if by rote, 'Thurgood Marshall, now Justice Thurgood Marshall of the United States Supreme Court, successfully argued *Brown versus Board of Education* in 1954. The Supreme Court decision led to the end of segregation in public schools and overturned the "separate but equal" doctrine of the *Plessy versus Ferguson* decision of 1896.'

'Absolutely right,' his father answered.

Jake Zignelik had been there in 1954 in the US Supreme Court when Thurgood Marshall had argued *Brown versus Board of Education*. In 1949, fresh from Columbia Law School, Jake Zignelik, a New York Jew, went to work for what would later become known as the NAACP Legal Defense and Educational Fund, later simply known as the LDF. He went on to be mentored by Thurgood Marshall. In a long career he represented Martin Luther King and many others, arguing numerous civil rights cases before the US Supreme Court. He represented black students attempting to gain admission to segregated colleges and professional schools, black men charged with the rape of white women and black servicemen subjected to racial discrimination in the armed services. He later became the director-counsel for the LDF.

'Very good,' Jake Zignelik said to his son Adam. 'Watch your suitcase. Always watch your suitcase, especially in the park. So these three years between the *Brown* decision and the "Little Rock Nine", they were really part of some ninety-odd years when people waited for the government to keep its promise. And that's exactly what Thurgood said. It was after the Arthurine Lucy case. He was asked if he was a gradualist. You know what a gradualist is?'

'Yes.'

'What's a gradualist?'

'Someone who wants change to come but gradually,' young Adam answered as he'd been taught.

'That's right. After the Lucy case Thurgood said he believed in gradualism but that he also believed ninety-odd years was pretty gradual. You think he was right?'

'Yep.'

'Yeah, so do I. Ninety-odd years is a long time to wait to be treated with the same dignity everyone else is supposed to be treated with, supposed to according to law. See, what good is it having great laws that protect people and help people to live the best lives they can if those laws aren't upheld, if they aren't enforced? It's really like saying there are some laws you have to respect and obey and others you don't really have to worry about. And it just so happened that the laws you didn't have to worry about always affected the same people. Which people?'

'Black people.'

'Right, black people. Right from the time their ancestors were kidnapped, taken against their will – can you imagine being forcibly separated from your family to be used as a thing, not as a person, just so other people could get rich? – right from that time there was never a time when black people didn't face discrimination, didn't find life harder than other people, just because they belonged to a group, a group they were born into. Of course, other people have had it very hard too, including your grandparents. All sorts of people suffer for all sorts of reasons at different times but black people are the descendants of people who didn't even choose to come here, who were often treated like animals just so that white people could make money out of them. And what did our government, their government, do? Despite the beauty of the Declaration of Independence, despite the beauty of the Emancipation Proclamation, even despite the Supreme Court decision Thurgood fought for in *Brown versus Board of Education*, the government turned its back on black people.'

'So is the government the enemy?'

'No, government can be an agent of fairness. That's what government is meant to be.'

'So . . . who is the enemy?' young Adam asked with one hand holding his sandwich and the other resting on his suitcase.

'The enemy,' Jake Zignelik explained, 'is racism. But, see, racism isn't a person. It's a virus that infects people. It can infect whole towns and cities, even whole countries. Sometimes you can see it in people's faces when they're sick with it. It can paralyse even good people. It can paralyse government. We have to fight that wherever we find it. That's what good people do.'

So much of what his father would always too hastily tell him on those visits to New York stayed with Adam Zignelik. The names and the dates of the people associated with the struggle; and always that article of faith would come back to him again and again. As a mantra, it would come to him at times when other people might rely on a religious incantation or injunction. 'That's what good people do.' It came back to him the first time right after his father had kissed him goodbye and put him on a plane to fly back to his mother. The very long flight to Australia allowed him plenty of time to repeat it over and over to himself as he sat strapped in his seat, a blanket on his knees, trying to hide the tears in his eyes from the passenger seated next to him or the flight attendants who always seemed to be on the lookout for such things from little boys who travelled alone on long flights. 'That's what good people do.'

When Adam would get home to Melbourne he would tell as many people as he could everything he remembered and he remembered everything his father had told him. He remembered about the work his father was doing, about the people his father worked with, the places, the dates, the laws, the cases, the various decisions of the various courts and what they all meant. He told his friends who didn't understand and didn't care. He told all his teachers who understood more and, for the most part, could have cared more, which alternately distressed or angered him. Adam's father was Jake Zignelik after all. Perhaps they had heard of him? Everyone young Adam met in New York had heard of him. Of course, the little boy was only meeting people his father introduced him to. Adam had met Justice Marshall, quite a few, even many, times. What were these people, adults, teachers; what were they doing with their lives? He was talking about Justice Thurgood Marshall for God's sake! He *knew* him. He told his mother, who understood everything and cared very much. She had cared enough long ago to seek out Jake Zignelik from the other side of the world.

In the decade after World War I, pockets of Eastern Europe shivered with outbreaks of feverish pogroms against its Jews. At the same time in the United States the passing of the Johnson-Reed Act slowed what had been a flow of Jewish immigration to a drip. Any eastern European Jews hoping to start a new life in the New World now had to consider the even newer world. In the early 1930s Adam Zignelik's grandparents on his mother's side arrived in Australia, a country so far away they were never quite sure it really existed until they docked at Port Melbourne. They moved to the inner-city Melbourne suburb of Carlton. They eked out a meager living making knitwear such as cardigans and sweaters, or 'jumpers' as these were called in Australia, on a single at first manual and then motorised knitting machine in their dining room and selling it at a stall in the nearby Victoria Market. They had two children, a son who died before he was five and a daughter on whom they lavished all the anxious attention their fragile health, language difficulties and precarious social and economic circumstances permitted.

Always the brightest in her class, she eventually made her way to the sandstone lecture theatres of Melbourne University Law School in the early 1960s. It was there she heard about the work of the NAACP and by the time she graduated she had decided to go to New York to see if she could obtain an internship there. When she met Jake Zignelik, an older still single man and by then the director-counsel of the LDF, she fell for him instantly. Mutual attraction, flattery and admiration blossomed in the hothouse of long hours and other people's problems into an office romance. It might have ended there but Jake felt obliged to marry the young Australian lawyer when she fell pregnant. 'It's what good people do.' Not long before Adam was born, his mother had to give up work at the LDF and she realised later that once she was out of Jake's work life she was out of what really was the part of his life he cared most about. With ageing sickly immigrant parents on the other side of the world and already a widow in all but name, she joked that if ever she were to leave Jake it would take him years to find out. Adam never knew the precise mechanics of it but by the time he was three the marriage had been dissolved and he was living with his mother in Melbourne.

Jake Zignelik admitted on more than one occasion that he knew he wasn't much of a father but the first admission, made privately during a US Supreme Court hearing, was not made to his ex-wife or to Adam. It was made to William McCray, his long-time friend and LDF colleague. A veteran both of the civil rights movement and of the segregated armed services during World War II, William McCray also had one child; a son. But he was a much better father to his son, Charles, than Jake was to Adam. It was not long after Jake had put his eight-year-old son on a plane to Australia that he found himself admitting as much to William over coffee during an adjournment in the hearing.

'It's not that I don't love him because, of course, I love him very much,' Jake Zignelik said, looking out beyond the steam that rose from his cup.

'Jake, if you can't be a good father to him, you could at least tell him that you *know* you're not much of a father.'

'I never see him.'

'Well that's not *his* fault. What did you talk about with him when he was here? You talked to him about the decision in *Brown versus Board of Education*, didn't you?'

Jake thought a moment and even when he remembered he didn't answer. He was thinking about his lunch with Adam in Bryant Park.

'So it's 1863 – you have to imagine it,' he told his son. 'It's the middle of the Civil War. It's a hot summer in New York. Lincoln had announced the Emancipation Proclamation the previous September but it had only been in effect since January. It was intended to free slaves in those parts of the country at war with the Union. By the way, any slave owner in any Confederate state that rejoined the Union between September 1862 and January 1863 got to keep their slaves. See, even the Emancipation Proclamation had a loophole. But now with the Emancipation Proclamation in effect, all sorts of people could blame the war on black people.'

'Why?'

''Cause now it could be said that the war was being fought on behalf of black people so if it wasn't for them there wouldn't be a war. You see how twisted that is, Adam? These people are being bought and sold like animals. Finally enough people agree that it's just plain wrong and that you can't do that to human beings. But there are vested interests, right? You remember who they are?'

'The slave owners?'

'That's right, the slave owners. Well, they don't want to give up what they regard as their property and they're willing to fight and even secede from the Union. You know what "secede" means?'

'Yes.'

'What?'

'They wanted to be a different country.'

'That's right. They wanted to be a different country and were willing to fight to achieve all this. The Union fought back and when people suffered because of the war there were those who thought this whole mess could be blamed on black people. A lot of poor white working people, a lot of Irish and German immigrants and their offspring, had been made to fear the effects of the Emancipation Proclamation.'

'Why did they fear it?'

'Because they'd been told there'd be a flood of former slaves from the south coming to New York and taking their jobs. They thought the slaves would be willing to work for even lower wages than they, the Irish and Germans, were getting.'

'Because the slaves had been used to working for nothing.'

'Good boy! That's exactly what they were told.'

'Who told them that?'

'Pro-slavery people.'

'Were there pro-slavery people in New York?'

'Sure.'

'Who were they?'

'Lots of people. People in the Democratic Party.'

'You mean the Democrats?'

'Yep.'

'I thought the Democrats were good? Aren't *we* Democrats?'

'They weren't always good. No one's always good. Listen, things got worse. So it's a hot summer in 1863 in the middle of the Civil War. Things aren't going so good for the Union and, in order to get more troops, Lincoln introduces a new draft law. You know what that means?'

'Not exactly.'

'When a government wants to force people to do things for it that people aren't volunteering to do, it "drafts" them. It coerces them into doing things against their wishes; in this case it drafted them into the Union Army.'

'Like forcing them?'

'Exactly. Lincoln introduced a federal draft law that was stricter than any before it. It was to be in the form of an enforced lottery. Any male citizen between twenty-five and thirty-five was liable to have his name drawn, and if it was, he'd have to join the army. That's a lot of men who ran the risk of being forced to join and fight for the Union army. That's a lot of men who were frightened they'd be called up, frightened or angry they might be called up.'

'Could they get out of it?'

'Thinking like a lawyer already! Yes, you could get out of it, but listen how. If you had enough money to pay a substitute to go instead of you and your name was called, the substitute would go instead of you.'

'But who'd want to do that?'

'Exactly. Not many people wanted to be someone else's substitute so it cost a lot of money to get a substitute, and who didn't have a lot of money?'

'Black people?'

'Right, but black people were exempt, which means they didn't have to go into the lottery. You know why?'

'Because Abraham Lincoln liked black people?'

'No, because they weren't even considered citizens. That's why black men were exempt from the federal draft law. But poor white men, the Irish and the Germans, they weren't exempt and they couldn't afford to hire substitutes. But there was another way out of it too. If you simply paid the government a fee you could get out of it. That sounds a pretty easy way to get out of it, doesn't it?'

'Sure, but what if you didn't have that money either?'

'Exactly! If you paid the government a fee of $300 you could forget the whole thing. But you know how long it took the average person to earn $300?'

'No.'

'A whole year. It took a whole year for the average person to earn $300. And it wasn't simply a matter of working for a year and hoping your name wasn't called while you were saving. What were you supposed to live on? In that year you had to eat, to buy clothes, to pay rent. Maybe you had a wife, maybe you had children to support. Where was the average working man going to suddenly get a whole year's worth of wages? So it's the hot summer of 1863 and many of the newspapers were run by people who were in favour of slavery.'

'Were they slave owners?'

'Probably not, but people with a lot of money often save much of their sympathy for other people who have a lot of money. So the sympathies of the newspaper owners were mostly with the slave owners. They would have known how well New York did from slavery. The slaves weren't here, they were down south, but all the cotton, all the crops – everything the slaves produced for their southern masters – it all had to be sold, traded or transported to some other market, even to some markets overseas.'

'Like Australia?'

'No, it was too early for anyone to be talking about Australia. This was 1863. I'm talking about Europe. If you had to ship goods to Europe, where would you do it from?'

'New York?'

'Exactly – greatest natural harbour in America. Everything the slaves produced, sooner or later, was coming into New York. At the least it *was* before the beginning of the Civil War. So the newspaper owners knew how much New York benefited from slavery and they started publishing articles, stories, pieces in their newspapers designed to make working-class Irish and Germans angry at the Federal Government for introducing the draft law.'

'But they were already angry.'

'That's right, they were. But the newspapers could stir things up, make them even angrier. And they did. They criticised the Federal Government for causing all this trouble just for what they called a "nigger war". They encouraged a climate in which white working-class men thought that their value was slipping compared to the value of slaves. Whereas a slave might sell for about $1000, the Irish and Germans thought now *they* could be bought for just $300 'cause it took $300 to buy them an exemption from the draft.'

'Yeah but they'd still be free. The slaves were slaves forever till they died.'

'That's absolutely right. But this is how grown men were thinking at that time because they were scared, poor, angry, and sick with that virus.'

'Racism.'

'You bet! Racism. Saturday 11 July the first New York draw was held to see who'd have to go to fight. The whole city was uneasy. It was hot. People, especially working people, were living crammed together in the tenements downtown. Whole families were living in one room. To get out, to get away, men went to the taverns and drank. They drank and they talked about all the things that bothered them. A lot of things bothered them so they drank a lot. Two days later, some time between six and seven in the morning, mobs of men started to form on the lower East Side. They moved west across Broadway and headed towards the draft office. They were armed with wooden sticks, planks and iron bars.

'As they moved uptown they collected more and more men, dissatisfied angry men who'd already been so humiliated by their circumstances, by their poverty, that they didn't know themselves any more. They had lost their individuality. You know what I mean by that?'

'Not really.'

'Each man had forgotten what made him different from the next guy. And now, added to all the chronic humiliation was his anger at the unfairness of the draft, at the possibility of becoming, not a man any more, but an animal in a pack of animals. There were thousands of men like this and they headed towards the draft office on 3rd Avenue. By the time they reached it there were 15,000 of them and they set to destroying the building. They smashed and burned it. They set all sorts of things on fire, other buildings, everything. They cut the telegraph wires so that reinforcements couldn't be sent to assist what few police were there. Remember that many of the regular police force were already in the Army. There was a small military detachment at the draft office and, even though they were armed with rifles, they were no match for the mob. It was too big. One soldier was disarmed, then beaten and kicked to death and then his body was thrown twenty feet to the ground. Train tracks were ripped up. Street cars were destroyed. The armoury on 21st Street was looted then destroyed.

'Columns of black smoke blotted out the July sun. They went after any policeman they could find, politicians, anyone who looked rich enough to pay the $300 needed to be exempt from the draft.'

'How could they tell?'

'By the way someone looked, the way they were dressed.'

'But they could be wrong. Maybe a poor person was wearing their best clothes.'

'They *could* be wrong but they didn't care. It didn't matter to them. Watch your case. Are you watching your suitcase?

'By eleven-thirty that Monday morning the draft, at least in New York, was suspended. But it was too late. The mob was in charge of Manhattan. At two-thirty that afternoon it reached the Colored Orphan Asylum. This was a charitable institution for black children who had lost their parents and who had no one else to take care of them. It had its own nursery, a school and an infirmary. There were 230 or so children. They were having a normal day when suddenly the building was rushed by the mob. Anything that could be taken, lifted, carried from the building was looted; sheets, blankets, clothes, even food. They took toys. Everything else was set on fire after someone in the mob yelled "Burn the niggers' nest!" They were black orphaned children. Was there anyone more vulnerable in all the city? The mob set upon the asylum. With clubs, brick bats, anything they had to hand. It only took about twenty minutes to destroy the whole place.'

'Did anyone try to stop it?'

'Actually, yes. It was reported that one man – he was Irish – pleaded with the mob to help the children but they set upon him too.'

'And what . . . what happened to the children?'

'The children, carrying whatever belongings they could hold, were led out through a side entrance by some staff and through the streets with a police guard. Some soldiers armed with bayonets came to escort them and keep them from the mob.'

'So none of them were killed?'

'One of them was, a ten-year-old girl.'

'What happened to her?'

'As she was being led away from the building, a piece of furniture hurled out the window of the asylum by the mob hit her in the head. It's horrible, Adam, what people can do, what they're capable of.'

'Did her friends see, the other children, I mean? Did they see her get killed?'

'I guess they must have.'

'And what happened to the rest of them, the children?'

'Well, I read one account that said they were taken to a police station on 35th Street and another version said they were put on a barge and towed out to the middle of the East River to keep them safe from the mob.'

'Which one's right?'

'I don't know. Maybe someone knows. Maybe it's one of those things . . . one of those things people don't know.'

'Why don't people know? Why are there two versions of the ending? Does that mean that one of the versions is wrong?'

'I don't know. That's what historians do, that's for historians. They take raw material and piece together the stories that make up history for the rest of us.'

'What do you mean, "raw material"?'

'Whatever they can find, eyewitness statements, police statements, newspaper reports – anything they can find. You want to see where it happened?'

'The Colored Orphan Asylum?'

'It's only a block away. You can probably see where it was from here. It's 43rd and 5th. Look, just there, that corner, you see? We'll go there but then we'll have to get a cab.'

The cab would take them to the airport where Jake Zignelik would say goodbye to his son Adam and put him on the long flight back to his mother. But before that the father dragged the son who dragged his suitcase to the corner of 43rd and 5th where the Colored Orphan Asylum had once stood. Young Adam craned his neck and looked up. He was looking in the air for furniture that might be thrown out of a window by people wanting to kill children, children who had already lost their parents. It had happened right there. It was no fairytale, not even a dark one with hidden meanings known only to grown-ups, known only to students of history, some sinister tale not really meant for children, a tale that had crossed the Atlantic from the thick forests of Europe. No, this was something that had happened right there on the corner of 43rd Street and 5th Avenue. It was New York where the Colored Orphan Asylum had been attacked. It was New York where a ten-year-old black girl had been killed when furniture pushed out of the window fell on her as she was fleeing the mob that had invaded the orphanage she'd been sent to after she was abandoned. This was the same New York his dad worked and lived in.

More than the Empire State Building or the Chrysler Building, the Statue of Liberty, Broadway or Times Square, this was the New York young Adam thought about when he got home to his mother. This was the New York he took with him on the plane. New York was the city where the orphans were attacked. Irrespective of whether Jake Zignelik thought he had turned the exercise of separation, first from his wife, then from his son, into an art, irrespective of the delis with wise-cracking old waiters who knew everything, irrespective of his dad's doting lady friends with their intoxicating perfume and cigarette cases that snapped shut with a crisp sound you wanted to try to emulate, pretty ladies who ran their fingers through a little boy's hair with the genuine but transient affection of someone temporarily engaging with a cat they were visiting, irrespective of shows he didn't always understand and museums and art galleries that were interesting up to the point where the back of his legs hurt, irrespective of the parks and *the* park, Central Park, and irrespective of kindly William McCray and his son Charles, who took care of Adam from time to time when their fathers had important work to do, New York was first and foremost to young Adam Zignelik the city with the Colored Orphan Asylum. This was the place of the orphans. Do you know about them, he would say, do you know what happened at the Colored Orphan Asylum? New York was the city of orphans.

'What was her name?'

'What?'

'What was the little girl's name?' Adam asked his father in the cab on the way to the airport, looking out the window at late 1970s Queens.

'Which little girl?'

'The little girl who was killed by the furniture the mob threw out the window at the Colored Orphan Asylum?'

'You know, I don't know.'

'Do people know?'

'I don't know that either.'

'But if the other children . . . if some of the other children saw it happen then . . . some of them would have known her name, even if she was shy . . . and they could have told the soldiers with the bayonets so some grown-ups would know her name.'

Jake Zignelik, whose thoughts had been elsewhere, realised how much his son had remembered of the story he had told him and he didn't know whether to be pleased, proud or perhaps alarmed.

'Maybe they did,' he said to his son in the back of the cab, now running his fingers through Adam's hair, 'maybe her name is known and it's just that . . . *I* don't know her name. *We* don't know her name. Maybe that's something you could look into next time you visit me. You could read up about it and tell me her name.'

William McCray was a better father to his son Charles than Jake Zignelik was to his son Adam. 'I never see him,' Jake Zignelik said to William McCray over coffee during an adjournment in the US Supreme Court.

'Well, that's not *his* fault. What did you talk about with him when he was here? You talked to him about the decision in *Brown versus Board of Education*, didn't you?'

William's son, Charles McCray, was now the Chairman of the History Department at Columbia. One of the youngest people ever to hold the position, he was also the first African American to hold the position. He had married a woman some ten years younger named Michelle. Uncommonly beautiful, Michelle was a social worker. Much as she tried to dress down, she found her looks hampered her work. Charles and Michelle had one child, a daughter, Sonia.

Adam Zignelik never forgot his father's account of the events leading up to the New York draft riots and the mob attack on the Colored Orphan Asylum in the summer of 1863. But he never found out the name of the little girl who had been killed by the furniture they had thrown out the window.

Shortly before 4.30 am that Monday morning, Adam Zignelik was to awake momentarily uncertain of where he was and experience a shortness of breath sometimes associated with a heart attack or at least with the tart panic of a nightmare. In the minutes before he woke a montage of images in his mind, mostly in monochrome, had induced a series of increasingly violent bodily tremors almost indistinguishable from a convulsion. The images, except for those of his father and of a white television newsreader on Australian television broadcast in black and white, were mainly of black people. They were from another time. He saw Emmett Till and Emmett's mother, Mamie. He saw Carole Robertson, Cynthia Wesley, Addie May Collins, all aged fourteen, and little Denise McNair, aged eleven, smiling, her braided hair tied tight with ribbons, the four little girls who had been killed when the Sixteenth Street Baptist Church in Birmingham, Alabama, was bombed by white segregationists. He saw

Arthurine Lucy. He saw Elizabeth Eckford and the others of the 'Little Rock Nine'. And he saw the Colored Orphan Asylum at the corner of 43rd and 5th. But he couldn't see the little girl from there who had been killed by the falling piece of furniture. He looked but could not find her. There he was, aged eight, alternately looking for her, looking out for falling objects, and looking out for his father, who had been there a moment ago. And whenever he thought he saw her it wasn't her but little Denise McNair, her braided hair tied tight with ribbons, smiling.

It was impossible to begrudge anyone trying to protect Denise McNair, impossible to begrudge anyone trying to help her people fight unmitigated evil, impossible to begrudge your father. But William McCray, who had fought both Hitler *and* Jim Crow, had managed to be a good father to his son Charles, now head of History at Columbia, and William McCray was someone his son *could* find, someone his son had *always* been able to find. But on the corner of 43rd and 5th Adam Zignelik couldn't find his father.

'Hold on to your suitcase.'

That was him, but when Adam looked around he wasn't there any more. Adam was there, trying to look out for Denise McNair as everybody else on 5th Avenue brushed past, oblivious to the danger. They were killing abandoned children on that very block. There had been Jake's legacy, but it was largely Charles McCray's example and later, his assistance, that had led Adam to the History Department at Columbia. He went there first as an undergraduate. He graduated with a history major but, uncertain what to do next and with some guilt at leaving his mother alone, Adam returned to Australia and tried to make a career for himself as a journalist. For almost six years he toiled away but it irked him that he wasn't progressing faster. It was Charles McCray, with whom he had kept in regular contact, who got him to consider a PhD in history with a view to becoming an academic historian. At twenty-eight, Adam moved back to New York and enrolled in the PhD program of the History Department at NYU. The fashion within civil rights history over the previous decade or so had been to eschew the 'great man' theory or school of civil rights history in favour of social history that focused on the nameless people who constituted the bulk of the movement.

Adam used his father as an inspiration for reacquainting scholars with the importance of the civil rights legal strategy. His argument was a reminder that without concomitant changes in the law there would have been no grounds on which the local activists could base their fight. It was because of the success of the legal strategy in cases such as *Brown versus Board of Education* that the local activists were able to galvanise black communities around the country, particularly in the south, and tell them the law was now on their side. The fight could be taken from there. Adam's dissertation served to remind historians in the area just how difficult it was in those days, in that climate, to win the cases from first instance all the way up to the Supreme Court and how hard it was to get civil rights legislation enacted. He wrote of the need to look again at the legal strategy, not as engaged in by one great man or great woman, but as the outcome of the concerted efforts of a group, a group of lawyers.

All the while he was at NYU he stayed involved in the Columbia community. He took classes at Columbia and once a month came uptown for a 'Twentieth Century Politics and Society' seminar. He met and maintained friendships with Columbia graduate students from the History Department. It was through one of them that he met Diana, the woman who had grown not unaccustomed to the rhythm of his recent nightmares. And of course, there was Charles McCray, who was for him a cross between a mentor, an older brother and a 'co-conspirator'. The 'conspiracy' was one between children of the movement. They could say things to each other that it was almost impossible to say to anyone else.

It was a game Charles and Adam used to play, alone and in private. It involved saying things that were unacceptable within mainstream political discourse. Sometimes the 'things' were statements or propositions many people knew to be true or likely to be true. At other times they were simply defamatory statements they came up with to amuse each other. But none of the 'things' could be said, at least publicly, without contravening political correctness. Often after a few drinks, the 'things' were just things they both knew the other didn't believe. This latter category of 'thing', even more than the former, would have them in tears of laughter by the end of an evening.

It was on the strength of his PhD and, again, with the assistance of Charles who, though not yet chairman, was already a highly
respected member of the department and a well-regarded scholar of the
Reconstruction, that Adam joined the faculty at Columbia. His dissertation became the basis for a book. As the telegenic son of Jake with a
Britishoid accent, Adam, for a time at least, was plucked up by the media
as 'the son' and, consequently, the book had sold better than anyone,
including Adam, had expected. He wrote a few non-scholarly articles in
newspapers and magazines and was even asked to be a 'talking head' in a
television documentary for public television.

But even as this was happening, he wondered whether other people
were wondering whether his public persona was going to his head. It
wasn't. His anxiety over what his colleagues might be wondering would
not permit this. It crowded out most other things. Whether they were
wondering this or not, colleagues did start to ask, 'So what's your next
project about?' More importantly, he started to ask himself the same
thing. When he didn't have an answer for himself it amplified a deeper
question he had long fought to silence. Was he an intellectual light-
weight? Perhaps he was only ever going to have one idea. He wondered if
he was capable of writing another book that would contribute to scholarly debate in any meaningful way.

But worrying if he would *ever* have another sufficiently good idea was
now a luxury he could no longer afford because it wasn't enough to have
a good idea one day. It probably wasn't enough to have one even now.
He really needed to have had one before now because, having spent five
years at Columbia with only one book to show for it, an untenured
academic seeking tenure was in very big trouble. It would take an internal
departmental committee to decide to put him up for tenure. That was
standard practice. If this happened, the matter would then go before a
university-wide committee, the 'ad hoc' committee, which consisted of
academics from all over the university. But the real cut-off point was
his own department, now headed by his friend Charles McCray, and
Charles had more than an inkling that Adam had nothing about to come
out. Adam would have discussed it with Charles if he had. What Charles
didn't know was that it wasn't a matter of simply buying time, even were

that a simple matter. Adam had hit a brick wall. He didn't have even the seed of something interesting. He felt he was finished and he didn't want to put Charles through the unpleasant task of having to confirm that he was indeed finished. Charles had been leaving messages gently suggesting that they needed to talk. Their friendship and history would allow only gentleness. But for how long? The days in which it was legitimate not to have yet responded to any of Charles' messages had evaporated till there were, so to speak, only hours left. Soon Adam's failure to respond would itself become the first topic of their next conversation. Perhaps, after all, that's what Adam wanted.

Adam was going to have to talk to him sooner or later about Diana, who lay beside him every night. He had almost struck her in his near convulsion shortly before 4.30 am that Monday morning, she lying asleep beside him, and he, in a time unrelated to real time, an eight-year-old boy craning his neck on the corner of 43rd Street and 5th Avenue. He had never discovered the little girl's name, the name of the orphan in the city of orphans, and even then, just before 4.30 am that Monday morning, only hours away from teaching, from assaulting a class with his particular version of 'What is History?', he was still, all those years later, replacing the missing picture in his mind of the little girl victim of 1863 from the Colored Orphan Asylum with the image of Denise McNair, who had been killed in the Sixteenth Street Baptist Church in Birmingham, Alabama, for the same reason by the same people a hundred years later.

Adam saw little eleven-year-old, feisty yet caring Denise McNair. He could have fixed on any of the other child victims. It was her eyes. More than anything else, it was her eyes. Not merely beautiful, they were expressive. They held more than a child's eyes should hold; mischief, warmth, intelligence, sweetness, yes, but also a kind of understanding, as though she understood things you were going to need to understand. That's who Adam saw when he saw the little girl victim of 1863 from the Colored Orphan Asylum.

'Dad!'

On a black-and-white television screen a newsreader read the news for the Australian Broadcasting Corporation. A little boy sat cross-legged in front of the television waiting to hear something to remember that might interest his father at the end of the week when he spoke to him over the telephone all the way across all those oceans. His father had once told him he 'liked the sound of this Hawke guy'. What was his name? Bob Hawke. Ever since then Adam had collected as many facts as he could about Bob Hawke to tell his father.

Bob Hawke, an Oxford University Rhodes Scholar, was the Australian Council of Trade Unions' first paid advocate before the Arbitration Commission, the body that determined the minimum wage for the whole country. Subsequently a president of the Australian Council of Trade Unions and a member of the governing board of the International Labour Organisation, he campaigned against apartheid in South Africa, among other ills. Jake Zignelik liked the sound of the guy.

Searching for something to tell his father that might interest him, Adam would phone him from his mother's house and talk about Bob Hawke. And Jake, when stretched for something to say to his son that mattered even a little, would often ask, 'How's your mate, Bob Hawke?'

The little boy sat alone cross-legged on the carpet in front of the black-and-white news broadcast and then ran around the house from room to room looking for somebody to tell. But each room was empty. Diana was still asleep. She wanted to have a child. She wanted to marry Adam and have a child with him.

'Dad!'

Charles had been leaving messages gently suggesting that they needed to talk. Adam had hit a brick wall. He wanted to spare Charles the embarrassment of having to tell him that it was all over for him. Diana wanted them to have a child. If you have a child you have to be able to feed it.

'Watch your suitcase! Always watch your suitcase.'

When the eight-year-old boy craned his neck to look up at the corner of 43rd and 5th he saw the face, the eyes, of Denise McNair. If you have a child you have to know its name. Don't you have to know the names of all the children? Can you have a child and not give it a name? Can it be done? Maybe someone would tell him because he really didn't know.

'Dad!'

By the time Hawke had been elected Prime Minister of Australia, Adam's mother had died of breast cancer and his father, Jake Zignelik, had died of a heart attack. Shortly before 4.30 am that Monday morning Diana woke up beside the writhing Adam, her Adam, and put her arms around him to try to calm him.

'Shhh! It's okay. It's okay.' She whispered it soothingly in the greyish-blue light of their Morningside Heights apartment in the north-west corner of an island in the city of orphans.

'Shhh!'

She warmed his back with her body and hugged him. Adam, exhausted, was gasping for air. His cheeks were wet. She held him tighter. She loved him. She wanted to have a child with him. Adam was awake now. In a couple of weeks they would be separated.

part three

THE BUS JERKED TO A STOP at a set of traffic lights on its way uptown. The sudden change of momentum woke Lamont Williams. He had made it through the day, his fourth day as a probationary employee in Building Services at Memorial Sloan-Kettering Cancer Center. He had even managed to find a seat on the bus, a window seat, on the first of the two buses he needed to catch to get home to the Bronx. For a moment he had fallen asleep, his head against the window, and in that moment he relived random snatches of the years he had spent in Mid-Orange Correctional Facility. He sometimes dreamed he was back there or in Woodbourne where he had spent three years before being transferred to Mid-Orange. Sometimes he dreamed of his daughter who, when he woke on the bus going home, was eight years old. Her age was one thing that didn't depend on whether he was able to find her or not. These dreams, the ones with his daughter in them, didn't require him to be asleep.

It was the end of his shift and the bus was crowded. His head was still against the window and no one watching would have realised he was awake as he looked around through almost closed eyes. The man seated beside him was reading the *New York Post*. An older white woman next to this man stood trying to read what she could of the man's paper while holding a small cage that contained a very docile cat. Lamont had trouble making out the age or breed of the cat but preferred not to risk looking more carefully in case the cat-lady, observing he was awake and taking an interest in her cat, attempted to press a claim to his seat.

Lamont's daughter might be anywhere in the city. Then again, she might not be in the city at all. She might not even be in the state. And yet, she could be on that very bus. It was too crowded to see everyone but even if Lamont could, he hadn't seen his daughter since she was two and a half, so who exactly was he continually looking for since his release? How many light-skinned black girls could he find on buses, on the subway and on the street if he looked hard enough? He knew he could get arrested for looking too hard, not that that was going to stop him.

Somewhere in the city there was another bus crawling through the streets, exhaling fumes and edging its nose tentatively between the traffic. This one was just moderately crowded and only a handful of people were standing. One of those standing was a child. A light-skinned black girl with braided hair tied tight with red ribbons, she was aged somewhere between seven and ten. On top of a red T-shirt she wore a mid-season jacket, unzipped, as if in anticipation of a change of season in the middle of her day. Seeing a newly vacant seat towards the back of the bus in the section with the row of seats that flip up to accommodate wheelchairs the young girl took it. She could not have been sitting for much more than a minute when she offered her newly acquired seat to a man she'd just noticed who was standing talking to a seated friend of his.

The standing friend had not by any measure been desperate to sit down and when the little girl actively volunteered her seat to him he was instantly arrested by her charm, her grace, her politeness, and by the warmth of her personality. She had delivered all this with the manner of her offer and with something inside her she was too young to realise she had and certainly too young to name. After engaging her in conversation for a few minutes he asked her whether she was travelling alone. Unfazed by this question, the young girl with the braided hair tied tight with red ribbons waved her hand in the direction of the other end of the bus as if to indicate she was not travelling alone. At this the man seemed relieved.

A stop or two after this, the young girl moved towards the exit. There were two older women, somewhere in their sixties, standing with her by the exit. They had made their way from the front of the bus. She talked freely to them and an observer of the whole scene could have been forgiven for thinking that one of these women was the little girl's grand-mother. The two women in their sixties and the young girl were among a number of passengers who got off at the next stop. Through the still open door it was possible to hear one of the women – they were in the street by then – ask the girl, 'Are you travelling alone, dear?'

There was a story Lamont had been told in Mid-Orange about a certain cat-loving Corrections Officer who had worked there some years before Lamont's time.

The CO had found a prisoner feeding cats that had strayed into the prison. Not only did he not write him a ticket that would have gone on the cat-feeding prisoner's record, he also let him continue feeding the cats. Then some of the other prisoners started helping this prisoner and the CO, seeing the effect caring for the cats had on these often embit-tered, angry men, started bringing bags of dry cat food into the prison to help them. Then one day, when the wrong CO caught the wrong prisoner with a bag of the dry cat food, all hell broke loose and what had been tolerated till then no longer was.

After a while there were not so many cats finding their way into Mid-Orange. But somebody in authority must have noticed the effect taking care of the cats was having on those prisoners involved because, by the time Lamont had been transferred from Woodbourne to Mid-Orange, a program had been established for prisoners to care for animals. It involved dogs, not cats, and the prisoners weren't simply feeding the dogs, they were training them. 'Puppies Behind Bars', the program was called. Prisoners were being taught to train dogs to be guide dogs for the blind. After September 11, some dogs were even trained for the New York Police Department and for the Bureau of Alcohol, Tobacco and Firearms. They were trained to sniff for explosives. Of course the dogs were not exposed to explosives in the prison but much of the training was the same as that for guide dogs. They needed to be socialised, taught how to be around people, and how to follow instructions even in situa-tions of stress. So did the dogs.

Like many of the prisoners, Lamont had applied to work in the dog program. But hardly anybody got the chance to work in that detail. It was a feel-good story. It was even a true story. But it didn't alter the fact that most of the programs existed in name only for the vast bulk of the Mid-Orange prison population. There just weren't enough places in any of the programs so you put your name down and waited like you waited for everything else. If you had something to trade or to sell, or you were well connected, you received preferential treatment. The saying went, 'It's not who you *know* but who you *blow*.'

'Well, you gots to be anatomically gifted one way or the other,' Numbers had explained to Lamont not long after Lamont had been transferred from Woodbourne to Mid-Orange, just as Numbers himself had been some time earlier. When Lamont sought clarification Numbers tried to explain.

'Well now, how else a *straight* brother gonna know how to give head? There's "trial and error", I guess, but you don't wanna go gettin' *that* wrong. And even "trial and error" don't apply at the other end. Know what I'm saying?'

'No.'

'Okay, there's some who so sensitive down there they tear up every second time they take a dump. These brothers frightened of roughage. But with some brothers it just slide up nice and easy like they was born already with Vaseline up there. So when the CO spreads your cheeks after a contact visit from family and such, this man can breathe easy knowing these dumb-ass lazy COs ain't gonna go that far up inside of him. Now *that* man truly blessed. He a rich man inside; a living, breathing, walking Fort Knox. Can't no one *learn* that. It's a gift from God.'

Lamont was not so anatomically, or otherwise, blessed. He put his name down for the puppy program just as he did for plumbing, carpentry and horticulture. He got none of them. Like almost half the prisoners in Mid-Orange he worked as a porter keeping the prison clean, sweeping up cigarette butts and other garbage the prisoners had left. But it was the dog program he'd really wanted to be in, particularly after he'd caught sight of a handful of other prisoners in the distance walking and then grooming some Labs not much older than puppies. Privately he'd prided himself on his capacity to limit his wants and expectations. That seemed to him the best way to survive his sentence. Whatever comfort even cigarettes might have provided he refused to smoke them in order to avoid being addicted to a currency he would have to trade for. But seeing the dogs hurt him unexpectedly. It cut through him.

He wondered if he would ever again hold his daughter in his arms, squeeze her tight, rock her to sleep. He told himself he would. He promised himself. What did she look like now? Did his daughter look like him? Did she look like her mother or like the combination of them that she was? Often in prison when he caught sight of his own reflection he tried to imagine different combinations of his face and that of his daughter's mother merging into the face of a little girl. He was in the yard at Mid-Orange sweeping up over by a puddle one day in spring when he thought for a moment that he had it perfectly. There in the puddle, as he narrowed his eyes to a squint, was finally, completely still, a little girl's face. That was probably how she looked. Had to be. He could summon up the image again if only he could find and hold a clear reflection of himself.

'Three years,' Numbers pronounced. 'No one come no more after three years. They give up on you . . . like you dead. You can cross Christmas off of your calendar too. Rip it out.'

'What's that "three years" bullshit?' Lamont asked.

'I'm just saying.'

'Ain't no law say people don't visit after three years.'

'It's a law o' averages, Lamont.'

'Well, if it's an average then some people stop coming *before* three years up and some still coming *after* three years, right? That's what average means.'

'I guess,' Numbers conceded before adding, 'I ain't never met no one here above average like that.'

Lamont spent the first three years of his six-year sentence at Woodbourne and the last three years at Mid-Orange. Of those few who came to see him from time to time at Woodbourne, it was only his grandmother who stayed the more than three-year course and continued to visit him at Mid-Orange. She wasn't able to come very often because of her work as a kitchen hand and the distance from Co-op City. And she was elderly and not well. His cousin Michelle visited him in Mid-Orange once.

'One good thing 'bout Mid-Orange,' Numbers told him when they re-met at the beginning of Lamont's time there, 'they got four coffee shops within a five-mile radius. That's more 'n usual for your average medium-security country correctional facility. Increase the chances someone come visit you. Problem is . . . they all Dunkin' Donuts. No one drive two hours eat that shit.'

During the early part of Lamont's time at Woodbourne some of the people from his neighbourhood made the trek to visit him. His old friend Michael couldn't come because he was serving time somewhere else. Michael had been the one to get Lamont to drive his van to the liquor store for what Lamont hadn't realised would become an armed robbery, the one for which he'd serve six years. But Michael's younger brother, who had only ever been an acquaintance, came quite a few times in the beginning. Lamont didn't understand why he was coming. He wasn't an unfriendly young man but he was a good deal younger and clearly didn't enjoy coming and, in any case, he had Michael, his own brother, to visit in another prison if he needed an excuse to visit a prison. He didn't like making conversation for conversation's sake much more than Lamont did but he came anyway and asked the usual questions with the usual, maybe even more than usual, discomfort.

After a while it became clear to Lamont that Michael's brother was coming because of Michael, possibly even on his instructions. That was the only explanation he could find. Lamont reasoned that Michael had never meant for him to become involved in the robbery. He himself had fallen under the influence of a much younger man, a reckless man with an addiction and a gun and a way of talking, a way of being, that made certain people want to be around him. The idea of robbing the liquor store was the younger man's and he'd arrived at it only once Lamont had driven them to the liquor store. Michael said that he hadn't known about it until he and the younger man had left Lamont in the van and gone into the store. Had Michael gone along with it? From the liquor store's security video footage it looked as though he had. The younger man had the gun on him. Michael hadn't known. That's what he said. There was hardly any interval between the younger man's conception of the plan and its execution. He was already carrying the gun. They had Lamont's van. It must have seemed to the younger man too good an opportunity to pass up. So, Lamont figured, Michael's younger brother had to be visiting him for Michael. It was an attempt to make things right as much as possible for the mess he'd unintentionally got him into, given he wasn't in a position to send him any money.

On the other hand, Lamont realised, it was also possible that Michael had set him up, that he and the younger man with the gun had planned all along to rob the liquor store without telling Lamont and then count on Lamont to drive them away. The simplicity of that hypothesis gave it a certain attractiveness. Lamont could drive and he had his own van. Not everyone in the neighbourhood had their own vehicle. This could have been why Michael had brought Lamont to meet the young gun-owner.

It was a possibility Lamont did not entertain for very long. He couldn't bring himself to believe that Michael had tricked him, not like this. It seemed more likely to him that when the kid decided on the spur of the moment to rob the store, Michael, not wanting to court his derision and put to risk a new and untested acquaintance, had abandoned all reason, not to mention a friendship that was almost as old as he was.

Michael too had grown up in Co-op City and they had been friends since grade school. Michael's mother had permitted him to go to Lamont's place after school even though she knew Lamont's grandmother would still be at work. She trusted Lamont. The two of them would grab a Hawaiian Punch or a High-C from the refrigerator and watch *Looney Tunes*, the *Electric Company*, old Tom and Jerry or Rocky and Bullwinkle, which Lamont enjoyed more than Michael. Lamont had always been more comfortable than Michael keeping his own company. Lamont's apparent self-sufficiency was something Michael had often felt envious of without knowing that this was what he was feeling. It had only made him value Lamont's time and attention all the more.

They had learned to ride their bikes at the same time and had ridden them together on the bike path along the Greenway all the way from Section 1 to Section 4 to the movie theatre or the Baskin-Robbins ice-cream store. They even spent time in the pet store choosing the pets they'd have bought if either of them had been permitted to keep a pet. When they got a little older and a little braver they went further to Section 5, the newest outlying section, taking what was called 'Killer Curve' to get there. Michael had once lost control on 'Killer Curve', going over the handlebars and requiring five stitches in his chest. It was Lamont who had taken care of everything. Afraid to call Michael's house for fear of getting him into trouble with his sometimes volatile mother and with his own grandmother still at work, he called his cousin, Michelle, from a payphone.

Although she was only two years older, her role in Lamont's life ranged between that of a friend and that of an older sister, according to the demands of the situation. When Michelle was convinced it wasn't a prank she said she would call an ambulance and told Lamont to stay with him. She arrived there herself on her bike before the ambulance arrived. She saw Lamont sitting beside Michael with his jacket draped across Michael's chest. The two of them went to the ER with Michael. While Michael was getting stitches in his chest, Lamont asked Michelle how she could have thought even for a moment that his call could have been a prank. If it *had* been a prank, it would have been Michael who had put him up to it, Michelle had explained as they waited at the hospital. He was about to protest that her explanation unfairly impugned his friend's character when he remembered a couple of instances she could use to substantiate her point if she needed to so he didn't press it, even though, in general, Michael had never really been able to exercise much influence over him. Sometimes he had done things out of boredom that he regretted but this was hardly due to Michael's influence. It had just been that Michael happened to have been there at the time.

It had been with Michael that Lamont had tasted the thrill of shoplifting at Cappy's, the local stationery store. Lamont liked to read the magazines but Michael had always been more interested in the candy. Michael was the first to steal and it had been candy, Now and Laters and Hershey Bars he'd stolen. Lamont had had his head buried in a magazine and hadn't known what Michael was doing until they'd left the store. Michael had said he had to try. No one saw a thing. It was too easy not to at least give it a try. The candy tasted better when you took it, Michael said. They'd ridden furiously to the Pine Island playground near Building Five and eaten the candy by the swings. But it hadn't tasted better to Lamont. On the contrary, the chocolate didn't seem as rich. Its taste was thinner on his tongue and on the roof of his mouth. It was as though someone had taken some of the chocolate out of the chocolate, as though the chocolate had been corrupted by shame. It had never really occurred to him before that his actions could dilute what should have been a standard almost manufacturer-guaranteed reward.

Without fully understanding why, he'd been momentarily angry with Michael, who was eating his chocolate like a hungry animal and in between bites grinning like an idiot. What would Michelle say if she knew? It was the magazines Lamont had wanted more than the candy anyway. Later on he would take some magazines and comic books. There was shame then too, but at least he'd really wanted them. He could never have afforded them. Shame vied with excitement and a sense of accomplishment. Eventually he was caught.

He wondered why he preferred the conversations he had with himself to most of the conversations he had with Michael. The self he would talk to understood things so much better than Michael did, better than anyone did. This self saw everything that happened to him and didn't forget any of it. It always saw his loneliness even if it wasn't always able to ameliorate it. When others misunderstood him this self did not. This self saw him *want* his grandmother to ask and want her *not* to ask how school was, both at the same time, when she'd come home in the evening. It saw him prefer to watch television than answer her question and then regret that he hadn't. He didn't want her never to ask. He couldn't admit any of this even to himself. But he could to this self.

Years later, while he was serving his sentence at Woodbourne, he thought about those times and wondered who was asking his grandmother about *her* day while he was in Woodbourne. He should have asked her about her day back then.

Michelle was infinitely better company than Michael, far more interesting and entertaining, though much worse at handball. Being two years older though and not living quite so close, it wasn't as easy to get time with her. 'Can I go see 'Chelle?' he'd ask his grandmother, who delighted in her grandchildren's affection for each other. It was Michelle who had introduced him to the Piers Anthony 'Xanth' books. She took him to the library where, as she explained, the books would always be waiting for him. He liked to read and to draw there but was unsure to whom it was safe to admit this. He had taken Michael to the library but Michael had quickly become bored. Michael seemed to feel there wasn't much in the library for him and he was bewildered and sometimes annoyed that Lamont wanted to go there.

Michelle had parakeets and she'd let him feed them. She'd let him hold them and place them on his shoulder. When her father was buying her sneakers she'd make sure it happened on a day when Lamont was with her so that her father would end up feeling obliged to buy Lamont a pair too. And he did. One year he chose the blue suede Pumas and he showed her how you were meant to wear the laces; two colours intricately woven together, left untied and stuffed under the tongue of the sneaker to raise it prominently. His grandmother was always at him to tie his shoes. She didn't understand. Michelle did.

It was better to go shopping with Michelle. She encouraged him to wear the right jeans; Sassoon, Jordache or Sergio Valenti and especially Tale Lord. It was hard to get his grandmother to buy what he wanted when she took him on the bus to shop for clothes on Fordham Road. The older he got, the worse these trips got. The love he had for his grandmother never wavered but the only thing worse than having her buy his clothes was having people see him shopping for clothes for himself with her. At these times he had to fight a desire to run away from her or even, literally, push her away from him. He never did, nor did he ever even permit himself to show his grandmother his frustration.

It was during this period of his life, he could recall, that he first began feeling a chronic low-grade nervousness, a restlessness coupled with an anxiety that was more or less constant, one that was still with him. It was always as though he was expecting a calamitous event that he was unable to identify and was therefore completely unable to prevent or avoid. The exhaustion this produced was such that no amount of rest or sleep ever relieved him of it. Because it had been so long a time since he had not felt this way, being anxious seemed normal to him and, in a sense, for him, it was. He might even have had it from earliest childhood. He couldn't be sure.

He had thought of discussing these feelings with Michelle because if anyone would have understood how he felt it would have been her. She was the smartest person he knew, maybe smarter than his teachers, because she seemed to understand things he hadn't wanted to say and even some things he didn't say. Maybe it was because she was two years older. Maybe it was because she was a girl or because both her parents lived at home with her and everyone – her parents, their grandmother, grown-ups in the neighbourhood – they all knew *she* was going to be okay.

He had told Michelle how he'd felt about the horseshoe crab incident and what had happened in class and just seeing the understanding written on her face helped him make sense of it a little more. At that moment, with all her concentration on him and her eyes so full of the story he was telling her, his love for his cousin was great enough for him to imagine it was possible that, just by knowing her, he might be all right.

Mr Shapiro had been teaching the class about dinosaurs, Lamont had explained. Over a few lessons he'd gone through the origins of life from the single-celled amoeba to plankton through to the various kinds of dinosaurs, reptiles, birds, apes and finally on to people. He was getting kids to name existing animals that might be easily identified as descendants of now-extinct species. Answers volunteered included zebras, elephants and lizards. But Lamont felt he had the best example and, from his response, it seemed Mr Shapiro agreed with him. Lamont hadn't known if he had ever felt so good. Horseshoe crabs! They're descended from trilobites. Mr Shapiro exclaimed, 'Man, that *is* a good answer!'

Encouraged, Lamont took the matter further.

'They're real big. They got long pointy tails. And they . . . They look prehistoric.'

Mr Shapiro said, 'Excellent! Would you like to come out to the front, Lamont, and draw one for us on the board?'

So Lamont got up out of his seat and went up to the front and started drawing a horseshoe crab.

'They have eyes but they can't see too good. It's their tails that's impor-tant. Maybe more than the eyes, not sure. They use their tails in the sand and dirt and stuff on the ground. I think they're really old.'

'Excellent!' Mr Shapiro said. 'You certainly know a lot about them, Lamont.'

'I seen 'em.'

'In a book?'

'Yeah, but I've seen real ones too.'

'Lamont, are you sure? I'm not sure about that.'

But Lamont had seen them. Near Section 5 en route from Section 1 where Lamont lived, it was possible, if you were sufficiently motivated, to make one's way down to the Hutchinson River. Lamont had done it often. There in the shallows of the banks of the Hutchinson River he had found a species of 'crab' that he'd learned at the library were horseshoe crabs.

'I could show you, Mr Shapiro.'

'That would be good. Maybe one day.' Mr Shapiro was packing his satchel.

'When? After school?'

'Sure. Maybe one day after school.'

'When? Next week maybe?'

'Maybe.'

'Next Wednesday after school?'

'Well, okay, maybe next Wednesday.'

'I'll draw you a map. Show you how to get there.'

'Okay, thanks. Thanks, Lamont.'

Michael was with him after school the following Wednesday afternoon on the banks of the river. An hour and a half had passed when Michael told Lamont what he already knew, that Mr Shapiro wasn't coming.

'He don't want to hear about that stuff no more. It's over.'

'Well, he mighta got held up or something. Mighta got lost. Maybe he thinks it's gonna rain. Michael, be bad if he comes later and I'm not down here.'

'He ain't never comin', Lamont.'

'Well, maybe. I don't know. But I *know* there are horseshoe crabs in here. I'm gonna show Michelle too. *You* see how they use their tails when they walk?'

'Shapiro . . . He ain't comin',' Michael insisted. 'He knows there ain't no dumb ol' horseshoe shit . . . but you get your cousin down here . . . I sure show her somethin' . . . real pointy tail!'

That was all he had a chance to say before Lamont landed a punch to Michael's face, the force of which pushed Michael on to the ground. Lamont stood there for a moment looking at him. It shocked him to think that he'd done that.

Lamont didn't know why he'd let Michael make him so angry. They rode their bikes home against the wind without speaking. They didn't see each other for a while after that. It didn't bother Lamont much.

He hadn't been seeing so much of Michelle at the time either. She was going to Bronx Science now and claimed to have more homework than ever. She made it sound genuinely heroic, like something to which Lamont might aspire, but she did it without ever being at all self-promotional or sounding in any way as though she thought herself superior to him, or to anyone else. At least that's how it sounded over the phone whenever he said a little sadly but without accusation, 'You sure are busy now, 'Chelle.'

But on his birthday Michelle's parents had taken him, Michelle and their grandmother downtown to a steak restaurant. He didn't remember now exactly where it was except that it was near Union Square. He remembered that. It had to have been around there because they walked through Union Square on the way to and from the place Michelle's father had parked the car. Lamont liked going out with Michelle's family. He'd wanted it to happen more often. Her mother, obviously on Michelle's instructions, had bought Lamont more books from the Xanth series, books only Michelle would have known he hadn't already read. Her father, again clearly guided by her, had got him a few action figures, Micronauts with translucent plastic limbs and a couple of accessories, which Michelle knew he admired. In addition, he got two of the original highly complex Shogun Warrior action figures, which Michelle explained later could only be bought in Chinatown. This was before Mattel started turning them out. Owning these could definitely enhance the social life of someone in Lamont's position. It was as though, recognising that she was seeing him less and less often and that this was the way it was going to be, Michelle had engineered the day by way of partial reparations. It worked.

Lamont had started spending time with Danny Ehrlich. This pleased Lamont's grandmother because Danny's father was a teacher at Truman High School. She thought Danny Ehrlich would be a better influence on Lamont than Michael was. Mr Ehrlich was said to be just about the most laid-back teacher there was, a mellow hippy throwback. That was partly why the story about him, the famous Mr Ehrlich story, spread as fast as it did.

The story involved a student in Mr Ehrlich's class, a skinny black kid from the neighbourhood known as the 'Valley' in Boston Secor outside Co-op City just across the highway. This student once drew a swastika on the blackboard. One of the worst-behaved kids in the class, he knew it was a bad symbol, one that shocked people, one that offended, even frightened some people, but he didn't understand why. On that day he learned why and so did everyone else in the class. Mr Ehrlich was said to have gone temporarily insane.

Of course there were various versions of the story that made the rounds. In one, he hit the boy repeatedly. In another, the kid peed himself because of the verbal lashing he got. In some versions it was racism that Mr Ehrlich talked about. Some said it was slavery. Some said he made the class write an essay about being different. Others said Mr Ehrlich gave a long talk about something called 'Nazism' after which he just calmed down suddenly and it was all over. What was common to all the versions was that there was a day, just one, when that old hippy teacher, Mr Ehrlich, absolutely lost it. That became the canonical story.

Lamont was in Danny Ehrlich's class and neither of them had ever been students of Mr Ehrlich. Danny too was a fan of the Xanth books. After spending some time together in class, Danny invited Lamont to come over after school. Lamont's grandmother first learned of the boys' friendship when Lamont asked her permission to go. He couldn't help but notice her pleasure at their association. Lamont took along one of the Shogun Warrior action figures Michelle's father had bought in Chinatown for his birthday. He chose one of the bad guys, a fabulous mix of dye-cast and plastic articulated limbs with ball joints in the shoulders, feet and even the neck. The paint job was smooth and clean. There was no bleeding of colours, just a well-defined fierce-red shield with yellow rib-like indents covering the chest. The head, disproportionately small and, by virtue of this, extra creepy, consisted of almost nothing but a skull with two blue stripes going from the front at the top of the eye sockets over the crown all the way back to where the skull joined the neck. Other than his feet, which were blue, the rest of him was a metallic silver. To see him was to want him because without even holding him he could set a boy's imagination on fire. The first time you actually held him you were smitten, you were in awe.

Lamont watched Danny's eyes as he pulled the bad guy Shogun Warrior out of his bag. Danny Ehrlich saw the Shogun Warrior and his eyes widened till they were as round as golf balls. Then solemnly, Lamont handed it over to Danny Ehrlich, who stood there for a moment perfectly still, just trying to get a sense of its weight. Danny gently ran the thumb and index finger of his left hand over the length of the Shogun Warrior. He inhaled deeply, exhaled slowly, and said quietly, 'Wow, I don't believe it!'

Still holding the Shogun Warrior, Danny Ehrlich turned suddenly and, without warning, ran down the hall to his mother in the kitchen yelling, 'Look, Mom! Look what Lamont gave me. Isn't it incredible?!'

Lamont swallowed hard. He hadn't expected Danny Ehrlich to think he'd given it to him and he didn't know what to do. He walked slowly down the hall towards Danny and his mother. He'd never been in the kitchen before. He'd never met Danny's mother before either. Danny Ehrlich had seemed to like his mother a lot. He stood in the doorway of the kitchen.

'Thank you so much, Lamont, for that incredible monster,' Danny's mother said kindly.

'It's a Shogun Warrior, Mom,' Danny corrected her with a momentary impatience. 'Look at the arms!'

Lamont couldn't go home without it. That just couldn't happen. His grandmother would miss it. He was sure she would. He'd asked her permission to take it to Danny Ehrlich's place and she'd permitted it only if he'd promised to be careful with it. He *had* been careful. He'd kept it safe at school all day, kept it hidden all day. All he had done at the very end of the day when he was alone inside the Ehrlichs' home was to show it to his new friend, Danny Ehrlich, and to allow Danny to hold it. That was all he'd done. And now he was in all sorts of trouble. Michelle might want to see it again one day too. She had told her father precisely what it was he should buy Lamont and even where to go to get it. This was one of the best things Lamont had. Maybe it was the very best thing he had. His uncle had got it in Chinatown for him for his birthday. There was no telling what it cost. There would be no telling what would happen if he didn't bring it back home with him. Should he say something to Danny Ehrlich? He couldn't. This was a calamity for which his anxiety had been rehearsing and for which it would rehearse long after the event was over. It was the flavour of his adult life to come.

Danny Ehrlich wasn't in the room when Lamont put the Shogun Warrior action figure back in his school bag. He was going to smuggle it back to his grandmother's apartment. No one saw him do it and Lamont wondered whether he'd get away with it. Perhaps Danny Ehrlich would forget about the Shogun Warrior action figure. No, this was not possible. Could it happen that Danny Ehrlich might think that he himself had lost it? After all, he had quite a lot of stuff. But this was unlikely, Lamont concluded. In fact, it was more than unlikely, it was impossible.

Lamont had felt sick from the moment he'd heard Danny Ehrlich telling Danny's mother that Lamont had given him the the Shogun Warrior. He felt even sicker when he secreted the action figure back into his bag. To the pain of his still possible imminent loss of the Shogun Warrior, to the expectation of his grandmother's anger at him for giving Michelle's gift away, and to his incredulity that something so inherently innocent had turned into such a nightmare was now added not only his gut-wrenching guilt for stealing the toy back but something even more powerful, more immediate, something that screamed like Danny Ehrlich's father had in the story about him and the kid from 'the Valley', screamed till there were globules of sweat on his palms. It was terror. Lamont was afraid he would be caught with the

Shogun Warrior action figure in his bag even though it was his. As it happened, he wasn't caught. He made it back home with the toy in his bag undetected.

Lamont said nothing about the incident to his grandmother. The next day Danny Ehrlich said nothing about it either. Perhaps he hadn't yet noticed it was gone, Lamont speculated to himself. But this was clearly wrong. Of course Danny Ehrlich had noticed. Lamont was never again invited back to the Ehrlich house. In fact, Danny Ehrlich hardly ever spoke to Lamont again after that day. On the few occasions he did speak to him it was in a strangely polite way, not at all like a boy of his age would normally speak but in the tone of a teacher or a parent or a social worker. It was as though Danny Ehrlich had been coached by an adult on how he should speak to Lamont Williams should the need to speak to him again ever arise.

Michelle never asked to see the Shogun Warrior action figure again nor did she ask to see anything else Lamont had been given for his birthday. Michelle wore perfume now and her feminine charm, the charm that had so engaged Michael's imagination on the banks of the Hutchinson River, was even more evident. Then there was her poise and her intellectual hunger for things just out of Lamont's reach, out of his then universe of awareness. It wasn't merely that he didn't understand these things – he didn't even know what they were, just *that* they were. She had a slightly different way of speaking. He felt that it was a better way of speaking. She didn't talk much any more about Jason and the Argonauts and any of the Ray Harryhausen stuff or about the Xanth books. She talked more and more like a girl who would any second now be a woman with a beauty she could no more hide than others could ignore. If she already had boyfriends she somehow managed to keep this area of her life away from Lamont. It wasn't as difficult as it might have been since they were seeing less and less of each other anyway. If their grandmother knew anything about any of Michelle's boyfriends she certainly never said. Michelle was the one, always the one, their grandmother didn't have to worry about. Maybe Michelle was studying too hard to have time for boyfriends. If she had boyfriends, maybe they knew all those things Lamont imagined Michelle wanted to know.

Sometimes seeing Michael was better than nothing. Often it wasn't. Sometimes Michael had to bring his kid brother along, the one who would years later visit Lamont in Woodbourne. Michael liked to talk about girls. Who he wanted, what he'd done, who he'd touched and where, what he was going to do – he talked about it all. A lot of it, most of it, was lies. He would talk like this even in front of his kid brother, which made Lamont uncomfortable. Lamont thought about girls too but he didn't much like talking about many of the things he thought about and he didn't see much point lying to Michael or anyone else about his achievements in this or any other area. His self would know he was lying and he would feel ashamed.

As his high school days sped to an end Lamont began seriously to consider what he should do after he left. He knew a few guys from the neighbourhood who had joined the Army. He didn't know them well but he liked the idea of being 'all that he could be', liked the sound of it. He was still thinking about this when school ended and he picked up some construction work, unskilled and off the books. He had done that off and on during school vacations for quite a few years. It had enabled him to help his grandmother with money. And it had felt good having a little money. It was a feeling that made him go back to construction work after he left school.

It was some years later that he happened to meet a young Hispanic man from Inwood on a construction site. They got talking and the man explained how he earned his living with the only thing the man had been left by his father when he'd died, his pick-up truck. It was old and needed a respect that bordered on pampering but it was taking care of him now just as the man's father had promised it would. The man explained how the pick-up truck played only cassettes but that there was even something comforting about that when looked at in the right way. He had found some mixed tapes his dad used to listen to. He didn't know who had made them for his father but he would drive around the city hauling things and making deliveries with his dad's songs turned up loud. When Lamont asked the Hispanic man how this man's father's truck was taking care of him, the man explained that there was more delivery work than he could handle.

'No reason it should stop long as I keep my dad's truck in good shape and stay competitive. A guy can make a packet on the IKEA run alone, Elizabeth, New Jersey, to Manhattan or wherever. People need help with that shit.'

Lamont listened to the man's description of what he did each day and liked what he heard. Later, over a beer, he asked him if he wanted another driver to take some of the extra work. The man said he needed to think about it. He could see that the two of them got on well. Nevertheless, as he explained politely, he felt he needed to be careful who he entrusted with his father's truck. Lamont said that he understood this and that he respected it.

'I hear every little purr my dad's truck makes. You know?'

'Sure, I understand. I bet you're a good driver too.'

'I'd like to think I am . . . most of the time.'

'Prob'ly not enough for you to know the driver; you'd prob'ly want to know the guy who *taught* him to drive.' The Hispanic man laughed.

'I mean it,' Lamont said.

'What do you mean?' the man asked.

'Well, you seem to know *yourself.* Teach *me* how to drive.'

'You don't drive?'

'I will if you teach me.'

'You don't drive?' the man repeated, shaking his head in disbelief. Why was this man wasting his time?

'I work construction. I live with my grandmother in the Bronx. And, no, I don't drive. You teach me how to drive the way you think your dad would want someone to drive his van. You teach me to listen out for its purr and wheeze and you can take a cut off of me while I'm working and you're resting.'

'Listen, Lamont, you seem like a nice guy but . . . I don't know.'

Lamont wrote his name and phone number on the back of a Samuel Adams coaster and told Ramón, the Hispanic man, to think about his proposition. Almost two weeks passed and then Ramón called Lamont early one evening. His grandmother interrupted her preparation of pork chops and yams to answer the phone. It was some Spanish guy for Lamont.

'What kind of music you like?' Ramón asked.

'Why do you ask me that?'

'I need to know whether to leave my father's mix tapes in the truck,' Ramón answered. This was how Lamont started driving for a living. But first he had to learn to drive.

When Lamont had suggested Ramón teach him to drive, he hadn't really expected to be taken up on it. But once Ramón had agreed it seemed a time of possibility was dawning like perhaps no other he had known. It didn't take him long to learn to drive. He liked driving and though it was Ramón's truck, Lamont felt he was his own boss. They were friends. It had happened naturally, organically, as though it was meant to be, in a way no other good fortune had ever made itself known to him. To win Ramón's trust, to learn to drive, to learn the vagaries of Ramón's father's truck – its throb and hum – to learn the streets of New York and even some in New Jersey that had been foreign to him and to have some extra cash in his pocket – it seemed like a new start. Over a period of weeks it felt to him as though his lungs had increased their capacity while his heart was able to beat more slowly, restrained for the first time by real calm as opposed to the calm he wore as armour, as protection. This new calm, the kind that can come from a sense of accomplishment, didn't diminish his excitement. Never in his life had Lamont been more pleased to get up in the morning. The excitement abated after a while but the calm persisted for years. If he was ever going to meet someone like Chantal it would surely be during this time. And it was.

In reality the biggest change in his luck was the way he was feeling when finally he spoke to her, rather than that a woman so attractive or so elegantly dressed should talk to him or even that she would appear at Cappy's where he had whiled away so many childhood and adolescent hours reading and occasionally stealing comic books and magazines. But Lamont would never see it that way. He thought *she* was his luck, the agent of its change, and its realisation.

She was only nineteen when they met. She was working at a cosmetics counter in an upmarket department store downtown. Only at this time would Lamont have approached a young woman who looked like Chantal. Only at this time would she have seriously considered the entreaties delivered in the quiet voice of a shy man who did not come on hard or strut like an inner-city peacock. At most other times in their lives – even had they been next to each other in a store, at a bus stop or at a movie theatre – they would not have even looked at each other. But the time was this time. He was buoyed by the promise of steady work and she was ready to try a man who had a job, no drug habit, no prison record, no children from another woman, and next to no money. So he asked her out.

Although it was not the first time they had been out when he took her to eat steak and drink from glasses meant only for wine, rounded and swollen at the bottom like over-grown tulips, Lamont still had not got used to the fact that this woman kept saying 'yes' whenever he asked her to go out with him. With each 'yes' he had grown a little more confident but that didn't stop him being nervous this time too. This nervousness, which showed no sign of subsiding, was almost a pleasant sensation so he didn't entirely mind it. He just had to check himself to make sure he didn't say or do anything inappropriate, anything he might regret when he replayed the evening over in his head at night in bed or else later in Ramón's father's truck. It was hard to resist the urge to touch her when she opened the door to her mother's apartment. It was hard to resist touching her as they walked along Union Square.

She knew the area better than Lamont because she worked near there. She knew people in the stores there – people on the day shift anyway – knew where to buy lunch. Best chicken salad sandwich ever was near the Flatiron Building. Famous. Real famous. Old Jew place of like a million years ago. On 5th. No, he didn't think he knew it. What did he know? He knew that the cafeteria at the IKEA store in Elizabeth, New Jersey, opened a half-hour before the rest of the store. You could get eggs, potato and bacon for under a dollar. Bus your own tray so there's no need to tip. That's how they keep the prices so low. Probably. That might be part of it. Also, they buy in bulk, everything. Started in Sweden, Europe. The whole thing. Ever been there? Sweden? No, IKEA. No. Elizabeth? Where is it again? New Jersey. No.

She had a friend who was trying to become a model. Surely that was something Chantal herself might want to do, Lamont had volunteered. Good money. She was certainly pretty enough. No, really. He had a cousin who was also very pretty, went to college and married a professor. Didn't see so much of her. Not lately. Not these days. Tight when they were kids though. They had a daughter. Not really his niece, a cousin's daughter, Sonia. He was thinking he might get his own van; set up on his own. Wasn't sure. Maybe. Chantal thought that was a great idea. They really should think of printing the wine list in English. She laughed, thank God. He meant it but he also meant her to laugh at it. Didn't know which he meant more. Didn't matter. She laughed. This meal was going to kill him but it was worth it. Maybe he could pick up a couple of days' construction work in addition to the driving. Didn't make any sense to fill up on the bread unless he was going to take home that part of the steak he couldn't finish. He wouldn't do that unless she did. And he couldn't know that in advance. Wasn't worth the risk. He just wouldn't do it. His grandmother loved a good steak, though. Shouldn't have said that. Shouldn't have mentioned his grandmother.

They walked through Union Square and he thought he might be in love with her. He'd never paid so much for food in his life. If only Michelle could see him now. He would look into making a down payment on a vehicle of his own. The bigger the vehicle the more it could haul but the more it would cost to run. He thought he might be in love with her. His grandmother would be pleased.

Look at all those other people walking or driving past. For once he could just look at them and not have to drink them in. Maybe as he and Chantal walked by there were people drinking *him* in; *him*, the man with *her*. How did they look together? Michelle would like it. She'd like the look of it. Maybe they would get married one day, have a cousin for Michelle's little girl, Sonia, to play with. He leaned in to hear Chantal as they talked and walked. He had to. She didn't lean in to him. It was the same crowd, same noise for her too. She faced the same thing. But she was younger. Perhaps her hearing was better than his? He didn't notice this imbalance too much. Not too much. But his self saw it. He tried to banish the observation, to deny he'd made it. A random smile of hers ultimately enabled him to convince himself that she just really hadn't heard what he had said to her. Maybe everything will pay off, maybe everything will work out? It could, he thought to himself.

Michelle would have seen the inequality in their body language, an inequality that might have suggested the young woman was just visiting Lamont's life. Their grandmother might have seen it too. But there was something more eventful his grandmother wouldn't have seen that Saturday night. Lamont was again staying with her while he looked for an apartment to replace the one he'd been living in, which was being torn down. His grandmother wouldn't have seen it because Lamont's bedroom door that night was closed in a way that let out less light than usual. And she wouldn't have seen it on the Sunday morning because she had gone to church, something she had long since given up trying to get her grandson to do. She had tried to talk to him about God when he was a boy. It wasn't that he wasn't interested but just that he didn't understand what she was talking about. She clearly liked it very much – God, Jesus and the Church. But he didn't really get it so he hardly ever accompanied her, not even when he was a boy. He particularly did not join her that Sunday morning. Instead, he smuggled Chantal into his room the night before and joined *her*. That was the time their daughter was conceived. Not long after she was born Lamont got his own van.

No one could ever take that night away from him, even if later it seemed they could take his daughter away from him. That was still to come. First there had to have been their night together at his grandmother's house, and the dinner in the steakhouse, and their walk through Union Square and how the men had looked at Chantal. It was the way men looked at her at the Visit Center at Woodbourne Correctional Facility a few years later. He was sharing a cell with a man named Darrell and he made the mistake one night of confiding in Darrell about the way he felt when he saw the other men look at Chantal. It had been a couple of months since she had visited Lamont but Darrell too had seen her then and, perhaps in an attempt to mitigate Chantal's absence or perhaps merely to amuse himself, Darrell painted a picture with words that seemed to hang in the dead night air of their cell.

'She got a life to lead. I don't wanna hear 'bout your innocence no more. Every dumb-ass nigga innocent in here. Think of *her*. Think of how things are for *her*. You leave anything behind for *her*? She the mother of your daughter but you left nothing behind for her. She gonna need more money as the kid gets older. She *had* a job when you went in but maybe she *lost* her job. She need take care of the little girl, your daughter. You in here. They out there. If she don't have anything to eat she gonna have to go to welfare. What do they wait there – forty-five days, sixty days, to get somethin'? You say she live with her mother but maybe she *don't* no more. Her *mother* want more babies?

'What she gonna have to do? Listen to me, once you go to prison, people gonna look at her, especially her – she a fine lookin' woman – you know, different. Now they look at her *different*. The guy in the store, the guy in the bodega, the super – everybody. Now she has a *need*, *not* because she wants to get out, *not* because she wants to party. She has needs, many needs, and you ain't satisfyin' none of 'em. You know what I'm saying? So she needs twenty dollars for milk and shit, kids' stuff. So she gotta go see the landlord. So she gotta go see the super and you gotta live with this knowledge. You don't know the "whens" and the "whos" but you know why. *You* did this. Lotta guys in here go crazy; call their wives "bitch", "whore". I hear 'em. I seen 'em. The woman's wrong, the landlord's wrong. Everybody wrong but you. Your daughter's growin' *all* the time. A good mother do whatever she has to. Credit will kill you. You know it. So think on it. How long you think it take 'fore she reach an accommodation with the man in the bodega? An' I *seen* her. All them things you first like about her back in the day – they speed up this man's thinkin'.'

This was the same man, Darrell, who on another occasion talked into the night about the joy he felt at seeing his own daughter when he came out of prison the last time. She was eight years old when Darrell was last out, about the same age Lamont's daughter was as he made his way home after day four of his six-month probation period in Building Services at Memorial Sloan-Kettering Cancer Center. Darrell described the scene of that homecoming. His daughter's school bus was slowing down to the stop at which she got off but Darrell knew it had to go a little past her aunt's house first, the house where she'd been living, in order to get to the stop. As chance would have it she was looking out of the bus window and the look of surprised delight, of unadulterated joy, on the little girl's face when she saw him waiting outside the house was something Darrell said he'd never forget. Then, he said, she ran from the bus stop towards him with her heavy bag, ribbons in her hair and eyes wide as the moon. She called out, 'Daddy!' and gripped him tighter than he'd ever been gripped; including the time the police caught him again a few months later. They caught him in an alley, having chased him from his daughter's aunt's front porch with his daughter chasing him too and the police between them. She had called out, 'Daddy!' then too. He was running and saw only what was ahead of him. So he didn't see her face then. But the look she'd had when she saw him from the school bus the day he came back the previous time and the grip she put on him, Darrell said the memory of it was what kept him going. That was what you lived for.

Lamont already knew what he lived for. When he got out of prison he was going to find his daughter, be with her and be a father to her. He was going to get a job and stay out of prison, he told Darrell, who took offence the way other people breathe, autonomically. He shot back, 'Yeah, that's right, you the smartest *nigga* ever drove the getaway car.'

But Lamont had to talk to someone. His stream of visitors was drying up. Chantal wasn't visiting him at Woodbourne any more and there was no one else to bring his daughter to see him. At first Michelle did come. She even brought her husband once or twice, the professor. On one occasion he came on his own, explaining that Michelle had wanted to come but had had to take care of Sonia, their daughter, who would have been about eight by then.

Perhaps it hurt Michelle too much to see her younger cousin in prison. Perhaps she was angry with him. Maybe it had just been too hard to get to Woodbourne, too unpleasant getting there or too unpleasant just being there. She was a social worker. She had to see people like this all day, five days a week. But this was Lamont and he hadn't always been someone like that, a case or a 'client'. He had been a little boy without parents living with his grandmother, a little boy who had loved her so much, looked up to her, listened to her. No wonder she didn't come.

There was a part of Lamont that hadn't wanted her to come, hadn't wanted her to see him like that, like the people she tried to help every day. If she came would someone tell her not to bring her husband or her daughter or her disgust or disappointment? Or the Shogun Warrior action figures? Instead, tell Danny Ehrlich it was a misunderstanding.

Tell Mr Shapiro there really *were* horseshoe crabs by the Hutchinson River. And bring our bikes. Bring some hope, if you come to the Visit Center. Would someone tell her, if she decided to come, not to bring that part of her that believed the prosecutor's version of the events of that night when Michael and some new friend of his went into a liquor store, robbed it and ruined his, Lamont's, life. He had always felt that she hadn't believed him when he'd said he hadn't known anything about it. Almost nobody believed him, not the jury, not his attorney, and not Michelle either; that was the worst. But if she ever did come he knew he wouldn't be able to refuse to see her.

It was best that she concentrate on her own life, on her husband Charles, her daughter Sonia, her career. Charles, the professor, was an important man, no doubt a busy man, whom Lamont barely knew. There was no reason the professor should trek out to Woodbourne to see his wife's cousin. It was good of him to have ever come. But it was natural he wouldn't keep coming. Lamont's grandmother came as often as she could. But she was elderly and it hurt her too much to see him there. He knew that and didn't blame her for not coming more often.

Michael's younger brother came to Woodbourne though, just a few times in the early days. They had never really known each other very well. What was he doing there?

'How you doin', Lamont?'

'Fine, I guess.'

'I could look in on your grandma sometime. You want me to do that?'

'Sure, I guess. Thanks.' What was he doing there?

'You want me to look in on Chantal . . . and the baby?'

'She's two.'

'What?'

'My daughter is two . . . almost two and a half.'

'Sure.'

Lamont heard Darrell's voice in his head and the words stayed there like a bad song, a stupid song that takes you prisoner. 'Once you go to prison,' Darrell had said, 'people gonna look at her, especially her – she a fine lookin' woman – you know, *different*. Now they look at her *different*. The guy in the store, the guy in the bodega . . .'

'You want me to look in on Chantal . . . ?' Michael's brother had asked. Maybe she would have stopped coming anyway. He'd tried to remember and thought she'd already stopped visiting by the time Michael's brother started coming. But as the months passed it became harder and harder to be sure of anything outside the prison or of anything that had happened outside the time he was in prison. Maybe they had overlapped once, come on the same day, taken the same bus. Who the hell knew and what did it matter any more?

'You don't know the "whens" and the "whos" but you know why,' Darrell had said. Woken one night by the echo of someone screaming in a distant cell in Woodbourne Correctional Facility, a not unusual occurrence, Lamont tried to think of happy times. His mind went to Union Square, walking around, floating, blowing around like a tumbleweed, watching himself with her, Chantal, only a few years earlier. Chantal. Look at her! Look at that woman! She was hot. She was smokin'. She didn't ever lean in.

Darrell gave him the good news and he gave him the bad news. The good news was that there were facilities at Woodbourne to help him trace his daughter. There was a prison library, other prisoners who knew the law and even programs of visitors, qualified well-intentioned people who come and help you. You give them your daughter's name and they'll check the local hospitals for records of her. Start with the hospital at which she was born. If she doesn't get sick or isn't taken to hospital, it's still possible to find her. Check the schools around the neighbourhood her mother lived in. It is possible to check school enrolments in other states. You can check school enrolments all over the country, if you have to. That was the good news.

The bad news, as Darrell also explained, was that if Lamont's daughter was too young for school, he was going to have to wait till she was of school age before getting any news of her. That's if her mother didn't want the girl to have any contact with him and it seemed that this was precisely what she wanted. So Lamont tried to keep his nose clean, tried to be a 'model prisoner', promising himself he would find his daughter as soon as she was of school age. He was successful in one respect. He *was* a model prisoner and the success was marked by a transfer to

Mid-Orange Correctional Facility. It was less violent there. Prisoners there could almost 'see the street' so they tended to behave better.

By this time Lamont's daughter was of school age. He could have started to try to track her down. If Chantal had married and given their daughter her husband's name it might well be impossible. But if that *hadn't* happened, now that she was at school it was at least possible for him to find her. It would have been possible for him at least to look for her. But where this would have been possible at Woodbourne, it was not possible at Mid-Orange. He hadn't realised that when he was transferred – the transfer being regarded by his fellow prisoners as an enviable improvement in the circumstances of his incarceration. He hadn't realised that just as his daughter was reaching school age he would be transferred to a prison from where it would be virtually impossible for him to locate her even without Chantal marrying some other man and taking her new husband's name for Lamont's daughter. Mid-Orange didn't have the facilities to help him track down his daughter that Woodbourne boasted. Things were tight for the Department of Correctional Services, resources stretched. They always were. Mid-Orange didn't really need these facilities, it was said, because by the time you got to Mid-Orange you could almost 'see the street'.

So for three years in Mid-Orange, after three years in Woodbourne, Lamont Williams swept up the cigarette butts and mess left by the prisoners and imagined a day when his daughter would look at him the way Darrell's daughter had looked at Darrell. But whereas Darrell's daughter knew what her father looked like, Lamont's daughter hadn't seen her father since she was two and a half. Unless she had seen photos of him, it was very unlikely that she would recognise him. And under the circumstances it wasn't likely Chantal had shown her any of the few photos of him she'd once had. Nor was there anyone else to show her a photo of him. Chantal had had no contact with Lamont's grandmother. The child was eight years old. She wouldn't know what he looked like and he wouldn't know what she looked like. But he could try to imagine.

In prison whenever he saw a reflection of his face – even in a puddle on the ground – he would try to fuse it and the image he carried in his mind of Chantal's face into a photofit of the face of a little girl. But for how long can you look for your daughter in your own reflection in a puddle on the ground of a prison yard before somebody steps in it? As long as you can. He was right to think he wouldn't have got the chance to explain it to another prisoner but wrong to think no other prisoner would have understood.

Now he was out. He had a job. He had survived his fourth day as a probationary employee in Building Services at Memorial Sloan-Kettering Cancer Center. The trick is not to hate yourself for what you've done or what was done to you. He was going to find his daughter. Where would he start? He could start by visiting Chantal's mother. He could go tonight. Surely she would know where Chantal was? Don't go tonight, his grandmother told him every night. Get yourself settled first. Start by surviving the six-month probationary period of the job.

Or he could visit Michael's mother. He could go there to enquire after Michael. Then when Michael's mother was assured he wasn't harbouring hostility to Michael, he could casually enquire after Michael's brother, who might or might not be with Chantal. Even if Michael's mother wanted to lie about this, Lamont thought he'd be able to tell. He'd learn something from the visit. He would find Chantal. Just don't go tonight. He would find his daughter sooner or later. And one day she would have that look on her face when she saw him coming, that look Darrell's daughter had when through the window of the school bus she saw Darrell sitting on the stoop of her aunt's house. He would take her to see her older cousin, Sonia, and to Sonia's parents, Michelle and Michelle's husband, the professor. Just don't go tonight. He would read her stories. He would tell her stories. Make them up. Just a matter of time. Get settled first. Wait just a little longer so you can start looking from a position of strength.

When he got to his grandmother's apartment he saw she had the Rice-a-Roni she used to make for him when he was still at school ready to heat up. She asked about his day. It was fine, he told her. Before going in to take a shower he took a photograph of his daughter from the time she was two that he'd had with him in prison and placed it carefully on the mantle so that it formed part of the shrine of photographs of family members his grandmother had created years ago. There was a photo of him still at school, a photo of his late grandfather, several of Michelle including one as a child with Lamont and one from her college graduation ceremony. There was a wedding photograph of Michelle and the professor. There were two photos of Lamont's mother. Leaning against one of these was now another member of the family, Lamont's and Chantal's daughter. He would find her. Don't go tonight.

Over dinner he told his grandmother that he thought he might go to see Chantal's mother after dinner. As usual, she didn't want him to go. Not that night. He didn't ask her why. He didn't want to make her say that as long as he didn't go he could always live in the hope that Chantal's mother might lead him to his daughter. Once he had seen Chantal's mother that hope was likely to vanish and his grandmother wanted him to have hope. He didn't want to make his grandmother say all that. He wanted to spare her telling him she thought it was futile to look for his daughter. So he asked her about her day and answered her questions about his. He told her about the strange old white man he had talked to, a patient. He told her how they would be increasing his responsibility over time, giving him more tasks and more demanding ones. He volunteered to clear the table and do the dishes. His grandmother accepted his offer and went to her room to watch television. She listened out and observed that he didn't go to Chantal's mother's place that night. She was relieved.

She usually slept well but that night she was awakened by a sound and after a few moments she got up to confirm that it was Lamont. It was around two-thirty in the morning. He was having a glass of apple juice in the kitchen. The fluorescent strip light hummed from the ceiling. He couldn't sleep but he assured her he was fine.

'Work okay? Really?'

'Yeah. It'll be fine. It *was* fine.' He started going over the events of that day in his mind. There were six months less four days to get through the probation period. His grandmother poured herself a tea cup of apple juice. She said they should both try to get some sleep.

'Grandma, what's a death camp?'

'A what?'

'That old white guy, the patient, he said . . . he said there were six death camps.'

'I guess that's where they take the deaf kids. Like a summer camp or something for deaf kids.'

'No, no, a *death* camp,' he said as she was washing her cup.

'I don't know. Sounds crazy,' his grandmother said and then she leaned in to him to kiss him on his forehead. 'Get some sleep,' she added, leaving the kitchen to go back to bed.

On her way back to the bedroom she noticed a photo of a tiny light-skinned black girl partially covering one of the photos of her daughter. It took her a few seconds to realise the identity of the child in the photo. This shamed her just for a moment.

Lamont had finished washing his cup and was placing it on the draining board when he heard his grandmother's voice from the hallway near her bedroom.

'He's prob'ly . . .' she said almost to herself.

'You say something, Grandma?' Lamont called to her.

'Prob'ly . . . That old white man . . . the patient in the hospital . . . He's a Jew.'

part four

'LISTEN CAREFULLY. A young man – a very young man – lived in a house with his elderly father whom he loved very much. His father had grown unwell to the point of being bedridden. The young man shared the responsibility for taking care of the ailing father both with his mother and with a long-time and loyal servant of the family. His care extended to giving his father the medicine he had been prescribed, even compounding different drugs at home when the situation required. He sat with him, dressed his wound, massaged his legs and generally did everything within his power to comfort him. He took pleasure in this even though, being a serious student at that time, he might have been forgiven for begrudging time away from studying in furtherance of his own future. It was all the more remarkable given the added stresses on him as a newly married young man living upstairs in the family home with his even younger pregnant wife. The desire to be a dutiful son competed with the desire to be a dedicated student and a devoted husband to his very young wife. Still, the young man loved taking care of his father. Is any of this true?' Adam Zignelik asked those of his students who attended his 'What is History?' course at Columbia University that day.

This particular lecture had been due some weeks earlier but when the students arrived on the originally scheduled day they had found a note attached to the lecture theatre door informing them that the class was cancelled because Professor Zignelik was unavailable for what the note described as 'personal reasons'. While it would have been harsh to have characterised his cancellation of that lecture back then as self-indulgent, harsh and unfair to Adam as only he was to himself, he now regretted not having given it because he was currently in a far worse state and he couldn't cancel it twice. He wasn't sure he was going to be able to make it through the lecture. Recently he'd been speculating that perhaps it was a bit late in their studies to be telling college history students what history was. But then the department liked the course being taught and it was popular with students, the latter possibly influencing the former. Anyway, if historians could argue over the definition of history, there was no shame in discussing it with students. Adam used to enjoy teaching it too, used to find it exciting.

But today the excitement would come only from seeing whether he could get through the lecture. Would he be able to make sense until the last student had left the room? There were always one or two who stayed back. Would he lose his temper and shout at the students if their ignorance mocked his choice of career, a career he had at times allowed himself to see as a vocation? Would he chastise them without humour or good grace because their silence in response to his questions, their failure to play their part in today's employment of the Socratic method, a method Adam seldom resorted to, would defini-tively confirm to Adam, on the very day that he was most susceptible to counting any lack of response as confirmation, that he was wasting his life? Would he be able to keep standing the whole time? Would he make it through the lecture without crying? This could be an exciting lecture after all.

'Is any of this true?' Adam repeated as though his students' silence might have been explained by the failure of each of them to hear the question the first time. Adam waited again but not for long. He had to make it through the silence. But even then it was possible that his mind could wander from the words he was giving voice to and leave it free to be colonised by those thoughts he most feared that day and would most fear for so many of the coming days in the silences between his words when his mind was completely unprotected. Breathe in but not too sharply, he told himself. The silences would get him. It might have been a mistake to adopt the Socratic method that day. The plan had been to have the students' contribution fill up the time so that even if he didn't get through all the material meant for that day he would at least survive the lecture. Surely he could count on these students to try to impress each other, flirt with each other, joust with each other armed with statements dressed up as questions, jargon from one or other discipline dressed up as knowledge, and vague political attitudes dressed up as considered positions within established schools of thought?

'I'm so pleased none of you tried to answer that question.' The class laughed. Adam breathed again. 'Your silence is almost the perfect answer. Really! Almost. How could you make it better? How could you make it an even better answer?'

There was more silence. Come on, kids, Adam pleaded with them to himself. Where are your libidos? Where are your egos? Help me. I made you laugh.

'Okay, I asked you if any of this is true. How can you know? How can you *possibly* know? I haven't given you enough information even to ask better, more sensible, more meaningful questions. The better question is, "Having heard what I told you about the young man, is it *likely* to be true?" Let me suggest these categories: true, untrue, likely to be true, unlikely to be true, and, there isn't enough known to answer likely or unlikely.'

*

Not far away, Diana, Adam's girlfriend for the last eight years, had taken that day off and was at that time on her knees in their Morningside Heights apartment folding cardboard sides and sticking them together with duct tape to make the last of the boxes she would need to finish her packing. They had spent the weekend together assembling boxes and packing but you always need more. As the last minute approaches you always need more. On Saturday afternoon they had started making boxes listening to Jonathan Schwartz play songs from the *Great American Songbook* on WNYC. By the time he had closed the show with Nancy LaMott, the boxes had formed a wall.

Soon a man she had found on Craig's List would come with a van and take Diana and all the boxes to an apartment in Hell's Kitchen. A friend of Diana, an actress whom she'd met in college, lived in the oldest of the new apartment buildings that some ten years earlier had started shooting up out of the concrete like a phalanx of fortified fungi spawned by market speculation and watered by the rain coming in off the ocean. They now stretched from the makeshift Falun Gong camp opposite the Chinese Consulate on the Hudson all the way along 42nd Street to Times Square. The actress friend had been cast in a play in London and after that was scheduled to appear in a movie to be shot in Eastern Europe and Diana had the use of her friend's apartment for six months. Beyond that she couldn't imagine her life. But she had never imagined that this day would come and now here it was. She couldn't cry. She wanted to cry but there wasn't time. She still had to assemble what she thought would be the last box. Soon the man would arrive with the van. Why was this happening? she asked herself. It made no sense. It was so unnecessary. As the last minute approaches you find you always need more boxes. You always need more time.

*

'Okay then,' Adam continued to his students, 'let me tell you a little more about the young man with the ailing father and the very young pregnant wife. The young man's father's condition was getting progressively worse and he was spending more and more time asleep. One evening the young man was massaging his father when an uncle came to the house and offered to take over from him for a while. The young man was glad to be relieved for the rest of the evening and his mind went straight to his young pregnant wife and where his mind went his body followed and he was soon with her in their bedroom. She was asleep but he woke her and only minutes after leaving his father's bedside he was intimately joined with her.

'What did she think? I won't pretend to know that, but within five or six minutes the loyal servant knocked at the young couple's bedroom door. He explained to the young man that his father was very ill. Of course, the young man realised from the fact that he was being inter-rupted at that time of night in the privacy of his bedroom by the servant only to be told that his father was "very ill", that his father's condition had become extremely grave. How did he know? Because everybody in the house had known for a very long time that his father was very ill. It wasn't new information. It was a description chosen in the middle of the night in delicate circumstances by a loyal servant who was himself likely to have been affected emotionally by what was going on in the house, an expression chosen hastily with due deference and without any pretension to medical expertise, an expression chosen to impart an urgent request, "Get up. Your father's illness has taken a turn for the worse".

'The young man sprang out of bed and ran to his father's room. His father was dead. His uncle, the father's brother, was with his father at the time of death. You know where the son was. You know what he was doing at the very moment his father was dying. Is this true, untrue, likely to be true, unlikely to be true or is there not enough known from what I've told you for you to say? Wait, don't answer! There's more. I'll throw in a set of steak knives.'

The students laughed again. At least he had their attention. But then he'd have had that anyway if they'd realised they were watching the youngish professor with the slight Australian accent dying before their very eyes. Perhaps they'd seen him in the public television documentary talking about the legal battles of the civil rights movement. Maybe that's why they'd enrolled in the course. It had been a few years earlier. He had been the one talking about his father.

*

There were a few photographs of Adam Zignelik around the apartment Adam shared with Diana and she looked at them as she was packing the last of the boxes. She knew the photographs and the stories attached to them so well and wondered if she was looking at them for the last time. It was a terrible thought, one she'd never entertained before, to add to the barrage of terrible thoughts that kept assailing her. Adam had been such a part of her life for eight years that it was no more possible for her to imagine the next phase of her soon-to-be separate life than it was for her to imagine the soil hitting the wood at her own funeral.

In the days to come she would replay Adam's ostensible reasons for ending the relationship and come to implicate his father in what she had described breathlessly and through tears as emotional vandalism. What couple did they know who loved each other more than they did? But she was in her mid-thirties and wanted children and Adam said he couldn't in good conscience bring a child into the world. He felt he would soon be out of work. You don't have a child on a whim the way you buy that jacket that you knew you really couldn't afford. It looked great in the store. You wanted it. You took it home, tried it on but kept the receipt. You don't have children by mistake, by accident, or even intentionally when a tide of uncertainty is welling up around you. Soon it will drown you. Adam felt that the biggest gift he could give Diana was a future, one with a child that she so badly wanted. But it was a future that wouldn't contain him.

*

'Okay,' Adam Zignelik continued, 'the very young man's father had died and he, the dutiful son, had not been there with him in his last moments. The guilt was immediate and it was unbearable. Some time later but not all that much later, the very young man's even younger wife gave birth to their first child. This newest, smallest member of the family fights to breathe but little more than three days after it was born it dies. The young man feels the child's death is punishment for his having gratified a sexual urge when he should have been taking care of his ailing father. Furthermore, he is troubled that he had gone to his wife like that when she was pregnant. Is this true, untrue, likely to be true, unlikely to be true or is there not enough known for you to say?'

A student, a young man, raised his hand and answered at the same time, 'It's true.'

'Why?' Adam asked him.

'Because you're telling us the story.' The other students laughed.

'I'm pleased you've never known me to lie or to be wrong but I have to admit both *have* happened.' The class laughed again. The student sought to explain his answer.

'No, but you wouldn't be telling us this story in class if it wasn't true.' The class laughed again.

*

'This is insane,' Diana had said many times since Adam had put to her that they separate. 'People who love each other don't split up.'

But as she looked, surrounded by all the boxes, at the photo of Jake Zignelik there was no one else in the room to argue on her behalf, on their behalf, no one else to put the case for them as a couple to Adam. Professionally, Adam described himself as a 'dead man walking'. When the wheels of administration within the History Department turned far enough he would be crushed into insignificance and have no choice but to put his career into boxes not unlike those he was forcing Diana to put her life into that day. He could get another job, Diana insisted, but he said he couldn't, not an academic job, not in New York, not in the city. He was convinced their relationship couldn't survive him losing his job.

'So you're killing it *now*?' Diana had asked incredulously. It made so little sense to her that it took her a long time to believe there wasn't another woman. 'What about an academic position *outside* New York?' she'd asked him. But he said he couldn't make her leave her parents, who were growing old in Westchester. And he didn't want to be the reason she left her job. She taught public school in New Jersey. He didn't want to be the reason she left her friends in the city. How could he, in good conscience, get her to uproot her life knowing he was about to slide downwards but not knowing where he would land?

'Uproot my life! Are you kidding? You *are* my life! I would change jobs for you in a heart beat.'

'What about your friends? What about leaving your parents?'

Her heart must have beaten more slowly because she paused at this. Leaving her parents was harder. She didn't say no but it was definitely harder. They both saw her hesitate at this. He told her that he didn't want to make her do it but he didn't tell her how much the decision was killing him. It robbed him of sleep and led him to find himself tearful in the middle of the street hoping no one he knew would see him. He cried in the street, went into bars, drank and didn't tell her any of it. If he had told her it would only have made things harder.

'Maybe they won't get rid of you?'

'They will. They have to. I've left them with no choice.'

'Can't Charlie save you?'

'Diana, there's nothing he can do. I'm finished. I've really fucked up. I'm sorry. I've nothing to show them, the committee. There are people from all over the country, all over the world, who would kill for my position, kill for a shot at tenure in this department, in *any* department at Columbia. And I'll tell you something, they'd deserve it more than I do. I've got absolutely nothing to show them and I don't know how it happened. I've given Charlie nothing to fight for me with. Yes, he's the chair of the department but I don't expect him to go out on a limb for me in some futile gesture that smacks of something bordering on nepotism. I've got nothing to show him or the committee or . . . anyone, and he can't save me.'

She would hug him whenever he'd say all this, which he would regularly in order to try to convince her they had to separate. Diana had raised the possibility of Adam writing history without an institutional attachment, without an academic position of any kind. There were examples of well-regarded historians who had done this with great success.

One of the historians much admired by Adam, the late Barbara Tuchman, had done this. Adam often cited Barbara Tuchman's work to his students in his 'What is History?' class, not least for her easy yet erudite literary style. But her times and her circumstances had been very different from those Adam was facing. Barbara Tuchman's first book came out more than fifty years before Diana needed to cite not Tuchman's work but her life to Adam in an attempt to save their relationship. Tuchman had begun writing history for the educated public at a time when women weren't expected to work outside the home and if they worked for paid income it was a bonus to the family's resources. Adam, on the other hand, was expected by everybody to earn a salary that would keep the nose of each member of a putative family permanently above the waves of economic vicissitude that were out there waiting to crash down on them. Perhaps Diana didn't expect this now, not while her thoughts were focused on a child. But she could not be relied upon never to expect it. A child was a deal-breaker, *the* deal-breaker, and Adam would not let her take the child off the table. He knew that if she did she would regret it and resent him for it for the rest of her life.

Barbara Tuchman had been married to a prominent New York physician. Diana would have Adam married to a New Jersey public school teacher. Barbara Tuchman was descended from a family of diplomats and friends of presidents on one side, the Morgenthaus, and from investment bankers, the Wertheims, on the other. Adam Zignelik was descended from parents who had left him with meagre savings, a passion for social justice or at least guilt for not realising their passion for it, and a lot of fear, including the fear of bringing into the world a child who might know a sense of abandonment from which he, approaching forty, had suffered from almost as a birthright. How do you argue with this? Diana didn't know and there was no one there to help her.

*

'The gentleman in the front thinks I wouldn't be telling you this story if it wasn't true. Okay, don't laugh; he might be on to something,' Adam told his class. 'He's judging the veracity and the accuracy of the story on the basis of its source, on the basis of its origin. He's using his powers of deduction, maybe even intuition, which I'll come back to later. He's got to start somewhere. Even if I'm only a secondary source for this story about the young man and his father, a secondary source can be your starting point. I'm a professor of history at Columbia University taking up my students' limited time here with a tragic story.'

'It's *likely* to be true,' another student announced with a vertically raised right arm.

'Well, yes, but it could all be part of some ingenious pedagogic trick,' Adam Zignelik answered.

'Not enough is known,' volunteered another student.

'I'm telling you this story in a fair degree of detail. If I were making it up as I went along I'd probably stumble more or I'd gloss over the details. Remember the details. Five or six minutes after the young man and his even younger pregnant wife started having sex the loyal servant interrupted them with a knock at the door and a euphemism, "Father is very ill". The child born later lived less than four days. Remember the details. Of course, I could have made the story up for some ill-conceived educational purpose and just have told it many times before.'

'It's *likely* to be true,' a young woman answered.

'Why?'

'Because . . . you're a professor of history at Columbia University taking up your students' valuable time with it.' The class laughed again. At least *they're* having a good time, Adam thought. Then he spoke.

'You'll find in your lives that giving somebody back an answer they've already given you will usually work well. It'll probably help you. But the answer you give might still be wrong.'

Adam wanted a drink. It was still morning. Although he felt his career was over, the lecture wasn't. He wasn't sure he was going to make it.

*

Diana was holding a photograph of Adam when he was not much older than a baby, a child between one and two. His mother had dressed him in quilted overalls. His parents' marriage couldn't have had much more than a year left to run at the time the photo was taken. Diana knew it was taken in only the second and last time Jake Zignelik had ever been in Australia. The three of them had visited during winter to spend the briefest time on the Australian summer with Adam's mother's family. There were really just her parents. Other people who were labelled family were not really family. There was a Mr and Mrs Leibowitz who had two sons, Bernard and another Adam. The two Adams were about the same age. Adam grew up with his grandfather pointing at the two of them when they were together saying, 'I don't know him from Adam.' It was never funny. It was only years later that its very lack of funniness became funny and this was only funny to Adam Zignelik and Diana, no one else. They said it to each other incongruously in restaurants, on buses, on the subway, as incongruously as it had seemed to the young Adam when his European grandfather had said it. This was an 'in' joke, one of many, that was about to lose its currency. With Diana gone it would join all those thoughts, comments, references and allusions no one else would know, understand or care about. No one would even remember it. Adam would. Along with so many other things, he would now have only himself to say it to.

*

'You're trusting the vetting procedure of Columbia University. And why not? You don't have much to go on. It's an Ivy League school. Is it bad for the health of a pregnant woman to have sex? Is it bad for the health of the baby? Let me go back a step. Without asking your assessment of any of the faculty here, including me, without asking your assessment of anyone in this room, is there anyone in any of your other classes whom you think is, well . . . an idiot? Thank you for smiling. That didn't take long. Well, somebody at Columbia let that idiot in. Columbia can make mistakes. It does. You've seen it. Are you going to say this story is likely to be true because it's told to you by somebody at Columbia who was vetted by somebody else at Columbia? The baby died and the man, convinced that the death was a direct consequence of him having sex with his pregnant wife, blamed himself. Is sex during pregnancy bad for the health of the mother or the baby according to the currently received view on that matter?'

'No,' a young woman answered.

'The young man's family had a servant. Whatever the family's social position, this tells you there were families of lower status than his. If he had access to the received view at the time about the effect on the foetus of sex during pregnancy and was still wrong, what does *that* tell us?'

'That he lived in the past,' the same young woman answered.

'If, from a family not without some social privilege or status, he married when so young a woman even *younger*, what does that tell us?'

'Also that he lived in the past,' the young woman repeated. Then a woman with straight jet-black hair, whom Adam couldn't remember having ever seen in class before, interjected.

'Not necessarily,' she said quietly. 'It might be a contemporary story about people living now but in another society, a contemporary society with other . . . *different* values.'

'Okay, yes. But I'm a professor of history at Columbia University. I'm a student of history. I teach history. Whatever that is, it has something to do with the past. So I ask again, is this story true, untrue, likely to be true, unlikely to be true or is not enough known?'

With her eyes lowered to Adam Zignelik's shoes, the woman with a straight jet-black hair spoke again. 'Columbia makes mistakes,' she said.

Not today, don't do this to me today, Adam thought.

*

Everyone makes mistakes. Diana was slow to answer when the moving man from Craig's List buzzed the intercom. She was holding the black-and-white photograph of Adam as a toddler in quilted overalls. She wanted to take it with her. She had looked at it over the last eight years, seen it every day and thought that if she and Adam ever had a son he might look like this toddler in the quilted overalls. She hoped he would. She wanted to be able to go back and hold him, squeeze him, pick up this little boy and protect him from all that was coming, so much of which she knew about. Adam and Diana were each other's historians. Their familiarity with each other's lives transcended their respective arrivals in them. In addition to being each other's historian, they were each other's best friend and, in a way, they were each other's guardian.

Diana held the photo in her hand. She could hear the man with the moving van, wheeling his trolley towards the front door of the apartment. She wanted to take the photograph. It wasn't really hers. Everything had been theirs. Only Adam had been hers. She looked around the living room.

For years they had read the weekend papers together sprawled on the floor in that room or lying on the couch listening to WNYC. There was a knock at the door. It was the man with the van. He had come for the boxes. This was a huge mistake.

*

Columbia makes mistakes, the student said. Yes, but sometimes Columbia can correct its mistakes. He was an asset in which it had invested unwisely. Adam had just been thinking there was a chance, a slight one, he could make it through the class without imploding, dissolving, expiring or unravelling until the honey-skinned woman with straight jet-black hair – where is she from? – until she reminded everyone and especially him that Columbia makes mistakes. Like everyone, Columbia makes mistakes: discuss. You will never again hold anyone the way you have held Diana: discuss.

'After the death of his father and then of his infant child, the young man was on a quest that was to last the rest of his life, a quest to rid himself of what he called "the shackles of lust". Okay, I'm going to go through the categories again and as I do ask each of you to write down your opinion on a scrap of paper. We will collect the scraps and see how many of you place the story into the various categories. Is the story true, untrue, likely to be true, not likely to be true or is not enough known for you to say?'

The students wrote their opinions on scraps of paper and Adam had one of them collect the scraps and deliver them to him at the front of the room. As this was happening he concentrated on his breathing. He could no longer remember the point of tabulating the students' opinions and then telling them the results. He couldn't hold on to the point of anything. If it was to demonstrate that the majority can be wrong, he knew that even *they* probably already knew that. He was just trying to make it through the lecture. If they left this class knowing only that Columbia made mistakes and that the majority can be wrong, who was it going to hurt? It wasn't what he was meant to be teaching them, not exactly, but he figured that in the gap between what he taught them and what he was meant to teach them was perhaps the most useful lesson of all: disappointment. In this way he was able to kid himself that he wasn't being irresponsible. Deep down though, he knew that he was just killing time until the time when he didn't care that that was all he was doing.

He put the scraps of paper into their various categories and announced with surprise that one of the students had, in fact, got the answer right.

'One of you has been brave enough to get off the fence and ought to be rewarded for this bravery. This student, and there is only one of you, has simply written "true". The story *is* true. Could that student please raise his or her hand?'

It was the honey-skinned woman with the jet-black straight hair. Everyone looked at her but instead of appearing proud to have been the only person to get it right, her discomfort at the attention was consistent with being singled out as the only person to have got it wrong. Who was this woman? Adam wondered. Was she foreign-born? She didn't appear to have an accent. What was her ethnicity? Was she incredibly beautiful or was she actually quite ugly? She was so far from plain but any seemingly definitive conclusion as to her attractiveness could be rendered completely unreliable by the slightest tilt of her head, movement of her eyes, shift in the disposition of her lips, or even by a change in the tension and extension of her neck. She was completely striking and yet it was to Adam as though she had appeared in the class for the first time.

'You said the story was true. You're right. There were others who said it was *likely* to be true but you didn't hedge your bets. What made you say it was true?'

'I put the last bit of information together with everything else you'd already said and I think I know who the young man was.'

'You gathered from the few facts you had that I was talking about a real historical figure?'

'Yes.'

'This is part of what the historian does, an important part. With the facts she knew were solid underneath her, she built a bridge into the unknown. Who do you think the young man in the story is?'

'I think it's Gandhi.'

'Wow! I was *indeed* talking about Gandhi. We don't tend to think of him as a very young man but this was long before he won an Oscar for his portrayal of Ben Kingsley.' No one even smiled. Adam concentrated on his breathing. 'We don't tend to think of him as lustful. In fact, we don't tend to think of him much at all. Let's, for a moment or two, think of him. Think of this guy, Gandhi.

'In the middle of the most violent century in the erratic, haunting, tragic, occasionally beautiful and frequently astounding history of our species, this physically timid, skinny, shiny-headed man, who made a point of getting around in drab spun cloth, galvanised millions of disparate, mostly uneducated people and became the spiritual father of the world's largest democracy. He did it by devising and then practising what we now call the techniques of non-violent civil disobedience. Would this have happened, would he have been the same or a sufficiently similar man without the earlier shame that led him for the rest of his life to want to rid himself of what he called the "shackles of lust"?

'Perhaps this is really a question better asked of sociologists or anthropologists. Or is it really perhaps a question for psychologists? Should they try to answer it first? Is this *ever* a question for us, for historians? When is it *our* business? What *is* our business anyway? It's history, isn't it? That's what we do, right? What *is* history, anyway? What is history? Let's spend a little time thinking about this. Not much. Don't worry, it won't take long. When you look back on your life, blink and you'll miss this bit. But let's consider it now, just before you take that long subway ride all the way downtown. You know the one I mean. This will take less time than it will take you to stop halfway at Staples, to choose the right cartridge for your printer to print off your resume and covering letter, less time than it will take to deliver them and get that job on Wall Street where you can pay off your otherwise crippling student loans in less time than it will take us here today to consider, "What is history?"

'Okay, let's go another round. Picture this. In Poland during the Hitler years, a group of German men gathered together and sang Negro spirituals.' At this the students laughed again. 'With the facts you know are solid underneath you, build a bridge to the unknown. Is this true, untrue, likely to be true, unlikely to be true or is there not enough known to you to say?'

A young man shot up his hand. 'It's untrue.' Another student, a woman, said, 'It's *likely* to be untrue.'

Adam asked, 'Is it braver to get off the fence or to hedge your bets after bravery has already been conspicuously praised, I wonder? Why is it untrue?'

The student continued. 'A few reasons. The Nazis were ambivalent at best, if not hostile, to religion. Their racial doctrines regarded African Americans as inferior and definitely not a group with a culture to celebrate and, anyway, they wouldn't have known any Negro spirituals.'

'I wouldn't disagree with any of what you just said. Does anything change if I add some information? Listen. In Poland during the Hitler years, a group of German men gathered together and sang Negro spirituals in the town of Zdroje. It's a town on the banks of the Oder River. In Poland it's known as the *Odra*.' Nobody said anything.

'Okay,' said Adam, 'I'm guessing a map of that part of Europe is not appearing in anyone's head right now. When were the Hitler years?'

'From 1933 to 1945,' said the student who had decided the story was untrue.

'And when and how did World War II start in Europe?'

'Germany invaded Poland,' the student shot back.

'I didn't say these German men were singing Negro spirituals in Zdroje *during* the war. Does that help? There were six pre-war years, a bit more, before the invasion of Poland for these men to sing the hymns in. The river's name is *Oder* in German, but *Odra* in Polish. What does that suggest?'

'The same river runs through both countries?'

'It does suggest that. Doesn't prove it but it does *suggest* it. What we call Paris, the French call *Paree*. Doesn't mean it's also in New York but I like the way you're thinking. If the river runs through both countries then it might be near the border of each country. The town or region within the town known as Zdroje was also known in German as Finkenwalde.'

'That makes it more likely this area is near the German–Polish border so maybe it was part of Germany before the war,' a student volunteered without raising his arm.

'Maybe it does. And if it does, what then?' Adam asked and got another student's answer.

'Then it's still unlikely to be true because of Nazi ideology with respect to religion and race. No self-respecting Nazi would be singing Negro spirituals, even before the war.'

'He's right,' Adam said. 'It is unlikely to be true. Sadly, it was terribly unlikely. But I didn't say that the singers were Nazis. They were Germans, German men. And it *was* true. In the years 1935 to 1937 as Nazism gripped Germany, re-militarised it and as the rest of Europe looked on anxiously, if you went to that part of the town of Stettin known as Finkenwalde in what is now Zdroje, you could have heard a group of German men singing "Swing Low Sweet Chariot" in English.

'They were being taught the words, the music and the style in which it should be sung by a man who had learned it about a mile from where we are now on West 138 Street. The German singers in Finkenwalde were members of a religious seminary that had been started by a German who had visited New York in 1930, although it was the Far East that really called out to him. He had always wanted to visit India because of his interest in the teachings of Gandhi. But instead he came here. I guess it was easier. What did he see in the New York of 1930? The Rockefeller Center hadn't been built, the Empire State Building was *being* built, he wasn't able to get a drink without breaking the law because of prohibition and the rate of unemployment was much higher here than it was even in Germany at that time. He was a student on a teaching fellowship just over there on Broadway at the Union Theological Seminary. He met the American-born, ethnically German theologian Reinhold Niebuhr, who wrote extensively on the need for Christians to work actively for social improvement. He devoured American literature and American philosophy and tried to absorb as much of the place as he could. He enjoyed taking excursions around the city and wrote, "If one really tried tasting New York to the full, it would practically be the death of one." He took a tour of Harlem. It was still the era of the Harlem Renaissance and this white German cleric started reading contemporary African American literature and publications put out by the NAACP.

'A black student also enrolled at the Union Theological Seminary with whom he became a close friend took him around Harlem and gave him a first-hand look at life there where 170,000 African Americans per

95

square mile were trying to live. It was through this friendship that this white German man became a regular attendee of the Abyssinian Baptist Church of Adam Clayton Powell, junior *and* senior, on West 138 Street, which was where he heard "Swing Low Sweet Chariot".

'He was terribly affected by the manner in which the congregation there worshipped. He'd never seen anything like it. The passion with which these people seemed to love their God and their religion contrasted sharply with the patterns of austere worship of the congregations he knew at home. He bought gramophone recordings of the spirituals, took them with him back to Germany and later, in even more difficult times, he taught them to the theology students under his supervision in Finken-walde. By the way, some of you will have met Professor Charles McCray, chair of the department. Well, his father, William McCray, knew the man who showed this white German cleric around Harlem in 1930.'

*

Approximately once a week, sometimes more, William McCray would come to his son's office at Fayerweather Hall on the Columbia campus. It was always at the end of the day. They would talk for a while about politics, economics, history, the state of the world, before going back to Charles' home to have dinner with Charles' wife Michelle and their daughter Sonia. William, a veteran of both World War II and the civil rights movement, was now in his eighties but he lived on his own in an apartment not far from Columbia and therefore not far from Charles and his family. Charles and Michelle worried about him living on his own but he valued his independence; indeed, he was proud of it.

It was quiet on campus that afternoon as it often was late in the day when he took his weekly walks to his son's office. He had arrived a little early and since the weather was mild he took the opportunity to sit on the bench by the grass before entering Fayerweather Hall to see his son. He had studied law at a time when most of the parents of the under-graduates who hurried past him had not even been born. He looked at the students as closely as their haste would permit, but so intent were they on themselves they didn't notice him. How was it, he wondered, that the sum of all his yesterdays did not amount to one moment of their todays?

William McCray had started work at the NAACP Legal Defense and Educational Fund, Inc, within months of Jake Zignelik starting there. It was in 1949 and from their office on West 40th Street the young attorneys could look out the window when they paused to think and seek inspiration from the awe-inspiring main branch of the New York Public Library and calm or solace from the greenery of Bryant Park. They and the handful of other assistant counsel were each on a salary of $3600 a year. There was a small room next to his office where two secretaries worked and on the other side was the office of Thurgood Marshall.

In the very early days William McCray shared an office with Jake Zignelik, a respectful yet fiery, somewhat wiry Jewish kid who had to be taught that while his passion for the work would help get the job done, anger would only get in the way. Anger could sabotage the benefit of the passion. It could be the enemy of a good lawyer. Thurgood taught him that. It was funny that the lawyer to whom this needed to be explained most often was also, at least at that time, the only white one. It was expected that each of the young attorneys would either know the law or know how to find it out. But, additionally, Jake had to learn what it meant to be black in America in the middle of the twentieth century. He had to learn how to feel it or at least how those who were black felt it, and to get the job done anyway. Of course he could never know it entirely but there was always something each of the attorneys had to learn and, calm as he was, Thurgood didn't shy away from reminding them of this. Each of them could always do a little better, know a little more.

In addition to teaching the practice of law by example, Thurgood made sure all the attorneys, including William McCray, knew the debt civil rights lawyers owed to Charles Hamilton Houston. He was the grandfather of civil rights law. Graduating in the top five per cent of his class, he was the first black person elected to the *Harvard Law Review*. As Dean of Law at Howard University he had taught and moulded Thurgood and many other black lawyers and in 1935 he was appointed special counsel to the NAACP. It was Charles Hamilton Houston who devised the plan to advance the cause of civil rights through litigation. He was tough on his students, including Thurgood, who enjoyed telling William McCray and the others how tough 'cement shoes' Charlie Houston used to be on them. 'No tea for the feeble, no crepe for the dead,' William learned he'd said.

William was also taught the backstory of the NAACP Legal Defense and Education Fund or LDF; how it came to be what it was, how it got its revenue. Everyone had to be schooled in what came before them. Back in 1943, during the war, six years before William started at the LDF, there had been a race riot in Detroit. A spontaneous strike had arisen without union sanction when three black workers were upgraded at the Packard plant. Thirty-four people were killed, over 600 people were injured and property was destroyed. Harold Oram, the former University of Miami football star who had a history of supporting progressive causes, organised a committee to raise funds for what would become the NAACP–LDF. The first and urgent task was to raise funds for the more than 1200 victims of the Detroit riot. In his tireless collection of signatories he collected those of Adam Clayton Powell Jr, Mary McLeod Bethune, a leader of the National Organization of Negro Women, Henry Sloane Coffin, President of the Union Theological Seminary, Mrs Louis D. Brandeis, James Bryant Conant, President of Harvard, Albert Einstein, Archibald MacLeish, Rabbi Abba Hillel Silver, Helen Keller, Reinhold Niebuhr and Rabbi Stephen S. Wise. They were able to raise approximately $15,000 in 1943. This was a long time before major corporations understood the public relations benefit of contributing to progressive social causes.

Then there were the people you were helping. It wasn't enough to know the law. Thurgood wanted his attorneys to know as much as they could about the clients who needed them. His attorneys had to know the clients' backstories as well. Young William McCray had it explained to him soon after he arrived that two years earlier, in 1947, there were thirty school buses for white children and none for black children in Clarendon County, South Carolina. He was told that when J. A. DeLaine, a black preacher and teacher at the school for over ten years, complained to the white chairman of the school board, the chairman took a break from the running of his sawmill to explain, 'We ain't got no money to buy a bus for your nigger children.' When DeLaine wouldn't let it rest at this, they fired him from his job at the school. Then they fired his wife, two of his sisters and a niece. Then they threatened him with assault. Then they found a spurious cause of action, sued him on it and left him with a judgement debt he was unable to pay and, as a consequence, an inability to obtain credit anywhere. Then they set his house on fire. When he called the fire department the white firefighters came just in time and watched as his house burned down. His church was stoned and shotguns were fired at him in the night. When he shot back, they charged him with felonious assault with a deadly weapon. This was about the time he fled the state. This was the beginning of one of the cases that became known collectively as *Brown versus the Board of Education*.

William McCray remembered the nervous excitement of his first day on the job. There might well have been better-paid jobs for lawyers in New York City, even for Negro lawyers, as they were called, but surely for him, he reasoned, there was no better job anywhere in the world. He felt this keenly even on his first day when he couldn't have imagined the momentous events in the nation's history and in the stop-start history of Western Enlightenment in which he and his colleagues would play a part. And, at twenty-five, he had already helped win World War II.

*

'The German cleric,' Professor Adam Zignelik continued his lecture, 'was an active opponent of Nazism. His name was Dietrich Bonhoeffer. Like Gandhi he believed that ethical behaviour required evil be confronted through action, not merely intellectually through writing, thinking and arguing. Having observed the flowering of African American culture in Harlem, felt the power of passionate black worship, and seen the conditions blacks were living in, he returned home. There, some years later, he saw what his country was doing to some of its own citizens, its Jews. While others joined in the persecution of German Jews or else looked away, he found that he couldn't.

'Gandhi, Harlem, Christ, Jews in Europe, a black man living over there on Broadway in the Union Theological Seminary in 1930: you never know the connections between things, people, places, ideas. But there *are* connections. You never know where you'll find them. Most people don't know where to find them or even that there's any point to finding them. Who even looks? Who's got time to look? Whose job is it to look? Ours. Historians. It's part of our job. The more you know, the more you read, the better will be your intuition. You can use your intuition as a first-order Geiger counter of likelihood, of probability, and also as a starting point for new lines of enquiry. But whatever you end up doing for a living, wherever you do it, you'll need intuition and curiosity, as much of it as you can muster. Develop these as an athlete develops muscles and impulses. You'll need them if for no other reason than to keep your mind going. Whatever happens on Wall Street, sooner or later you're going to want your mind back for yourself.'

*

Prison had honed Lamont Williams' intuition but his curiosity predated his time in prison. Now he wanted to survive his six-month probation period and become a full-time employee at Memorial Sloan-Kettering Cancer Center. He hoped the people around him couldn't see how hard he was trying.

He was collecting trash on the ninth floor when he reached the room of a patient; an old man he had spoken to before. He had tried to look in on the man a couple of times since then but he had not yet managed to find the man alone. Once the patient seemed to have family visiting him and on two other occasions it was the man's oncologist, a tall fearsome-looking young African American woman who was visiting him on her rounds.

Lamont thought she would be pretty if she weren't so officious-looking, like a stern no-nonsense schoolteacher, someone waiting to catch him doing the wrong thing. Anyway, if she had found Lamont in the patient's room when there had been no garbage there to collect and she had asked him what he was doing there, he wouldn't have been able to say. He didn't really know what he was doing there. He had read the name on the old man's chart after they had spoken the first time and he'd remained curious about him. It was at the time Adam Zignelik was stumbling through his 'What is history?' lecture uptown that Lamont

Williams looked in on the old man again. Alone and awake, the patient cocked one eye at him with what could be mistaken for an almost comical surreption. Not that the man had much cause to be amused. He was old and had cancer. Would he complain about being disturbed? Did anybody see him go in? Maybe someone *he* hadn't seen had seen *him*. Perhaps he could lose his job for this. No. But why not? Who would stop it?

'I'm sorry, sir . . . Mr . . . er . . . Mandel-brot, I didn't mean to wake you. We . . . um . . . we talked before. You don't . . . maybe you don't remember. I was . . . I'm sorry, I didn't mean to –'

'You're not really a doctor, are you?'

Lamont smiled. 'No, sir, I'm in Building Services. Remember?'

'The other one is, you know . . . the tall one.'

'The other what?'

'The other one – the one who frightens you, the girl. She's a doctor. She's my oncologist . . . one of them.'

'Uh-huh. You mean Dr Washington?'

'Yes, like the city . . . and the first president.'

'Uh-huh.'

'You know her?'

'No, I mean I seen her 'round.'

'Ever talked to her?'

'Dr Washington?'

'Yes. She talks.'

'No, I never actually –'

'*She* reads my chart too, like you. Why are you afraid of her?'

Lamont smiled. 'I ain't . . . I'm not afraid of her. I . . . It's just . . . we work . . . you know . . . in different departments.'

'Different departments,' Mr Mandelbrot repeated quietly.

'I prob'ly . . . I should prob'ly go, Mr Mandelbrot.'

'Ever been to Washington, Mister . . . ?'

'Washington DC? No, I never been there. Listen, sir, I'm sorry if I disturbed you . . . I should prob'ly go.'

'You *should* go. You'd like it but not in the summer 'cause in the summer it's too hot. Like here. But there's no ocean there what there is here. What's your name?'

'*My* name? Williams, sir, Lamont . . . Lamont Williams.'

'What is it? Laront?'

'Lamont. I should prob'ly go.'

'I've been to Washington, Mr Lamont.'

'Yeah?'

'I went there with my family once . . . in the summer . . . when it was too hot. I live now with my family, not in Washington, in Long Island. Sometimes it's too hot there too but they have the air-conditioning. When I'm not here dying, I'm with them there living. What about you, Mr Lamont?'

'I gotta be gettin' back to work, Mr Mandelbrot.'

'Don't be frightened of that lady doctor. She won't hurt you. She is too busy trying to kill *me*. What about you? You live with your family, Mr Lamont?'

*

When Michelle came home from work she got to washing vegetables in preparation for the dinner she was making for her family, her father-in-law William and an old family friend, Adam Zignelik. Her daughter was meant to be doing her homework but she was bored and came into the kitchen. Sonia turned the radio on. A spurt of music sprang out of it, loud, too loud for her mother. She had a book in her hand.

'Can you turn it off, please?'

Sonia rolled her eyes but did as she was asked.

'Don't tell me you can read with the music on *that* loud.'

'Okay, I won't tell you,' Sonia said, reaching for a carrot.

'Is that for school?' Michelle asked, nodding in the direction of Sonia's book but her daughter ignored the question, preferring to let her thoughts roam to dinner.

'Who's coming for dinner?' she asked, crunching on the carrot.

'Your grandpa and Adam.'

'What about Diana?'

'No, I don't think she's able to come.'

'Why not?'

'I don't know.'

'Is she sick?'

'I don't know. Adam left a message on your dad's answering machine at work saying she wouldn't be able to come tonight.'

'Why?' Sonia persisted.

Michelle took in a breath and held it for a moment.

'Sonia, is this a hormonal thing? I don't know why she's not coming. I'm not holding anything back. I guess Adam will tell us. I know you like her.'

She tried to identify the book Sonia was holding but couldn't see it well enough from where she stood at the sink. It hadn't been an easy day. None of them were. Then suddenly, for no reason a third party might have been able to ascertain, she looked at Sonia again but as if through a different lens and she felt grateful that her daughter, though bored, was at home with her, eating carrots, wanting conversation with her mother despite pretending not to, enquiring about the wellbeing of a family friend and carrying a book. Her daughter was home with her, talking to her.

*

Somewhere else in the city a little light-skinned black girl aged between seven and nine was battling to stay upright on a crowded bus. She wore her hair in braids tied tight with ribbons. She grimaced involuntarily. Everyone was bigger than her. Squashed and gasping for fresh air, she wondered if she'd ever get a seat.

*

Pay attention to the small details. It is the mark of a professional. When Adam Zignelik said this to his students he was referring to the craft of a professional historian. More than fifty years earlier William McCray learned the same thing as it pertains to lawyers. He learned it from Thurgood Marshall not merely through it being said but also by simply watching him and the way he worked. Thurgood taught all the attorneys working under him what Charles Hamilton Houston had taught him; they were going to have to be twice as good as lawyers arguing *against* the extension of civil rights to non-whites. William noted the way Thurgood argued in court and the firm but unfailingly polite manner in which he addressed all judges, even those he knew were opposed to his most passionate beliefs. He noted the total absence of any crossing out in his boss's written arguments as they appeared in court documents, in the briefs handed up. If Thurgood changed so much as one word the whole document would be retyped. It was a part of his punctiliousness that he passed on to William and the others. Later, William would pass this on to his son Charles, the historian.

An astute observer at the US Supreme Court in Washington on 17 May 1954 might have suspected before the commencement of the actual proceedings that something was up. He would have noticed the enthusiasm of the recently appointed Chief Justice Earl Warren during the usually formal and staid preliminary admission ceremony welcoming the new members of the bar. And what was a frail-looking Justice Jackson doing sneaking into the building through a seldom-used side entrance so soon after suffering a severe heart attack, and why did he stop off to knowingly advise some of the other judges' clerks without explanation, 'I think you boys ought to be in the courtroom today'?

Thurgood knew to be there that day. Two-thirds of the way through Chief Justice Warren's reading out of the majority opinion it wasn't yet clear which way the court was going to find. Thurgood fixed a stare on Justice Stanley Reed, a native of Kentucky, whom he thought the most likely to lead a push in favour of retaining segregation. He would have to appear before him again so he needed to be careful with the way he looked at him but he continued to look for what gamblers call a 'tell' in Justice Reed's eyes. The Chief Justice continued reading aloud. He had been reciting the majority's review of previously decided cases when Thurgood heard him read the sentence that suddenly showed the majority's hand. Referring to black children, Chief Justice Warren said, 'To separate them and others of similar age and qualifications solely because of their race generates a feeling of inferiority as to their status in the community that may affect their hearts and minds in a way unlikely ever to be undone.' Thurgood just had to keep still and keep breathing. When the Chief Justice reached the paragraph that began with 'we conclude', he added a word that was not found in the printed text. The word was 'unanimously'. At around this time Justice Stanley Reed, a native of Kentucky, had tears in his eyes.

Whatever was churning inside him, Thurgood Marshall, the gradualist, maintained his composure as he listened to the Supreme Court unanimously decide in *Brown versus Board of Education* that it was wrong and illegal to segregate school children on the basis of race. It was not only morally wrong, it was also unconstitutional.

Thurgood was numb. He found the nearest payphone and called the LDF office in New York. Jake Zignelik took the call and William McCray stopped what he was doing after the third time he heard Jake say the only thing he had said after 'hello' up till then in the conversation: '*Oh my God!*'. Everyone in the office wanted to speak to Thurgood after he had spoken to William, who had grabbed the phone off Jake. Thurgood instructed them to phone Roy Wilkins and Walter White and Kenneth Clarke too. As soon as Thurgood's call had finished the switchboard began to light up with calls from all over the country. Exactly the same thing was happening at the same time at the office of the NAACP.

Thurgood took the first plane back to New York. The first call he took when he got back to the office was from John W. Davis, the 79-year-old one-time Democratic presidential candidate, counsel in the Brown case for the state of South Carolina, and, while only one of a large group of lawyers who had argued the case for retaining segregation, he was its unofficial leader. Davis had called to congratulate Thurgood. Work stopped for everyone. Champagne flowed freely in the LDF office. People were laughing, walking in and out of each other's offices. No one could quite believe it. The drinks session grew more festive. From the board members to the receptionists, everyone was celebrating the decision. Reporters arrived and quickly joined the group. More than by alcohol, people were intoxicated and numbed by history so fresh its full effect could not even begin to be divined. Before long people adjourned to Thurgood's favourite restaurant, the Blue Ribbon, where at some stage Thurgood interrupted the celebrations with a sober and prophetic reminder. 'I don't want any of you fooling yourselves; it's just begun, the fight has just begun.' While they knew he was right, Jake Zignelik and William McCray were part of a large group of revellers still celebrating at the Blue Ribbon after 1 am.

*

'And what of Dietrich Bonhoeffer?' Adam Zignelik asked his 'What is History?' class rhetorically. 'His visit to New York in 1930 played an important part in the evolution of his thinking. In addition to that friend-ship with a black student at Union Theological Seminary, he befriended a French theology student, the pacifist Jean Lasserre. Lasserre's pacifism and his insistence on the centrality – to all branches of Christianity – of Christ's Sermon on the Mount affected him deeply. In conversations in the streets around here where you walk, Lasserre led Bonhoeffer to the conclusion that this was it; the Sermon on the Mount was the whole point.

'This stayed with Bonhoeffer when he returned to Germany in the summer of 1931 and found seven million people unemployed. It was still with him on 30 January 1933 when, shortly before noon, Adolf Hitler was sworn in as Chancellor of Germany. You can safely assume it was with him on 1 April of that year when it became government policy to boycott Jewish stores and businesses. You will have seen the photos of the store windows with the Jewish Star of David painted on the windows and the stormtroopers from the SS and the SA patrolling the streets outside, enforcing the new law. It wasn't difficult to enforce. It met with little resistance.'

*

There was a knock at the door of the apartment Diana shared with Adam Zignelik. It was the man with the moving van. He had come for the boxes. Diana was holding a photo of Adam as a toddler in quilted overalls. Was there something she should have said? Was there some form of words that she hadn't thought of, a form of words that could have made Adam see that they were never likely to love anyone else more than they loved each other so questions of jobs and salaries and location were all second-ary? The man knocked on the door again. It was only for so long that it was polite to pretend not to have heard the knock. She couldn't pretend to be surprised he was there. They'd already spoken over the intercom. She looked around the living room. What about the bathroom? What about the bedroom? She'd been through each of them several times since Adam had gone to work but should she look one more time? Could she take the photo? 'Just a minute,' she called. Could she take the photo? For a moment she thought to ask the man who had come for the boxes.

*

Professor Charles McCray, Chair of the History Department, was on the phone in his office with the door slightly ajar when his father William arrived to see him. William looked at the young woman who sat outside his son's office and who stood to greet him.

'Hello, Mr McCray,' she said warmly. 'Lovely to see you. How are you today?' Not only could he not remember her name, he also couldn't even remember her title. Was she his son's secretary or his personal assistant? Did she work for him, for a few professors or for the department generally? None of this mattered as much as her name when greeting her but since he couldn't remember any of it and there wasn't time to look for clues around her workstation, he just smiled before shaking her hand with an enthusiastic hello. She would be able to guess at his age to within ten years and would therefore go on to assume he was declining intellectually and she would therefore deem him incapable of offending her. Everything was just fine.

'I'm sure he won't be long. He's just on a call at the moment. I'll tell him you're here.'

'Thank you,' William said. The thought occasionally crossed his mind on these visits that Charles didn't hurry with the tasks he had to complete before he invited him into his office. But even as the thought would cross his mind he was aware he had no evidence to support this and was ashamed of ever thinking it.

'Sorry, Dad, I couldn't get off. It was someone from the President's office and I –'

'Bush?'

'No, the President of the university. Nearly as big.'

'What have you done now, Charlie? You in trouble again?' his father asked through a gentle smile.

Charles stretched in his chair. 'Yeah, there's always something going on around here and I always seem to get dragged in. It's like they want to stop me from getting my work done. Somebody does. That's the *real* conspiracy around here.'

'What do you mean?'

'Someone's invited one of those 9/11 conspiracy theorists to give a talk.'

'What, one of those guys who says the Neo-cons were behind it and when he says Neo-cons he means "the Jews"?'

'Kinda . . . That and a bit more. Apparently this guy says 4000 Jews stayed home from the World Trade Center on 9/11 'cause they got tipped off.'

'Oh, I hadn't heard that one.'

'You're slipping, Dad. That one's not so new.'

'Tell me nobody involved with this is black.'

'I wish I could.'

'Oh no, they *are* black?'

'Well, that phone call is the first I've heard of it so I don't know. But –'

'Let me guess. The President wants you to look into it?'

'The President's asked me to be on an ad-hoc subcommittee to look into this thing so you can bet your bottom dollar *somebody* involved in this is going to be African American. You can sort of hear it on the phone even before they say it. I'm telling you, this is the last thing the university needs right now. This is the last thing *I* need right now.'

'Well, you just got to stop this guy from coming, Charlie.'

'It's not that simple, Dad; you of all people know that.'

'Yes, it is. It *is* that simple.'

'There's a little thing called the First Amendment, which I know you've heard of.'

'Freedom of speech doesn't mean freedom to intimidate and whip up racial hatred.'

'Then there's academic freedom to consider.'

'Don't tell me this guy was invited by a faculty member?'

'I don't know yet but I'm going to know soon, like it or not. The President's going to make sure I know and,' he said, leaning back in his chair and stretching again, 'that's why I already know that somebody in this picture is going to be, just *has* to be, African American.'

'All the more reason you've got to stop it, Charlie.'

'All the more reason?'

'We don't need another nutcase. Stamp it out, Charlie, if it is as it sounds. Do what you can to stamp it out fast.'

'I don't know. Maybe the sheer absurdity of this guy's argument is the best weapon against it.'

'Yes, I've heard that one. But that's allowing it to cloak itself in the respectability of the university. Don't mess around. Pull it out by the roots, Charlie.'

'Oh, the roots go much farther and much deeper than I've got time to dig. I'd have to quit my job and go digging deep as a coalmine to look for all those roots. And that's assuming I have any real sway in this anyway.'

'Don't shirk it, Charlie.'

'I could just be the spokesperson here.'

'Well, there's precedent for that, I guess. Give an African American a PhD, make a mess and get him to clean it up, like they did with Condi and Colin.'

'I think you're letting *them* off a bit lightly. And no one *gave* me anything!'

'It's a figure of speech, Charlie, especially when it comes from me. I'm just telling you not to be anybody's patsy and definitely don't be the guy who shirked it.'

'Dad, I've just had the phone call about it now, only one brief phone call. I hardly know anything –'

'Do what's right here, Charlie.'

'Geez, now I've made a rod for my back with *you*, haven't I?'

'A rod for *your* back?'

'Another one.'

'Are you serious?'

'I don't know. I'm tired, Dad. Just let me find out what this is all about first. There's no way 'round it though. I'm their man. There will be plenty of time for us to argue about this. Let's just have a nice dinner tonight. Okay?'

*

'In April 1933 with the boycott of Jewish businesses already under way,' Adam explained to his class, 'Bonhoeffer was asked to deliver a talk to his clerical brethren. He chose as his topic "The Church and the Jewish Question".

'The country was a sea of swastikas. It was in this environment that Bonhoeffer wrote what was in fact really a challenge to the Church, his own Church. He said that the Church had three possible courses of action. First, it could question the State as to the legitimacy of the State's actions. Second, the Church could help the victims of the State's actions. The Church, he said, was unconditionally obliged to do this. Remember, anti-Semitism was now State sponsored and opposition to the State was extremely dangerous.

'On 7 April 1933 legislation was passed promoting an "Aryan Church" that excluded not only Jews, whom Martin Luther had, from the time the German Church was established, wanted to convert but also Christians of Jewish descent. They were now to be excluded too. Luther's problems with the Jews had been doctrinal. Now Hitler added the insurmountable layer of racism. It was in the midst of all of this that Bonhoeffer wrote and delivered his challenge to the Church with its three possible courses of action, the third of which was really quite astonishing. The third possible course of action for the Church, Bonhoeffer wrote, was not merely to bandage the victims of the wheel, but to stop the wheel. Imagine saying that. We could stop the wheel. We *should* stop the wheel. That's what he was saying.'

'I'm sorry,' Diana said, opening the door to the Hispanic-looking man with the moving van who had come to move her boxes, 'I didn't hear you. I mean, I heard you on the intercom. I didn't hear the . . . the knock. I'm just . . . you know . . . not quite . . . nearly though.' The man looked at a piece of paper that he'd taken out of his pocket.

'You're . . . Diana, right?'

'Uh-huh.'

'So how many you got?'

'I haven't counted. You can come in and take a look.' The man took two steps in and didn't seem to need to count the boxes to be able to ask, 'Can I start taking them down to the van now?' She didn't want to go. Other than having children, she thought her life with Adam had been close to all she had wanted as an adult woman. 'Yes,' she said. 'Okay.' Her breathing sped up.

'Anything fragile?' the man asked.

*

'Adam and Diana coming tonight?' William McCray asked his son Charles later that day as they sat trying not to argue in Charles' office in Fayerweather Hall on the campus of Columbia University.

'Adam is.'

'Something wrong with Diana?'

'I don't know. He left a message saying she wasn't going to be able to make it.'

'Is she unwell?'

'I don't know.'

'Maybe she has an after-hours school obligation. They're working teachers harder than ever these days. But they still won't pay them any more.'

'I don't know. He didn't say on the message. You know, I think he calls me on this line when he knows I'm not here.'

'Why doesn't he call you at home?'

'I don't know. I think he's avoiding me. I don't think he wants to talk to me.'

'You two have some kind of problem?'

'We haven't had an argument but we're going to have a problem. He has a problem all right. It's professional. It's . . . it's awful. Dad, he is . . . Adam's in big trouble.'

'What is it? You know you've got to give him the benefit of the doubt. Start that way at least –'

'No, no, no one's accusing him of doing anything unethical. Problem is, for the longest time, he hasn't really done anything . . . at all. I mean he *is* fulfilling his teaching obligations, gives lectures, grades papers, turns up to departmental meetings. But he's not doing any of his own work. He's not doing any original research.'

'Well, people have their ups and downs, Charlie. No one can be productive all the time. Has he got a project?'

'No, that's part of the problem, I don't think he has.'

'Haven't you talked to him about it?'

'I've tried but . . . Dad, he's not going to be offered tenure.' William didn't seem to hear the end of the sentence.

'What do you mean you *tried*? You're chairman of his department. And you're his friend, a very old friend.'

'Dad, there's a lot going on around here . . . as you can see. I've tried to talk to him but he's not the easiest person to get a hold of these days.'

'Neither are you so I guess that ought to bode well for his academic career.'

Charles tilted his forehead into his right hand. 'I know there's *some* kind of subtext here, Dad. I don't know *exactly* how you're attaching the blame for Adam's predicament to me, but I've got a feeling you'll tell me. Or are we talking about something else?'

'No, *I'm* talking about Adam. Listen, you'll see him tonight, take him to one side, explain the situation, how urgent it is for him to get something on paper and then give him extra time.'

'Dad, you don't understand. It's not like that.'

'Charlie, you must have some discretion at least as far as time is concerned. Cut him some slack. It's Adam.'

'I can't do anything for him that I couldn't do for anyone else. You're a lawyer. You ought to know that better than most people.'

'It's *because* I'm a lawyer that I understand the nature of the decision-maker's discretion. I'm sure you have some discretion in all this. I'm just suggesting you apply it favourably, especially since it would appear you're late getting on top of this. It's Adam, Charlie.'

'Dad, I couldn't do anything for anyone in his situation. He's been here for over five years. One book in five years won't cut it. And he knows that. I think that's why he's leaving messages for me when he knows I'm not here.'

'At least he wrote about his father in his one book. He wrote about *your* father too in that book. It's a fine book.'

'You're not a hundred per cent kidding with this, are you?' William waved his hand dismissively. 'I'm a historian of the Reconstruction. If you'd been around then I'm sure I too would have got around to writing about you by now. Sadly, you're just not that old.'

'I nearly am. I feel it . . . sitting here.'

'Dad, between the administration, the teaching, the departmental politics *and* the university politics, I'm having trouble getting round to doing my own work too. All I want to do . . . Hell, I'm a historian of the Reconstruction and I –'

'Yes, you said, Mr Chairman.'

'Dad, what do you want me to do? I just want to be left alone to do . . . to read and write on my own area. But I keep getting waylaid and blindsided by all this other crap all the time.'

'Adam's not "other crap"!'

'Dad, please, how can I confide in you if you're going to be like this? Please, you know what I'm saying.'

'I *do* know what you're saying. You're saying things are very hard for you and you wish someone would cut you some slack.'

'Why do I feel like you've just boxed me in?' The phone started to ring. 'Don't worry; I'm not going to take it.'

'You can take it.'

'I'm not going to.'

'You can take it.'

'I'm not going to.'

'Take it!'

'I won't.'

'Charlie, it could be Adam. You're here *now*. Take it!'

The phone stopped ringing. The two men looked at it and neither of them spoke for a few moments.

'Charlie, listen to me. You talked about a coalmine before. Remember, a little while ago you said something 'bout a coalmine? The canary in the coalmine gives you its life and you don't even know.'

'Oh, here we go,' Charles said to a third person who wasn't there. 'A canary!'

His father continued. 'Did you even know it was dead? It looks dead but actually it isn't. It's you now. You're the canary. You think you're out of the coalmine but you're not. No doubt about it. You're still in the coalmine. Only question is: who're *you* going to save?'

*

Adam continued the lecture. 'The Lutheran Church in Germany was divided in protest against the "Aryan Church" legislation. By May 1934 a breakaway group had established a new church, the Confessing Church. Bonhoeffer, then only twenty-eight, was one of its leaders.

'Badly needing to train new pastors, the Confessing Church established an illegal seminary. It was led by Bonhoeffer. Where was it? In Finkenwalde in Stettin on the Oder River in what is now Zdroje in Szezecin on the Odra. This is where between 1935 and 1937 a group of German students were taught, among other things, "Swing Low Sweet Chariot". Bonhoeffer talked to his students about his experience in New York and about the position of African Americans, saying that he saw parallels between the situation of blacks in the United States and the Jews in Germany.

'In 1937, the Gestapo closed Finkenwalde. In 1938, equating Jews simultaneously with Bolshevism *and* with international finance, and then attributing to them super-human conspiratorial powers, Hitler threatened that "If the international Jewish finance people inside and outside Europe, if they succeed in getting the nations of the world into a world war, the result will not be the Bolshevism of the world and so the victory of the Jewish people. No, the result will be the destruction of the Jewish race in Europe." After *Kristalnacht*, the night of broken glass, on 9 November 1938, a pogrom in which Jews were killed, taken away and Jewish property was confiscated, not even the Confessing Church would dare protest and its members remained silent. All but Dietrich Bonhoeffer, who said, "Only he who cries out for the Jews may sing Gregorian chants." He continued to maintain the centrality to Christianity of Christ's Sermon on the Mount but now, when confronted with the evil of Nazism, he jettisoned Jean Lasserre's pacifism and Gandhi's belief in non-violent resistance. He felt that in this situation he had no choice. His brother-in-law, Hans Von Dohnanyi, had already by this time recruited him to the *Abwehr*, the office of military intelligence and the secret centre of resistance to Hitler.'

*

Towards the end of the day at the time when afternoon and evening vied for ascendancy, Michelle McCray stood in her kitchen as her fourteen-year-old daughter Sonia, crunching into a carrot, made what Michelle considered the loudest sound she'd ever heard involving a vegetable, an almost ostentatiously loud sound.

'No problem with your teeth, I see,' Michelle said to her daughter.

'What?' she said, crunching.

'No problem with your teeth . . .'

'I can't hear you when I'm eating this –'

'That was my point . . . sort of . . . What are you reading?'

'Nothing,' said Sonia, having now swallowed the last of the carrot.

'What's the book?'

'Oh, it's not one *I* chose. It's for school.'

'That doesn't mean it has to be bad. What is it?'

'Oh, it's bad all right. It sucks . . . It's boring and . . . unrealistic.'

'What is it?'

'You wouldn't have heard of it. No one has. It's old and . . .'

'Sonia, what is it?' Her daughter held up a copy of the book and Michelle read the title. It was *The Jungle* by Upton Sinclair.

'Sonia, are you kidding? That's a classic. *The Jungle!*'

'Have you read it?' Sonia asked.

'As a matter of fact I have, a long long time ago, but I remember thinking it was fantastic; interesting, moving, enlightening. It certainly wasn't boring. *I* didn't think so. Thousands, probably hundreds of thousands of other people didn't think so.'

'My class thinks so.'

'And why'd you say it was unrealistic?'

'Well, I'm not very far into it but . . .'

'Yeah?'

''Cause it's so boring.'

'Yes, you said that. But why'd you say it's unrealistic?'

'Well . . . it's set in Chicago, right?'

'Yes.'

'Well, it's set in Chicago and there ain't any *ni. . .*' Sonia stopped herself from finishing the word. She froze, saw her mother's eyes widen and knew she was in serious trouble.

'Don't . . . you . . . *ever* –'

'What? I didn't say anything!'

'I know what you were about to say. Why would you say that? That word has hurt so many people, your people, your family. Don't you ever say that word around Grandpa William.'

'He's deaf.'

'Sonia, I'm deadly serious about this. I don't know where to start. People gave their lives, I don't just mean their careers, I mean they gave their lives so that you might have the kind of life that you have.'

'Mom, I understand what you're saying but a lot of African Americans use that word now. You know they do. Black people say it on TV, in the movies . . . Your clients use it and you know they do.'

'My clients are mostly disadvantaged, disenfranchised, disillusioned and uneducated. That's why they use it. What's your excuse?'

'I don't know, Mom. It's only a big deal if you make a big deal of it.'

'Well, you listen to me 'cause I'm making a big deal of it. I don't want you ever using that word in this house. You understand . . . Sonia. I'm serious. You understand?'

'Yes, Mom.'

'I'm surprised at you, coming from this house, with all that you know.'

'Mom, I'm sorry, okay! I didn't even actually say it.'

'I wouldn't pursue that line of argument if I were you, miss. I'd go back to sorry if you want an easy life around here.'

'They say it on the radio.'

'Not the radio in this house.'

'Yes, they do. I heard it on NPR.'

'Oh really?'

'Yeah, that day I was home sick. They were talking about it on one of the morning shows. African American listeners called in and they said we can use it if it's . . . if it's . . . what is it? . . . ironic.'

'Sonia, do you know what "ironic" means?'

'Yes.'

'Well, then?'

'Ironic is . . . er . . , sort of funny . . . It's when something's funny in a kind of grown-up way.'

'That's not really what "irony" means. You look it up. You want me to get your dad or maybe Grandpa William to talk to you about the meaning of "ironic"?'

'No thanks.'

''Cause they'd want to know how we got started on the topic . . .'

'Sorry, Mom.'

'Let me say this without the slightest trace of irony. I don't want you ever using that word in this house, Sonia. Ever. And you can drop those "ain't's" too. It *ain't* "acting white" to speak your own language properly. People fought for you to get the best possible education. It would break your grandpa's heart to hear you talk like nothing had changed.'

'Sorry, Mom.'

*

'That's it. That's the last of them,' the Hispanic man with the van said to Diana. 'I've got room up front if you want to ride with me. Save you getting a cab.'

'Sure. Thanks. I'll just have one last look around. I . . . um . . . I'll be right down.' The man went down to wait in his van. Diana was alone in the apartment. All her possessions were in boxes in a van on the street. This was it. She was still holding the photo of Adam as a toddler in quilted overalls. Perhaps he would change his mind. But the plan was to not be in touch for a little while to give each of them time to adjust to life without the other. Neither of them asked for nor offered a definition of 'a little while'. She took the photo with her as she walked through each room of the apartment. She was breathing quickly. They'd hugged when Adam had left in the morning. Neither of them had wanted to end the hug but Adam had a lecture to give that he'd already cancelled once.

On the street the man waited for Diana to come down. He'd thought this job was going to be easy. He'd only had to come from Inwood and the final destination was Hell's Kitchen. There were not too many boxes and all of them seemed to be well made. What could be simpler than this? But the woman was taking a long time to come down. He couldn't hurry her. He almost never hurried them. This woman looked like she might cry. Then what would he do? All he could do now was wait. He got into the driver's seat and and inserted a cassette of a compilation tape of some music someone had once made for his late father.

Diana held what she could in her arms and stood on the outside of what had been her front door. It was a quirk of the door that even once it was closed you had to pull it closed a second time for the deadlock to align properly in order for the lock to work and secure the apartment. She felt sick. She was holding the photograph. She was going to take it. Would he blame her? She closed the door once. Could Adam just come home and stop this? Now the door was closed. But it was still possible to get in. She still had to give it one more pull. She could hear her own heart beat. What was she waiting for? There was no one in the hallway. What did she think was going to happen now? No one was coming. There it was. She heard the click. The door was locked and she couldn't get back in.

Adam continued his lecture. 'As a member of the *Abwehr*, Bonhoeffer was given permission and the necessary documentation to travel outside Germany, ostensibly to spy for the Nazis. In reality he was a double-agent working for the resistance through the *Abwehr*.

'It seems unlikely now and hard for us to understand given all that was to come, but, at the time Warsaw surrendered on 27 September 1939, the conspirators in the *Abwehr* felt they had cause for hope. I know it's hard, almost impossible, to believe in hindsight. Why did they think this? They thought this because news of SS atrocities in Poland had begun to make their way back to Germany. The conspirators hoped that neither the public nor the generals would put up with this barbaric cruelty which, in addition, flouted international law. General Blaskowitz, the senior German military commander in Poland, for instance, appalled by the atrocities, made it known to other generals that "What the foreign radio stations have broadcast up to now is only a tiny fraction of what has actually happened".

'Following a failed assassination attempt on Hitler in March 1943, the Gestapo raided the headquarters of the *Abwehr* on 5 April. Dietrich Bonhoeffer, his brother, his sister and her husband, and another brother-in-law were arrested. Their interrogation included torture.

'On 24 July 1944 one last attempt was made by the resistance to assassinate Hitler. Claiming that his hearing had been impaired in the North African campaign, Col. Klaus Von Stauffenberg asked to be seated as close as possible to Hitler shortly before a military strategy meeting was to start. The briefcase he carried contained a bomb. In the eventual explosion the bunker was damaged and some officers were killed but Hitler was only wounded. There were arrests and interrogations.

'At 3 am on 16 April 1945, the Soviet's Marshal Zhukov began his assault on the German line on the Oder, their defensive line before Berlin, with a massive artillery barrage. After the artillery came the tanks and then the infantry. The German Ninth Army there was massively outnumbered. Zhukov had 3,000 tanks against the Germans' 500. It took three days for the Russians to break through. In the battle for the Seelow Heights the Germans lost 12,000 troops. But such was the strength of the German fortifications on the slopes that the Soviets lost 33,000 troops. Nevertheless, by 29 April the Soviets had won the battle of the Oder. Eight years earlier there had been singing on the Oder. "Swing low sweet chariot. Comin' for to carry me home."

'With the forces of Marshal Zhukov meeting those of Marshal Konev, the German Ninth Army was encircled. Forty kilometres away were the suburbs of Berlin. Although it had lost 120,000 men captive to the Soviets, Hitler still deluded himself into thinking the Ninth Army could regroup under the youngest of his generals, General Walter Wenck, of the Twelfth Army, to defend Berlin. But with US forces reaching the Elbe on 25 April and Zhukov at the outskirts of Berlin, it was all over. Hitler commited suicide on 30 April and on 7 May Germany surrendered unconditionally.

'Dietrich Bonhoeffer was one of the many tens of millions of people for whom this was too late. The previous month, Hitler had ordered the execution of all remaining conspirators. On 9 April Dietrich Bonhoeffer was marched naked to the gallows. "Swing low sweet chariot. Comin' for to carry me home."'

*

'Okay. Now you were saying *The Jungle* is set in Chicago and is unrealistic. Why is it unrealistic?' Michelle McCray asked her daughter.

'Well, I'm not very far into it, I admit, but it's about these foreign-born meat-workers and I don't think one of them – or maybe just one of them – is African American. Now that's just not realistic, not in Chicago. Right? And then you find out the book's written by some white dude –'

'Sonia, this *white dude*, Upton Sinclair, when did he set the book?'

'I don't know . . . twentieth century some time.'

'When?'

'I don't know. Does it say?'

'Have a look at the front of the book and see when it was published. Unless it's fantasy or science fiction it's not likely to have been set after it was published. Do you see the date there?'

'Yeah. "*The Jungle* was first published in 1906".'

'Okay, so it's likely to have been set in Chicago during or before 1906.'

'Okay, so?'

'So when was the Great Migration?' Her daughter didn't answer. 'Okay, *what* was the Great Migration?'

'I know, Mom,' Sonia said with a hint of impatience for which any external observer might see little justification. 'It's when African Americans moved from the rural south to the urban north.'

'Do you have any sense of the size of this migration?' Again her daughter was silent. She looked at the back of the book either as though she might find the answer there or else in the hope that her apparent sudden interest in the book might end this lecture with its small humiliation. For all her adolescent affected nonchalance, she didn't like wearing her mother's disappointment. Growing up, she had always enjoyed her parents' admiration for her intellect and her grades. Now she was trying to find a happy middle path between continuing to court this admiration and asserting her independence. Although her mother's strictures annoyed her, a part of her almost always knew she wanted to be like her mother when she grew up, even if she didn't want to start being like her now.

'You're not really thinking you'll find the answer on the back of the book, are you?'

'I don't know! You're going to ask me to look this up, aren't you?'

'I should but you'd probably go looking for the answer from a Facebook friend.'

'That's a good idea!'

'Oh yeah, a great idea! I wouldn't see you till dinner and they'd be wrong.'

'I might come back for another carrot.'

'The Great Migration didn't get under way until World War I but it took World War II to really hit full swing. Five million African Americans moved north between 1940 and 1970, the largest mass movement of people in the history of the country. Do you know why they moved in such numbers then?'

'Cotton?'

'What do you mean, "cotton"? Is that really a serious answer?'

'I don't know. It's something to do with cotton, isn't it?'

'Well, yes, it does have a lot to do with cotton but that's no answer. You can't give a one-word answer. You really *should* look this up.' Michelle thought for a moment before continuing. 'Listen to me. The labour of southern black sharecroppers was always pretty inexpensive, but by the 1940s they'd been priced out of their jobs by machines that could do the work of fifty people per machine. So, looking for work and hope of a new and better life, southern blacks moved north to places like New York and Chicago. That's a simplified version of it, anyway. But now you know that at the time *The Jungle* is set the Great Migration hadn't happened yet. So the substantial African American community in the urban north that you're thinking of – correctly – wasn't there yet. You're accusing *The Jungle* of a lack of realism when the fault lies with you for not knowing what's real, not knowing your history.'

'Oops!'

'Oops indeed! Pass me that book. I remember it being magnificent, very powerful, very moving. Isn't there . . . ? There's a wonderful description of the first time they go to the slaughterhouse. They're being shown where the hogs are killed and someone there says, "They use everything but the squeal." Let me have a look at it.'

*

'What is history?' Adam Zignelik asked rhetorically in winding up his lecture. 'Barbara Tuchman addresses this question in a number of illuminating essays. In one she writes, quoting historian G. M. Trevelyan, ". . . ideally history should be the exposition of facts about the past, in their full emotional and intellectual value to a wide public by the difficult art of literature". She and Trevelyan suggest that the best historians take a thorough knowledge of the evidence of their subject and combine it with a sharp intellect, the warmest understanding of people and the highest imaginative powers. Why imagination? Not because you should be making up your own evidence but to help you leap into the lives, into the skin of the people who came before us. The chronological narrative might be the spine of the body of knowledge we call history but psychological insight and a vigorous imagination will help us get not merely the "what" of history but also the intensely satisfying "why".

'Should you find some attractive school or philosophy of history and attach yourself to it? No. Why not? If you do, it will be tempting to manipulate, coerce, cajole your evidence to fit the interests of the school or philosophy when you should instead be concentrating on the questions of what happened and why it happened. You might see patterns emerging before you but it's better to let the historical theory or grand generalisation emerge from the facts rather than contorting the facts to fit the theory. You'll be busy enough doing all of this and simultaneously keeping your bias away. "Bias?" you say with alarm. If you're human, you will have some. If you are not human, my congratulations to you for getting this far.' Nobody laughed.

'What do you do with your bias?' Adam Zignelik continued. 'Acknowledge it and fight it but have the intellectual honesty to admit that temporal distance is no guarantee of immunity from the bias that is woven into the fabric of our humanity, sometimes imperceptibly. To be as objective as we can be is not the same thing as being neutral. The passage of time *can*, however, confer perspective which a historian needs as much as oxygen. But even in the choice of what to tell, in the choice of the order in which to tell it, there is bias.'

*

'What about you? You live with your family, Mr Lamont?'
　'I can't be . . . I really gotta –'
　'Why are you frightened?'
　'I really gotta go, Mr Mandelbrot.'
　'I know who you are.'
　'What?'
　'You saved me.'
　'What?'

'From the street. I remember. You were the one who brought me up from the street that day.'

'Mr Mandelbrot. I can't afford to lose my job. I'm new here.'

'I'm old here.'

'I'm on probation. They can fire me like that,' Lamont said, snapping his fingers. 'So I gotta go now. You gotta understand.'

'I'm telling you something, Mr Lamont.'

'What?'

'I'm telling you I know who you are and . . .' The old man's mouth was dry and he spoke softly, almost hoarsely. 'You can come back.'

It was towards the end of the day and Lamont Williams had finished his shift. Instead of going straight home he returned to the room of a patient he had seen earlier and was getting to know. It had nothing to do with his work. Had anyone asked him why he was visiting a patient he hardly knew he would not have had an immediate answer.

The old white man with the wispy hair and the foreign accent looked up from his bed as Lamont Williams stood in the doorway.

'Mr Mandelbrot, I was here before. I just wanted to –'

'I know who you are.'

*

Sonia handed the book by Upton Sinclair to her mother and Michelle started leafing through it. She read in silence for a while and Sonia watched her mother reading. Then Michelle began to read out loud.

' "They had chains which they fastened around the leg of the nearest hog, and the other end of the chain they hooked into one of the rings upon the wheel. So, as the wheel turned, a hog was suddenly jerked off his feet and borne aloft.

' "At the same instant the ear was assailed by a most terrifying shriek; the visitors started in alarm, the women turned pale and shrank back. The shriek was followed by another, louder and yet more agonizing – for once started on that journey, the hog never came back . . . There were high squeals and low squeals, grunts, and wails of agony; there would come a momentary lull, and then a fresh burst, louder than ever, surging up to a deafening climax . . . Meantime, heedless of all these things, the men upon the floor were going about their work. Neither squeals of hogs nor tears of visitors made any difference to them; one by one they hooked up the hogs, and one by one with a swift stroke they slit their throats."'

As Michelle McCray continued reading *The Jungle*, her daughter Sonia listened to a purity in her mother's voice that she had first heard when she was a tiny girl being read to in bed. ' "Was it permitted to believe that there was nowhere upon the earth, or above the earth, a heaven for hogs, where they were requited for all this suffering? Each one of the hogs was a separate creature. Some were white hogs, some were black; some were brown, some were spotted; some were old, some were young . . ."'

Sonia looked at her mother with something that Michelle identified as a respect strong enough to free her from the shackles of studied adolescent bravado and sullenness, even if perhaps just for a minute or so. 'It's a lot better when you read it,' she told her mother quietly.

*

'Can we use history to predict the future?' asked Adam Zignelik. 'It's tempting to say we can but I don't think so. The lighthouse of history might suggest flashing glimpses of the way ahead but it's imprudent to count on history for a precise illuminated map replete with synclines and anticlines of the terrain ahead. We shouldn't count on history to tell us with accuracy what's going to happen next.

'Why can't history tell us what's going to happen next? It's because it deals with people and they are, as much as if not more than most animals, unpredictable. They can't even be relied upon to do what they *themselves* did previously in similar circumstances, or to do what is obviously in their own interest. People are unpredictable, individually and collectively, ordinary people and powerful leaders.

'How do you explain the following?' Adam continued. 'When Joseph Stalin was informed in advance of the precise date of the planned German invasion of the USSR in 1941, he ignored it, feeling certain there wouldn't be any German attack without Hitler first issuing some kind of ultimatum. The reports he was sent detailing the date of the German attack were rejected as "doubtful and misleading information". Did Stalin, that monstrously paranoid, brutal megalomaniac suddenly trust Hitler? No, of course not. This was a man who had been tempered in the flames of a place and time charged with suspicion, with factions within factions, with secrecy and espionage, and with betrayal and murder, a man whose suspicion, once awakened, could not be put back to sleep, a man who, according to his own daughter, "saw enemies every-where. It had reached the point of being pathological . . ." No, he didn't trust Hitler. He just trusted the organs of his own intelligence services even less. And so fearful of Stalin was everybody around him that nobody would contradict him. Even once the German attack had started Stalin thought that perhaps certain German generals were acting on their own without Hitler's knowledge or approval. Even when his own generals sent back reports of the invasion and of Russian troop losses he didn't order the Red Army to fight back. He had to wait until Berlin had confirmed that it really was at war with Russia.

'Who in their right mind would have predicted a response like this from Stalin? People are unpredictable individually let alone collectively, too unpredictable for history to be able to tell us what's going to happen next. There are now some six billion of us. Each of us has 100 billion neurons, each neuron has a thousand or more synapses and all of this gives rise to our own individual consciousness, to our own emotions and thoughts, and to the actions these determine. Don't ever let anyone fault history for being unable to predict the future when the natural sciences have trouble getting tomorrow's weather right.'

*

A young girl, a light-skinned black girl aged between seven and nine, her hair in braids tied tight with ribbons, struggled to stay upright on a crowded bus in Manhattan. As she stood there, engulfed by the odour of the squash of people, she heard snatches of conversation, many of them one side of mobile phone dialogues. 'Well, at least I got my resumé done before work . . . so that's good,' a young man said. Two older men she could barely see were talking loudly enough for others to hear. '. . . Just takes votes away from Hillary . . . like Nader,' to which the other man replied, 'What're you, an idiot? What're you talking about? It's the primaries.' A woman spoke into her mobile phone. 'She said there weren't any appointments till November . . . November! . . . I don't know . . . and the freakin' bus isn't moving.' The little girl listened to every word as the bus trip dragged on. Her school bag was weighing her down. At times when her view of the passing street names was obstructed she referred to a map of her route in her head. She thought she might be the smallest person on the bus. It was getting late.

*

Lamont Williams stood in the doorway.

'Mr Mandelbrot, I was here before. I just wanted to –'

'I know who you are,' Mr Mandelbrot said to Lamont Williams.

'I just wanted to say . . . I'm sorry . . . you know . . . I'm sorry about before.'

'What are you talking about? What are you saying sorry about?'

'I had to rush off like that. I didn't . . . I didn't mean to . . . like . . . show you . . . disrespect.'

'You had to work.'

'Yeah, but it's more than that . . . for me. See, I'm . . . new here. I only just started. I'm kinda part of a program.'

'A program?'

'See, I'm on probation here, Mr Mandelbrot.'

'Probation?' Mr Mandelbrot propped himself up in bed and as he did the sleeve of his left arm was pushed up towards the old man's elbow. This was when Lamont Williams saw a series of small bluish-green numbers tattooed on the patient's arm.

*

'So, with the unpredictability of human beings,' Adam Zignelik continued, 'with all these caveats, qualifications and limitations, what's the use of history? There are a few and none of them are unimportant. While history can't tell us exactly what's going to happen next, it can suggest certain things we should or should not do the next time something similar happens again. That history hasn't been used in this way more often is not the fault of history. Either we *fail* to see that it *is* something similar to that which has happened before, or we don't even know what happened before because we don't know any history or else our vision of the present is so clouded by our national, ethnic, racial, political, religious or even personal mythologies that we're unable to recognise even the shape of the outline of the suggestions history is providing.

'History can provide comfort in difficult or even turbulent and traumatic times. It shows us what our species has been through before and that we survived. It can help to know we've made it through more than one dark age. And history is vitally important because perhaps as much as, if not more than biology, the past owns us and however much we think we can, we cannot escape it. If you only knew how close you are to people who seem so far from you . . . it would astonish you.

'Also, it's a way of honouring those who came before us. We can tell their stories. Wouldn't you want someone to tell your story? Ultimately, it's the best proof there is that we mattered. And what else is life from the time you were born but a struggle to matter, at least to someone?'

'Sweetheart,' he heard Diana whisper, 'you're meant to be talking to your students. You're talking to yourself. There'll be time for that.'

*

Holding his satchel by its handle, Adam Zignelik put the key inside the front door of his apartment but was afraid to turn it, afraid to open the door to his own home. He didn't know how he would be when he opened it and saw how the place looked without Diana or any of her things. There was so much he didn't know. He didn't know that on 23 June 1940, the day Hitler entered Paris, Barbara Wertheim married Dr Lester Tuchman in New York City. When Dr Tuchman looked about him at the state of the world he saw nothing to recommend it as a place for bringing up children. But the new Mrs Tuchman met his argument with her own. It was wrong, she argued, to wait for things to improve because it might mean waiting forever. If they were ever going to have children they should have them now and to hell with Hitler. Her view prevailed and they had three daughters. Adam didn't know any of this and there was no one to tell him. Both his parents were dead and he had no siblings. So, notwithstanding his admiration for Barbara Tuchman, this aspect of her life was unknown to him and therefore incapable of inspiring him to take a chance and have a child with Diana irrespective of what was to happen to him professionally. Armed with this ignorance, he stood, almost forty, with the key in the front door of his apartment, afraid to go inside and see how it looked without Diana.

Eventually, he turned the key and went in. Inside it was far worse than he had imagined it would be. The absence of the walls of boxes revealed a greater, more gaping absence. He had done this. He had caused it. The bookshelves looked like bomb craters. He flung his briefcase on the couch. He could still smell her. How long would that last? How long would he want it to last? He went to the pantry, poured himself a Scotch as fast as he could and began telling her about his day.

'I did the "true, untrue, likely to be true, unlikely to be true" one today. I took them from Gandhi to Bonhoeffer, Adam Clayton Powell Jr, Jean Lasserre, Blaskowitz, Hitler, Zhukov, Konev and Stalin. And guess what? Somebody guessed Gandhi! Really! A woman, I think she might be subcontinental, ethnically anyway. I'm guessing. She looks older than most of the others. I have to go to Charles' and Michelle's. Do you think I should change? I don't have to change, do I? They won't even notice what I'm wearing. We'll be so busy talking about you.'

He arrived at Charles' and Michelle's apartment slightly late and slightly drunk but no one noticed. Nor did anyone other than Sonia mention Diana that evening. Everyone there had earlier come up with their own private explanation for her absence and, thinking they knew the reason and that it was pleasantly trivial, they didn't check with Adam for confirmation. They were in any case too preoccupied, too thrown, too shaken by other news. Adam joined in this conversation and because of the primacy and immediacy of it he didn't even have to discuss his stalled career with Charles. When Sonia, about to go to bed, quietly asked him to say 'Hi' to Diana for her, Adam briefly shut his eyes and nodded once. She went to hug him as she said good night and, holding her in his arms slightly longer than usual, his torso moved as though in spasm and he thought he might be about to break down.

*

Earlier that day Professor Charles McCray had sat at his desk in his office in Fayerweather Hall on the Columbia campus talking to his father. They were just about to leave to go to Charles' home to have dinner with Michelle, Sonia and Adam when the phone rang. Charles let it ring out. It rang again and this time Charles took the call.

'Hello, Charles McCray. What? What? No, I don't know anything about it,' he said to the person on the other end of the line. 'Well, I haven't checked my email in a little while . . . okay, let me check it now.'

Charles put down the phone without saying goodbye to the caller, and without any apology to his father checked his email. Numerous emails had come in since he had last checked. They were all on the same topic and reading the first one was enough to tell him what had happened. The others merely confirmed it. What he read strained credulity. The distress it delivered had the immediacy of a long past hurt recalled by a scent or odour. His pain battled with his need to hide it from his father, and the battleground was his face. He was angry. He wasn't going to be able to keep this from his father. It shouldn't be kept from him. Probably he should be the one to tell him but he was completely unprepared for this and didn't know how to tell him. The news could literally kill him.

*

'I'm on probation here at Sloan-Kettering as part of a . . . sort of . . . what they call a program.'

'A program, what kind of program?' Lamont swallowed. He felt he wasn't making much sense and, anyway, what was he doing there visiting a patient he didn't know? He didn't really know anyone there, not even his co-workers. He didn't want to lose his job. The point of his life now was to get to a position where he could try to find his daughter, if not that day then one day soon. There would be many steps to take and he'd take them one day at a time as he had now for years. But right now it was time to go home. This was another day and he'd made it safely through to the end. Things were okay. So get out, go home, he thought to himself. But when he saw the numbers tattooed on the old man's arm he couldn't move. The numbers held him there where he stood. Lamont had seen tattoos of all kinds in prison but never anything like this. It wasn't decorative, it was functional. This looked like the old man had been catalogued, as though he woke up every day wearing a primitive kind of bar-code waiting to be scanned, as though the man had been the product of an assembly line.

'It's a . . . like a pilot program. See . . . I . . . I done time, Mr Mandelbrot. I was –'

'Time?'

'Yeah, I was . . . I was in prison. So this is . . . This job . . . They're kinda giving me another chance here and I –'

'Did you do something wrong, Mr Lamont?'

'They *said* I did . . .' Lamont Williams' words hung in the air of the cancer patient's room. 'But I didn't.'

They looked at each other for a moment without speaking. The old man's eyes seemed more alive than the rest of him. Not old, not sick, they vigorously took in all of the visitor from Building Services, sized him up, measured him and his words, swallowed what they saw and then fed them back to a sick old man who some weeks earlier had been mistakenly left on York Avenue to get some air while everyone around him tried to smoke away their particular anxieties. He had been cold, coughing, ignored and alone on the street when he first came into contact with the man who now stood before him. This man had taken a risk for him. Now he caught the man trying not to look at the number on his forearm. He had invited him to come back and he *had*. Neither of them fully understood why. Someone, some people had said that this man had done something wrong. He said he hadn't. He wasn't believed and he went inside for six years. Then he came out and had six months to make it on his own. They'd be watching him. This was the system and he was one of the lucky ones. They both were.

'A program . . . I understand a program,' Mr Mandelbrot said.

*

'What's wrong?' William McCray asked his son. Charles was going to have to tell his father. He had no choice but to tell him but he decided to wait till he got him home and made him a drink. He was going to have to be quick on his feet and make something up to distract his father's attention from the truth on the way home. He knew his father had had a nose for the truth all his life so it would be a mistake to say something too fanciful. He had to think fast. But he was having trouble coping with his own distress. As they walked from the campus to the apartment everything seemed a little surreal. He waved to some colleagues in the distance. There were some students walking down the street in the same direction as Charles and his father. If they were to strike up a conversation with them it might distract his father for at least some of the way home. But then the students might want to talk to Charles about the very thing he was trying to keep from him till they got home. The students had just acknowledged him with a wave. They were catching up. Any second they would be within speaking distance. If Charles was able to recognise them he wondered if he might be able to pre-empt the conversation, steer it towards a topic of his choosing. He looked at his old father walking steadily, determinedly. The students were getting closer. Charles couldn't place them precisely enough to ask a sensible question. However this unfolded was going to be out of his hands. 'Good night, Professor.' 'Good night,' he answered uncertainly. The students walked past them. As soon as they got home Charles checked *The New York Times* online. Michelle and Sonia greeted William. Soon Adam Zignelik would arrive. But first Charles sat his father down in a room alone.

*

A number of people had trouble sleeping that night in the city of orphans. Surrounded by the boxes containing her life that followed her from the living room to the bedroom of her absent friend's Hell's Kitchen apartment, Diana stared at the ceiling in numb disbelief. In Co-op City Lamont Williams lay in his bedroom in his grandmother's apartment thinking about a set of small numbers he'd seen on an old man's arm at Memorial Sloan-Kettering Cancer Center. In Morningside Heights Adam Zignelik, on his way to the pantry to pour himself another drink, tripped over a space that once held something he already couldn't remember. On his way back to bed he stopped off in the bathroom to pee and saw a comb she had left. He picked it up, held it, saw her hair and then put it back down. Michelle McCray was woken by her husband's tossing. He was thinking about his father. William McCray got up in the middle of the night. He switched on a small table lamp. He walked over to a chair by the window and sat down. He looked out the window. He rocked slightly. Then he began to howl.

True, untrue, likely to be true, unlikely to be true or there just isn't enough known to say? Under Chief Justice John G. Roberts, a majority of the United States Supreme Court had reversed the decision in *Brown versus Board of Education* making it again permissible to segregate schools on the basis of race. After fifty-three years it was very unlikely to be true and yet it was true.

part five

SHE HEARD THE KNOCKING at the door of her apartment. It was tentative and slightly muted by the sound of the television and she was at first able to convince herself it was for another apartment. Then came the voice on the other side of the door. It belonged to a man who knew her name. The knocks grew louder and more insistent but she wasn't going to open the door.

The trouble was, and always had been, that despite the thick electronically operated glass doors, anyone could get into the building. There were so many tenants legitimately coming and going, such a constant stream of children, young mothers, maintenance workers, cable installers, pizza delivery guys and repairmen that an unauthorised visitor barely needed any guile or even any patience to slip inside.

For all that, when she heard the knocks at the door she was startled and when she heard the voice on the other side of it she was frightened, not because she didn't recognise the voice but because she did. She knew he would come sooner or later.

'It's Lamont . . . Lamont Williams,' he said after knocking.

His grandmother had advised him against going there. Michael Sweeney's mother is a fool, she'd said. No, he had countered, she's just one of those people who are afraid of everything. Lamont explained quietly that he had only to convince her she had nothing to fear, and she would talk to him. Lamont didn't want anything from her or from either of her sons, Michael or the younger brother, Kevin. He didn't even want anything from Chantal. All he wanted was to find his daughter. Perhaps Michael's mother could help? Perhaps she knew something? Lamont was fairly confident that Michael's brother Kevin had spent some time with Chantal, the mother of Lamont's daughter. He didn't know the precise nature of the relationship nor its duration but Kevin and Michael's mother could be the first link in a chain that might lead him to his daughter. He told himself each day that to find his daughter he would need to take one step at a time and not be daunted by obstacles. The thing to remember, he told himself, was that at any one time he needed to take only one step. This was one of them.

Lamont stood on the linoleum floor in the alcove formed by the three adjacent apartments. He could smell competing cooking smells and hear the muffled sounds of television through and under the door of each apartment. From under one door he heard that 'Zoloft is not for everyone. Talk to your doctor about Zoloft. Because no one should have to feel this way.' There were side effects but they were mentioned too quickly to hear. From another door he heard Ryan Seacrest trying to keep things moving, and from the third door he heard that somebody had just saved a bundle on car insurance. What were the side effects? His mouth was dry. His palms were moist. Most nights he woke some time between three and five. During the day at Memorial Sloan-Kettering Cancer Center he would be sleepy and afraid his supervisor might notice it and take it as a lack of enthusiasm for the job. He knocked again. No one should have to feel this way.

'It's Lamont . . . Lamont Williams, Mrs Sweeney.'

'I know who you are.'

'I wanted to talk to you. Can I come in?'

'He ain't here.'

'Who?'

'Neither one of 'em.'

'I know Michael's . . . He's still inside, right?'

'That's right.'

'And Kevin?' She didn't answer. Maybe she didn't hear him. The televisions were talking to one another.

'He ain't here neither.'

'Mrs Sweeney, I don't want nothin' from them . . . or from you. I'm tryin' to find my daughter is all. See, I thought Kevin might be able to help me locate Chantal and . . . Mrs Sweeney, do you think you might wanna open the door? You known me since I was a kid.'

He stood there for a while with his hands in his pockets. He had visited this apartment so many times as a child. Michael's mother had welcomed his friendship with Michael. She had trusted Lamont to take care of her son even though they were the same age. Now, many years later, Mrs Sweeney and Lamont stood on opposite sides of her apartment door. Neither of them spoke and the televisions ravaged the air. Zoloft was not for everyone. Side effects may include dry mouth, insomnia, sexual side effects, diarrhoea, nausea and sleepiness.

Lamont hadn't known that his grandmother had tried to contact Michael's mother several times while he was in prison to try to help him locate Chantal and find his daughter. That woman, Mrs Sweeney, was a fool. When Lamont came to her door she was terrified and she wouldn't let him in.

*

The telephone rang in Charles McCray's office in Fayerweather Hall on the campus of Columbia University. Adam Zignelik sat slumped in a chair on one side of the desk, the supplicant side, and watched his old friend, his one-time mentor, now the chair of the department, take the call. Charles made a gesture with the flattened palm and straightened fingers of his left hand as though taking an oath of some kind and apologised for having to take the call. The words of the apology were the last words Adam really heard for a while as he took the opportunity afforded by Charles' phone call to let his mind wander from the day he was stumbling through.

There were photos on Charles' desk and a few on one of his bookshelves. The ones on his desk were of his wife Michelle, his daughter Sonia and of his parents, the latter taken not long before his mother's death. There was also an old black-and-white photo of a group of people, most of them men, whom Adam recognised. It was a photo of the LDF, what had been known as the NAACP Legal Defense and Educational Fund, taken at the time when Thurgood Marshall was still running things. At the centre was Thurgood flanked by Charles' father, William McCray, Constance Baker Motley, Franklin H. Williams, Robert L. Carter, the sociologist Annette Peyser, Adam's father, Jake Zignelik and some others. He squinted to try to see better the expression on his father's face as his boss continued the phone call. The photograph had once sat on Charles' desk, Adam registered, but it had been moved to one of the bookshelves. Desks get cluttered and, from time to time, often at the start of the academic year, they have to be cleared.

Adam and Charles had just about come to the end of a conversation that for some time they had each been dreading. The phone call had allowed them to delay its conclusion. Notwithstanding that they had known each other for several decades, notwithstanding that Charles had years ago steered a younger Adam towards a career as an academic historian, had employed him and then championed him within the department, and notwithstanding that what had looked like a promising career had now come to a standstill, the conversation had been easier than either of them could have expected. Adam wasn't looking for any favours and Charles explained bluntly that the biggest help he could offer was to make sure Adam understood, fully and immediately, that there was nothing Charles could do for him. Once they had agreed that Adam would see out his teaching obligations for at least the next semester at a minimum, Charles felt as though the burden that came with the superiority of his position had been lifted and that they then were free to talk as friends. But talking to your friends in the middle of a busy work day was a luxury, especially for somebody so diligent. And how much time can anyone in a position of responsibility spare a friend in the middle of a weekday before the friend's vulnerability is transferred to the carer?

How had it happened that Adam's research had just stopped, that he hadn't even been able to come up with a topic to research? And how had it happened that he and Diana had ended their relationship of so many years? They had looked so good together, so comfortable with each other, not at all like a couple on the verge of splitting up. It had all the hallmarks of a midlife crisis, Charles remarked, but Adam was too young for that. This was when the telephone had rung.

At another time, Adam observing himself with Charles in that office under those circumstances might have asked a few questions himself, at least to himself. How had Charles, a friend of over thirty years, failed to intervene, failed to enquire about Adam's professional stagnation? How had he let things for Adam go so far off the rails without showing much greater interest? It wasn't that Charles' feelings for his friend had diminished. Rather it was that they were swamped, overwhelmed, by other needs, even sometimes other passions. He had the department to administer now, he had his own teaching obligations and, most importantly to him professionally, he had his research to prosecute. Had he known the extent to which his research would be hijacked by university politics and departmental administration, he might never have accepted the position of chair of the department. His research, his writing, was everything to him. There hadn't been enough time for his writing *before* his promotion. Now the demands on his time had become intolerable.

But in accepting the promotion and by being the first African American Chair of the History Department he was giving his father immense pride and that counted for a lot. He was also, consciously or otherwise, competing with his father. It was a competition he could never win. A World War II veteran and a veteran civil rights lawyer, William had participated in his own times in the *making* of history. He had done this twice, with barely enough time between the two endeavours to draw breath. As exalted as Charles' academic career might be, he would only ever *write* about history, he would not participate in it. At least he hoped not. He did not have his father's taste for it. And anyway, good sons, *really* good sons, don't make history. They're more inclined towards making families and carving careers that require less ambition than that possessed by those with a disposition to make history.

But as far as Charles could read himself, it was enough for him to write history or, as historians would say, to 'do' history. He didn't need to make it. He didn't want to make it. To be as highly recognised as he was for what he did and to know as much as he knew about his chosen area – the Reconstruction – he thought would satisfy him enough for two lifetimes. There were times when he had thought himself every bit as fortunate to have the job he had as his father William had considered himself to have been back when William first started working for the LDF not long after the war. This sense of his own good fortune was perhaps one of the reasons why Charles hadn't properly registered the extent to which his friend, the young untenured professor Adam Zignelik, was in the process of derailing his own career. Charles had genuine difficulty imagining *not* having more to write about than time permitted. How does this happen to a real scholar? At another time Adam might have wondered whether Charles honestly considered him a real scholar any more. Perhaps he never really had. Adam was not up to pondering this at this time in his life, at this time on this day, the day the consequences of his decline began to be formally, institutionally, planned.

Was the man on the other side of the desk holding the telephone the same man who had held Adam in his arms when Jake Zignelik had died? Sometimes Charles' wife Michelle called at work either from home or from her own chaotic workplace and thought her husband sounded different from the way he used to sound. She thought he sometimes sounded like a man who had forgotten he was talking to his wife, like a man who, whenever she called, was at a meeting at that very moment. His father, obliquely but not infrequently, had complained that Charles didn't have enough time to spend with him. More than anything this had the capacity to make Charles feel guilty because he felt William was responsible, through the way he had brought him up, through his concerted, conscious, pedagogic effort and also by his own example, for much of his success. It was in part this success that saw a quiet bookish academic able to attract a quite beautiful well-educated woman some ten years younger who would eventually agree to marry him. His contemporaries had married much earlier but Charles had waited patiently for a woman he had called his 'jewel', a woman who now sometimes felt her calls to him were interrupting a perpetual committee meeting.

Though Charles and Adam had never had anything remotely amounting to a falling out, their friendship had ebbed and flowed over the years as was natural, especially given the age difference between them. It had helped them, though, over the last several years when Diana and

Michelle had got along so well and when Sonia had been so fond of both Diana and Adam. The two couples and Sonia and William had been like a small but extended family. Adam and Diana's friendship had sometimes even served to distract Michelle and Sonia when Charles, as he frequently did, lost himself in his work. But they were now all entering a new era. In fact, they had already entered it. Unrecognised by any of them, except perhaps Diana, their many group interactions had come to an end, which they would soon be mourning.

'Sorry, Adam, but if I don't take these calls I have to return them later. Then the list mounts up till I can't face it. Same with email. It's a curse.' Charles scrawled a note to himself on a pad beside the phone.

'How's your dad?' Adam asked. 'After the Supreme Court decision, I mean.'

'I'd be lying if I said I didn't worry about him . . . which he doesn't like. Frankly, he's been pretty shaken by it. Terribly shaken, actually. We're going to try to see more of him for a while. I know you're going through a rough time yourself, obviously, but if you can spare any time –'

'Of course, I was worried about him too.'

'Well, one good thing to come out of it . . . you can see how mentally acute, how sharp, he is. He's been on the internet reading all about it, reading the decision. It's all he wants to talk about. He wants to write letters.'

'I can only imagine how he must feel.'

'He's so angry at the Supreme Court. Don't get him started on Clarence Thomas. I'm worried someone in the media's going to find him and get him to defame somebody. He's good copy when he's angry.' The telephone rang again. Charles looked to the ceiling, apologised again and took the call.

'Sorry, Adam,' Charles said, putting the phone down and scribbling another note to himself.

'It's fine . . . really,' Adam half whispered to Charles, to Diana and to himself.

'Have you had much to do with anyone from MEALAC?' Charles asked.

'What's MEALAC?'

'Middle East and Asian Languages and Cultures Department.'

'No, I don't think I know anyone from there. Why?'

'There've been some . . . complaints . . .'

'From MEALAC?'

'Complaints *about* MEALAC.'

'What do you mean?'

'There've been complaints from students – complaints of harassment . . . of anti-Semitism. Jewish students have reported being harassed.'

'By other students?'

'No, by faculty.'

'Oh shit. Is there any validity to it?'

'I don't know . . . but I'm going to have to find out.'

'What does it have to do with you?'

'I'm the President's go-to guy on stuff like this, *one* of them, anyway. I'm on a committee, yet another one.'

'You're the black one, right, the black go-to guy for stuff like this?'

'You got it, boy wonder!' Charles stood up. 'That's why I'm going to have to wrap this up. Sorry, Adam, I really am. The meeting I have to go to now . . .' Charles exhaled.

'That's about MEALAC?'

'Yeah,' said Charles, shaking Adam's hand. 'We got to have you for dinner again . . . soon. Thanks for looking in on Dad. We really appreciate it.'

'No, it's fine. You know how much I . . . It's . . . No . . . really no . . . problem.'

Adam had planned to call William. He promised himself he would call him just as soon as he was able to do anything. But he couldn't predict when that would be. Even doing his laundry seemed to require a capacity for organisation that was beyond him and he couldn't imagine a time when it would not be this way. The author of his PhD thesis, of his successful book on the lawyers of the civil rights movement, the person who had spoken on public television documentaries and who had successfully applied for a position in the History Department at Columbia, who had years before worked as a journalist for several newspapers and magazines in Australia, that had to have been somebody else.

'I know you always said I shouldn't ball my socks when they come out of the dryer. I know it stretches the elastic and shortens the life of the socks,' he told Diana, who was not there, 'but it keeps the socks together better than tying them. Laziness exists along a continuum. You always knew that. And we always knew that lazy is my default position but it's not laziness now. I can't go looking for the strays any more and as for their lifespan, well, they're going to outlive me anyway.' No one else was ever again going to care about the state of the elastic in his socks so why do anything about it, or about anything?

He really had planned to call William McCray because even a finished man has moral obligations, however hard they might be to fulfil. All conversation was hard now; whether trivial or significant, superfluous or necessary, it was hard like lifting rocks, boulders, hard like lifting the phone. But when the phone rang for him he answered it. It could have been anyone. It could have been Diana. It was William suggesting they meet for coffee. So they met where they always did, at the Hungarian Pastry Shop at 110th Street and Amsterdam.

When Adam arrived he saw William already sitting there, looking out the window staring up at the spires of St John the Divine. The place was quieter than usual, sparsely populated with people reading newspapers, magazines and their laptops. William must have been the oldest person there by around sixty years until Adam sat down and reduced the gap by twenty years.

'Sorry I was late.'

'You weren't late, I was early.'

'How you doing?'

'I could ask you the same thing.'

'I asked you first.'

'But I'm older.'

'So then I'm allowed to be more impatient.'

'No, after eighty all bets are off. Hasn't Charlie told you; I'm regressing?'

'Humour me. You first. Are you feeling any better?'

'You mean about the Supreme Court decision? I could lie to you but . . . I can't get it out of my mind.'

'Charlie said you read the decision online.'

'I read the decision, I read *about* the decision, all from my own home. The internet; what a tool! All these technological advances giving people ringside seats to the world's regression. This was the final day of John Roberts' first full term as Chief Justice. And this was how he marked it, by trying to turn back the tide of desegregation. Can you believe it? And, you know, he has the temerity to say that he and the other four majority justices are being *faithful* to the 1954 decision in *Brown*. Faithful! He wrote that the way to stop discriminating on the basis of race is to stop discriminating on the basis of race. The evil in the sophistry!

'There is racism in society, right? Always has been. Among its myriad ways, it manifested itself traditionally, institutionally, formally and legally in substandard education for African American children. The decision in *Brown* sought to change this. But Roberts and the majority deliberately confuse *negative* discrimination with the *positive* discrimination that seeks to be its antidote.' Adam smiled to himself. Whenever the conversation turned to injustice William sounded as if he were still addressing the full bench of the US Supreme Court.

'You see, when someone first hears that "the way to stop discriminating on the basis of race is to stop discriminating on the basis of race", it sounds like a simple tautology so you can't argue with it. Its simplicity is beguiling. And it's pernicious.'

'Well, what about the dissenting judges? They must provide some hope. There are four of them.'

'Justice Breyer, Stephen Breyer, wrote the principal judgement for the dissenters and he saw it for what it is. He got it right. He described the majority's decision *not* as in line with *Brown* but as a radical departure from it. He said that its effect would be to remove from local communities their capacity to prevent resegregation. Stevens, also a dissenter – and he's been on the bench since Gerald Ford – he went even further. He talked about the *cruel irony* of the majority's decision. Listen, I wrote this down, listen to this.'

'You carry it on you?'

'It makes me feel better, lowers my blood pressure. Stevens wrote that the majority opinion "rewrites the history of one of this court's most important decisions . . . It is my firm conviction", he wrote, "that no member of the court that I joined in 1975 would have agreed with today's decision." See, he's not just talking *stare decisis* there; he's having a dig at Roberts right there because Bill Rehnquist was one of the members of that court.'

'So? I don't get it.'

'So, early in his career Roberts clerked for Rehnquist. It won't do us any good, not one black child gets a better education from it but still it . . . Well, it wouldn't have been lost on Roberts. This radical right-wing shift in the balance of the court now makes it the very monster the conservatives elected Bush to create. Now they've got it and we're going to pay; not just African Americans, the whole country. Scalia's been let loose completely. Scalia's like a junk-yard dog. He even attacks Roberts when the two are *concurring*. Really! He says that while Roberts is agreeing with him, he's being too coy about it. Can you believe that? Poster boy for the Neo-cons, our Italian friend! You know this all goes way back. You can see the pattern beginning in decisions of the '70s and '80s in cases like *Bakke* and *Patterson*.

'Charlie thinks it goes back even further than that, as far as Nixon, to Nixon's "Southern Strategy" to get southern whites to vote Republican.' William took a sip of his coffee.

'Well, I guess after Johnson signed those civil rights acts in the '60s he pretty much knew he'd given the south to the Republicans for at least a generation. I think he said as much. So, as with most things, I guess Charlie might be right. But none of that excuses this current crop.

'And as for Clarence Thomas . . . I don't know where to start with that man. He was always a fool but now he's an unbearably smug fool. I mean, listen to this. A black man in the process of overturning *Brown* writes, "If our history has taught us anything it has taught us to beware of elites bearing racial theories." This is a black man who buys the conservative line that those with a liberal disposition are, by definition, the elites, while the ruling oligarchy he works for are on the side of the dispossessed. You want to talk about Uncle Tom? Let me introduce you to Uncle Clarence.

'This man is unbelievable. And listen to what he says to one of the other dissenters, Justice Stephen Breyer, what he says *about* Breyer. I mean he didn't just say this, he *wrote* it in his opinion, in a footnote, he wrote, "Justice Breyer's good intentions, which I do not doubt, have the shelf life of Justice Breyer's tenure." Vicious! See, Breyer's soon to retire, on his way out in a few months I think, and Clarence Thomas, the plantation owner's favourite Negro, is saying the force of Breyer's dissenting opinion will evaporate when Breyer's time is up. There's a viciousness there that he's too stupid to hide. It's not enough for Clarence Thomas to sell out his own people; he has to go so far as to put on record his character assassination of an honourable man who has the audacity to disagree with him. I tell you, the best argument against affirmative action *is* Clarence Thomas himself. Did you know a Jesuit school in Massachusetts took him in as part of a black recruitment program? And then after that he got into Yale Law on a minority program. He's a hypocrite, one willing to turn his back on his people and worse, to fight *against* his people while *benefiting* from their previous victories, which he does his best to overturn. This is the man George W. Bush's father appointed to the Supreme Court to replace Thurgood Marshall! I tell you, Adam, it makes me hope against hope there's no heaven, just so Thurgood doesn't have to see this. What kind of a world is it we're living in? I ask you.'

'I have no answer to that,' Adam said quietly.

'I'm sorry to go on about this, Adam.'

'No, William, I agree with everything you say. It's just that I have no answer, not one that would please you.'

'Well, then at least I know you're committed to telling the truth. I shudder to think what your father would be saying right now. Speaking of the truth, tell me it isn't true about you and Diana. I was talking to Michelle about you two. I know this is personal and if ever anything is none of my business this is it. But you're like a son to me. Tell me it isn't true. Is it really over? What happened?'

'There's a lot to say but . . . she wants children and –'

'Don't you want children?'

'Well . . . under different circumstances I do . . . I would.'

'What do you mean?'

Adam took a moment to draw breath and to formulate the words to best express what had once seemed so eminently logical, prudent and even kind.

'More than anyone I know,' he began, 'you knew what kind of a father my father was. I don't mean what kind of *man*; I mean what kind of *father.*'

'Adam, you mustn't doubt how much he loved you but, yes, he was a pretty terrible father and he knew it. Jake was a special man but part of what made him special made him unsuitable for being a parent. You suffered for this. But that doesn't mean *you'd* make a bad father. You don't think that, do you? Is *that* what this is about?'

'William . . . I felt I needed to give her a chance to have children.'

'With someone else?'

'Yes.'

'Why not with you?'

'I'm . . . I'm . . . Where do I start? I'm probably going to lose my job. They can't give me tenure. My work, my research has stopped.'

'What do you think it is?'

'I don't know. It's partly confidence, I guess.'

'What do you mean? You've done so well. The book was a huge success and there's the television . . .'

'That was all a while ago and anyway . . . William, I feel . . . perhaps I've always felt kind of . . . fraudulent.'

'Fraudulent?'

'There is a part of me that feels I've been living off my father's name. I feel that I have to constantly, albeit with varying degrees of subtlety, defend my professional interest in civil rights. I'm white, I'm Jewish . . . Even the way I talk requires an explanation.'

'Your Australian *accent*? People love that accent.'

'Some do and, frankly, most of *them* think it's British anyway. But it all adds up to a feeling that I need to constantly justify my professional interest, even my position.'

'At Columbia?'

'Yeah, it's like people are thinking I'm only here because of who my father was. He's Jake Zignelik's son. It's like I haven't earned anything myself.'

'Now you know how Charlie must feel.'

'Because he's *your* son?'

'No, I didn't mean that. Not exactly.'

'Because he's black?'

'Sure. He's the first African American chair of the department. He's watching people looking at him and he's wondering if they're thinking he's really earned it or if it's just that it's time. Are they thinking that he's the lucky one, the black man who happened to be there when the liberals' guilt or shame got too much?'

'He's said that to you?'

'Not in so many words.'

'Really? With complete justification, he's a pretty confident academic. William, I'd be very surprised if he said that in *any* words.'

'Adam, he doesn't have to say it.' William took a sip of his coffee and turned his gaze briefly outside and up to the spires.

'Adam, I hope you won't mind, I don't think it will surprise you but Charlie and I *have* talked about you. I do know a little about your professional situation. Actually, it's one of the things I wanted to talk to you about . . . as well as about you and Diana. After all, your personal situation and your professional situation are connected. Now look, I know that your research has stopped. Charlie told me. I think he's let you down –'

'Oh no! William, there's nothing he can do. He's been a great friend and –'

'Adam, I may have something for you.'

'What do you mean?'

'I mean that I think I have a topic for you, something important, something that needs to be written about.'

'But it's . . . William, you're kind even to give it some thought but . . . No, it's too late for me.'

'Adam, you're much too young to know how much time you've got left.'

'No, I mean the committee meets soon. They won't, they . . . they *can't* give me tenure and –'

'You're a historian, aren't you?'

'Yes.'

'Well, I've got something you might want to consider researching. I didn't say anything about tenure. I didn't say anything about Columbia, did I? Someone will pay if you do good work. You think you're in a difficult position? As I understand it you *are* in a difficult position. But I would have thought that in your life you'd studied and written enough about people in difficult positions to be ashamed to throw in the towel so easily. Are you really going to tell me you won't even hear me out? There'll always be time to quit, I promise you.'

Adam Zignelik took the old man's hands in his hands for a moment and squeezed.

'You're somethin' else, you know that?'

'I *know* what *I* am. We're talking about you. What kind of man are you?'

'All right, councillor, I'm listening.'

*

Lamont Williams talked very little at work, even to his colleagues in Building Services. Most of the time as he made his rounds, however far his thoughts might have roamed, he kept them to himself. He often thought of his daughter as he collected the garbage, mopped the hallways and swept the floors. Where was she? Was she at school? What was she learning? But now he was thinking about cancer. It was all around him. Sometimes it went for children. In every room at Memorial Sloan-Kettering Cancer Center there was a patient who had some kind of cancer. There had to have been a time, he thought, when they didn't have it. Then the moment came when they were told that they had it and everything was changed for them. The moment of the telling would become something the patient would never forget. It was the moment at which a wall descended with the speed and terror of the blade of the guillotine to instantly divide time in two – the time he had been well, and the time his life was on notice. Where do you go with the news? Where do you take it? Do you take it home? In each room was a patient with his or her own set of answers. It reminded him of the time he was sentenced.

The moment he was convicted everything changed. Even after he was arrested with his childhood friend Michael and another younger man he barely knew, there had been the possibility that his version of events would be believed and he would be found 'not guilty' of armed robbery. He'd had that hope. But the moment he heard the word 'guilty' a wall appeared in his life dividing his days forever between the days he only suspected he might not be believed and the day his suspicion proved to be warranted and he was deprived of his liberty.

He was thinking about this as he collected the garbage and reached the room of a patient with whom he had, in a short space of time, become fascinated. This old man, with his unusual way of talking, seemed to have singled out Lamont as no one else in the institution had. The man was an odd mix of humour and tired, almost sad, resignation. Many of their respective words were lost on the other yet he felt in a way strangely understood by this odd old white man. Visiting and listening to the man was somehow calming. It was critically important for Lamont not to get distracted during his shift but at the end of the day, before going home, it was a huge relief to have this man take him away from concerns about money, about the security of his job, about the way the day had gone and whether the way his supervisor had looked at him bode good or ill or nothing at all for him.

The old man looked at everything, including Lamont, unlike the way any other people Lamont had ever encountered did. It was as though the old man didn't live in the real world of traffic on crowded streets, buses, subway stations, police, lawyers, courts, upstate penitentiaries, social workers, welfare, television, advertising, bodegas and supermarkets. Even the medical staff didn't seem to genuinely permeate this man's world. From what Lamont could see, it was as though the man was humouring them. He tolerated them. He played with them even though, surely, Lamont reasoned, he needed them. With his wispy hair and frail body the man floated through all this or perhaps above all of it, like someone in a fantasy. If, sitting on a bus for instance, Lamont's mind turned to the man, he appeared almost mythical, no more real than a creature of Ray Harryhausen's making he remembered from childhood. But the old man in the bed in the ward was certainly real. And though his cancer was real too, he never seemed afraid. More than anything he had said to Lamont up to then, this was what was most seductive about time spent in this man's company. No one else Lamont had spoken to since leaving prison had seemed so intoxicatingly unafraid.

When he came again the old patient was being visited by the tall young black woman he'd seen in Mr Mandelbrot's room before, the seemingly no-nonsense young oncologist, Dr Washington. He knocked once on the door just to announce his presence and, without making eye contact with either of them, went straight for the garbage. There were some candy wrappers in the bin. The bin was too far from the bed for the wrappers to belong to the old man and, he reasoned, the strictly business young oncologist was unlikely to be eating candy with him so Lamont interpreted the signs as suggesting the old man had had at least one visitor. The tentative conclusion pleased him. He didn't like to think of the old man as lonely and the realisation of this made him smile to himself. He was, himself, often lonely. He tried to creep out of the room without drawing attention to himself. What kind of cancer did the old man have?

'There he is!' he heard Mr Mandelbrot say. 'He doesn't visit me when you're around.'

Lamont Williams turned back to face them with the smallest hint of a smile before urging his trolley on down the corridor away from the old man's room.

*

'In 1948,' William McCray told Adam Zignelik, 'President Harry Truman issued Executive Order 9948 declaring that from then on there would be equality of treatment and opportunity for all persons in the armed services regardless of race, colour, religion or national origin. You would know this and you'd know that he did it about three years too late for me and for men like me who fought in World War II. There were young black men in Europe and in Asia fighting for a country that segregated them from the majority of their countrymen even as they fought the same enemy for the same country. We were fighting for values fundamental to the very essence of what it means to be a human being. I want to say we were fighting for freedom but now, when I talk about freedom in this context I'm not talking about it as a concept debased by virtue of its appropriation by conservative economic and political ideologues over the last twenty or thirty years. I'm not talking about freedom to ignore Jim Crow laws or freedom to ignore the separation of Church and State or freedom from government intervention in the alleviation of chronic poverty or freedom to carry semi-automatic weapons around your neighbourhood or freedom to incite racial hatred under cover of the First Amendment.' Adam loved this man. He was forever fighting the good fight. William barely took time to draw breath before continuing.

'I'm talking about the inalienable freedom to live as a citizen of a country with rights equal to those of all other citizens of that country. In some cases I'm talking about the very first freedom: the freedom just to live. This is what we were fighting for.

'We started off doing menial chores; cleaning, cooking, lifting, hauling, delivering equipment, driving and waiting on white officers. But as the needs of the armed forces grew they were forced to confront their own prejudice. They badly needed men to fight the Nazis. They had access to a pool of healthy strong young men but they'd always considered these men inferior, inherently inferior. But now Hitler was calling, and the needs of the war demanded that black men be permitted to fight, and fight we did.

'When we got the chance, hell, did we fight! In towns right across Europe we fought the Nazis; sometimes it was street-to-street combat. We fought them hard and close, street by street. But when the streets were liberated and under Allied control, the liberating black soldiers were banned from them, forbidden to use those same streets we had just taken. We saw our friends maimed or killed taking those streets, maimed and killed taking German prisoners of war. Some of us were put under the command of vicious white — often southern — officers. It was thought that these men knew how to get the best out of coloured men. They even had us sit behind the German POWs at the USO shows. We were fighting and dying every day but you never see us in the war movies just like you didn't see us in the newsreels. Our own grandchildren barely know what we did.

'Adam, somebody's got to tell them. Somebody's got to tell people what we did. You see, when we got home a lot of us couldn't let things go back to the way they were before the war. We just couldn't after what we'd been through, after what we'd done. A lot of the impetus for the civil rights movement came from these returned soldiers and I don't think people know this.'

'No, you're right, there hasn't been all that much written about it, not that aspect.'

'You want to trace the steps of certain individuals from their war experience to their work in the movement after the war. Nobody's done that, have they?'

'No, I don't think anyone *has* done that. But, William, that doesn't mean *I* should be the one.'

'I don't want to hear that. There isn't time. These are old men we're talking about and already there aren't many of them left.'

'Look, you're right, it's very important work, but you should probably talk to Charlie about getting somebody else because —' The old man took Adam Zignelik surprisingly firmly by the wrist and changed his tone to one of force.

'I'm talking to *you*. Listen to me; I got a friend in Boston, a black man, a veteran of the civil rights movement and a veteran of the Second World War. Now you want to talk to him and don't tell me you don't. You didn't know what to write about. That's what stopped you. You split up from Diana. Well, this man was in the outfit that liberated Dachau. Do you know what he saw? Do you know what he thought when he saw it and do you know what he did when he came home with those thoughts? What does a man do with those thoughts? I think you want to talk to him. Don't you look at me and tell me you don't want to tell the story of a man like that.'

*

What kind of cancer did the old man have? The question stayed with Lamont throughout the day. He wondered how he could find out. Since

153

starting work there he'd learned that some days a patient you had seen just the day before could, without any announcement, suddenly no longer be there the next morning and the thought had arisen that this could happen to his strange old new friend, Mr Mandelbrot. He imagined it happening and imagined it too well. He felt a sadness at the prospect of the old man's passing that he hadn't expected. At the end of the day, when he had completed all his duties, he quietly made his way back to the old man's room. Mr Mandelbrot was there and alone.

'Mr Lamont, come in. You don't want to take any chances. You have to take chances in this life. Come in, come in.'

'Hey, Mr Mandelbrot. How you doin'?'

'You are not someone who takes chances in life. Sit down.'

'What do you mean?'

'You won't come in when she's here.'

'Who?'

'You know who.'

'The doctor?'

'You don't come in when she's here. There's space in this room for two opinions but you don't come in. What are you so afraid of?'

'I don't get you, Mr Mandelbrot.'

'She might be a doctor but she's still a woman. The man has to take the chance, even these days. You're the man, Mr Lamont. You got to take chances.'

Lamont smiled. 'You still takin' chances, are you, Mr Mandelbrot?'

'Let me tell you, I've taken chances all my life, many chances. If I hadn't been someone to take chances I wouldn't be lucky enough to have cancer here. You don't know me. I know more about you than you know about me.'

'Prob'ly. If you're feelin' up to it you can tell me about you, before I have to go home.'

'Wouldn't you like to go home with Dr Washington?'

'Now we're talking about you.'

'Are you married, Mr Lamont? No ring what I can see.'

'We're talkin' about you, I thought.'

'You want to hear about me?'

'If you want to tell me.'

'I want to tell you if you're really going to pay attention. No one pays attention; even Dr Washington. Pay attention, otherwise I can have other appointments.'

'I'm paying attention.'

''Cause I'm going to test you, Mr Lamont.'

'Okay, I'm listening. I'm paying attention.'

'My father was a butcher in Poland.'

'You Polish?'

'I'm a Polish Jew.'

'My grandma said you might be a Jew.'

'Your grandma? Is she a Polish Jew?'

Lamont smiled. 'I was talking to her about you.'

'Did she think she was in my story? I'm not remembering her.'

'I'm sorry, Mr Mandelbrot.'

'Pay good attention. I've got cancer. I'm going to test you.'

*

Adam sat alone at his kitchen table poring over a miscellany of take-out menus. None of them inspired him. Nor did the cold chicken in the fridge. The chicken hadn't inspired him two days earlier, when it was hot, either. He got up to pour himself a Scotch and soda, the soda in a concession to an inner voice whose message he was having trouble making out.

'You thought he was going to talk more about us, didn't you? And you're disappointed. You were waiting for somebody to convince you to contact me and William had been your best bet,' he heard Diana's voice say in his head. He took his drink over to the couch and turned on the television.

'Do you *want* me to contact you?' he asked her. 'I don't have your new number.'

'You have my work number, my cell and my email address.'

'You didn't answer the question. Do you want me to contact you?'

'What would you be saying?'

'I don't know . . . I bought some raisins today.'

'Yeah?'

'The ones you like . . . from that health food store you like, the one run by successive refugees of successive totalitarian regimes.'

'Yeah?'

'I bought too many for the jar.'

'Really.'

'Yeah.'

'What are you going to do?'

'I don't know. I thought maybe we could get back together. You could tell me what to do.'

'With the raisins?'

'You could start with the raisins.'

'You've got to talk to William's friend, you know that, the one who liberated Dachau. You know that, don't you?'

For about an hour Adam had been imagining them talking in this way while he flicked through a stream of television channels without ever focusing on any of them. When the intercom buzzed the transition to a reality outside his head was slow. 'Is that you?' he asked Diana.

'Why don't you answer it?'

'What if it's you?'

'Do you want it to be me?' Adam picked up the receiver.

'Hello?'

'Adam?'

'Who is this?'

'Is that Adam?' asked a female voice so young-sounding it might have belonged to a child.

'Who *is* this?'

'If you could just say it's Adam I could tell you.'

'Okay, it's Adam. Who *is* this?'

'Sounds like you but you might just be saying it. Guess I should have thought of that.'

'Sonia?'

'Can I come up?'

'What are you doing here?'

'Is it bad that I came?'

'No. Is everything all right? Come on up.' He let her in and she was soon standing in his apartment.

'What's wrong?'

'Nothing.'

'Where are your parents?'

'At home still, I guess.'

'What are you doing out at this time of night?'

'It's not so late. I felt like a walk. I was in the neighbourhood so I thought I'd stop by.'

'Do your parents know you're here?'

'Maybe. Prob'ly not.'

'Probably not! Where do they think you are?'

'I don't know. They prob'ly think I'm in my room . . . when they get to think about it. I thought I'd hang out here for a while. Is that okay?'

'It's okay with me but don't you think we should tell your parents where you are?'

'They wouldn't care.'

'Now I know *that's* not true. I'm going to call them and tell them where you are. If they don't mind you being here I certainly don't but –'

'You'll just be interrupting them.'

'Sonia, what's going on?'

'They're just fighting . . . again . . . and I got sick of it. Do you think maybe I could have a beverage of some kind?'

'I'm going to call your parents. You help yourself to whatever's in the fridge. I think I've got Coke Zero.'

'Do you have Diet Coke?'

'What's the difference?'

'Coke Zero's for guys and Diet Coke's for girls.'

'What are you, six?' Adam picked up the phone to call Sonia's parents.

'That's not what *you're* drinking,' Sonia called from the refrigerator. 'I could smell it. You're all liquored up.'

'Now I'm *really* calling your parents.'

'I don't *mind* that you're all liquored up,' Sonia said, taking a can from the fridge.

Michelle took the call. Neither she nor Charles had realised that Sonia hadn't been in her room and Adam heard their reaction to their ignorance of this as itself either a new source of trouble or an instance of an old one. Michelle explained the call to Charles with her hand obviously but ineffectively over the mouthpiece of the phone. 'See, that's what I'm talking about,' Adam heard her say. 'This is exactly the kind of thing. She's out roaming the streets. And you didn't even know,' to which Charles responded with slightly less regard to volume, '*You* didn't know!'

'Is she okay?' Michelle asked.

'She's fine,' Adam said looking at Sonia on the couch flicking through the television channels.

'She's not going to be okay when I'm through with her,' Adam heard Charles say. Michelle thanked Adam for taking care of Sonia and said one of them would be around soon to pick her up.

'Do you want to talk about it?'

'About what?'

'About your parents arguing.'

'It's fairly complicated as these things go.'

'Really . . . as these things go?'

'Nothing to do with me. Hey, where'd all your books go? Oops, sorry!'

'It's okay.'

'You know . . . I really like Diana. Do you think I can still be friends with her?'

'Can't see why not.'

'Think *you* will be?'

'I hope so . . . eventually.'

'Where'd she move to?'

'Hell's Kitchen.'

'That's not so far.'

'No, someone like you could walk there for an evening stroll.'

'Why'd you guys break up?'

'It's fairly complicated . . . as these things go.'

'Was it about children? You should have children, you know. Mom said –'

'Do you mind if we talk about something else?'

'What do you want to talk about?'

'Haven't you got some teenage stuff we can talk about? Haven't you ever thought of setting fire to your parents' apartment, taking lots of hard drugs and running away with the worst boy in school?'

'No! Did *they* say that? All I said was I was thinking of maybe getting a job, part-time, like in a Duane Reade or something.'

'Sure, I could see that. You already know how to act bored.'

'Were they mad on the phone?'

'Little bit.'

'Who more?'

'Hard to say.'

'Was it Dad?'

'By a nose.'

'Find out what's wrong with her,' Diana whispered. But there wasn't time to find out much more.

Both Charles and Michelle arrived to pick up Sonia from Adam's apartment. For a moment Adam thought he saw fear in Sonia's eyes. He wondered if she were afraid of getting into trouble or of something else. Charles was the first to speak.

'Sonia McCray, what in God's name has gotten into you? Are you out of your mind?'

Sonia rushed into her mother's arms and then buried her face in her mother's chest. Michelle gestured to Adam to take Charles into another room, which he did.

'Adam, I'm so sorry you're getting dragged into our daughter's prime time adolescent dramas.' Charles was furious.

'Charlie,' Adam whispered, 'you know how much I love Sonia. But whatever's going on at your place – and it's none of my business – I think it upset her to a point where –'

'What did she say?'

'Not very much at all.'

'Really?'

'Yeah. You should be very proud of her –'

'Proud!'

'Yeah, as upset as she was, she was still incredibly discreet. I tried to find out all that goes on behind the closed doors of the McCray household but she really wasn't giving anything away. If you hadn't shown up I was going to have to waterboard her.

'Listen, I know she shouldn't have run out like that. She does too. You don't think she didn't know it even as she was doing it? And I know you'll need to satisfy yourself of that but while you're doing that, remember there had to be something going on inside her to make her do something like this. It's just a cry for attention. She gets upset and what does she do? Does she really run away? Does she do drugs? Does she drink? Does she steal? Is she hanging out with boys? She's not even smoking cigarettes. She walks a couple of blocks to my place and drinks a Diet Coke. She knows the first thing I'm going to do is see if she's okay, right after which I'm going to call you. This is not really what anybody would call running off the rails.'

'You're a good friend, you know that?'

'To her or to you?'

'To her; I was ready to kill her. You saved her from a good whoopin' that would have made me feel a whole lot better. So you see, you're no damn good to me.'

'Charlie, you've never hit her in your life.'

'No, I haven't. Maybe that's the problem.'

'Maybe you ought to drink more. You want a beer?'

'That's not what you've been drinkin'.'

'You want a Scotch?'

'I'd love a double but I don't think we're goin' to get the time.'

'Sure . . .' The two men looked at each other in the room Adam used to share with Diana. The bed was unmade. Adam hadn't expected any company.

'I caught up with your dad today.'

'Oh, thanks, Adam. That's great. I really do owe you. How do you think he's doing?'

'About the Supreme Court? Well, he seems more fired up than

depressed or even resigned. I think he thinks the decision might've been different if *he'd* been arguing it. He said he wanted to talk to me about . . . me, my situation.'

'Well, that's good I guess, as long as you don't mind. It means he's able to think of something besides himself.'

'I don't think his feelings about the Supreme Court decision should be characterised as him thinking about himself.'

'No, you're right. It was unfair of me to put it that way.' Charles let out a breath and put his hand on Adam's shoulder. Looking out in the direction of Michelle and Sonia, he continued, 'It's been a long day.'

'He said he wanted to talk to me about a friend of his. I . . . gather you talked to him about my tenure situation.'

'Yeah, Adam, I hope you don't mind but for all his passion, when it counts he's discreet and he cares about you very much. I'm sorry if you think I've betrayed your confidence. I was worried about you and –'

'Charlie, I don't mind. Really. I thought he'd want to talk about me and Diana but –'

'Didn't he?'

'Not so much. He kind of got sidetracked by this friend of his he was telling me about.'

'A friend?'

'He was trying to encourage me professionally. He said he thinks he has something for me to write about. Charlie, don't look so worried. I know where things stand as far as Columbia's concerned. I tried to explain to him that it's over for me there but he was urging me to write my way into another job or to write a book or something. He wants me to write again and he thinks he can help me.'

'I'm sorry, Adam. I didn't mean your kindness and his therapy to spill over into your career. You don't have to humour him any more than you already have.'

'He wants me to talk to a veteran friend of his.'

'Not what's-his-name, the guy from Boston? Is this about the liberation of Dachau?'

'Yeah, that's right. I take it he's talked to you about this.'

'You got that right.'

'I'm not getting you. You're sceptical about this or is it just that he talks about this too often?'

Michelle stuck her head in the door. 'Sorry to interrupt but I think we need to get little Miss Night Stalker home.'

'You around late tomorrow afternoon?' Charles asked. 'If you want to pick this up we could talk then.' It was agreed that next time Sonia wanted to visit Adam she would have to both tell her parents and ask Adam beforehand.

'Sorry I have to go. I'll come again another time,' Sonia said.

'Well, that's good. I'll count on it,' Adam answered.

Leaning on his door, Adam watched the three of them as they walked away. 'There's no one else there but him . . . ever!' he heard Sonia whispering to her mother as he was closing the door to his apartment.

*

'I was born 15 December 1922 in the town of Olkusz.' Lamont Williams sat in a chair and listened. 'It's a little town what is near Krakow but when I was four years old we moved to Zabkowice. My father was a butcher and *he* took chances too. He had, with my mother, three other children after me. We didn't have much money. During the school vacation I took work with any farmers in the area who had work what they needed doing. I also helped out my father with the butchery.

'The times were very hard in Poland between the wars. People didn't have money. My father took debt from people instead of money.'

'You mean like credit?'

'Yes, credit. People took their meat on credit. They took a long time to pay or else they didn't pay at all. So my father's butchery went out of business from this.'

'Bankrupt?'

'Yes, bankrupt. Being the eldest in the family I had to do what I could to help out the family. I would go to the train tracks to collect coal from the tracks, anything what I could. A lot of the farmers in the area knew me because when my father would buy cows and other animals from them he sent me to take it from the farmers. I was a strong boy so

I could handle the animals. The farmers knew me and liked me from all the business what we did. I knew them and their farms. I knew the roads there and also the short cuts through the fields where I could take the animals. I looked for places, hidden places where maybe I could take a girl if I could ever be lucky. I found some places, more places than girls. It was not like now. But I had a lot of friends in the area. You know?'

'They all Jews?'

'No. I was like a leader of a group of boys, all of them Polish, not Jews, except me.'

'You're Polish too though, right?'

'You are black, Mr Lamont, yes?'

'Uh-huh.'

'You are American too, yes?'

'Gotcha.'

'Listen and remember. When was I born?'

'Nineteen twenty-two.'

'What day, what month? Remember me. There is no one else like me, and your Dr Washington thinks I have cancer so you have to remember. I will test you. I was born 15 December 1922 in the town of Olkusz. Say it!'

'Fifteenth December 1922.'

'Where?'

'I don't remember.'

'No, you *have* to remember, Mr Lamont. Otherwise what are we talking?'

'I'm sorry.'

'I was born 15 December 1922 in the town of Olkusz. It's a little town what is near Krakow but when I was four years old we moved to Zabkowice. Say it: Olkusz.'

'Ol-kooz.'

'Say Zabkowice.'

'Zab-kov-itz-ay.'

'My father?'

'Your father was a butcher. Sold meat on credit in hard times. Went bankrupt. You were the leader of a gang, the others were all Polish, you were the only Jew. You got no trouble, as a Jew, I mean?'

'Others did, yes. Not me. Maybe sometimes. If anyone called me a Jew I hit them. I was strong. There was one boy from the area. I remember his face. I can see it. A boy from the area but not really in the group, with hair like it was so straight from a ruler making angles, sharp angles on the ears; I remember him. He wanted trouble; called me dirty Jew so I hit him. He cried in front of the other boys and that was that for him.

'I was working in a stone yard when the Germans invaded Poland to start the war.'

'Stone yard, you mean . . . like a quarry?'

'Yes, a quarry. I had work there. When they set up the ghetto it was 1942.'

'What do you mean a ghetto . . . for Jews?'

'You know what is a ghetto, Mr Lamont?'

'Yeah.'

'When the Nazis invaded, sooner or later they set up ghettos all over Poland for the Jews. Jews were expelled from the villages and towns and sent to the nearest ghetto. My family was sent with the other Jewish families from around the area to Dabrowa Gornicza. You say it: Dabrowa Gornicza.'

'Dab-rov-a Gor-nitch-a.'

'We were in the ghetto at Dabrowa Gornicza and I had a special pass what let me come and go from the ghetto.'

'How come you got that pass?'

'Because I was chosen to work outside the ghetto in construction. There was a lot of building going on at the time and the Nazis needed labour. They used the Jews as slave labour. You see, they were settling that part of Poland, the west, with Germans. From Germany German people and families along with the soldiers were coming. They called them *Volksdeutsche*. For the *Volksdeutsche* they needed buildings, houses, roads, renovations to old buildings and they used Jews what came from the nearest ghetto to where they were. I was lucky and took my chances with a pass that let me leave the ghetto every day to work in the construction.

'Leading out of the ghetto from the street where my family lived in the ghetto in Dabrowa Gornicza there was a street where was an SA man living there with his wife in a house they were building. I saw them and I saw the man every day when I went off to work.'

'What do you mean, "an SA man"?'

'SA means *Sturmabteilung*, Storm Troopers. It was a German paramilitary organisation. Each day when I went off to work and I would see him I would say hello, good morning and things like this to him. Even though he saw me with the yellow star he would still answer back, good morning. I said it in German.'

'What do you mean the yellow star?'

'They made all Jews wear the Jewish Star of David, a yellow one sewn onto your clothing. If you were caught without it you could be shot where you stood.

'Because of my work permit for the construction works I heard things from outside the ghetto and I heard many things before other people. Lots of things were said. You couldn't always believe them. I heard that when Jews left the ghetto they didn't always go to another ghetto. Sometimes they were sent to be killed. I wasn't sure so I didn't want to tell my parents what I'd heard. What for would I tell them when it might not be true? I heard that they were going to be moving the Jews of Dabrowa Gornicza to a ghetto in Sosnowiec. You can say it.'

'Sos-nov-ietz.'

*

It was six o'clock the following evening when Charles and Adam resumed their conversation. 'The more I think about it the angrier at him I get,' Charles said. 'He really has no right –'

'Angry?'

'Adam, the sweet old man is taking advantage of you, of your situation. He knows you're not in good shape professionally and he thinks this is his chance.'

'Charlie, what are you talking about? The more *I* think about it the more I think it might be worth a *little* time at least.'

'You can't be serious? All my professional life he's been trying to get me to use my education and then later also my position to explore the role of black World War II veterans and now he's trying it on you because he thinks you're his best chance.'

'But he might be onto something. People know that when black World War II veterans came home to the Jim Crow south they weren't going to take it any more. They weren't going to say "Yes, sir, yes, ma'am", they weren't going to be addressed as "boy", they weren't going to be addressed by their first names when they had to address white people as "Mister" and "Missus". They weren't any longer going to step off the sidewalk when a white man went past. These are all small acts of resistance that veterans introduced. Their experience in the war gave them the courage for it that they hadn't had before. Look, Charlie, I don't know of any study by anyone that actually links black soldiers' specific experience abroad with their post-war civil rights activities back home. If I can get the people who were there on the ground, including at the liberation of concentration camps, if I can put together a map of exactly where black soldiers were . . . it might well be the first piece in making that concrete link. Charlie, you might remember, I copped flak, at least from certain quarters and quite wrongly in my opinion, for studying the role of lawyers because lawyers don't constitute a social movement. But what we're talking about now is a social movement, a classic example of one. Maybe I can do it, get the black soldiers there and bring them home, then show what they did back home.'

'Adam, I'm telling you, don't get involved with this.'

'Why on earth not?'

'Okay, first and foremost, the subject is a veritable minefield. There was a PBS documentary made around the early '90s on the role of black soldiers at the liberation of Dachau. Did you know about this? As a consequence of the documentary all sorts of people came out of the woodwork saying there were no black troops at the liberation of Dachau. The military records are said not to back up the claim.'

'Charlie, since when did you take the official government line as the beginning and end of anything? I've started looking at this and one is entitled to start asking questions about the accuracy of the records. There are obvious reasons why the records might not tell the whole story. Even without bias the records might distort the truth. Did you know black outfits were frequently split up and "lent out" to other outfits? Take the 761st, for example; it was often referred to as a "bastard outfit" because it didn't seem to belong to anyone. This meant that nobody "officially" knew where they were at any given time so, of course, no formal record of their service would be complete.'

'Adam, whether or not they were there, the topic, especially the Dachau example, aroused intense passions, not to mention the attention of some virulent racists, who seemed to feel the need to protect the record of the military as though having black troops there somehow tarnishes the US Army's record. Adam, it's a minefield.'

'Isn't this precisely the sort of topic we should be researching?'

'Who's "we"?'

'Historians.'

'Adam, is that what you're looking for – controversy, or maybe some kind of glory? You want to be a hero or do you want to be a scholar? And anyway, have you ever considered the consequences of concluding that black troops were *not* there?'

'Are you suggesting there are some conclusions only a black historian can reach?'

'For God's sake, Adam, I'm trying to protect you! Can't you see that?'

'Does this mean that you've already formed a view? You think black soldiers weren't there.'

Adam knew that it was possible for William to see him as his last chance to get something written about the specific role of black veterans in the civil rights movement, for it to be controversial and for the suggestion to be offered as both a measure of hope and as a legitimate scholarly idea. There was nothing inherently wrong with all these purposes being served simultaneously. But he couldn't help feeling a little disturbed by William's failing to mention the PBS documentary and the surrounding controversy. Adam turned over in his mind the pros and cons of raising this with William. On the one hand it might put the old man on the spot. On the other hand to deny William the opportunity to explain the omission would be to deny him the intellectual respect he would accord a younger man. He was still mulling this over when William called him and, though he hadn't reached any firm decision, he found himself succumbing to a childlike lack of restraint and asking with a hint of complaint how William had kept the saga of the early '90s PBS documentary from him. Then before he knew what he was saying and before giving William a chance to respond, he added as a younger brother might that Charles had been trying to dissuade him from taking up the topic.

'I was going to tell you about that documentary, of course I was,' William told him. 'You were going to find it within minutes of starting your research anyway so what would be the point of keeping it from you? But it's not the first thing I wanted you to know, that's true. We don't know who it was who apparently definitively dismissed the claim that black soldiers were part of the liberation of Dachau. I certainly don't know who it was and Charlie's never given me a satisfactory answer as to their identity and that's 'cause he doesn't know and could not be bothered looking into it.

'And, yes, it's also true that I *have* been trying to get Charlie to write about this. For years, frankly, I've been trying to get him to write about it. I don't mind admitting that. What's wrong with that? My son is a highly respected historian and my generation is dying out. One could say, given his position and what I, and other black men of my generation lived through, that I have an obligation to at least try to get him to write about it. He holds a privileged position in a society where black men are still over-represented in most of the negative statistics and under-represented in most of the positive ones. More than 50 per cent of black men in this country don't finish high school and, of that more than 50 per cent, 72 per cent are unemployed. They've got no pride, no hope and very few positive role models. They should know what men like my friend did, black men of my generation. The world should know what we did. But Charlie's not going to tell anyone. He's got a block on this, a mental block when it comes to this.

'Now take this story for instance. My friend is a black veteran who, among other things, served his country at the risk of his own life, liberating victims of one of the worst regimes that has ever existed, and ever since then people have been saying he wasn't there. Don't you see what this is, Adam? This is what happened when the invisible man went to war! But my son is a historian of the Reconstruction and he doesn't want to rock any boats now that he's risen to the top.'

'William, I think you're being a bit hard on Charlie. I completely agree that the role and experience of black servicemen abroad and at home are worthy and under-researched topics but they fall more into the realm of twentieth-century political history. That's my area, not Charlie's. At least it was what I took to *calling* my area.'

'So you're still interested?'

'I'll certainly talk to your friend in Boston.'

'That's great, Adam! You're a good boy. You won't regret this. I've left a couple of messages for him but he hasn't returned the call. I hope he's all right. At our age . . .'

Later that day William's friend did return the call, which led to William calling Adam again. This time though he sounded deflated. William's friend in Boston did not want to speak to Adam or to anyone.

'He's tired, he's old and he's not well,' William explained. 'He suffered racism as a kid at home before the war, risked his life in a segregated army fighting Nazism in Europe, came home to fight the civil rights battles we fought and now he just wants to be left alone. He can no longer bear the indignity of having to prove anything to anyone. He said he's given all the interviews he's ever going to give about any aspect of his life. He thinks the controversy generated by the PBS documentary has taken years off his life. I can well imagine it has, Adam. He feels as though, even after all these years, nothing much has been achieved. The Supreme Court decision didn't exactly make him want to get up and do the quick-step, either.'

'There was nothing you could say?'

'Adam, how well do you know me? Don't you think I tried? I told him all about you, that you weren't just anybody, told him you were Jake's son.'

'Jake's son,' Adam said almost to himself.

'He liked the sound of you, really he did but . . . he's just done fighting. He's not well. So I'm afraid if you're still inclined to run with this you're going to have to rely on the interviews he's already given.

He said he could get his daughter to send them or at least a reference to them through the internet.'

'Email?'

'Yeah, he said she's got email. He doesn't want to be bothered with computers. Said he gave up trying to program the TiVo. Want to read the interviews?'

'Well, there's no harm looking, but his critics will just say they're versions of the same self-serving story anyway told by the one source.'

'That's pretty much what he said too. I guess that's it, Adam. We tried. That's all you could do.'

'It's a shame. I have to admit I was getting more and more interested.'

'Well, thanks for humouring an old man but we've come to the end of the road. He won't talk any more. Much as I tried to talk him out of it, I understand completely. He's been really hurt. "Let him read the interviews I've already done," he said. Oh, he also thinks there might've been a survivor who mentioned seeing African American soldiers at the liberation of Dachau but he doesn't remember exactly where he saw that. It was a long time back, just after the war. He raised this back when they were testing the makers of the documentary but it didn't go anywhere. Some guy in Chicago, a historian, got something about it from a survivor in the years immediately after the war. My friend said he wrote the guy's name down at the time on a scrap of paper and forgot all about it till the hullabaloo about the PBS documentary. Then he went looking through his records, personal files, found it and gave the name and even the name of the academic's institution to one of the researchers working on the documentary but nothing came of it.'

'Why not?'

'Well, he was embarrassed to admit this just now but, reading between the lines, I think he got the names wrong, either the historian's name or the university's name or both. I'm guessing that when he offered it up to the researchers so that they could find the interview with the survivor, they couldn't find it. The producers wanted to believe him but they were drawing a lot of heat from the press, from the channel, from a lot of people by all accounts. He said he never thought it would ever be so important. After all, it had only been by chance that he'd copied down the Chicago guy's details in the first place. He said this was something he read about in the first year or two after demobilisation and he clipped it out of the paper because it was about a time and place he was familiar with – Dachau concentration camp in April 1945. There was a lot going on but he said he made a note of the Chicago professor's name . . .'

'Do you think he'd still have the Chicago guy's details?'

'Well, he had them twenty minutes ago.'

'There's an Australian expression you might want to use on him. Ask him if it would be "stretching the friendship" to pass on to me via you any details of the Chicago historian he read about after the war. I mean the guy's name, his department, the institution, anything.'

'You want to check it out?'

'It shouldn't take long to confirm that he did indeed have the name wrong. But it's always possible he got it right and that the researchers made a mistake or perhaps they were just lazy. It only takes one person to be fed up, lazy, busy . . . who knows?'

'I go back a long way with this man. I know this is still important to him. I don't think it would be "stretching the friendship".'

William called Adam again ten minutes later. The name on the scrap of paper his Boston friend had written down all those years ago was Professor Boardman. That's all that was written on the paper, 'Professor Boardman, Chicago Institute of Technology'.

*

'One day when they had brought us back to the ghetto at Dabrowa Gornicza,' Mr Mandelbrot continued, 'I saw a gap in the security and took the chance to escape the ghetto. I had no time to think. If I was going to act I had to do so immediately. It was what they call now a "window of opportunity". I tore off the Jewish star what was stitched to my jacket and walked into the street leading out of the ghetto. It was very late winter, maybe early spring, and late afternoon and already it was getting dark outside. The street was completely deserted. I didn't know where I was going or if I was doing the right thing. Although I did not look the way they thought Jews look, I still had to think of some story to tell if I was pulled up. I was walking away from the ghetto when a man stepped out in front of me and stopped me. It did not matter whether I looked like a Jew or not. This man knew that I was a Jew. It was the SA man.'

*

Professor Adam Zignelik learned that the US Army Center of Military History, while not surprisingly aware of the PBS documentary on the liberation of Dachau and the controversy it had provoked some fifteen years earlier, would neither confirm nor deny that African American troops were involved. That was its official position on the matter. Additionally, within thirty-six hours of learning from William what was written on a scrap of paper by his veteran friend in the mid- to late 1940s in Boston, Adam had established that there is no Chicago Institute of Technology, not now nor back then, not ever. There was and is, however, an Illinois Institute of Technology but it has never had anyone named Boardman on the faculty, not in the 1940s or later. It has never even had a history department.

Adam made notes of the places he checked. In the mid-1940s the University of Illinois had two campuses, at Navy Pier and at Urbana-Champaign. History was taught at Navy Pier from the time it opened in 1946 to cater for the huge influx of veterans returning home. According to the 1947–48 catalogues, there were ten history courses on offer and nine members of faculty to teach them. But not one of them was named Boardman. As for the Urbana-Champaign campus, there was a Department of History within the College of Liberal Arts and Sciences there during the 1945–46 academic year. According to the Board of Trustees Report of 29 August 1945, there were thirty employees in the Department of History of whom fourteen were faculty, all of them with only 'indefinite tenure'. None of these fourteen academics was named Boardman. Adam even checked the University of Chicago simply because it was in Chicago. He found that it had had a history department right from the time of its establishment in the 1890s but there was no Boardman there, not in the 1940s or before or after. Without asking himself whether he was motivated by scholarship, desperation or some combination of both, Adam checked DePaul, North Park and Loyola universities. He thought to check Northwestern. But while some of them may have existed at the relevant time, there was no Professor Boardman teaching history in the 1940s, '50s or '60s at any of them.

Adam had to conclude that there really was nothing to follow up. William's Boston friend was either lying, mistaken or sending him, advertently or inadvertently, on a wild goose chase. He might have had his reasons to lie about the broader issue, about being at the liberation of Dachau – perhaps to ingratiate himself with liberal Jews who were active in the civil rights movement, Jews like Jake Zignelik. He might have lied perhaps because he had Jewish friends, because he *wished* he'd been there for quite noble reasons or perhaps he could have lied just to have a story to tell.

But why, Adam wondered, make up a story about some Chicago historian and the interviews he'd conducted in the mid-1940s? This was so easy to check and yet, some sixty-odd years later, the man was still mentioning it. Whatever motivated William's friend from Boston, it was looking less and less like the business of a historian. With this knowledge came the sinking re-emergence of the dread that the business of a genuine historian was not really the business of the man whom Adam Zignelik found roaming his apartment alone aimlessly in the middle of the night, his own insensate face looking back at him pathetically from the bathroom mirror. He opened the mirror cupboard and found the comb that Diana had left still entwined with strands of her hair and he wondered how he became the man that held that comb.

'So that's it, is it?' Diana whispered to him in the middle of the night.

'I looked everywhere I could, did everything I could do . . . everything I could think of.'

'Yes, you did. And didn't it feel good? For a minute there you had something to do.'

'Yeah, it did feel good. I could stop thinking about the future and allow myself to become intoxicated with delusions of adequacy.'

'Wasn't there someone at the Illinois Institute of Technology?'

'No, they don't even have a history department, never did.'

'But there was a Boardman, a Professor Boardman.'

'No, there was no Boardman.'

'Yes, there was.'

'No, there wasn't. Believe me, I'd remember.'

'Have a look at your notes.'

'Is it not enough that you visit me and talk to me when I know you're not here? Now you even read my notes. And what's more, you misremember them.'

'Check them, Adam.'

'And if I'm right?'

'If you're right I'll tell you what to do with the surplus raisins.'

'Will you forgive me . . . for what I've done . . . to us?'

'Sweetheart, check your notes.'

Adam went to his desk as he'd heard her direct him and started flicking through the pages. He could see in his own handwriting the fleeting moments of his fragile enthusiasm. 'Illinois Institute of Technology. No History Department. Not ever. No Professor Boardman. Not ever. Once a Professor Border on the faculty but not a historian. No Boardman.'

'Sweetheart, are you sure you're finished?'

*

'I said good evening to the SA man, trying to act calm as though maybe, if I talked like someone who was permitted to walk those streets at that time, he might be tricked by my confidence. I was eighteen or nineteen then and I had confidence. He said good evening back to me and I walked on no more than three steps before he said "stop". He had known what I was and in my three steps each of us had considered our positions. When he said "stop" I thought for a moment to run but this man who said good morning could have had me shot or he could be the best friend I had for many streets. What would you do?'

Lamont Williams didn't know what he would have done and so said nothing. He did not want to delay hearing what happened.

'I didn't run. I turned around to look at the SA man and saw that he had the beginning of a smile on his face. "You are outside the ghetto after curfew," he said. I told him I was strong. I could work. What did he want? I looked up at the second floor of his house, which was still not finished, and I told him I worked in construction and that I could work on his house to help finish it. He shook his head a little bit, not far but very slowly and said that the work on the second floor of his house was work what was being done by civilians. There was nothing in it for him to take the risk of them turning me in.

'But when he said this, I saw for the first time that it was possible, maybe, that he could let me go. If he was already imagining the civilian workers turning me in, it meant that in his head I was living past these few minutes standing there on the street with him. I knew then that there had to be something I could offer for him to let me stay alive. What could he want what I could give? I didn't know but I knew I had to think of something quickly. But I had nothing. I had just before slipped out of the ghetto, like they say, impulsively. I said to him I could do things for him around his house while he was at work in the day, told him I was strong but he laughed. He could see my mind going, running, running while my body stood there on the spot. My heart beat like the heart of small rabbit. He told me to wait there outside while he went inside his house and I said I would wait. Should I run or should I stay? I didn't know. Someone else could have seen me in the light of the street lamp while I waited. The streets were still quiet but I didn't know if they would stay quiet. I didn't know how long he would be gone. What had he gone to do? If I stayed there and waited and no one else saw me and then he came back, what would he do when he came back? This man had said good morning to me every day but he could come outside and shoot me dead in the street with no consequences for him. What was "good morning" worth to this SA man?'

*

What would it take to determine which faculty at the Illinois Institute of Technology had this Professor Border as a member? It took a ten-minute phone call the following day to determine that Professor Henry S. Border was a professor of psychology in the 1940s and the

1950s. This couldn't be the man William's Boston friend was talking about. This man was a psychologist. Exactly what kind of work did this Professor Border do? No one at the end of the phone in Chicago knew offhand. Why should they? The man worked there long before the computer age so there was little that Adam would be able to learn about Professor Border online. Someone on the phone from the School of Psychology told Adam he was welcome to come out there and take a look at Border's files, if he was interested and had the time. They were sorry but, unfortunately, no one there had the time. Of course they didn't have the time. These people were real academics. Only Adam had time. Adam had only time.

What was to stop him flying to Chicago and going to the Illinois Institute of Technology? He could leave for the airport immediately after his Monday morning 'What is History?' lecture. Who would it bother? Who would even know? Adam stood on the street with a little suitcase and his laptop safely packed away. Maybe he was going to a conference. Maybe he mattered. No one he knew saw him. He had no trouble hailing a cab and an immigrant from the subcontinent took him to the airport, no questions asked. He stood in Hudson News at JFK looking at magazines. He looked at cigarette lighters though he didn't smoke, looked at gum and at playing cards. He bought a pen that he didn't need, a copy of *The New York Times* and some peanuts.

The lines at the airport were longer than they used to be, more slow-moving, the security checks more invasive. New York was still on a code orange alert. Or was it yellow now? He didn't know and wondered if anyone there knew. Which was worse? Orange had more red in it so that was probably worse, he figured. No fluids were permitted on the flight, not enough to be useful for anything. Before your legs got crammed under the seat in front of you, you had the opportunity to be shamed by worn, torn or mismatched socks, courtesy of the shoe-bomber. Diana had warned him about the elastic in his socks. 'We appreciate you have a choice of airlines and we thank you for choosing United.' It flew to more than a hundred destinations and in and out of Chapter 11. On a flight to Chicago, towards the rear of the cabin, there was a man impersonating an academic historian. Could anyone tell? Would someone report it?

Adam opened the *Times* and tried to read it. There was an article about the Turks, the Kurds, the US and Iraq. He read the same two sentences over and over, trying to take a running start into the article, but could not get engaged.

Adam thought he might be hungry. He was having trouble opening his peanuts. In disgust with himself he ended up tearing violently at the pack and some of the peanuts flew towards the front of the plane as though more serious than Adam about getting to Chicago. With salt on his hands, Adam watched them fly and then crash-land. He had no children. His parents were long dead. He'd tell people at the Illinois Institute of Technology that he was a historian from Columbia University in New York but soon that wouldn't be true. When wouldn't it be true? How fast did the plane fly? A man across the aisle and one row ahead turned back to look at Adam and what was left of his peanuts. Adam smiled weakly. He felt there were bits of peanut caught between his teeth. What was he doing flying out to Chicago to examine the sixty-year-old work of an unknown mid-western psychologist whose name was a little bit like the name an old man in Boston once wrote on a scrap of paper? This was absurd. Adam looked at his salty fingers and thought, Fuck, I hate me.

*

'He came back out into the street. It seemed to me I had been waiting for an hour but it was only really a few minutes. I don't know how long it was. He looked around the street, which was still empty. With his finger he beckoned me to come inside to his house. I didn't know what he was going to do but I did as he wanted. I could have tried to run away, but to where? And, anyway, he could have shot me in the back with a pistol. It was still chilly at that time and he wore a coat. Perhaps he had a pistol inside the coat. I didn't know.

'We went inside, he closed the front door behind him and he told me to wait in the hall. He walked away from me into a room, maybe it was the bedroom, and he closed the door. I listened but I couldn't hear much what he was saying. It was more like loud whispering between him and a woman. This woman was his wife. After some minutes he came out of the room alone. He told me that I could sleep in the unfinished upstairs part of the house but in the day I would have to go somewhere else. I thanked him and then he went and got his wife. She looked at me like I was something she had never in her life seen before, a strange animal. She seemed fascinated. Maybe she was even a bit afraid of me. I don't know. It was not how the guards who took us from the ghetto to work looked at us. They looked at us with contempt but it was different with her. It was a kind of fearful fascination; I would describe it like that. I nodded to her, not knowing whether I should shake hands with her or even with him.

'He showed me upstairs and told me that he would come in the morning to make sure I was awake before the sun came up. I had to leave there before the builders came to start work on the upstairs. Then his wife came up behind him with some bread. They used a ladder. I don't know what he had told her. I didn't even know for sure if she knew I was a Jew but I guessed because of the way she looked at me that she knew. Perhaps this was the first time that the reality of what the Germans were doing there was getting through to her. I didn't know what she knew. It was hard to imagine that she couldn't know what was happening to us in the ghetto a few streets away from her new house, but perhaps she didn't know. Even outside the ghetto they had hanged some Poles, non-Jews, and made their neighbours watch. But if she didn't see this and nobody told her . . .'

*

Adam Zignelik checked into what looked like an out-of-the-way truck stop passing itself off as a hotel in a neighbourhood that had been described on the internet as downtown Chicago but which felt more deserted than any downtown should feel. A website had lied. A few days earlier he had not ever heard of the Illinois Institute of Technology. Now he was instructing a cab driver to take him there on Chicago's south side. Though he had little time to observe his surroundings and was concerned not to look an idiot to the young professor he was due to be meeting in the office of the School of Psychology, Adam couldn't help but notice that, with its unusual variety of greenery among a mix of very old and very new buildings, some almost ostentatiously modern, the campus was unlike any he had ever seen before.

'That's the Mies van der Rohe touch, amazing, amazing architect, very famous,' the young psychology professor waxed lyrically, walking Adam out of the building and escorting him to the Galvin Library, the institute's largest library. 'You should take a tour of the campus, if you've got the time. We often get people visiting just for the architecture. I hate to do this to you but I've got to rush. It was . . . What did you want to see again? It was the Border stuff you wanted to see, yeah?'

Within minutes Adam was in a dimly lit basement with some boxes filled with the files and papers of an academic psychologist who had worked there some fifty to sixty years earlier. Alone, Adam started to question the sense of the expedition. Not knowing exactly what to do next, he took out a pen and notebook and started jotting down whatever random facts of interest he could find while at the same time trying to shut out the voice in his head, his own voice, telling him in sharp and shrill bursts that he was a charlatan.

So . . . It wasn't until 1939 that Armour College and Lewis University merged to become the Illinois Institute of Technology or, as everyone seemed to call it, IIT.

Adam had heard of Armour. An important Chicago figure or family, yes, but who was Armour, exactly, again? Then he read that Armour College was the bequest of Chicago's Armour meat slaughtering, processing and packing dynasty. The Lewis money came from real estate back in one of Chicago's booms.

Henry Border had been there from at least the time of the merger in 1939 in what was then the Department of Psychology and Philosophy. Before 1939 he had taught part time at Lewis, whose students were working class and/or immigrants, mostly men who, for various reasons no document of the time would make specific, were unable to get into the University of Chicago or Northwestern. Border himself, though, got his PhD from Northwestern some time in the 1930s. Adam read that he was a 'student of Wundt'. Who the hell was Wundt? Wundt, he discovered, was the 'father of experimental psychology'. That sounded impressive. What was Wundt's student doing teaching workers and immigrants part time at a nascent mid-western university? And how deep was the interest in psychology, experimental or otherwise, of the no doubt numerous workers and immigrants enrolled there as students? But Border could have been Wundt's 'student' only in the sense of following Wundt's methods or belonging to some Wundt-inspired school of thought because Wundt's famous proto-typical experimental psychology laboratory was in Germany, in Leipzig. Furthermore, Wundt died in 1920 so Border can have been his student only in the way he was also a 'student' of Francis Bacon who died in the seventeenth century. What an embarrassing waste of time this could be.

'You're such an idiot,' Adam whispered to himself. 'The only saving grace here is that no one can see you wasting your time like this.'

*

'I fell asleep in their second floor what was not yet finished,' Mr Mandelbrot continued. 'The cold came in through the missing windows but I was exhausted and fell asleep very quickly. The next thing what I knew was the SA man standing over me in the dark. I didn't know where I was. It was morning but the sun was not yet up. He looked down at me and said good morning. He had come to wake me before the civilian workers came to start work on the second floor where I had slept. He told me I had to go. If I made it through the day I could come back there. I said good morning to him.

'I went down the ladder and away from the house into the streets. I didn't know what to do. I thought maybe I should go back to the ghetto. My parents, my family, didn't know where I was but I heard and then saw the work detail from the ghetto being led from the streets of the ghetto on the way to work. I hid and watched them go past under guard, none of them talking or they could be struck. I looked at them and saw what I must have looked like the day before this. What should I do?

'I spent that day hiding in the streets around the ghetto wondering what should I do. At night when the sun was gone and when I knew the civilian workers would be gone, I went back to the house of the SA man and his wife. Had I done the right thing? I didn't know. Every day I didn't know what was the right thing to do from one minute to another minute, but if you were still alive it means it was the right thing to do. But you only knew when the minute had passed and then you had no time to relax; you had to think of the next minute. I heard that they had started taking the Jews of Dabrowa Gornicza to a ghetto in Sosnowiec. Perhaps my family had already gone or would go the next day. Should I go to try to find them? Were they still all together? Maybe it was too late to find them in Dabrowa Gornicza. Would I be killed just trying to get back into the ghetto? I stayed like this upstairs in the house of the SA man every night for five or maybe six weeks until one day the SA man and his wife invited me to supper.

'They sat me down at a table in their kitchen. He was on my right side, she was on my left. I was in the middle of them. The table, I remember, had a white lace tablecloth. There was more food on the table than I had seen since the war started. Chicken, cabbage, everything was there. They told me I should eat. I wanted to eat everything on the table but I started off slowly so that they would start to eat and not see how hungry I was. In the ghetto I was hungry every minute. I could see them looking at each other, the man and the wife. They kept looking like they had something they wanted to tell me and then he said it. The second floor would be finished very soon and this night was going to be my last night there. After this dinner the wife couldn't look at me.

'By now they had definitely begun the process of collecting the people what were at the ghetto at Dabrowa Gornicza to take them all what were still alive to Sosnowiec, those who had not died of starvation or of some disease. I thought that if my family was still alive they would be now probably in the ghetto at Sosnowiec. You can say it, Sosnowiec. Mr Lamont, you say it.'

'Sos-nov-ietz.'

'I could not stay any more at night in the second floor of this *Volks-deutsche* SA man and his wife and I decided to go to Sosnowiec. So I began this journey to Sosnowiec. Through my father and the butchery business what he had and my own dealings I knew a lot of farmers and a lot of the people around from the villages what were in the area. There were many places I could go where the people, Poles –'

'Not Jewish?'

'Not Jews, of course not. Jews then, all Jews in Poland were in a ghetto or hiding or they were dead. These were non-Jewish Poles, Polish farmers, and I knew them but I was ashamed to see them like this. I was wearing the same clothes what I had on. They knew what was happening to the Jews; some of them were sad about it, some were happy to see it and some didn't care so much but they liked me. I couldn't stay with any one of them for too long because it was dangerous for them.'

'Why?'

'Because the Nazis were killing Poles what were caught helping Jews and they made sure all the Poles knew this. I decided I would try to get into the ghetto at Sosnowiec to see if I could find my family. Maybe it was stupid but I didn't ever know what might be clever and what might be stupid and I wanted to see my family. There was a part of Sosnowiec, a suburb, called Szrodula and the Germans moved all the Polish Christians out of Szrodula and made it a gated ghetto for the Jews of Sosnowiec and other Jews what came from around there. But by the time I got there they had already some time even a year or more earlier begun the deportations from Sosnowiec and I was told about this. The SS, you know what that is?'

'I know . . . I've heard of it but –'

'The SS – it stands for *Schutzstaffel* – was the elite armed force of the Nazi regime, an armed force on top of the regular army, and they had responsibility for the Nazi program against the Jews. From time to time the SS would order a large group of Jews from the ghetto to assemble in the town square with their families. These round-ups, what was called an *Aktion*, was repeated till there were no Jews left in the ghetto. Each Jew was made to pass in front of what was called a deportation commission who sent the Jew into one of four categories. You could be employed in a factory what was considered essential to the German war effort. Such a Jew would stay in the ghetto. This was one category. You could be transferred to Germany as slave labour for a labour camp. This was another category. You could be sent to another different camp or you could be in a category what they hadn't decided about you yet. These were the four categories.

You can imagine, Mr Lamont, that people from the one family would be split up into different categories. People would try to stay together with their family members so they would try to go into some other category other than what was selected for them. When this happened the person trying to cross to another category would be shot on the spot in front of the family members what they were trying to join. The bodies would just lie there. These *Aktions* could last till midnight.'

*

Deep in the Galvin Library at IIT in Chicago, Adam found a reference to a psychological museum, the Chicago Psychological Museum. What was a psychological museum and what did it have to do with Border and why should Adam Zignelik, a professor of twentieth-century political history, care? There was an article from *The Chicago Daily News* dated 27 March 1944. Dr Henry Border was inviting the public to attend the newly established Chicago Psychological Museum to see 'exhibits and demonstrations of psychological apparatus testing vision, hearing, taste and smell'. There was something called a driver's clinic testing perception. It was all situated in the Lewis Gymnasium at IIT. Border had established the museum and was its curator.

'Look, sweetheart, your psychologist has the instincts and the tendencies of a historian,' he heard Diana whisper.

'You're clutching at straws,' he replied.

'No, the man was a collector. Whatever this museum was, Border recognised that the methods, the practice and research of this discipline examining human behaviour in the middle of the twentieth century deserved recording. It deserved historical documentation.'

'Oh, okay. And when I die will you find someone to research *me* researching *him* to show the last desperate flailing of a soon-to-be out of work early twenty-first-century historian? You're not helping me.'

'No, I am.'

'No, you're really not. It doesn't help to encourage me to waste my time and make a fool of myself.'

'Time is something, just about the *only* thing, you've got. As for making a fool of yourself, you said it yourself before, no one can see you. Who even knows you're here?'

'That junior psych academic and the Chief Librarian, they know I'm here. He told her I was here, told me to go and see her if I had any questions.'

'Do you remember their names?'

'His name is Phil something. I've got his surname written down in my notes and her name is . . .'

'You don't remember her name.'

'It began with an "S". It was unusual sounding. What's your point? I'm wasting my time.'

'Keep reading. She doesn't remember your name, doesn't even remember you're here. Forget about shame.'

But the Chief Librarian clearly did remember that Adam was there because he saw her walking towards him with some papers in her hand.

'Are you Dr Zignelik?'

'Adam, yes.'

'Phil Tolson told me I'd find you here. I'm Sahera Shukri. I'm the Dean of Libraries.'

'I'm sorry, Sahera, I meant to introduce myself to you earlier but I . . .' Adam trailed off as they shook hands.

'No, *I'm* sorry. I'd meant to show you round the library but the day has gotten away from me. Phil said you're a historian from Columbia.'

'Yes.'

'And you have an interest in Henry Border.'

'Well, I might have an interest in him.'

'You know, this isn't everything we have of his. It's all we have here in the Galvin Library but the university might have some more that's not here yet.'

'Really?'

'Yeah, Eileen Miller, the Dean of Psychology, told me she thinks there might be more of his papers somewhere in their department but she hasn't got around to checking if they're all his and then sending them to us. And as you can see we haven't really begun sorting out what she's already sent us. No one thought there was any particular urgency to it so I'm afraid your visit finds us a little embarrassed.'

'Oh there's no need to be embarrassed on my account. Believe me! Do you know much about Border's work?'

'No, almost nothing. By now you'd know more about him than I do. No, I guess Eileen knows more about him than anyone else here. Have you spoken to her?'

'No, Phil Tolson said she's away till tomorrow. My timing's not great. I came out here sort of on a hunch.'

'Well, I received something in the mail a little while back from a retired colleague of mine who used to work here at the library and your visit prompted me to remember it.'

'Yeah?'

'My colleague's uncle used to work at IIT back in the '50s and he passed away not long ago. My friend was cleaning out her uncle's attic and she found some pages from an old IIT newsletter. I think it's from some time in the early '50s. You'd have to look. This one says 1951. There's a bit here about Border and a psychological museum and I've meant to add it to the pile. Your visit has prompted me to get down here. Do you want to take a look? I can leave it with you if you'll just add it to the pile when you're done. I'm going to have to leave soon. It was nice to meet you. Love the accent, by the way. Are you British?'

'No, my mother was Australian. My father was a New Yorker. The accent comes from my mother.'

'It's very nice. Good luck, Adam. I hope you find what you're looking for.'

*

'Like always, I didn't know what to do. If I went to live in the ghetto I could get caught in an *Aktion* but I wanted to try to find my family. I had a chance of being selected to work in a local factory for the German war effort but also a chance of being selected in the other categories. I decided I would try to live outside the ghetto but I would try to survive smuggling things into and out of it. The people what were left there were always hungry. There was never enough food. Never. As people became more and more desperate to have food they were more and more willing to give up something what they had brought with them into the ghetto.'

'Like a piece of clothing or something?'

'Yes, clothing, a watch, a child's toy; something like this. What I did was take these things out of the ghetto and –'

'Smuggle them?'

'Smuggle them, yes, out of the ghetto and sell them to the people what my father and me had known from in the country and in the villages. I could get money. I could get food and bring it back into the ghetto. This is what I did.'

'And your family?'

'My family? When I got to Szrodula, to the ghetto at Sosnowiec, they were not there. What I needed to be able to smuggle out urgently was some good clothes that were not too torn or too old.'

'Why?'

'Because outside the ghetto I couldn't be invisible and if people saw me they had to think I was a Pole.'

'A Christian Pole?'

'Yes. From what was left from Jews what were already gone I got some clothes what were in better condition than what I had from Dabrowa Gornicza which I had been wearing completely every day and even a brief case. So when someone saw me outside the ghetto they wouldn't notice me.

'I smuggled like this for some time when one day I was at a tram stop outside the ghetto.'

'In Sosnowiec?'

'Yes, I was in Sosnowiec. I had to go maybe four tram stops and then quite a distance on foot. I was already outside the ghetto and I was just standing there waiting for the tram. I was looking left and looking right, trying not to look to anyone, you know, suspicious. On the other side of the tram stop there was something like a small hill. Suddenly, there is a meeting of eyes, a face-to-face meeting of eyes; my eyes and the eyes of someone looking out at me from over the other side of the small hill. I knew who this was. It was the boy from Zabkowice. He was older and now he was in Sosnowiec but I knew straight away that this was the boy who had called me a Jew what I had to fight when I was younger. We looked at each other, each with probably the same memory of the past. He had seen me so there was no point looking away. I had to stare right back in his eyes hoping that the memory would frighten him away. Who knew what had happened to him in the years since I had made him quiet in front of the other boys? He looked and thought and I looked and I thought for about two or three minutes. Then he disappeared. I thought maybe I had scared him away with my look and the memory it was meant to deliver but even so I wanted very much for the tram to come and take me away. Other people were now waiting for the tram and I thought that maybe I could blend in but within maybe five minutes a very tall well-dressed man came from behind the small hill. He had with him a huge dog and behind them both was my schoolyard colleague with the very straight hair. The man walked up to me in the middle of the crowd with his dog. He did not even look at the other people what were waiting also for the tram and, in German, he told me I was under arrest.'

'Was he a soldier?'

'No, he was a civilian.'

'Was he a . . . *Volksdeutsche*?'

'Yes, Mr Lamont, he was *Volksdeutsche*.'

'How could he arrest you if he was a civilian?'

'He was a German, I was a Jew and I had been caught outside the ghetto and without the yellow Jewish star what they made us wear. If it wasn't for the dog I would have run. But the dog was very, very big. The tall man with the dog took me to the civilian police.'

'German?'

'Yes. The civilian police took me to an interrogation room to find out how long I had been out of the ghetto and especially where I had been hiding. If I had told them about the people my father and I knew what had let me stay in their barns and on their farms and properties, all these people, they would all have been killed. So I wouldn't say who gave me shelter. They ordered me to undress to my underwear and made me get down sitting on the floor with my legs out. They got two sticks and put one between each elbow and each knee so that I was bowed in a semi-circle with my head touching the ground. Then they beat me.'

*

Sahera Shukri, the Dean of Libraries at IIT, left Adam alone with the papers she'd given him from the colleague's late uncle's attic. He watched her walk away and wished he had somewhere he had to be. He didn't know whether to go back to the pile he'd been examining before she came or to look at the much smaller one she'd just given him. He chose the new smaller one because he'd get through it faster and then might possibly have some small feeling of accomplishment. This was the ration-ale behind his decision, the only rationale for it.

The first few pages were things he'd seen before concerning the psychological museum but the next page was new to him. It was an IIT newsletter from 1947. In an article written by Border himself, it referred to a recent expedition Border had made to Europe as part of his research. The article said the research trip had led to Border's then current work, particularly a paper titled 'The Adjective–Verb Quotient: An Investi-gation of the Speech Patterns of Displaced Persons'. Who were these 'displaced persons'? Could this be the source of the interview William McCray's veteran friend from Boston was talking about? After a little research on a different floor of the Galvin Library, Adam learned that it wasn't until 1980 that post-traumatic stress disorder was accepted as a psychopathology in the Diagnostic and Statistical Manual of Mental Disorders. The timing of the inclusion had a lot to do with the by then frequently reported experience of Vietnam veterans. But what kind of work was Border doing in the mid-1940s?

*

'I knew I had to give them something so I told them I would tell them where I had been hiding. From when I was younger bringing animals to my father I knew the roads and also the short cuts through the fields and farms in the area and I knew where there were the ruins of an old castle. A place I had hoped one day to bring a girl but I never did. Now I could still try to make use of it in a way I had never imagined. It was quite a long way from Sosnowiec but I had thought that if I needed to go there I could. I never got around to going to these ruins but I told the criminal police that this was where I had been hiding. They didn't believe me and they took me back to the cell and left me there.

'You might not believe it now looking at me here in this room that I was ever twenty-one but that is how old I was at that time. And I was in a prison in my own country just for being what I was when I was born. It hadn't been so much of a crime when I was born, maybe a bit sometimes, but now it was a capital offence. I didn't know exactly where my family was and I had been beaten by the criminal police for not betraying the people what had helped me. After four days they took me again to the interrogation room and asked me again, "Who has been hiding you?" I said to them that I already told them the truth. I was living in the ruins of an old castle. I said, "I could take you there and show you and you can check." Even this might have been bad for me because I was afraid that maybe they would ask me to take them there. Then, Mr Lamont, they would see that there was nothing there what showed a person had been living there; no bits of food or any scraps from a life. Unless, of course, some other Jew had been hiding there but two Jews were never so lucky in Poland at those times. And then if they didn't believe me they might just shoot me in the fields. Yes, why not? But they didn't want to travel so far or maybe they didn't believe me in the first place. They didn't beat me this time, just threw me back in the cell. After one or two days they took me to the Gestapo headquarters.

'A car came for me, I remember. It was still in Sosnowiec.'

'What was the Gestapo, more police?'

'Yes, it was the German Secret State Police. The criminal police took me to Gestapo headquarters and the Gestapo asked the same question, "Where have you been hiding and who has been hiding you?" I told them the same what I had told the criminal police. I was living in the ruins of a castle in the fields. I can show you where it is. They didn't believe me and they also beat me. They smashed me in the face with the butt of a rifle. I said the same thing again and again but they didn't care. Blood flowed in a line in the centre of my face from the top here to my chin. They hit me in the same place again and again and after a couple of hours the Gestapo put me in a car. They took me to a prison. I remember it; I can see it on Ostrogorska Street. They took me to a cell on the fourth floor of the prison building and put me in a cell what had in it six Jews and ten Poles; sixteen people in one cell. The Poles, most of them were older than the Jews. The Jews were about my age. When I saw there were young Jews we all started to ask each other questions to see who might know something new what had to do with one of our families, anything we might learn.'

'Do you know where your family was at that time?'

'My parents,' Mr Mandelbrot sighed, 'my parents were probably by that time already sent to where I was going.'

'Where were you going?'

'To Auschwitz.'

'What is *Owswich*, I mean, exactly?'

'Auschwitz.'

'*Owswitz.*'

'Auschwitz.'

'*Ausch-vitz.*'

Mr Mandelbrot slowly nodded once with his eyes half closed to convey assent to his student.

'What exactly is *Ausch-vitz*?' Lamont asked quietly.

'This,' Mr Mandelbrot said, tapping the number tattooed on his left forearm with two fingers of his right hand, 'this, what you've been staring at, this is Auschwitz.'

*

Back in the first of the two piles of documents, the larger one, Adam found drafts of grant applications by Henry Border to a myriad organisations for funding to take him to Europe, some of them dating back as far as 1945. It looked as though Border had attempted to get to Europe almost as soon as hostilities had ended there after the war. There were so many applications and rejection letters that it was clear Border was not making any progress, yet he didn't quit. Application after application, he just kept going. Somehow Border seemed to have got there in 1946. It wasn't making sense to Adam. It seemed absurd to think that this man's professional interest in linguistic analysis, something Border was calling 'The Adjective–Verb Quotient', would necessitate that he go all the way from Chicago to recently liberated war-ravaged Europe in 1946 simply to gather data for his hypothesis with respect to the relative rate at which distressed people used adjectives and verbs. Something was wrong with this picture. Who in particular among these displaced persons did he want to interview? And who on earth was Henry S. Border?

'You have to talk to Eileen Miller, the Dean of Psychology. You have to examine the other papers. You have to stay longer,' Diana whispered. But Adam was due to fly back to New York the next morning. The lights might be left on over night but most of the eight million people who lived there would be trying to get some sleep. Many of them wouldn't sleep. Some of them couldn't. They would do what they thought they had to do to get to the next day. One of them was up talking to himself under the strip light in the kitchen of his grandmother's Co-op City apartment in the Bronx. Not one of them would know if Adam Zignelik changed his flight.

'You have to stay longer,' Diana whispered to Adam Zignelik. 'You know you do.'

*

Lamont Williams' grandmother woke in the middle of the night to check on a sound, a dull sound. She looked over at the digital clock and saw that it was 2.47 am. She had wanted a good night's sleep. Her granddaughter was to be taking her out to lunch in the next few days. She always looked forward to these lunches and wanted to be well rested for it but something was keeping her up. The sound she heard was the muffled voice of a man talking to himself out loud. It was her grandson. He was speaking quietly, at times in a particular rhythm, single words most of which she could not make out, and what she could make out she couldn't understand, words that seemed to be from a language she hadn't known he spoke. He said them as though they were an incantation of some kind. His grandmother put on her robe and opened the door of her bedroom to better hear what it was her grandson was saying to himself in the middle of the night. Was she going to need help with him? Maybe she could finally prevail upon Michelle to help her with him. He was out now. He had a job; he'd paid his debt to society. What in hell was he saying? It was best to know the worst as soon as possible, however much it might hurt. You lessen the hurt that way. Had he learned a new language in prison? That would be a good sign. Was that even possible? Was it some kind of relaxation technique? Even that would be good. Please let that be it, she said to herself.

'He was born 15 December 1922 in the town of Olkusz. His father was a butcher,' Lamont Williams said, sipping a teacup of Seneca frozen apple juice.

Whose father was a butcher? Who was born in 1922? his grandmother wondered. She heard him take a few sips more and put the cup down again.

'Ol-kusz. Zab-ko-vitz-ay. Dab-rov-a Gorn-itch-a. *Volksdeutsche*. Sos-nov-ietz. Sosnowiec.'

Was he using drugs now? she wondered. Was he high? What on earth was he saying? She made her way as silently as she could down the hall past the shrine of family photographs, which included one of her then two-and-a-half-year-old great-granddaughter, and continued to listen as he whispered to himself above the hum of the strip light and the refrigerator.

'Dab-rov-a Gorn-itch-a . . . Dabrowa Gornicza.'

It was just after 3 am in Co-op City, the Bronx. Lamont Williams, the new guy, still on probation in Building Services, kind of quiet, a nervous guy, was sitting in his grandmother's kitchen under the strip light talking softly to himself. Lightly he rubbed two fingers from his right hand over his left forearm. His grandmother pulled her robe shut tight with one hand in the darkened hallway and tried to listen to her grandson. What was going to happen to him? He spoke in a curious whisper. She thought to pray that she might understand him.

'Sos-nov-ietz. Sosnowiec. SS *Shutzstaffel*. Ausch-vitz. Auschwitz.'

part six

THE WAITER HELD OUT HER CHAIR FOR HER and, once she was seated, pushed it back in towards the table. Then he did the same for Michelle. This only ever happened to her when she was taken out by her granddaughter. Doubtless, she speculated, watching the waiter push in Michelle's chair, it happened to Michelle all the time. This discrepancy in their experience didn't bother her. On the contrary, watching the waiter lavish attention on her granddaughter filled her with pride. Michelle could have been an actress or a model, her grandmother used to tell her. But Michelle was never interested in drawing attention to herself. When people complimented her on her looks it would embarrass her. It was not an attribute she had worked hard to achieve like good grades, which she got but which never garnered her anywhere near the same praise.

At college the men who were most likely to ask her out were vacuous and shallow, uninterested in the person she really was and what she thought about things, and she·thought a lot about most things. They were either arrogant jocks or else delusional desperadoes who had no idea of the way the world saw them. Sensitive men, she had always felt, were intimidated by her looks, thinking that rejection was so likely that, as rich as the prize might be, they were too flawed, too certain to fail, to do anything but admire from a distance. Men like these pursued women just slightly prettier than plain and then married whichever of them they were next to when suddenly the music stopped to announce that graduate school was over. A single guest at weddings, couples would admire her appearance almost excessively and, in so doing, embarrass her, never for a moment dreaming she might know loneliness every bit as well, every bit as sharp, as they ever had.

A bright student, she graduated with a Masters in social work because helping people had seemed like the best thing she could do with her life. She got a job doing just that, dispensing help to people in need and teaching others to do the same. She dressed down both for her colleagues and her 'clients' but still her appearance didn't go unnoticed by either her male clients or her female clients, though not in the same way. She was well liked and highly regarded by her colleagues but even with them there had been problems that she had needed to overcome. The women, suspicious of her motives for working there, had to be won over since, for the most part, had they looked like Michelle they would not have been social workers earning a relative pittance. Michelle's male colleagues weren't susceptible to this kind of suspicion but they were vulnerable to moments of mistaking the friendliness of someone as attractive as Michelle for something more.

For at least the last year or so Michelle had wondered if she hadn't chosen the wrong career. Nobody can be asked to display limitless compassion and especially not to people who so often didn't even heed her advice. She had to stop herself from blaming them. When she had been a student it had been a lot easier to blame history, society and free market fundamentalism, the Federal Government, the City and racism. Now it could take all her strength not to shake some of her clients when they came back with the same problems again and again. She and her husband Charles would go to dinner parties in Westchester, Brooklyn Heights and Park Slope and dine with liberal academics, white and black, Hispanic and Asian, and she would envy their capacity to continue thinking exactly as she had as a student. Theory always trumped experience at these occasions and she envied the time they seemed to have to find peer-reviewed evidence to support their long-held views.

Despite all of this she worked on herself to exhibit kindness in all her dealings with people both professionally and in her private life. This was how she came to be taking her grandmother out to lunch one Saturday.

They had gone to a place the family had at times gone to on special occasions in the past. It was a steak restaurant in the city, downtown near Union Square, and this was one of many times the two of them had had one of their 'special' lunches there since those now distant occasions when Michelle had been a little girl.

'Sonia didn't want to come?' Michelle's grandmother asked tentatively.

'Are you kidding, Grandma? She was desperate to come. I wouldn't let her. She had soccer this morning and has to study for a test she's got on Monday and then another one she's got on Wednesday. No, she really wanted to see you and we even had words over it. She was especially mad at me for not letting her come since we got you a little present and it was her idea.' The last time they had met downtown Michelle's grandmother had left home without an umbrella and when it had rained suddenly but emphatically she'd had no choice but to go against her New Yorker's instincts and buy the nearest cheap umbrella proffered by an African immigrant who had materialised on the street with the first drop of rain and was in a new line of work by the time the last drop hit the sidewalk. She had known that the umbrella was likely not to last very long and it hadn't, succumbing to the wind on its very first outing. It was for that reason that before meeting her grandmother at the steak restaurant Michelle had stopped at a specialist umbrella store on East 45th Street and bought her a distinctive Guy de Jean umbrella with a shiny black wooden handle and a houndstooth-like design in charcoal grey topped by a wraparound frieze of Scottish terriers with bright red bow ties as a gift ostensibly from Sonia.

Michelle was all the more attuned to her grandmother's financial circumstances since her cousin moved back in with her grandmother after his release from prison. She knew that her grandmother's household expenditure would have suddenly risen dramatically without any corresponding increase in income. She wasn't counting on Lamont being in a position to contribute anything despite, as her grandmother had told her with pride, his having got a job in Building Services at a hospital. But it was difficult to give her grandmother money without embarrassing her.

The best way would have been to slip a cheque or, even better, some cash inside her grandmother's purse when she was distracted but this wasn't practical and, in any event, Michelle had wanted her to know that there was extra money to help her through the week or through the month. To accomplish this she hit upon the idea of presenting her grandmother with a gift from Sonia accompanied by a card with some cash inside the envelope about which Michelle wouldn't comment.

'Oh, my goodness it's beautiful!' her grandmother said, examining the umbrella at the table in the restaurant. She leaned over to kiss her grand-daughter. 'You really shouldn't have done this,' she said opening the card from Sonia. It read, 'Dear Nanny, I hope you like the umbrella. I wanted to give it to you myself since it was my idea but Mom wouldn't let me 'cos of my tests and soccer. Sorry she did this. Hope to see you soon. Love, Sonia.' Then Michelle's grandmother saw the cash that waited in the envelope behind the card.

'Now before you say anything,' Michelle pre-empted, 'we know, Charlie and me, we know that things might've got a bit harder now that Lamont's home and we just felt that, you know, since we could, we wanted to try to –'

''Chelle, he's doin' real well.' She used the diminutive version of her name that her cousin had coined in their youth. It wasn't lost on her granddaughter.

'That's good, Grandma.'

'*Real* well. They talkin' 'bout givin' him extra duties.'

'That's good.'

'He's still hoping to see his little girl but . . . I don't want to crush his hopes 'cause I think that maybe . . . maybe they help him get up in the morning.' She looked out into the middle distance and then returned her gaze to the umbrella and then to Michelle.

'Do you think he'll find her? Maybe you . . . ain't that the kind of thing . . . will you see him? At least *see* him.' She took her grand-daughter's hand.

'I will, Grandma.'

'Really?'

'Sure.'

'You will?'
'I will.'
'When?'
'I don't know. I can't right now.'

*

In 1945, immediately after the end of the war in Europe but before the war in the Pacific was over, before the atom bombing of Hiroshima and Nagasaki, a civilian, a little-known professor of psychology at the Illinois Institute of Technology on Chicago's south side by the name of Henry Border began tirelessly to make what seemed like an endless succession of grant applications in an attempt to get himself into the heart of Allied-occupied Europe. Why? Searching through the Galvin Library at IIT, Adam Zignelik found, from a 1947 university newsletter, that Border's stated purpose was to gather data from 'displaced persons' to further his research into what Border, the psychologist, called the 'Adjective–Verb Quotient'. Border's at least tentative hypothesis was that people in 'distress' will use adjectives and verbs in a different ratio to each other than will people who are not in 'distress'.

However valid or even however significant this hypothesis might or might not be, Adam had little difficulty imagining the psychologist Henry Border taking it seriously. This was, after all, Adam reasoned, the sort of research a psychologist might well undertake. Border, it seemed, even had some of his students look into the subject with him as part of the work on which they were assessed. But there were plenty of 'distressed' people in the US, in Chicago, even right there on the south side of Chicago where the Illinois Institute of Technology was situated, without his needing to go to all the trouble and expense of trying to get to Europe to find them.

From the numerous drafts of unsuccessful grant applications seeking financial assistance to get him to Europe and the fact that the 1947 IIT newsletter contained an article by Border himself in which he tells of having eventually managed to get himself there, it was clear that this trip was by then the most important professional goal he had set himself.

Adam found no record of Border having done any work on what had previously been his big project, the psychological museum, after early May 1945 and from May onward the only references to the psychological museum were in work Border had already done.

Clearly, Border's plan to travel to Europe had hatched with the final defeat of Germany in very early May 1945. After that, at least professionally, there was no matter more important to him than getting to Europe to conduct field research on people in 'distress'. These people were thick on the ground; there were literally millions of them. Indeed, it would have been hard to find people in Europe *not* in some kind of distress. By the early summer of 1945, as a consequence of the most brutal war in history, there were something of the order of seven million civilians in Western Europe, travelling or temporarily housed somewhere other than where they wanted to be. Swelling the roads or the makeshift under-resourced camps dotted throughout Western Europe there were Poles, Germans, Russians, Slovaks, Jews, Slovenians, Italians, Frenchmen, Belgians, Greeks, Ukrainian Cossacks, Croatians, White Russians and many more besides. Were they all using adjectives and verbs in the same ratio? It wasn't enough for Border to seek answers with respect to his 'Adjective–Verb Quotient' from 'distressed' people right there on the south side of Chicago. For some reason he had to go to Europe.

The article Border had written for the IIT newsletter explained that when he had got to Europe he had gone to 'Displaced Persons' or 'DP' camps, as they were called. There was a reference to a book Border had written based on his research there. Adam thought there was a good chance that at least one of the libraries at IIT would have the book. His knees in pain from squatting there in the basement of the Galvin Library, Adam stood up for a moment and kneaded the muscles around them and around his thighs with his thumbs and fingers before sitting back down on the ground, this time with his legs stretched out in front of him. To better effect this position he fanned out his arms with the intention of resting his palms on the floor for balance. But in the process, his right palm inadvertently hit the bottom bookshelf, tipping over a cardboard box that was next to where Border's documents had been before Adam had removed them and spilling some of the contents onto the floor.

Before returning the loosely bound documents to their box, he stretched, yawned and picked one of them up and glanced at it without thinking, almost as a matter of course.

In the half-light of the library basement the words on the cover of the document formed tiny black islands of printed meaning that lay one on top of another amid a sea of grey that had once been white. It was a sea Adam Zignelik's eyes were too tired to swim, especially when there was no apparent reason to, and he was about to put the loosely bound document back in its box with the others when his eyes stumbled upon and then fixed on the name 'Henry S. Border'. No one had directed Adam to the box he had knocked over, the box *beside* the Border piles, but Adam found this box also contained documents relevant to Border. The document in Adam's hand was headed 'Topical Autobiographies of Displaced People, recorded verbatim in Displaced Persons Camps, with a psychological and anthropological analysis, by Henry S. Border, PhD'.

Adam opened it at random and began reading.

'Then they took us to Oranienburg.'

'What was Oranienburg?'

'It was a *Konzentrationslager.*'

'Where was it, exactly?'

'Near Berlin. This was Sachsenhausen.'

'What do you mean it was Sachsenhausen?'

'Oranienburg was what they called later Sachsenhausen.'

'And Sachsenhausen . . . Oranienburg . . . was a . . . a concentration camp?'

'Yes.'

'And why were you there?'

'They took us there.'

'Who took you there?'

'The SS took us there.'

'Why?'

'It was just after *Kristalnacht* in November 1938 and –'

'1938?'

'Yes, of course. There were about 2000 of us there, Jews, and the SS took us to Oranienburg. It was night, completely dark, you see, and because there was a sharp . . . a steep slope there, the people at the front stumbled and tripped. They fell and the people behind them could barely see them, and the people behind these people couldn't see the people at the front at all. Those people, the ones at the front, those of the ones at the front who could not get up fast enough, they were crushed. They were completely crushed. We did it. We crushed them. The SS forced us to run down the ravine in the dark. It was chaos and we crushed some of them. We were not expecting this, not expecting anything like this. They forced us with guns and dogs in the dark . . . faster and faster and . . . We crushed them ourselves immediately on arrival there and they died just like that. In the dark you heard the sound of the screams, human screams in your ears and the crushing of people, the crushing of bones under foot. You heard it but it was too late. You were being pushed and you had to keep moving and not fall. There were people behind us, pushing, and people behind them pushing those people.

The SS left the corpses lying there in the ditch waiting for us to see them when it got light. Then we had to clean up the mess made by the corpses. We had to clean up the corpses. We had to drag the corpses away. But they had just before been people and we knew these people. Some knew them well. For some of us these corpses were colleagues, our friends, old friends and sometimes family. Sometimes they were family. These were our first corpses . . . I had never before seen a dead person.'

'It was 1938, yes, before the war?'

'Yes.'

'Jacob, we need to go back to the beginning.'

'The beginning of what? I'm telling you what happened –'

'I need to ask you certain basic questions like your full name and where you were born.'

'But I've barely started and now you . . . I want to take you much past Oranienburg. You said –'

'And I want you to. Jacob, I want to hear everything, but we need to start at the beginning.'

These had to have been the transcripts. Adam thought that in the box he had knocked over he had found the transcripts of the interviews Border had conducted with the 'distressed' people in the Displaced

Persons camps from Border's visit to Europe in 1946. Keeping the loosely bound folder on his lap, Adam picked up another one, opened it at random and started reading.

'We had built a bunker. It was deep, very deep, completely underground with no windows. In fact, it had no ventilation at all. We weren't able to build it with any ventilation because we had to build it in secret. We weren't builders.'

'Even in the ghetto it had to be a secret?'

'Yes. Now at that time, this must have been about the middle of January –'

'Nineteen forty-three?'

'Yes. At that time all the workshops were gone.'

'What do you mean they were gone?'

'They were closed.'

'You mean they had been shut down?'

'Yes, the Nazis had shut them all except for one. Schultz's was still operating.'

'What did Schultz's do?'

'If you were skilled in shoemaking or maybe if you were a furrier, maybe you could get work, but of course everybody was saying that they and their children and their mothers and their grandmothers, everyone was a shoemaker. I remember someone said to me . . . it was a sort of sick joke in a way . . . every last Jew in Warsaw is a shoemaker.'

'A joke?'

'Yes. Of course it wasn't true but to have some chance at surviving in the ghetto at this time it helped either to be a shoemaker or to say that you were a shoemaker. It didn't really help much at all actually. The joke helped more, if you know what I mean.'

'You mean that even dark humour helped people cope with the conditions?'

'Yes. Anyway, everybody knew it was only a matter of time till even this last workshop –'

'Schultz's?'

'Yes, even Schultz's would be closed down and because we felt this had to happen and could happen at any time we moved underground to the bunker.'

'How many people went to the bunker?'

'I would say about thirty. Nobody in the ghetto who was still alive and wasn't already mad, nobody who hadn't completely lost his mind from hunger or disease or the loss of their family, could think that the Nazis had any other plan.'

'Other plan than what?'

'Than they wanted . . . they wanted Warsaw completely Jew-free.

'Then they led us all to be registered. They knew what was going to happen and they did a better job than the Germans. They knew and they were happy.'

'Who do you mean when you say "they"?'

'The local police. They were happy, everyone was happy that they were going to be rid of the Jews. People were already going into our homes and taking whatever they wanted.'

'Who, the police?'

'No, just ordinary people, some of them we knew. Some were our neighbours. They said they would live off all the Jewish possessions they'd heard about and they . . . they just . . .'

'Your neighbours looted your homes?'

'Yes.'

This was the third of three of Border's transcribed interviews of 'distressed' DPs perused at random by Adam. All the interviewees so far had been Jews. Where were the other nationalities? Where were the Poles, the Germans, Russians, Slovaks, Slovenians, Italians, Frenchmen, Belgians, Greeks, Ukrainians, Croatians and White Russians? Had Adam's spilling of the contents of the box resulted in him reading a biased sample? What exactly had Border brought back from Europe in the summer of 1946? Adam closed the transcript he was reading but didn't put it back. He kept it out of the box and placed it in his lap with the first two transcripts he'd read. He estimated there might have been fifty or sixty of them, maybe more. Perhaps this was the Jewish section, he wondered. Perhaps all those years ago they had been placed in the box according to ethnicity and Adam had by chance taken out the transcripts of Jewish DPs. Maybe Border's hands had been the last to hold the transcripts until now. Adam took another of the loosely bound manuscripts, this one from the far end of the box, the opposite end from where the first three manuscripts had come.

'We didn't know but when the train finally stopped and they opened the door we were in Auschwitz.'

'Now where exactly is Auschwitz?'

'It's in Poland, in Upper Silesia.'

'Upper Silesia. And that's where you got the number on your arm?'

'Yes.'

'Now tell me, what exactly was Auschwitz? What happened there in this camp in Upper Silesia?'

Adam tried to imagine this American, the Chicagoan, Henry Border, in a DP camp hearing all this somewhere in the hot and sunny exhausted bloody mess that was Europe in the summer of 1946. The pages resting in Adam's hands in the dimly lit basement of the Galvin Library at IIT quarantined the time when Border had captured before the ink on the ribbon on his typewriter ran out. Border had gone to Europe to record and measure the verbal consequences of distress and it was beads of distress that rolled down Adam's cheeks with each adjective, with the verbs, and all the silences held between the words that Border had included. What had Border known about Auschwitz, before then? Here in Adam Zignelik's hands one could see an American professor of psychology learning about this place for the very first time from someone who had been there months before. How many people really knew about Auschwitz back in 1946? How many knew precisely what went on there and the scale of it?

'By this time I was in Grimma, near Leipzig. I had walked twenty-five kilometres to get to where the Americans were. The Germans had blown up the bridge over the Rhine but the Americans had put up ladders on it so it was still possible to use the bridge to get across. That's when I saw my first American soldier and I went up to him and I spoke to him in English. I could speak English from before the war. Like everybody else at that time, I wanted to get across to the American side.'

'What did you say to the American soldier?'

'I asked him if I could get across to the American side.'

'And what did the soldier say?'

'He asked first if I was a member of any military unit of any country.'

'You were not.'

'No, I wasn't so I said no. So then he said that I wasn't a prisoner of war and that he had orders only concerning prisoners of war. Prisoners of war could be let through but he didn't have orders to let other people through. So I tried to explain my situation.'

'What was your situation?'

'I had no papers, no food, no money and my leg was quite badly injured. I didn't know what to do. He seemed sympathetic when I said this and he asked again whether I had been in an Allied army or an Axis army. Well, I'd been in Drancy and Auschwitz and then I was in Ravensbrück but I was never in any army. So the American soldier asked me what I was.'

'And what did you say?'

'I explained that I was a . . . I said I was . . . a political prisoner.'

'A political prisoner?'

'Yes.'

'But he said he was very sorry, he didn't have any orders about political prisoners. He could try to get some orders but he wouldn't have an answer until the next day at the earliest.'

The woman Border was talking to was a Holocaust survivor before such a category existed within any language on earth. Of all the languages the world has given birth to since time began, not one of them had a word to describe what this woman was or what she had just experienced. Not one of these languages had ever before needed such a word. It had only just happened and there were no words for it yet, so, as she spoke to the American soldier, she had to come up with something on the spot. She had just lived through the Holocaust but couldn't possibly have had a word for it. Even if she had had a word for it, the American soldier wouldn't have known what it meant.

Adam placed the box of transcripts back where it had been before he had caused it to tip over but he kept hold of the few transcripts he'd already partially read, taking them with him as he went to look for the Dean of Libraries, Sahera Shukri. He wanted to tell her what he thought he'd discovered. In the stacks, on the bottom shelf in the basement of the Galvin Library, he thought he'd found at least a few, but possibly fifty or sixty, of the earliest ever systematic, at-length, in-depth interviews conducted with survivors of the Holocaust. Whatever their significance to psychology or to the history of psychology, they gave every appearance of being of remarkable, irreplaceable significance to twentieth-century political history. IIT was the custodian, if not the owner, of a collection of transcripts of tremendous historical value. The transcripts would need to be specially housed and protected. They would need to be delicately copied with the utmost care. If this was what it appeared to be, scholars from all over the world would be clamouring to see it.

Adam was told by the librarian at the front desk that Sahera Shukri was away from her office but was due back at any time. Unable to hide his excitement at the potential significance of the find, Adam explained to the librarian on duty precisely what it was he thought the library had in its basement. This was, he said, a 'once in a career' find. The librarian asked if he wanted to wait there or in the basement for Ms Shukri but Adam explained that the very next thing he wanted to do was to try to track down Henry Border's book. This wasn't difficult. The library had a copy, one copy, of Border's book and, fortunately, it was exactly where it was meant to be, unread, perhaps untouched for half a century. Its cover was tattered. This was a first edition. Perhaps there was only ever a first edition, Adam speculated. Published in 1949, a copy now rested in the hands of Adam Zignelik. Adam, now for the first time, registered the title of the book: *I Did Not Interview the Dead.*

*

Lamont Williams' grandmother sat across the kitchen table from her grandson in her Co-op City apartment while they had their dinner. He had the usual serving of macaroni and cheese but the serving she'd given herself was tiny. She denied she was feeling unwell when he asked her but he didn't seem to believe her. He had known she'd been out that afternoon, even known that she'd been to the city. What he hadn't known was that his cousin Michelle had taken her out to lunch to a steak restaurant off Union Square, a place with particular family significance.

He went over to his grandmother and put his hand to her forehead because he'd found her protestations of perfect health unconvincing. She was weighing up telling him the truth, telling him that she wasn't hungry because she was still full from the steak she'd had with Michelle. If she told him, she reasoned, it would explain why she wasn't hungry and allay his concern for her health but it would raise all sorts of other issues and memories that were so likely to distress her grandson, even if he said nothing about them, that she had wanted to get through the day without mentioning the true nature of her excursion downtown.

He would be hurt to be reminded that Michelle seemed to have turned her back on him a long time ago, not long after he first went into prison, that he didn't know her family any more, that she wasn't interested in his progress after he'd served his time in prison. It would remind him of the times when they had all gone to that steak restaurant, times when there had been hope, not merely for Michelle's future but for Lamont's as well. His grandmother was right. But a frank account of why she wasn't hungry would have triggered not only these thoughts in her grandson but others as well. He would have given some thought to the evening he had spent with Chantal, the mother of his daughter, and the night he had taken Chantal there. He would have remembered how she'd made him feel both in the restaurant and then later, walking around the crowded surrounds of Union Square. Everything had seemed so close to perfect that night, closer than it had ever been. He hadn't wanted to let anything that was within his control go the slightest bit wrong. He couldn't control the traffic or the weather or the noise of the street, but he was going to get her anything she wanted, be the perfect gentleman, and he was going to hang on her every word. He would have remembered that such had been the noise on the street that he'd had to lean in just to make sure no single word of hers failed to reach his ears. And he would have remembered that when *he* spoke to *her*, she never leaned in, not once.

His grandmother sat there thinking. Should she tell him about her lunch with Michelle at the restaurant or quickly make something else up? She had to think fast. He seemed so concerned about her health. Then, as if gripped by the devil, she sat back bolt upright in her chair at the very moment his hand was on her forehead and, without being able to control herself, she called out, 'Christ!'

Lamont jumped back. There was silence between the two of them under the strip light in that Bronx kitchen. He had never before, not once, heard his grandmother swear. He thought perhaps it was something he'd done and was at once a small boy again trying to please his grandmother, the only person on earth who loved him unequivocally, unconditionally, the only person who was always there for him. What had he done to make her so angry that she would swear at him? She looked up at him mournfully. She was ashamed. Now she was going to have to tell him about her lunch. It wasn't directed at her grandson but at herself and she was going to have to explain this. In remembering her lunch from earlier that day, she remembered how sweet Michelle had been to bring her the beautiful umbrella with the houndstooth-like design in charcoal grey with Scottish terriers with red bow ties and this was when she realised that she had left the umbrella in the restaurant.

*

On the front inside flap of *I Did Not Interview the Dead* was a photograph of its author, Dr Henry Border. Wearing the sort of round glasses often associated earlier with Vladimir Lenin and much later with John Lennon, he looked to be in his late fifties. He had a neatly trimmed beard that he'd restricted to his chin and an equally neatly trimmed moustache and, in the photo, he wore a dark suit jacket covering a white shirt whose collar was fastened with a tie, all of it ordered. The picture was of an older conservative-looking European gentleman. Perhaps Border *had* studied in Europe with Wundt after all? Adam speculated. For the man in the photo, this wouldn't have been impossible, at least not by reason of his age.

From the brief introduction and from the even briefer acknowledgements, a clearer picture of Border and the task he had set himself began to emerge. Despite his unsuccessful draft grant applications, Adam saw that Border did get some assistance. He thanked a number of people from IIT: its president, vice-president, the dean of what was called 'Liberal Studies', the chairman of what was then the Department of Psychology and Education and also someone from the Department of Engineering. He thanked a number of people, mostly unnamed, at various voluntary or charitable agencies in Europe: the ORT, the OSE, the JDC for their assistance in making contact with the people in the DP camps and the various safe houses he visited as well as people from UNRRA, the United Nations Relief and Rehabilitation Administration. He thanked the National Institute of Health, the Chicago Psychological Museum, which, since he was its president, must have been like thanking himself, as well as someone from *The Chicago Tribune*, someone from the University of Illinois Press, the publisher of the book, and he thanked the DPs themselves. As far as Adam could tell, Border thanked only one member of his family, his daughter Elise.

In the introduction Border described the process by which he obtained the interviews and how the idea had come to him. A few days before the end of the war in Europe, the then Supreme Commander of Allied Forces, General Dwight D. Eisenhower, issued a call to American newspapers to come and see the liberated victims of Nazi concentration camps. Border observed that while newspaper reporters were heeding Eisenhower's call and newsreel footage was being taken of the emaciated survivors in the camps, no one was actually conducting systematic, in-depth interviews with these people and recording their testimony. Serendipitously, at around the time this realisation dawned on him, Border learned of the development of a new recording device developed by a certain Marvin Cadden of the Armour Research Foundation (which was later incorporated into IIT). The recording device Cadden had developed was a wire recorder, an electronic device on which sound was magnetically recorded on to strands of carbon steel wire. Border sought out Cadden and established a professional relationship with him. Securing one of Cadden's wire recorders and 200 spools of carbon steel wire along with assorted transformers, he then lugged it all across the Atlantic to Europe to various DP camps.

With the assistance of representatives from the various refugee agencies operating under Allied auspices, he would ask to be permitted to sit in on a meal with a group of DPs in the mess hall. After the meal he would bring out Cadden's wire recorder, show it to the assembled DPs and ask if anybody there would agree to sing a folk song from their home town or village or else a nursery rhyme from their childhood into the wire recorder. He would record one or more tunes from some of the assembled DPs' past and then play it back to the group. Of course the people there had to have been astounded to hear the voice they had just heard singing played back to them through this box. They would never have seen anything remotely like that. By this time Border would have the unequivocal attention of everyone assembled and this was when he explained that he was gathering information about the experience of prisoners in concentration camps to take back and disseminate to people in America so that they would know better what had happened. He said nothing to them about research into the relative use of adjectives and verbs. Indeed, he said nothing at all to them about psychology.

Sometimes people working for the particular relief agency in charge would recommend a certain person because the person's story had made the rounds of the camp and the relief workers considered it exceptional. But Border hadn't wanted exceptional stories. He wanted and asked for what he described as 'rank and file' experiences. But he quickly learned that the rank and file experiences of anyone who was there to tell of them had to be, by definition, exceptional. Surviving had been the exception.

Border explained that he began each interview the same way. He would take the person away from the mess tent or from wherever else they had gathered with others. Despite what must have been a very recent and only cursory knowledge of his surroundings, he would look for a place to talk that was as quiet and as private as the circumstances allowed. Adam Zignelik tried to imagine the circumstances; a noisy makeshift camp where the weather followed you under doors everywhere you went and the dirt on your feet knew the rest of your body every bit as well as it had ever known your feet, where a cacophony of sounds approximating a myriad languages jostled fiercely with each other from the mouths of people of disparate ages and origins who shared only that, en masse, they were more broken from their first-hand experience of what humans are able to visit on one another, more broken from their unasked-for and unusually refined understanding of life's jagged extremes than perhaps any other collection of people on earth. Corralled again inside a camp, this one overseen by their liberators, they waited for a future almost as unimaginable to them as their recent past was to everybody else. Exhale too fast and you'd blow them over and with them their memories would spill out onto the very European ground their families now fertilised.

Border, the conservative-looking mid-western psychologist, would patiently get the person to sit down at a table with a microphone in front of them. Then, in order for the subject not to be influenced by anything Border did other than his asking of questions, he would sit behind the person seated at the table so that they were unable to see him without turning around. The interview subjects were not allowed to refer to notes or to any other stimuli and no other people were permitted to be present. When the person was ready to begin, Border would switch on the wire recorder and introduce the interview with, 'In the United States we don't really know very much about the everyday lives of the people who were forced to live in concentration camps during the war. With your help and with the help of other displaced persons, I am hoping we can change that situation. Thank you for agreeing to tell your story. Please can you begin with your name, your age, where you were when the war started and then go on to tell what has happened to you since?' This was, according to Border's Introduction in his book, exactly what he said every time.

Returning to Chicago, Border wrote in the introduction to *I Did Not Interview the Dead* that the purpose of the expedition to Europe was not to gain a comprehensive account of all the displaced persons there but to collect data from personal reports for future study by psychologists and anthropologists. He described a method of analysis he had developed for interpreting the DPs' experience which he called the 'Traumatic Index'. He listed twelve categories of traumatic experience in the Introduction but he made a point of informing the reader that this list was abridged. He didn't state why it was abridged and so the reader was left to speculate both why and what the other categories might be.

Border then went on to provide a relatively detailed history of the general experience of the Displaced Persons to whom he'd spoken. Two things struck Adam as he read on. Border had been forced, either by his publisher or by the dictates of time and/or space, to abridge his

Traumatic Index and yet he devoted the rest of the introduction to the general experience of Displaced Persons despite the stated purpose of his book being to provide data for study by psychologists and anthropologists. Additionally, Adam noticed, the Displaced Persons, those in the book and those whose accounts Adam had read in the loosely bound files, had all been Jewish. They were all what would later come to be known as Holocaust survivors. In fact, the potted but still relatively detailed chronological account of the experience of Displaced Persons was perhaps the first ever attempt at a history of the Holocaust gathered from primary sources before the genocide even had its own name; indeed, before even the term 'genocide' itself had been coined. How did it come about, Adam wondered, that by the end of the summer of 1946 a certain Henry Border, Professor of Psychology at IIT, had put together perhaps the first account based on detailed interviews of survivors of Hitler's systematic attempt to kill every last Jew in Europe?

It looked as though in the introduction itself Adam might find, if not the answer, then a clue to the answer. As Border described the stages of the Nazi genocidal process he wrote that at each stage the property of the local Jewish population was appropriated, stolen sometimes in front of them, largely by the Nazis but also by the local non-Jewish inhabitants of the area. It was not the fact of this, which Adam was aware of, that jumped out at him from the pages of Border's introduction when he read it but the language Border had chosen to describe it. Was Border's own choice of words as telling to Adam as the 'Adjective–Verb Quotient' was meant to be to psychologists?

Border had written, 'From 1933 onwards there had been a race to steal the raiments of the crucified.' Adam read the expression again and then again, '*the raiments of the crucified*'. This was the language of a Christian, not a casual Christian, not someone who just happened to be Christian, but of someone fairly familiar with scripture. Perhaps this was why Border had gone to such great trouble to go to Europe and collect these people's stories against all odds. Adam wondered if the psychologist, the man of science, did not have a religious motivation to save the stories of these people. There was no necessary reason why the student of Wundt could not also be a student of Christ.

The digital age made it much easier to check registries of births, deaths, marriages and charitable organisations to see whether Border or his family had ever been affiliated, even nominally, with any local church. Among those of Border's papers that Adam had already examined there was an apparently random receipt for a donation Border had made to a church. Adam had looked at it and put it back in the pile but perhaps it would lead him to Border's congregation. The church was probably near Border's home. How long would it take to find out where the psychologist had lived? Even if Border himself wasn't a practising Christian, perhaps he was married to one and perhaps his wife had influenced him. But the only member of his family to be thanked in the book's acknowledgements was his daughter.

More likely then, Adam considered, Border was himself a practising Christian or, if not himself religious, then Border's parents had been devout Christians and, whatever his beliefs and practices as an adult, the language of scripture poured out of him at times of emotional torment of the kind any reasonable person might have been expected to experience when hearing these stories, especially hearing them raw and unfiltered directly from the people who had so recently lived them. Border would not have been the first secular humanist, the first scientist, to lean on religion when all else failed. Surveying the world in the mid-1940s, Border might well have concluded that all else had indeed failed.

Who was this mid-western, mid-century psychologist who, when no longer young, dropped everything in his life to fight his way into Europe apparently, according to the failed grant applications, largely on his own money, to record the stories of traumatised Jews when the rest of the world wanted to focus on the future? Adam was growing ever more curious about him and his undertaking. There was more he needed to find out. He was due to be meeting with Eileen Miller, the Dean of Psychology. She might know something of Border's background.

On his way he chanced upon Sahera Shukri, the Dean of Libraries.

'One of my junior colleagues told me, quite excitedly, that you think you've made some kind of discovery from the papers of our Dr Border. This is a library, Dr Zignelik. We do our best to keep excitement out of the building,' she joked. But her smile receded somewhat when she learned directly from Adam that her colleague had not been exaggerating. Adam explained just what it was that he thought the library had, taking her down to the basement to show her the transcripts. There in the half-light she began reading them. He watched her reading, turning page after page, said nothing for minutes so that she could read and then realised that she had begun in silence to cry. He didn't want to embarrass her and so didn't say anything until she looked up and, without any attempt to hide the effect on her of Border's transcripts, wiped away her tears with the back of her hand. The quality of the light would have allowed her to pretend that she wasn't crying but she made no attempt to avail herself of it. Adam knew that she understood perfectly what they had on their hands.

'Have you told Eileen Miller about these?' she asked.

'No, she was away yesterday and this morning she's been teaching. But I'm due to see her at any moment. In fact, I should probably call her now,' Adam said, taking out his mobile phone.

'Reception's lousy here. Come with me back to my office and we'll try Eileen from there. This is astonishing stuff. We're going to need to protect it, to preserve it. It's just been sitting there. No one here . . . So you don't think that anyone at all knows about this? It's all unpublished?'

'As far as I've been able to ascertain all but eight of them are unpublished.'

'And the eight, where were they published?'

'In Border's book.' Adam held up the copy of Border's *I Did Not Interview the Dead* as they walked. 'And as far as I can tell, the book was pretty much ignored.'

'Why publish only eight?'

'I don't really know. I could guess.'

'Why do you think?'

'I think it would have been a consequence of a commercial consideration made in light of the times by the publisher.'

'The times . . . you mean people weren't interested?'

'Not really. It was just after the war. Some people knew a bit of the story but most people just wanted to focus on the future. There wasn't much of an appetite to know about these experiences and the book would have been a risk for the publisher. I'll bet they didn't pay him anything and it still would have lost money. My guess is they thought eight would be enough. I don't know this. I'm speculating.'

They had reached her office and she asked him to wait while she went over to her crowded but ordered desk and phoned Eileen Miller.

'Ellen, hi. It's Sahera. I've got Dr Zignelik with me . . . The historian from Columbia.'

*

'But the gun was not yours, Mr Lamont. You said it was not yours. You didn't have a gun,' Mr Mandelbrot said indignantly from his bed on the ninth floor of Memorial Sloan-Kettering Cancer Center.

'I know that,' Lamont said quietly.

'He was not even your friend, the young one with the gun,' Mr Mandelbrot added.

'I know that too. But it didn't seem to matter to them.'

'To who?'

'To the jury . . . and the judge.'

'And so this is why you went to prison?'

'Yep.'

'Because the jury and the judge didn't believe that you had nothing to do with the gun?'

'Yep.' Mr Mandelbrot shook his head slowly. 'Hey, I don't even think my own lawyer believed me,' Lamont continued. 'Public Defender. Busy man, overworked. Didn't have time to believe me.'

'So nobody believed you. Why didn't anybody believe you, Mr Lamont?'

'I didn't have the money to pay someone, a lawyer, to get them to believe me. Two young black guys did it and they confessed that they did it. Lookin' at a plea. Now it takes a whole lot of money to slow things down long enough for people to look differently at the third guy. I was the third guy and I didn't have that kind of money.'

'I see. So you went into prison and this is where you lost your daughter.'

'Yeah.'

'And you're looking for her now?'

'I'm taking steps all the time to find her.'

'How old is your daughter?'

'She's eight.'

'And your wife –'

'Chantal. We weren't married.'

'I see. She didn't let you keep any contact with your daughter?'

'No.'

'Because you were in prison?'

'I don't know. I don't know why. I haven't seen her to ask her why. So . . .'

'And you're living again now with your grandmother.'

'Yeah, back in the Bronx.'

'In the place where you grew up?'

'Yeah.'

Mr Mandelbrot considered his interlocutor carefully. 'You like your grandmother?'

'I *love* my grandmother.'

'And she loves you?'

'Sure.'

'You are good to her?'

'Sure.'

'Of course you are; you're good to *me*. I'm a stranger.'

'Well, not any more. I know you now.'

'Yes . . . you know me . . . and I know you. I know that things are getting better for you now, Mr Lamont. No more in prison, you're free to look for your little daughter now, you have this job here.'

'Yeah and they said they're gonna give me extra duties so I'll learn a whole lot of –'

'Extra, you mean instead of –'

'No, no, not *instead* of anything. Extra, as well as. Extra duties will help me to keep my job. The more I know how to do around here . . .'

Mr Mandelbrot turned towards the window.

'Yes, it's true. Extra duties. Sometimes . . . extra duties can save you.'

Adam listened to Sahera Shukri, Dean of Libraries at IIT, describe over the phone to Eileen Miller, Dean of Psychology, the full significance of Henry Border's transcripts and the effect reading some of them had had on her. There was a lot to do but he still hadn't figured out just what. What should he do with the material? Should he at least read it all himself or should he notify specialist historians of the Holocaust at Columbia and elsewhere about the transcripts and leave it to them? He didn't have an answer but nevertheless he felt that sense of calm that comes with achievement or at least with vindication. If you'd asked him what exactly he'd achieved, he would have been stuck for an answer other than to say what it was he'd found and to explain their historical significance and perhaps even their importance to psychology. Could someone else have found the transcripts and surmised their importance? Yes, but nobody had. Adam had saved these transcripts from eventual degradation and ultimately destruction. In doing this he had preserved the stories of the survivors and enlarged the record of precisely what had happened. As he'd told his students, this was no small thing.

'Don't give this to somebody else,' Adam heard Diana say. 'Have you lost your mind . . . again?'

'It's not my area and, anyway, how long will it take me to read fifty or more transcripts in the hope of finding a reference to black troops at the liberation of Dachau? Look, when I'm not seeing out my time teaching I need to be looking for a job.'

'You need to be looking for a wife. *This* is your job: Henry Border and his transcripts.'

'I don't know, I'll ask him,' Adam heard Sahera say over the phone. 'Eileen asks who translated the transcripts into English.'

'You know, I hadn't got to that yet. Mentally, I'd just assumed that Border had translated them himself but of course that's not so likely. Firstly, I don't even know if he spoke any language other than English and, secondly, the survivors would have been speaking different languages. Border couldn't possibly have spoken them all.' Adam started flicking through the book.

'No, he's looking through the book now . . . Okay. Great. See you,' Sahera Shukri said before putting the phone down. 'Eileen's coming here to pick you up and take you back to her office.'

Adam was reading through Border's introduction again. He found that Border's self-effacing language hid the most likely, albeit unexpected, origin of the translations, namely that Border had indeed translated the transcripts himself. Nowhere in either the acknowledgments nor in the introduction did Border thank or even refer to a translator and the copyright was held by Border alone. It wasn't shared with a translator. Border had written, 'A technique of translation was developed to assist me with the recording of adjectives and verbs.' In writing 'A technique was developed', Border had used the passive form so often employed in the sciences to suggest objectivity and to remove the observer from the report. On balance though, one had to conclude that Border himself had been the translator. Could he really have spoken so many languages so well? Adam flicked through the eight transcripts translated in Border's book. At the end of each interview it had, in italics, the language spoken by the interviewee. The first interview was translated from German, the next from Polish, then German, then French, then Russian, Polish again, then German. Could Border really have spoken all these languages himself? The next interview finished with the words *translated from Yiddish*. 'Yiddish!' Adam exclaimed under his breath. That was impossible. Surely Border couldn't have spoken Yiddish? Either the interviewee spoke a language other than Yiddish and it was mistakenly reported in the book as Yiddish or else some other person had translated it. Did Border have help that he didn't want to acknowledge? Did he have someone with him whom he hadn't mentioned anywhere in the book, someone who could speak Yiddish? Only Jews spoke Yiddish.

On this realisation a third possibility occurred to Adam Zignelik. Perhaps Henry Border was himself a Jew? But what about the allusion in his writing to Christianity, '*the raiments of the crucified*'? What about the donation to the church? Which church was it? Adam would check. Suddenly, though, a lot of things started making sense. Border had to have been around sixty when the book was published in 1949 but he had received his PhD from Northwestern University only some time in his forties. How many Jews was Northwestern graduating in the 1930s? Had he converted for the purpose of smoothing the pathway to a PhD from Northwestern? He claimed to have studied under Wundt but Wundt died in 1920. By the time Adam met Eileen Miller, the Dean of the School of Psychology, he was convinced that, whatever Henry Border might have been telling the world about who he was, Henry Border was in fact a Jew, a European Jew.

'I know him as a psychologist, one of the earliest members of the faculty here, the person who established the Chicago Psychological Museum,' Eileen Miller said. 'I don't know whether you've come across them yet but he reported his research in papers on the use of different devices designed to test people's visual acuity using both eyes in coordination.'

'What kind of device?'

'A dipthometer. This was the early research that laid the groundwork for understanding the different sides of the brain, how different information received by each eye gets coordinated, assimilated, by different sides of the brain into a single image.'

'So he was an important psychologist?'

'I'd say he was. Look, a lot of the artifacts that he collected for the Chicago-based psychological museum are now held in Akron.'

'Akron, Ohio?'

'Yeah.'

'Why there?'

'After he retired the Chicago Psychological Museum folded and all the equipment and documents that he collected went to Akron where the American Psychological Association houses its collection of historical psychological apparatus. Border had the foresight to collect and preserve these things. Nobody else did.'

'Did he get sufficient credit for this?'

'I'd have to say no. If you read his papers, if a psychologist reads his papers, and I have to admit there's an awful lot in those boxes in the storeroom that I haven't read, I think you'd have to conclude he was under-recognised.'

'At the time?'

'Both at the time and now. Are you interested in his work? He really should be better known, at least by psychologists.'

'Well, however important he was as a psychologist, and I'd be in no position to say, he was perhaps even more important as a historian.'

'A historian?'

'When you read the transcripts of his interviews with DPs, people we would now call Holocaust survivors, you have to conclude that he might well be the father of oral history. However he arrived at the idea – and perhaps he stumbled on it through his work on the "Adjective–Verb Quotient" – he's one of the first people to have realised the importance of recording people's testimony in their own words in the interests of historical research. I don't know of anyone having done that before him, certainly not recording the testimony of Holocaust survivors, perhaps not of anyone. He hasn't paraphrased these people. You read the transcripts and you get every stumble, every verbal tic, albeit in translation.'

'And you think he translated them himself?'

'I don't know. My hunch is that he did but I can't say for certain. Do you know whether he was Jewish?'

'I don't know. Why?'

'Because Yiddish was one of the many languages it appears he spoke. It's easier to imagine one person speaking all these languages than it is to imagine a gentile in the mid-west of mid-twentieth-century America speaking Yiddish, especially someone with a church affiliation.'

'What do you mean, a "church affiliation"?'

'Well, I might be putting it too highly but he did at least once make a donation to a church. He kept the receipt. I made a note of it.'

'That doesn't mean he worshipped there, doesn't mean he was part of the congregation.'

'No, I guess it doesn't. But why make a donation to a church you have no connection with?'

'What's the name of the church?'

Adam consulted his notes. 'It was . . . the Pilgrim Baptist Church.'

'Oh, that's just around here. But he wouldn't have been a member of that church. I'm confident of that.'

'Why do you say that?'

'The Pilgrim Baptist Church is a black church, one of Chicago's oldest black churches. There was a fire there last year but it's still there, sort of. Border might have made a donation just in passing on his way to and from work.'

'Sure, he could have. And if that was as far as his connection went there's nothing to say he wasn't Jewish, which would help explain why he was so keen to get to Europe and record the experiences of Jewish victims of Nazism. It's not possible that you have contact details for any of the faculty who knew him, if they're alive?'

'No, I doubt if any are. But we have lists of his students. Some of them might still be alive.'

'I'd only need to speak to one person who knew him.'

'But that person might not know whether he was Jewish or not.'

'No, but I suspect he was a European Jew and I want confirmation of some kind of accent. Although it might be easier just to check his birth certificate.'

'Dr Zignelik –'

'Adam.'

'Adam, why are you interested in him? What is it in particular?'

'I guess it's not really him that's going to be of interest to historians but his work. But if he really is one of the first oral historians he does deserve some biographical record himself. Is there much known about Marvin Cadden, the sound engineer he worked with?' Adam Zignelik asked.

'Yes, there is – a shameful amount – shameful to us in the School of Psychology considering the way we've ignored our Dr Border. The Engineers held a huge exhibition not long ago concerning his life and work. Everybody went. It got all sorts of attention, not just on campus but also in the media. They're very proud of him and his accomplishments.'

'You don't know if there's anyone in the Faculty of Engineering who could talk to me about him, maybe show me some of his equipment? I'd really love to see the wire recorder Border took to Europe in 1946. You don't think there'd be anyone here who knew him?'

'He died some time in the 1990s so it's not out of the question that someone from Electrical Engineering met him or even knew him a little,' Dr Miller said.

'Died in the 1990s, that recently?'

'Well, he was much younger than Border, twenty or thirty years younger. Someone there can probably tell you a lot about Cadden's work, maybe even a little about his life. I'll give them a call for you. I know you don't have a lot of time and we're keen to do anything we can to assist you with your research into Border. But it's not likely they'll be able to tell you anything about Cadden's interaction with Dr Border.'

'No, probably not, but I'd still be very interested to see Cadden's wire recording device, the one Border took with him. It must have been state of the art.'

'Must have been. They'll be falling over themselves in Electrical Engineering to help you. Cadden put them on the map. But we've got a lot of material from Border himself in the reading room in Psychology that no one's ever been through, as far as I know. I don't know what it all is. I'll give Engineering a call now and at least see when someone can see you.'

'You mean *if* someone can see me.'

'No, I mean *when*. They really put us to shame. Whenever it is you see them, and it might be now for all I know, don't let them dazzle you with the history of twentieth-century sound engineering.'

'No, don't worry. The devices aren't of themselves of interest, not to me. It's Border's importance in the development of oral history that might well be my subject.'

'Might well be?'

'I need to see the full extent of what's here before deciding exactly what to do with it. It might well be that I simply pass on the transcripts to historians of the Holocaust.'

*

On the ninth floor of Memorial Sloan-Kettering Cancer Center, Dr Washington, the young African American oncologist, was finishing her visit to her patient Henryk Mandelbrot. Her professional demeanour seldom wavered. It served to protect her from the pain that might be occasioned by the daily attempt to tame cancer. But with some patients it was harder to maintain than with others. As she was leaving

Mr Mandelbrot's room she said, 'I guess I'd better be leaving now. This is about the time when your family comes to visit, isn't it?'

'No, I asked them to come later,' he said. 'They will avoid the traffic. But I have another appointment.'

'I see.'

In truth it was not so much an attempt to save various family members their battle with the end-of-day traffic but to space out his evening visits as much as he could to avoid loneliness. The first regular visitor came in the late afternoon and did not have to battle the traffic to get there since he worked at Sloan-Kettering and so was already there. Somehow a routine had developed in which, at the end of his shift, Lamont Williams, an employee from Building Services, would visit the old man before taking several buses uptown to his grandmother's apartment in Co-op City, the Bronx.

Initially Lamont had thought his visits to the patient would need to be brief for he didn't know how they would be viewed by the hierarchy within the hospital. As much as Mr Mandelbrot assured him nothing negative would come from these at first brief visits, it took a long time for Lamont to act calmly on these assurances. The consequences for him, the breach of rules or even of some perhaps unspoken institutional protocol before the end of his probation period – the loss of the job with its attendant economic consequences, the setback to his post-prison adjustment, his concomitant decrease in confidence, and the disruption to his search for his daughter – all of these made him slow to accept the old man's assurances that no harm would come to him if his visits were discovered. But despite his unease Lamont would come anyway.

Such was the regularity of the visits that it was evident that not only was Mr Mandelbrot getting something out of them but that Lamont was too. And, bit by bit, Lamont was coming to the view that, at least as long as the visits were at the end of his shift, no one at the hospital would care, indeed, that no one would even notice them.

But the one person who definitely did notice them was the visited patient himself, and he took comfort from them not only because they helped consume otherwise dangerously undistracted time but because he too came to conclude that his incongruously regular visitor was gaining some sustenance from them and this realisation in turn multiplied many times the sustenance Mr Mandelbrot himself got from them. So, one day, at around the time when Lamont Williams was normally due to stop by the room on the ninth floor but did not, the old man noticed it, not merely in passing but acutely. There was no one there to see him crane his neck from his bed in his room at each passing sound beyond the door, no one there to see him, while nervously smoothing the sheets on his bed, look at the alarm clock and speculate why it was that the quiet young black man wasn't there. What could have gone wrong?

*

Eileen Miller set up an appointment for Adam with someone from the Electrical Engineering Department who not only had met Cadden several times but also could show him through the remains of Cadden's laboratory there and then. He could even show Adam a wire recorder of the type that Border had used. Since Cadden was the archetypal engineer, it was explained to Adam, he was constantly cannibalising his earlier work for later models so it couldn't be said definitively that the wire recorder Adam would be shown was the precise one Border had taken to the DP camps of Europe in the summer of 1946.

'Well, this is it or certainly one like it,' Arturo Suarez, the academic from Electrical Engineering explained. Adam looked at it.

'Do you mind if I pick it up?'

'No, so long as you're careful. Might be a good idea to stand with it over the table so it won't have too big a drop if you slip. But don't let it slip.' Adam held it. It was heavy, heavier in his arms than he had expected. He tried to imagine a man close to sixty dragging it in and out of DP camps immediately after the war.

'You know, prob'ly still works,' Arturo Suarez said with quiet admiration.

'How exactly does it work?' Adam asked.

'Okay, let me tell you the whole thing, from the beginning. You want to put it down there for a moment?' Arturo Suarez asked him. Adam gently placed it down. Eileen Miller had been right to predict the enthusiasm that the Electrical Engineers had for Cadden. Arturo Suarez continued.

'So Marvin Cadden, born right here in Chicago, was tinkering with things in his parents' house from the time he was five, you believe that? He's in his early twenties when he gets to studying electrical engineering at the Armour Institute of Technology, which is what we were called before we were IIT. Well, bear in mind that he could have done anything; I mean anything, he was that kind of guy. You know? But it turns out that his cousin is some kind of opera singer or somethin'. I mean, I don't know if he was any good as an opera singer but he was trainin' to become an opera singer and Marvin was close to his cousin and the whole thing was Marv wanted to give his cousin a chance to hear what he sounded like – as an opera singer, I mean – a chance for his cousin to hear himself sing. So he remembers something he learned here about Poulsen's idea. Valdemar Poulsen? You may not know of Poulsen, but no matter.

'So Poulsen had come up with what he called a telegraphphone wherein he recorded sounds magnetically. Never been done before. Marvin Cadden had learned about this and wanted to do somethin' similar for his cousin, the opera singer.

'He tried using piano wire. He was able to record a range of sounds by converting them into a range of magnetic fields and to use these to induce a range of degrees of magnetisation in a travelling wire. And by reversing the procedure, he was able to reproduce the original sounds. He found, however, that the wire would twist during the process and distort the sound on playback. That's when Marv revolutionised sound recording forever. To avoid the distortion due to the wire twisting, he came up with a magnetic recording head, see? By surrounding the wire with this recording head, but without them touching, he was able to induce the degree of magnetisation appropriate to a particular sound uniformly around the circumference of the cross-section of the wire passing through the head at that time. That was his idea and it worked. This was genius. The guy was still in his twenties.

'I don't know what happened to the opera singer cousin but Marvin got a position at Armour and started taking out patents and he was off and running. During the war the Navy used his technology to train submarine pilots. It was 'cause of Marvin's work they were able to simulate the sounds made during depth charge attacks. In this way the crew in the sub could acclimatise, could get accustomed to operating with the pressure of that sound, the noise of being attacked. The US Army used his work too. They used the Model 50 to spook the enemy with decoy attacks, attacks that existed only aurally. It was his equipment, Marv's equipment developed right here, that blasted out the prerecorded sounds of an infantry attack, high volume, on D-Day during the landing. Confused the enemy and saved lives. The guy was a hero and a genius innovator.

'And it didn't stop after the war, either. After the war he turned his attention away from wire and on to tape. All the magnetic tapes and magnetic coatings, magnetic sound for motion pictures, multi-track tape-recording, high-frequency bias, you know, of the kind that reduces the signal to noise ratio; that's all Marvin. By the time he died he had something like 500 patents to his name and they'd get licensed to companies like GE, 3M and Eastman Kodak. Sony made a packet out of Marv but he never really saw any of it.'

'When did he die?'

'I wanna say . . . mid-'90s, I think about 1995. I can check for you if it's important. His widow is still alive.'

'What kind of man was he?'

'Friendly, regular guy, one of nature's gentlemen. He was very . . . what do you say? Unassuming, no airs or graces. Liked a joke, always smiling.'

'Did you meet him?'

'Sure, I was just an undergraduate comin' up but everybody knew about him and if you wanted to meet him you could and anybody who had any interest in electrical engineering wanted to meet him. He was approachable. He used to play harmonica, I mean really play. He was a virtuoso with that. Played every week in one of a couple of bars. He was doin' it for years. People asked him to tour, he was that good, show tunes as well as blues. Black guys asked him to play with them. Really! He could've made a living off of *that*.'

'Did he play with them, black musicians?'

'I don't know. If I had to guess I would say no.'

'Why?'

'People didn't tend to mix so much in those days. So I'm told.'

'I don't suppose he ever mentioned anything at all about the psychologist, Henry Border.'

Arturo Suarez shook his head. 'No, never.'

When Adam had finished looking at Marvin Cadden's wire recorder, Arturo Suarez, the electrical engineer, escorted him back to the School of Psychology inside the Life Sciences building. Everyone at IIT was being quite unexpectedly helpful. Adam thought about this and wondered if it was because of his connection to Columbia. When he permitted himself to think that this was the reason, he felt a fraud. Would these people be so helpful if they knew the true state of his career?

Adam Zignelik was to be meeting up with Eileen Miller again but his visit to the Electrical Engineering Department had taken longer than he'd expected and now she was unavailable, teaching or at a meeting. Adam wondered if he hadn't pushed his luck. Perhaps she'd done enough and was due back in her own world. But she'd left instructions for a staff member to show Adam to the reading room where Border's materials were kept. Now he was alone there with some more boxes and his own voice telling him to quit, insisting he stop pretending he had something valuable to contribute. He told himself he should just hand Border's transcripts over to experts, Holocaust historians, to nod once politely when these experts thanked him, to pack up his office at Columbia and start looking for another job. Somebody would eventually go through all of the transcripts. Sooner or later they'd all be digitised and it would be easy enough to see then whether there was any mention of African American soldiers participating in the liberation of Dachau.

As for Border, the man himself, what did it matter if he had been Jewish? It might well have been his religion or his ethnicity that accounted for the motivation of this little mid-western psychologist becoming one of the pioneers of oral history but what did his motivation matter? One of Adam's inner voices told him it was enough for Adam to have found the transcripts. But another voice countered that this was something that could have been done by anyone who'd cared to look. This voice told him there were two good reasons no one had cared to look before him. First, because everyone else had real work to do and, second, because Border was, in himself, of no interest to anybody. So what should he do now? he asked himself, as he sat there in the reading room alone, just the way he sat in most places. You'll look at some unread, barely published papers on arcane aspects of psychology to do with the word choice of trauma victims before catching a cab to the airport where you'll buy more peanuts to throw around the cabin of the plane on your way home to an empty apartment that you'll soon have to give up.

'Why can't you look at this man's papers,' Diana whispered, 'without looking at yourself looking at them?'

A draught seemed to be coming from the storeroom that was off the reading room and Adam got up to close the door. Maybe I could get sick while I'm here, Adam thought to himself.

There was a tiny window in the storeroom that looked on to an expanse of grass outside. Adam stepped over a crate covered by some kind of sheet to check whether the tiny window could be more tightly closed but he realised it was too high for him to reach and he'd have to make do by just closing the storeroom door. That was the best he was going to be able to do. Careful not to knock over either of the two ladders, the bucket, the mop or the broom stored there, Adam bumped his shin against the covered crate and swore. The crate had cut him.

When he got back to New York he would have a bruise as a souvenir of this storeroom off the reading room in the School of Psychology inside the Life Sciences building at IIT. The sheet covering the crate was itself covered with a layer of dust about as thick as the sheet itself. Adam thought he might sneeze. Though the dust wouldn't follow him back to New York, he felt it was best to get out of this miserable storeroom as soon as possible. He was closing the door when he thought to go back in.

It was probably cleaning materials or carpenters' equipment but since this was the room that had housed the remaining boxes of Border's papers, he thought perhaps he should at least lift the dust-caked sheet that someone had once draped over the offending crate before he left.

He took hold of a corner of the sheet and slowly lifted it off. By the time it was a third of the way off the crate Adam had the first inkling of what the contents might be. There were white plastic cylinders, thin in the middle and expanded at each rim. At first glance there had to have been easily over a hundred of them.

'Oh, Jesus!' Adam said out loud. These were the spools of wire given to him by Marvin Cadden that Henry Border had taken to DP camps in Europe in the summer of 1946 to record people who would now be called Holocaust survivors. Adam looked at the spools. All around him was silence. Inside the crate there were people waiting to get out, people who had experienced unimaginable events, the remnants of communities that had been silenced through annihilation. Inside the crate there were voices. This was as close as anyone had ever got to interviewing these people at length while the trauma was being occasioned to them. Civilian Germans had not stopped it, the other Axis powers and their citizenry had not stopped it, nor had the Allied governments, their armies or their citizenry stopped it. The Jews of Europe had tried desperately to tell the world what was happening to them but their voices went essentially unheard until they were completely silenced, all except voices such as those of the few just-freed survivors on the spools of wire in this crate in the storeroom off the reading room in the School of Psychology at the Illinois Institute of Technology.

At first Adam didn't know what to do. He wanted to shout, to tell someone, but he didn't know who to tell and, anyway, he needed to confirm that he was right about the contents of the crate. He picked up one of the spools and looked at it. It was numbered. How could he confirm its contents? He hunched over, placed the dusty sheet back over the entire aperture of the crate and dragged the thing out of the storeroom and into the reading room. He picked up the phone on the desk there and made an internal call to Arturo Suarez, the electrical engineer. At first he couldn't reach him. The calls were being caught by a departmental answering machine. In a garbled message Adam left both the extension of the phone in the reading room and his mobile phone number. He put the phone down. The room was quiet. Adam was almost too frightened to peek under the dusty sheet again in case he'd dreamed the whole thing or in case, in shifting the crate, he'd somehow been responsible for ruining the wire recordings.

Having paced the hall outside the reading room for no reason whatsoever, he took to calling Arturo Suarez every sixty seconds. Suarez might have gone for the day, he might have been teaching, he might have been at a meeting or he might have had a heart attack and died. Adam didn't know what else to do while waiting for Suarez to call him back other than call him. In one of the sixty-second breaks Arturo Suarez called him back. It took Adam, who could barely contain himself, about five minutes to explain to Suarez the possible significance of the wire on the spools. Could Suarez bring the wire recorder he had shown him to the reading room of the School of Psychology as soon as possible? Adam thought he was probably going to miss his plane. Had it not been for a teaching obligation he wouldn't have cared. Arturo Suarez took a little over twenty minutes from the time they got off the phone to carefully bring around to the Psychology reading room Marvin Cadden's wire recorder. He was out of breath and mildly perspiring when he got there and he had to agree that the wire spools had every chance of being what Adam hoped they were.

The wire was as thin as nylon thread but much more fragile. Adam didn't want to unwind it but it needed to be partially unwound before it could be threaded into the machine.

'I can't do it. I don't trust my fingers,' Adam said.

'I'll do it,' Arturo Suarez volunteered, taking a spool from Adam that Adam had chosen at random. Adam watched him plug the wire recorder into the wall and then begin to thread the wire with the delicacy of a surgeon.

The first sound they heard was a crackling sound, which became the sound of a crowd of people talking, a set of voices of different tones and shades and volumes melding into a wall of languages. Then came a solitary 'shoosh', which was quickly joined by so many others that the chorus of them overpowered the wall of language and then all was quiet but for some hiss and crackling. Then Adam heard a solitary voice. The sound it made was a song, a lullaby familiar to him, and it shocked him to be catapulted back to his own childhood. This was the last thing he expected, to hear a fragment of his own childhood.

As a little boy growing up in Melbourne he had heard his grandparents sing this song to him many times when they babysat while his mother was out. When he grew a bit older his mother found a place that would transfer the song from the 78 record his grandparents had it on to a cassette when 78s were superseded by LPs. Now he listened to it in the reading room of the School of Psychology of IIT on the south side of Chicago. He listened and was astonished at how immediately he lost his professional distance. With both Adam and Arturo staring at the wire recorder, Adam felt his eyes well up and they listened to the lone voice of a young man sing amid the crackling sound. Adam thought of himself as a child, of his Polish Jewish grandparents, of his mother who never remarried and then of the young man singing in a DP camp. What had been done to this young man just before he sang into the machine Marvin Cadden had taught Border to use? He wondered if Border, assuming he had been a Jew, had been able to hold on to his professional detachment better than he had. What was Border thinking when the thin voice of this thin young man, new to manhood, new to liberty, sang for him as it now did for Adam Zignelik?

Shlof mayn kind, shlof keseyder,
Zingen vel ich dir a lid.
Az du mayn kind vest elter veren
Vestu visn an untersheid.

Az du mayn kind vest elter veren
Vestu vern mit laytn glaych.
Damolst estu gevoyre veren
Vos heyst orim un vos heyst raych.

'What's he singing? Do you know what language that is?' Arturo Suarez asked Adam.

'It's Yiddish. It's a lullaby. The singer is telling the child to sleep. "Sleep, my child, sleep peacefully".'

This was it, Adam thought. These were Border's wire recordings. He had found them. Other than Border himself, Arturo Suarez and Adam Zignelik might well have been the first people to hear this since it was recorded. Adam was going to miss his plane but he couldn't leave the room. He looked at his watch.

'You're going to have to teach me how to thread the wire.'

'I thought you didn't trust your fingers?'

'I don't. But you have to teach me anyway. First, if you don't mind, I'm going to need to get a later flight, if I can.'

Arturo Suarez needed to make a call himself. He needed to call his wife to explain that he would be home a bit late. It took Adam longer than it should have to change his flight and it cost him more than it should have. But now that he had a later flight he was free to learn how to thread Henry Border's 1946 wire into Marvin Cadden's wire recorder. There had to be more than a hundred hours of interviews to listen to. He was going to start then and there.

*

Late one afternoon before even the earliest of the dinner guests had arrived, two waiters in waistcoats and bow ties were preparing the tables from the floor plan as the first of their duties on their shift in a venerable downtown Manhattan steak restaurant just off Union Square. One of them was setting tables with glasses and cutlery and the other was running a vacuum cleaner under the tables his colleague hadn't yet reached. Preoccupied alternately with work-related and more personal thoughts, with the pressure of the time remaining before the first guests were due to arrive, and distracted by the noise of the vacuum cleaner, they didn't notice Lamont Williams, fresh from his shift at Memorial Sloan-Kettering Cancer Center, walk past the unattended greeting station at the front of the restaurant and stand in the middle of the dining room.

How many years had it been since he had been there? The most recent time he had been there was almost a decade earlier on his first date with a young woman with whom he had had a daughter. His thoughts went around the room to the different tables at which he'd sat at different times, all as the two waiters and then others he vaguely heard but couldn't see went about their business.

'Side entrance, bud,' somebody called over the vacuum cleaner.

Chantal was the name of the woman he had taken there and everyone had looked at her. She was beautiful.

'Side entrance.'

'You done yet?' someone called to one of the waiters.

'Almost.'

'Side entrance.'

Lamont remembered looking at the size of the wine glasses next to the water glasses and thinking it was going to take all the money he had ever seen to fill those wine glasses even once. But if anyone had been worth it, he'd thought she was. He remembered leaning in to hear her against the noise of the traffic in Union Square. And that she never leaned in, not once.

'Side entrance, bud. Hey, I'm talkin' to you!' a man with authority within the hierarchy of the steak restaurant barked at Lamont. 'Deliveries to the side entrance!'

'I ain't here to deliver anything,' Lamont said quietly, causing the maitre d' to approach him in order to hear him.

'What did you say?' he said, looking Lamont up and down.

'I ain't here to deliver anything. I'm here to pick something up.'

'What're you talkin' about?'

'My grandma was here last Saturday. She left her umbrella. Special umbrella. I'm here to pick it up for her.'

'Lotta people leave their umbrellas here,' the maitre d' said suspiciously.

'No doubt they do. She's one of 'em. Last Saturday. Table for two, reservation made under the name of McCray.'

The maitre d' thought for a moment.

'Special umbrella, you say?'

'That's right.'

'What's it look like?'

'It's got Scotty dogs on it . . . Scotty dogs with red bow ties around the edge . . . and it's grey . . . charcoal grey. It's got . . . she said it's . . . it's got a dog's-tooth design pattern.'

'Dog's tooth?' the maitre d' said sceptically.

Lamont pulled out a slip of paper from his pocket. 'Houndstooth, it's got like a houndstooth design pattern in charcoal grey.'

Again the maitre d' thought for a moment before he spoke. 'Come with me.'

Lamont followed him to the coat check room and was told to wait. After about a minute, the maitre d' brought out a kind of shopping cart that held a collection of some twenty or so umbrellas.

'See any Scotty dogs with red bow ties?' the maitre d' asked him. Lamont took his time and looked carefully inside the trolley but he couldn't see any umbrellas matching the description his grandmother had given him.

'I'll take that one,' Lamont said, pointing at a large and sturdy-looking umbrella with a shiny black handle.

'That ain't the one you described,' the maitre d' said.

'I'll take that one,' Lamont repeated quietly.

'Well, what am I gonna do when the owner of this one comes in lookin' for it and it's gone?'

Lamont beckoned to the maitre d' to lean in over the counter as he picked up the large sturdy-looking umbrella with the shiny black handle and spoke to him almost in a whisper.

'You tell 'em whatever shit you gonna try on me.' He turned slowly towards the greeting station and walked in no hurry past the other waiters and then on in the direction of Union Square, the umbrella with the shiny black handle tucked firmly under one arm.

*

It was 9.15 pm when Adam found himself alone, not merely in the reading room but also alone in the building. Arturo Suarez had gone home to his wife long ago. Adam had left messages on the office answering machines of both Sahera Shukri at the Galvin Library and Eileen Miller explaining that he had found Border's wire recordings, the source of the transcripts. Eileen Miller would have to ensure they were kept safe. The wire recorder should be returned to Arturo Suarez in Electrical Engineering. He thanked each of them and promised to call them from New York. He looked at his watch again and wondered if he had time to listen to one last wire recording before trying to find a cab in the dark to take him first to his hotel downtown and then on to the airport. Not knowing how long the journey would take at that time, let alone even how difficult it would be to catch a cab, Adam was playing with fire. He picked another spool anyway and, with clammy hands, started to thread the wire into Cadden's machine. He chose the one nearest the right wall of the crate. Each spool was labelled but Adam hadn't yet started paying attention to the markings. For now he was just listening.

This interview – it turned out to be the last one Border recorded – was in Yiddish, a language Adam didn't speak but recognised and partially understood from his maternal grandparents. He recognised also the name of the interviewee because the interview happened to be one of the eight included in Border's book, *I Did Not Interview the Dead*. In the book Border had described the woman. The interviewee, a fair-skinned Jewish woman with light hair, who had been in both of the two ghettoes established for the Jews of Grodno on the ethnic border of Poland and Belarus, had told Border how her husband had convinced her that their newborn baby's only chance of survival lay with the woman trying to pass as a Christian at least long enough to get the baby to the door of the local church-run orphanage. It snowed the night she set off to try.

She told Border, seated with her back to him, that it was minus twenty-six degrees Celsius, which Adam calculated to be about minus fifteen Fahrenheit. After ripping off the yellow star from her coat and being handed the baby by her husband, the woman tried to make it out of the ghetto gate with a group of other Jews, but she was unsuccessful. Shots were fired and sixteen Jews lay dead in the snow on the street at the side of the ghetto. Holding her baby against her chest in an attempt to balance its need for air and for protection, she stifled a scream as she looked down at the corpses of the people next to whom she had stood moments before. She and the baby kept quiet as blood trickled out of five of the escapees and coloured the snow. But she must have shuddered at the sight of a twitching leg on one of the corpses because the tiny girl started to cry. The mother tucked the baby into her coat and ran back into the ghetto proper.

Later with the help of her husband the woman tried again, this time through the wire fence, which in this ghetto was not electrified at the time. Her husband raised the wire and, holding the baby wrapped up in swaddling cloth, the woman crawled through. There was a curfew even outside the ghetto for the non-Jewish residents and the woman had an hour to save her baby daughter's life. She went to the home of a Polish Christian woman whom she'd liked but had met no more than twice and she begged the woman to take her child to the local orphanage. But the Polish woman was afraid and explained that she could be shot merely for speaking those few words to her. All of it in whispers, all in shadows, all of it in the snow, the two women looked at each other, pleading with each other to understand the other's position.

Then the Polish woman came up with an idea. She told the Jewish woman to leave the baby wrapped in the swaddling in the street a little bit away from the door, maybe thirty paces, and then to go. She would come out a few minutes later with a neighbour. They would come out together and, as if by chance, the Polish woman would find the baby in front of her neighbour. The neighbour would then be a witness. Then in the morning the Polish woman would take the baby girl to the orphanage.

There was nothing else the Jewish woman could do. She spoke into Cadden's wire recording device and explained what it is like to leave your newborn baby in the snow in the streets not far from a ghetto. She told of how she gently placed her daughter on the ground, how she kissed the baby's forehead, knowing how unlikely it was she would ever touch her daughter again, how unlikely it was she would ever see the child again. She told of how she hid across the street and watched her baby lying in the snow, waiting for the woman to come out of her house with the neighbour as a witness. She described her anguish in the minutes as she waited hidden, her only hope being that a virtual stranger would come and pretend to find her baby, how in those minutes which seemed to last an eternity she wanted to run out into the street and grab the baby and keep her with her and how the pull of the child screamed against her reason, which said that in this strategy lay the best chance of the child's survival. She described the bitter-sweetness at seeing the Polish woman come out with her neighbour and 'discover' the baby, just as she'd promised.

Border listens, occasionally interjecting a question without any emotion, although the woman often broke down in tears, sometimes sobbing uncontrollably for minutes. Adam found it hard to breathe as he listened, following along with the transcript as it was translated and printed in Border's book, *I Did Not Interview the Dead*. The woman described unspeakable horrors, including the beating and then the death of her husband, her own suffering in the ghettoes, and then in Auschwitz, until she was finally liberated.

Throughout all of it, and indeed throughout all the interviews Adam had heard thus far, Border had betrayed no emotion at all once the interviewees had started their stories. As far as Adam could hear, Border remained always the scientist, the academic psychologist interviewing these people in a range of languages simply for the raw data they provided. Then, when it appeared that this woman had finished her story, Border asked about the fate of the woman's daughter. The woman explained that she had been in that DP camp in Wiesbaden for a year. There was silence on the wire but for its own hiss and crackling and the faint background sounds of the other displaced persons. Then the interviewee spoke.

'The Polish woman had come out . . . with her neighbour . . . and she picked up my daughter. It became known that she picked her up from the street. There was an investigation . . . The authorities determined that the child was Jewish and –' At this point Border interrupted.

'How could they determine that?'

'I don't know, perhaps because my daughter had my husband's colouring not mine, perhaps because my husband's family was well known in the town. I . . . really can't say. Perhaps it was because the woman had not given my daughter to the orphanage after all.'

'Why not?'

'I suspect it was because she loved her. The woman was childless. It was just three weeks before the Russians came that . . . they buried her . . . my daughter. She is in the Christian cemetery. I would . . . the Jewish one was completely desecrated. There is a woman in Lodz, the wife of a doctor there, and this woman . . .' Again the interviewee collapsed into uncontrollable sobs.

'And this woman . . . the wife of a doctor in Lodz?' Border asked. The woman took in deep breaths before answering in a tiny voice.

'The woman in Lodz . . . she has photographs . . . of my daughter.' After this, Border had lost her. She had disappeared inside her own agony and he spoke directly into the machine for the first time, not to an interviewee or to anyone else in the vicinity but to Cadden's machine. As the woman continued to cry Adam heard Border speak in an English with a strong European accent. Now for the first time, Adam hears emotion in Border's voice.

'You are lighting a cigarette,' he says, even though the woman doubtless doesn't speak English. 'Well, we have to conclude . . . Wiesbaden, September 1946, in the synagogue that was desecrated in 1937 or '38 and which has its holiday service for the first time . . . although it has not been rededicated . . . What we have heard from this woman . . . is the story we have heard from everybody . . . I'm concluding my project in Germany . . . I want to thank the UNRRA, Jack Thompson from *The Chicago Tribune* . . . and . . . I can't speak. I don't remember the names . . . now . . . because I'm too emotional . . . this woman's report. I'm concluding this project. The automobile is waiting. I am going to Frankfurt.'

Then the crackle, the hum and the hiss of the wire recorder continue without competition from any other sound for a few moments with Border remaining silent. He was just sitting there, exhausted, behind the now silent woman. The moments pass and his voice begins again. Adam hears that it is the voice of a man who feels unutterably alone. He hears, '. . . Who will sit in judgement over all this?' Again there is another long silence save for the hum and the crackle of the equipment. Then Border speaks again. 'And who is going to judge my work? . . . Who is going to judge . . . me? IIT wire recording. Leaving tonight for Paris. This project is concluded.' That was the end of the wire. A little over sixty years later Adam Zignelik too had a plane to catch.

*

Some time between 9.30 and 10pm on a Saturday night a young African American girl kept herself upright by holding on to the pole of a very crowded subway car going uptown on the Number One line. She had got on at the Lincoln Center stop and was tired enough to have fallen asleep, had it been possible to sleep where she stood without falling down.

There was a bit of a racket going on at the other end of the car but it seemed far enough away not to concern her. She listened to a nearby conversation to try to keep herself awake so she wouldn't miss her stop. A man and a woman who, from their tone, clearly knew each other were talking.

'You know the One and the Nine were voted the dirtiest trains.'

'No kidding?'

'Yeah, I read about it.'

'They're *voting* for that now? I remember the Nine. They don't have it any more.'

'No, you know why?'

'Too dirty?'

'Gotta be.'

At the other end of the carriage the ruckus was being caused by a man the young girl deemed obviously deranged. He was talking at an inappropriately high volume to people he was treating as friends but who, their response made it clear, did not know him. With difficulty he tried to maintain his balance as he slowly made his way over to her end of the carriage. He had matted hair and torn clothing and moved the fingers of one hand rapidly and consecutively like a consummate pianist passing through an arpeggio. He swayed on another axis entirely to the one that had him shuffling towards the young girl's end of the carriage. A tourist might have thought he was drunk but she knew better. He slurred his words and spoke too loudly. His non-arpeggio hand was more or less outstretched. One had to quickly formulate a policy with respect to each mendicant. Did he warrant any money? Did you have any change? Did you have easy access to the change? Did he have a story that was sad enough? Did you believe it? Could you make the slightest bit of difference to him? Her mother would have known what to do. Were you afraid of him? Were there other people around to help you if your policy had unforeseen consequences? What was the young girl doing on that train?

The previous day she had made arrangements to go to the movies. She was to be meeting a group of friends at Loews Movie Theater but, with the alacrity and the logic that seemed acceptable only to the collective judgement of a group of fourteen-year-old girls, the plans had been altered drastically at the last moment and then suddenly none of them were to be meeting at the movies. But since it had taken Sonia so long to convince her parents to let her go in the first place and since she was intent on spending the evening away from them, she didn't tell them that her plans had fallen through. She didn't want to hear them pretending they hadn't just been arguing. Instead of staying home, she had gone ahead with the original plan and seen the movie on her own without telling her parents that she would be out on her own. She'd been planning to look at the CDs and magazines in Tower Records but had forgotten that it had closed down so, tired and disappointed, she spent some time in a Starbucks watching people, before making her way to catch the train that arrived carrying the broken man now coming towards her.

He made a lot of sounds but it wasn't always clear what he was saying. The outstretched hand was contorted. At the other end of the car he'd been causing a few people to laugh but no one was laughing around him now. A dishevelled African American man, he looked to be in his early fifties. Sonia thought he had to have been around her father's age. Discreetly she put her hand in one of her pockets to see if she had any change. She wondered as she did this whether giving him change would be the right thing to do or the smart thing. It might move him along faster or it might win her unwanted attention. Her mother would have known the right thing to do. He dragged his body past the people near Sonia, mumbling and slurring most of his words until they were too incoherent to be understood. He seemed to know on some level that no money would change hands without a story but he wasn't able to get the story out. Sonia had reached into her pocket and was ready to give him something when he dragged his body past her and everyone else without stopping long enough for anyone to give him anything. Still mumbling, he made his way through the carriage door into the concertinaed section between that carriage and the next one. The train continued on its way uptown.

*

One night, early in the Chicago May of 1945, a man aged about sixty but who felt older, and whose manner was entirely of another time and place and whose heavy coat was of another season, walked alone on the city's south side. He travelled from his home some ten miles away to this neighbourhood five days a week in order to get to work and, although he had at times worked late into the night, he was certainly not accustomed to being at work this late at night. His normal route home took him from his office in the Main Building at the Illinois Institute of Technology to the Elevated train station at 33rd and State streets. He was certainly not accustomed to being in the surrounding streets in the dark. With the bearing of a Europe that had vanished, less at this moment an immigrant and more a refugee, he kept glancing at a piece of paper in his hand and then up at the street signs, from one to the other again and again, looking for assurance that he was headed in the right direction.

There were a lot of people, men and women, old and young, passing him on the street. In passing them he caught snippets of conversation but understood none of it. All of the people he passed were black. It was their neighbourhood and when they looked at him what they saw was an oddity. So many people out at night, he thought, as he walked past the rib joints and funeral parlours, the storefront churches, pawn shops, bargain shoe stores and liquor stores. The people swirling all around him were of different ages but most were much younger than him. The men wore suits that can't have been theirs when the suits first were sold some time in the previous decade. The women's clothes were of more recent vintage, often obviously homemade. So many of them were recent arrivals to Chicago from the south. Many had arrived more recently than he had and to a casual onlooker not a few of them might have seemed lost but it felt to him that every man, woman and child belonged there more than he did.

When he got to the corner of 35th and State streets he went through a narrow entrance to a place whose name he had been given over the telephone a few days earlier. Not only had he never been there before, he had also never been to any place remotely like it before, and on taking a few steps inside, he felt that he was on another planet.

A tall and solidly built black man stood between the end of the hallway and the entrance to the room proper and pointed at a sign advertising the cover charge. 'Whoa! You gotta pay to hear the music.'

'I'm not here for the music. I'm here to meet someone.'

'Don't matter why you here, Dr Goldberg. You still gotta pay if you want to come in.'

'I am Dr Border.'

'What?'

'I am Dr Border, Henry Border.'

'I don't care *who* you are, mister.'

'I'm not Dr Goldberg. How did you know I was a doctor?'

'You either a doctor or the landlord and either way, mister, you gotta pay if you want to come in. Look behind you there! See, I got people waitin' to come in.'

Henry Border paid the man as he was asked and walked tentatively into a rectangular room, which was, in all other respects, unlike any he had ever been in. Several of his senses were assaulted simultaneously but it was perhaps the sound of the music, its volume and its style, that most immediately confronted him. It seemed to him louder than traffic, as loud as a steam engine when one got too close to it but, unlike a steam train, it never moved on. Its very intensity, its very proximity to the audience, seemed to be the point. Then there was its style; it pulsated, throbbed from the rudimentary stage with flattened thirds and sevenths within its chords making for a dissonant gathering of tonalities, played in four four time and all of it amplified against an incessant back beat from a kick drum. Along with the drum were a bass and an electrified guitar, which took turns with a harmonica, also amplified through a microphone, to wail with a piercing brashness.

The smoke of tobacco and reefers made a wall that kept reconstituting itself as soon as anyone broke through it; and people did break through it, some to get near the pool table at one corner of the room and especially near the furthermost wall where young men and women danced, all of them black, at least as far as Dr Border could see, but for this one young white woman dancing. Already perspiring because of the effect on him of the heat of the crowded room, the heat from the rapidly moving bodies and from the fact that he was dressed in a suit and tie and an inappropriately thick coat that he wore buttoned up, he took the slip of paper out of his coat pocket and squinted in the dim light to read again the address he had written down. He thought that he could not possibly be in the right place despite the fact that the building's address corresponded with that written on the paper in his own hand. He thought that the combined effect of the volume of the sound and the close atmosphere was going to lead him to pass out and he walked against the flow of ever more people coming in towards the entrance where the tall man he had paid in order to get in told him that he would have to pay again if he wanted to re-enter. Henry Border didn't care and mumbled something about the doctor not being there. It was something the tall man would have ignored but for the fact that at the moment Border said it he started to buckle at the knees and the tall man was forced to prop him up if for no other reason than to prevent a blockage in the crowded narrow entrance hall.

'Who ain't here?' he asked Henry Border.

'I was coming to meet a colleague but he's not here so I wish to leave,' Border tried to say over the crowd noise and the music.

'Who is it you want?'

'Dr Cadden, Marvin Cadden.'

'That's Marvin right there,' the tall man said, pointing at the white man on stage playing the harmonica. Henry Border turned around, squinted up at the stage against the far wall for a moment and then went right back in.

'You are Dr Cadden?' he said to the man when the musicians' set was over.

'*Mister* Cadden. I have a masters but I don't have a doctorate.' They shook hands and Marvin Cadden led Border to a seat at one of the few unoccupied tables.

'Mr Cadden,' Henry Border began, looking around him before continuing, 'I hadn't expected . . . this. It's part of your work?'

'This? No, it's music. I play with these guys, sometimes anyway.'

'Music?'

'Uh-huh.'

'Are you good with this . . . ?'

'The harmonica?'

'Yes, the harmonica.'

'Good enough for them to let me sit in sometimes.'

'Mr Cadden, I came to see you about something connected to my research. It's about the wire recorder that you have made. You invented this?'

'Yes.'

'And it works like you told me over the phone?'

'Yes. You want to know if it can record voices, interviews. Sure it can. Dr Border, I don't understand why you needed to come here to discuss this.'

'Have I offended you in some way, Mr Cadden?'

'No, not at all. Please . . . Can I buy you a drink?'

'No, no thank you.'

'Please, you have to let me buy you a drink. You can't come here and not have at least one drink. It's rude. People here will think you won't drink with them.'

'It's rude?'

'Sure. Let me buy you one drink. Beer?'

'Will you allow me to pay for it and to buy you one?'

'No, the first one's on me. What'll it be?'

'Do you think they might have vodka?'

'They've got bourbon or gin or beer. Can I get you bourbon?'

'Thank you, Mr Cadden. It's kind of you. Can I just tell you first about my project and how I thought you might be able to assist me, before we drink?'

'You want to record interviews with DPs?'

'Yes.'

'In Europe?'

'Yes, that's the plan.'

'How will you get into Europe?'

'I am already under way with applications. It's difficult but I don't need to trouble you with that part of it.'

'Okay, sure. Look, I'm going to help you if I can but I have to ask you something. Why did you feel the need to come down here in the middle of the night to talk to me about this when we could have discussed this on campus during the day? Forgive me but you're clearly not comfortable here.'

'Mr Cadden, I think I might be more comfortable discussing my project with you here than I would be on campus.'

'Why?'

Henry Border shifted slightly on his chair from one side to the other and then leaned in over the table, causing Marvin Cadden to lean in as well in order to hear Border's quiet voice above the surrounding din.

'Mr Cadden, I am a psychologist and my interest here is to interview displaced persons to investigate their speech patterns, the way people use language when they have experienced trauma. But it's not just any displaced persons I want to speak with. It's Jews. These people were the most targeted victims of the Nazis.'

'I see.'

'Perhaps you have read something about what they have been through in Europe under the Nazis?'

'Yes, I have. But I still don't understand why you need to come down here at night to talk to me about it when you said you live uptown.'

'Mr Cadden, I am a European Jew, born in Poland. In all my grant applications for this project and also in my attempts to get to Europe I have said that I wish to speak to displaced persons but I never specified in any of the paperwork that the displaced persons I wish to speak to are Jews.'

'You thought it would count against you? This is not Europe, Dr Border. This is America.'

'I know America is not Europe. I came here already qualified. I had studied at Jagiellonian University in Krakow and then in Germany, in Leipzig under Wilhelm Wundt, a man considered the father of experimental psychology. I made this known when I applied twice to get into the doctoral program at the University of Chicago and was rejected. I made it known again when I tried once at Northwestern and was rejected. I tried again at Northwestern, only this time I made it a point on the application to tell them I was Episcopalian. Now I have a PhD from Northwestern University. Only one variable changed in the four applications. But this is not Europe, I know.'

'Are you Episcopalian?'

'Technically now I am. But I thought that if I were going to ask you for your help with the technology you have invented and if we were, at least for a time, going to work together just enough so you could teach me how to operate the equipment, if you are going to let me take one of your machines with me all the way to the DP camps – well, I thought you should know more precisely what are my intentions with this work.'

Marvin Cadden shook his head. 'I would be surprised if your difficulties getting funding for the project would be increased if people knew the DPs you're interested in are Jewish.'

'Mr Cadden, three years ago a poll was conducted in this country. You may have heard something about this. A group of Americans were asked about a series of national or ethnic groups. They were asked about each group, are they "as good as we are in all important respects", "not as good as we are" or "definitely inferior"? The category of Jewish immigrants came in tenth. Germans came in significantly higher and this country was at war with them. Germans had been fighting and killing the sons of the people being questioned. But this is not Europe, I know.'

'What about these people?' Marvin Cadden asked, gesturing to include the people around him.

'The black Americans?'

'Yeah, where were *they* ranked?'

'They were not even an option. This is not Europe.'

'Dr Border –'

'Mr Cadden, I am a scientist, like you. But I am a psychologist; I do not work with machines. I work in a very new science, the science of the human mind. The mind, Mr Cadden, exists inside the brain but is not the brain. You could dissect an infinite number of human brains and still you would never find the mind, not one, not ever. This is psychology. People don't know much about it. They are sceptical about it. Some are even fearful of it. Our progress within this science, it is slow and small. Now, with all this in mind, how would it be if I come along and tell them: hello, I am a Jew and I want your help to study Jews? Can you imagine? My project would have even less chance than it has now. With all due respect, Mr Cadden, this is perhaps something you might understand better if you were a Jew.'

'Dr Border, how do you know I'm not?' Marvin Cadden responded.

Taken aback for a moment, Border looked up to see the one white woman in the club, the one he'd seen earlier, dancing, come over to them. Sixty-two years later this woman spoke over the phone from Chicago to Adam Zignelik, who was back in New York.

'That was where we met,' the widow of Marvin Cadden told Adam over the phone from Chicago.

'So he became an Episcopalian to improve his chances of getting into Northwestern?'

'That's what he told Marvin. Look, it worked. He got his PhD from Northwestern, right? Anyway, he thought that's what had made the difference.'

'Sure. It's funny though. I mean, I understand why he might've thought he needed to do that and perhaps he did. But in going through his papers I found a receipt for a donation he made to a Baptist church, the Pilgrim Baptist Church.'

'Oh, that's a black church on the south side, near IIT,' Marvin Cadden's widow said.

'Yes, I found that out.'

'Well, that was probably 'cause of Callie.'

'Who was Callie?'

'Callie was his housekeeper. She was black. He met her through us, through Marvin, from people Marvin played with. You see, when Border did finally get permission to go to Europe he needed someone to take care of his daughter. He couldn't leave her on her own. I don't know exactly how old she was at the time but she was quite young. It wasn't just the wire recorder Marvin helped him with. Marvin found him Callie through his contacts at the club where they'd first met. She needed the work, lived at the Mecca. She was probably trying to raise money for the church and that would be how Border came to make the donation. Of course I'm guessing. I don't know this. It was such a long time ago. You see, Marvin might have been important to Henry Border but Border wasn't important to Marvin's career.'

'Sure. What's the Mecca?'

'The Mecca Flats. Dr Zignelik, if the south side of Chicago is a world within Chicago, on the south side the Mecca was a whole other world again.'

The light was flashing on his answering machine when Adam Zignelik looked at it later and though he didn't know who was calling him he didn't want to listen to the message. He stood there for a moment just watching it blink.

'Is this because you think it's me or because you think it isn't me?' he heard Diana whisper.

'I don't know.'

'Which would be harder?' she asked him.

'Depends what you'd say.'

'Looks like you'll never know,' she said as the answering machine blinked on, oblivious to the anxiety it was capable of provoking. Finally after staring at it and hovering above it he let his finger press 'play'. It was a woman's voice, a familiar one, and it cut through him before he'd had a chance to listen to its words or even to place the voice. But the fourth word was her name.

'Hey. Adam, it's Michelle. How you doing? Hope it's not too late but Charlie said that William said you might be in Chicago. Is that right? Gone to follow something up? Sounds interesting. Anyway, I wondered if you wanted to catch up some time soon. We haven't seen you for a while. You could come for dinner but . . . also, I was kind of thinking . . . Am I going to run out of time? Better speak much faster. Okay. Let me know if you want to meet for coffee some time. As *well* as dinner I mean, not *instead*. Talk soon. Hope Chicago's good. Call –.' Then the machine whistled and then clicked to indicate that it had granted Michelle as much time as she was going to get.

'She's going to want to talk about you, about us. She's going to tell me how you're doing, isn't she?'

'How do you want me to be doing?'

'Well, if she says you're doing well I won't believe her.'

'And if she convinces you?'

'I'll feel terrible.'

'And if I'm not doing well?'

'I'll feel worse.'

'So coffee with Michelle has now become something you dread, one more example of collateral damage from the stupidest thing you've ever done in your life?'

'Why does she want to have coffee? We've never met for coffee before, not just the two of us.'

'Well, Charlie's probably working or taking care of Sonia or seeing his father so he can't come and you banished me to a far better life, so I can't come.'

'At least see the logic in the decision.'

'Adam, I never could. You're trying to turn your fear of the future, your panic about parenthood and professional failure into something noble that you've done for me. I never bought it.'

'Diana, it's possible at the one time both to be afraid *and* to act nobly for another person. Come on! Look at where I've come from. You know what my father was like. You know what my childhood was like.'

'I know exactly where you've come from. I rubbed your back and held you after nightmares. I'm the one who took the black-and-white photo of the little boy in quilted overalls. I took him with me even as you were kicking me out. You have to follow up this man Border and write on him and his work. It could be your salvation.'

'Are you saying that if I had something to work on, to write on, if I had some hope of professional viability, we could get together again . . . try to have a child?'

'No, I've always said that something to write about is not something you should need for that, but if you do need it, I'm saying Henry Border's just given it to you.'

'But I can't know that yet. Look, there's incredible stuff there but it's for someone else, experts in the area. I don't know if I've really got anything that *I* should be following up with Border. I can't tell you to come back just because I've got a hunch or rather because I have these moments where I imagine that *you've* got a hunch that I've found something to write about.'

'Follow Border! Hang on to him and don't let him go.'

'And if he leads nowhere? What then?'

'Then ask Michelle what to do with the raisins.'

*

It was the end of the day and Lamont Williams sat down in a chair, tired but ready.

'How you doin' today?' he asked.

'You got your grandmother a nice umbrella, yes?' the old man asked in turn as his answer.

'Yeah.'

'A good one?'

'Yeah.'

'Very nice. Is there any water left in that thing? If yes, give it here please. You want? No? Sure? All right. Now, where are we?'

'You'd just got there.'

'Got where?'

'Auschwitz,' Lamont Williams reminded him. 'Most of the Jews got there by train but you didn't get there by train.'

'No, I didn't. Almost everybody else did from all over Europe but I was on a truck. You remember!' he said, impressed. 'Good. You have to remember.'

*

Adam Zignelik thought of the Pilgrim Baptist Church and remembered why it had sounded so familiar to him. This was the Chicago landmark, the one-time south side Kehilath Anshe Ma'ariv synagogue. It had become the Pilgrim Baptist Church in 1922. It was in this guise that it became the birthplace of gospel music under the musical directorship of Thomas A. Dorsey and was, in 1946, where some 2500 people made their way inside while outside thousands lined the surrounding streets, all of them there to pay their respects at the funeral of Jack Johnson, the first African American heavyweight champion of the world, the man who defeated every great white hope they could throw at him and a lot more besides. The Staples Singers, Mahalia Jackson and Aretha Franklin had all sung there. Martin Luther King had preached there at the height of the civil rights struggle. That was the Pilgrim Baptist Church to which Henry Border had made a donation in 1946. Now Adam remembered. He kept hearing Border's voice at the conclusion of the last wire recording at the point where the woman had finished the story of the loss of her daughter. It had sounded as though the man's voice was held up by only the hum and the crackle of the recording, as though without that surface noise to support it, the voice would not ever have made it on to the wire. And this was the way it sounded in Adam's mind as it followed him around his Morningside Heights apartment in the middle of the night in the city of orphans.

'What we have heard from this woman . . . is the story we have heard from everybody . . . I'm concluding my project in Germany . . . I want to thank the UNRRA, Jack Thompson from *The Chicago Tribune* . . . and . . . I can't speak. I don't remember the names . . . now . . . because I'm too emotional . . . this woman's report. I'm concluding this project. The automobile is waiting. I am going to Frankfurt. Who will sit in judgement over all this? And who is going to judge my work? . . . Who is going to judge . . . me? IIT wire recording. Leaving tonight for Paris. This project is concluded.'

*

A lot of people were in attendance at the Workmen's Circle cemetery in the very late winter of 1982 when they buried Jake Zignelik following his sudden heart attack; more black folks than Jews as far as William McCray could tell. This might have been surprising to a casual onlooker at a Jewish cemetery, especially because by then relations between African Americans and Jews had passed what some might have called their golden age. But anyone who had really known Jake Zignelik would not have been so surprised. At the time of his death he was still director-counsel of the LDF and he had socialised with African Americans as much as if not more than with Jews or with anybody else. The frozen ground made it hard for his son to navigate the shovel around the soil to begin the process of covering the plain pine wood coffin dictated by Jewish tradition. William McCray stood near the grave and watched the stick of a kid, Jake's son, Adam, trying to keep himself composed long enough to get a few shovels' worth of soil on to the coffin. The kid was sixteen and had just got off a plane from Australia. The cemetery was crowded but the kid, Jake's only child, knew hardly anyone and when he heard the first 'thud' of hard earth hit the coffin William McCray thought he might be about to buckle at the knees and collapse in the grave on top of his father's coffin.

That's when William's son, Charles, who had been standing at the graveside beside his father, caught Adam and hugged him, held him very tight. This was Charles' first Jewish funeral but it hadn't been the first for William and, later, Charles asked his father whether Jake had died with so little money that he couldn't afford more than the most rudimentary pine box for a coffin, a coffin so lacking in ornamentation that the best that could be said for it was that it was fit for its service. William explained that while Jake didn't die a wealthy man by any means, it wasn't impecuniousness that explained the pine box coffin. It was Jewish tradition, he explained, that all people, irrespective of their wealth or status or achievements, should leave the world as equals before their Creator.

William McCray found himself thinking about Jake's funeral as he walked on the grounds of Columbia University. He made his way past the library towards Fayerweather Hall where his son was Chair of History and it wasn't until he was seated outside his son's office that he retraced the route by which his memory had arrived at Jake's funeral. Usually at this time he met his son for a cup of coffee, a chat and, depending on the weather and on how he was feeling, maybe a walk. Today though he had a medical appointment and, as medical appointments always did these days, it focused his mind on his own mortality. Additionally, he'd heard from Charles that Adam had been to Chicago to follow up some information from his veteran friend in Boston that he, William, had passed on to him. Perhaps Charlie knew what had come of it. What was going to happen to Adam? He should never have let Diana go. These were the paths taken by William's mind that afternoon to arrive at Jake Zigne-lik's funeral. He could still hear that skinny kid trying to get through *Kaddish*, the mourner's prayer.

'Hello, Mr McCray,' said the young woman warmly who was either his son's secretary or his personal assistant, as they now called them, or else she was a secretary all the department could call on. Who the hell knew what she did when she wasn't greeting him cheerfully?

'Lovely to see you. How are you today, Mr McCray?'

'Fine, thank you, and you?' William could never remember her name.

'Your son has just stepped out of the office but he isn't far,' she said before whispering, 'I think he's gone to the bathroom but he won't be long,' before adding more audibly, 'He's locked the office and he has his coat on.'

'His coat?' William enquired.

'Oh, I always have to remind him to take his coat. Did you?'

'I don't follow you.'

'When he's going out,' she explained.

'He's going out?'

'You have a medical appointment today, don't you, sir?'

'I do.'

'Downtown isn't it? He asked me to cancel his appointments. He's going with you.'

It was night again. In Co-op City, the Bronx, Lamont Williams' grand-mother looked over with a discomfort she would have found difficult to articulate at a large and sturdy-looking umbrella with a shiny black handle. Then she looked over at her grandson who was reading the paper. She hoped her granddaughter would never ask to see the umbrella she had bought for her and given her at the steak restaurant off Union Square. At least, she contented herself, she hadn't lost the envelope that contained Sonia's card. Putting the money from its envelope in her purse, she looked over at her grandson and hoped with all her might, to the point of mouthing a brief impromptu prayer, that he was going to be all right. He noticed her looking at him. He saw her lips moving without any sound coming out and he asked, 'You okay, Grandma? Can I get you something?'

Many hours later that night, a few miles south across the Harlem River in his Morningside Heights apartment, Adam Zignelik was unable to sleep. He could not quieten his mind. Deciding to take a sleeping pill, he went into the bathroom and, opening the mirror cabinet, saw Diana's comb, the comb she had left that held strands of her hair. He picked it up, looked at it, and gripped it tight till the skin on the palm of his hand was white and indented. He didn't want to put it down. He didn't see why he ever should put it down. Looking at it there in his hand and at his face in the mirror, he was overwhelmed by a wave of self-loathing, panic and a sense of loss that, in staccato bursts, flushed the air from his lungs till the moisture in his sleep-starved eyes formed a vitreous glaze that mercifully blurred his reflection in the mirror. Everything else, though, everything else in his life, every regret, every flaw, every mistake he'd ever made was clear, all 3 am-sharp, and he gripped the comb still tighter. Where were the sleeping pills?

'Did you take them?'

Diana's reply was drowned out by Henry Border's anguish through the crackle and hum Marvin Cadden hadn't yet been able to eradicate. 'Who will sit in judgement over all this . . . And who is going to judge my work? . . . Who is going to judge – ?'

part seven

'ELISE . . . ELISE!'

Henry Border stood at the bottom of the staircase and called up to her but there was no answer. The once-grand house had been built at the turn of the century when the land around there could be snatched up for a song. A number of similar places had been built just in time for the rumour to calcify into the incontrovertible fact that the North-western Elevated Railroad was coming to Uptown. It was a large house with more rooms than they needed just for themselves. There had been a number of reasons Henry Border had chosen it at the time he and his daughter had moved in but a major attraction had been the extra rooms that he had planned to sublet to help with the rent and perhaps even to help with their other living expenses. There had been a shifting cast of subtenants for a time but the war had eventually taken them all away and by the summer of 1946 when he and Elise were living there alone the house had almost none of the grandeur it had once had.

For such a reserved and, by nature, private man, subletting had been a necessary accommodation to the uncomfortable economic realities from which he tried to shelter his daughter as he sought to make his way in America. By both his instruction and example his daughter had learned to find a self-contained richness within the walls of the room she had been allocated when they had moved in years earlier. She could lose herself in her books – her own or from libraries – or even in her school homework. It was perhaps in one of those books that her mind sojourned that summer's day when the sound of her father's voice eventually reached her through her closed bedroom door. Her father, who could appear formal to the point of being curt to strangers, was not usually this way with her. If anything, even his brusquest admonishments were almost always delivered as appeals to reason and had, if not a sugar coating, then at least the flavour of cinnamon. But the tenor of the voice that found her through her now-opened bedroom door, and which had grown ever more urgent with the mounting evidence of its impotence, suggested to her that her father was calling out to her in the presence of another person. When she got from her bedroom to the top of the stairs and looked down she saw that she was right. Standing beside him at the bottom of the stairs was a black woman she had never seen before.

'Elise, I want you to meet Miss Ford.'

'How do you do, Miss Ford?' she said, shaking the black woman's hand. The woman glanced down at the twelve-and-a-half-year-old girl's hand clasping hers and said with a tentative smile, 'Please, miss, call me Callie, miss.'

'Callie?'

'Yes, miss.'

'Please call me Elise, Callie . . . or Elly, if you like, or Lissenka, my father sometimes calls me that . . . Sort of foreign, Polish, I think,' Elise said shyly, briefly lowering her head while she tried to work out who this woman was and what she was doing there.

Henry Border ushered his daughter and Callie Ford further into the living room and bade them sit down.

'Miss Ford is going to be staying with you.'

'With *me*?' Elise said, surprised that his sentence permitted the possibility of a separation from her father.

'Yes, when I go to Europe. Why don't I make us all a cup of tea while you two get to know one another? You drink tea, Miss Ford?'

'Yes. Thank you, Dr Border.'

He left the room for the kitchen and Elise smiled nervously as her feet moved back and forth slightly in what was the most immediate and obvious sign of her rising nervousness. Her father had mentioned a trip to Europe for his work. In fact, he had mentioned it many times but it had seemed like it was never really ever going to happen.

'You at school, miss?'

'Yes,' Elise said, continuing to smile. 'I mean not at the moment though . . . summer and all.' She noticed what her feet were doing and the movement gave way to embarrassment for having been caught out being a nervous twelve-and-a-half-year-old girl. Adults didn't move their feet that way in company and she was grown-up enough to know that.

Callie Ford had worked as a housekeeper before, originally in the south where she'd been born and raised and then for a time in Detroit before moving to Chicago. The work had involved her taking care of other people's children even when she had still been a child herself. So it wasn't the child-minding that made her every bit as anxious as the fidgeting girl on the couch with the jet-black, wavy, shoulder-length hair and huge black eyes trying to smile her way through this situation, a girl with skin the colour of alabaster, white as if it had never been outside, had never seen a minute of this or any other summer. Callie Ford had thought the position was for a visiting housekeeper. She hadn't known how many days a week she was going to be required and, depending on the pay, she would have been prepared to come every day. But she hadn't realised the doctor wanted her to stay there overnight too. Was that really what he had in mind, just her and the girl in that otherwise empty house?

'Here we are . . . tea for everyone!' Henry Border said with a hurried and forced bonhomie as he placed a tray down on the table in front of Callie Ford's chair and the couch.

'Do you take milk, Miss Ford? Or perhaps sugar? I'm afraid we have no cake.'

They were treating her like she was a guest, not someone they were interviewing to be the help, but still she couldn't stay there.

'Perhaps she takes both, Daddy.'

'Both what?' Henry Border asked his daughter.

'Both milk *and* sugar. Do you, Callie?'

Callie Ford looked at her, the girl with her jet-black wavy hair and eyes ever wider, the same colour as her hair, almost a woman but not quite yet. What could she say to this girl?

'Milk *and* sugar, please,' Callie replied hesitantly.

She was twenty-nine years old. Since moving from Detroit three years earlier she had lived in a series of wooden tenements on the south side of Chicago until moving into one of the rooms in one of the 176 apartments that housed more than two thousand black men, women and children inside the grey brick monolith that took up half the block between State and Dearborn streets just north of 34th Street known as the Mecca Flats. She needed money as badly as anyone she knew there and she knew a lot of people, or at least had met some and had seen the rest living out their lives, many in public, right there in front of her; a mass of people herded together by their circumstances. She saw them, some in families of varying and changing sizes, some of them alone, some old, some young and some of an indeterminate age that kept increasing as you looked, their youth draining from their bodies. She saw them trying to help one another, giving to each other, saw them coming home from work or going out to look for it, saw them in various states of undress, some hollering, laughing, spitting, drinking, fighting, cursing, loving, smoking, dancing, singing, starving, bleeding, stealing, begging, washing up and sweating; all of it on top of her. But Callie Ford didn't know anyone who lived in the part of town this old foreign white man and his daughter with her various names did. And she certainly had never before been there herself.

She had worked for women before but never for a man. Women could grind you down mercilessly with the hours they would make you work. From her own experience and from the stories of other black women who worked as domestics she knew that sometimes the ladies of the house didn't care how young or old you were or what shape you were in. They could work you worse than a mule. Even a mule got to sleep but in some houses you might be expected to be on call twenty-four hours a day.

258

Men, however, harboured their own dangers. Callie had once been chased by a boss's drunken husband. She had been asleep at the time and so half undressed. The first she knew of it she was feeling warm licks of this strange man's flammable breath on her face and woke to a nightmare feeling his drunken hand inside her nightgown fumbling for her breast. She had got out from under him, out of bed still half asleep, and had run out of the room and down the hall. Was it better to keep quiet about it in the morning? Would it happen again? Would the woman blame her, disbelieve her or would she recognise the husband from the details of the assault but make Callie pack her few belongings and leave anyway? On another occasion back when she was barely out of childhood and still in the south, a woman's son had come back from boarding school for the weekend only to make rough advances when the rest of the house was asleep. The son, who was growing stronger with each visit home, thought of only one thing. Fortunately he wasn't there that much.

But this man here didn't seem that kind of man. It wasn't so much that he was foreign, old or educated, although perhaps that helped. Not that she could know. She'd never met anyone like this. He wore a three-piece suit though it was the beginning of summer. She knew he was a doctor of some kind but, as he hastily showed her around the house, he appeared to need a doctor himself. In his hurry to show her each room he quickly became out of breath. In the kitchen pantry, and again in his bedroom, he didn't take the opportunity to see how close she would let him get. It looked as if the thought had never occurred to him. He was exceedingly polite but he seemed like he wanted to get the tour of the house over and done. His explanation of the workings of the house didn't extend beyond pointing out what she could already see just standing there. What could she see? It was a big house with many rooms that would take a long time to dust but it was almost empty. There was no one living there but the old man and the girl, whom at first she had mistaken for the doctor's granddaughter. He was offering her a wage that exceeded the market rate. Why? Was he too old or too foreign to know the going rate? Well, she thought, it was a rate set unofficially by a marketplace of white women and perhaps the only woman in his life was the little black-haired dolly sitting there lonely on the couch.

Henry Border and his daughter Elise waited for her to say something. She had survived on her instincts and in the faded glory of that living room her instincts were telling her that this was possibly the best or at least the easiest job she would ever be offered. Unless she was missing something, it was the kind of job no one in her position, no one in their right mind, would turn down. But she was going to have to turn it down much as it would hurt her, and it would hurt her a lot. It would hurt her for days and even weeks back in the foyer, on the stairs and in her room back in the Mecca as she remembered the chance she'd had. But there was no way around it. She couldn't possibly stay there as the Borders' live-in housekeeper. They looked at her expectantly. No, it was out of the question, just not possible. Who would take care of her son?

*

'I knew Callie. We all did,' Arch Sanasarian explained to Adam Zignelik over sixty years later as he took a sip of iced water in the lounge beside the Chi bar in the Chicago Sheraton. Adam couldn't afford to stay there but he decided it was better to meet people there than in the hotel in which he could afford to stay, especially since it looked like he was going to need to travel to Chicago quite a few more times even after this visit. Arch Sanasarian was the first of Border's graduate students still alive when Adam had been able to track down. A list of the graduate students who had written their dissertations on Border's 'Adjective–Verb Quotient' had not been too hard to come by, not with Eileen Miller's assistance. But in addition to this, Adam had managed to find contact details for three of the survivors Border had interviewed in DP camps in the summer of 1946. He didn't know if the contact details were still current, if the interviewees were still mentally coherent or even if they were still alive, but just finding them gave Adam the feeling that it might be possible to come to know something more about the man who had pioneered oral history, this man who seemed to need to record these people's stories at great cost to himself at a time when barely anyone else wanted to know.

Adam caught himself feeling a certain excitement about his work that only a short time earlier he had relinquished hope of ever recapturing.

He couldn't remember how long it had been since he had experienced any emotion that was remotely positive. The best he had been able to achieve since Diana had moved out was numbness, usually alcohol induced. In the weeks, even months, leading up to her leaving, it seemed to him impossible that he would ever again feel any pleasure from anything short of the temporary absence of pain. But more recently it had dawned on him that it was possible, from time to time, to feel some stirrings of hope but only as long as he thought solely of pursuing his interest both in the possible role of black troops in the liberation of Dachau and in Border and those whom the Chicago psychologist had known or interviewed. His own personal life remained the disaster he'd engineered.

Arch Sanasarian was the first person Adam had met face-to-face who had known Henry Border. Border was now very slowly coming back to life and this encouraged Adam even more. A gentle, thoughtful man, a distinguished psychologist himself, now in his eighties, Arch Sanasarian's long fingers moved slowly when carefully attaching the tiny microphone that went from the lapel of his shirt to Adam's digital audio recorder.

'We didn't know Callie at that time because *none* of us knew Dr Border then, not in 1946. Not even Wayne knew him then. He went to Europe in 1946 to conduct the interviews but we didn't meet him till about 1950 or perhaps late '49. Elly was sixteen or seventeen by the time we met her and *I Did Not Interview the Dead* had already been published. As I understand it, Callie started working for him when he went to Europe back in '46. That's how she became involved with the Borders. Do you want to make sure you're picking me up on this thing?'

'Thank you, no, we're good. Who was Wayne?'

'Wayne Rosenthal, he was one of the other graduate students. Didn't they give you his name too?'

'Yes, but I wanted to make sure I knew which Wayne you were referring to. You seemed to single him out.'

'I think Dr Border singled him out.'

'In what way?'

'I think that of all of us – the five or six or was it seven of us – Wayne was the closest to Dr Border, even closer than Amy was. He reserved a special – what should I say – tenderness for Amy. But it was probably

Wayne; I mean I think they had the closest relationship. You had to look carefully to see it because Dr Border was a very proper man. He had a way about him that was warm while still being formal, in that way of a European teacher, a little strict, sometimes even intimidating. What was I saying? Oh, Wayne, right. Dr Border would have hated anyone to think he was showing favouritism to any of his students but I think Wayne was his favourite.'

'Eileen Miller at IIT gave me the impression that *you* were his favourite.'

'Really? I don't know why she would say that.'

'She said when he finally finished at IIT and moved house –'

'He didn't just move house. He left Chicago.'

'When he retired he left Chicago?'

'Eventually, he did.'

'She said that you helped him pack up his house.'

'That's right, I did. But that was right at the end.'

'Is that how you came to know his housekeeper, Callie, and his daughter, Elise?'

'No, I met them, we all met them, when we started work on our Masters dissertations on "The Adjective–Verb Quotient" back in 1950. Or we might have started talking to him about it in 1949. You see, it was the same year *I Did Not Interview the Dead* came out and there was a certain celebrity around campus that attached to Dr Border because of it.'

'That celebrity, it didn't last, did it?'

'No, but . . .' He thought for a moment about things that came to him too fast for words. 'Yes, it was only on campus and it didn't last long at all but it lasted just long enough for us to hear about it, about Dr Border and about his work. That's probably why we all wanted him to be our thesis adviser.'

'Can I ask you, if he was strict in manner, almost to the point of being intimidating, if he was formal in an old world sense, how did you and the other Masters students come to know him so well that you knew his daughter Elise and even knew his housekeeper Callie?'

'Sure, I can explain that easily. We were often at his house.'

'All of you?'

'Yeah, the six or seven of us. He would hold evening seminars for his Masters students at his home.'

'At his home . . . in the evening . . . why?'

'Well, most of us, perhaps all of us . . . oh no, not Evie Harmon, but most of us had jobs, at least part-time ones. So it was a great help to us that he agreed, no he *offered*, to hold our seminars at night at his house.'

'And why at his house? Why not on campus?'

'I think he thought it was safer than going down to the south side at night. And it was more convenient.'

'For him.'

'Certainly it was more convenient for him. Also for me. I lived right near him, two blocks away. In that respect I was luckier than the others. This might be why Eileen Miller told you I had the closest relationship with him, because of the proximity of my place to where he lived but . . .' Arch Sanasarian looked wistfully above his interviewer's head for a moment. 'I think Wayne Rosenthal was the closest with him. Not that he wasn't terrific to me. He was, right from the first time I went to talk to him about doing my Masters under him.'

'How did you first hear about him, about the possibility of doing that kind of work?'

'You know, I can't quite remember. Perhaps one of the others told me.'

'Told you what?'

'Well, he was actively recruiting.'

'Border was?'

'Yes, he wanted students to work on "The Adjective–Verb Quotient". I remember his office and his lab too; they were both in the Main building. They were next to each other with adjoining doors. You know the Main building? It's the red-brick nineteenth-century one. I think it's the oldest on campus.'

'And that's where you first went to see him to talk about the prospect of your dissertation assisting his research on "The Adjective–Verb Quotient"?'

'Yes, it's not just that I was nervous, of course. But I remember I even had trouble finding his office. That might sound crazy because the Main building houses – or at least it used to house – the university administration.'

'I think it still does. No, it's not hard to find.'

'No, it's not, and was then even less so. Fewer buildings then, you see. But I had trouble finding him because he was the only faculty member from Psychology with an office in that building.'

'Oh, why was that?'

'Originally the Department of Psychology and Philosophy had been housed there but they had all moved. They needed more room and they moved. Everybody but him.'

'Why didn't he move?'

'I don't know. I could speculate but I don't really know why.'

'Speculate then.'

Arch Sanasarian smiled. 'Where do I start? If you're thinking of intra-departmental politics or ructions of some kind, yes, though he would never discuss them with us, not with me at any rate, I suspect there were some. But they wouldn't have been severe enough, not significant enough to him for him not to move with everybody else. The thing you really have to remember about Dr Border was that his work was every-thing to him. I mean it really was *everything*. Of course none of us knew him till after he'd interviewed the DPs in Europe and *I Did Not Interview the Dead*. Why didn't he move with the rest of the department?' Arch Sanasarian smiled again in his chair in the lounge beside the Chi bar in the Chicago Sheraton Hotel thinking of his teacher of over half a century ago. 'I suspect he didn't have time.'

*

Lamont Williams' grandmother was, as usual, home before her grandson. This would have been the perfect time to speak to her granddaughter Michelle. She had left a message for Michelle and was hoping she might call back at that time. That was why she kept looking at the phone as though simply by looking at it, by an act of will, she could impel it to ring. But the phone wasn't ringing so she had to come up with another strategy to get it to ring. She put the television on so that the phone might be distracted and not see her waiting. Michelle had always been a dutiful granddaughter and she wondered now if it wasn't her imagination or was Michelle of late taking increasingly longer to return her calls? Or was it that Michelle knew what her grandmother would want to talk about and had become tired of her concern for Lamont?

But to Michelle's grandmother the concern made sense. She had thought that if Lamont didn't make even the smallest progress with respect to finding his daughter, if he didn't have so much as a plan or even a first step, sooner or later something in him would give. He would snap, lash out, do something against his best interests and lose that job. Or he might implode; he might be overwhelmed with despair and stop trying to make a new life for himself. The sad truth was that she didn't really believe he had much chance of finding his daughter. Chantal, the little girl's mother, seemed to have taken steps a long time ago to keep her from Lamont and if that was really what she wanted, Lamont's grandmother admitted to herself there would be little Lamont could do about it.

For Lamont's grandmother, finding his daughter wasn't really the point. What he needed, all he needed, was just to have a plan, have steps to take, at least just long enough for him to get past the six-month probation period at the cancer hospital. This might just be enough for him, enough to keep him on the right track towards his reintegration into mainstream society. If he had a good job with benefits, money coming in every week, if he started to make some friends at work, friends who had never been to prison, who didn't have to know *he'd* been to prison, he might be in a position to meet a woman. He might be in a position to start a family, a new family, a proper one where the child had a mother and a father who were married to each other. He would never stop longing for the little girl Chantal was keeping from him but, if he had a job and another family, the sharp pain of losing her might turn into a dull ache. Lamont's grandmother knew all about turning sharp pain into dull aches and felt that the capacity to do this determined who among the people she knew were successful and who slipped through the cracks.

The telephone rang just as a man from a small South Carolina town on *Antiques Roadshow* was explaining to the antiques expert that his great-grandmother had bequeathed his mother a spinning wheel. The call was not from Michelle but from a telemarketing company. Was Michelle slow to call because she had given up on her cousin? At the very least, she could offer some practical advice to help him search for his daughter, advice that might extend his hope beyond the six-month probation period. Was that too much to ask? their grandmother found herself thinking.

'Well, I'd say you come from one lucky family,' the antique spinning-wheel expert said on television to the man from South Carolina. 'Would you care to take a guess how much your great-grandmother's spinning wheel is worth?'

Then she started to worry that maybe Michelle had problems of her own. Maybe she should worry more about Michelle? Even were Michelle to call right now there wouldn't be much time left for them to talk freely, not now. Lamont was due home soon.

*

Professor Henry Border was looking into a small mirror that sat on top of one of the many filing cabinets in his office. He was trimming his beard when he heard a knock at the door. He put down his trimming scissors, looked at his watch and called, 'Come in.'

The young man who entered the room trying to hide his nervousness was Arch Sanasarian. Seeing the professor seated at an old roll-top desk, he walked over to him and stretched out his hand to introduce himself.

'Thank you for agreeing to see me, Dr Border. I'm Arch Sanasarian.'

'Please take a seat, Mr Sanasarian,' Border said, turning his chair and gesturing to the seat nearby, which, once the student relieved it of a pile of papers, creaked when he sat down on it. The room was filled with books both on shelves and in piles on top of the rows of filing cabinets that hugged every inch of wall that did not have a wall-to-ceiling book-shelf in front of it.

'Arch?' said Border, considering the name. 'It's an abbreviation of some kind, Mr Sanasarian?'

'Yes, my full name is Archibald.'

'It's an American abbreviation, is it?'

'Yes.'

'Were you born here?'

'Yes, Professor, I was.'

'Archibald becomes Arch. I see. I wasn't born here so I'm always needing to learn these things. You want to write your Masters dissertation on "The Adjective–Verb Quotient"?'

'Yes, that's right. I've read your book and –'

'You know, Mr Sanasarian, even if you have read the book, even if you think you are interested in the analysis of speech patterns, this is only a necessary condition, not a sufficient one.'

'I'm sorry, sir, I don't think I'm following you.'

'I mean that this kind of material, the interviews from distressed people, it's distressing itself and . . . well, it's not for everyone.'

'No, no, of course, but I think it's for me. Frankly, Professor, I can't think of any other topic that's of greater interest to me. In fact, having read your book I can't stop thinking about the material, about the experience of these people.'

'I see,' said Border.

'Sir, if this is about my academic record, if you'll allow me to go through it with you there are certain grades that I think I might be able to put into some kind of context that –'

'I haven't looked at your academic record.'

'Well, if this is about –'

'What is the "this"? Why do you think there is a "this", Mr Sanasarian?'

'Professor Border, I . . . I can't think of anything more important than the work you've been doing and if you'll just hear me out, sir –'

'Arch is an American abbreviation of Archibald,' Border interrupted. 'Sanasarian, that's an Armenian name, is it?'

'Yes, sir, it is.'

'Your parents were born overseas?'

'Yes, Professor.'

'When did they come to the United States?'

'In the early twenties.'

'The twenties? From where did they come?'

'My father from Van and my mother from –'

'Your father was from Van?'

'Yes.'

'Both your parents are from Armenia?'

'Yes.'

Henry Border looked at the young Armenian American man who sat on the other side of his desk. 'Do you have any family left there now?'

'No, none that my parents are aware of. They were all killed.'

'I see,' said Henry Border, cupping his right hand around his goatee. The two of them sat in the room in silence for a moment. Only the workings of a grandfather clock covered their breathing.

'There's course work too and seminars, you know that. Do you want to ask me anything about the course work, Mr Sanasarian?'

'Well, nothing I can think of, I mean not at the moment, Professor, but I thought perhaps . . . Don't you . . . want to see my academic record?'

'No, Mr Sanasarian.' Henry Border stood up from behind his desk and shook the young man's hand. 'Take this form away with you, fill it in and return it. It's not for me. It's for the departmental office. I already know enough.'

*

When Callie Ford first saw James Pearson it was at a rent party on the third floor of the Mecca Flats, the floor on which she lived in a room with her son, Russell. Though the hosts of the party were, at least technically, for a time her neighbours, Callie hadn't known them at all. She had gone there seeking company and inexpensive entertainment. It was not uncommon for recently arrived Bluesmen to play, sometimes solo, sometimes in ad hoc groups in the nearby tenements and also in the Mecca. Since the party was going to keep you awake you might as well join it, if you could. James Pearson was there not because he couldn't afford more expensive entertainment. He had a good job at one of the meatpacking houses. She already knew of him by reputation. A quiet man, not tall but broad-shouldered and clearly strong, he was known to certain people in the Mecca as 'Mr Anything-You-Want'. Some time later it transpired that Mr Pearson moved into the room next door to Callie's room within the same apartment. Tommy Parks was another single male neighbour of hers from the same apartment, also a packinghouse worker but of an entirely different temperament, a vulgar, short-fused, irascible man. When Tommy Parks saw Callie Ford smile at her new neighbour as James Pearson was bringing in his cases, he made a show of welcoming him for Callie's benefit.

'Well,' said Tommy Parks, leaning against his doorway, 'if it ain't "Mister Anything-You-Want"! Ever you need somethin' now, Callie, you don't need to be botherin' me in the middle of the night. You can come to "Mister Anything-You-Want". Might give you anything you want *whenever* you want it but you just remember, Callie, I give it *how* you want.'

The comment embarrassed Callie, as was intended, and James Pearson, moving in his possessions in a trunk and a few cases, chose to act as though he hadn't heard it. The irony in the comment was that, both drunk and sober, it was Tommy Parks who had come to Callie at night a few times, not the other way around. She had had to rebuff his advances firmly yet without making an enemy of him because he lived in a room in the same apartment. It was uncomfortable enough having a civil Tommy Parks as a neighbour. It would be much harder if he turned hostile. It was bad enough that Russell had already had to see Parks' amorous advances on his mother. She didn't want him seeing her pushed or hit.

James Pearson had earned the nickname Mr Anything-You-Want when he had arrived in Chicago and made his way to Armour and Company. Tommy Parks was already working at the Armour plant and he had witnessed the whole thing. In fact, he had contributed to the growth of Pearson's reputation. They were killing over a thousand hogs an hour at Armour when James Pearson walked in looking for a job and was asked by the man in Personnel, 'What can you do?'

'Anything you want,' James Pearson answered without wishing to convey anything but the truth.

'Anything?'

'Yes, sir.'

'Hear that?' the Personnel officer said to his colleague. 'This man can do anything we want.'

'Can you head a hog?'

'Yes, sir.'

He was taken out of the office and led straight on to the killing floor where the Personnel officer suddenly decided to increase the difficulty of the task and asked him, 'How about three of 'em?'

'Yes, sir.'

The Personnel officer smiled and looked over at his colleague who had followed to watch this new man who, although quiet, was altogether too confident for anybody's liking to be telling the truth. The first man pointed to a chain. Tommy Parks, who had followed the action to the killing floor from its beginning in the Personnel office where he had come to argue about his hours, watched as James Pearson picked up the chain and headed three hogs in a manner differently from the way it was commonly performed there. Differently, but perfectly. There was not a single scratch or a scar anywhere on any of the three hogs. The two men from Personnel, and Tommy Parks, whom they hadn't noticed, could not help but be impressed but not one of them said anything to indicate this. Then thinking maybe this was James Pearson's specialty, that perhaps he had been lucky to be asked to head hogs, the one thing he could do superbly, the first Personnel officer asked, 'What about splittin'? Can you split a hog?'

'Anything you want, sir,' Pearson answered just as he had before and they all moved en masse to where the hogs were split. The Personnel officer told one of the existing splitters to stand back and give his cleaver to Pearson. They all stood around, the process moving on relentlessly and waited till an especially large hog came down the line, which is when the Personnel officer said, 'I want you to split that one for me.'

Without saying a word James Pearson split the hog perfectly down the middle without a scratch, a scar, a tear, without breaking a loin. Even the bone was split perfectly. It was as though this hog had been created like this since surely it could not have arrived in this state by virtue of human intervention. The men, including Tommy Parks and some other packinghouse workers who had cottoned on that something special was going on, looked on in genuine admiration. Pearson was asked to do it again on the very next hog and he repeated the task just as perfectly.

'If I asked you to come on over to fancy meats . . .' the Personnel officer trailed off.

'Anything you want, sir.' Pearson was hired on the spot and, with Tommy Parks' assistance, the story of Mr Anything-You-Want went around the plant and even around parts of the Mecca Flats in a very short time.

Although they were very different men, Tommy Parks had to admire James Pearson and was not unhappy to spend time with him or to be seen with him. Tommy was a much louder man and liked to enjoy himself in ways that held no interest for James Pearson. It was through Tommy Parks that Pearson heard about the room going at the Mecca so, when Pearson arrived with his cases, Tommy Parks was only pretending to be surprised in order to have some fun at Callie's expense. He had known Pearson was coming to take the room and when ultimately James Pearson left Armour and Company for Swift, Tommy Parks followed him. Such was the regard in which James Pearson was held at Armour that the head of Personnel there wanted to know why he was leaving and when unable to talk him into staying even promised him his job back should he ever change his mind. This was unheard of and had there not been witnesses it wouldn't have been believed.

Tommy Parks had seen the man work and he had no trouble believing it. The two didn't socialise much, theirs being an uneasy friendship, bordering on professional collegiality and a certain mutual respect for the work they each did, rather than shared interests. Tommy gambled, drank a lot and chased women, sometimes literally at the same time. James Pearson, on the other hand, kept to himself and showed no interest in any of these things. It was said that he was putting money away in order to move somewhere better when the time came. Certainly, like Tommy, he earned more than most of the people who had no choice but to live in the Mecca. But whereas it might have seemed that James Pearson was heading towards a better life, Tommy Parks was doing nothing to stop himself heading away from the best life he had ever known, or would ever know. He fed his appetites where he could and when they dictated his behaviour the entertainment that produced gave him a measure of popularity with people desperate for some distraction from the desperation of their own lives.

James Pearson earned simply a quiet respect, and from almost as many people, but nobody ever called out to him as they did to Tommy Parks, nobody except Mrs Sallie. On the day Tommy Parks tried to embarrass Callie as James Pearson was moving into the apartment, old Mrs Sallie, who moved even when she stood still and who, unlike Callie, did not know him even by reputation, called out to him, 'Have you met my friend, mister? Have you met, met my friend, Jesus? He gonna take me out of here and, and if you will but extend your hand to him . . . he do the same kindness for you.'

Both Callie Ford and Tommy Parks looked on as James Pearson put down the case he was carrying, took the right hand of Mrs Sallie in his hand, and said, 'My name is James Pearson, ma'am. I be pleased if you let me know ever I can extend a kindness to you . . . while you waitin' on your friend.'

Everything Callie Ford saw of him from then on and the few words they exchanged in the coming months was consistent with what she saw in him the day he moved in. Tommy Parks was a little less forward to her when James Pearson was around and she felt generally safer having him there in the next room. This was why, one evening about two weeks after someone had been shot and killed at the extreme end of the floor above, she was able to summon the courage to knock on James Pearson's door and ask if she could talk to him. She had been offered an excellent job for a couple of months over the summer but it was some ten miles away uptown and required her to live at her place of work. Her son Russell was for the most part a good boy. If she took the job and gave some portion of her wages to James Pearson, would he look in on the boy at night? Whatever James Pearson might be eating on any particular night, could he maybe share some of it with her boy Russell?

*

It was the end of Lamont Williams' shift and he was running late for dinner with his grandmother. He had intended his visit with the old man on the ninth floor to be very brief but he got caught up yet again. The hospital had been promising him extra duties for a while now but they didn't seem to be following through with them. The more he could do around the hospital the more opportunity he would have to show his capacity and enthusiasm for the work. He thought it might make them less likely to get rid of him. Extra duties were good but they didn't seem to be coming. Maybe the hospital administrators had changed their mind about him or about the principle of hiring ex-cons. He didn't want to let those kinds of thoughts gain the upper hand in the arm wrestle that was forever taking place in his mind. But you had to wonder, didn't you? Was it his supervisor? There was more than one. Which one of them liked him least? Did any of them like him at all? How do you make them like you? Everyone was always so busy. That was probably all it was that was keeping him from the extra duties. It probably meant nothing. You didn't want to let these sorts of thoughts gain the upper hand.

But a colleague from Building Services, a man named D'Sean, younger than Lamont but who had worked there for four years and in whom Lamont had briefly confided, had told him what a good sign it was that there had been that talk of extra duties. D'Sean had seen men come and go from Building Services throughout his time there, many of them never making it past the six-month probation period. But he had never seen the hospital give this opportunity to an ex-con. 'They give you extra duties yet?' D'Sean kept asking Lamont. 'No? Not yet! What'd you mean "not yet"? They talkin' 'bout it, why they don't give it you? They got a problem with you, you needa fix it soon as you can. Ain't sayin' they do but if'n they do you needa fix it. But if it's they just forget 'bout you, you need to get up in their face so they remember. You all quiet and shit, Lamont, like you ain't even there, sweepin' up like you gotta sneak 'round to do it, like you wasn't *supposed* to do it. You all like "Excuse me for livin'. I ain't even here." Ain't never knowed a brother like you, finish his time then back on the outside live like he still in solitary. Well, you back on the outside now, Lamont, an' you gotta take care you own self. I don't mean be up in your business or nothin'. I'm just sayin', lookin' out for you. You know?'

Lamont regretted ever having told D'Sean that he had served time in prison or even that he had been offered extra duties. Whatever D'Sean's intention, his life lessons fed Lamont's anxieties. They were the rabbits his hair-trigger imagination hounded down black holes of anxiety. In his youth he had let his imagination run wild and it had kept him entertained when not much else did. In prison, though, he'd develop a strategy for keeping the worst excesses of his imagination in check, for repressing negative thoughts that were only going to hurt him or sabotage his progress, and he'd become very skilled at it. It was a skill D'Sean was now, out of the blue, forcing Lamont to put to use again.

*

It was the European summer of 1946 and nobody around was paying much attention to a somewhat bewildered-looking man slowly making his way around the camp, looking intently, almost reverentially, at everything as though his eyes had been starved of whatever it was they were seeing and now could not get enough of. The man was lugging around a heavy box, with cords, transformers and plugs, some sort of recording device, he explained when asked. But he was not often asked. He was a Pole, someone said, no, a German, a doctor of some kind. Well, good, they needed doctors. They needed everything but typhus and TB. No, he's a Polish Jew. But he looked too well to be a Polish Jew. Someone else said he was from America. Henry Border, once from Poland, now from Chicago, Illinois, was accustomed to being taken as someone to be dealt with after other people. He had been to a number of Displaced Persons camps before arriving in Föhrenwald but each time he looked at the inmates in any of the DP camps he visited it was as though he were seeing a new life form for the first time that he could not take his eyes off. His breath came too quickly and he had to calm himself. It happened every time and he castigated himself for it. Erratic breathing was a luxury no one around there could afford, not even him.

As he carried his equipment around with him, leaning for a while to one side and then to the other to try to spread the wear and tear on his body, he came upon a makeshift hut filled with children, Jewish children. He knew they were Jewish because the language they were being instructed in was Yiddish. He put down his equipment in order to get a little closer to the window to hear what was being taught. The children were of different sizes and so, he surmised, probably of different ages. While he was standing there another group of children of wildly different sizes walked past him in a formation so orderly it was almost a march. They were led by an adult and they were singing what sounded to Henry Border like a Hebrew song. Then as if to give a lie to the notion of order, another group of children, also randomly sized and also singing in Hebrew but a different song, almost walked into the path of the first group of singing children. Instinctively the two groups deviated from their paths to avoid a collision.

Henry Border was mesmerised by these children. He wanted to stop each one and ask what had happened to their parents. What had happened to *them*? In those first few minutes in Föhrenwald he had seen almost no adults. He wondered what these children had seen and how they had survived without adult supervision then and even now. He stood in the middle of this tiny gathering, a little town of children, a city of orphans, when this flood of private imaginings was drained by the barking of the adult instructor of the second group of marching singing children, who now left the group and asked him who he was and what he was doing there.

It took a little while to explain. Border could never predict the response of the person in authority. This person, a man in his thirties, was an American Jew from the American Jewish Joint Distribution Committee, known as 'the Joint'. His young charges had marched away still singing but he didn't seem to mind and was now satisfied with Border's reasons for being there, even slightly encouraging. Henry Border placed his equipment on the ground and wiped his moist brow with the back of his hand.

'So many children?'

'So many and not enough,' the man from the Joint answered.

'Yes, of course, but . . . right here it's –'

'They are in class. It's a school. And we're getting more all the time. We got some more just yesterday.'

'Where have they been? Why are they coming only now?' Henry Border asked.

'The violence flushes them out.'

'What do you mean "violence"?'

'What do you mean "what do I mean violence"?'

'You mean by the Nazis?'

'No, the Nazis were defeated last May, that's . . . fourteen months ago. I'm talking about two weeks ago.'

'What are you talking about? I'm sorry, I don't understand.'

'A young boy, a Polish boy . . .' The man from the Joint stopped in disbelief at the story he was himself about to tell. He took a deep breath and continued. 'He'd run away from his parents and by all accounts he'd been gone three days. When he came back home people, his parents, wanted to know where he'd been. They were furious with the boy. So he told them the Jews had kidnapped him and taken him to a cellar where he'd had to watch fifteen other Polish boys, Christians, murdered by them so that they could use their blood to make matzah. The story got around very quickly and a group of men in the uniform of the Polish military herded the rump of the town's returned Jews into one place and then, egged on by some members of both the local militia and the local clergy and – and I've heard there was also a factory director newly installed by the Socialists – these Jewish survivors fresh from Hitler's camps were thrown to a wild crowd baying for blood said to be about five thousand strong.'

'A pogrom? Even now?' Henry Border asked incredulously.

'Yes.'

'This was two weeks ago, a pogrom two weeks ago? Where?'

'In Kielce. Most of the Jews who managed to get away went to Zeilsheim but we have a few here including a couple of orphaned children. In fact, quietly, look. Come here. If you can look without drawing attention to yourself, look into that classroom where the children are sitting. You see that little boy on the end?'

Henry Border looked in through the window where the children were facing side on to him and looking at their teacher. He saw a tiny boy somewhere between three and five holding the hand of a girl who looked about eight.

'They came here yesterday?' Border asked. 'How did they get here? This is just . . . They're both from Kielce?'

'No, only the boy.'

'So how does he know the girl?'

'He doesn't. He can't have met her before yesterday. But there's no one alive he's known longer than her. If you'll excuse me I have to get back to my children. I wish you luck with your project. Don't forget to talk to the children.'

The man from the Joint walked away leaving Henry Border quite shaken. He just stood there for a moment and then, drawn by the thought of the little boy, he looked in through the window again. He saw that there was a bandage on the boy's free hand that stretched all the way up to his elbow.

'So when she heard that,' the teacher was saying to the children, 'she took her son down to the river and placed the baby Moses in a basket amidst the bullrushes and set him to float down the river. And some time later the Egyptian princess discovered him in the basket and took him in. Do you think it would have been hard or easy for Moses' mother to do this?'

The girl who was holding the hand of the newly arrived little boy from Kielce put up her hand and answered. 'She was hoping someone would pick him up and save him. I saw mothers throw their children out of a train to save them. Maybe it saved them. It can work.'

'I was saved that way,' a boy called out.

'I saw a mother throw a baby over a fence during an *Aktion*,' another boy called out, instigating a flow of uncontrolled conversation from the children in a myriad tongues.

'Children! Children! Quiet please. Quiet! Do we think Moses' mother did the right thing then? Was she a good mother?'

'Yes,' all the children answered in unison, all except for the newly arrived little boy from Kielce. Henry Border watched him and saw that he gripped the little girl's hand tightly with his unbandaged hand and remained silent.

*

Outside the Mecca Flats two white men looked at each other as if to say, 'Can this be it?' The sidewalk in front of them was pockmarked with fissures and at one point the gaps gave way to a tunnel. Under the street light they saw an old black man pushing a cart. 'You fellas goin' in there?' the man called out. One of the white men nodded. 'Don't mind me sayin' but I think you in the wrong neighbourhood,' and as he was moving on, as if to underscore his point, for the first time they noticed the tunnel. A small boy who had poked his head out of it took one look at them and ran inside the Mecca. They followed him but he had disappeared by the time they had taken a few steps inside the court-yard. There was no longer even a pretence at concrete underfoot any more. Neither were there plants or grass, just cans, broken glass and milk cartons. The white men continued walking undeterred.

Russell Ford slept alone in a room that he had until recently shared with his mother. So when the nightmares came now, and they came almost every night, there was no one in the room to settle him down. This meant it took him longer to realise where he was and that he was no longer in the setting of the nightmare. His mother hadn't mentioned the nightmares to James Pearson when she had asked Mr Anything-You-Want to look in on Russell while she was working as a live-in house-keeper for Henry Border. But not only had James Pearson heard the boy from the hall, he had also heard him from inside his own room. At first he thought there was someone else in there with him. The sounds hadn't sounded like Russell. They didn't last long but they visited him so often at night that James Pearson would hear them despite the perpetual emanation of one kind of noise or another from some part of the Mecca Flats to compete with whatever you wanted to hear.

Pearson had asked Russell about his interrupted sleep but the boy had seemed reluctant to talk about it. Over time he realised that Russell was less shy when he chose the topic of conversation himself. The chosen topic might be any of a number of things as long as it wasn't himself. More than once Russell had chosen Pearson's work at Swift's as his preferred topic. He had wanted to know about life in the meat-packing house. Gentle but persistent cross-examination from James Pearson revealed that Russell really had nothing to do over the summer. Sometimes he had played with the other kids in the building but their games were too chaotic for his liking. It emerged that he'd spent some time getting in the way of the Icer across State Street and had even tried several times unsuccessfully to get in to the Railroad Men's Social Club. Occasionally Tommy Parks would throw a ball with him but this never lasted too long and, in any event, Tommy Parks would share his limited attention around at the slightest provocation. No, essentially it seemed that Russell had been spending much of his time alone with nothing to do. On this realisation James Pearson hit upon the idea of asking whether he wanted to come to work with him one day. There was nothing better Russell could have been offered.

Somebody – and James never found out who – told Personnel that someone was bringing in his kid. When they found out it was James Pearson they said that he could stay as long as he didn't get in the way. By the end of the week they had Russell sweeping up and even salting. It didn't occur to Russell to ask for money for his work. He was happy just to be there but James Pearson spoke to a few people and got him nine cents an hour, making him promise to give two-thirds to his mother.

'She gonna be real proud of you when she gets back.'

James Pearson was in the hallway nearing Russell's bedroom door when he came upon Mrs Sallie with her ear cupped listening at Russell's door. She saw Pearson approaching but wasn't at all shamed by being discovered and she continued to listen.

'He fightin' them demons again,' she said turning to James Pearson. He knew what the sounds signified even if he didn't know where they came from night after night. He opened the door and stood at the entrance to the room where Russell was in bed. He'd never intervened like this before.

'You all right, son?'

'What?' The boy was waking up.

'I . . . I heard somethin' from in there and I thought to check if you all right.'

Russell knew what had happened. He was embarrassed to think that his cries had been heard outside his room and by James Pearson, of all people. Russell knew what the dreams were about because whenever he woke from them they stayed with him more like memories than dreams. They *were* memories. They had their origins in events he had witnessed. It was going to be just another Detroit summer in a boy's life. He hadn't known about the unrest at the Packard plant where 25,000 white workers who had been employed producing engines for bombers and for PT boats went on strike upon learning that a handful of black women had started work there. He was young but he would have understood what it meant to hear a white worker outside the plant say that he'd rather let Hitler and Hirohito win than stand beside a *nigger* on the factory floor. He hadn't heard that said but he knew the city in which he lived with his mother and his father, childhood sweethearts now reconciled who had, with some slips, some gaps and a lot of difficulty, stuck by each other since Mississippi.

He had been with his father that morning. It had been a stinking hot Monday morning towards the end of the school year, June 1943. Because of the events of the previous day, the Police Commissioner had met with the Mayor and the US Army colonel in charge of the Detroit area at four o'clock that morning. Mayor Jefferies had a lot of meetings that day and made a lot of phone calls. He was a very busy man and it wasn't until seven-thirty that evening that he made his own inspection of the streets of his town only to see what he could have seen eleven hours earlier, which was more or less what Russell Ford had seen.

Russell had walked his father to the stop at which his father normally caught the bus to work at the Ford plant. His father wasn't the first black man Russell saw pulled off that streetcar by a crowd of white men but he is the man he would see the longest. Night after night he now saw his father being dragged off the streetcar, saw him trying not to let go of the satchel he always took with him to work. Russell doesn't remember what his father used to put in that satchel but he remembers how his father kept hold of it during the first few blows. A mob of men pulled him on

280

to the street but there were too many to hit him all at once. In a brutal display of collectivism they took turns, waiting and jeering while one man after another tired himself out on Russell Ford's father. The first man hit him in the head while someone else held him. Another man kicked him in the abdomen. No sound came from Russell's mouth though he tried to scream. A fresh man punched his father in the stomach so many times he tired himself out and then, breathing like a wild stallion at the peak of its run, went on to another black man who had also been dragged off the streetcar. By this time no one any longer cared to hold up Russell's father for his next assailant but this didn't lead to the end of the assault. It was not nearly over. Lying on the ground, more of the mob could get to him at any one time. He was kicked and jumped on. By the time his skull was crushed he might already have been dead. No one will ever know, not his wife Callie nor his son Russell, who saw the whole thing from start to end and sees it most nights of the week. When he wakes in a sweat his father is still gone and it has all still happened just as he had seen it. It's not really a dream at all. In the dark he gets his breath back but never does the terror completely go, never does he not feel ashamed that he hadn't been able to save his father and never does he stop missing him. He still has his father's satchel. Callie cleaned it out after the funeral, cleaned off the blood, and Russell keeps it.

'I . . . I heard somethin' from in here and I thought to check if you all right,' James Pearson asked.

'Yes, sir. I'm all right.'

Mrs Sallie would have liked to have kept listening to what was going on in that room between James Pearson and the boy whose mother had left him but there was a knock at the front door of the apartment that was too insistent to ignore. She went to the door before anyone else could get there and opened it. There stood the two white men. Mrs Sallie looked them up and down slowly in a questioning manner not untouched by anxiety.

'Good evening, ma'am,' the older of the two white men said. 'Sorry to disturb you at this hour. We're looking for –'

'Have you met, met my friend?'

'Well, we're looking for –'

'Have you met, met my friend, Jesus?'

Russell's bedroom door was slightly ajar and James Pearson heard a man say, 'Ma'am, we're looking for Mr Pearson, James Pearson. We understand he lives here.'

'I understand that too,' Mrs Sallie said without taking one step back.

'Do you know him? Is he here?' the other man asked.

'He a friend 'o mine. But I . . . a lot of friends. My best, best friend is Jesus. He bring the bright, bright light you know . . . bright, bright sun. He bring it ever'day just like today and . . .' she said, thinking as she spoke, looking these two white men straight in the eye, first one then the other, before continuing, 'just like tomorrow. He bring it tomorrow. I tell you 'bout him then, tomorrow,' she said, beginning to close the door on the men when the younger one of the two stuck his foot in the doorway. She was unable to close the door.

Elise Border, who normally slept well, was awake. Something was going on outside. She wasn't sure but she thought she'd heard something. Was it worth troubling Callie? It might have been just the wind knocking over the lid of a garbage can. There it was again. Would Callie be asleep by now?

Tommy Parks was on State Street heading back in the direction of the Mecca. It hadn't been a bad night at all and if he could just make it up to his room without anyone bothering him he could sleep off the night's diversions smiling to himself at the entertainment he'd been able to call up at such short notice and at such a reasonable price. He could see the doorway to the State Street entrance by now and that was when he suddenly sobered up a little. He saw two white men walking from the building and with them was what looked to be his neighbour, James Pearson, Mr Anything-You-Want. He decided to hang back and watch the direction they took. But he hung back too long. They were walking fast and by that time of the evening he wasn't in any position to walk nearly so fast. The two white men and James Pearson were gone.

*

A man and a woman were about to meet casually, but by arrangement, for coffee. It was with a sense of foreboding that Adam could see Michelle approaching on Amsterdam Avenue. He feared that she might give him news of some kind about Diana that would underscore just how much he had let her down. The pain from expected news of how Diana was faring in her life after they parted had rendered him almost physically incapable of making this arrangement, even after Michelle had left a message on his answering machine requesting it, and it was his procrastination that shamed him as they approached each other, coming closer and closer until he saw her smile. It wasn't her best smile but it was better than most anyone else's.

When she hugged him outside the Hungarian Pastry Shop he remembered what a good friend she had always been and thought for the first time ever that perhaps in some way he loved her. That she was strikingly attractive wasn't news to him but to know it intellectually is not the same as to register it viscerally. She was his friend and also the wife of his friend but still her beauty hit him like a gust of wind by which no man could remain unmoved. When she hugged him he felt a certain pride he was sure he hadn't earned or, at least, not recently. They were both tired. Adam saw her tiredness in her smiling eyes and realised how good of her it was to nudge him into this casual meeting for coffee, this exchange.

That's what this was – an exchange, an exchange of information. There was certain updated information about Diana that the maintenance of his self-flagellation required. Not long after the exchange of niceties they got right down to it. Michelle had seen Diana. That was good. She had visited her in Hell's Kitchen, Diana's new neighbourhood. How was she? For the first two weeks Diana had barely eaten anything, almost nothing at all. She had lost a lot of weight and grown weak. She had forced herself to go to work. But she hadn't gone out to buy food, hadn't even wanted to explore the neighbourhood. She'd felt numb, briefly angry, but mainly numb. She'd told Michelle that she'd heard about this sort of thing happening to other couples but she had never imagined it would happen to her and Adam. But somehow, after about two weeks, as if it were a virus that she had defeated, she began to be able to think, at least tentatively, about the future. She started calling people, exploring the stores in the area, and taking advantage of her new location to see some shows.

'Did you see her apartment?'

'No, we met at a café on Ninth Avenue.'

Adam tried to picture the area but he didn't know it very well. 'Ninth Avenue; what's around there?'

'Oh, there's a lot going on there, 'round the high 30s, 40s and 50s.'

'Really?'

'Sure, a lot of restaurants and bars.'

Adam sat there trying to process it all. Diana had almost starved for two weeks after which she was calling people, going to shows, eating out and hanging out at Ninth Avenue bars. Starving herself was excessive grief. It suggested depression. Two weeks wasn't very long.

What exactly had he wanted Michelle to say? If Diana was suffering it would hurt him, if she was coping it would hurt him. What he really wanted, although he wasn't fully aware of it, was for Michelle to somehow convince him that he and Diana should be together again and then to arrange it. Nor was he aware of both just how unrealistic it was to expect this from Michelle and of how this was the only thing she could have said with respect to Diana that would *not* have hurt him.

Adam thought about Diana on her own in an apartment he didn't know, he thought of her looking gaunt, he thought of Ninth Avenue, he thought about how many hours were contained in two weeks as opposed to the number of hours that were contained in almost ten years. Michelle had wanted to know how he was faring but she had felt he couldn't have been coping too badly because her husband and her father-in-law had mentioned some new project that seemed to have him inspired and kept taking him to Chicago. She didn't seem to want to know why he'd ended the relationship. Presumably she'd heard some version of it from Diana. She hadn't wanted to talk him out of it or to pass on any messages. She'd simply wanted to give him this limited information. Had there been anything she'd wanted from him, from Adam?

A beautiful woman, the wife of the Chairman of History at Columbia, a man who even Adam had observed, no longer had time for anything that didn't involve more than one person at a time, is sharing a coffee with a mutual friend. She is smiling through tired eyes and pleading for someone to talk to. But the pleading is there only in her eyes. It remains unsaid.

'Adam,' Michelle said after providing the latest news on Diana, 'when Sonia came over to your place that day, uninvited, and we came to pick her up –'

'Uh-huh.'

'What did she say?'

'What do you mean?'

'Did she say anything . . . about Charles and me?'

*

The white men had introduced themselves at the doorway to the apartment at the Mecca and although James Pearson had known they were looking for him and that they had tried to talk to him before, he hadn't expected them to suddenly arrive at the doorway of his home one hot summer night. Since he knew who they were and knew that they weren't going to give up, he agreed to go to a nearby bar with them.

'I'm real sorry to drag you out of your home, Mr Pearson, but as you can imagine, we couldn't exactly have had this conversation with you at the plant,' Herbert Marks said, skilfully placing three glasses of beer on the table of the bar. It was a local bar and Herbert Marks and his older colleague, Ralph Hellerstein, were the only white men there.

'You got me out this late to talk about business. I was fixin' to go to sleep. Nothin' against nobody, Mr Hellerstein –'

'It's Ralph.'

'I ain't lookin' for no trouble . . . Ralph.'

'Can I call you James?' the younger man, Herbert Marks, asked.

'I don't see why not.'

'There's already trouble, James.'

'Now, I admit things can be . . . difficult at times,' James Pearson said. 'But we already got a union, independent union.'

'James, that's not an independent union, that's a company union.'

'It's a union . . . we got a union.'

'You got grievance procedures that are going to take care of you . . . every last one of you?'

'I guess.'

'Every last one? You think the company union really takes care of the workers? Does it take care of the Negro workers?'

'No more 'n no less than anyone else do,' James Pearson said, sipping on his beer.

Herbert Marks leaned in close. 'You work with Billy Moore, don't you?'

'Yeah . . . so?'

'You like him?'

'Sure I do.'

'Not a bad splitter, is he?'

'He one hell of a splitter. Everybody knows.'

'Slowed down a bit lately though,' said Ralph Hellerstein almost to himself.

'He's a friend of yours, you said? Ever meet any of his kids?'

'No, I only ever see him at the plant but –'

'Not *one* of his kids? 'Cause he's got five kids. He's slowed down a little. You know it and you know why.'

'I don't know what you talkin' about.'

'It's his back, James,' said Herbert Marks. 'He's got a problem with his back. Sounds like a lower disk problem but, hey, I'm no doctor. He doesn't want anyone to know but he's confided in you.'

'I ain't sayin' . . . I don't know what you talkin' about.'

'James, *we* know about it 'cause the company knows about it and they know about it because his numbers have dropped.'

'Billy Moore, he's a master splitter,' James said quietly.

'He suffers back spasms. The company's noticed he's slowed down. He's slowing down the whole line. You've tried to cover for him but he's slowed down.'

'Not much,' James countered.

'No, not so much. Enough so they noticed. Some time in the next week –'

'We don't know exactly when,' Ralph Hellerstein interrupted.

'Some time in the next week they're going to send him to see the company doctor. He won't have a choice, James, he'll have to go.'

'Now the doctor's going to give Billy a series of tests, physical tests, and Billy's not going to make it. They're goin' to keep testing his back until it spasms.'

'And then?' James Pearson asked.

'Then they're going to fire him.'

'But he can still work. Might of slowed some but . . . I mean I know the man. He's right next to me every day.'

'Well, he won't be soon,' Herb Marks said.

'He's got five children, James, worked there eleven years and they're going to ease him on out the door with nothing in his hand after the handshake leaves him cold with his arm stuck out and his palm facin' up. They give you that handshake and you're ready to beg.'

'But he can still work,' James protested.

'James, if the hogs could process *you* do you think they wouldn't round *them* up, pay *them* what they're paying you? They'd corral them, spy on them . . .' Ralph Hellerstein trailed off and Herb Marks took off.

'They'd even kid those hogs into thinking they had an independent union. The only reason they don't do that is that they can't think of any way to make money out of getting people to eat you.'

'James,' Ralph Hellerstein began, 'they hire and fire as they wish; they pay as little as they can get away with.'

'Mr Hellerstein –'

'Ralph.'

'Ralph, there ain't nothin' we can do about any 'o this.'

'Who's we?'

'We . . . I don't know; the workin' man, the workin' black man.'

'Well, see, if you meant "we", the men on the floor, *all* the men on the floor, I'd say that's where you're wrong.'

'That what you want, *all* the men on the floor?' asked James Pearson.

'We want you to consider, now just to *consider*, no undertakings, just to think about joining the Packinghouse Workers Organising Committee.'

'What!'

'We're not asking you for an answer now. We're not asking you to join tonight. We're asking you to consider joining. We're going to come back and talk to you about this another time after you've given it some thought. Please just think it over. We need someone like you. A lot of people do. In the meantime, if you want to talk to us, you call this number.'

James Pearson looked at the card and put it in his pocket. 'Mr Hellerstein –'

'Ralph.'

'I like to get me my sleep at night. No offence but how do I know when you comin' back?'

'When Billy Moore tells you they're done with him and that he doesn't know what he's gonna do, doesn't know how he's gonna feed his kids; very soon after that you can expect to hear from us.'

*

Ten miles away Elly Border thought she knew the sounds of her house very well. She had lived there alone with only her father and he was a quiet man. The noises around her home weren't something she had given conscious attention to. It was rather that they were the dots in a pointillist aural landscape that had been etched into her unconscious. This was different; something was going on outside. It was louder than any cat or any wind could have made and there had been no wind to speak of all that night. She couldn't avoid the feeling that the something that was out there was a person. What was he doing around her house? Maybe he was drunk.

'Callie,' she whispered as she knocked on Callie's door.

'Elly, go back to bed.'

It took a few more attempts. 'Callie! Callie!'

'You sure better hope you sick or somethin', young lady,' she said, opening her door and putting on a bathrobe.

'There's someone here.'

'No, there's not. Go back to bed. I'm not jokin' with you, child. You gettin' me mad.'

'Callie, I'm serious. Listen!'

But now Callie heard something too. She went downstairs and Elise followed her. Whatever the source of the sound, it was hovering around the front porch. Through the frosted glass at the front door Callie could see a figure right outside. She went to the broom closet not saying a word and, with Elly close behind, she picked up a broom and took it out. She switched on the outside light and could see the shape of a human figure unambiguously. Holding the broom she called to the person, 'What do you want?'

No spoken answer came, only a little knock at the front door, almost timid.

'Who is it? What do you want?' Again no answer came from the other side of the door, nothing but a knock.

Elly stood right behind her at the front door and for the first time she doubted the wisdom of her protector as in horror she watched Callie, broom in one hand, slowly open the door. Elly had been right. She really had heard noises that hadn't belonged at her home. They had come from a human. Now standing behind Callie, Elly Border saw who it was that had made those sounds. She saw a black man with a crazed look in his eyes. She was terrified. Callie Ford, standing in front of her, saw something quite different. She saw her fourteen-year-old son, Russell. He was terrified.

'Momma,' he said, breathing heavily. 'They taken away Mr Pearson. Two white men took him away. I saw it.'

*

It was unusually good luck for Henry Border that almost immediately upon entry to the Stuttgart West DP camp the first person he came across was a DP named Gruenberg who seemed to be some kind of camp elder, a spokesman or communal leader of some kind of the Jewish inmates. This man knew the camp and understood the way things worked there.

'What is this?' Gruenberg asked Henry Border, pointing at the heavy recording equipment the older man lugged with him. When Border explained that he was there to record the experiences of the Jewish DPs, Gruenberg nodded encouragingly.

'You can record people on this? How does it work?' he asked but before Border had a chance to reply, a young man walking so briskly he was almost running interrupted them. 'Very soon, Mr Gruenberg, very soon. I think it will be today.'

'You come and get me as soon as you think she's ready. You won't forget, Shmuel?' Gruenberg answered.

'I won't forget, Mr Gruenberg.'

'Promise me?'

'I promise,' the young man called back, now running away from where Gruenberg and Henry Border were standing. They watched him go.

'That young man there, Shmuel, he and his wife are expecting a child.'

That Shmuel himself looked like a child, that neither of them knew how long it would take, if ever, for the remnants of European Jewry to numerically replace the ones they had just lost but that there was no greater impulse than to try, all of it went unsaid by Gruenberg and by Henry Border as they watched this man Shmuel run back to his wife.

'Well,' continued Gruenberg, 'anything you can tell the Americans about what we have been through can only help. Initially they made no distinction between us and any other DPs. In fact, it's still this way in the British Zone and also in the French Zone.'

'What do you mean?'

'You had a situation where, for example, they would put all DPs together, no matter where they came from. So you might have Ukrainians who had fought on the side of the Nazis, but who now don't want to go home for fear of retribution from the Russians, living in the same camp with us. These Ukrainians are as anti-Semitic as anyone we have ever seen. A few Jews said they recognised some of them.'

'Recognised them from where?'

'From Auschwitz.'

'I don't understand. If they were fighting on the side of the Germans what were they doing in Auschwitz?'

'They were working there as guards, Dr Border.' Gruenberg looked at Henry Border as if for the first time. He was perplexed. 'You are American, you said. Are you here from the Joint?'

'No.'

'You're not? Who are you with?'

'I'm not with anybody.'

'But who sent you?'

'Nobody.'

'What do you mean "nobody"? Who's paying you to be here?'

'Nobody's paying me.'

'But how did you get here, on whose money?'

'My own money.'

'Just for these interviews on your machine?'

'Yes.'

Gruenberg looked at him for a moment without speaking. 'Well, as I said, anything you can tell the Americans about what we have been through can only help. I imagine it will, I hope it will, but who knows? With some of them . . .' he trailed off.

'Maybe it will encourage people to give us provisions, supplies. We need men's clothing, everything; shirts, trousers, jackets, socks, shoes, underwear. Women's clothing too. If we had the material and sewing machines there are people here who could make it for us themselves. Better than nothing. Much better, actually. There are tailors here in the camp. If we only had the fabric and of course the sewing machines. We need writing equipment for the children and also for letters. People here write letters all the time, sending them to people they don't know, to people they've never met, sending them into every corner of the world looking for the latest news, the freshest news they can get of the dead. Well, we need everything. There's nothing we don't need. Men walk around here, like that young man before, Shmuel, and –'

Border interrupted him. 'What did you mean before about the Americans? You said "With some of them". What about some of them, the Americans?'

Gruenberg seemed reluctant to go on. 'You know, the way your General Patton felt about us is not very different from how the Nazis felt.

It's true. He said the Jewish DPs are lower than animals. He described the Jews as a subhuman species without any of the social or cultural refinements of our time. Really, that's what he said. You have to wonder if these views were based on the starved, wretched, barely alive Jews he'd seen in a just-liberated concentration camp. Or were his views older than that? You have to wonder when exactly he developed these views.'

Henry Border didn't know what to say to this. He wasn't used to being part of the 'you' that possessed a victorious four-star general, now dead, a hero to the country that helped liberate the remnants of the people some of whom he saw all around him even now in ill-fitting rags surrounded by wire.

'I didn't know that,' Henry Border said quietly with a shame that might have suggested that he himself felt responsible for what Patton had said. There were so many thoughts rushing through his mind at any one time, all of them rushing too quickly to be caught and catalogued. But worse than this for him, as each thought passed the upper reaches of his consciousness they would not dissolve or evaporate. Instead, each thought he'd had since arriving in Europe and seeing his first Displaced Person stayed on his mind and backed up, congregated and concertinaed into the next one as it jostled for attention as *primus inter pares*. Each recollection, each anecdote, each missing family member of someone to whom he had spoken cried out to be his only thought. The enormity of what had befallen these people, his people, weighed down on him far more heavily than a thousand Marvin Cadden wire recording devices. It was taking every ounce of his mental strength to remember what he was doing there. And this was before he had even turned his mind to what had happened to his own family and friends.

'Tell me,' said Gruenberg, as they walked towards a building to which Gruenberg clearly wanted to take him, 'you said you're American but you speak Yiddish like a Polish Jew.'

'I *am* a Polish Jew.'

'When did you get to America?'

'Before the war.'

'*Before* the war! And your family, what do you know about . . .'

Gruenberg's attention and then Border's too was abruptly transferred from their conversation all the way to the other side of the camp by a man shouting. DPs often shouted at each other in a babel of languages but this was different. It came from the side of the camp from where they had come, the side where the gates were. There was some sort of commotion. A lot of trucks had arrived and were parking in a row beside the long line of trees outside the camp. A visible wave of anxiety rippled through the inmates nearest the gates. Gruenberg turned away from Henry Border mid-sentence and walked hurriedly over to the DP who was shouting.

'You have no right,' the man, whose short sleeves revealed the number tattooed on his arm at Auschwitz, yelled. 'Get out of here at once!'

Henry Border, carrying his recording equipment, hastily followed Gruenberg to see that the man was shouting at two armed German policemen. The crowd of inmates was growing bigger.

'We are not *asking* you. This is an order.'

'We don't follow your orders any more. Your thousand-year Reich is over. You lost.'

'What seems to be the problem here?' Gruenberg asked as a crowd of DPs started to gather.

'They want to search the camp! Can you believe this, Mr Gruenberg?'

'Why do you want to search the camp?' Gruenberg asked.

'What is your name? What authority do you carry here?' the older of the two policemen asked.

'Where are the Americans?' an old man in the crowd called out. 'How come they let them in? They're never here when you need them.'

'Get the man from UNRRA. Where is *he* now, *any* of them from UNRRA?' a woman called out.

'The Americans took so long to get here and now –' the old man continued.

'How do you think these thugs got in?' someone else shouted in reply to the old man. 'It's the Americans who let them in.'

'My name is Gruenberg,' he said over the top of the sounds of the growing crowd. 'What authority do I have? I have moral authority.'

'We are not obliged to explain anything to you,' the younger policeman said.

'Well, that depends on where you look for your obligations,' Gruenberg said.

'I am not obliged by law to explain anything,' the younger policeman said.

'How well do you know the laws of the occupation?' Gruenberg asked the policeman.

'Mr Gruenberg, there's no point arguing with them. They're Nazis out for a last frolic,' shouted the man in the short-sleeved shirt.

'Stand back, all of you. We are going to conduct a search of the camp. You are advised –'

'Are you up to date with the laws of the occupation for this Zone, officer?'

'Yes,' the older of the two policemen answered.

'It is changing all the time and –'

'We don't need to answer to you.'

'Oh, you will answer to us. You will. More than you know, you Nazi thug,' the man in the short-sleeved shirt called out.

'If you tell us what you're looking for,' said Gruenberg calmly, 'we might be able to save you some trouble.'

'We are here because of black market activities,' the younger of the two policemen said.

'You think there are black marketeers in this camp?' Gruenberg asked.

'Listen, there's a black market flourishing all over Stuttgart,' the man in the short sleeves said. 'The German civilians are up to their necks in it and you know it. The Americans soldiers too. They're selling cigarettes, stockings and everything else under the sun and you know that too. Everybody here knows it.'

Border looked at the policemen in their perfectly fitting uniforms. How fast they make themselves uniforms, he speculated, or were these the same uniforms they wore during the Hitler years, and on the same men but now serving different masters? More and more DPs were gathering around the policemen. In contrast to the policemen, the DPs wore an odd assortment of ill-fitting clothes of various weights for various seasons. Border looked at them too, these people arriving on the scene trying to understand what was going on. 'What now?' they wondered, bewildered in their misshapen clothing, dragging themselves around, running from themselves, looking for the past with every mail truck and now rediscovering anger. 'What is it? What do they want? Criminals, you said, black marketeers? What kind of police are they? Who do they want?' came the whispers, the murmurs from around the crowd, now of women and men of all different ages.

'Mr Gruenberg!' Border heard a voice calling from far away.

'So with a black market selling goods from all over the world flourishing in every inch of occupied Europe why do you come *here* looking for black marketeers? Everybody here knows the answer to that too,' the man in the short sleeves continued passionately.

'I'm sorry but you are not meant to come in here like this,' Gruenberg said.

'This is Stuttgart and we are the police investigating illegal activity. We can go wherever it's necessary for us to perform our duty,' the younger policeman said.

'Mr Gruenberg!' came the voice from the distance again, now getting closer.

'No, actually not,' said Gruenberg. 'As of March of this year only the American police are entitled to enter and search here and even they are answerable to the camp police.'

From the corner of his eye Henry Border noticed column after column of armed German policemen dismounting from the trucks lined up outside the perimeter of the camp by the fir trees. He wondered if Gruenberg had noticed and, if Gruenberg hadn't yet noticed, whether he should alert him. But he was a scientist there to record, not to participate. He was an American, not a DP. He was an Episcopalian and also a Polish Jew. He glanced down at his feet to check on Marvin Cadden's wire recording equipment. It was still there untouched.

'What camp police?' the younger policeman asked.

'The camp's Jewish police here,' Gruenberg said and at this the younger policeman started to laugh. The laugh was not quite to himself but nor was it bravado. It was involuntary.

'Mr Gruenberg!' a man was calling, running now out of breath.

'You don't laugh any more,' the man in the short sleeves yelled and at the same time the older of the two policemen blew a whistle, which was the signal for tens of policemen from outside the camp to enter the camp. Approximately two hundred of them came in through the gates, running in predetermined directions. The older policeman started shouting, 'Everybody stay where you are! Nobody is to move.'

'Mr Gruenberg!' said the man out of breath, now level with the crowd; but only Border noticed him. It was the man Gruenberg had earlier called Shmuel. Gruenberg either didn't hear him or ignored him. The crowd was in panic. People started to shout. Women were screaming.

'Jews defend yourselves! Throw stones, anything you can find!' Hearing this, the younger policeman drew his pistol and this was the last straw for the man in the short sleeves and he lunged at the younger policeman.

'Get his gun!' the short-sleeved man called as the older policeman tried to pull him off his colleague.

'Filthy Jew!' the younger policeman said as the three men struggled. Other policemen ran in the direction of the first two and, at seeing this, a number of DPs started throwing stones and whatever was at hand at them. Henry Border moved away from the scuffling men, now on the ground. He hugged his recording equipment to his chest.

'Mr Gruenberg! It's time! My wife, she's started!'

Henry Border heard the first shot fired just as everyone else did. People screamed. A man lay bleeding on the ground. Gruenberg cradled the man on the ground of Stuttgart West DP camp. The young man, Shmuel, the expectant father, now had Gruenberg's attention.

*

A man went into a bar. It wasn't a joke. It might have been funny but it wasn't a joke, not even a bad one. And he wasn't trying to get a laugh. This was just as well because nothing seemed particularly funny to Adam Zignelik that night as he walked alone among people who, unlike him, had some place in Hell's Kitchen they wanted to be. He must have walked along each side of Ninth Avenue between 38th and 53rd streets two or three times, just looking at the neighbourhood, Diana's new neighbourhood. He looked in the windows of the Mercury Bar, the Marseille, the Greek Bakery and the Kemia Bar.

He walked into the Film Center Café and saw small groups of people in booths and at the bar talking, laughing, checking their mobile phones. And at the end of the bar he saw a man who sat waiting, looking expectantly at the entrance. In Rudy's Bar & Grill he saw a man in a suit sitting alone at the bar singing to himself while he got steadily older and more tanked. At the other end of the bar it was 'A Man Walked into a Bar' night. People were lining up to tell a joke that had to begin with the line 'a man walked into a bar'.

Adam had to get several drinks down in a hurry if he was to maintain the pretence to himself that he had come down there simply to explore a neighbourhood he didn't much know. By subway, by chance, by metrocard he had ridden the downtown express via denial to an existential crisis in the city of orphans changing at Times Square, which is how he'd landed in Hell's Kitchen. He had come to Ninth Avenue in the crushingly forlorn hope that he might run into Diana by chance and then they could begin talking again. He could tell her about his work, about Border and Chicago and the DP camps, and maybe he could erase what he'd done and start over again. It was a hope he was dimly aware he had harboured ever since she had closed the door to the Morningside Heights apartment he used to share with her.

So he went inside Zanzibar where the clientele ranged between twenty-five and forty and the waitresses and female bartenders had the figures of dancers and the striking looks of actresses for whom every new order placed was an audition. Asian American, African American, mid-western farm types, Hispanic and Scandinavian-looking women gracefully served people amid a chaos that only they could navigate and when one of them asked Adam if he would like a seat at the bar, he noticed that the bar stool at the very end of the bar, the one furthest from the street entrance, was freshly available and he went for it as though it represented his last chance at something he couldn't quite name any more. The bartenders were women, all with designer jeans they'd been poured into, all with exposed midriffs and then up above, all with cleavages from the designer who had given the world the Grand Canyon. Adam didn't know what he was doing there and was trying to hide behind the menu when one of them half spoke, half called to him, 'What can I get you?' A shiver coursed through him because he shouldn't have been there and because she couldn't get him anything he wanted, let alone anything he needed, and so he heard himself above the din ordering the first thing his eyes could cling to that wasn't the bartender herself.

'I'll have a Mango Mojito, please,' he said, aiming a disconjugated gaze along the bench top of the bar.

'One Mango Mojito coming right up, Professor.'

It was the honey-skinned woman with jet-black straight hair, the student who no longer attended his 'What is History?' lectures; the one who had correctly guessed Gandhi. True? It was unlikely to be true but beneath the palm fronds as the past and present wilted, beneath the candlelight where shadows snuff the sidle of evening, beneath the tropical motifs, thatch-clad walls and thud of the speakers there to help drown out people's private internal, soon-to-be-publicly-misunderstood celebration of themselves, it was true.

*

Callie Ford had taken her son Russell into the kitchen of Henry Border's house. How he had managed to find the house and at night might have been something she would have commented on had she not been so intent on absorbing and understanding the details of his story, the taking of James Pearson from his apartment in the Mecca Flats by two white men in the middle of the night. Elise Border was stunned to not only learn but to see that Callie Ford had a son, and to see that he was as old as he was. Elly's father was old enough to be Callie's father and yet here was Callie with a son older than Elly. Callie had never mentioned that she was a mother and for a moment that soon passed she felt a terrible sense of loss, almost a sense of betrayal, that Callie, for whom she had so quickly developed such strong affection, had failed to tell her so important a biographical detail. It indicated to Elly that they were not as close as she had thought. While the hurt was not to last, what was to recur intermittently, even as she got to know and like Russell, was envy, envy that he had a mother.

But by the time the three of them were drinking lemonade in the kitchen, the dominant emotion was a fascination with Russell, with the world from which he (and now quite clearly Callie) had come, and with the story he told of James Pearson being taken away by the two white men. She had seen black children on the street, on public transportation, seen them working in the back of restaurants and shining shoes but she had never socialised with any. Now here was one in her home in the middle of the night. To add to her fascination he was a boy, an older boy, made harmless both by being Callie's son and, at least temporarily, by his obvious vulnerability and distress. Elly listened to Russell's account of what had happened to James Pearson and watched as Callie attempted to calm her son. In truth, though, she didn't understand what had been so distressing to Russell. Had she been taken out of the kitchen and asked to retell Russell's story to a third party, she would have said that a man named James Pearson, a friend of the family, had been seen leaving their building late at night with two men. The men happened to be white. It seemed that it was this that most distressed Russell, although at first she had thought that it was that Russell had been abandoned by the man who was meant to take care of him, just like Callie was meant to take care of her.

For all he knew, Callie told Russell in reassuring tones, Mr Pearson could be back at the Mecca safe and sound. The white men weren't man-handling Mr Pearson, she got Russell to concede. Perhaps they were men he knew from the packinghouse. Despite Russell's avowal that he hadn't seen them there, mention of the packinghouse enabled her to change the subject by asking him about his new job and praising him for it. He told her how Mr Pearson had made him promise to save some of his wages for her. Mr Anything-You-Want had more than come through for her, she thought.

She finished the evening's kitchen summit by suggesting a strategy. She would make up a bed for Russell in one of the vacant rooms and in the morning all three of them would go downtown to the Mecca Flats to try to find out what had happened to James Pearson. And when Russell would go to work, maybe Mr Pearson would be there. Elly Border would come with them because Callie didn't want to leave her on her own and didn't know where else to take her.

*

For a while James Pearson didn't give any serious thought to his meeting with Herb Marks and Ralph Hellerstein and their request that he consider joining the Packinghouse Workers Organising Committee. For a start, all he wanted was a chance to put a little money away until he had enough to get out of the Mecca Flats. Then maybe he could think of finding a woman. But additionally, it seemed to him far-fetched to the point of farcical to think that any group of white packinghouse workers was going to accept or take seriously any organisation with a Negro on its peak body. Anyway, how comfortable would he be working long hours at a physically demanding job only to spend his off hours going to meetings where he was the only black man? The more time that passed after his evening meeting with Hellerstein and Marks the crazier the proposition appeared to him.

It was at the end of his shift at Swift and Company a few weeks later and James Pearson was in the locker room, the one used by the black workers. There were a lot of men in there, some far off in their own worlds and some talking while they tried to get clean before leaving to go home or anywhere else they might care to go to unwind on the south side. That's how it was that, despite his time at the plant, despite being well liked among his colleagues, nobody noticed Billy Moore come in. But James Pearson caught him from the corner of his eye wearing an expression that brought Pearson in an instant back to his meeting with Ralph Hellerstein and Herb Marks.

'Billy?' James Pearson said to him quietly but Billy Moore was in no mood for talking. He was experiencing something far worse than the back spasms he had been unable to hide from James and ultimately from the management at Swift. He was experiencing dread. Eventually James managed to get from Billy a story that confirmed that everything

Hellerstein and Marks had predicted had come about. Billy Moore was finished splitting hogs at Swifts.

'But you can do other things,' James Pearson said.

'I can do other things. I can still split hogs. I told 'em that.'

'What'd they say?'

'They said they'd keep the doctor's report in their records. Said they contact me somethin' come up.' The two men looked at each other and then, without James Pearson having to say a word, Billy Moore said what the other man was thinking. 'Ain't no one ever gonna contact me.'

The next morning James Pearson went in to the Personnel Office before the start of the shift to make enquiries on behalf of Billy Moore. Hellerstein and Marks had been entirely right and so had Billy Moore. It was clear that, even should a position somewhere else in the plant arise, Billy Moore was considered damaged goods. No one at Swifts was going to contact him. Why should they, when a younger man without any history of back trouble could take up the newly vacant position? And as James Pearson immediately realised, there was nothing to stop an injustice like this one to Billy Moore and his wife and children happening to him too. One company-observed back spasm, one soft tissue injury and Mr Anything-You-Want could also be let go. Who was there to stop it?

Seeing Tommy Parks leaning on the railing of the balcony outside their apartment at the Mecca having a cigarette late one night, James Pearson approached him.

'You hear 'bout Billy Moore?' James asked.

'Yeah, I heard. He looked all right to me. They say he got nothin' now.'

'Nothin' but a wife and five kids.'

'Yeah, well, them five kids, they his fault. Wife too.'

'I'm talkin' 'bout Swifts.'

Tommy Parks took a drag on his cigarette and let it out slowly. 'I know what you talkin' 'bout.'

Through gesture alone, Tommy Parks offered James a cigarette, which Pearson declined. The two men stood there for a while without talking.

'While back I had a visit from two men.'

'Two white boys,' Tommy Parks interrupted. They were standing beside one another but James Pearson used his surprise to turn and look at Parks straight on.

'How you know that?' he asked.

Tommy Parks smiled. 'Now I wondered when you gonna tell me 'bout that. Even you break some time. You got a story for me?'

*

Sixteen men got off a truck one by one. Shouts accompanied the sound of their feet hitting the ground. They were in a place unlike any they had ever been before. The sixteen men ranged in age from their teens to their late forties. Some had heard the name before. Some had not heard it – Birkenau, the largest of the more than forty camps and subcamps that made up the *Konzentrationslager* in the Polish region of Upper Silesia known as Auschwitz-Birkenau, or just Auschwitz. They were told to wait. A physician was coming and they had to wait for him. Of the sixteen, the four oldest were Polish Catholics, the twelve youngest were Polish Jews. One of the twelve was Henryk Mandelbrot. Why did they have to wait for a physician? Nobody explained why. Questions were forbidden. Talking was forbidden.

Two SS men guarded them, which meant they too had to wait for the physician to arrive. The guards were bored. They knew the men they were guarding would have to have been afraid but since these men weren't allowed to do anything but wait without speaking, their fear wasn't very entertaining. One hour went past, then came another moving even more slowly. The two guards spoke to each other quietly in a voice too soft for most of their prisoners to hear.

'You know what would break this up?' the first guard whispered to his colleague.

'What?'

'Shooting. We could shoot one of them.'

'They've been counted already,' the second guard said, yawning as he stretched.

'Yeah but who'd care?'

'They're not all Jews.'

'Well, we could shoot one of *them*.'

'We've got our orders,' the second guard objected.

'Well then . . . perhaps they tried to attack us, to disarm us?' at which the other guard rolled his eyes.

'Well, *you* think of something,' the first guard said. Then with the excitement of hitting upon a good idea, 'We could order two of them to race each other and shoot the two of them as they were running away. You choose one, I get the other. We give them a count of ten or fifteen if you want to make it interesting.'

'And what were these two runners doing, escaping?'

'Sure.'

'You think they'd believe it?'

'Oh God-in-heaven, no one's going to worry about two of them. They'll get two more.'

'And what if there's something special about these prisoners? What if they know something, if they're to be interrogated? Maybe they have some special skills. You go looking for trouble. You shouldn't. Enjoy the rest.'

Henryk Mandelbrot heard every word they said.

The sixteen prisoners and the two guards waited almost three hours before the physician arrived. He was harried. There was always too much work to do. He spoke quickly in a monotone to the guards.

'Four Poles and the rest Jews, yeah?'

'Yes, Doctor,' the second guard said.

'So,' the overworked doctor called to the prisoners in a slightly weary, matter-of-fact tone, 'Poles to the right, Jews to the left.'

Henryk Mandelbrot didn't see what happened to the Poles. He and the other eleven Jews were taken to a place known as the *Bekleidungs-kammer*, a vast warehouse full of clothes and personal effects of all types. There were rows of shelves as far as he could see. It was a vast store of everything from all over Europe. This was what each Jew had taken with them when told they were being resettled. It was a physical answer to the question, 'What do people consider most important for a long journey?' Parents had packed for their children. In addition to clothes of all sizes for men, women and children, in addition to cutlery, eyeglasses, books, toothbrushes, hairbrushes, artificial limbs and religious materials there were items of sentimental value, photographs, teddy bears. Here at the *Bekleidungskammer* it was collected, sorted into categories and cleaned of vermin in miniature gas chambers before being sent to Germany for distribution to the German people. Assignment of prisoners to this area of Birkenau provided them with access to goods that could be traded for food and it became known among them as *Kanada*.

This was where Henryk Mandelbrot was sent. A man, a prisoner functionary of some kind, poked his head through a window and told him and the other eleven Jews who were lined up in single file to wait there while he got them each clothes from the shelves. There were two men in front of Mandelbrot. He wasn't able to see what the first man was given but he was able to compare the clothes given to the second man with the clothes the prisoner functionary gave him and he felt cheated. The pants he had got had legs of different sizes.

'I can't wear these.'

'What?'

'I can't wear these.'

'You'll wear what you're given.'

'No, I can't wear these. One leg is bigger than the other. I'd hate to see the man these once fitted.'

'Yeah, well, no one will see him again so shut up. You'll wear what you're given,' said the prisoner functionary, looking up and down at the man behind Mandelbrot and going back to the shelves to find clothes for him.

'Let me look for some better-fitting clothes,' Mandelbrot called to the prisoner functionary.

'No, you've got your clothes.'

'Mister whoever-you-are, I told you I can't wear these clothes. They make me look ridiculous. I can't move properly, I –'

'You think you look ridiculous! Don't worry how you look, you stupid fucking Jew! You'll be dead inside the week!'

'You'll be dead sooner than me,' Mandelbrot said and then lunged at the prisoner functionary, pushing him back in the shelves nearest him, and proceeded to rain blow after blow on his face while the others looked on in astonishment.

'Help! Help! This man's killing me,' he yelled between Mandelbrot's blows, his lip now split and his face bleeding.

'You let me get some better clothes or by all that's holy you'll die right now.'

The prisoner functionary raised his arms up to his face and continued to call for help.

'What's going on here?' a new man asked. Also a prisoner, it was clear to Mandelbrot and the other five, though they had never seen him before, that this man was in another category, a higher category of prisoner. It was there in the way he carried himself and in the way he spoke. He was tall, thin and blond and had come out from further beyond the shelves than any of the others could see.

Mandelbrot let go of the prisoner functionary and looked at this new man.

'He was going to kill me, *Ober-kapo* Fritz.'

Ober-kapo Fritz looked Mandelbrot up and down.

'What is the problem here?'

'The clothes he's given me don't fit. I wanted to choose better-fitting clothes that I can work in and this man refuses to let me look and insults me into the bargain.'

Ober-kapo Fritz looked at Mandelbrot with surprise, which grew into something bordering on admiration. Then he looked slowly at the other men standing silently in a row and then back to Mandelbrot.

No one else said anything. The prisoner functionary was still panting. The *Ober-kapo* waited for him to wipe the blood from his face. Then he turned back to Mandelbrot.

'I will stay and watch you while you choose some clothes that better fit you.'

Henryk Mandelbrot hurried to the shelves to look for pants that would fit him. The *Ober-kapo* watched him with a smile.

Then he spoke slowly to Mandelbrot while Mandelbrot searched through different pairs of pants.

'You don't seem to have any understanding of where you are now. You are now in Birkenau and you don't seem to know what that means. Do you have the slightest idea . . . where you are?' Mandelbrot stopped his searching to turn around and answer the man directly.

'*Ober-kapo*, sir, I know exactly where I am.'

*

The excitement of the evening's events would not let Elly sleep and a short while after they'd gone to their separate rooms Russell heard a knock at his door. It was Elly standing there with a glass of water for him.

'I hope I'm not disturbing you,' she said in a manner combining both formality and kindness that no one had ever accorded him before. 'It's just that I thought you might get thirsty in the middle of the night and not know how to find the kitchen in the dark so I brought you this . . . um . . . it's just a glass of water. 'Cause you know . . . it's so hot and all.'

Now for the first time since arriving at Henry Border's home, Russell was embarrassed. Perhaps she hadn't realised that under the covers he wasn't wearing any clothes but he knew it all too well.

'Thanks,' he said uncertainly.

'Your mom's been great to me. You're very lucky to have a mom like her.'

'Uh-huh,' Russell agreed cautiously. 'You live here with your daddy?'

'Yeah.'

'Just you and him . . . here?'

'Yeah.'

'You sure got a lotta rooms.'

'Yeah, we used to have boarders but . . .'

'Borders . . . like your name, ain't it?'

'Yeah,' she laughed.

'Your daddy's away?'

'Yeah, he had to go away for work . . . overseas to Europe. That's why Callie, I mean your mom's here.'

'Your daddy . . . he in the military?'

'No.'

'What work does he do?'

'He's a psychologist at IIT,' Elise Border said matter-of-factly.

'Uh-huh,' Russell said uncertainly. He didn't know what any of that meant.

Elly's eyes had adjusted to the dark. When she saw Russell's clothes folded on the chair she realised he must have been naked under the covers. Then she began to feel shy and foolish for not having felt this way sooner. Curiosity, loneliness and an attempt to bring comfort to a stranger had taken her to the very edge of her twelve and a half years. But that was all she had.

'Well, I guess I better let you get some sleep then. Good night.'

'Thanks for the water . . . Miss Elly.'

'Oh you're welcome,' she said, opening the bedroom door to leave and then adding, 'Oh . . . um . . . It's Elly . . . just Elly.'

'Elly?' Russell began. 'You got a momma?'

'She died when . . . before we came here.'

'Where you from?'

'Poland.'

'Poland! You Polacks?'

'We're Jews.'

'Jews,' Russell said, considering it as he heard himself say it.

'Uh-huh,' Elise Border said, still standing at the slightly open bedroom door. She stood there for a moment not knowing whether their conversation had ended until Russell spoke again.

'My *daddy* died.'

'Oh, I'm . . . I'm sorry. How long ago?'

''Bout three years now.'

Three years suddenly didn't seem very long ago to Elly.

'You must miss him a lot.'

'Yep,' he said from under the covers.

She stood there in the dark, not leaving. After a little while he broke the silence.

'You miss your momma, Elly?'

'I was very small . . . when she died . . . very small.' Then, deliberately, as though she was aware that her next comment would have the effect of automatically ending the conversation, she added, 'It was back in Poland.'

Whether they were simply tired or had reached a mutual understanding, those were the last words spoken in Henry Border's house that night. There was, however, a long causal chain that linked their conversation to another night, in another place a long time before that. In Poland, before the war, before Hitler had become Chancellor of Germany, in the town of Ciechanow, as autumn turned into winter, a woman waited under a gas-lit street lamp on a windy street corner hoping no one would see her out at that time of night, hoping no one would see her but her lover.

part eight

IT HAD BEEN RAINING ALL DAY but now, as though the night was offering at least the hope of a reprieve to anyone foolish or desperate enough to be out so late, the rain had finally stopped. Had she looked up she would have snatched glimpses of the moon between black clouds that had come in from the Baltic Sea and were passing fleetingly over her on their way to Bialystock and then to Minsk and on still further east into Russia. Heartened only by the light from the street lamps and occasionally from the moon through the gaps in the clouds, a young woman stood waiting anxiously in a street in Ciechanow. The still-wet cobblestone pavement in the Polish town, where Jews quite like Rosa Rabinowicz had lived since medieval times, struggled to glisten for more than a moment now and then that night in the interwar years when news of the growing popularity of a new German politician, Herr Hitler, was beginning to seep through in the newspapers her father read. She read them too at her father's urging and discussed them with her friends, the young men and women at the youth movement gatherings. But for Rosa, then seventeen, there were more urgent matters clawing for her attention that night.

She was waiting for her love from childhood, Noah Lewental. There had been rumours about many of the boys she knew and Rosa Rabinow-icz had heard all of them, believed some, disregarded others, but now for the first time one of the rumours concerned her Noah. The rumour was similar to all those she had heard about the other boys but they hadn't mattered to her. She would react to them with shock or titillation as the mood moved her. But this one concerned Noah. Could it be true? It would certainly be out of character if it were. Still, she knew that boys had urges and she knew there were things that he wanted to do, that they all wanted to do, wanted to the point of portraying the want as a need, things that she felt unable to provide, not then, not yet. None of her girlfriends were able to provide those services to their intendeds either, at least that was what the girls told each other. But this left a gap in the market for the satisfaction of young men's needs and this was where Ada, the shoemaker's daughter, came in. This was where the rumours were born, right where the shoemaker lived with his strange young daughter. And this was where Noah had been seen, with Ada, the shoemaker's daughter.

For all that Ada was referred to as the shoemaker's daughter, it was widely known among the Jews of Ciechanow that she was not really his daughter, not biologically. She had been barely three years old when both her parents were killed in a pogrom in Luban just south of Minsk. The little girl was passed from one Jewish community to another until the shoemaker of Ciechanow, a childless widower, found himself taking on the role of her father. He never knew and so she never knew whether her parents' murderers were demobilised soldiers of the then newly formed Red Army or a band of anti-Semitic Ukrainian nationalists, but whoever they were, it was noticed from the time of her arrival that Ada was different from the other children. Like the other artisans and small traders of Jewish Ciechanow, Ada's father travelled a lot, in his case to sell his shoes. To Golomin, to Preshitz, to Makow and to Churzel he went to sell his shoes and Ada was often left alone. It was said by some that being left alone so frequently was the source of her strangeness. Others said it came with her from Luban, came from what the tiny girl had seen; a lasting gift from the pogromists.

It was not clear whether Ada was simple or just touched. She wanted to be liked and from an early age she would read the palms of the children around her, offering to tell their fortune. She would trace the lines in the palms of their hands with the tips of her fingers and in a quiet soothing voice tell them what they wanted to hear. Eventually some of the adult women started coming around in secret while their husbands were working and while her father was away. They brought food for the young girl but they too came to have their palms read. The boys of the town had always discounted Ada's palm reading as the nonsense of a simple girl until suddenly, in her and their teenage years, they discovered she had other talents. There were differing degrees of religiosity among the Jews of Ciechanow, differing degrees of need for other-worldly prognostications, but nobody that had seen the stop-start stream of young men furtively making their way to the shoemaker's home while he was away could seriously have believed that these young men were in the grip of some mass infatuation with palm reading.

There, at last, was Noah. Rosa Rabinowicz could see him coming in the distance. Soon she would know. Noah spoke in a whisper even before they were within arm's length of each other.

'Sorry I was late. My father was up. He couldn't sleep. He got up and was reading and –'

'Is it true?' she asked, holding on to him with all her strength for what she feared might be the last time.

'Is what true?' he asked, only serving to worry her even more. He knew exactly why they were meeting there at that hour. They had met in secret before and at night too but never anywhere near as late as this.

'Have you been too?'

'Have I been where?'

'Have you been . . . to the shoemaker's house?'

'Rosa, you know I have. I had to go.'

'Noah, don't try that again. You didn't *have* to. You don't *have* to do anything. You pretend you have this need. I'm sick of hearing about it. Admit what you are! You're no better than an animal! And I'm stupid and gullible. I kept saying you haven't been.'

'Rosanké, listen to me. I *had* to go there and I *had* to see Ada. She was the only one there.'

'What?'

'My father sent me.'

'Your father?'

'My father sent me to the shoemaker's house to pick up his shoes. They'd been repaired and –'

'But what about Ada, why did you have to see Ada?'

'Because her father was away. My sweet Rosanké, listen to me. She was the only one there. My father sent me to fetch his shoes. It had been arranged between him and the shoemaker. You can ask my father.'

'Noah, you know I can't do that.'

'Why not?'

'I can't ask your father if he really sent you to the shoemaker's house . . . to fetch his shoes. How could I ask him that? He'd know what I was really asking and I couldn't possibly ask your father that.'

'And yet . . .' Noah said, moving a pace back from her and looking at the full length of her, 'yet you seem to have no trouble asking me.' He exhaled his disappointment. They looked at each other under the street light. Soon the milkman's cart would be joining them.

'I'm telling you. I went there to fetch his shoes. My father had arranged it with the shoemaker. She was expecting me. The shoes were waiting, they were ready. Why don't you ask my father next time you see him?'

Rosa raised the palm of her hand dismissively.

'All right, don't ask him. Compliment him on his shoes. I'll come and fetch you after *shabbos* dinner and, in passing conversation, you can casually compliment him on his shoes.'

She thought for a moment. 'What if he's not wearing those shoes?'

'He always wears those shoes on *shabbos*. They're his favourite shoes, had them forever. That's why he was so desperate to have me collect them from the shoemaker.'

She so wanted to believe him that she did. Still, she would go with him to visit his parents the very next Friday night. She was very fond of Noah's family; his brothers and sisters were almost like hers. His parents were such intelligent and kind people; his father had always seemed so wise. And it happened just as Noah had promised. She complimented Mr Lewental, Noah's father, on his shoes and he, smiling, praised the work of the travelling, never-prosperous, hardworking shoemaker. In fact, when Mr Lewental started waxing lyrical on the topic of the quality of the shoemaker's work, she exchanged glances with Noah, who was now rolling his eyes at his father's verbosity as if to say, 'Now look what you've started.' It was a beautiful evening in Ciechanow for Rosa Rabino-wicz but such evenings were already numbered.

Rosa was eighteen and still with Noah Lewental when the news came like a flood from a river that had burst its banks. Ada, the shoemaker's daughter, was pregnant. It was an undeniable fact. When the simple Ada, the palm reader, identified Noah as the father, Rosa wasn't around to hear the heated conversation between him and Mr Lewental. Whatever the simple girl's circumstances, Mr Lewental had argued that if no one else came forward to own up to the child's paternity, Noah had to do the right thing by the poor girl. That it was impossible for him to have been responsible for the pregnancy was not a lie Noah was able to tell his father.

'What about Rosa?' Noah argued. What would become of Rosa if he was made to marry Ada? Rosa would be free to find a genuinely honourable man, Mr Lewental told his son.

Rosa lost not only Noah but with him her self-confidence. Of all the romantically paired young people in their circle, she and Noah had been regarded as among the most compatible. Certainly their relationship had lasted the longest. The scandal had robbed her of confidence not only in herself but in others too. For a time she didn't want to leave the house or see anyone. She was sure people were talking about her.

In truth, many did talk about her and Noah, about his betrayal and her subsequent self-imposed isolation. Although in no version of the story was she anything less than innocent, it did not prevent her from being a ripe topic of conversation. Some just wanted to talk about how unlucky this striking and gifted young woman had so suddenly become. Even well-intentioned people pondered the meaning of it almost as a religious or philosophical exercise. Others asked how Ada could be so sure it was Noah who was the father when there were so many other young men it could have been. Did she just choose the boy she considered most likely to do the right thing? Perhaps she was not so simple after all.

Rosa's parents, inreasingly concerned for her wellbeing, and having tried without success everything they could think of to return her to her old self, in desperation agreed with someone's suggestion that she spend

313

time away from Ciechanow. Still numb and without saying goodbye to Noah or even to many of her friends, it was a shattered Rosa Rabino-wicz who went to stay for an unspecified duration with distant relatives in Warsaw.

*

It was the honey-skinned woman with the jet-black straight hair, the student who no longer attended his 'What is History?' lectures, the one who had correctly guessed Gandhi, this was the person who served Adam Zignelik a Mango Mojito inside Zanzibar on Ninth Avenue in Hell's Kitchen. She had recognised him despite the unfamiliar context. Professor Zignelik was from another part of her life.

'You don't remember me, do you?' she asked him.

'Yes,' he said, trying to place her.

She smiled. 'Boy, we really *are* all the same to you guys!'

'No, of course not. It's just that . . .' He tried not to look at her cleavage.

In truth, he remembered the student as somewhat older than the usual undergrad. But he had never seen her made up like this and he now found his mind toggling between a half-remembered image and the woman now in front of him, this alluring, suggestively dressed maker of Mojitos. No student had ever looked like this, at least not on campus, not that he had seen.

'I was a student in your "What is History?" class. My name is Mehrzad Yazdi.'

'Right! Mehrzad, of course!' He had never known her name. 'You dropped the course.'

'I dropped every course. I had to leave college.'

'Oh, I'm sorry.'

'Yeah, me too.'

'I hope everything's okay,' he said tentatively, trying to get right the balance between concern and prying.

'Well, I guess it is now . . . sort of. Look, I'm not really supposed to be talking now –'

314

'No, of course not,' he said, looking around at all the other customers milling around the bar impatiently, waiting to be served, 'I'm sorry.'

'Look at you!' she smiled. 'I don't mean you to apologise but if you could come back some other time.'

'Some other time? I only just got here.'

'No, listen. What I mean is . . . I'd *like* to tell you what happened. I kind of wanted to explain 'cause . . . yours was my favourite class.'

'Really?'

'Yes and I just thought if you live around here –'

'I don't.'

'Professor Zignelik, you're not making this any easier, are you?'

'Mehrzad, I won't . . . embarrass you but if you want me to act like I don't even know you . . . Are you trying to ask me . . . to leave?'

'No, I'm trying to ask if you'd like to meet me for a drink . . . one night when I'm not working.'

'You mean here?'

'Sure, unless you don't like your Mojito.'

On the night he was to meet Mehrzad Yazdi for a drink Adam stepped out of the shower and began to dry himself with a towel that hung on a hook at the back of the bathroom door.

'The towel dries faster now there's only one of them hanging on the back of the door,' he heard Diana's voice say in his head. Adam ignored the voice but she went right on talking. 'You already shaved today,' she said.

'Yeah, so? I'm not shaving again.'

'You're putting on aftershave.'

Mehrzad Yazdi was dressed less provocatively than she had been when she was working. She'd arrived first and got them a table of the kind, Adam realised, tended to be reserved for well-connected people. Standing up to greet him, she put her hand on his arm just below the shoulder and offered him her cheek, which he half met with his lips but mostly with the slightly percussive sound he thought was meant to accompany the gesture. Halfway now between bartender and student, she appeared so unexpectedly attractive that it made him nervous. He didn't know what he was doing there. He looked around the bar. He had for a while been focusing on his work to pull him out of his hole. He was making progress. He now had more strands to follow than he had ever had when researching any other topic thus far in his career. There might well be more than one person could handle. He didn't need any other distractions and there was a part of him that recognised this. But now here he was, nonetheless, sitting in this bar in Hell's Kitchen with Mehrzad, the 'Gandhi' girl. This was Diana's neighbourhood now. Surely she wouldn't walk into this bar. But what if she did? Was he ever going to feel comfortable again anywhere other than in the stacks of the Galvin Library at IIT or else interviewing someone in Chicago? Mehrzad was very comfortable there. She knew what to order, how to order, where to sit, how to dress, even how to modulate her voice. She was 'in the know'. He wasn't. Despite this, it didn't feel too bad to be there with her. Would Diana understand that? For all that Mehrzad Yazdi was alluring both in appearance and in manner, and for all that Adam had what amounted to a historian's treasure trove to unpack, in the ongoing, never-ending, private, almost hallucinatory conversation he was in with Diana, it still mattered to him that Diana could understand what he was doing there. He needed her approval and wondered if that was ever going to change.

'My parents felt this was the best way to exercise their control over me.'

'To refuse to pay your tuition?'

'Yep.'

'But didn't they want you to finish college?'

'Yes, but they wanted even more to be able to influence all these other areas of my life.'

'Your boyfriend?'

'Him, yes . . . Actually, they were right about him although for totally different reasons . . . but even the way I dress, for God's sake! Like it's their business at my age! They might have left Iran but they sure took a lot of it with them. They might appear to have adapted to life here but they're still very traditional people with very traditional values when it comes down to it. That's their default position: tradition. This is where they go in moments of peril.'

'Peril?'

'Perceived peril. Immigrants smell peril where others smell roses. Especially those coming from the Middle East. Everyone here either thinks you're a terrorist or else they're liberals who fetishise "orientalism" and suck up to you because of it. That was part of the problem with my ex-boyfriend. Edward Said was right on the money with that. You're English, sorry, Australian, I know the accent. So perhaps it's different with you. You're a different kind of migrant, less alien. My parents will always feel very alien here. They have a different standard when it comes to my brother, which doesn't always help things between us. I mean, it's not *his* fault but . . . Not that I'm saying you're like my parents' generation. Am I talking too much? Do you want another drink?'

They got another drink and another after that.

'Mehrzad, have you talked to Columbia about financial aid? There are all sorts of options if you –'

'Believe me, Professor, I've –'

'You really gotta call me Adam.'

'Adam,' she smiled, 'I looked into everything, talked to everyone. I will go back. I really want to but right now I've got rent to cover and . . . but I will go back. I promise. I don't want to spend my life mixing Mojitos. Will you be there?'

'Columbia?'

'Yes, I really . . . I really do want to finish your course.'

They stood on Ninth Avenue. It was late. He kissed her on the cheek properly this time. When their heads parted she smiled at him intriguingly and walked off down the street. As he stood there with people brushing past him, Adam wondered whether she had wanted more, and whether he had.

*

It seemed that there was never a good time for Michelle McCray to speak to her cousin Lamont even over the phone and offer him whatever advice she could. As often as her grandmother had asked her, had urged her, to speak to Lamont and as much as Michelle had always intended to speak to him in the near future, that future never arrived. At any given moment she found that she couldn't bring herself to make contact with him to apologise for not having stayed in touch while he was in prison, and to undertake to see him, not only with her family but also professionally in order to help him wade through the mire that no doubt his search for his daughter presented. No task she could think of so filled her with guilt or laid her so open to inertia as counselling her cousin on the best way for him to find his daughter. Navigating between her guilt, her inertia and her grandmother's pleading, she eventually gave her grandmother the name and the direct extension of one of her colleagues, a Ms Linh Tran, to whom she had explained her cousin's situation.

Accustomed to the problems he experienced in life invariably becoming somebody's case, Lamont Williams now needed to call Linh Tran, the colleague his cousin had recommended, in the hope that his search for his daughter might become her next case. The call would need to be made during business hours, which would likely mean during his lunch break.

Not being able to afford a mobile phone and not wanting to parade his past in front of his colleagues by phoning from the employee lunch room at Sloan-Kettering, he considered trying the payphone on 68th Street but abandoned the idea because of the traffic noise as soon as he'd left the building.

With his pen and notepad in his hand Lamont walked slowly into the St Catherine of Siena Church, which was also on 68th Street. The church was dark, cavernous and seemed empty. He was beginning to panic. His lunch hour was being used up and he hadn't begun to talk to Linh Tran. Eventually he found the priest who, after some explaining by Lamont, was very understanding and offered him the free use of his phone from his private office. Aware that he would soon need to go back to work, he managed to speak to Linh Tran and arrange with both her and the priest of St Catherine of Siena a time and date for a long phone call.

At the agreed time the following week Lamont returned to the church, found the priest and made the call from the priest's office with the priest intermittently standing there watching and listening to Lamont's side of the conversation.

Was Lamont already legally recognised as the father? He wasn't sure. What exactly did that mean, 'legally recognised'? Was he married to the mother when the child was born? No, he wasn't. He's never been married to the mother. Did he get his name on the child's birth certificate? Lamont didn't remember. Wasn't it meant to contain his daughter's name? The parents too, yes, of course. He couldn't say. Has the mother ever applied for child support? No, she hasn't.

'I used to give her money but . . . you know, nobody *made* me. I just did it. She was my daughter and I was working then but . . . never . . . you know . . . like, official child support.'

'Did you or your daughter's mother ever sign a form and submit it to the Department of Vital Statistics?'

'No, I don't think so.'

''Cause you could get on the birth certificate that way.'

'I don't know if I ever did sign a form for the Department . . . Vital Statistics. Let's say I didn't.'

'So then you're telling me you're not sure you've established legal paternity?'

'I mean . . . I'm the father. I know that. But I don't know what's been established like that.'

'Would you say you had a close relationship with your daughter prior to going into a correctional facility?'

'Yes. I did. Very close, definitely.'

'Did you ever change her diaper?'

'More times than I could count.'

'Did she ever call you Daddy?

'She always called me Daddy.'

'If a court were to ask her if she ever visited her daddy in jail, what do you think she'd say?'

'She did visit me but only at the beginning. She was about two and a half then. She's eight now.'

'You haven't seen her at all since she was two and a half?'

'No.'

'I see.'

'So I don't know what she'd say. I mean, I don't know what she'd remember.'

'And you don't know where the mother is?'

'No, I tried to find out but . . . ain't had no luck yet which is why I needed to speak to you.'

'Mr Williams, I think you're going to need to go to court and file a visitation petition.'

'Okay, well, how'd I do that?'

'Your sister said you're working at the moment?'

'You don't mean my sister. You mean Michelle? She's my cousin.'

'Oh yes, I'm sorry, your cousin. Are you still in employment, Mr Williams?'

'Yes, I am.'

'In the Bronx?'

'No, I *live* in the Bronx but I *work* in Manhattan.'

'Okay, 'cause you're going to need to go to court during business hours, say between nine and five to file the petition.'

'See, Miss Linh Tran, how can I do that? I can't leave work. I'm still on probation at my job. We get put on six months' probation and I can't just . . . you know, I can't just leave. Where is the court?'

'I think you'd need to go to the Family Court, which is down on Lafayette Street. Maybe you could get help from the Legal Aid Society, which is right by there on Church Street.'

'I know a lot about the Legal Aid Society. Lot of time inside for the stories to get around 'bout the work they do.'

'Yeah . . . well, they do have a horrible caseload. Come to think of it I'm not even sure they do this kind of work.'

'What are my options if they don't?'

'Well, you could always see a lawyer in private practice who specialises in this sort of thing but it costs.'

'What does it cost?'

'I couldn't say exactly.'

'Well . . . Miss Linh Tran, could you maybe give me a ballpark figure?'

'You could probably find someone who would do it for between $150 and $350.'

'So if I could come up with $350 I could get someone to take care of it for me? I don't know how long it would take me to find that kind of money.'

'No, I mean between $150 and $350 an hour.'

'An *hour*?'

'I'm afraid so.'

'Well, how many hours it gonna take to file these documents?'

'I really couldn't say. You could probably find a lawyer who'd do the whole thing for between about . . . let's see . . . maybe $3000 to $5000.'

'Miss Linh Tran, my daughter's gonna be twenty-one before I get that kind of money. Do I have any other options?'

'Well, like I was saying, you could go to the Family Court and do it yourself.'

'So if I took a day off of work to do that, what would I have to do?'

'Well, it shouldn't take a whole day. You'd just go down there and file a visitation petition. You'll be told to come back about six weeks later and then they'll give you the relevant paperwork –'

'So that's like another day off of work?'

'Well, you'd have to go there for some time; again it shouldn't take the whole day. They'll give you the relevant paperwork and explain the correct procedure for effecting service on your daughter's mother.'

'Effecting what?'

'Effecting service; that just means there's certain specified ways she's to take delivery of the documents.'

'But I don't know where she lives.'

'Well, see, that's a problem. You don't seem to have what a court would call "standing" with respect to your daughter so that's why you need to file the petition in the first place.'

'Yeah, but I don't know where Chantal is in the first place and in the second place . . . I mean I can't be takin' all these days off of work, not while I'm still on probation. I got to get through probation before I can even think about cuttin' any corners.'

'And you're not in a position to engage a private lawyer?'

'No, I'm not currently in that position.'

'Mr Williams, I don't know what else to say. Do you think you can wait till after your probation period with your employer is done?'

'I can't see no other way, Miss Linh Tran. But even then if I could get down to the court on those days, that still won't mean I know where Chantal is livin'.'

'I know this might seem hard but if you could wait till you're finished your probation . . . you could call me again then.'

'Well, I thank you, really I do, but even then . . . What if I still don't know then where Chantal is livin'?'

'Won't you be in a better position to find out?'

'I guess so but . . .'

'You don't have any evidence of your daughter being in any kind of danger, do you?'

'No. I mean I don't have any evidence of her at all.'

'Well, if she's not in danger . . . I don't mean to sound harsh because I know how much you want to re-establish contact with your daughter but maybe your best bet is to wait until your employment situation is more secure. Don't you think? You've already waited so long. I don't know what else to advise. Maybe you'll need to hire a private detective to track down the mother but I really don't know what they'd charge. Mr Williams, I really think it might serve you and your daughter best if you can secure your employment beyond the probation period. It will look good to a judge and it will help you or at least make it easier for you to get any time off you may need. It will probably help you in lots of ways.'

The priest who had been listening, initially coming and going on the pretext of needing things from his office, eventually gave up pretending and just stood at the doorway watching Lamont, listening as hard as he could. When Lamont got off the phone he put down the receiver and said, automatically with his mind far away, 'Thank you, Father,' and began walking out in a hurry to avoid being late back to work.

'Good news?'

'Pardon me?' said Lamont, walking quickly through the darkened church towards the exit on 68th Street. The priest was trailing behind him. Lamont had to get back to work. That seemed to be what Linh

Tran was saying. Just get through the probation period. Everything starts from there. Hope starts from there. The soles of his shoes made quick sharp noises on the stone floor of the church. The priest hurried to catch up to him.

'I said "good news?"'

'Pardon me?'

'Good news?'

'Glad *you* got some. I gotta get back to work, Father.'

*

In Poland, in the years between the war to end all wars and the war after that, one in three inhabitants of Warsaw was Jewish and at least one of the other two felt it was much more than that. So persistent and widespread was this feeling, particularly among the intelligentsia, that the universities instituted what was known as a *numerus clausus* or *closed number*, a quota on the number of Jews permitted to study at university. At some universities those Jewish students who came within the quota were made to sit in special 'Jewish' seats in the classroom. At certain universities right-wing student activists instituted 'Jew-free days' and sometimes 'Jew-free weeks'. A Jewish student caught on campus during those times was more than usually likely to be assaulted by the student activists or else by thugs from outside who would go looking for them. Those Jewish students who wanted to undertake postgraduate studies or to study medicine, engineering or law were forced either to study abroad or to consider other ways of earning a living. The Polish civil service was similarly closed to them and an increasing number of intellectual Polish Jews sought the modest but economically secure path of teaching school children. Some felt fulfilled by teaching while for others it represented a painful compromise. Many of them dreamed of something beyond their schools and some of them even worked in their chosen fields in the hours their school obligations allowed.

Two such Jews sat drinking coffee in a Warsaw café at the end of a day at school. One of them wanted more than anything else to earn his living as a historian, the other felt the same way about psychology.

This other was Chaim Broder, a man who had studied under Wilhelm Wundt, the pioneer of experimental psychology, what seemed like many years earlier.

'Emanuel, you're an inveterate optimist, you know that?'

'I have to be,' said the younger Emanuel Ringelblum.

'You're a historian who works on his own trying to learn all he can about this wretched history of ours. The Jews themselves don't care to know even though it's their history and the Poles definitely don't want to know. You and your Jewish colleagues are afraid to give papers on Jewish history at professional conferences and –'

'We're not afraid. As a rule they won't let us because they don't consider us to be a "nation". But sometimes they do. It's not all as hopeless as you think.'

'Sometimes they do!' repeated Chaim Broder with gentle mockery. 'And that's why you're an inveterate optimist?'

'No,' said Emanuel Ringelblum, 'I told you, I *have* to be an optimist. You want to ask why?'

'Would it make any difference if I didn't?'

'Of course not.'

'All right then, so why?'

'Because I have to see *you* every day. Anyone forced to see you every day needs to be an incorrigible optimist.'

'I'm not a pessimist, Emanuel. Science is neither for nor against hope.'

'I know. You've mentioned it a couple of times before. In Leipzig you studied under Wundt and now you're a scientist of the mind.'

'Well, I . . .' Chaim Broder paused to sip his coffee before continuing, 'and every day I go and teach little children. I teach children, Jewish children. What am I doing this for? Why?'

'You need to earn a living like the rest of us and you teach children so they can grow up and –'

'Emanuel, the best of them will be lucky if *they'll* be allowed to teach little children.'

'But Chaim, you're preparing them. If it changes who will be –'

'If it *changes*? If it *changes*?'

'Gentlemen, I see you're sitting here arguing as usual,' said a third man who had just arrived at their table. 'Good to see, anything else would be a quite disconcerting change and, anyway, I have someone charming for you to meet. It would be wrong to give her an atypical impression. Better she should have an honest and unfavourable one.'

The man was Rafal Gutman, the head of the Jewish community education system for all of Warsaw, and with him stood a young woman.

'This is Miss Rosa Rabinowicz, originally from Ciechanow. She will soon be a qualified teacher. And I thought part of her training really should include learning to put up with people like you two. May we join you?'

The two seated men stood up to greet Rafal Gutman and more particularly the slip of a girl passing as a woman, Rosa Rabinowicz.

'Rafal, we must have done *something* right. I can't remember the last time you introduced us to someone so charming,' said Emanuel Ringelblum, briefly taking the young woman's hand.

'Never,' said Rafal Gutman, 'I have never introduced you to someone so charming. But the better question is, "What has Rosa done that is so wrong that she deserves to meet the likes of you two?"'

'And what *have* you done that is so wrong, Miss Rabinowicz?' asked Emanuel Ringelblum.

'Me? Well, nothing I'm sure,' she said a little nervously to the two cosmopolitan intellectuals.

'Rosa already knows a little about both of you.'

'Well, only a little. I know one of you is also a historian and the other is . . . is it a psychologist? But I might as well confess that I don't remember which of you is which. I'm sorry. And, at the risk of embarrassing myself further, I'm not really even all that sure what a psychologist is.'

'No need to be embarrassed at all, Miss Rabinowicz,' said Emanuel Ringelblum. 'I am the historian and Chaim here . . . well, it really doesn't matter what Chaim does. He's such a pessimist about everything, even *he* doesn't really think he matters much. And since there's no one who thinks Chaim matters more than Chaim thinks he does, you can immediately see how much validity there is to his pessimism.'

Rafal Gutman and Emanuel Ringelblum had been flattering and amusing. But Chaim Broder had not uttered a word. It had taken him only one look at this young woman to begin to experience things he had not lately experienced; excitement, even hope. He must not allow this introduction to be all there was to this chance meeting with this girl, Rosa Rabinowicz. He had to see her again. But rendered too embarrassed and shy by grainy memories of past romantic disappointments to know what to say, he had not yet said anything.

'Please forgive my ignorance, Mr Broder, but what exactly is psychology?' Rosa Rabinowicz asked Chaim Broder while Rafal Gutman ordered coffee from a waiter for both Rosa and himself.

'Miss Rabinowicz, there is nothing at all to be embarrassed about,' Broder said, embarrassed at the quiver in his voice. He cleared his throat and, trying to steady himself, continued, 'Admitting ignorance about something is a virtue, not a fault.'

'Oh dear, had I known I was being virtuous I might not have asked.' Rosa smiled.

'It's neither a virtue nor a fault to ask questions about the nature of psychology,' interjected Emanuel Ringelblum. 'But it is a folly if you're asking a curmudgeonly pessimistic psychologist like Chaim.'

'He makes fun of me, Miss Rabinowicz.'

'He does,' said Rosa. 'But from the way you take it, I can see that it's not at all true.'

She was as charming as Rafal Gutman had said. She had a sense of humour and, worse still, she was kind. What was Rafal doing introducing this beautiful young thing to him, a single man whose loneliness he tried to wash off each morning before getting dressed for work? He wanted to touch her. The soft skin he could see on the top of her hand would do. What on earth was wrong with him? he wondered. He had thought of himself as an educated, cultured man, a man of science. It was this image of himself that had got him through most things most of the time; his loneliness, the professional obstacles and the various indignities and humiliations he had endured throughout his life. Now in an instant he'd been reduced to a tingling adolescent boy.

'You see how they argue,' offered Rafal Gutman. 'It's back and forth, positively Talmudic.'

'Talmudic?' asked Ringelblum rhetorically. 'Well, only God could have been crueler to Chaim than I've been. And judging by what Chaim has to say, He *was*.' The waiter came to deliver the most recently ordered coffee.

'Charm and beauty and an enquiring mind, Miss Rabinowicz,' said Broder, ignoring Ringelblum's jibe. He wondered if he wasn't being excessive in his praise.

'Thank you, Mr Broder.' Rosa blushed.

'Please call me Chaim. Psychology is,' Broder continued, 'to put it very simply, the scientific study of the human mind. It's a very new discipline so it's not at all surprising that you're not familiar with it. But tell me, how do you find Warsaw?'

'It's beautiful but I've never lived in a place with so many people. Sometimes it's a bit daunting. It's a far cry from Ciechanow.' There was the opening he had hoped for. Now was his moment to push himself forward or forever damn himself to solitude for nothing but cowardice.

'It would be my pleasure to show you around, if you have time.'

This was how it happened that Chaim Broder managed to take on the role of tour guide, caregiver and confidant to young Rosa Rabinowicz. He showed her around the city, took her to both the Yiddish and the Polish theatre, took her to meet writer friends of his at the Writers' Club, took her for walks and for meals for which he always paid. Not one zloty, not a groschen of her own did she ever spend when she was with him. He took her for walks past the religious bookshops on Franciszkanska Street so that he might initiate conversation about religion in order to get a sense of whether she had sufficiently distanced herself from what Broder considered outdated provincial religiosity. If she hadn't it would not have dampened his enthusiasm for her. It would have meant only that he was going to have to work on her beliefs to bring them closer to his. But although her values might have derived from a religious background, by the time Rosa was living in Warsaw she was at most 'traditional' in her religious adherence.

She knew very few people there and quickly grew quite dependent on him. Broder was aware that some of her evident feeling for him was simply gratitude. But then isn't gratitude a constituent component of affection? Chaim Broder asked himself. However, that was some time later. On that first day, the day they met, their attention had returned to the conversation Emanuel Ringelblum was having with Rafal Gutman.

'Hundreds of thousands of Jews all over Poland toil away in misery. They're barely able to survive on the pittance they're earning. They don't own any property. They're lucky if they own a cow. Look, even here in Warsaw there are Jews who live in frightening poverty yet –'

'Emanuel, you won't get any argument from me on this,' said Rafal Gutman. 'But I don't understand what you think you can do with it. How do you think your historical studies will help?'

'If the Polish historians, the establishment, better understood the truth of the Jewish historical experience it would help us to be seen without prejudice and as we really are.'

'This is where he loses me,' said Chaim Broder.

'No, no, it's not as hopeless as you make it out to be, Chaim. Already there's a professor at Warsaw University, Jan Kochanowski, a Pole, and he has some time for my arguments. He's quite open to me and a few of my colleagues.'

'No, it's not the existence of one sympathetic Polish historian here or there, an existence I admit you'd know more about than I would,' interjected Broder. 'It's that Emanuel here seriously thinks this piecemeal process will eventually lead to a radically different perception of Jews throughout Polish society. I'm sorry but it's just . . . it's fanciful!'

'Don't both successful and *un*successful undertakings begin with small bands of enthusiasts?' asked Rosa Rabinowicz. Despite her partial support for Ringlblum, Chaim Broder smiled with a pride in her he had not earned a right to. Nor was he going to argue with anything she said. The discussion might have continued for the rest of the day had not Rafal Gutman, with Rosa Rabinowicz in tow, left for a meeting at the Jewish Orphans Home on Krochmalna Street. For him it was a routine event but for her it was so stirring an experience that she subsequently started going there to help with the teaching in a voluntary capacity.

Some weeks later Chaim Broder asked Rosa Rabinowicz out for dinner for the first time. He had reserved a table at an expensive restaurant. Arriving to pick her up from the orphanage after work, a young boy mistakenly took him to the office of the director, Dr Janusz Korczak, who, after apologising for the misunderstanding, personally accompanied him to where Rosa was teaching. They talked as they walked.

'It's never been my good fortune to actually meet you in person, Dr Korczak. I'm pleased the young boy's misunderstanding has given me the privilege.'

'You're kind to say that, Mr Broder, but it appears to me that your good fortune far exceeds meeting me.'

'I'm sorry, Dr Korczak, I'm afraid I'm not following you.'

'I'm referring to Rosa, Mr Broder. She's a gift to us all but especially to you, I understand.'

Chaim Broder blushed. Janusz Korczak had assumed an intimacy between Broder and Rosa Rabinowicz that Broder dreamed of but one that, in reality, had not yet developed. Fortunately for him they reached the room where Rosa was working with the children before candour would have required Broder to disabuse him and he left the assumption hanging in the air unchallenged. As they stood looking through the open door at Rosa at a table surrounded by children, Korczak explained that she was chairing a meeting of the editorial board of the children's newspaper. Sitting to one side of her a young girl of about fourteen was speaking quietly to the group without making eye contact with any of them.

'My grandmother had wanted my mother to marry a scholar, a Torah scholar . . . My troubles started before me. He was . . . he was a mean man. I think my mother's life ended on her wedding day.' The assembled group sat in silence listening.

'But what were *your* first memories?' asked Rosa quietly with her hand casually resting on the young girl's hand. 'If we all agreed that the pieces should start with your first memories and end with your hopes for your future then we do need to be strict about where we start and where we stop. Avram, how many words do we have in each autobiography?'

'No more than two thousand,' said a boy of around fifteen.

'It might sound like a lot but as we've seen everybody at this table has quite a story to tell. Remember, the idea in the first place was to provide examples and encouragement to the others, to get the others writing.'

Rosa looked up and saw Chaim Broder and Janusz Korczak just outside the door.

'I think that's all we have time for today but next time we can continue where we left off. Keep your notes. Everyone will get a chance. Have a good night, children.'

'Thank you, Miss Rabinowicz,' some of the children said.

'Good night, Miss Rabinowicz,' said some others, packing up their things and leaving the room.

'My father was poor. I hadn't realised we were so poor until I got to public school. The other kids didn't have to wear rags. They had white bread. This must have been part of what made him so angry all the time,' said the fourteen-year-old girl to Rosa as the others filed past.

'You can write everything you want, you know. Talk about your parents and your grandparents, everything, and if it's a longer piece we'll use it for something else. But we can talk about that next time.'

'Miss Rabinowicz . . . Maybe I could talk to you . . . alone some time?'

'Of course you can, my darling. I have someone waiting for me now but we will talk. I promise you. As much as you want.'

'Hello, Dr Korczak,' two students said in unison as they left the room.

'Good afternoon, Dr Korczak,' said other departing students, one after another.

Rosa's smile as she greeted him when the last child, the fourteen-year-old girl, had left the room gave him a courage that evening that he had been waiting for. Almost a child herself but not a child, not an orphan but she might as well have been for all the help her parents in Ciechanow could give her in Warsaw, Rosa took his arm in the street. He would protect her. It was this promise of his that she heard that night back home in her bed as she considered the offer he had made when saying goodbye. Would she agree to marry him? he had asked her.

Although he was kind and worldly, although she felt safe with him, he was not the man she had dreamed of. But a plant grows towards the light and he was her only light. This was how between these two people there came to be a coincidence of wants for just long enough for Chaim

Broder, once of Krakow, and Rosa Rabinowicz, once of Ciechanow, to marry. The way he saw her didn't change but by the time their daughter Elise arrived, the pull of the light he carried counted for less with her and he sensed this. He tried to blame it on the pregnancy, then on the birth and then on the demands of their baby daughter. But in the dark of the Warsaw night as they lay in bed together, Rosa always tired, always silent, always as far away as a shared bed would allow, there was no longer any light at all pulling her towards him. If she only knew, she didn't have long to wait for her unhappiness to turn to fear, not of him, but of what was happening in Poland, in Europe.

*

William McCray sat outside Charles' office waiting for his son's receptionist to permit him to enter.

'Turning chilly already,' she said to him.

'Pardon me?'

'I said it's turning chilly already. I don't remember being cheated out of fall this early, do you?'

'It is a bit chilly but when the sun's out it's not too bad.'

'Charlie, you want to come for a walk?' William asked his son. 'I'll treat you to a coffee. Do you good to get some fresh air.'

'No, I'd better not, Dad. I'm up to my ears in work here. I'll only feel guilty if I go out.'

'Guilty? Is it true what I hear about the meeting of presidents?' William McCray asked his son Charles.

'What meeting of presidents is that?'

'Your president, the President of the University, what's his name –'

'Bollinger.'

'Right, Bollinger. Is it true that your President Bollinger has invited the President of Iran to speak at the university?'

Charles ran his palm over his forehead and closed his eyes. 'It's true.'

'I want to see that I understand this. Bollinger has actually invited Ahmadinejad to speak at Columbia?'

'Yes.'

'Hitler all booked up?'

'Dad!'

'Dad what?'

'Well, he's not Hitler.'

'Hitler wasn't perceived as Hitler when Chamberlain tried to engage with him.'

'What do you want me to say, Dad? It's a university. If diversity of opinion and free speech aren't welcome here then –'

'Diversity of opinion! The man is a brutal dictator who kills people whose opinion differs from his. As for freedom of speech, you're a historian. If you had a colleague on faculty who blatantly falsified history and propagated manifest falsehoods, would you encourage it or not object on the grounds of diversity of opinion or free speech? Would you promote it? Would you create a platform for it where otherwise there would be none?'

'Dad, of course, you're right. What can I say? I wasn't thrilled to learn he'd done this but I thought . . . at least this one's not *my* fight.'

'Not your fight?'

'Well, thankfully, it's not. No one's asking my opinion, for once.'

'No! Not your fight, huh? Well, I don't remember Jim Crow being Jake Zignelik's fight either. And I don't remember the "Freedom Summer" being Andrew Goodman's or Michael Schwerner's fight either.'

'Oh God, Schwerner and Goodman again! Dad, I have a lot of Jewish friends, just as you always have had, but I have to tell you, I don't always agree with everything Israel does.'

'Who does? Find me a Jew or even an Israeli who does. We're talking about Ahmadinejad being given a platform at your university to spread hate and fear. This man denies the Holocaust happened but promises to deliver a brand new Holocaust of his own making as soon as he gets nuclear weapons. This man is not looking to promote a solution to the Arab–Israeli dispute. This man is not looking out for the Palestinians. He's using them for his own political ends. The man is talking hate, pure and simple. It's good old-fashioned hate. What does Bollinger think he's doing?'

'Dad, not all criticism of Israel is anti-Semitism.'

'No, you're definitely right there, not all criticism of Israel is anti-Semitism. But *none* of it should be. And while you permit that part of it that is, you're just a coward or an anti-Semite . . . or both.'

Michelle McCray came home from work a little later than usual, a little later than she'd expected but no less tired than experience had taught her was likely. She found a note from her daughter Sonia on the kitchen table. It read, 'At Adam's. Called first. Okay with him. Watching DVDs. Love, me. PS. Done my homework so don't even ask and this is educational anyway.'

'Called first!' Michelle said to herself. 'What chance did he have? What about dinner?'

She kicked off her shoes, flopped down into a chair in the living room and called Adam.

'Well, we've got *The Shop Around the Corner* and *To Be or Not To Be.* Your daughter hasn't seen either so I figured we'd go for one of those.'

'We could get through both,' Michelle heard Sonia suggest.

'*To Be or Not To Be*, is it the original or the remake?' Michelle asked.

'It's the original; Lubitsch. We're having a Lubitsch festival here.'

'We could do both,' Sonia advocated again.

'I don't know, Sonia, we haven't even had dinner yet,' Adam countered.

'I haven't had dinner either,' said Michelle.

'You want to come over?'

'Are you making dinner?' Michelle asked.

'Well, the finely honed selection of take-out menus *are* mine, if that's what you mean.'

'Could we watch *To Be or Not To Be*?' Michelle asked.

'Let me check on that. Sonia!'

'Yeah,' Sonia answered.

'Your mum would like to come over and watch *To Be or Not To Be* with us.'

'We could do both.'

'You sure I won't be cramping her style?' Michelle asked.

'Your mum wants to know if she'd be cramping your style.'

'I like how you say "mum". Makes her sound like she's the Queen or something.'

'She's not cramping anybody's style, is she?'

'Why am I hearing silence?' Michelle asked.

'She's having an adolescent moment.'

'She can come,' Sonia answered. 'But tell her we've already decided we're watching *both* movies. They're educational. I mean, they're black and white for God's sake!'

'Heard from Adam?' William McCray asked his son Charles at their weekly meeting in Charles' office in the Fayerweather Building at Columbia.

'A little, not much. He seems to be very busy with this research project he's got going in Chicago. Spends a lot of time there.'

'Oh, I know all about that. He's uncovered recordings of some kind from Holocaust survivors. I led him to it, well, indirectly. He's looking for the evidence my friend spoke of, evidence of black troops at the liberation of Dachau.'

'I don't think he is, Dad.'

'Oh I *know* he is.'

'No, I think it's gone beyond that. He's looking into the life of the man who made those recordings.'

'Maybe, but he's still on the trail of the evidence –'

'That might be where it started but –'

'Is it really so important to you that he *doesn't* find it?' William snapped. They sat there, neither of them believing what William had just said. How had it come to this?

Charles McCray went home that night and opened the door to a silent apartment, silent because it was empty. On the kitchen table lay a note from his wife Michelle. She was having dinner and watching a movie at Adam Zignelik's place. Beneath the note was a note from his daughter Sonia. She was there too. Charles stood there looking at the notes. Then he looked around the room. There was no doubt about it. He was the only one there.

*

The little girl, Elise, not much more than a baby, had finally gone to sleep and, although it was only early afternoon, Rosa Broder, born Rosa

Rabinowicz, was already tired. Just attending to her daughter and the cooking and cleaning, on top of repeated nights with little sleep, had made her feel like taking a nap too. She had taken off her house slippers and her clothes and had put on her robe when she heard a knock at the front door. He husband was not due home for hours and she wasn't expecting anyone. She thought it was probably somebody trying to hawk their wares door-to-door. If she just ignored the knock for long enough the salesman would think there was no one home and move on to the next door. But the knocking continued. She waited for it to stop, which it did, but then after a very short break it began again. This was no ordinary hawker. She went to the door and looked through the peephole. She couldn't believe what she saw. Standing outside the front door of her Warsaw apartment was Noah Lewental. She hadn't seen him since she left Ciechanow. Nor had there been any contact between them.

Nervously, she looked at him as he stood there, now a little older, looking at her front door then turning around to face the foyer and the stairs as though expecting something of interest to appear there, and then turning back to her door again. Just an inch or two of wood separated them. He wouldn't have realised that. He knew it was her apartment. He didn't know she was there. But why did he stay there knocking? Why didn't he just leave? Perhaps a neighbour downstairs had assured him that Mrs Broder was at home with the little one; a little girl she was.

'Mrs Broder has a daughter?'

'Yes, a little girl, Elise.'

She had thought of him from time to time since she'd left Ciechanow, often, in the early days. Sometimes it was in anger, sometimes in sorrow. Sometimes she had even been angry at herself for not having been more accommodating with respect to his urges. As a married woman now she had accustomed herself to satisfying another man's needs. Where would the tragedy have been in learning earlier to satisfy someone she'd loved since girlhood? She'd thought these thoughts in the middle of the night as her husband Chaim Broder lay beside her, sometimes asleep, sometimes pretending to be asleep so as not to invade the privacy of her regret. What did she regret? Broder didn't know all of it but he knew she probably regretted marrying so hastily and marrying a much older man. His adoration of her hadn't diminished. But he was not oblivious to his wife's true feelings. He could accept that she didn't have the *same* feeling for him that he had for her but not too easily that she barely had any at all.

By day he fought the intellectual dissatisfaction delivered by his job, by the lack of opportunities to study further, by his inability to work as a psychologist. By night he lived with the knowledge that if his wife kissed him, if she held him, if she permitted him to touch her and to take her in bed, it was her loneliness and poverty that had delivered her to him. It was these thoughts, these feelings, that day after day chipped away at his sense of self.

Rosa looked through the peephole at the man she should have married and memories of other times flooded back. Noah should have been able to wait. He should have understood. He should have resisted simple Ada. Suddenly he turned away and started to walk towards the stairs. He was leaving. Without understanding why, she opened the door. Had he heard the door open over the sounds of his footsteps? Should she call to him before it was too late? She wouldn't be able to chase after him. Her daughter was asleep in the next room. Where was he going – back to Ciechanow, back to Ada? Why had he come? He stopped and stood still at the top of the stairs.

'Noah . . . Is that you?'

He turned around on the top stair, leaned on the banister and said sadly, 'I knew you were home.'

She asked him in and took his coat. They just stood there and stared at each other. Gathering herself together, she invited him to sit down and asked him whether he'd like a cup of tea.

'You'll have to speak quietly. My daughter's asleep.'

'I'd heard you have a daughter. How old is she now?'

'She's two, almost two and a half.'

'How are you?' he asked.

'How am I? I'm fine, I'm well.'

'Good,' he said uncomfortably.

'How old is *your* . . . child . . . now?' she asked.

'Oh,' he said even more uncomfortably. 'You didn't hear? Ada . . . um . . . She lost the child. It wasn't born alive.'

'Noah, I'm sorry. How is . . . Ada?'

'About the baby?'

'Yes.'

'She's the same. Very quickly, almost immediately, she went back to being the same strange girl she ever was. You see, she thinks the baby's not dead.'

'What?'

'She thinks it's not with us now but it will be. She says we'll see it soon and that eventually we'll see it along with her parents, her real parents, the ones who were killed in the pogrom in Luban when she was a baby. She's not a bad person but she's . . .'

'Simple?' offered Rosa.

'And she's crazy. I think it probably helps her.'

'You don't have a baby,' Rosa said almost to herself. 'So everything . . . the whole thing was for nothing. You needn't have married her.'

'No, I needn't have.' They looked at each other. Both so young, and both already so bruised.

'Rosa . . . I don't know how she could have known I was the father. I only ever . . . *saw* her once. There were others who visited her many times and who –'

'Noah, I *know* . . . how many boys went there. We all knew. Perhaps Ada isn't so simple after all?'

'What do you mean?'

'She chose the one, perhaps the only one, who would admit what he'd done and marry her,' Rosa said, not with anger but with resignation and sadness.

'I wasn't so good, so strong, so moral. Rosa, I'd have lied as quickly as the rest of them to cover up what I'd done and get on with my life, go ahead with my . . . with our plans.

'It was my father who got me to admit that I could have been responsible and it was my father who got me to marry her and live with the consequences.'

'Did he say anything about me, your father?'

'Yes, he said I would be giving you the chance to find an honourable man.' At that Noah looked around the apartment. 'And is he, your husband, an honourable man?'

'He is unquestionably an honourable man,' she answered. Noah had known her since childhood and the way she said this, coupled with all she did not say, told him everything she'd meant.

'Why have you come to Warsaw?'

'There's no work in Ciechanow. I've come here looking for work, or else to train for something. I heard there's work for electricians.'

'And if you find it?'

'If I find it I'll leave Ciechanow . . . move here.'

'And your wife?'

'Ada can be Ada anywhere. Rosa, I ruined both our lives.'

'I'm not angry at you, not any more.'

'No? Well, I am. Every day I punish myself . . . and then God adds some too.' Noah looked around the apartment and said quietly, 'An honourable man.'

Whether he was speculating on the character of her husband or commenting ironically on his own character, Rosa didn't know, but something about this last remark made her close her eyes and when she opened them again crushed tears stained her cheeks. Seeing them, he went over to hug her. Brushing her tears away with the back of his hand he then broadened the scope of his attention to sweeping away the hair from her eyes to the side of her face and behind her ears. Then he kissed her gently on the top of her head and with equal softness on her temple all the while continuing to stroke her hair. She didn't move when he kissed her softly on the lips except to surprise him when she opened her mouth. It was as though kissing him passionately in this Warsaw apartment while her daughter slept in the next room was the most natural thing in the world to her. And while it was not the most natural thing in the world, she moved to it as though, natural or not, it was the thing she most wanted.

They stood kissing and when he pulled her robe off her shoulders he saw her breasts for only the third time and for the first time in the light. Kneeling, he took her robe off entirely and let it fall at her feet on the floor. She stood there completely naked, still with tears in her eyes, and let his mouth wander all over her body. The little girl Elise stayed asleep in her parents' bedroom and Noah led the girl's mother to the couch.

He entered her for the first time ever just as he had wanted to years before when then, as now, it had been forbidden, though for different reasons. How much time did they have before the world closed in on them? They were not to know.

It was twelve minutes later when Chaim Broder, sent home early from the school where he taught by a migraine, turned the lock in the front door quietly and unexpectedly and saw them just moments before Rosa saw him. He was to always remember the scene, and even more vividly than the sight, the sound of his wife's moaning before she saw him from the corner of her eye. She sat up and instinctively tried to shield her husband from their nakedness with a blanket that lay at one end of the couch, a movement that led Noah Lewental to turn around and see the back of Chaim Broder's head as Broder, without saying a word, made his way back briskly towards the front door. He opened the door, walked out and closed it without slamming it, returning some four hours later. Noah dressed hurriedly and left, leaving Rosa to pace the apartment sobbing, sometimes with hysterical gasps of breath and sometimes in silence. When the child awoke Rosa sang her little songs in a vain attempt to hide her distress while she fed her.

Ten days later the little girl Elise was gone. Her father had taken her and a small collection of their things without Rosa's knowledge or permission on a long journey that would deliver them both ultimately to Chicago. His anger would eventually subside but never the pain or the sneaking suspicion that he was in some way, through some potent cocktail of failure, responsible for what he had found in his home that migrainous afternoon. This sense of comprehensive failure clung to him wherever he went and with every change of clothes and every change of season in Chicago, Illinois, where he was known, mainly to his students, as Henry Border.

*

To phone her or not to phone her?' That was the question that Adam Zignelik was toying with. Finally, things were beginning to go well for him, at least professionally, Adam told himself. His work was looking promising. In Chicago, Sahera Shukri, Dean of Libraries at IIT's Galvin Library, and members of her staff were, of their own volition, digitally storing Henry Border's transcripts of the wire recordings he had brought back from the DP camps of Europe in 1946. The contents of the transcripts, the voices, followed these staff around, into their homes, their cars and into their sleep and some had to report after a while that they were unable to continue. Waiting for Adam in Yiddish and other languages were wire recordings that Border had never got to translate or transcribe. There were people to interview and people to search for in the hope of interviewing them. In addition to Arch Sanasarian, at least two of Border's postgraduate students, two who had worked on the 'Adjective–Verb Quotient', Amy Muirden and the reputedly much-loved Wayne Rosenthal, were still alive. There might have been others too. Adam wasn't sure where the work was going to take him but there was no doubting that it was the bona fide work of a genuine historian and it was buoying him. If any of Border's interviewees were in Dachau when the war finished their transcripts might even mention being liberated by black American troops just as William McCray's friend from Boston had said. Nothing like this had been on the horizon when Diana had pulled shut the door to the Morningside Heights apartment that had been theirs.

So did he really want to phone his ex-student, the one who knew it was Gandhi, for a date? However one defines 'want', the feeling attaching itself to him right then was qualitatively different from the one that had engulfed him after Diana had – true, at his insistence – left him to stumble about alone in the apartment that Columbia University would sooner or later require for someone else's life.

'Should I call her?' Adam asked himself, sitting alone in the dark of his apartment.

*

'Welcome home, Dr Border,' Callie Ford said when opening the front door for Henry Border. It was 1946 and he had returned to his uptown Chicago home from Europe. He had to make several trips from the cab up the steps to the stoop and through the front door because he had a lot to carry. Not only was there his luggage to bring inside but also Marvin Cadden's wire recording device and all the wire recordings themselves.

'Dad!' Elise Border cried as she ran down the stairs to greet her father and throw her arms around him. The top of her head came to a little higher up his chest than it had before and it required only a slight bow from him to kiss her on her forehead. He closed his eyes. He was not the same man who had left.

He would teach just as he had before the trip to Europe, he would pay his bills and his taxes, he would smile and even joke, especially in the years to come with his students – the favourite ones, Arch Sanasarian, Amy Muirden, sometimes even Evie Harmon and especially Wayne Rosenthal, who would go on a few years later to research his thesis on the 'Adjective–Verb Quotient' from the transcripts he would make laboriously day after day, night after night from the wire recordings – but Henry Border had heard things on his trip to Europe that had shaken his core understanding of mankind. He had heard things that had happened to people, his own people, including some he had walked out on, which had left him with an enveloping guilt that would in a very short time take hold of him, grip him under each arm, reach over his shoulders and down his back and would never let go, a guilt that would clamp his heart a little at every single beat from that time on. There were siblings and cousins, aunts and uncles. There was Rosa, his wife, the woman he had abandoned in a fit of jealousy, abandoned and stolen her child. All of them gone.

'Dad! I thought you were *never* coming home,' Elise cried.

What else was there for him, apart from Elise, but to take the stories of the broken people in the DP camps and disseminate them as widely as possible? The world had to know what had happened to these people, not that, as he was to find out, anybody really wanted to know in those years immediately after the war. Driven, Henry Border was to work tirelessly, weekdays and weekends, day and night, listening and patiently transcribing and then translating every word, every nuance, every sound those wire recordings held. There was nothing else worth doing with his life and nothing more to live for but this and Elise. Fit of jealousy or not, act of cruelty or not, it could not be disputed that what he had done in leaving his wife was to save not merely himself but also his daughter. He had saved his daughter. Then why did he feel like a criminal, like an accomplice?

'Elly! My Elly!' He kissed his daughter again. Callie Ford saw that as he did this he had tears in his eyes. She heard the cab pull away. Henry Border was still gripping his daughter tightly when there was a slow creaking on the stairs. He looked up, still with moist eyes.

'Dr Border, sir, this is my son Russell. You come down here and shake Dr Border's hand.'

Callie, supported by Elise, then proceeded to recount to him the events that had first led her son Russell to stay in his house. She had been afraid to tell him but she realised she really had no choice. She could neither ask nor expect Elly to lie to her father about Russell. But she hadn't expected Elly to have the sway over her father she had nor to have the desire to exercise that sway so doggedly on Russell's behalf. Elly told him about a man called James Pearson who lived where Russell lived, at a place called the Mecca Flats on the south side, not too far from IIT. Elly had been there with Russell and Callie that first morning after Russell had arrived on the doorstep of her home. She hadn't been able to clear her mind of what she had seen there.

Elly would take her father there. Twelve and a half years old, she insisted both on taking him there and on not revealing her reasons until they were there. He had always found it hard to stop himself letting her know quite how precious she was to him. Now, only recently back from the DP camps of Europe, she was even more precious so, though he was at a loss to understand why she wanted to take him there in those first weeks back home when he would take hold of her suddenly and weep silently above her head, he said little but would have done much more for his daughter than travel the ten miles to 34th Street between State and Dearborn. He had seen the building nearly every day but never like this.

Elly showed him the hole in the pavement outside the front entrance that formed a tunnel where children crawled in and out as though life spent partially underground was normal. She showed him the broken tiles and the children running around with crazy eyes playing makeshift games that suddenly turned violent while up above on the third floor a small child casually urinated down at them through the cast iron grating. The smell was an assault to the uninitiated, especially in the warmer weather. A dog with garbage in its mouth was being chased by a gang of children. There were no towers with armed guards surrounding the Mecca, the malnutrition that the children tearing around the foyer screaming at one another suffered was subtle, and no one was being shipped off to be exterminated, but this was unequivocally a ghetto. It was the ghetto one got in a country pretending to be at peace with itself. Where did you put your slaves when you were no longer allowed to keep them? Henry Border knew a ghetto when he saw one. He had seen enough. They could go. 'No,' Elly Border insisted. He had to see more.

She took her father to the apartment she had visited, the one where James Pearson lived, where Callie and Russell lived. She remembered where it was and, determined that her father see the conditions in which they lived, she knocked on the door.

'Do you remember me, Mrs Sallie?' The old woman thought for a moment. She didn't remember the skinny white girl with the black eyes but since the girl knew her by name she pretended she did.

'Yes, child. Yes, I do.' Elly pushed past her on the pretext of looking for Callie and entered the apartment.

'She ain't here now, child. Who this man with you?' Mrs Sallie said, looking Henry Border up and down.

'This is my father, Mrs Sallie. Can he come in?' Elly beckoned to her father to follow her and as he entered, Mrs Sallie asked him, 'Have you met, met my friend?'

'Miss Callie Ford? Yes, I know her.'

'She doesn't mean Callie,' Elly explained.

'Have you met, met my friend, Jesus?'

The smell was almost unbearable to Henry Border. Mrs Sallie explained that neither Russell nor Callie was there, which Elly already knew. She looked at her father and could see her work was done.

This was the new chapter in the life of the shy motherless Jewish girl, a girl whose after-school world had until then been largely confined to her homework and to her books, that Henry Border had returned to. It starred Callie Ford and her son Russell and increasingly the man whose apparent disappearance had started it all, James Pearson, Mr Anything-You-Want. After that first night when Russell had arrived terrified from having witnessed what he had taken to be the abduction of James Pearson, Callie had let him stay in that spare room each night. At the end of a day at the packinghouse he returned to his mother and Elly at the Border home. Sometimes James Pearson was with him. Callie made dinner for the four of them and suddenly a makeshift and unlikely family emerged from disparate origins. A deep bond, begun in the Mecca Flats and cemented in the packinghouse, had developed between young Russell and James Pearson. Callie had always been taken by James Pearson's quiet manners but now in addition she felt a gratitude to him for caring for her son of a kind she had never again expected to experience after the death of her husband.

Russell had not needed James Pearson to accompany him to Sheridan Road, Uptown, and Callie knew that each of them well knew this. It became clear to her that this was a shy man's courting. James Pearson, who had independently taken a shine to her son to the extent of getting him a job and guiding him within its blood-soaked carcass-ridden floors, was now showing a gentle but committed interest in her. And it was all happening at the Borders' kitchen table where there sat a mother, a father figure, a son and a white Polish-born Jewish girl who lapped up the benefits of this impromptu family. She had never known anything like this.

Callie and Elly would talk about what they had done during the day and Russell and James Pearson would talk about the day's events at the packinghouse. All of a sudden, Elly Border was hearing talk of heading and splitting hogs, of characters like Tommy Parks and old Mrs Sallie back at the Mecca. Early on, she even heard what she was not supposed to hear, the story behind the late night visit of the two white men who had come to the Mecca the night Russell had fled to tell his mother what had happened to James Pearson. Those men had not taken him away to hurt him. They respected him; in fact, they had been trying to court him, all for something called a union. Whether or not it was going to be of any benefit to black folks, there was nothing to be afraid of, Russell had been told.

What does a union do? Elly Border asked Russell Ford, breaking an unusual silence one night when they were sharing the washing up. In answering her, he came to understand it himself.

It was into this world that Henry Border came home, returning from the DP camps of Europe, gatecrashing his own home. It was Elly who hatched the plan that would solidify and codify the radical change that had come about naturally during Border's absence. Callie and Russell would live with them, each with their own rent-free room. Callie would continue as a permanent live-in housekeeper and save the rent she had paid for their room at the Mecca. Russell would take the 'L' in time to go to work with James Pearson who would continue to come calling the ten miles to Sheridan Road. And of course, Callie remained wonderful to and for Henry Border's daughter. Essentially it was only this that really mattered to him.

A man who valued his privacy, now that he had two new people living with him, one a teenage boy, surely he should charge them rent? The thought didn't occur to him. Elly was growing into her womanhood every day and now there was a strange young man, almost fifteen, who worked at a meat works downtown, living, showering and sleeping a few doors away and under the same roof as his daughter. They went for walks together. She was going out downtown with him, Callie and James Pearson at weekends. Where exactly were they going? What exactly were they doing? Should he have been concerned? Elly was happier than he could remember. She came home safely and on time and when school started again she showed no sign of any diminution of interest in her school work. She was coming out of herself. Whatever qualms he might have had should these changes have been put to him in prospect at any time before his recent trip to the DP camps of Europe, Henry Border now gave the appearance of letting life wash over him. It was not that he was carefree. Rather, he cared now about only one thing. If his daughter was safe and not unhappy it would leave him completely free to concentrate on getting the story out. If anything, these changes helped him with his work. With the wire recorder stopping and starting he took down every word, every syllable. The house was often empty leaving Border free to work on the transcripts, the first eight of which became the book *I Did Not Interview the Dead*. It would take him years to find a publisher.

'Can I get you something, Dr Border?' Callie Ford asked late one night as he sat under a desk lamp in his study surrounded by wire spools. What was he doing till late at night, every night, so intently? What were those wire recordings that he sat listening to night after night, stopping and starting, playing and replaying? She looked at this ageing man. He looked right back at her as if he didn't know she was there. She wondered if perhaps *he* was not quite all there. She hadn't really known him before he went to Europe but it looked to her as though part of him was still there. What had he seen there?

*

At the very end of the day Lamont Williams walked into the ninth floor room of the Memorial Sloan-Kettering Cancer Center occupied by the old patient he regularly visited. His visits had lately been less frequent and the old man was unable to leave this uncommented on as soon as Lamont had sat down.

'You don't come now so much, Mr Lamont,' and then seeing the bandage around Lamont's hand, he asked, 'Is it because of your hand? What is it with your hand?'

'It's nothin' really. Just hurt it doin' the extra duties. That's why I haven't been around so much. It's the extra duties.'

'The extra duties . . . well, it's bad that you got hurt from them but it's good that now you have them. Yes?'

'Yeah, it's good.'

'What are they, the extra duties?'

'Well, it's to do with waste disposal. They got me –'

'You already are collecting garbage. This is how I met you. They give you more to collect and call it "extra duties"?'

'No, no, they're teaching me how to work the incinerator; huge incinerator gets rid of toxic waste, all sorts of things. You don't want to know.'

'I already know.'

'I don't get you.'

'The incinerator, it's an oven, yes?'

'Yeah, huge oven. They make us wear protective clothing. Dirty work but . . . you know . . . kinda interesting, I guess.'

'I used to work with an oven . . . in the Birkenau section of Auschwitz-Birkenau, where a Frenchman gave me this,' Mr Mandelbrot said, indicating the tattoo on his left arm. 'I told him, "Small, I want it small as you can make it." One, Eight, One, Nine, Seven, Zero. That was the number what I got when I came to Auschwitz.'

'When was this?'

'Mr Lamont, you're supposed to remember these things. I won't be here forever. I won't be here in a couple of days.'

'What do you mean? Don't talk like that!'

'They letting me go back to Long Island.'

'Back home?'

'Yes. Either I'm better or I'm very sick and soon to be dying. I don't know which but it doesn't matter. Dr Washington's keeping it to herself. You see, if you knew her better . . . One, Eight, One, Nine, Seven, Zero. I got it in April 1944. You need to remember. They put us – you remember I came with eleven other Jews?'

'From Sosnowiec, you came in a truck. You hit a man to get clothes that fit you.'

Mr Mandelbrot smiled. 'Yes, you remember. It was April 1944. I was almost four weeks in Quarantine. That's where I saw my first *Muselmann*. You know what that is?'

'No.'

'It's a person what is finished with life before life is finished with him. They live because their bodies haven't died yet. They are skeletons but they still move. They move, they're hungry all the time like an animal but otherwise they are dead. I saw them and I promised myself I would not become one of them. But it's easier said than what it is done. These *Muselmänner* didn't want to become *Muselmänner* when they got to Auschwitz. Four weeks in Quarantine in Auschwitz. I thought I'd seen everything what a man could see. I was wrong. My education was only beginning.

347

'Twelve Jews got off the truck with me and went to the *Bekleidungs-kammer* where they stored the clothes. After maybe four weeks three of us were chosen for the real education. We were the strongest three. Do you know what is the *Sonderkommando*?'

'No.'

'The *Sonderkommando* was the work detail what worked the gas chambers and ovens in the crematoria. I was in the *Sonderkommando*. I'll tell you about it and you'll see why it doesn't matter what Dr Washington says about why I go home.'

*

Birkenau, by far the largest of the component camps that made up Auschwitz *Vernichtungslager*, extermination camp, lay between two rivers. All around were scattered birch trees that, nourished as they always had been by the sun and watered by the rain, endured wind, frost, snow in the winter, scorching heat in the summer and everything else there was to endure in an upper Silesian Polish swamp. Day after day, month after month, year after year, they grew taller and saw everything that went on but, like all trees, they could not speak, not one word. Other than that, nothing about this place was like anywhere else on earth.

Henryk Mandelbrot's first day in the *Sonderkommando* came at night. Nothing, not even the ghetto, could have prepared him for this, and for the rest of his life each day for him would be without the sun. In the middle of the night he and two other Jews who had arrived with him on the same truck and had also been previously selected were summoned to report urgently to the *Sonderkommando*, the 'Special Unit'. They had been chosen on the basis of their apparent physical strength. Henryk Mandelbrot hadn't heard of the *Sonderkommando* and had no idea what it was. He and the two others were taken hastily to a barrack by two SS men where the next of three shifts of *Sonderkommando* were getting ready to start their shift. The barrack was filled with men, all busily getting dressed; Polish, Dutch, Greek and French. All apart from a handful of high-ranking German prisoners, *Kapos*, were Jews. Henryk Mandelbrot saw that none of these men was talking. They were just putting on their clothes. The three new men stood among the others not knowing what to do and Henryk Mandelbrot asked a man who was busily getting ready for work, 'We're supposed to join you. What do you do?'

'You've come to burn bodies.'

One of the two SS guards who had brought them to this barrack came inside and told them that since they were already dressed they could start ahead of the others.

'What do we do?' Henryk Mandelbrot asked.

'You look pretty strong for a Jew. Come on, I'll show you. All of you come with me. Hurry! You've got a lot of work to do.'

Henryk Mandelbrot and the other two Jews who had arrived with him followed the SS guard. Joined outside by the second SS guard they were taken to what they would learn was Crematorium V. It had its own gas chamber and outside the gas chamber there lay a mountain of bodies. Mandelbrot shuddered momentarily. So it was true, and here he was, face-to-face with the truth. He had seen people die in the ghetto but he had never seen anything like this. So many bodies, inert, stacked hurriedly one on top of the other, a vast hill of them, a small mountain, so recently people. Here, Mandelbrot thought, was the end of every slur, racial or religious, every joke, every sneer directed against the Jews. Every time someone harboured the belief, or just the sneaking suspicion, even when it shamed them, that the Jews, as a people, are dishonest and immoral, that they are avaricious, deceitful, cunning, that they are capitalists, that they are communists, that they are responsible for all the troubles in the world, that they are guilty of deicide, that belief or suspicion, sometimes barely conscious, adds momentum to a train on a journey of its own; this is where the line finally ends, at this mountain of corpses. The prejudices, the unfounded states of mind, that grow from wariness to dislike to hatred of the 'other', they all lead to where Henryk Mandelbrot now stood.

This was his first shift, his first day on the job, but it was the middle of the night. Suddenly it was neither day nor night for him but some new time he had never experienced. If day followed night there would be an end to it as there was for other jobs but there had never been a job like this, not ever. Seeing the mountain of corpses that waited for him, Mandelbrot knew that *day*, as he had known it, had ended forever. It had ended not just for him but also for the world.

He had heard the rumours but this was far worse than the rumours.

'What is this?'

'This is you if you don't get to work. The others are coming but you're already dressed so you can start now.'

'But . . . what?'

'Look, Jew, I can shoot you and throw you on the heap and get another one or you can start work and stop asking questions.'

'But what do we do?'

'What do you think? The three of you are to start dragging the pieces to the pits over there. Welcome to the *Sonderkommando*. Start now or I'm taking aim. Tell me you understand?' he said, lifting his rifle.

'I understand.'

'Okay, start now. We're getting very behind. I'm watching you. Move! Move!'

Henryk Mandelbrot bent down to pick up his first body. The floodlights shone down from the towers. In the middle distance dogs were barking at the next transport of Jews, which had already arrived; a fresh trainload of people to be converted into corpses as soon as the system could process them. Terrified, bewildered, thirsty, exhausted, dirty, unsteady on their feet, and with the dogs leaping and barking at them, they stumbled and fell out of the cattle cars they had been packed in for days. It sounded to Henryk Mandelbrot, still with a rifle trained at him, not like the barking of a pack of dogs but like the barking of all the dogs of Europe.

Transports were being unloaded inside the camp for the first time that very month instead of at the *Judenrampe* outside, the rail line extension inside the camp having just been completed in time to facilitate the extermination of the Jews of Hungary. But now the crematoria were unable to cope with so many bodies quickly enough and, to take the pressure off them, pits had to be dug and the corpses burned in these. It was to the extra labour that had to be found to boost each shift of the *Sonderkommando* that Mandelbrot and his two companions had been assigned.

'Move!' the SS man shouted above the sound of dogs and the terror of the transport being unloaded in the middle distance. Mandelbrot heard the exhausted Jews getting off the train and he saw the mountain of corpses. He knew the two were separated by an hour or two at the most.

For all his revulsion, he had to move quickly because the guard still had his rifle trained on him. The first corpse he touched from the top of the mound belonged to a child, a girl of no more than ten. His two companions saw him and went for bodies next to the dead girl. The corpse Mandelbrot reached for should have been easy to drag. The child had been starved and there was nothing of her. But when he picked up her hand he couldn't get a grip of her. The girl's skin was coming off in his hand. He reached further up her arm as the guard watched but her skin was coming off from her upper arm too. It was like nothing he had ever experienced. These bodies had been lying there for hours. They'd been gassed and the previous shift had been unable to get them through the crematorium because the ovens couldn't cope. There were just too many bodies to get through in the time allowed and they kept coming. The previous shift had had to leave them there for the next shift and the first members of the next shift were the three new prisoners who had never worked a single shift, one of whom was Henryk Mandelbrot.

Seeing the flesh come off in their hands, the SS guard said almost by way of explanation, 'That's not how they're usually stored. But you better figure something out. I want them moved. Now!'

Henryk Mandelbrot saw where the victims' clothes were waiting to be sent to *Kanada* where the murdered Jews' property was stored and he walked over to the heap with the guard still watching him. He picked up a shirt from within the pile and tore it into a long strip out of which he fashioned a crude rope. He walked back with it, intending to slip it around the girl's body to better drag her. When he bent down to lift the girl's head with one hand he inadvertently pressed down on her chest with the other, leaning on her slightly and causing a profusion of human gases to come out of her, startling him, arousing fresh revulsion in him and causing the guard to let out a little laugh. With the cloth rope partially around her he stood back upright and began to drag the girl. The other two Jews hurriedly went to get strips of cloth to do the same. But in their fear they went too quickly to observe the full effect of Mandelbrot's experiment. It had barely made any difference. After a few paces friction was causing the parts of the body in contact with the ground to detach from the rest of it. The girl's body was coming away in pieces as he tried to pull it. They were never going to get this hill of corpses to the pit this way. Then Henryk Mandelbrot remembered something he'd seen in his father's butcher shop. He got a bucket and filled it with water, splashed some of the water on the young girl's body and the rest of it along the ground that was to be his path to the pit. This worked. Now she would slide.

'This Jew's strong *and* clever,' said the first SS man to the second. 'He'll make a good recruit.' Then as Henryk Mandelbrot made his way towards the vast open pits with the bucket in one hand and the girl's corpse dragging under the crudely fashioned rope, the SS man called out to him, 'You'll do well here.'

part nine

'LAST NIGHT THERE WAS A MASSACRE outside the brush-maker's shop. Who has heard about it? Anyone?'

Emanuel Ringelblum asked this question to the assembly of carefully chosen people seated around the crowded front room, some on chairs, and some on the floor. The door behind them in the second-storey flat on Leszno Street was closed. On the staircase side of the door a teenage boy, Nahum Grzywacz, was keeping watch. This was a meeting of a clandestine organisation. A few people had already heard about the massacre outside the brush-maker's shop. Someone from inside the room would be assigned the task of finding witnesses. They were to learn and record as much as they could.

It was 1942 and the walls of the Warsaw ghetto had been sealed since November 1940. A third of Warsaw's pre-war population, its Jews, had been forced into two and a half per cent of the city's area and then, as the months went on, more and more Jews from all over Poland were added to their number. Hunger was everywhere. While the weather could perhaps be temporarily kept out of a room, even a damp mouldy room within a crumbling building, poor, dilapidated to begin with and made worse by the aerial bombing that accompanied the German invasion of Poland, the sharp, piercing, cunning, relentless hunger followed you into the room. If you had a blanket, it found you under your blanket. If you went to sleep, it went there with you. And when you woke up it was there first thing, even before you knew where you were. Before you knew who you were, you knew only that you were hungry. If you could not sleep it was there anyway, eating you, eating away at whatever was left inside you, eating the core of you, your hope and your cells. You might try to not think of the pain but you can't. It laughs. It wins every time. This was how you knew you weren't dead. You were hungry.

Everyone was always hungry. The poorer you were, the hungrier you were, and with the hunger came weakness and irritability. It became difficult to think clearly and you needed to think clearly to work out how to survive the next day, how to get food. You were sure you could still work if you could find work, and you could look for it if only you could eat. But how were you going to get food, for yourself, for your children, for your wife or husband, for your parents? There were simply too many people within those walls for the calories that were let in. How were you to get food when there just wasn't enough of it? What were you going to have to do? With hunger of this severity came fatigue, a weakness that transcended tiredness and permeated your sinews and bones. As your limbs got ever lighter, they felt progressively heavier with each new day.

With so many hundreds of thousands of people so hungry, so weak, desperately pressed up next to each other, disease swam about the population with reckless abandon, lethal and unchecked. Disease licked your face like a dog unrestrained. Here is a lick from dysentery. From around the corner comes a kiss on the lips and then into your mouth from typhus. Tuberculosis lusts after you insatiably. Too weak to resist, you are burning up as the marriage is consummated right there on the street. You lie there on the ground, unrecognisable, a nuisance to those still able to make their way to the soup kitchen. Will someone notice your absence there today? They might. You will never know. But you do know what's going on over there. They all have a fever of their own. It holds their gaze and whispers to them in voices unheard and unheard of outside the ghetto. They are not them and you are not you. Is that you, friendless? Is that you, dying? Is that you, naked in the filth of a grey city street? Among the slowly dying, new thieves are born every day. When did you last speak to anybody, who did you still know who might bury you once your clothes have been stolen?

In the middle of all of this, Emanuel Ringelblum had set up an underground organisation, a group that numbered variously between fifty and sixty people chosen from the ranks of historians, teachers, journalists, economists and other intellectuals, business people, political activists of various hues, administrators, and leaders of youth groups. He chose them carefully and vetted them over time on their quality and aptitude for the work. Their task was to collect, document and preserve a record of what was happening to the Jews of Warsaw and of Poland generally. He had begun recording his observations when the war started but by 1940 he had realised that the scope of the task he envisaged was way beyond that which any one person, no matter how dedicated, could hope to achieve on his own and that was why he had established his *Oneg Shabbas*, a group dedicated to recording the torment of a once-bustling civilisation that had existed precariously there within another civilisation for a thousand years. When, on his own, he had first begun recording the life of Jewish Warsaw under Nazi occupation his aim had been to spread word of what was happening in the hope of persuading the outside world to intervene. But now it was 1942 and it had long been apparent to Emanuel Ringleblum that no historian had ever undertaken a more futile task. The community he knew, the people he saw, the once dynamic, vibrant, seemingly inexhaustible world he was trying to record and save, was vanishing. Any day now it would be completely gone and there would be nobody left to save. He knew that. All he could still try to do, against all odds, was to save their memory.

Some members of his clandestine *Oneg Shabbas* group were charged with interviewing people; people from the streets, the shops and the work details. They interviewed nurses, housewives, smugglers who risked their lives to bring food from outside the ghetto walls, undertakers, artisans reduced to begging, former factory workers, the people who ran the soup kitchens and the people from within the hungry tens and tens of thousands who patronised them, everybody. Other members, better known from before the war for their writing skills, were to write their own accounts of what they saw, what they heard, what they had been told and what they felt. Some *Oneg Shabbas* members were dedicated solely to the transcription and copying of documents. At a meeting of the group's Executive Committee Emanuel Ringelblum asked who knew about the previous night's massacre outside the brush-maker's shop.

'Cecilya, tomorrow you should go and talk to Czerniakow.'

'Emanuel, he'll tell me –'

'I know he'll tell you that he's the Chairman of the Jewish Council and that among many other things he's trying to organise soup for over 100,000 people, many of whom will die that day if they don't get it. He'll tell you this and your problem will be that it's completely true. You can't argue with that. But when they die, there will be no way of telling the world they had even existed if we don't bother him.'

'But Emanuel –'

'Cecilya, don't be afraid of him.'

'But Emanuel –'

'Cecilya, he *will* be annoyed at first. Be ready for that. But you will very quickly have him eating out of your hand. Listen, I saw something yesterday that's remarkable even for here. It involves Czerniakow and when you raise it with him I guarantee that he will stop what he's doing and tell you about it.'

'What did you see?'

'Last night I saw him walking a way ahead of me on Grzybowska Street back towards his office. He must have forgotten something. When he got to the doorway of the building he stepped over something without giving it much thought. Perhaps, unconsciously, he registered the obstacle in the pavement as a corpse but one gets so accustomed to stepping over nameless corpses on the street . . . anyway, perhaps his mind was elsewhere. He definitely stepped *over* the obstruction, not *on* it, but his mind must've been somewhere else because he didn't really examine what it was. He just stepped over it. I saw this myself. He stood outside the building for a moment fumbling in his coat pocket for something when suddenly the pile of broken wooden crating at his feet burst open and in the half-light of the street a small boy, perhaps eight years old, stood up. The boy, clearly starving, was completely naked. Czerniakow was startled. He lost his composure and he screamed in shock. It must have seemed like some kind of apparition to him.

'The boy kicked at the crating beside him with one foot and another boy, about the same age and also completely naked, got out of it and stood up. Both small boys then started to remonstrate with Czerniakow, albeit addressing him respectfully, as Mr Czerniakow. They knew he was the Chairman of the *Judenrat*, but they weren't at all fazed by that. They'd been waiting for him and were complaining about the food rations. They were orphans. They said they were the last of their families and they tugged on Czerniakow's coat. 'We've been waiting for you! Are you going to let us die also, Mr Czerniakow?'

'What did he do?'

'They were covered in dirt and excrement and God knows what else but Czerniakow knelt down to look at them, to look them in the eye. He took these two skeletons in his arms. He said something I wasn't able to hear and then he began to sob quite uncontrollably. Really, Czerniakow . . . I saw this. Then he took them into the building. Go there tomorrow and ask him about it. You can tell him it was me that saw it. Tell him I sent you there. I don't care. If he won't write his own account of this for you then get him to dictate it. I'll bet you two things: no matter how busy he is, he will quickly become acquiescent when you tell him what you know of this. He knows what we're doing here.'

'What's the other thing?' Cecilya Slepak asked.

'The wood those boys had used to hide themselves, even if you leave for Grzybowska Street right now, it won't be there when you get there.'

'Who's covering the soup kitchen?' Eliyahu Gutkowski asked. But before anyone could answer there was a knock at the door. Nobody said anything as Emanuel Ringelblum stood up and walked to the door. He opened it partially to see the young watchman, Nahum Grzywacz, standing next to Rosa Rabinowicz, the deserted wife of Henry Border.

'She told me to knock,' the boy, instantly ashamed for blaming her, blurted out by way of explanation. He liked Rosa and would normally have cut many corners for her. He had stolen for her, delivered smuggled food to her and had even fantasised about her but to interrupt the meeting might have been going too far.

'It's all right, Nahum. Rosa, you don't need to knock. Just come in.'

She was out of breath. 'I'm sorry I'm late but –'

'Are you all right?'

'Yes but –'

'Then just come in.'

'No, before I do I need to tell you something that I wasn't sure I should say in public, I mean not even in front of the Executive Committee.'

'Rosa, can't it wait?'

'Please forgive me if it can, but I'm not sure it can.'

'Nahum, go inside and tell them everything is all right but that I need a couple of minutes to attend to something. Then wait inside for me to come back in,' Ringelblum told him.

Once they were alone Rosa proceeded to tell her story. 'A smuggler brought a man into the ghetto just now.'

'Somebody wanted to get *into* the ghetto! What kind of man could *he* be?'

'He's a Jew,' said Rosa, still out of breath. 'He says his name is Jacob Grojanowski from the shtetl of Izbica. He said it's near Lublin. But he hasn't come from there now. He says he's escaped from a camp where he was working as a grave digger.'

'Rosa, I have to get back inside. You can take down his story but . . . Surely this can wait.'

'No, no, it can't. He's in hiding now with some people who know me and they stopped me on my way to the meeting. They told me his story. I don't know why they chose me to tell. I swear I haven't mentioned a thing about our work here but . . . Anyway this man, Grojanowski . . . He wants to see Czerniakow but when I heard his story . . . well, I thought you should know everything as soon as possible. Even before Czerniakow.

'He says that at the camp he was in the Germans aren't working the Jews at all. Instead they take them in groups of sixty or so and they put them in hermetically sealed trucks. Then they drive the trucks into the forest. The exhaust from the trucks is channelled back into the sealed part and the Jews are gassed.'

'They're gassed?'

'That's what he said. He was working there as a grave digger. He saw everything.'

'What's the name of this camp?'

'Chelmno.'

Emmanuel Ringelblum cut short that evening's *Oneg Shabbas* Executive Committee meeting and that night, with the assistance of Rosa Rabinowicz, he learned from a witness that, when taken away from the various ghettoes around Poland, the Jews were not being resettled and sent to labour details but were being gassed. At least, this was what was happening at a camp called Chelmno. Immediately a document was prepared in various languages and smuggled out of the ghetto so that the world might know what he and Rosa and then the Executive Committee now knew.

Sometime in early August 1942 a member of Emanuel Ringelblum's *Oneg Shabbas* group, a man called Israel Lichtenstein, summoned two of its youngest members, the young man, Nahum Grzywacz, who had kept watch the night the Executive Committee had learned of the gassings at Chelmno, and another young man, the nineteen-year-old David Graber. Ringelblum had entrusted no one but Lichtenstein with the task of burying the *Oneg Shabbas* archives and the older man took the two younger men to Number 68 Nowolipki Street. There in the height of summer the three of them dug and dug as far into the earth as their strength, their tools and their courage permitted, fuelled by the belief that they had in their safekeeping the last, most comprehensive record of the soon-to-be entirely obliterated Jews of Europe. There at Number 68 Nowolipki Street, a building that had once been a school, they buried the two giant milk cans and several tin boxes whose contents comprised the first part of the *Oneg Shabbas* archives of the historian Emanuel Ringelblum.

It took them two days, and before they had finished, before they had filled in the hole, a tomb for the last words in the thousand-year history of the Jews of Poland, they each added a brief personal autobiographical note. The last to finish his note was Nahum Grzywacz who apologised to the future reader for the poor quality of his handwriting, explaining that his family was poor so he hadn't had much education. He wrote furiously not merely because they were all in a hurry to accomplish their task but because he had recently heard that both of his parents had just been taken away and he needed to get back to check on the veracity of the report. This was the scene on 3 August 1942 on Nowolipki Street inside the Warsaw ghetto. By then Rosa Rabinowicz, mother of Elise Border of Chicago, had not been seen by any of the few remaining members of the Executive Committee for some time. Since her body had not been found in any of the places she used to frequent, it was suspected by some of those remaining who knew her that perhaps she had left the ghetto. But in that place at that time dead bodies went missing too. So perhaps she had died after all. Who could be sure? And who could be sure to remember to give it any thought?

Young Nahum Grzywacz, who had always thought she was pretty and had many times taken comfort from her kindnesses, liked her very much and had often thought of her when he was alone in the corner of a room he shared with his parents, sisters and two other families. But even he had not thought of her in a while and was not thinking of her at all as, at 68 Nowolipki Street, within earshot of a man pleading then screaming amid a blur of bullets, in a shaky hand he wrote his last sentence for a reader he would never meet. And then along with the leavings of a people's thousand-year history, he buried it. The earth weighed heavy on all the words, including this young man's plea to the reader: 'Remember, my name is Nahum Grzywacz.'

*

The secretary, receptionist, personal assistant or whatever she was to Charles McCray had gone to the bathroom leaving Charles' father, William, alone and unguarded. Seeing that the gatekeeper was not there and that neither was his son, William McCray took the liberty of going into his son's office uninvited. He looked around, picked up some journals, flicked through them but could not get interested. His mind would not be calmed. He was too upset. He sat down in a chair opposite his son's desk chair and waited.

The day before, someone had left a noose hanging on the door of a black professor from Columbia University's Teachers College. The professor, a woman who hailed from a disadvantaged southern background, now a professor of psychology and education, was known for her particular interest in the psychological effects of racism on victims. Now she was a victim of it herself. The targeting of this woman in particular, with her professional interest, and in multicultural, liberal, ethnically diverse New York, at Columbia University of all places, in William's own neighbourhood, filled him with a mixture of fury and sadness, impotence, fear and despair at what he was tempted to see as the futility of his life's work. He hadn't been able to sleep since he had read about the incident in the *Times*; in fact, it had been all he had been able to think about. Startled by his son when he got back to his office, it never occurred to William how affected Charles might be by the incident, how hard it had been for him not to rage at people around campus for what he felt was their collective failure to learn anything from history.

'This isn't Money, Mississippi, in the fifties! This is New York in the twenty-first century. This is a university. This is Columbia University. What the hell is happening here? One moment you got Jim Gilchrist and the Minutemen coming out here stirring up hate against illegal immigrants, that is until your students restore order with a riot. Then Bollinger invites Ahmadinejad to come up here and say the Holocaust didn't happen but it's okay, there's no need to panic 'cause he's going to make his own Holocaust for the Jews in the twenty-first century. Then your good President Bollinger thinks he can redeem himself by getting up on stage and publicly ridiculing Ahmadinejad in order to be everyone's new favourite superhero. How pathetic. How shamefully pathetic. Then I saw you got some good old-fashioned anti-Semitism going on over in Lewisohn Hall. Someone's gone over there and drawn a swastika next to a caricature of a Jew in a yarmulke and now, yesterday I read about this. A noose is found hanging on the door of a black professor's office over at the Teachers College. I've seen a lot in my time, you know I have. But when it comes out of the blue in a place like *this* . . . This is *your* university. This is where you work. What in God's name is going on here?'

'Dad, what can I say?'

'I don't know, Charlie, what can you say?'

'The university's a microcosm of society.'

'Is that what you can say? Is that *all* you can say?'

'Well now what exactly are *you* saying? How exactly is all or even any of this my fault?'

'Charlie, I don't mean you personally. I'm mean you academics. You all sit there watching the flames as the barn burns down crying, "How's this *our* fault? We didn't do it!"'

'What exactly would you have us do, me or any of us?'

'Charlie, how did you get to be this age, sitting in this office with your name and title on the door, Chair of the History Department, and you're not ashamed to be asking me that?'

'Dad, leaving the question of my shame to one side, what the hell *would* you have me do?'

'You should be speaking out publicly about these things. You guys should be writing letters. You should be organising like-minded people to do these things. You should be giving encouragement, comfort and support to those people, students, faculty, people around the city who don't have the chance to be heard like you do but who fear this institution is going to hell in a hand basket instead of . . .'

'Instead of what?'

'Instead of staying back late in this office leaving your wife and daughter at home so you can write narrowly focused arcane academic articles to be read by a handful of people just to keep your quota up and all of it merely in the service of your own aggrandisement.'

What does a good son do when the man you've most admired, the man who is responsible for all that you've ever felt was good about you, the man who has fought injustice all of his life, berates you for not actively protesting against the contemporary state of the world, which he views with ever-increasing powerlessness and horror? When this dear man, who has only you left in the world, is so eloquently delineating just how fully you've failed him, when his version of your fundamental failings are coming at you like a torrent downhill, what do you do?

If in doubt, keep quiet. There's a rule for you, probably one he taught you. Don't speak in anger lest you say something you might regret, something he'll never let you take back. If in doubt, keep quiet. Hold your tongue even if he takes your silence as proof that he's right. After all, in keeping quiet and letting him hurt you, in loving him and wanting to protect him even against your own anger, are you not the very essence of the man he wants you to be even if he doesn't realise it?

So Charles McCray let his father speak. He didn't hurry him, he barely argued with him. But now it was late. William said he was too tired to come over to have dinner with his daughter-in-law and his granddaughter so Charles walked him home. He told Charles once again that Charles was the canary in the coalmine. He hugged him, which was how they always parted, and then the canary walked home.

The keys being turned in the door of the house where the son lived made a series of clicking sounds. These sounds once signalled that a father, a husband, had come home and a wife and a daughter would acknowledge it with a greeting. The sounds were the same in the door as they ever were. He closed the door quietly and put the keys in his pocket. He was late. Should he explain then or later? Now all three people who lived there were home. Nobody called out to greet him. A copy of *The New York Times* lay open on the kitchen table. Charles McCray, Chair of the History Department at Columbia University, the good son, just not always good enough, the good husband seemingly a little deficient here too, the canary in the coalmine, stood alone in his kitchen, briefcase in hand. For a moment he didn't know what to do. You cannot demand that someone greets you when you come home. He looked down at the newspaper and, still standing, started to read. The headline always calls first: 'Turks Angry Over House Armenian Genocide Vote. Turkey reacted angrily Thursday to a House committee vote in Washington to condemn as genocide the mass killings of Armenians in Turkey that began during World War I . . . The Bush administration . . . vowed to try to defeat the resolution on Capitol Hill.'

He looked over towards the telephone and saw the pen and a notepad he and Michelle kept there. They had always, since they started living together, kept a pen and paper near the phone for messages and shopping lists. Two educated, responsible people with similar values and aspirations had married and were raising a daughter. He had always thought they made quite a team. But a team is not a couple. He kept reading. 'President Bush's chief spokeswoman, Dana Perino, said, "We have national security concerns, and many of our troops and supplies go through Turkey."' Charles McCray reached for the pen and paper and, still with his coat on, he sat down at the kitchen table. You cannot demand that someone greets you when you come home, not your wife, not your daughter. Maybe they hadn't heard him come in. 'In Turkey, there was widespread expectation that the House committee vote and any further steps would damage relations between the countries.' Leaning on the newspaper he began to compose a note to the professor from Columbia University's Teachers College who had two days earlier had a noose left hanging from her door. Maybe someone would need something from the kitchen and see him there.

*

James Pearson, Mr Anything-You-Want, had a story for Tommy Parks, the meatpacker who lived in a room in the same apartment as Pearson at the Mecca Flats, the same apartment that Callie and Russell Ford had shared before they moved to the Borders' Uptown house. It was the story of the events of the night the two white men appeared from nowhere looking specifically for him. These men, Ralph Hellerstein and Herb Marks, were union men. They had accurately predicted the dismissal of James Pearson's colleague, Billy Moore, when Billy Moore had become unable to hide a soft tissue injury in his back. They had invited James Pearson to join them on the Packinghouse Workers Organising Committee.

'You don't want no trouble? You stay the hell away from them white unions. They got some shit goin' on but they won't be tellin' you nothin' 'bout it. Anyways, whatever shit they up to, it don't mean *you* no good,' Tommy Parks advised Pearson as the two of them drank a beer late one night on the broken steps outside the Mecca Flats.

'But they asked me to join 'em, not just the union but the Organising Committee.'

'Join 'em?'

'On the Packinghouse Workers Organising Committee.'

'What that mean?'

'It mean I be the same as them.'

'Same as them?' Tommy Parks laughed. 'You the same as them, how come you ain't getting them two white boys join you and a group o' black men on the Packinghouse Workers Organising Committee?'

''Cause they already started it.'

'Yeah and they started it for themselves.'

'Well, why ever they started it, now they askin' me to join. Ain't no rank and file thing, they askin' me to join the Organising Committee.'

'You ask some of them old boys. They tell how them unions do for the black man back in the day. It were more an' twenty year ago but ain't none of 'em there forget it.'

'What happened?'

'There's union trouble so the meatworks go and hire a whole lot of black folks.'

'What do you mean "union trouble"?'

'You know, the usual, union lookin' for higher wages as they do. Meatworks flat refused as *they* do. So the union go on strike and the meatworks go and hire a whole lot of black folks. Negro men come up from the south, bring their wives, children and all, for the best job they ever had 'cause ain't no white man want it. Then the union say we stealin' their jobs. Lot of black folks' blood spilt before the meatworks and the union reach a deal and the black man left with his wounds and not a pot to piss in. Bunch of Polaks and Irishmen do real good out of it. That's the union you want to join.'

'Yeah, but that's the difference between the twenties and now. These men tell me they want black men in the union so they won't be workin' for just the Polaks and the Irishmen no more.'

Tommy Parks smiled and slowly shook his head. 'Man, I took you smarter 'n that, I really did. Can you see all them Polaks and all them Irishmen workin' for *you*? You be their nigger. You be their union nigger. Now how that feel, "Mister Anything-You-Want" union nigger?'

'Tommy, we just talkin', right? Now I ain't sayin' I'm smart or nothin'. But I'm smarter 'n you if you don't think maybe, just maybe I seen that possibility and I searched 'em out on it.'

'Yeah? How you do that?'

'They say they want a united union, black and white, all together, all equal. That's why they ask me to join the Organising Committee.'

'James Pearson! They got you dreamin' of no place ever been on earth. They give you a fancy title, put you on the "Organising Committee" and you think you died and gone to heaven. Maybe they even want coloured workers to join. Maybe they do. So what if they do? They ain't interested in the problems of a black man. They don't even *know* the problems of a black man.'

James Pearson took another sip from his bottle. Then he smiled. 'Tommy, you be surprised what they know.'

'I be surprised!'

James Pearson turned to face him. 'You know 'bout the stars?'

'The stars? What you talkin' 'bout?'

'Ever wonder how when things get slow and the foreman gotta lay off people, he call out their name?'

'Yeah, I seen it.'

'They all Negro men.'

'I know that.'

'Yeah, but how the foreman know whose name to call? He don't know everyone by their name. Too many there for that.'

'What you talkin' 'bout?'

'Each and every man at the plant got a time card.'

'I know that.'

'The time card of every Negro worker got a little star on it, a little black mark. It tell the foreman who's who.'

'The union men tell you that?'

'Yes, they did. They say if I join and if we can get enough black men to join, their first campaign be the removal of that black star off of every Negro worker's time card.'

'The whole union going to fight for that?'

'That's what they say . . . if we can get enough black men to join.'

'Well, they good talkers, I give you that,' Tommy Parks said, lighting up a cigarette.

'That all you give me?'

'You starting with me, ain't you? Jesus, boy! If you don't have a hide

366

and a half! Get me talkin' just so I agree every week to give a cracker-ass union some of my pay. How dumb you think I am?' Tommy Parks laughed.

'Don't blame me; I know how dumb you are. It's them union boys, they got no idea how dumb you are, much as I told 'em.'

'What you told 'em?'

'I told 'em you don't give a shit 'bout no one but your own self.'

'Wait a minute; this thing ain't got nothin' to do with me –'

'I told 'em you squirm every single way God made just to get out of doin' one thing for someone else, even for your fellow Negro meat-packer.'

'Don't put this shit on me, nigger. You let them sell you shit and all of a sudden I'm the bad guy.'

'No, you the fool, Tommy. I told 'em that. But they want to meet you anyway. Insist on it.'

'They want to meet *me?*'

'They know how folks round here like you, here *and* at the plant. They want *you* to join the Packinghouse Workers Organising Committee. They want you to join with me.'

A meeting was arranged. Tommy Parks was to be meeting Ralph Hellerstein and his younger offsider, Herb Marks, at Goldblatt's Discount Store at the corner of 47th Street and Ashland Avenue. But given that it was still daylight, Hellerstein reconsidered his original choice of meeting place and later thought it wise to change the venue to the union hall at 48th Street and Marshfield Avenue, a mere five- to ten-minute walk from Goldblatt's. He had tried to get a message through to Tommy Parks during the day but wasn't sure Parks had got it. He talked it over with James Pearson later that day and Pearson had volunteered to meet Parks at Goldblatt's, give him the message and walk with him to the union hall.

James Pearson, who had finished his shift and had young Russell Ford with him, was having his own second thoughts about the change of venue. It was not that it was so far from the original meeting place but in a way it might as well have been. The half-mile walk from Goldblatt's Discount Store to the corner of 48th and Marshfield would put them in an all-Polish neighbourhood. James Pearson was himself far from delighted to be going there but he knew Tommy Parks would be even less happy to go there. James Pearson was contemplating calling Hellerstein and suggesting they switch it back to somewhere around Goldblatt's. He would argue that the detriment in discussing union business in broad daylight in a public place was smaller than the likely harm achieved by getting Tommy Parks riled before the meeting had even started. When James Pearson and Russell Ford arrived at Goldblatt's, they found that Tommy Parks was already there and, although nobody was late yet, it appeared everyone was already too late for the meeting of Hellerstein, Herb Marks and Tommy Parks to achieve its purpose.

Tommy Parks was sitting alone at one end of the lunch counter waiting to be served. Between his seat and the next person in the row of seated customers were four empty seats. All of these customers had either been served or were being served. All those customers were white. James Pearson, with Russell in tow, walked over to Tommy Parks. He knew that while black workers and their families might have shopped at the store, while they might even have had accounts at the store, they didn't eat there. This was where white folks ate.

'You get the message? They changed the meetin' place,' James Pearson asked him.

'Yeah, I heard,' Tommy Parks said, looking around.

'Well, you wanna go now? It's the union hall over on 48th and Marshfield.'

'I know where it is,' he said distractedly, still looking around the room.

'I got the boy here with me but . . . I mean . . . we don't gotta go there if you prefer it some other way.'

'Some other way . . .' Tommy Parks repeated, still looking around the room when he wasn't tossing a spinning coin into the air and catching it. 'Yeah, I do prefer it some other way.' James Pearson shifted uncomfortably from one foot to the other.

'You want me to get them come here? We could maybe meet up with them here and –'

'No, it don't matter. I go there.'

'Yeah?'

'Yeah, just as soon as I get me some of that soup.'

'What?'

'That's right. Can't talk business on no empty stomach,' he said standing up for a moment and craning his neck, feigning a need to better examine the contents of the bowls of the people down the other end of the row.

'Tommy, what you doin'?'

'When you come in –'

'Tommy –'

'When you come in you mighta seen that there soup them good folks eatin'. Looked like chicken soup, far as I can tell.'

'Tommy –'

'You *see* the soup I'm talkin' 'bout? Got them dumplin's. Ever seen that, boy? You ever seen them Jew dumplin's they put in their soup?' Russell Ford kept quiet. He looked up at James Pearson, who squeezed the boy's shoulder.

'Tommy, they ain't gonna serve you no soup here. Let's go to the union hall.'

'No, what you talkin' 'bout? They got the soup. I seen it. Now it all hot already. I drink it down real quick then we be ready meet your pals at the union hall. Miss!' he called out. 'Miss!' The waitress, a young woman, the only person serving the customers, turned around. She walked over to the end of the counter where Tommy Parks was sitting. On her lapel she wore a name tag that read 'Esther' and she took in the sight of the two black men, one sitting and one standing next to the young black boy and she said quietly, 'Sir, we don't want no trouble. Okay?'

'Trouble! I don't want no trouble neither. Ain't no one ever *want* trouble but just 'bout everybody get some. Now I'm just looking for some service here, Esther. See I'm lookin' for some of that fine soup with them dumplin's.'

'Sir, we're not lookin' for any trouble here,' the waitress repeated. She became aware that all the other customers at the other end of the counter were now watching their interaction.

'Tommy, come on. We got business take care of.'

'I know,' Tommy Parks said casually, 'I just gonna have me some soup 'fore we go. I'm talkin' 'bout the soup what those people got.'

'Sir, I don't make the rules,' the waitress said.

'Look like you do, Esther.'

'What do you mean by that?'

'Well, now, you the only one here.'

'My uncle's back in the kitchen.'

'So why don't you go on back there and ask him for some of that nice soup you people make?'

'Tommy, we gonna be late. Let's go!'

'Can't keep them white union boys waitin'.'

'Tommy –'

Then Tommy Parks swung around on his stool to face James Pearson and he fixed a threatening stare on him. 'You call them union boys and you tell 'em Tommy Parks be right there soon as he can get his self some soup.'

'Tommy –'

'When I gets the soup I go to the union hall. It's a simple proposition. They understand. You tell 'em that.'

'This is just some stunt, ain't it, Tommy? You ain't got no intention of comin' to this meetin'.'

'You can walk there or you can call 'em but you gotta tell 'em. This ain't Mississippi or wherever the fuck you from. This here Chicago, ain't it, Esther? When I gets the soup I go to the union hall. It's a simple proposition.'

Everyone was staring at the group of black men and the waitress as James Pearson took Russell Ford with him outside into the street. He took a piece of paper out of his pocket and dialled the number written on it from a nearby payphone.

'Yeah, Ralph, it's me, James Pearson.' Then he explained everything that had happened. Ralph Hellerstein was relaying every word of it to Herb Marks.

'He's screwing with us, James. For Christ's sake, one thing at a time! He can't expect me to desegregate every lunch counter, restaurant and drugstore in Chicago before he'll agree to meet with us. We gotta start

370

with the union. Tell him we want his help so we can help each and every one of the workers at the plant but . . . Jesus, one thing at a time!'

James Pearson went back into Goldblatt's to try to explain Ralph Hellerstein's position and heard Tommy Parks continuing to argue animatedly with the waitress.

'We always have to come in the sideways entrance to the movie theatres. Pay the same price for the same ticket though. How you explain that, Esther?'

'That's nothin' to do with me.'

'It's all nothin' to do with you. Ain't nothin' to do with you. If it ain't nothin' to do with you, how come all those good people over there lookin' over at you in your family's business right this very minute? Ain't nothin' to do with you!'

'We don't own any movie theatres.'

'They *all* owned by Jews. All of 'em, far as I knowed.'

'I wouldn't know about that.'

'Well *I* know about it. You take our money but you make us come in the sideways entrance and now here you won't give me no soup.'

'Tommy, they ain't buying it, the union men,' James Pearson explained. 'You can come with me now for a meetin' in the union hall or you can forget it.' He turned to face young Russell Ford after he said this and wondered what the boy was thinking. Which side of this argument was he leaning towards? Tommy Parks, aware the boy was interested in what they were saying, continued, 'That's what your union worth. It ain't worth shit, Pearson. And look at what you showin' the boy here, runnin' round doin' white man's business tryin' to talk me down from my stool here.'

'Tommy, one thing at a time!'

'All right, I see that. I make the one thing to be one them bowls of soup with the dumplin's, just like they got,' Tommy Parks said, pointing at the people at the other end of the counter.

James Pearson took Russell outside again and made the call to explain to Ralph Hellerstein that it was all over with Tommy Parks. He wasn't going to budge.

'Yeah, well fuck him then,' said Hellerstein over the phone.

'I'm sorry 'bout this, Ralph,' Pearson said as the young boy looked up at him.

'James, it's not your fault. You've done everything you could do. Anyway, it's not like you didn't warn us he was a hot-head. It was worth a try. Go home and get some rest. See if you can think of anyone else who might be the right type, someone with . . . I don't know . . . charisma.'

James Pearson had put the phone down and he and Russell were about to walk back into Goldblatt's when he heard a familiar voice from behind him.

'I heard we got trouble. Anything I can do?' The man put his hands on Pearson's broad shoulders. It was Herb Marks. The two men shook hands.

'Who's the young man?'

'Russell, say hello to Mr Marks.'

'How do you do, Russell?' he said, shaking the boy's hand.

'How do you do, sir,' Russell answered.

'You work in the plant too, don't you?'

'Yes, sir, I do.'

'Well, if you're old enough to work perhaps you don't need to call me sir. My name's Herb Marks. I'm from the union and I'd be pleased if you called me Herb.'

'How'd you do . . . Herb?'

'Well, I'd do a lot better if we didn't have this problem with Mr Parks. I heard he wants a bowl of soup before he'll consider coming to our meeting.' Russell nodded gravely.

'Let's go and talk to him.'

'Won't do no use, Herb,' said Russell Ford.

'Oh, I don't want to talk him out of it. I want to see if we can't get him some soup. With *kreplach*, if possible. You ever had *kreplach*?'

The three of them walked in to see everybody at the counter still watching Tommy Parks arguing with the waitress, Esther. Herb Marks walked over to them and stuck his hand out to the waitress and introduced himself.

'Mister, I keep telling him, we don't want no trouble.'

'No, of course you don't. Whoever wants trouble? Why don't you attend to your other customers while I have a chat with Mr Parks here? Okay?'

The waitress was pleased to have an excuse for a respite from the argument with the stubborn man whose repeated requests for a bowl of soup were making her more and more uncomfortable. As she was leaving, Herb Marks stuck out his hand to introduce himself in a quiet voice to her antagonist.

'Hello, Mr Parks, I'm Herb Marks. I'm one of the two union men hoping to meet you tonight to invite you to join the Packinghouse Workers Organising Committee. The other man, my partner Ralph Hellerstein, can't be here right now because he's furiously busy back in the union hall cursing you to the heavens.' At this Tommy Parks smiled and took the man's hand.

'Yeah, what's he sayin'?'

'Well now, bear in mind that I'm a good ten minutes out of date but when I left the union hall he had just called you a useless cunt.'

At this Tommy Parks smiled even more broadly. 'Now you sure he didn't throw the word nigger in there somewhere? You ain't holdin' nothin' back now, are you, Mister –'

'It's Herb and, no, he doesn't use that word. 'Bout the only word he doesn't use. None of us on the Packinghouse Workers Organising Committee use that word.'

'Well, I'd raise my glass to you, Herb, but Esther over there, she won't give me one.'

'You want a bowl, don't you, a bowl of chicken soup, is that right?'

'That's right.'

'And if you got that bowl of soup you'd come to the union hall to meet with me and Mr Hellerstein?'

'I sure would.'

'Well, that sounds fair.'

'Glad you find it so, Herb.' Tommy Parks considered this white union man from his shoes up to his deep-set eyes. 'You ain't from here?' he asked the union man.

'No, I'm not.'

'You one of them Brooklyn Jews, ain't ya?'

'Yes, that's right.'

'You gonna get me some of that soup?'

'Well, what kind of a union would it be if we couldn't even get you a bowl of soup?'

Herb Marks managed to get the waitress alone as she was coming out of the kitchen with somebody's burger and he convinced her to give him a minute or two to talk to her in private away from other people. But she wasn't having any of it.

'I know who you are, mister. You're one of them unionists and you don't care about making trouble for ordinary people because you like trouble. Well, we don't! If we serve him he's gonna tell his friends and then they're all gonna come in expecting to be served. There's already two of 'em waiting to see if he can get service. Then they'll all come in.'

'And if they all come in then it's more business for you.'

'Mister, I don't make the rules. If the coloureds come in then those folks won't,' she said, pointing to the customers at the other end of the counter. 'Mister, I don't make the rules. This is a family business. We're just trying to make a living.'

'So is he.'

'Yeah, well, I ain't stoppin' him. Mister, if you don't all leave I'm goin' to have to call the police.'

Herb Marks was walking back in the direction of Tommy Parks, Pearson and Russell Ford. Feeling a sense of triumph at seeing the union man walking away, Esther quite unnecessarily called out, 'That's right, mister, the police. So you get the hell out of here or else that's what I'm goin' to do.' Then she went to clear plates from the end of the counter that had been getting her service. But the damage was done. She had called out too loudly in too close a proximity to the kitchen and this was when her uncle heard her and he came out. He walked out on to the floor and over to the counter and stood about midway between where Herb Marks was confessing his failure to Tommy Parks and the others and where his niece was wiping up someone's mess.

'What's going on here? What is there to call the police?' asked the old man in an accent coated in Europe.

'Your waitress, Esther –' Herb Marks began.

'She's my niece. What about her?' the old man asked.

'She doesn't seem to want to serve my friend here.' Everyone stopped to see what the old man was going to say, including people who were too far away to hear the conversation.

'What does he want?' the old man asked.

'He wants a bowl of soup,' Tommy Parks announced about himself.

'What kind?'

'Chicken with dumplin's,' said Tommy Parks. The old man stood with his hands on his hips, looked around the restaurant at the customers looking at him. He drew breath and let it out.

'Esther, get the man his soup.'

'Uncle Nate –'

'Get the man his soup.'

'Uncle Nate, people ain't gonna come here if –'

'Get the man his soup! Don't argue with me!'

Esther walked towards the kitchen shaking her head and muttering under her breath. What didn't her uncle understand?

'I'm sorry for this, mister,' the old man said to Tommy Parks. 'It shouldn't have happened. You come in here for my soup whenever you like. And you can tell anyone you like . . . about our soup.'

'I'd like to order another three bowls for me and my two companions, with *kreplach*,' said Herb Marks. 'We have to go to a meeting and we need our strength. We got a lot to talk about.'

The old man went back out to the kitchen and it was clear he was having words with his niece.

'Let me duck outside for a minute to call Ralph. He thinks this meeting's cancelled.'

'Next meeting, I want you to get me Saul Alinsky. I wanna meet with him,' announced Tommy Parks. 'I wanna talk with him about housing . . . for my people. Can you fix that?'

'Sure, we know Saul.'

'I thought you might.'

'Who's Saul Alinsky?' James Pearson asked.

'He's what you might call a "community organiser",' Herb Marks said before Tommy Parks interjected by way of further explanation,

'He organised all the housing for them folks in Back-of the-Yards.' Then turning to Herb Marks and pointing at James Pearson he added, 'See, *I* know more 'n *him*.'

After a few minutes the old man himself came out with a tray containing four bowls of soup. He put the tray down on the counter, and allocated each man a bowl, a spoon and some crackers and a napkin. Then, as if sharing a confidence, he spoke quietly to Tommy Parks.

'You come here whenever you like but forgive the girl, please, mister, I ask you. Don't make trouble for the girl. She was born here so . . .' The old man seemed unsure how to finish the sentence.

'So what?' asked Tommy Parks.

'So she thinks she's white.'

That evening Tommy Parks joined the Packinghouse Workers Organising Committee. Some time much later he stood in the Pilgrim Baptist Church not far from James Pearson and Russell Ford as Pearson, Mr Anything-You-Want, took the vows necessary to marry Callie Ford. The daughter of Rosa Rabinowicz, Elly Border, was there too, dressed in a crisp white shirt with a frilly collar and a perfectly pleated skirt, all of it painstakingly made by the bride. Elly, who had never been to a wedding before, was beaming as she stood beside her silent father. To fully absorb as much of the occasion as possible she turned around for a moment to glance behind her and this was when she first noticed Ralph Hellerstein and Herb Marks standing a little farther down the back on the groom's side of the aisle, right opposite Mrs Sallie. She wondered who these white men could be.

*

Lamont Williams' grandmother had grown accustomed to his arriving late home from work sometimes. Increasingly, she didn't ask why, assuming it was because he had been able to secure some overtime and this had to be good news. It was good news because it meant extra money for her grandson, extra self-confidence, and extra hope for a future where he had found himself a place in the world, and because it suggested that his supervisor, or the Human Resources Department, or whoever it was that made the hiring and firing decisions, was looking at Lamont favourably. But Lamont's occasional lateness had nothing to do with overtime and nothing to do with how he was regarded by anybody but an old man, a patient with no apparent power to influence anything in Lamont's life. Nonetheless, at the end of his shift, Lamont Williams had become, yet again, drawn into this old man's world, the world of this man's past. Mr Mandelbrot, without explaining why, had said he was soon to be discharged from his room on the ninth floor of Memorial Sloan-Kettering Cancer Center. Lamont didn't know how to ask whether the patient was being sent home because he was in remission or whether he was being sent home to die. Fearing that this might be his last opportunity to talk with him, he stayed back late yet again and quickly found himself enthralled in the next chapter of this man's history, almost to the point of disbelief.

'But . . . I mean . . . How was . . . ?' There was no other way of asking other than directly. 'How did it work?' That's how Lamont Williams asked the old man on the ninth floor.

'How did it work? Listen. It worked like a factory, smooth like a factory, a factory that turned living people into corpses. I mean this. Really, this is what it did. Once the SS chose you for work in the *Sonderkommando*, you had no choice – other than your own death what would come immediately in a way you didn't know – you had no choice but to work in one of five groups. Remember it, five different types of work the *Sonderkommando* did.'

'Five kinds of work,' Lamont Williams said quietly.

'Five kinds of work,' Mr Mandelbrot continued. 'The work of the *Sonderkommando* was broken into five different kinds of work. Sometimes we swapped but mostly not. I did all five kinds of work in my time in the *Sonderkommando*.

'A transport of Jews would come in cattle cars, cattle wagons, from anywhere in Europe, anywhere, *everywhere*. You know what it means, cattle cars, Mr Lamont?'

'Like a train?'

'Yes, but it was a train of wagons what they had used before the war to transport cattle. Since the transport of people –'

'Of Jews?'

'Yes, of course Jews. Since it could have come to Auschwitz-Birkenau from anywhere in Europe, the people could have been on it for days; one, two, maybe three days on it without food, without any water, without medicines, without any possibility of cleaning themselves. You know what it means? They were packed in with whatever belongings they could carry and before even arriving some of them would be dead. If the transport was coming from one of the ghettoes they were already weak, some of them sick and *ready* to die before they even *got* on the train. Some would be crushed inside the cattle cars; old people, sometimes small children got crushed.

'So the train would arrive at Birkenau, the doors would open and the people what had been packed inside would have SS men shouting at them to get down.'

'Off of the train?'

'Yes. They had dogs barking like in a hunt, hunting dogs barking at the people on the trains. The people got off the trains but some got off slow if they were old or sick. Some didn't get off at all. These were the people what had died on the cattle trucks, on the trains. The ones who got off, fell off, their belongings in their hands, were greeted by the SS and the dogs, shouting, barking at them. These people didn't know where they were. They didn't know about Auschwitz, they had never *heard* of Auschwitz. It's only famous now because of what was about to happen to them then, them, and all the ones before them and all the ones after them.

'The inside of the cars were emptied of the dead by members of the *Kanada Kommando*. You remember I told you about *Kanada*?'

'Yes.'

'The *Kanada* workers had to climb up on to the cattle trucks and pull off the bodies of the Jews who had died on their way to Auschwitz. The rest of the transport who stood exhausted with their belongings – and there might have been as many as two thousand from all the cattle cars – might be met with beatings straight away.'

'From the SS men?'

'Yes. And if it was night – because the transports arrived day and night – they would be blinded by floodlights. They see only white light; they hear only screaming from the SS, barking from the dogs and the crying of their children. They feel the beating. Yes? Hurry, hurry! Sometimes they were beaten as soon as they got off the trains, before they even knew the name of the place they were in. They were told to give the prisoners from the *Kanada Kommando* all what they had so that they could be transferred to where they were being relocated.'

'Relocated?'

'Yes, that's what they were told. Then it was time for what was called a *Selektion*. An SS officer, a registrar and one of the physicians, a doctor, would be there.'

'A Jewish doctor?'

'No, no, an SS doctor. The women were separated from the men and then each person had to walk past the SS man and the doctor and they would select if you were to go to the left or the right. The doctor would wave a stick to the left or to the right. Usually he didn't say anything, just looked at the person and pointed. The people didn't know whether it was better to be sent to the left or to the right. To the right meant you went into some work detail, some slave labour detail. To the left meant death, gassing. If they needed more slave labour a higher proportion might be saved. A good *Selektion* was when maybe as many as thirty per cent were sent to work in some part of the camp.'

'So seventy per cent were gassed?'

'Yes, that was a good *Selektion*. It was never less than that. Sometimes one hundred per cent of the transport what came in was gassed immediately. The doctor would wave his stick left or right as each person walked up to him for inspection. It could take a long time with so many people. Sometimes the doctor got tired and would give one big sweeping wave of the stick to the left. This meant anybody what he hadn't got to see yet, all the people what were still waiting, they were to go to the left.'

'To be gassed?'

'Yes, to the gas chamber, yes.'

'You said there were five groups, five kinds of work.'

'Yes, there were five kinds of work what the *Sonderkommando* did. It's good you remember. You have to remember it.

'First there was the undressing phase and the transport of the clothes to *Kanada*.

'Then came the removal of the bodies from the gas chamber.

'There was the shaving of the hair –'

'From dead bodies?'

'Yes, shaving of the hair and extraction of gold teeth from the dead bodies after they were gassed.

'There were the stokers.'

'Stokers?'

'Yes, this was those *Sonderkommando* members what worked with the ovens cremating the people what had just been gassed.

'Then was the disposal of the remains. This means disposing of the ashes and the crushing of bones, also to be disposed. After you burn a body there are bones and teeth left. We had to grind them into dust.'

'You *did* this?'

'Yes, this was all the work of the *Sonderkommando*. At times I have worked in each of the different sections.'

'Why did you do it?'

'I had no choice if I was to keep living. None of us had a choice. It was "live in this hell, a world like no human being had ever known before, or not live at all". At first you don't believe it even as you see it. You don't know where you are and you don't think you're going to be able to get through it.'

'Did you ever want to die . . . instead of doin' that . . . work?'

'Yes, many times. At the start of your shift you want to die. You can't imagine that you're going to get through even one hour. And you're carrying around this heaviness, a weight in your chest like you're going to split open, your heart is going to burst. But all the time you're thinking that somebody has to survive just to tell what happened. Somebody has to get the story out. Maybe that will be me what gets the story out so that the world will know. Otherwise, how will anybody know what they did there?'

'You wanted to survive to get the story out?'

'Yes, for what other reason was there to live?'

'Your family?'

'When I saw what they were doing I knew my family must be already dead. If any of them survived the ghetto, I knew they wouldn't survive the transport, the cattle trucks. And if they survived the cattle trucks they wouldn't survive the *Selektion*. In the *Sonderkommando* you learn more than you ever wanted to know about death. You stood at the door between life and death. You saw everything.

'When a transport arrived we had to immediately report to the undressing room of the crematorium complex what we were assigned to. We would be waiting there for the victims, for the Jews. They came from all over Europe: Greece, France, Hungary, *everywhere*. There were in Birkenau, not counting two little houses what they sometimes used, what was called the "red house" and the "white house", there were four crematoria each with its own gas chamber: Crematoria II, III, IV and V.'

'What about number one?'

'Number one was in Auschwitz I but the others were in Birkenau, all of them. Birkenau was Auschwitz II.'

'Where you were.'

'Yes. Each crematorium had a yard, closed in so that no one from outside could see what was going on. The Jews had to cross the courtyard to get to the crematorium building, the building with a huge chimney like on a factory that housed also the gas chamber as well as the ovens. But before that, the victims were often made to stand in the courtyard while an SS officer, someone like *Oberscharführer* Moll . . .' Mr Mandelbrot shook his head slowly at the mention of this man's name. '*Oberscharführer* Moll, a terrible man, would often make a short speech, not always, but the speech was always the same meaning. He would tell them they were going to be given a shower and after this they would be sent to work. Then they were sent to what was called the "undressing room" attached to that crematorium. There would be numbered hooks in the undressing room, he would say, and they were to leave their things near one of the hooks and remember the number of the hook so they could get their things when they came out of the showers.'

'Were there really hooks with numbers?'

'Yes, there were hooks with numbers and in the gas chamber there were even . . . What do you call it, where the water comes out in the shower?'

'Shower heads, faucets?'

'Yes, they had some shower heads, faucets in the ceiling of the gas chambers but they were not connected to anything. They were just shower heads. No water came out of them. It was all just to trick them. Everything was to trick them so they wouldn't panic, to keep them as calm as possible so it would all run as smoothly as possible like clockwork. They wanted it all done efficiently and they had to have it like this. There were times when more than ten thousand people were gassed and burned in one day.'

'Ten thousand?'

'Yes. You cannot imagine it. It's just . . . worse than your worst nightmare. They needed each step of the process to operate efficiently. Well, yes, the Germans always like order. You know this. They got the people to go down the stairs of the building –'

'What did it look like?'

'What, the building?'

'Yeah?'

'It looked like a normal building, red brick with red shingle roof and a huge chimney. Nothing . . . you know . . . if you didn't know . . . There was nothing what would tell anybody from the outside that inside is a gas chamber and another room with five ovens for no other reason than burning people. Sometimes, when the ovens couldn't keep up, the bodies were burned in open pits. I remember the chimneys on Crematoria II and III were taller than the others. It was the design.'

'Who dug the pits?'

'We did.'

'The *Sonderkommando*?'

'Yes, we dug the pits, we took the bodies of the gassed Jews and threw them into the pits and there was a way to do even this, an order how the Nazis wanted it . . . to make the burning better. They liked order.'

'Yeah, you said that . . .'

'People know this about them. They had the people go down the stairs into the undressing room in files.'

'Like in rows?'

'Yes, rows of maybe five at a time. Five people would go down the stairs and then another five and then another five. Like this for the whole transport. It might be up to two thousand people this way.'

'Why did they listen, the Jews? Why'd they do it?'

'I told you, they were told that it was just for a shower, disinfection before being sent to a work detail and also they did it because there were SS standing around all them and even right up to the stairs at the entrance of the building, the SS stood around them with guns. A few of the SS even went downstairs into the undressing room where we were.'

'Didn't people suspect what was down there?'

'How would they know?'

'I don't know . . . rumours?'

'Yes, there were rumours and some people did suspect. You are right. When there were people who suspected they might move slow down the stairs but then would come down on them a storm of beatings from the SS so hard it could kill you on the spot, so hard that the people went down the stairs away from the beatings they knew were real for sure down to the fate that was still only for them just rumours. People hang on to hope as long as they can, Mr Lamont. Maybe down there is better than up here? Even the ones who suspected, they didn't know for sure. It had never happened in the history of the world what was about to happen to them. No other people ever had this happen to them. But it didn't really matter what they thought. This was what was going to happen to them and what they thought only had to do with how long it took. If the Jews could be fooled until they were in the gas chamber it all went along a lot quicker, a lot smoother.'

'Did you talk to them?'

'Not much. We weren't allowed to talk much, only to say certain things the Nazis had told us to say.'

'Like what?'

'"Get undressed. You're going to have a shower. Remember where you put your clothes." This sort of thing.'

'You lied to them? How could you –'

'Look, what should I do, tell them the truth? Mr Lamont, they are downstairs. They are defenceless. They are undressing then they are naked. For what should we tell them the truth? We wanted to try to take their fear away. Can you see them? You have to see them; mothers with small children, sometimes with babies at their breast, young girls, teenage girls, people ashamed to be naked, old people what we had to help undress –'

'You had to undress them?'

'Yes, sometimes when they were too slow for the Nazis, we had to undress them; people like our fathers and mothers, our grandparents, already sick and weak, frightened. Why frighten them more? What good would it do? We could provide the last comfort what they were going to get on earth before the gas chamber. What good would it do to tell them the truth?'

'What would have happened to you if you told them the truth? I mean, didn't you ever want to warn them? Why didn't you ever warn them?'

'Why didn't we warn them?'

*

The first five came down the stairs. No one wanted to look at them. Henryk Mandelbrot was one of approximately twenty *Sonderkommando* members standing in the undressing room of Crematorium II. He stood in the middle of the room. The floor was grey concrete and the walls were white. Around the entire circumference of the room were smooth pine benches and above these there were hooks with numbers next to them. It looked like a very large, very narrow, but otherwise unremarkable gymnasium locker room. When the number of *Sonderkommando* men outnumbered the victims, as it always did for the first minute or so, it was hard to find an excuse not to look the victims in the eye. What made it worse was that, unless for some reason it was an all-male group, the first to come down were usually women. In addition to whatever the women had just been through and in addition to whatever they suspected they were about to go through, they were exhausted, confused and very ashamed to have to undress to the point of complete nakedness in front of strangers. There were married women who had only ever been naked in front of their husbands. There were old women, little girls and teenage girls from small villages, *shtetls*, girls who had only ever been naked in front of their mothers years earlier. They found it hard to imagine even being married to a man who was permitted to touch their bodies and to see them naked. Now here they were being told to undress in brusque, sharp tones by SS men whom each one knew meant them no good; men of the type that had put them in ghettoes, men who were fully dressed, armed, uniformed soldiers of Hitler. And it wasn't enough to simply undress. They had to undress very quickly. The SS men greeted the women's naked bodies variously, at best with short-tempered indifference, usually with harsh words sometimes further humiliating them, and frequently with violence.

The first five women were spoken to firmly in a no-nonsense manner by the SS men in the undressing room. Some of them wondered why armed SS men had to watch them get undressed for a shower. Something was not right. And who were these other men, seemingly prisoners, also interested in getting them undressed as quickly as possible to go to the shower room next door? These men, the prisoners, seemed to be Jews. They were speaking to them in Yiddish but they would not look at them.

'Come on now. You have to hurry. Leave your things by a hook and remember the number on it,' Henryk Mandelbrot said to a woman whose shame seemed to be paralysing her. He couldn't look her in the eye as he spoke but he saw an SS man looking at him as he was speaking to the slowly undressing woman and then, with small relief, he saw the officer's gaze shift from him to other *Sonderkommando* men, to Schubach, Ochrenberg, Touba and Raijsmann, as another five women came down the stairs, then another five and another five followed by another and still another. Very quickly there were more victims than *Sonderkommando* or SS men in the undressing room even though once undressed the women were ordered down the hall to the room with the shower faucets. Now some men started coming down the stairs in rows of five. They were being screamed at by the SS men upstairs or was it the five people immediately behind them or the five behind them? Already the beatings had started up the stairs to make things go faster and five pushed five to escape the beatings. The first five men saw women undressing and clothes left in piles around the room.

'You can pick your things up after the shower,' Mandelbrot said to an old man who seemed to have trouble believing what he was seeing. The man moved slowly, too slowly. Henryk Mandelbrot knew the man would be beaten any second if he didn't start making progress undressing.

'You have to hurry!' A baby was crying, which set off another baby. A mother tried to comfort it but she had to undress both the baby and herself quickly. An SS man was watching her and she saw him. With the baby in her arms, she turned her back to him.

'The showers . . .' the old man asked Mandelbrot. 'They're the same ones for men *and* for women?'

'Yes, they're the same,' Mandelbrot said to the old man without emotion, at the same time helping him with his coat. Five more came down, followed by another five, some of whom were freshly bleeding from their heads, all of whom were pushed by the five behind them. Then another five . . .

'You're a Jew?' the old man asked Henryk Mandelbrot.

'Yes. You have to hurry. They'll beat both of us if you're too –'

'It's gas, isn't it?'

Mandelbrot turned away from this old man as five more people came down the stairs into the undressing room, followed by another five, then another five and another five after that. Henryk Mandelbrot had to look away from the stairway. But where could he look? Another five came down followed by another five and then another five. A girl of around twelve was carrying her brother who looked to be no more than three. Mandelbrot went to her and her brother.

'Don't touch him, you Jewish murderer! He'll die with me . . . in my arms.'

Then came another five, then another, a carpenter whose wife used to say he worked too much, a tailor came, then a man with a singing voice that all his neighbours had enjoyed since he was a child, a teacher was there who had hoped to be a principal some day, a widow who sewed clothes, a nurse who had had an affair with a patient, a slightly overweight boy of eleven with wavy hair who felt he had never been able to live up to his parents' expectations, he was also there. The fattest man of his village was going to have to undress in a hurry too. A newly graduated doctor was there and, unbeknown to him, way off in the corner there was one of his professors from medical school. A man who had been unfaithful to his wife once in another town while on business was there, a pharmacist who had always gone out of his way to help people, a girl who kept calling out for her sister, a woman who had brought food to widows in the hope of pleasing God, a thief, a man who sold candles, a prostitute who had run away from home, a man who failed to get into art school but who had kept drawing all his life never showing his work to anyone, the wife of a man who hawked spices, an engineer, a fishmonger, a woman whose husband often embarrassed her was there, a man who worked with his brothers in a foundry, the daughter of a stonemason, a man whose blindness was not evident to others, a mathematician, a woman who loved fashion magazines was there with her daughter who dreamed of one day being in them. Then another five came down, including a rabbi and a chazan and a woman who had tried to see every movie that came to her town, and still the Jews kept coming. They heard the command to undress and began to do what everybody else was doing before being forced by SS men into the other room to wait for the shower. Then another five.

The undressing room was crowded and hot. Schubach, Ochrenberg, Touba and Raijsmann were there with Henryk Mandelbrot. Spread out, they and the others in the detail were saying the same things to the Jews who kept coming in wave after wave of five. Under the eye of an SS man, a *Sonderkommando* member, Wentzel, began to use his fists on a woman who undressed too slowly. An undressing man looked at him in disgust and the woman undressed faster. This was a full transport of close to 2000 people. The undressing room was filling up even as it emptied when the naked people went to the room next door. There was going to be a huge mound of clothes to clear; clothes of all types and sizes as well as all the little, small, last-minute things people took with them in their clothes or on their person. There would be small photos of loved ones, a letter of commendation from the German Army from World War I, a comb, a grandparent's wedding ring, a page blank but for someone's signature, a miniature teddy bear, some cash imperfectly hidden in the lining of a coat, a pen, a love letter, something small for the baby to eat, a telephone number scrawled on the back of a bus ticket and a yarmulke for after the shower.

Henryk Mandelbrot saw Ochrenberg go over to a beautiful young woman with dark eyes and thick black hair who was there with a child, a sister or a daughter. Mandelbrot couldn't tell. What was wrong? Ochrenberg was there too long. Was he talking to her? He was taking too long. The woman stopped undressing, looked at Ochrenberg and started shouting something. Suddenly Ochrenberg moved away from her as fast as he could. From a distance Mandelbrot saw the mood of tension and anxiety change around this woman to one of unequivocal panic. The SS men saw it too. Like a ripple spreading across a pond after a stone has been thrown in, the closer to Ochrenberg's woman, the greater the panic.

'It's not water in the showers. It's gas! It's gas!' the woman shouted.

'Gas?'

'They mean to gas us!'

A rain of blows came down on this half-undressed woman. People, even the child, moved away from her as the SS men clubbed her to the ground, beating her furiously. She lay there, panting, her torn slip leaking blood from her lacerated breasts and head. What had Ochrenberg hoped to achieve? The last of the transport were being shoved down the stairs as the young woman lay unconscious. Mandelbrot had to take the clothes off her child, who was now hysterical. The child struggled violently, twisting in every direction to break free, twisting in Mandelbrot's arms like a creature possessed. If he let her go they would beat her too.

The last few rows of five could not help see how terrified those ahead of them were. They saw the young woman collapsed amid the piles of clothing. A mother from among the last in was calling out, 'My son! My son is missing! He is in a blue coat. He's wearing a blue coat. He's three years old. I just want to find my son. He was holding my . . .' The woman started to go back up the stairs, explaining that she wanted to find her son, but an SS man grabbed her around the waist, threw her to the ground and shot her in the head. By then most of the transport were out of the undressing room and either in the corridor that led from the undressing room to the gas chamber or already in the gas chamber.

Undressed, they went through the door, the only door, with the sign 'To the Disinfection Room'. Strangers stood naked together in this room where the ceiling was markedly lower than in the undressing room. It was warm, warmer than the undressing room. At first they stood apart but as the room filled with more and more people they were forced to get closer and closer until they could not help but touch each other. Children cried. Adults tried to comfort them. Adults cried. Children looked for their parents. They called out for them as the room filled.

'Where are you? Are you here? Take my hand.'

Some were too ashamed to look at one another. Some looked in astonishment. What world was this? This was wrong. It felt wrong. Some looked at the shower faucets in the ceiling. Some looked for the God they and their parents and their grandparents had tried so hard to please. Some called out to the Germans in anger. They looked around the room as other people called out, called to each other, to their children, to the SS, to God. There were lights along the centre of the ceiling encaged for protection. Families, if they could, stayed close together. They hugged. When a father suspected the truth he would hug his wife and his children, not voicing his suspicion, but they would see him crying silently and they would cry. Soon everyone around them was crying. In the middle of the room were four pillars made of layers of metal mesh.

People in the room with the shower faucets were too disoriented and distressed to notice the pillars immediately. Who thought about the architecture of the room? Would the water be hot? Would it be warm? Were there really enough faucets for all these people? But soon, any moment, everyone in the room would notice the pillars. People were packed into this room and at the door someone screamed with an unmatched urgency. This scream came from the last person, beaten by the butt of an SS rifle and pushed in. There was no longer any space left in the room. The truth was becoming clearer. They were all of them in a gas chamber. Many now knew what was going to happen after an SS man closed the sealed door.

In the undressing room Henryk Mandelbrot and the other *Sonderkommando* men in this detail, including Schubach, Ochrenberg, Touba and Raijsmann, looked at each other and at the mountains of clothing. They were numb. They were always numb. Sometimes they were grateful they were not inside the gas chamber but mostly now they felt nothing.

'What are you waiting for, you pieces of shit?' an SS man shouted at them. 'Pick up the clothes!'

Pointing with the toe of his boot to the mother of the missing three-year-old boy in the blue coat, the SS man who had shot her said to Mandelbrot, 'Here's another one for you,' and, putting his pistol away, he began to leave the undressing room hurriedly to try to see the gassing from the upstairs window outside. Suddenly he stopped and turned around to speak to Mandelbrot.

'If the ovens are still backed up, take her to the pits while the others are getting the clothes. Be quick. I have another job for you men.'

Outside the crematorium complex, a truck deceptively bearing the symbol of the Red Cross had arrived and from the back, sealed metal canisters were taken out. An SS man donned a gas mask and with a hammer and a knife he opened a canister. Its contents, Zyklon B, consisted of pellets of very porous rock saturated with hydrogen cyanide. The SS man in the gas mask now opened the hatches on top of the projections through the roof of the four metal mesh pillars in the gas chamber and poured in the Zyklon B. A man with this duty got extra cigarettes and, provided there were not too many officers crowding out the view, he got to watch the gassing through a sealed peephole in the door. It was a very popular task.

The green pellets of Zyklon B fell to the bottom of each of the hollow pillars and, warmed in the preheated and now overcrowded chamber, the volatile hydrogen cyanide with which the pellets were saturated started to vapourise and diffuse out through the metal mesh. People nearest the pillars gasped first in shock but, very soon after, for breath. Then the coughing started all over the room and within minutes people were not any longer themselves. Their cells were being deprived of oxygen by the cyanide and they were being asphyxiated. As the cyanide took effect and their very organs screamed out for oxygen, people experienced a terror unlike any they had ever known, an instant unfiltered prerational auto-nomic primeval panic. But they were physically unable to stifle the reflex to breathe and so they breathed in more of the poison.

The cyanide vapourising out of the pellets at the bottom of the pillars spread into the room through the metal mesh and rose upward. The lowest points in the room were initially the most toxic but with every second the rest of the room was catching up. It was in the seconds before the gas had colonised all parts of the room equally that the climbing started. People were not any longer remotely like the people they had been all their lives up to the time the pellets started taking effect. As consciousness began to leave them they behaved not like parents or husbands or wives or friends or brothers and sisters but like the most basic organisms without the capacity to do a single thing in their struggle not to die except try desperately to get away from the gas as it made its way upward and filled the room. The smallest, the weakest, the most frail were being crushed as the man with the beautiful singing voice, the carpenter, the younger of the two doctors, the engineer, the thief, climbed over and then stood on the body and sometimes then on the head of the woman whose husband used to embarrass her, the eleven-year-old boy with the wavy hair, the teacher, the prostitute, the daughter of the stonemason, the man who never showed anyone his drawings, the old man who was slow to undress, the woman who liked fashion magazines, her daughter. And on the children, and the old.

The pain was quickly extreme. People drooled like animals. Their eyes bulged. Their bodies began to jerk in wild spasms as the gas rendered completely useless whatever oxygen they could find. After three minutes they were bleeding, some from the scramble, the struggle to the top of the heap, but all from the effect of the gas. They bled from their noses. They bled from their ears. People lost continence and many were pushed down into a mess of blood, urine, vomit and excrement as people with memories, affections, ambitions, relationships, opinions, values and accomplishments all merged into a tangled phalanx of human beings a metre deep covered in their own fluids, all of them gasping, their bodies jerking, their faces distorted by their agony. With their brains and their organs increasingly depleted of oxygen with every second, it was in a state of unimaginable terror and pain that they had their last thoughts. They were already no longer people.

The *Sonderkommando* men in the undressing room heard the screams and knew well their pattern; louder and louder and louder until they reached a peak and then began to subside. They continued working, each man desperate for the arrival of the silence. They knew it was coming but they couldn't wait for it. Then when the silence came, the agony from the next room would be over, leaving these men, the last to see the victims alive, to deduce it from the hellish distortions of their faces and from the contorted positions of their bodies within the tangle of bodies when the door was opened.

Henryk Mandelbrot undressed the murdered mother of the three-year-old and threw her clothes on the pile. Knowing the ovens were still backed up, he dragged her by the arm to the burning pits outside where the corpses of a previous transport lay piled up waiting for *Sonderkommando* men to throw them on the pile in the ditches. As he got closer the flames rose higher than his eye could see. He coughed and almost choked on the smell. The men working here had tied material around their mouths and noses but Mandelbrot was there only to drop off one corpse. This wasn't his detail. His eyes watered. He let go of the dead woman's hand to rub his eyes and that's when he saw the other men around him stop. He saw they were looking at *Oberscharführer* Moll standing at the edge of the pit.

Oberscharführer Moll had in his arms a three-year-old boy with dark brown hair bundled up in a blue coat crying out for his mother. He let the boy drop from his arms to the ground so that the child lay winded on his back. The boy was in shock. Then with one recently polished boot raised high, Moll stomped down on the boy's face. The child screamed in terror at what he saw coming towards him, and then wailed in agony. *Oberscharführer* Moll bent down to pick up the disfigured boy. He took the blue coat off the whimpering blood-soaked child, tossed the coat over his shoulder and then threw the boy like a sack of wheat on to the top of the pyre of burning bodies. Henryk Mandelbrot heard the child screaming from the top of the fire. The boy had not been dead when he was thrown in. Mandelbrot picked up the naked corpse of the child's mother and slung it on the pyre next to her son, as close as he could. Then he hurried back to the undressing room.

Schubach, Ochrenberg, Touba, Raijsmann, Wentzel and the others were working through the piles of clothes in the undressing room when he got back. The gas chamber should have been opened by then but, for some reason, that seemed to have been delayed. Mandelbrot was just realising this when *Oberscharführer* Schillinger appeared surrounded by a group of SS men.

'Are they all here?' he asked one of the SS men.

'Yes, sir.'

'Each one?'

'Yes, sir. The other one just got back.'

'Good. All of you go immediately to the ovens in Crematorium III. Now! Hurry! All of you!'

Henryk Mandelbrot and each of the others who had been with him in the undressing room knew that all of the ovens at Crematorium III and indeed all of the ovens at all four of Birkenau's gas chamber and crematoria installations had no capacity for extra bodies. The ovens were not keeping up with the corpses they already had and were falling behind. This was why the mass pits outside were being used again. It didn't make any sense for these men to report to the ovens in Crematorium III, especially when their work on the most recent transport's clothes in the undressing room of the Crematorium II complex to which they were assigned had not been completed. Additionally, the gas chamber next door to the ovens where they now stood still held the 2000 people, now corpses, just freshly gassed. It needed to be cleared and cleaned for the people who were already waiting outside listening to an SS officer tell them about their need to be disinfected before being transferred to their new work detail.

But whatever their misgivings about the reasons behind the order, no one would delay obeying *Oberscharführer* Schillinger. Better they should run straight to the electric wire fence and end it that way. So they all went, unaccompanied by SS guards and without hesitation, to the ovens of Crematorium III. The smell of the burning flesh was nauseating. A few of them gagged. Among the stokers there was Zalman Gradowski who saw these men arrive as he was laying the corpse of a young man, the last of three people, onto the metal stretcher tray and was sliding it into the oven. Then he closed the heavy semi-circular oven door and the bodies started burning.

'What are you all doing here? We're not ready for any more. Look!' he said, directing their attention to a pile of corpses waiting to be pushed into the ovens. 'Mandelbrot, what's going on?'

'I don't know. Schillinger ordered us to come here. He didn't tell us why.'

Hearing Schillinger's name caused Zalman Gradowski to stop what he was doing. He looked at Mandelbrot for an explanation from within his eyes if one was not to be forthcoming in his words. And it was then that he saw *Oberscharführer* Schillinger walk into the crematorium accompanied by a number of SS guards.

'Take your pieces out,' *Oberscharführer* Schillinger ordered Gradowski, referring to the corpses in the oven. Nobody had ever heard an order like this before. The men working at the other furnaces stopped working and looked around at the scene before them.

'Did anybody tell you to stop working? Get on with it!' Schillinger yelled at the other stokers and they went back to work without hesitation.

Zalman Gradowski had no intention of chancing Schillinger's wrath but, nonetheless, he couldn't believe he had heard the order correctly. Was it more dangerous to stop burning the corpses he was working on when he and the others were constantly ordered to 'speed it up' or was it more dangerous to check his understanding of the order? For a moment everyone, including the SS men who had come in with Schillinger, stared at Gradowski. Only minutes earlier he had been quietly attending to his work, burning people, numb to the task after so many bodies, after so many shifts. His mind had escaped to an event in the past before the war, which is where all of him but his body resided. Now suddenly *Oberscharführer* Schillinger had appeared, was standing there, singling him out in front of *Sonderkommando* men who weren't even supposed to be there. Schillinger was giving him an order that defied the rationale for his continued existence. Did they think he was working too slowly? What was going on? Zalman Gradowski was confused, which meant, in his present circumstances, that he was terrified.

'Take them out, sir?'

'Take them out, Jew!' Schillinger roared.

Gradowski opened the door to the oven and, with a metal rake-like implement, pulled the three bodies out of the oven and onto the iron stretcher tray. Now the smell was unbearable and two of the SS men gagged. The hands and feet of the first two bodies, red in some places, charred and badly blistered in others, had already started to shrivel, curving to arch upwards.

'Put them on the floor,' Schillinger said, calmly this time.

Using a rake as a pitch fork, Gradowski emptied the tray of the corpses one by one. Nobody said a word as he did this. Nobody knew what was going on. Gradowski was completely at a loss when suddenly Schillinger turned to Mandelbrot, Schubach, Ochrenberg, Touba, Raijsmann, Wentzel and the others who had come from the undressing room on his orders and he began to address them calmly. The other stokers strained to hear what was being said without being conspicuous about it.

'We had some problems with the last transport in the undressing room, didn't we? It slowed us down. Sometimes we have delays beyond our control. I understand this. We're all up against it. There's so much to get through. But we just now experienced a problem that, fortunately, *is* easily overcome.'

He stopped for a moment and turned back to the direction of the oven. He took a step towards it, peering in to examine the fire that never went out. The unearthly heat, even from a distance, made his face perspire. He continued calmly, wiping his forehead with a handkerchief from a pocket.

'Listen, men, when you warn them, they panic. When they panic it slows us down and that's bad for all of us,' he said, stepping back from the oven and wiping his forehead again and then examining the extent to which the moisture had been absorbed by the otherwise pristine white cloth. 'We tell you this all the time. You can't say we don't. Just say what we tell you to say. It's not difficult to remember and it will make your work much easier. Don't warn them. Please, don't warn them,' he said softly. Then he closed his eyes as if exhausted and nodded slightly, just once, whereupon, before the *Sonderkommando* realised what was happening, three SS men grabbed Ochrenberg, one at each arm and one at his legs and they shoved him head first into Gradowski's yawning oven. The sound of Ochrenberg's screams from inside the oven made everybody in the room stop their work but now this sudden unscheduled break from their labour didn't seem to bother *Oberscharführer* Schillinger at all. The short time lost was an investment in efficiency. Now they could all go back to the undressing room before emptying their gas chamber and a new man could be brought from a new transport to join the ranks of the *Sonderkommando* to replace Ochrenburg.

All of this took place within the first seventy-five minutes of one shift of one day of Henryk Mandelbrot's term in the *Sonderkommando* at Birkenau.

'Why didn't you warn them?' Lamont Williams had asked. Sixty-three years later on the ninth floor of Memorial Sloan-Kettering Cancer Center in Manhattan, on the day before he was due to be discharged, Mr Mandelbrot told the man from Building Services about the death of a man called Ochrenberg.

A number of months would pass before they would see each other again. The older man would spend some time with his family in Long Island before eventually coming back to the city to be part of the hospital's outpatient program. Then as the seasons turned colder he would be readmitted, which is when the two men would find each other again. But in between their meetings, few days passed without Lamont Williams thinking of this man and of what he had told him. There were a lot of questions he wanted to ask the absent patient. On several occasions, at night, on his way home from work or just walking down Second Avenue on his lunch hour, Lamont Williams found himself wanting to tell somebody about the death of Ochrenberg, the man who had warned the young woman in one of the undressing rooms at Birkenau. There were often a lot of people in the Gristedes supermarket, a lot of students around Rockefeller and quite a few people in the bank. There were a lot of people in the nail salons and the drycleaners and always a lot of dog-walkers in the area too. But he found himself with no one to talk to about Ochrenberg.

*

Each week in New York, Adam Zignelik received from Sahera Shukri, the Dean of Libraries at Chicago's IIT, one or sometimes a number of the newly digitised transcripts of the interviews Henry Border had conducted with Holocaust survivors in the DP camps of Europe in the summer of 1946. He did his best to keep up with them but he still had teaching responsibilities to discharge. He read the transcripts to learn more about Henry Border, the little-known psychologist who, without realising it, was one of the pioneers of what is now known as Oral History. He also read them in the hope of discovering the very thing that had led him to Border in the first place; the prospect of finding evidence to support the proposition that African American troops had been involved in the liberation of the Dachau concentration camp.

He had met William McCray for coffee several times and he knew the old man was always restraining himself to allow a decent interval to elapse before it became polite to ask, 'What news from Chicago? You find anything in those transcripts about black troops at Dachau?' Adam hadn't found anything yet but, as he told William, he had plenty of Border's transcripts still to read. Not only that, and this especially cheered William, there were many of Border's wire recordings that had still not been digitally recorded for preservation and translation. There were also wire recordings that Border hadn't made transcripts of. Who knew what information was waiting to be unearthed?

Adam thought of this from Border's point of view. Not only had Border been unable to generate much interest in his lifetime in the wartime experiences of the DPs he had interviewed during his summer with them, but he hadn't even been able to transcribe all of his recordings of these interviews. He died without knowing whether anyone would ever hear or read the bulk of the most important work he had ever done. And perhaps they never would unless Adam, having stumbled upon them and having realised their importance and the glimmer of inarticulated salvation they held for him, decided to study them.

The work was delivering Adam hope in spasmodic spurts and arrhythmic drips. He had just returned from yet another trip to Chicago. The cost was mounting. Out of his own pocket Adam was paying students of the IIT electrical engineer, Arturo Suarez, to digitise Border's unheard wire recordings. It was expensive but Adam reasoned that paying for it himself would help tie him to the project ahead of any other historians, tenured academics who might not have to be pondering a life without the protection and kudos of a university. So, despite the cost, he was finding it worthwhile to travel to Chicago rather than simply to call or email there. His most recent trip had been to interview another of Border's former students, a woman, Amy Muirden, who had been one of those whose Masters' thesis had concerned Border's 'Adjective–Verb Quotient'.

A charming, delightful woman in her eighties, a psychologist all her professional life, Amy Muirden had provided Adam with further insight into Border as a teacher, an intellectual and as a man. She was also able to talk, to a certain extent, about Border's home life, about his daughter Elise, and the live-in housekeeper, Callie, a young black woman who, though not much older than Amy had been at the time, had a teenage son. Amy had met Elise, Callie and even Callie's son Russell, on many occasions because Dr Border used to hold evening seminars for his post-graduate students at his home. She remembered that Callie got married and that for a time all three of them – Callie, Russell and the new husband, a meat worker – lived in the Border home with Dr Border and Elise, whom everyone called 'Elly'. The son, Russell, worked at the meat works with his step-father, she remembered.

Callie used to serve refreshments at the end of the seminar and Elly would help her. Sometimes Elly, who would have been about seventeen or so then, would even sit in on the seminars. The male students showed Elly particular attention, none more than Wayne Rosenthal. Everybody was aware of this. Occasional teasing by the other male students would provoke protests of innocence from Wayne Rosenthal and Elly but there was no denying their interest in each other. Amy didn't remember Dr Border being at all concerned by Wayne's attention to his daughter. On reflection, when Adam put it to her, she would have to agree that Wayne Rosenthal was probably Dr Border's favourite male student, perhaps just ahead of Arch Sanasarian. Who was his favourite female student? Amy Muirden was too polite to say but Adam gauged that it had been her. By all accounts Dr Border had tried not to show favouritism and sometimes his wicked sense of humour was directed against Wayne Rosenthal too. But Wayne never seemed to mind. The bond between Dr Border and Wayne might have been particularly strong because Wayne was able to assist Dr Border with his work more than anyone else.

'You see, not only was Wayne Jewish but his parents were Eastern European immigrants who spoke Yiddish at home. Wayne's first language was Yiddish so he was able to work on the wire recordings more than any of the others. He didn't just help with the technical side of things like Arch had; he was able to listen to the recordings and to translate them. He spent many hours on them both on campus and at Dr Border's home. Well, it was another opportunity to see Elly, wasn't it?' Amy Muirden smiled.

'I remember there was a party. Yes! That's right; Evie Harmon's brother had a twenty-first birthday party or maybe it was a graduation party but it was a very grand affair. The Harmons were terribly wealthy, certainly by the standards of those days. Oh, I'm getting ahead of myself. I'm sorry. Evie Harmon was one of the group. She was one of the Masters students who was also working on Dr Border's "Adjective–Verb Quotient". Sometimes Dr Border would tease her, just gently.'

'What would he tease her about?'

'Well, she'd gone to all the right schools, you know, and she didn't mind letting people know. Her father was the Harmon from the organs. You know Harmon organs? There used to be a Harmon organ in every movie house in Chicago, probably one in practically every movie house in the country. That was her father, interested in any technology that had to do with sound, and I think it was this that led him to be friendly with Marvin Cadden. You know about Marvin Cadden? He was the engineer at IIT who developed the wire recording device Dr Border recorded his interviews on. Of course you would know about him. I vaguely recall that it was the Harmon family connection with Marvin Cadden that led Evie to Dr Border.

'Anyway, the Harmon family was very well-to-do and when her brother had a party, I forget the occasion, Evie was able to invite some of her own friends. I remember she invited the group, all of Dr Border's Masters students. We were a bit surprised because none of us had the kind of money to invite people who were, you know, not very close friends, to family functions. Not only that but she invited Dr Border too, and even Elly, who had become . . . what would you call it? She was like a mascot, if that doesn't sound too insulting. I mean that she was almost a de facto member of the class, encouraged in this by the boys of course and particularly by Wayne. I remember this because Evie had told me that she was going to invite Elly and Dr Border and I really hadn't expected him to come. I mean, for all that he provided a light supper for us in his home after the seminars, I'd never seen him do anything . . . you know . . . nothing that you might call in any way social, nothing, you know, frivolous.

'But he came, possibly because Marvin Cadden was going to be there. Mr Cadden was an important man on campus and I remember being surprised not so much that Elly came but that Dr Border came. You know, I just remembered, even Callie came. Of course she wasn't a guest. That's right! Evie's family needed extra help with the catering and she ended up hiring Callie and her son to help out with the serving and whatever. The Dr Border group didn't know any of the others so we all sort of hung around together. Elly was with us and Dr Border was never too far away. The house and the garden, it was all terribly impressive but once Evie had given us all the grand tour we tended to stay together not far from where they'd set up the bar. I don't mean that we were drinking heavily or anything but . . . There *was* some incident. I was barely aware of it. There was something. Something happened between Dr Border and Wayne Rosenthal. I don't know what it was. They might have had words over something. I know that sounds unimaginable because he was always terribly respectful to Dr Border, as we all were, but there *was* something. None of us knew exactly what had happened but I remember it affected Elly. I'm sorry, I don't really know the details.'

'Well, it was a very long time ago.'

'It wasn't appropriate to ask Dr Border and Wayne clearly didn't want to talk about it with any of us. You have to remember in those days . . . Well, people were a lot more private about . . . their feelings. Look, I don't even know how much Elly knew. I remember thinking that it had to have something to do with her but I don't know now why I thought that then. I think Wayne Rosenthal is still alive. Have you made contact with him?'

'I've tried to arrange an interview but he won't talk to me. His son sent me an email to say that he doesn't want to talk about Dr Border or his work.'

'Perhaps he's not in good health. I haven't seen him in over twenty years but I know he lost his wife.'

'Possibly, but I don't think that's it. The son's email doesn't offer any of those excuses. He just states quite specifically that his father, Wayne Rosenthal, doesn't wish to talk about Dr Border or his work. Amy, I wondered whether perhaps you might approach him, as an old class-mate? Maybe –'

'Oh no, Dr Zignelik –'

'Adam.'

'Adam, I'm sorry, I couldn't. I mean, I haven't seen him in so long. I wouldn't feel comfortable. Maybe Arch could get him to come 'round? I know he's been in touch with him a lot more recently than me. Every-body likes Arch. Who could say no to him, such a lovely man?'

'Wayne Rosenthal.'

'I beg your pardon?'

'Wayne Rosenthal could say no to him. He's already asked on my behalf and Wayne gave him the same answer his son's given me. All I could do was leave his son with my contact details in case he changed his mind. It might not have anything to do with any of my research. It's just the way the son made it clear. It was as though if I'd wanted to interview Wayne about something, anything other than Henry Border, he'd be up for it.'

Then Amy Muirden seemed to study Adam Zignelik's face with a seriousness she had not yet displayed before she spoke again.

'So you don't think you're going to get to speak to Wayne . . . at all?'

'No, it doesn't look that way.'

'I don't really know if I . . . It was years ago, but . . . I promised Wayne I would never say anything . . . because he swore me to the strictest confidence.'

'Anything you can remember might be helpful.'

'After the incident at Evie Harmon's family's party, he came to see me. He was in a terrible state. He didn't want to say anything, but I got it out of him by promising never to tell a soul – a promise I'm about to break – and by advising him that he needed to tell someone if he wanted a chance to feel better about it. We were all psychologists, after all. I said it didn't have to be me, but . . .'

'What did he tell you?'

'He said . . . He said that he thought that he had stumbled on a wire recording that revealed what had happened to Dr Border's wife . . . during the war. He'd raised it with him at the party or just before. That's where the trouble started . . . at the party.'

'Do you know what the story was, what happened to his wife?'

'No, Wayne wouldn't tell me that.'

'Really?'

'No, really. I would tell you now.'

'Do you remember anything else?'

'No, that's it . . . except her name. He told me her name and I never forgot it . . . isn't it funny . . . because of a T.S. Eliot poem, an anti-Semitic poem, actually. Her name was Rosa Rabinowicz. In the poem it's Rachel, not Rosa, but it was enough for me to remember. Do you know that poem, "Sweeney Among the Nightingales"? It always makes me think of young Elly Border. Isn't it funny what you remember?'

There were other leads to Border and his work. One in particular was potentially even more fruitful than Wayne Rosenthal might have been but it was much further away than Chicago and so more of a problem. Adam was already using what little savings he had to go back and forth from New York to Chicago and while he felt confident he could get a project and possibly a monograph out of his research on Border and his transcripts that would be of historiographical importance, he hadn't begun to put together a proposal that could land him an imminent academic job offer. Soon he was going to have to go into debt just to keep flying to Chicago and back. As for his original motivation in connection with the role of black returned servicemen in the civil rights movement, namely his search for evidence for the involvement of black troops in the liberation of Dachau, although it was far from exhausted, nothing had turned up yet.

The distant, potentially fruitful lead was in Melbourne, Australia. It presented not merely a financial challenge but an emotional one too. Melbourne, his late mother's home town, was the city he'd grown up in after his parents had separated when he was three. It was where his grandparents had helped his mother bring him up, where he had gone to school before college and where he still felt he should have been when his mother had died. But then surely this lead, more than any he'd found since stumbling upon Border and the wire recordings, was too tantalising to ignore. Adam had tracked down to Melbourne a Holocaust survivor, one he definitely knew to be still alive, who claimed to remember being interviewed by Border in Zeilsheim DP camp. He had come across the woman's name in Border's papers but he hadn't yet come across the transcript of her interview. It might have been one of the transcripts that Sahera Shukri and her staff hadn't yet reached or the Melbourne woman could have been on one of the wire recordings that nobody had heard since Border had recorded it.

'Sweetheart, you can't wait for this woman's transcript to turn up. It might not turn up until you get all the recordings digitised and transcribed and translated,' he heard Diana's voice tell him. 'In the meantime, the woman might die.'

'I'm already shelling out money on this thing left, right and centre.'

'Adam, you're not *shelling out money*, you're investing in a project that might be very important both for your career and for what we know about those times.'

'"Might be", are the operative words.'

'Adam, are you seeing a pattern here . . . in your life? You've got to show a little faith.'

'Of course you're right. Now if you could just meet me at the corner of 109th and Broadway, we can sell the faith I'm meant to have to my Chase personal banker and then I can go to Melbourne to interview this woman.'

'So you're still with Chase?'

Suddenly the buzzer to the intercom rang.

'You expecting someone?'

'You know I'm not. You live in my head.'

'I might live there but sometimes I go out.'

The buzzer rang again and this time Adam answered it. 'Hi, I think you've pressed the wrong buzzer.'

'No, I haven't. It's me.'

'Sonia?'

'Can I come up?'

'Sure.'

'Do your parents know you're here?'

'Comin' up!'

Adam stood around with his hands in his pockets waiting for Sonia to knock at the door. When she knocked he opened it. She came in, a little out of breath, and they hugged as they always had since she was a child, but this time he noticed she was slower to let go.

'Do your parents know you're here?'

'Yep.'

'Really?'

'You don't think I'm gonna lie, do you?'

'No, of course not. You're not capable of lying. Other people are but *you're* not.'

'Hey, what do you mean by that?'

'So your parents really do know you're here?'

'I've answered that.'

'That's true. It's just that . . . Weren't you meant to call before coming over?'

'Are you . . . *entertaining*?'

'Ooh that hurts! You really know how to hurt a guy. I could've been working.'

'Are you?'

'I *was* actually.'

'Sorry, Adam. You want me to go?' She looked at him plaintively.

'No, I'm nearly done. Why don't you grab a soda and I'll be with you in a few minutes? I've got to finish reading something.'

She walked over to his refrigerator and opened it. Adam was about to go back to his desk when he noticed that she was just standing there, seemingly transfixed by something inside the refrigerator. She had her back to him and wasn't moving.

'Sonia, you don't have to defrost the fridge.' She didn't move. It was as though she hadn't heard him.

'Sonia?' She stayed still and silent, just staring into the refrigerator. He walked over to see what it was she was staring at.

'Sonia? What are you looking at?' She turned around and he could see tears rolling down her cheeks.

'Hey, little one, what's wrong?' He took her in his arms and hugged her again. 'Was I meant to save the last Dr Pepper? What's wrong, sweetie?'

'Everything's all different now. Nobody says anything, like it's all still the same. But it's not.'

'What do you mean?'

'Are you and Diana ever going to get back together again?'

'Is that why you're crying? You're not s'posed to cry about that. That's *my* job.'

'Do you cry about that?'

'All the time.'

'Really?'

'Sure, what else have I got to do? But why are *you* crying?'

At this question she began to cry harder, her shoulders rising and falling involuntarily in time to the internal rhythm of her sadness.

'Adam, they're always fighting. I hate it. I really hate it. Grandpa didn't come for dinner tonight like he was meant to. Nobody said why. It didn't used to be like this, did it?' And then from a space between his arms and inside his chest she asked, 'When did it get like this?'

*

It was night and Henryk Mandelbrot, again on the day shift, was in one of the barracks used to house the *Sonderkommando*. Zalman Gradowski, one of the stokers, wanted to talk to him but Mandelbrot was going to have to wait. Gradowski had still not finished his evening ritual. Each night at the end of his shift, after the *Appell*, the roll call, and after he had eaten, Zalman Gradowski would put on a *tallis*, a Jewish prayer shawl, that had been found among a victim's possessions and he would recite *Kaddish*, the mourner's prayer, for all of the people he had just incinerated. He did this every day. Every day he also recorded in secret a running account of the work of the *Sonderkommando* and of all that he'd witnessed. Henryk Mandelbrot knew what he was doing and why. He'd had to know. Mandelbrot was one of two other men with whom Gradowski shared a wooden bunk and it would not have been possible to hide his writing from them. The other man, also named Zalman, was Zalman Lewental, a Polish Jew from the town of Ciechanow. Zalman Lewental was also keeping a record of the work of the *Sonderkommando*.

Gradowski and Lewental, who had been in the *Sonderkommando* longer than Mandelbrot, had explained to him their purpose. These writings, they had said, were acts of resistance. Since it looked to them as though no Jews would survive the war and it was close to certain that none of the *Sonderkommando* would, they had decided to produce a written account of the destruction of European Jewry down to the last detail and to bury it in the hope that it would survive. This was the whole point of surviving as long as they could. News, or, more accurately, rumours, had spread that the Russians were getting ever nearer and that the camp would soon be liberated but rumours of all sorts had always spread throughout the camp every bit as fast as lice, typhus and dysentery. The Nazis might sooner or later lose the war against the Allies but they would win their war against the Jews. The two Zalmans, Gradowski and Lewental, would record as much of what they saw as they could despite the certainty of immediate death if they were discovered. When they thought the time was right, they would bury their testimony as securely as was possible somewhere near the crematoria where they worked . . . This was what kept them going – the need to tell what would otherwise have been unimaginable.

It wasn't his writing that Gradowski wanted to talk about to Mandelbrot. While Lewental looked out, Gradowski took Mandelbrot outside the barrack and when he was certain no one was paying them any attention, he spoke to him very quietly. 'You know Lewental has a brother here?'

'Yeah, I know, an electrician, right?

'Right . . . an electrician,' said Gradowski. The flames from the pits lit up the night sky. The work of the night shift was well under way. Not every one of Birkenau's slave labour details were divided into day and night shifts. The *Sonderkommando* was. Its work never stopped.

'So . . . Lewental's brother is an electrician, that's what you wanted to tell me?'

Whatever it was Gradowski had wanted to tell him, he now seemed extremely reticent about it, almost as though he were having second thoughts about taking him aside. The smell of charred flesh hung in the air even as a new transport was being unloaded. 'Lewental . . . thinks we ought to tell you . . .'

'That his brother is an electrician?' Gradowski looked around them again. It was still safe to talk. It was almost a whisper.

'Henryk, have you heard anything about a resistance movement?'

'In the *Sonderkommando*?'

'Throughout the camp.'

'No, is there one?'

Gradowski nodded that there was.

'Yeah?' questioned Mandelbrot. 'Zalman, what exactly have they achieved? Look over there. It's business as usual.' Henryk Mandelbrot pointed up at the night sky lit up by the flames from the pits where the night shift was trying to hurry things along. 'This resistance, whoever they are, they're doing a great job.'

'Yeah, well, so far, yes, they've spent too much time arguing with each other to be of much use to anyone but themselves,' Gradowski had to admit, 'but there's been a change recently. We're hoping for better.'

The dogs were barking in the distance. The work of the night shift was progressing without diurnal variation. The sun was irrelevant to this work. The blinding lights were on. The screams had started right from the unloading ramp. The more screams the more the beatings. It was a rough equation, all the more true the earlier the screams began. If the people were already panicking there was no point trying to keep them calm. It was already too late. So the SS would just want to hurry them up. Spare the deception and hope to save time with more than usual beatings. This was going to be an especially difficult shift. Not only were too many people panicking too early, but the victims were going to have to wait. There were still corpses to be unpacked in the gas chamber of Crematorium III. They were falling further behind and it made the SS especially irritable.

'Who are these people, these resisters? Where are they?'

'Shhh! Listen to me carefully. I'll tell you what I know. There's an Auschwitz-Birkenau branch of the Polish underground, the Polish Home Army. They act in coordination with the Polish underground outside the camp.'

'The AK?'

'Yeah, the AK has a branch inside the camp. There's another resistance group in the camp, the *Kampfgruppe Auschwitz*, made up of leftists of all different nationalities, including some of the Jews in the different work details. Then there are various small groups of Jews who've formed resistance cells on the basis of . . . I don't know . . . ideological grounds or just based on their hometown ties.'

'So much resistance all over the camp!' interrupted Mandelbrot. 'It's a wonder anyone has time to be gassed.'

'Well, it's only the Jews who get gassed, isn't it? Okay, some Gypsies and homosexuals too, but the rest of them, the Poles, the Russians, the French, all the leftists and everyone else, they have time to make all sorts of plans, argue with each other about every detail, ditch the plans and start over again.'

'And they hate each other more than they hate the Germans.'

'Yeah, maybe. Perhaps that's why you've never seen any of their plans bear fruit.'

The filing had started in the dressing room of Crematorium III. The first five came down the stairs; all women – a hairdresser, a widow, a photographer's assistant, a teacher, and the cousin of a violin teacher well known in his town who played very well herself. The first of the next five pushed into the back of the violinist. She turned around and already another five were coming down.

'There seems to have been a change recently,' Gradowski whispered. 'The Auschwitz branch of the AK and the *Kampfgruppe Auschwitz* have put aside their differences.'

'I'm happy for them.'

'Well you might be. They've established what they're calling the joint Auschwitz Military Council . . .' Gradowski leaned in closer, 'with the intention of planning and executing an uprising.'

'An uprising?'

'Yes and the *Sonderkommando* are to be included in this uprising. Not only is the plan for there to be a mass escape from the ranks of the entire camp, it's planned that the gas chambers and crematoria be blown up and destroyed.'

'So that's where the *Sonderkommando* comes in?'

'Well, we have the privilege of living and working here. And we're going to die here anyway. Plans have been made and in fact efforts are already being made to enable prisoners to acquire weapons.'

'Weapons?'

'What do you know about the *Weichsel Union Metallwerke* factory?'

'Nothing, what is it?'

'One of the labour details is dedicated to the *Weichsel Union Metall-werke* factory. It's a munitions factory near the main camp. You passed it when they brought you in. We've wanted to acquire gun powder from there for the purpose of making our own incendiary devices, bombs or grenades of some kind. There's a Russian –'

'Who are *we*?'

'Henryk, so many questions! I need to get this over with. Some time ago we made contact with two Jews who work in the *Weichsel Union Metall-werke* munitions factory, Israel Gutman and Joshua Leifer, Polish Jews.'

'They're part of the resistance?'

'Yes, they were trying to make contact with the women who worked in what the Germans call the *Pulverraum*, the gunpowder room. Only women work there, no men. But the women in the *Pulverraum* are under the strictest supervision imaginable so they haven't been able to even contact them and sound them out about getting hold of gunpowder.'

'And they work in the same factory?'

'It's a big factory. They're under tight supervision.'

'So no gunpowder.'

'We don't even know if they'd agree to do it.'

'Well, if no one can even contact these women it's off, this part of it, right?'

'Not necessarily. No man can get to them but what if there is a woman from within the resistance who could contact the women in the *Pulver-raum* or even if there is another woman who works at the munitions factory who could?'

Inside the undressing room at Crematorium III the men had already started coming down. They were well advanced and most of the women were already at least partially undressed but for a mother and her two daughters, aged about twelve and fourteen. These three, all well dressed and clearly from a very comfortable background, did not move at all. Terrified, they looked around them in disbelief. Then the twelve-year-old said something to her mother in French and it happened that the *Sonderkommando* man nearest them, Chaim Neuhof, spoke a smattering of French.

Hurriedly in the middle of the chaos, trying to make sure the SS didn't notice him talking to her, he asked, 'Vous êtes française, madame? Madame? Are you French, madame?'

'De la Belgique, monsieur,' the fourteen-year-old replied shyly, her mother apparently totally unable to speak out of fear. The undressing room was filling up.

'Madame, you must all of you undress immediately! If the SS see you dressed they will beat you. They will kill you and the girls with their clubs! All of you . . . undress now!' he said in rapid whispered broken French while pretending to help an old man undress.

But a combination of shyness, shame, pride and terror rendered the mother and both of her daughters seemingly physically unable to comply. They just looked at the scene they were in with horrified disbelief but as though they were not a part of it.

'Hurry, madame! Please!' Chaim Neuhof insisted, still in a whisper with his head bowed as he helped the old man struggling to remove his trousers. An SS guard had now noticed the scene from the corner of his eye.

'I will stand in front of you, madame. Please! For the young girls, you have to hurry! They will beat you!'

The *Sonderkommando* man, Chaim Neuhof, stood up and placed himself in front of the mother and her two daughters with his back turned to them but, because they were standing near the centre of a crowded room full of frantic movement, he could only partially cover them on one side and could guarantee nothing other than that he himself wouldn't watch them undress. But somehow this act was itself enough to get them started. Neuhof provided seconds of cover from the SS man watching the mother and her daughters from the corner of his eye and by the time the guard's view was no longer obscured, they were largely naked and the guard turned his attention elsewhere around the undressing room. Chaim Neuhof turned around and saw that finally they had complied. Fortuitously he'd been able to save them from a brutal beating in the last minutes of their lives. He usually worked the day shift, and had only swapped that shift with a man who was ill, a man who, like almost every other *Sonderkommando* member, spoke no French.

'Thank you, madame,' he said when he eventually turned around. The three of them moved a little towards him as though he was in a position to protect them, not realising that what little help he could ever offer had just in those few seconds been spent. The mother was about to touch him, an involuntary consequence of this mix of his kindness, her fear and her gratitude. For a moment, quite dangerously, he stopped in the middle of everything. This was when he saw them anew, each of them by now naked, each of the three of them to Neuhof so beautiful, their round eyes pleading with him, their unblemished pale skin, their thick shoulder-length auburn hair. Would he ever get this image out of his head? Different-sized versions of female perfection had appeared before him in the middle of hell, the very middle. Tears welled up in his eyes. He bent down and picked up their clothes. 'Look at them!' screamed a voice from inside his head. This was death talking. He had to turn away.

Gradowski continued his explanation to Henryk Mandelbrot. 'A man was found who could make contact with a woman who could in turn make contact with the women in the *Pulverraum*.' He looked around to see if they were being watched. 'Lewental has a brother, Noah, who is an electrician.'

'Ah yes, Noah the electrician!'

'Being an electrician, the younger Lewental has access to parts of the camp ordinary prisoners never get to.'

'Yeah, but he still has to find the right woman. He can't interview for the job.'

'He has already found the perfect woman, so he says. She works in the *Effektenlager*, in *Kanada*.'

'That's great; she'll be in good shape.'

'Yeah, and she's from the Ciechanow group. That's where the Lewentals are from. She was his girlfriend before the war. Zalman knows her as well. She's going to be the contact between the women in the *Pulverraum* at the munitions factory and the *Sonderkommando* resistance. We'll receive the gun powder, store it and, with the Russian, figure out how to convert it into weapons. Then when the signal comes from the Auschwitz Military Council, when they're ready for the camp-wide rebellion, we'll try to use everything we've got to destroy the gas chambers and crematoria. Who knows, maybe some of us will even escape from here.'

'Do you think any of this is going to work?'

Gradowski turned to him. 'Henryk, we're all going to die anyway.'

'Who in the *Sonderkommando* knows about this?'

'Only those in the resistance know.'

'Well, I assume if you're telling me then –'

'Yes, Henryk, I'm asking you to join. So will you join?'

'Yes, of course. What's there to think about? I don't understand why you took so long to ask me.'

'It's just that . . . if we can . . . it will be the most dangerous enterprise undertaken in the entire history of this death camp.'

'What here isn't dangerous?'

'That's true, but you've never had any choice in anything that's happened to you since you first came through the gates. This now would be your choice.'

'Still, Zalman, can you seriously imagine me choosing not to be involved? And even if I did decline your invitation, there's sure to be others here you could approach.'

'Yes, but they're not all trustworthy and, anyway, I really didn't want to have to tell Lewental you'd declined.'

Now it was Henryk Mandelbrot's turn to smile. 'Since when were you so scared of Lewental?'

But Gradowski didn't smile, in fact he turned away.

As they spoke quietly and still undetected, the last of the people from the transport were pushed naked inside the gas chamber attached to Crematorium III and an SS guard slammed the door shut. People began to cry at the sound the door made. A signal was given and within minutes the green pellets were being dropped in from above. A woman who had shown some considerable skill at the violin looked around in terror, realising she had become separated from the last person there whom she knew. She called out for her friend. It was drowned out by the screams of 2000 strangers. She was going to die alone and she knew it. A young mother from Belgium, quite unusually beautiful, hugged her daughters as tightly as she could with both arms. It had started.

'No, I'm not scared of Lewental,' said Zalman Gradowski, looking away from him in the direction of the burning pits.

'So? I don't get it,' Mandelbrot asked.

'Henryk, I didn't really think you'd decline. But . . .'

'So why'd you wait to ask me?'

'What does it matter now?'

'No, I want to know.'

Inside the gas chamber of Crematorium III the climbing had started.

'If you had declined,' said Gradowski, 'given how much I've had to tell you . . . Well, I don't know what Lewental might've done.'

The dogs had started barking again. Another transport had just arrived.

part ten

It was night. The interminable *Appel*, the roll call, was over and the rations that masqueraded as the evening's meals had been distributed when Rosa Rabinowicz, hoping she hadn't been detected, reached the entrance of a block that was not hers within the women's camp at Auschwitz-Birkenau. Looking around furtively, she spoke to the *Block-älteste*, the senior female prisoner responsible for a block within the barracks.

'You have women here who work in the *Weichsel Union Metallwerke* factory?'

'What if we do?'

'Can you let me in?'

'What do you want?'

'I'm looking for a Jewish woman who works there in the *Pulverraum*, the one who lost her parents. I have a last message for her from them.'

'What are you talking about? There's not a Jewish woman *in* here that hasn't lost her parents.'

The disingenuousness of Rosa's approach had been as disarming as she had intended it to be.

Rosa Rabinowicz kept looking around. She was in danger just being there. 'Can you let me in? Then I can explain.'

'Why can't you explain out here?' Looking her up and down, the *Blockälteste* saw that Rosa seemed less starved than most of the other prisoners. What had this Jew done to be better fed than the average prisoner? the woman wondered. Perhaps she shouldn't be trusted? Or was she somebody with influence worth befriending? No ordinary Jew trying to find another Jew in Auschwitz-Birkenau would describe the person being sought as *the* one who had lost his or her parents. Who was she? Was she dangerous? What did she really want?

Rosa reached inside a pocket and pulled out a silver watch, which she showed the *Blockälteste*. 'It's yours if you let me in.'

'Where did you get that?' the woman said in astonishment.

'You get the watch if you let me in. You don't ever get any explanations.'

'You're from *Kanada*, aren't you?' the *Blockälteste* said, letting Rosa inside the block. In *Kanada* one could find food, or goods from the gassed victims' belongings to trade for food.

Finding Noah Lewental had given Rosa the courage to make this approach. Not only was there someone left alive who had known her from before the start of this nightmare, but that someone was Noah. Her parents were almost certainly dead and in all likelihood Elise, her long-lost daughter, was also dead. Her siblings, if not already dead, would sooner or later be killed because that was the logic of the place. To be alive there was an aberration that would be corrected as soon as you had outlived your utility to the Third Reich. But Noah was still alive. He had found her in this vast factory of death and he had enlisted her in a plan to try to sabotage the killing machinery. Most people there could not bring themselves even to imagine fighting back. The SS were fully armed and equipped, well fed, strong and healthy. To try was to commit certain suicide and though most knew that death in this place was inevitable, few could bring themselves to hasten it. What if a husband, a child, a parent was still alive? Didn't you want more than anything else to see them? Your good friend suicide, your best friend, would wait for you. Suicide was the one card always up your sleeve. It was just a matter of choosing the time to play it. But resisting the SS? Better to dream of fleeing to America. It was more realistic.

But now Rosa was not alone. Noah Lewental's presence there had rekindled her sense of self and she was going to resist. It was with this resolve that she had bribed her way into the block. Of course, as the *Blockälteste* had spat out with a mix of suspicion and contempt, Rosa knew that almost everybody there had lost their parents. But coupled with the silver watch from *Kanada*, of value as barter, the approach had got her into the block housing two girls employed, she'd been told, in the *Pulverraum*, the gunpowder area, of the *Weichsel Union Metallwerke* munitions factory, who might be prepared to help smuggle out quantities of gunpowder.

Rosa observed that a not uncommon evening ritual in many of the blocks of the women's camp had already begun in this one too. At the back of the room, next to a woman picking the lice off another woman's scalp, maybe half a dozen young Jewish women were sitting or lying listening to another woman whose turn it was to regale them with descriptions of food from home, dishes she remembered from before the war. Beside them a woman with glazed eyes and parched lips breathed through her mouth and shook with fever. Dysentery or typhus, who among them could tell? She could have been anyone and, live or die that evening, tomorrow it would be someone else. There was no one there who knew her full name, no one close enough to hear this woman wheezing who spoke her language. She'd been like this off and on for days. Nights were the worst and this was the worst of the nights. She'd never make it through another *Appel*. Falling out of and then back into consciousness long enough to hear a babble of languages she didn't understand, long enough to see the lice being flicked from another woman's scalp nearby, she was terrified. Surrounded by people who ignored her, she knew in her rare sentient moments that she was utterly alone and that this was how she would die. Who would be able to tell anyone after the war what had happened to this nameless woman?

'She would use a kilogram of beef and cut the fat off. Then she would add one tablespoon of paprika, one tablespoon of crushed garlic –'

'My mother added onions.'

'I'm not up to the onions. You interrupted. *My* mother used onions . . .'

'And the beans?'

'Yes, red beans, of course.'

Rosa approached the two girls whom the *Blockälteste* had pointed out to her.

'Are you Estusia?' she asked.

'Yes, who are you?' the young woman answered.

'Are you the Estusia who works in the *Pulverraum* at the *Union Metallwerke* factory?'

'Yes. Who are you?' she asked again, her sister, a girl of no more than fifteen, close beside her.

'My name is Rosa Rabinowicz. Can I talk to you . . . alone?'

'What's this about?'

'I'll tell you if we can talk . . .' She looked around the block. 'Can we talk . . . alone?'

'This is my sister, Hannah. She'll come with us.'

'No offence, but it might be better if she didn't.'

'Better?'

'Better for everyone.'

'I tell her everything.'

'Well, you may want to reconsider that.'

'She works with me.'

'In the *Pulverraum*?'

'Not in the *Pulverraum* but in the *Union Metallwerke* factory.'

'How old is she?'

'Old enough to answer questions put to her by strangers when she thinks there's a good reason to answer.'

'How old are you?' Rosa asked the younger of the Weiss sisters, Hannah.

'I'm fifteen. What do you want from us?'

'Come with me, both of you.'

Rosa Rabinowicz suggested they move to a corner of the block that was, at least temporarily, less crowded and that Hannah keep watch while she talked to Estusia, explaining that what she had to say was of the utmost importance and needed to be kept secret.

Rosa spoke almost in a whisper. 'What do you know about the resistance?'

'What do you mean "resistance"?' Estusia asked.

Estusia Weiss had every right to find it difficult to believe that any resistance movement existed in Auschwitz, a place where daily she saw people she was housed with die on their bunks or drop dead where they stood in front of her during the *Appel*, a place where, day and night, transports of newly arrived people, nearly all Jews, were gassed and cremated in their thousands, the smoke and the unmistakable smell from the crematoria chimneys filling the sky and the air. But when Rosa explained that not only was there a resistance movement within the camp but that its members wanted her and her colleagues at the *Weichsel Union Metallwerke* factory to assist them, Estusia felt stirrings entirely alien to most inmates in the camp. To learn that there were prisoners, Jewish prisoners too, who were planning to sabotage the killing process, to fight back, to attempt escape, was to experience something akin to a religious revelation. Perhaps someone would survive all of this. Perhaps the world might get to know even a tenth of what had gone on there. Despite the risk, she needed no convincing to join them and she was certain that some if not all of the other Jewish girls of the *Pulverraum* also would. She pointed at one of them, her friend Ala, who she was sure could be counted on.

It was arranged that Rosa would make regular visits to the block housing Estusia and Hannah Weiss using goods from *Kanada* as bribes wherever necessary to facilitate entry and egress. There she would receive the tiny packages of gunpowder and see that they were delivered to the resistance within the *Sonderkommando*.

How they would get the gunpowder out of the factory was still to be worked out.

The woman Rosa had seen lying shaking with fever had died by the time she walked back out of the block. Nobody had noticed. Within twelve hours she would be on a pile of corpses that Zalman Gradowski would burn with the transport of Jews that would arrive after the transport that was arriving now.

The stratagem they used to get the gunpowder out of the factory and into their block was devised by Estusia together with her fifteen-year-old sister Hannah and their friend and fellow *Pulverraum* worker, Ala. Only four women at a time and Regina, their supervisor, worked in the *Pulverraum*. All of them were Jews. Hannah was one of a group of prisoners assigned to maintenance in the factory. The women of the *Pulverraum* used presses to insert measured amounts of gunpowder into shell components that were delivered to them from somewhere else in the factory. The number and location of these munitions components were constantly checked by the Germans and there was no way any of these shells could be smuggled out of the *Pulverraum*. It was Hannah who thought of utilising the garbage collection system for smuggling out just the gunpowder. There were numerous small metal boxes throughout the factory for the purpose of collecting garbage to be emptied into large garbage bins that lined the walls and the corners of the factory. Prisoners in Hannah's group were variously given the task of sweeping the floor of a section and emptying the small metal boxes as well as the piles of swept garbage into the large garbage bins.

Hannah took it upon herself to convince the German civilian forewoman that she was required to regularly collect the small metal boxes in the *Pulverraum* containing garbage, empty them into the big bins in the factory, and then bring them back filled with strips of cloth from other parts of the factory for emptying into a big bin in the *Pulverraum*. It was in these small pieces of cloth that Estusia and Ala and later others, including Regina, would wrap and knot tiny quantities of gunpowder that they would drop into the returned small metal boxes. Hannah would make her rounds with an air of confidence that suggested to anyone watching her that somebody in authority must have ordered her to do this. She would always come and then leave the *Pulverraum* with two of the smaller metal boxes. One would be legitimate; the other would be used in the smuggling, either to deliver the cloth strips to Estusia and Ala for them to wrap the gunpowder in, or else to collect the wrapped gunpowder. Once Hannah had the tiny cloth packages of gunpowder she would distribute them to a few trusted colleagues who worked with her.

None of the *Pulverraum* workers themselves ever left the factory with gunpowder on them. It was Hannah and her colleagues in other sections of the *Metallwerke* factory who carried the cloth parcels, which they hid in their clothes, back into their barracks block in the women's camp in Auschwitz I. Their practice at the end of each shift was to position themselves in the middle of the formation of prisoners returning to their barracks in the camp so that in the event of one of the random searches by the SS they would have valuable seconds in which to untie the cloth parcels and empty the gunpowder onto the ground before they were reached. But in the normal course of events, the gunpowder parcels were picked up from Estusia and Hannah's block by Rosa and, later, another female prisoner from *Kanada*. From *Kanada* they could be picked up by members of the *Sonderkommando* when they were delivering the belongings of the freshly gassed transports. Every person involved knew the danger they were putting themselves in. But death there was certain. Only the way it came to you was not. And when.

*

When the Co-op City Express bus arrived at its final stop from Manhattan there were only three passengers still on it. The last one to get off was Lamont Williams. He had fallen asleep somewhere around 120th Street after another long day at work. He would have remained asleep on the bus had the driver not called out to wake him. Lamont was not more than two steps away from the bus when it pulled away from the kerb. The driver was in a hurry. It was dark, and since the other two passengers were already inside their respective buildings, Lamont started on his way home in what looked to be a deserted street. He didn't see anyone else around until suddenly he felt a man's forearm holding him around his collar bone and the blade of a knife against his neck.

'Don't turn around,' said a voice.

Instinctively, he turned his head slowly to see who was attacking him.

'Don't move,' said the voice.

From the little Lamont had been able to see there was only one person, a man wearing gloves and a balaclava under a hoody. Judging by his voice, the man was African American.

'Listen, man,' said Lamont, 'I ain't got no money and this whole place is crawlin' with cameras so you gotta ask yourself if this really what you wanna be doin'.'

'This ain't about money,' said the voice.

'I ain't got no drugs, no weapons neither. So you got yourself the wrong man.'

'No, you the right man.'

Lamont drew a breath through his nostrils and with all the strength he could muster threw off the man's forearm and ducked slightly so that when the knife moved in as he had known it would, it came in contact with the skin of his skull rather than into his neck. Feeling the blade against his head made the anger rise up in him and he fell onto his assailant who in turn fell onto the ground. The man still had not relinquished his grip on the knife but now Lamont at least had an even chance. As they rolled on the ground Lamont felt the knife cut his right hand. With his other hand he took a swing at the man's face. The connection wasn't perfect but the man felt it.

'What the fuck you want?'

'I want you to stay the fuck away from my mother!'

'Mister, you got the wrong man.'

'She told me you come around.'

'I don't know what you talkin' 'bout.'

'You leave her alone, you know what's good for you.'

'Show you what's good for you.'

'Leave her out of it, Lamont.'

When he heard his name he rolled away from the man slightly. His assailant's hoody had come off by this time and Lamont stood over the man, panting.

'You a damn fool! You cover up your head so's I won't know who you are. But you don't want me comin' near your mother.'

'That's right,' said the man, also panting, and now slowly getting up off the ground.

'So I *have* to know who you are, fool. You the son of your mother.'

'Yeah? Everybody the son of their mother.'

'Take off the balaclava, Kevin, you damn fool.'

'You scare her, Lamont. Why? She never done nothin' to you,' said Kevin Sweeney, the younger brother of Michael Sweeney, Lamont's childhood friend, the one whose armed robbery had led to Lamont's incarceration. Now his head was uncovered to reveal a bloodied ear where Lamont had hit him.

'You're comin' with me, shithead.'

'Where we goin'?'

With Michael's little brother in tow, Lamont flagged a gypsy cab to take them both to the Emergency Room at Jacobi. Lamont explained why he had visited Michael and Kevin's mother those months ago.

'So you sayin' you all about Chantal?'

'No, relax yourself, Kevin. I'm lookin' for my daughter. Chantal's her mother so that's where I start and I thought you might know where Chantal might be at.'

'I don't know where Chantal –'

'I don't care if you damn well married her, fool! I'm just lookin' for my –'

'Lamont,' Kevin said sadly in the back of the cab, 'I ain't seen Chantal for years, like five or six years. She never wanted me, not really. I admit, I thought she was fine but . . .'

'I can't tell my grandma I'm sittin' in the hospital. She don't need to hear that. Damn you, Kevin! Fuck! How am I gonna work now?' Lamont said, looking at his injured hand. 'They might have to put stitches in my damn hand. This gonna need stitches! You dumber n' your brother!'

'Yeah, I heard that,' Kevin said quietly.

'He still inside?'

'Yeah.'

'Listen to me, you gonna put *your* hand in your pocket for this here cab ride. You know that, don't you?'

'Yeah, I help you out. I like to do what's right. Think maybe they could look at my ear? You fierce, man!'

Lamont had to have several stitches put in his hand. He made a call to his grandmother telling her that he'd injured his hand at work and was waiting in ER for treatment.

'No, it's not too serious but I don't know how long I'll be so don't wait dinner and don't wait up . . . Well, I'll just warm up what's left when I get home.'

She was the only one in his life who cared enough about him to be lied to, it occurred to him as he put the receiver down and went back to the line he'd been in. When he got home he saw that she had left a note for him on the kitchen table explaining that there was a plate for him in the refrigerator. Beside the note was a glass of Seneca apple juice she'd left for him just as she used to when he was a child. Over the stitches they had put a bandage and that's what his grandmother saw the next morning before they both headed out to work. For quite some time nobody at work noticed his injury or thought to comment on it. He was making his rounds collecting the garbage from the patients' rooms as quietly and as inconspicuously as possible when he heard a voice coming weakly to him from inside one of the rooms.

'The hand, Mr Lamont, it's *still* not healed? It's the same one?'

'Hey, Mr Mandelbrot!' he said quietly. 'Yes, it's the same one. How you doin'?' He asked the question as a matter of form and without thinking. The old man had been readmitted but he was dying. Lamont could see that. It was a different room from the one on the ninth floor the old man was originally in. That, and the old man's health, were all that had changed.

'You find your wife yet?'

'We weren't married but –'

'Your daughter?'

'Not yet.'

Henryk Mandelbrot wanted to test him to see what he remembered of the chapters of his life but Lamont had to make his rounds and wasn't able to stop.

'I remember it, Mr Mandelbrot. How could I ever forget it?'

'All of it?'

'I think so.'

'So we'll see.'

'I can't stop now. I'll come see you at the end of my shift.'

'Don't take too long. You know I'm dying.'

'No you're not,' Lamont Williams said perfunctorily, as a matter of course.

'You'll see; that's what I'm here for.'

'I'll come back at the end of my shift.'

He was true to his word and when he came back at the end of his day he noticed that the patient looked even thinner, not merely than he had been in the other room, but thinner than earlier in the day; thinner, weaker and more vulnerable.

'So we have to continue where we left off before I got interrupted.'

'Interrupted?'

'A few months of life . . . in Great Neck . . . It interrupted us. You have to tell me what you remember.'

Lamont Williams smiled. With the exception of a few minor details, which Mr Mandelbrot wasted no time correcting, Lamont had remembered everything the patient had told him.

'That's all you told me. You got to stick around 'cause I don't know how the story ends.'

'It ends in a few days, maybe a few hours,' the old man whispered. 'I will tell you the end.'

'No, Mr Mandelbrot, you should save your strength.'

'What should I save it for?'

'For your family?'

'They were here. Already they came. You see that? Bring it here.'

Lamont went over to a shelf on the opposite wall where a vase full of red and yellow roses sat beside a silver *menorah*, a nine-branched candelabrum and, as requested, he brought the *menorah* over to the bedside.

'Do you know what this is, Mr Lamont?'

'It's a candleholder, a Jewish candleholder. For Christmas, you use it at Christmas, right?'

'You know about the Maccabees? Probably not.'

'No, I don't –'

'If I live long enough I'll tell you about them, but it's more important I finish about what happened to me.'

'You want me to put this back on the shelf?'

'Not yet. It's silver.'

'It's very nice.'

'My son and daughter-in-law brought it here. I'm glad now they did.'

'Sure.'

'When I die I want you to take it.'

'No, Mr Mandelbrot, I –'

'You have to remember what I've –'

'Mr Mandelbrot, I don't need this to remember you.'

'It's not me, it's *all* of them, all what I told you. This is your responsibility now. Do you understand this?'

'But I don't need this to remember –'

'But how will I know you remember? You take it and I'll know.'

'Mr Mandelbrot, I can't take it. It's yours.'

'Yes, it's mine so if I want to give it to someone I can.'

'But Mr Mandelbrot, I can't.'

'You keep saying that. Do you remember the first day I met you? You brought me up from the street where they were all smoking. Do you remember?'

'I remember.'

'You said the same thing that day too.'

'What?'

'"I can't." But you *did*. If you hadn't done that we wouldn't be here now talking like this. Like two old friends.'

'Like two old friends,' Lamont Williams repeated quietly.

'Old people don't make many new friends, Mr Lamont. Think about it. So a friend can give another friend a gift, right?'

'Right.'

'Of course right. Look, I haven't come all this way . . .' The old man swallowed and, as though talking for his life, he took Lamont's hand in both of his before continuing.

'You think I'm joking, Mr Lamont? They'll put it in a cupboard as soon as they get home from the funeral. And don't ever have grandchildren. Your death will only interrupt them. Their whole life is a party. They don't listen to me when I'm *alive*. They understand suffering like they understand . . . like . . . like they understand Chinese. You're a quiet man, Mr Lamont, but you . . . *you* understand Chinese. You understand? You'll take it home and put it somewhere where you can see it, maybe every day. When you look at it you'll know I'll be asking you, "Did you tell someone?" It won't be easy. At first they won't listen, and if they do listen, they won't believe you, but you'll keep going and you'll tell them what they did to your friend and his people. It's my gift.'

*

The tide of events outside Auschwitz-Birkenau often affected what went on inside the camp. In July 1944 the Hungarian Head of State, Admiral Horthy, in response to international pressure halted the deportation of Hungarian Jews to Auschwitz. More than 400,000 Hungarian Jews had already perished in the gas chambers there and although the deportations were to continue elsewhere after a German-backed putsch later that year, by October the transport of Hungarian Jews to Auschwitz had ceased. No group of prisoners was better placed to realise this than the *Sonderkommando*. In September some 200 members of the *Sonderkommando* were murdered by the SS without the knowledge of the remaining members. Tricked into believing they were being transferred to a subcamp at nearby Gleiwitz, they were instead taken to the gas chambers normally used for disinfecting clothes at *Kanada*. But it was impossible to keep this from the *Kanada Kommando* whose members included a young woman in the resistance, Rosa Rabinowicz. The remaining *Sonderkommando* would have learned the fate of their colleagues within days had they not learned of it even sooner.

For the only time ever in the history of the operation of the gas chambers and crematoria at Auschwitz-Birkenau, the SS ordered a lockdown of the *Sonderkommando* that day and took it upon themselves to perform the usual tasks of the *Sonderkommando* on the pretext that it was the bodies of the civilian casualties of an air raid that were being burned. The pretext for the lockdown made no sense since the *Sonderkommando* had always been forced to work no matter who it was that was being burned. When the lockdown was over, men on the next shift were able to confirm the worst fears of the *Sonderkommando* men. Being inexperienced at the burning of corpses, the SS had done a poor job. When Zalman Gradowski started work he found the incompletely burned bodies the SS had left behind. In horror Gradowski opened the oven door to find the charred body of a *Sonderkommando* member he recognised. It was a Greek Jew only recently dragooned into the *Sonderkommando*, one of the 200 men Gradowski knew had been selected ostensibly to be rehoused at Gleiwitz. Other stokers too were able to recognise their colleagues from the partially charred remains they found and within hours of the beginning of the very next shift after the lockdown the news had spread.

The SS were exterminating the *Sonderkommando* and before the end of the very next shift everybody knew it.

On learning of the murder of these 200 *Sonderkommando* men, the two Zalmans, Gradowski and Lewental, each buried the record they had been keeping of the precise nature of the mass killing operation they had been forced to participate in, so certain were they that, since fewer of them were going to be needed, more if not most of the *Sonderkommando* were in danger of imminent liquidation. Gradowski, Lewental and the others within the *Sonderkommando* resistance yet again urged the camp's combined resistance groups, or, as they called themselves, the joint Auschwitz Military Council, to start a general uprising of the kind they had been talking about for months. When faced with the usual response, namely that the time was still not right, the *Sonderkommando* resistance sent two emissaries to plead personally and with the greatest urgency with representatives of the joint Auschwitz Military Council one more time.

Chaim Neuhof and Henryk Mandelbrot were dispatched to argue the case for the *Sonderkommando*. They were in effect pleading not merely for a chance to save their own lives but also for a chance to put a spoke in the wheels of the killing machinery. Each day a cart would go around the camp collecting the corpses of the slave-labour prisoners who had died in the previous twenty-four hours. On this day Neuhof and Mandelbrot were designated by the *Sonderkommando* resistance to be in charge of the cart. This was how they managed to secure a secret meeting with three delegates of the Auschwitz Military Council, a man known only as 'Rot' and two other men, Dürmayer and Kazuba. When the cart was sufficiently full of corpses, Rot, Dürmayer and Kazuba approached it carrying a corpse of their own. They had found a convenient pretext to be in contact with the *Sonderkommando* men.

'You are Rot?' Neuhof asked, looking at Dürmayer.

'No, he is,' Dürmayer explained, pointing with his head.

'What's all this about?' Rot asked.

'You know what this is about. We've been sent to urge you once more to start the action now.'

'What do you mean "now"?' Rot asked.

'Now! As soon as possible. You let us know when you're ready and we'll –'

'To have any chance of success we need support from outside. We've explained that to you people countless times.'

'Whether that's true or not –'

'Trust me, it's true,' Rot interrupted.

'Trust you!' Henryk Mandelbrot said under his breath. Whether they heard or not, all three of them ignored the comment. He seemed the junior of the two *Sonderkommando* men after all. They had never seen or heard of him before.

'We hear the rumours too. The Russians can't be very far away,' Mandelbrot said.

'No, they're not so far away. But they're not so close either,' said Dürmayer.

'I don't know how many times we have to tell you. For this to work we're going to need all arms of the operation to be functioning,' Kazuba said.

'What does that mean, "all arms"?' Henryk Mandelbrot asked.

'It means that the Russians must be almost here before our people on the outside will work with our people on the inside and the internationals.'

'What do you mean, "our people"?' Mandelbrot asked.

'Who brought this Jew?' Rot asked.

'He means the Polish Home Army,' said Neuhof.

'What about us?' Mandelbrot asked.

'Of course this will be the time for you people to join in too.'

'We can't wait for everything to be right with you!' countered Mandelbrot, at which point Kazuba noticed an SS man coming towards them and he alerted the others with a facial gesture.

'This is one we bribe,' said Rot quietly.

'Well, we're about to see if it's enough,' said Chaim Neuhof.

'You men. Wait there.' The guard was now level with the cart of corpses. 'What are you doing?'

'This man died during the night and we're getting rid of his corpse before he causes disease among the other prisoners . . . so they can keep working,' answered Dürmayer.

The guard looked carefully at all five of them. 'Why does it take five of you for this?' he asked.

'I saw these men bring him over to the cart and . . . well, I knew this man, sir –'

'So you've come to say goodbye. He might be dead but the uniform is still useful.'

'The Jews save the uniform before they cremate him.'

'Be sure you do,' he said. Turning to leave, he struck Mandelbrot to the ground with the butt of his rifle and walked off. Neuhof and Dürmayer helped Mandelbrot to his feet. He was bleeding from the side of the head. When they were sure the SS man had gone they continued their meeting.

'We can't wait,' said Neuhof.

'They'll run out of transports soon and then they'll liquidate *us*,' said Mandelbrot, wiping the blood from the side of his head.

'Liquidate who?'

'The *Sonderkommando*, and we're the only ones who can tell what really happened here, how they killed twenty-four hours a day.'

'Look,' said Kazuba, 'the longer we wait the more support we'll have from outside. The Germans still control the area surrounding the camp. As long as this situation prevails the prisoners are safer *in* the camp than they are on the run *outside* it.'

'Not all of them.'

'You mean not the Jews.'

'That's exactly what I mean.'

'I can't risk the whole operation only for the Jews.'

'But we're the only ones who can't wait.'

'Exactly, as you say, the only ones. I accept that the Jews are in a special position. You're unlike anybody else here. I'm sorry. I didn't put you in this situation. This is what happens when you live in someone else's country.'

'In someone else's country? I'm a Polish Jew. We've been here a thousand years!' countered Neuhof.

'From Poland, Greece, Belgium, France, Italy, from all over Europe,' Kazuba continued almost in a whisper, 'they collect you people, put the yellow stars on you. Have you noticed – they place you together, not with others from Poland, Greece, Belgium, France and Italy? They put you together with each other. Wherever it is you're from, you're Jews. That's why your position here is different from everyone else's.'

The SS man had noticed now that the five of them were still together and that the cart laden with corpses had not moved. The guard had been bribed but he was coming back, his annoyance evident in his every step. As he got closer Rot made a point of shifting the corpse further towards the back of the heaped pile as though he were finalising the task. Then still looking at the oncoming SS man, but with the distracted air of a nineteenth-century nobleman at rest who suddenly signals to his carriage driver, he gave the side of the cart two swift raps of his knuckles and said, 'Gentlemen, time's up.'

*

Memory is a wilful dog. It won't be summoned or dismissed but it cannot survive without you. It can sustain you or feed on you. It visits when it is hungry, not when you are. It has a schedule of its own that you can never know. It can capture you, corner you or it can liberate you. It can leave you howling and it can make you smile. Sometimes it's funny what you remember.

It was 3.23 am in the Morningside Heights apartment Adam and Diana used to share. Adam was awake again. There was a tap dripping in the bathroom. He heard it but for a while did nothing about it. Perhaps he could kid himself into thinking he wasn't really awake. It didn't work. He found himself calculating something, nothing complicated, but it was enough to put paid to all pretence at sleep. Thoughts about his mother, about her childhood, about her ill-fated attempts to meet someone after her divorce from Jake Zignelik, attempts that Adam had tried but failed to shield himself from seeing, had segued into a trivial middle-of-the-night calculation. Almost exactly fourteen years to the day separated Henry Border's trip to the DP camps of Europe and the visit to Australia of the renowned African American historian and civil rights activist, John Hope Franklin. He had come to Australia to give a series of lectures at the invitation of Professor Zelman Cowen, the then Dean of Law at the University of Melbourne.

It was six years after the US Supreme Court decision in *Brown versus Board of Education*, a case Franklin had worked on with Thurgood Marshall and the NAACP Legal Defense Fund, and despite having heard negative reports about Australia's de facto immigration policy, often referred to as the 'White Australia Policy', and despite what he knew about the history of Australia's treatment of its indigenous population, he was amazed to find himself treated like a celebrity everywhere he went. Hotel porters, academics, journalists, they seemed to recognise him and everywhere he went he was treated with a reverence almost approaching awe. No Australian held the historian in higher regard than a young woman, a law student who came to all his Melbourne University lectures and then followed him to Sydney in order to hear him lecture further and to talk with him more. The young woman, the daughter of Eastern European Jewish immigrants, even struck up a correspondence with him when he returned to the US. It was this that eventually led her to the NAACP-LDF office in New York. There she would meet another civil rights lawyer, Jake Zignelik, and later give birth to his only child, Adam, who, still unable to sleep, speculated that had John Hope Franklin declined Zelman Cowen's invitation that summer he, Adam, would never have been born. Would the earth have spun any differently? he asked himself in his bed in the glare of an uncaring clock radio.

John Hope Franklin had also been a colleague of William McCray and even then, in his early nineties, he was still in touch with him. Adam wondered how disappointed William would be if he failed to come up with anything new concerning black troops at the liberation of Dachau. When last they'd met, William had been disconsolate over the trial of six African American teenagers in Jena, Louisiana. Adam had wanted to distract him from the trial with reports of his progress concerning the role of black troops in the liberation of concentration camps but he had had very little to tell him. He did tell William about Henry Border, however, and William was very much taken with the story of the Chicago psychologist.

'Are you telling Charlie all about this?' William asked. Adam didn't seem to think there was much point.

'Nonsense! You've got to tell him. I will if you don't.'

He lay in bed and looked at the clock radio. Now it was 3.47 am. The tap in the bathroom hadn't stopped dripping. It was this that had first woken him and it was this that he eventually got up to turn off. Once up, Adam, still half asleep, opened the bathroom cabinet and took out the comb Diana had left there. He held it in his hand and looked at the strands of her hair against his palm. This was becoming a ritual.

'Are you lonely?' he said inaudibly. 'What do you eat? Do you cook or do you live on take-out because cooking for one is . . . pointless, isn't it? How can you be bothered cooking for one? All those leftovers, they can make you sick if you're not careful. And then there are the shopping lists, tiny scribbled lists on scraps of paper, urban survival lists, *they* can make you sick just looking at them. I'm so sorry. Do you know that? Do you ever think about what I'm thinking? I was never unfaithful to you. That doesn't count for anything now, does it? I should have been unfaithful and then confessed it. The end result might have been the same but it would have at least been understandable. Do you ever think about me? Or have you already let go? Sometimes I picture two clasped hands slowly loosening their grip. Slowly, slowly, where once they held on to each other they merely touch each other. Then through the agency of inertia, or something, or gravity, the gravitational attraction of neighbouring bodies, so to speak, they begin to drift apart. One barely moves at all while the other drifts away.'

Diana didn't say anything.

'I've taken out a personal loan. I went to the bank and got a loan to fund a return trip to Melbourne to speak to a woman there, one of Border's women, one of the Holocaust survivors he interviewed in the summer of '46. It might be a complete waste of time and money. I didn't tell the bank that I already know that my employment is limited. Is this the kind of confidence you want me to have? I think I have it now . . . in my work. It's to do with the black troops at Dachau I'm following up and with other things that Border has led me to. I've got something now, quite a lot. It's almost too much. If only I'd found this sooner. It goes around and around in my head. How do you sleep? Do you wake up knowing I'm sorry? Or have you let go?'

From his office the next morning Adam called Diana's mobile phone. It was turned off. Perhaps she was already teaching. He left a message. He wanted to meet up with her. Dinner, a drink, whatever she wanted.

'Choose a place, somewhere in Hell's Kitchen is fine with me. I really want to talk to you.'

*

The *Sonderkommando* resistance members had not held out much hope of Henryk Mandelbrot and Chaim Neuhof succeeding in their attempt to persuade the joint Auschwitz Military Council to agree to bring forward its plan for a camp-wide uprising. The murder of 200 *Sonderkommando* men in September had done nothing to change the thinking of the non-Jewish resistance. In early October the situation grew even more urgent when the *Sonderkommando Kapos*, the SS-appointed prisoners in charge, were commanded to furnish the SS within twenty-four hours with a list of 300 *Sonderkommando* men. *Scharführer* Busch, an SS Lance Sergeant, announced that the chosen 300 were to be taken out from Auschwitz-Birkenau to clear rubble and debris from a nearby town that had been badly damaged in an Allied air raid. Not one member of the *Sonderkommando* believed this.

Scharführer Busch had in effect given the *Kapos* twenty-four hours to make a list of 300 of their colleagues to be murdered and left the *Kapos* to their own devices to sort it out. Each man wondered to himself, 'Have I ever done anything to offend one of the *Kapos*?'

The men of the *Sonderkommando* stayed up all night. They argued with each other. They pleaded with the *Kapos* and with anyone they thought capable of influencing the *Kapos* such as the two Zalmans, Lewental and Gradowski, two of the longest serving members of the *Sonderkommando*. The two were impressed by the criterion that Henryk Mandelbrot suggested should be used in drawing up the list. The *Kapo* they had known best, Kaminski, had recently been shot on suspicion of sabotage but they went to another *Kapo*, one who was part of the *Sonderkommando* resistance, a man named Kalniak. To Kalniak they put Mandelbrot's suggestion.

'Surely,' Mandelbrot had suggested, 'the first men to keep off the list are the ones who are most likely, mentally and physically, to be able to fight in the event of an uprising.'

'That would make sense,' Kalniak commented, 'if there was any realistic hope of an uprising.'

'But still –' and this was all Gradowski got to say privately to Kalniak before a prisoner fought his way past Lewental to plead with Kalniak. Whatever Kalniak's real influence with or standing among the other *Sonderkommando Kapos*, the fact that a fight had broken out just for the opportunity to plead one's case to him suddenly elevated his stature with tens of desperate men who had seen it. Perhaps talking to Kalniak could keep you off the list.

The next day two of the *Sonderkommando* prisoners whose task it was to bring food to the *Sonderkommando* were told to give a message to a certain prisoner in the kitchen detail. This prisoner was in the resistance and he was told to get a message urgently to the Auschwitz Military Council explaining the situation concerning the 300 men and to plead one last time for the camp-wide uprising to begin that day. The message came back within an hour and a half. Not only would the Auschwitz Military Council not participate in an uprising that day but it urged those *Sonderkommando* resistance members who were not on the list of 300 also not to take part in any uprising. The 300 men, whoever they were, on the list to be given to the SS, were to go to their deaths knowingly, without fighting back and without any assistance from anyone, not even from the other *Sonderkommando* men. That was the message from the camp-wide resistance, the Auschwitz Military Council.

'Perhaps Kalniak was right,' Henryk Mandelbrot heard Zalman Lewental say to Zalman Gradowski.

They were lining up in formation in front of Crematorium IV as they had so many times before but they were doing it very slowly. Had the SS noticed? Everyone was twitchy. No one had slept. A list had been made. One of the *Kapos* had it. Which *Kapo*? All anyone knew was that it was too late to influence anybody now. *Scharführer* Busch was there with a group of SS guards. Did these SS men really think that any of the men lined in front of them, men who had day after day, month after month been forced to witness and participate in the deception and in the mass murder of so many hundreds of thousands of innocents, did any of these SS men really think that a single *Sonderkommando* member thought for a moment that the 300 men whose names were about to be handed over were going to go out to clear rubble?

Neither Lewental nor Mandelbrot saw any of the *Kapos* hand a list to anyone but somehow one of the SS men had it and they saw this SS man hand it over to *Scharführer* Busch. There were men there who knew for certain that their names were on the list. Some of these men had made preparations. They might have trembled lined up there but they had secreted implements, crude weapons of various kinds on their persons. Those there who had worked the night shift in Crematorium IV had, in what they knew to be their last hours, wedged and crammed rags soaked in wood-alcohol and in oil in whatever spaces they could in the crematorium, between the rafters, in the coke room, everywhere. The soaked rags were even placed under some of the three-tier wooden bunks in their barracks block. They hadn't forgotten that not only people burn, wood burns too. Then there were the tins, small tins partially filled with the gunpowder stolen by the women of the *Pulverraum* and smuggled out by Rosa Rabinowicz and later others. If an uprising started, if a building used for killing was set on fire, perhaps other prisoners, not just *Sonderkommando* men but prisoners all across Auschwitz-Birkenau and maybe even prisoners in some of the subcamps would see it. Maybe others would rise up too. Could that happen? How could they know? This was like no place they had ever known.

How many minutes did they have left to live? *Scharführer* Busch began calling out names from the list. How did Chaim Neuhof's name get on it? As doomed men began stepping slowly forward, it occurred to *Scharführer* Busch that the formation in its entirety seemed somewhat short, that men were missing. Suspecting that some of them must have been hiding, he dispatched several SS men to Crematorium IV to search for the missing prisoners. The rags, the weapons, men who may have been hiding there, everything was about to be discovered.

There was nothing to wait for any more, nothing. Whether Chaim Neuhof was the first to realise this no one will ever know. But he was the first to act on this realisation. From the ranks of the condemned men he called out 'Hoorah!' and with an axe that he had managed to hide in his pants he lunged at one of the SS men about to search Crematorium IV. Suddenly a torrent of stones, gravel and assorted objects came flying at the SS men from the ranks of the prisoners chosen to be 'transferred'. Some of the SS retreated from the attacking *Sonderkommando* men, two fleeing on bicycles. Others began firing indiscriminately at both the condemned and the other *Sonderkommando* men.

Nobody now was waiting for anything. *Sonderkommando* men from both groups began attacking the SS and before long smoke could be seen coming from Crematorium IV. This was not the usual smoke from the burning of corpses. This smoke was unprecedented. Crematorium IV was on fire. Not Jews for once, it was the building itself that was burning. There were explosions too. The Jews were tossing grenades of some kind. And even as *Sonderkommando* men were falling before a rain of bullets, people, prisoners of all nationalities from other parts of the camp, stopped what they were doing to look up. Jews were fighting back. Inconceivable though it was, this was no fantasy. Somehow these *Sonderkommando* men were destroying one of the crematoria even amid a ceaseless hail of bullets.

Over at Crematorium II the *Sonderkommando* men heard the wail of a siren above the non-stop gunfire. In astonishment they saw that Crematorium IV was on fire. Believing that this was the start of the long hoped-for uprising, they attacked the SS men guarding them. Hidden caches of weapons including the homemade grenades were retrieved in the commotion. A pair of long-hidden insulated pliers was dug up and a hole large enough for people to get through was cut in the electrified perimeter fence. The SS were so shocked to be attacked in what appeared to them to be an organised uprising that in the time it took them to implement a coordinated response a large number of the *Sonderkommando* were able to reach the hole in the fence. To stem the firing the SS were now directing in that vicinity, the prisoners there lobbed grenades at them. By this time there were *Sonderkommando* men on the other side of the fence. Not knowing which way to run they followed the first to escape and headed towards the nearby town of Rajsko.

Shot at by the SS pursuing them, many were killed or wounded, but some of them made it the two kilometres to Rajsko where, in terror, in exhilaration, they took shelter in a barn they'd come upon. Those Poles in Rajsko who in the middle of an October afternoon saw these men run into the barn could not understand what they were witnessing. They saw the SS arrive with dogs and try to break into the barn but the *Sonderkommando* men had had just enough time to bar the very stout door. Temporarily safe, the escapees inside the barn reassessed their position. What to do next depended on what was happening outside. Perhaps other parts of the fence had been breached. Perhaps prisoners were resisting all over Auschwitz. Perhaps the Russians had finally arrived and were engaging the SS. Maybe this had been the moment when the Polish Home Army had joined with the Auschwitz Military Council and the SS were under siege. Perhaps this was the beginning of the end of this nightmare. They looked at each other. The Nazis seemed to have given up their attempt to get into the barn. Had the local Poles, the men and women of Rajsko, taken up arms? No, there was no resistance from the people of Rajsko, not that afternoon, none that these panting men could hear over their own breathing and the barking of the dogs outside.

The people of Rajsko were civilians. They didn't fight. The *Sonderkommando* men inside the barn at Rajsko smelled a burning smell, not of corpses but of wood. The men of the Auschwitz Military Council were not on hand, nor the local branch of the Polish Home Army. The SS had set fire to the barn. As the flames gained control and the heat and smoke became unbearable the *Sonderkommando* men were forced to open the door and run for their lives. The Russians were not there, but some of the townspeople of Rajsko were there to see these men run as fast as they could out of the flame-filled barn, only to be gunned down by the machine guns of the waiting SS.

Back inside Auschwitz, some of the night shift from the *Weichsel Union Metallwerke* factory came out of their barracks blocks to see smoke coming from Crematorium IV. It had really happened. In *Kanada* Rosa Rabinowicz was able to see it too. In the furthest parts of the camp they saw it. Others just heard about it but they all exulted in it. The

Sonderkommando, Jews, had fought back. One of the crematoria, its gas chamber and its ovens, had been destroyed. Across the camp an almost surreal pride rippled through the prisoner population.

Once the SS had received reinforcements the uprising was quickly subdued. Those *Sonderkommando* men not already killed either at the Rajsko barn or in the area of the crematoria were made to lie face-down on the ground. True: the fence had been cut, explosives made of smuggled gunpowder had been used, SS men had been wounded, some had been killed. But while all this had been going on, nobody other than the *Sonderkommando* had so much as cursed the SS. Henryk Mandelbrot lay face-down on the ground as did all the surviving *Sonderkommando* men. No longer in shock, the SS were merely furious, intent on revenge. Mandelbrot listened to the sound of the gunshots getting nearer. He heard the sounds of the feet of the SS man, the designated shooter, getting nearer. With his face in the dirt he listened and calculated that the SS were shooting every third *Sonderkommando* man. One, then two, then a shot. Then again, one, then two, then a shot. Who would be left to tell the world what had happened here on the afternoon of 7 October 1944? One, then two, then a shot. Who would be left when this was over? One, then two, then a shot.

'Will it be me?' wondered Henryk Mandelbrot with soil in his mouth. One, then two, then a shot. The footsteps grew louder and then so did the shots. One, then two, then a shot. Another man was dead. One, then two, then a shot. Another witness was silenced.

Chaim Neuhof was killed along with Dorebus, Panusz and Handels-mann. Kalniak, one of the *Sonderkommando Kapos* who had been responsible for making the list of names, had also been killed. Kalniak, though not himself on the list, had helped secrete the explosives in Crematorium IV the night before. He had known what was going to happen and that he would die.

Crematorium IV, its gas chamber and its ovens, had been so severely damaged it was never used again. When finally the shooting stopped, Henryk Mandelbrot was allowed to stand up. Before the uprising there had been 663 *Sonderkommando* men.

Afterwards there were 212. When Henryk Mandelbrot took his face out of the dirt and stood up he saw the two Zalmans, Lewental and Gradowski. They were both dead.

*

'Don't I need to know the end of the story?' Lamont Williams asked the old man in Manhattan's Memorial Sloan-Kettering Cancer Center.

'You are here for the end of the story.'

Lamont smiled but gently persisted. 'What did you do when the fighting started?'

'There was chaos in the yard. Prisoners –'

'*Sonderkommando* men?'

'Yes, *Sonderkommando* men were running in every direction as the SS fired at them. The ones what ran to the fence where the wire was cut –'

'The ones who ran to the barn at Rajsko?'

'Yes. When they ran and the SS chased them I saw there was a chance to do something but I didn't know what. There were men, men what I knew being shot and dying, their bodies hitting the ground all around me.'

'So what did you do?'

'You will think this is crazy, and it was, but it was what saved my life. I ran towards Crematorium IV and –'

'But that was the one that was on fire.'

'Yes, exactly, it was. But I thought that if I could get there without being shot, it might be the safest place.'

'But what about the fire?'

'At that time there were bullets flying everywhere and I was more afraid of the SS bullets than of the fire. They were shooting at me and twice I hit the ground and just lay there so they would think I was dead. Once I had hit the ground they stopped shooting at me. I waited a little bit and then I got up and ran. I did this twice and I made it to Crematorium IV.'

'But why did you want to go there? It was on fire.'

'Because it looked like they were going to shoot everybody they could see. Who knew what they would do even though they still needed *Sonderkommando* men and they knew it? They were so angry, so enraged, maybe even frightened, that they were just going to kill anyone they saw, so I had to try to not be seen. I had to hide. That was my instinct, to hide. Where should I hide? Where were they least likely to look? Crematorium IV.'

'Because it was on fire?'

'Yes, because it was on fire.'

'But how did you know you could survive the fire?'

'I didn't know anything, Mr Lamont. I could try now to pretend to be a hero. I was not a hero. There were plenty of heroes. I was not one of them. The heroes died. Look, when a building is on fire sometimes not all of it is on fire.'

'But how did you know that you'd even make it through the door?'

'I didn't know anything. All around you is shooting and you are in a panic and afraid. Where is the least shooting? Near where the building is on fire.'

'So you got to the door?'

'Yes, I got to the door. I had run and I was completely out of breath. The doorway was on fire but if I got through it . . . no more bullets. So I jumped through the flames and I got in. We knew the building better than most of the guards and I knew there was a place inside what the bullets couldn't reach and that was what I was looking for.'

'If it wasn't on fire.'

'Exactly, yes, if it wasn't on fire.'

'Where was it?'

'It was the flue. You understand? The flue, it was cast iron. It led from the ovens to the chimney.'

'That's where you went?'

'Yes, I hid there . . . while others fought and some tried to escape.'

'But how did you know the building wouldn't collapse on top of you and kill you?'

'I didn't know. I took a chance. Look, Mr Lamont, there was no logic to the place but death. We were all meant to die. The men who escaped from the camp and ran to Rajsko, they all died, all of them killed, and they were the heroes. The coward who ran into a burning building and hid, he lived until now.'

'And the two Zalmans, Gradowski and Lewental?'

'I told you.'

'Yeah, but you said you hid, so how did you – ?'

'I crept out of there. When the shooting had stopped I crept out.'

'The shooting had stopped?'

'Yes, because they were lining up everyone what had not yet been killed and they made them all lie face-down on the ground.'

'You too?'

'Yes, of course. I chose the wrong time to get out of the building but then maybe the fire would have got me, or the falling shingles, if I had stayed. They lined all of us up face-down in the dirt and they shot every third one. When I got up Gradowski and Lewental . . . I saw them on the ground. I survived but they didn't.'

This was the last time Lamont Williams would learn about the *Sonderkommando* from Mr Mandelbrot. Lamont hadn't known it but Mr Mandelbrot, it seemed, had. It was at the end of this visit that Mr Mandelbrot smiled as he saw Lamont take the silver *menorah*. That night when Lamont's grandmother saw it in their Co-op City apartment and asked him about it, Lamont told her a little of the story of the *Sonderkommando* uprising.

'If he'd followed the others out through the hole in the fence to Rajsko they would have shot him.'

'So he only survived by running into a burning building?'

'That's about right. He hid in the cast-iron flue in Crematorium IV.'

'What a story!' Lamont's grandmother said, getting up to clear the kitchen table. That night before going to bed she picked up the silver *menorah* and examined it.

'He must have really liked you . . . give you this. What do you think it's worth?'

Lamont didn't hear her and when she leaned in to kiss him goodnight she didn't repeat it.

'I'll try to come see you tomorrow,' Lamont had said to Mr Mandelbrot that night as he left him.

'Yes? Good,' the old man said. That was the last thing he ever said to Lamont. Lamont wasn't able to get back to him the very next night or the night after that. Three nights after their last conversation he was startled to see another patient when he walked into what had been the old man's room. Lamont realised what had happened but he found himself unprepared for it, and for all that it was really no surprise, still, he had to hear the end of the story from someone who really knew. The next day when he chanced upon the old man's treating oncologist in the hallway, he took the unusual step of approaching her.

'Excuse me, Dr Washington,' he said nervously. 'That patient, Mr Mandelbrot, was he moved to another – ?'

'He died,' she said, looking at her watch, and kept walking. Lamont Williams stood alone in the hallway for a moment with his mop in his hand and a bucket of grey soapy water at his feet and thought of the old man. Who else knew his story? Who else knew all of it? Anyone? The man from Building Services had to finish mopping the floor.

*

Adam still had not discovered anything that remotely connected black troops to the liberation of Dachau and, for all the intrinsic value of his discovery of Henry Border's transcripts and 1946 wire recordings of DPs, he felt himself getting pulled away from the topic that had initially led him to them. But he did find something in one transcript that offered him at least a glimmer of hope with respect to the role of African American troops in the liberation of another concentration camp. Border had interviewed a DP, a Holocaust survivor, named Taussig. It seemed that Mr Taussig had for a time been a prisoner at one of the satellite camps of a concentration camp named Natzweiler-Struthof. In the course of describing his liberation he mentioned to Border that among the first Allied troops he saw were black soldiers. Mr Taussig told Border that when he saw these armed black men, black soldiers, he knew that these had to be the Americans. There could be no doubt as to who these men were and he knew he was finally free.

Discovering this immediately sent Adam off to find out what he could about Natzweiler-Struthof. He quickly learned that Natzweiler-

Struthof was situated near Strasbourg just west of the Rhine. It was the only concentration camp the Germans ever established in France. The main Natzweiler-Struthof camp was abandoned some months before the Allied armies got to it but many of its satellite camps on the east side of the Rhine, some very close to it, were used by the Germans till only weeks before they surrendered. Adam discovered that in the last months of the war these satellite camps contained prisoners transported from camps in the east, which included Auschwitz, that were in the path of the advancing Red Army, and prisoners from Dachau and other camps in order to relieve the pressure on those camps too.

The abandoned Natzweiler-Struthof main camp was first entered by units of the French 1st Army which, together with the US 7th Army, constituted the combined Allied 6th Army Group commanded by the American Lieutenant General Jacob Devers. Adam was soon able to ascertain that the 6th Army Group reached the western bank of the Rhine around 24 November 1944. The 6th Army Group was the first Allied army to reach the Rhine and it was Devers' plan to cross it and advance north along the Rhine valley.

There were two aspects of this that particularly piqued Adam's interest. First, one of the divisions of the US 7th Army was the 79th Division and one of the battalions in that division was the African American 761st Tank Battalion. Adam had already come across reports, albeit not reports officially verified by the US military, to the effect that the 761st Tank Battalion had been involved in the liberation of a concentration camp. Second, in determining the viability of an assault across the Rhine in the Strasbourg region, Devers, Adam found, had sent scouting parties across the river to probe the German defences there. They reported back that the defences were quite surprisingly weak.

What excited Adam about all this was the possibility that members of the 761st were in the probing parties that crossed the Rhine in late November and that they were involved in skirmishes in the vicinity of a Natzweiler-Struthof satellite camp not far from the river. If he were able to confirm this then he would have established that black troops were among the first Allied troops on the Western Front to have encountered, or even perhaps to have entered, a functioning Nazi concentration camp, a very signal accomplishment.

Whatever the improbability of this speculation, Adam was for a time obsessed with looking into it further to see whether there could be anything to it.

What records might there be of the combat experiences of the 761st, official or otherwise? Who were the men of the 761st? There had been six white officers, thirty black officers, and 676 black enlisted men. Activated in 1942 in Louisiana, the 761st Tank Battalion had received intensive training in Texas. To his delight he found that they had landed at Omaha Beach, Normandy, on 10 October 1944. They would have been in Europe at the relevant time with more than a month to get to Natzweiler-Struthof. From a group of over 700 men surely someone had recorded his war experiences? Were there written accounts that had not been uncovered, that were known only to family members? Perhaps there were veterans of the battalion Adam could interview. There was so much to discover. Adam finally had something positive to offer his friend, William McCray.

*

The orders came all the way from Berlin. The war had turned increasingly against the Nazis with the American, British and Free French armies reaching the Rhine in the west and the Russians entering Poland in the east but still they had to know. The Reich looked about to collapse but still they had to know. Find out how they did it. How did these half-dead Jews, isolated prisoners in a death camp, get hold of weapons? How did they get hold of gunpowder? A delegation was sent from Berlin to Auschwitz-Birkenau. It was inconceivable to the SS that the gunpowder could have come from the women of the *Weichsel Union Metallwerke* factory. Just as they didn't consider and then dismiss the possibility that Churchill, Stalin or perhaps Roosevelt had personally delivered gunpowder to the men of the *Sonderkommando*, neither did they bother to consider that it could have come from these starved young Jewish women. Then during an examination of the destroyed building that had housed the gas chamber and ovens of Crematorium IV a little tin was found. It was round and metal and had once contained shoe polish. Now it contained braided strands of cotton, a wick of some kind and gunpowder. It was a homemade grenade that the *Sonderkommando* never got to use and the gunpowder it contained was recognised as that coming from the *Weichsel Union Metallwerke* factory.

It was around this time that a woman, a prisoner who had once been housed in the same block as Estusia and Hannah Weiss, was caught with a whole loaf of bread. Beaten but unwilling to betray the origins of the bread, she offered other information that might be of value, information about the prisoner Estusia Weiss who used to receive visits from the prisoner Rosa Rabinowicz of the *Kanada Kommando*. The smuggling of the bread was forgotten about.

Block 11, the camp's 'prison within a prison', was in Auschwitz I, the part of Auschwitz-Birkenau with the gate adorned by '*Arbeit macht frei*'. The *Kapo* of Block 11 was a Jew, an unusually tall and strong man known by many more prisoners than had ever seen him as *Kapo* Jakub. It was on the basis of his strength and size that the SS had chosen him to be the *Kapo* of Block 11. Some said he was simple; others made allegations of cruelty about Jakub. Still others who had got out of Block 11 swore that only his timely acts of kindness had saved them. When prisoners locked in the cells of Block 11 heard Jakub approaching their cell they recognised that it was him by his walk and if, from the sound of the footsteps, they believed he was alone, they would call out to him from the dark of the punishment cells.

'Help me, *Kapo* Jakub. Please help me.'

The call of the prisoners would follow the sound of his footsteps down the blackened concrete corridor. 'Help me, *Kapo* Jakub. Please help me.'

The year 1944 was coming to an end when Estusia Weiss and her friend Ala, two of the *Pulverraum* workers from the *Weichsel Union Metallwerke* factory were taken to Block 11 for interrogation. Their foreman, Regina, was taken there too, and soon after so was Rosa Rabinowicz. All four of them were beaten viciously, repeatedly. News of their incarceration in Block 11 reached Noah Lewental and others of the resistance movement. So certain were they that under interrogation they would be betrayed that many of them considered suicide.

Rosa Rabinowicz, her face, torso and legs lacerated and bleeding, lay on her back alone in her cell fresh from a beating. Struggling to breathe through broken ribs, she heard the prisoners in the distance announce the movement along the corridor of *Kapo* Jakub.

'Help me, *Kapo* Jakub. Please help me,' she heard them call. Without getting up or even trying to get up, she crawled along the floor to the cell door and waited for his step to come closer to her door. Then she started to call out, 'Help me, *Kapo* Jakub. Please help me.'

Jakub could not go past the cells alone without hearing this cry from inside the cell of every prisoner. 'Help me, *Kapo* Jakub. Please help me.' Even prisoners who had never been helped by him at all, who had never spoken to him and who had no reason to expect that he should suddenly risk his life to help them, even these prisoners called out to him from their cells, almost as though in prayer. They called out to him as though to fail to call when he went past would be to limit one's chance of survival. Those who didn't call out to him were no longer conscious.

Jakub heard the cries as he made his way along the basement corridor of Block 11 and when he got to the door of Rosa Rabinowicz he heard the broken woman's feeble cry and he stopped. Far from the loudest cry for his attention, he could have been forgiven for not hearing it, but he was walking slightly more slowly as he approached this particular cell. He knew exactly who it was that lay bleeding there. He had brought bread and water to this cell when its inmate had been unconscious. Jakub knew that this cell contained the woman Rosa, the woman who had smuggled gunpowder to the *Sonderkommando*, gunpowder used in the uprising, the only uprising in the history of the camp. Whatever privilege his position brought him he would try to share with this woman, Rosa Rabinowicz.

When she stopped hearing his steps she wondered if he was still there. Then she heard the keys in the door of her cell and within seconds there stood towering above her the hulking frame of *Kapo* Jakub. The man took a step over her and into the tiny cell. He crouched down and brought to her the bowl of water in the cell. Cradling her head in his lap, he told her that when he counted to three she should swallow and she did. He placed her head gently back on the ground and, still on his knees, he reached over to the bread he had left for her earlier and broke off a piece to feed her but she was unable to take it in her mouth. Her mouth, swollen and bloodied, could not accept anything solid. The blood from her mouth, fresh from her latest beating, dripped onto his leg. He took some of the bread, softened it in the water and began to feed her.

'Look at you,' he said quietly to himself, not expecting any response. But the broken woman with her head in his lap spoke to him between intakes of breath.

'Bring me Noah, Noah Lewental. Bring me Noah, Jakub, will you?'

'Who is he?'

'He's an electrician . . . from Ciechanow. Ask around . . . someone will know him . . . *They* will know him,' she whispered. 'Can you get him here before I die?'

Some three days later the *Kapo* Jakub received the electrician from Ciechanow, Noah Lewental. It was night and he came to the entrance of Block 11 with two bottles under his arm.

'Who's this?' asked the sleepy SS guard on duty.

'This is my cousin and this is for you,' Jakub said, placing the bottles in front of the SS man.

'What is it? Give it here. Egg liqueur!' the SS man laughed.

'Two bottles . . . for you,' repeated Jakub.

'*Ach*, you Jews! Even here, even *now*, you can get anything.'

Noah said nothing and watched to see what he would do. The guard opened one of the bottles and took a swig.

'Jakub, they love you around here. Even the dead send you their tributes. Well, you can have a drink too.'

The SS man gave the bottle to Jakub who pretended to drink from it and then handed it back. Before long the guard had finished the first bottle and quickly moved on to the second.

'From *Kanada*, yeah?' said the SS man, now affected by the liqueur.

'Wherever it's from, sir, it's yours now, isn't it?'

'Yeah, yeah . . . it's mine now. That's exactly right, Jakub. Mine now, isn't it?'

With a small amount still left in the second bottle, the SS man had fallen asleep and Jakub led Noah Lewental towards Rosa's cell. He walked so silently behind Jakub that the prisoners on the other side of their cell doors, assuming Jakub was alone, cried out as the two of them passed by.

'Help me, *Kapo* Jakub. Please help me.'

When they arrived at Rosa's cell Jakub unlocked the door quickly.

'Don't be long. I don't know how long the guard will sleep. It could be half the night or he could be already waking now,' he whispered. Pushing Noah inside, he closed the door on them and left, a chorus of prisoners' cries trailing away after him.

Noah Lewental looked down at the naked body at his feet. It was unrecognisable. Noah wondered if the giant *Kapo* had led him to the wrong place when a voice arose from the badly torn naked body with open wounds that lay without even a blanket or covering of any kind on the grey concrete floor.

'Noah, is that you?'

'Rosa?'

'How did you get here? Are you really here or am I delirious?'

Noah bent down. The voice was hers. This was the woman he had, since childhood, planned to marry, the woman he had lost through an act of adolescent impatience, the woman he'd hurt so much. And now this. What had they done to her?

'I'm here, of course I'm here,' he whispered. 'You sent for me, didn't you? Is this water?'

'Yes. I didn't think Jakub would find you. I didn't think you'd even get the message before they –'

'Shhh! Save your strength.' He cradled her head in his lap and gave her some water. That was when he saw that most of her teeth had been smashed.

'There's nothing to save it for,' she said.

'Don't talk like that. We'll do everything we can to . . . help you.'

'Noah, I'm not delirious and time is short. We mustn't lie to one another. They're going to kill me. We both know that but I had to tell you –'

'Shhh! Don't be so –'

'Noah, darling, don't talk down to me. Is it true that your brother died in the uprising?'

'Zalman? Yes, that's what I was told.'

'I heard that too. That's the only one I gave them.'

'What?'

'That's the only name I gave them when they interrogated me. I heard he was killed so I told them he was my contact, the only one I had.' Noah Lewental gently stroked the hair on the top of her head and felt it matted with dried blood.

'Tell them, Noah, tell them, the others in the resistance, tell them Zalman is the only name I gave them and the only one I'm going to give them. Tell them it stops with him. Anyone still alive is safe.'

'My Rosa! I don't know if anyone here is safe, not even Jakub.'

'But tell them, Noah, no one will be killed because of anything I say. Tell me what you know.'

'About what?'

'Are the Russians coming?'

'That's what we hear. That's what we always hear . . . but they never come.'

'And the uprising, did anyone escape?'

'As far as I know anyone who escaped was caught and killed. But they destroyed one of the crematoria.'

'Really?'

'Yes and they killed some SS men before it was all over.'

'Noah, you have to survive this.'

'So do you!'

'But I'm not going to. You might. You have to survive and make sure the rest of the world knows what happened here.'

'Who will believe it?'

'Yes, but you have to keep telling people till everyone knows. Promise me you'll survive and –'

'Rosa, you want me to promise something that's out of my hands.'

'Yes. Okay, but promise me that if you survive you will tell people what went on here. You have to tell –'

'Yes, of course. Shhh! Of course I will. What about the others? Do they have any of the other girls?'

'Yes, they have Estusia and Ala from the *Pulverraum* and Regina too, their foreman. But no one needs to worry about anything they might say. Estusia cares only for her sister and, anyway, I'm the only one they were in contact with outside the *Union Metallwerke* factory whose name they know.'

'Do you have a message for the sister?'

'For Estusia's sister, Hannah?'

'Yes, maybe I could –'

'No. Jakub is going to try to smuggle out a letter from Estusia,' Rosa whispered.

'Okay.'

'Noah?'

'Yes.'

'Why would *you* need to get a message to her sister?'

'What do you mean?'

'I thought you said we're going to be all right?'

She had caught him out and when she managed to lift her hand up to his face she found he was crying. They sat in close to perfect darkness in Block 11 knowing that at any moment Jakub could come back and that Noah would have to leave immediately. He might even be caught on the way out. He didn't care. He would give his life for her. She knew that now. But they both knew that the SS wouldn't take his life in exchange for hers. They would simply take both.

He cradled her head as they whispered about their childhood, about Ciechanow, their parents and their siblings. She said her father had seen this coming but then agreed that nobody could have imagined the enormity of what did come. Even when it is over, nobody will quite understand just how bad it was, the scale of it, the relentlessness of it. No, she had to agree, whatever it was her father had predicted, it hadn't been this. She had a daughter, Noah remembered. The little girl, her name was Elise. Her father had taken her away. Before the war she had tried all that was within her power to find her but could find not a trace of her or of her husband.

'Maybe she's alive. Do you think she is?' Rosa whispered, suddenly like a little girl.

'Perhaps she is,' Noah Lewental answered.

'It was so long ago –'

'Yes, but don't you see that helps. It was so long ago that by now she could be anywhere. She might be safe in Russia or England . . . even America.'

'Do you think so?'

'Yes, there was time for –'

Suddenly there was a knock at the door. They had been speaking non-stop for four hours. Now it was 2 am and the *Kapo* Jakub had crept back too quietly for the prisoners' pleadings to announce him. He knocked once and then opened the door to Rosa's cell.

'He's awake. Come on, you have to go.' It had come too suddenly for Noah to know what he should say to her. This would be the last time they saw each other and they both knew it. What should he say?

'Come on!' Jakub whispered insistently.

'Rosa, I love you. I've always loved you.'

'Noah, promise me you'll tell everyone –'

'Come on!' Jakub insisted.

'Tell everyone what happened here.'

'I will.'

'Promise me.'

'Come on!' said Jakub.

'I promise you I'll tell –'

'Tell everyone,' she whispered, 'everyone.'

Noah had placed her head back down on the ground.

'What if they find me with her?' he asked Jakub suddenly with his heart beating furiously. 'Let them take us together. I can't leave her . . . I can't . . . I don't care what they do to me.'

'Maybe *you* don't but they'll kill *me* too. We had a deal. Come on!' Jakub said, dragging him from the cell.

'Tell everyone!' Rosa Rabinowicz insisted.

'I will, I promise.'

'Everybody!' she called out, no longer in a whisper but with whatever strength she had. 'Tell everybody what happened here!'

Jakub had closed the door and now he and Noah were back in the corridor.

'Tell everybody what happened here,' Rosa called out. She was hysterical now and had given up any pretence at whispering.

'Tell everybody what happened here,' she called out and hearing her say this, her neighbour in the next cell woke and instead of the usual call to Jakub to save them the neighbour repeated Rosa's cry as though it had never occurred to him.

'Yes, tell everyone what happened here.' And the neighbour was heard by the prisoner in the next cell along who in turn repeated the plea.

In the middle of the night, some time just after 2 am, prisoners in the basement of the prison block were woken by the call as it progressed from prisoner to prisoner. One by one and then more and more of them together they were calling out to anyone who might hear them, 'Tell everyone what happened here,' and as Noah and Jakub made their way along the dark stone basement corridor the call followed them. At every cell they passed, each prisoner repeated the same incantation. No one there could hope to be saved but this made sense to call for; this made sense to pray for. That was how it came to pass that late one night in the cold of early winter, 1944, the prisoners in the basement of the prison block in Auschwitz cried out together to whoever might survive, 'Tell everyone what happened here.' 'Tell everyone what happened here.' 'Tell everyone what happened here.'

*

Over a number of sleepless nights Adam permitted his mind to run riot with the possibility that he might uncover something really solid about the role of the men of the 761st Tank Battalion, a black battalion, with respect to their role in the liberation of the most westerly of all the Nazi concentration camps, Natzweiler-Struthof. But when reason intruded into his nocturnal speculations he realised, just on the basis of numbers alone, that it was really very unlikely that of all the troops in the Allied 6th Army Group, it was members of the 761st that were in the probing parties. And he soon learned that, in any event, scouting parties were under orders to engage with the enemy only in self-defence. To compound the improbability of the scouting troops encountering a satellite camp of Natzweiler-Struthof, Adam found that the closest one was ten to twenty kilometres to the east of the Rhine.

Nor did the 761st cross the Rhine near any of the Natzweiler-Struthof satellite camps in the assault by the entire 6th Army Group that General

Devers had planned because, by order of the Supreme Commander of the Allied Armies in the West, General Dwight D. Eisenhower, and to the dismay of Devers, the assault did not proceed. This was despite the weak German defences on the other side of the Rhine and the opportunity that presented for Devers' Army Group to cross the river and attack the German 1st Army, which was at the time engaging Patton's 3rd Army, from behind. The very same advance would also cut off the German 19th Army.

Whether Eisenhower's order had been influenced in any way by the rumoured troubled personal relationship between him and Devers or whether it was entirely strategically based was a question that occupied Adam's mind only for a short time. It appeared that Eisenhower treated Devers with far less regard than other generals of Devers' rank. Nor was Devers overly respectful of Eisenhower, but the matter was not of real interest to Adam.

A related question, however, did keep coming back to him. Had Devers' 6th Army Group crossed the Rhine in November 1944, might that have stopped the Germans launching their offensive in the Ardennes further north just weeks later and might that have led to the war ending months sooner? And if it had, how many lives might have been saved?

In the event, the Germans did launch their Ardennes counter-offensive some weeks later and the Allied 6th Army Group was ordered to take part in the ensuing Battle of the Bulge. It was to cross the Rhine only in March 1945.

Ultimately, what killed Adam's Natzweiler-Struthof hypothesis stone dead was his discovery from US Army records that the 761st was attached to the 79th Division of the US 7th Army for only a week or two and this was between late February 1945 and early March 1945. In the time relevant to Devers' probe across the Rhine in late November 1944, the 761st was attached to the 87th Division of the US 3rd Army and was nowhere near Natzweiler-Struthof or any of its satellite camps. So far as the role of black troops in the liberation of concentration camps was concerned, Adam was back to where he had started.

*

They were to meet for a drink at the Film Center Café on Ninth Avenue in Hell's Kitchen, not far from where she now lived. The arrangement was made via a series of voice messages on their mobile phones. Adam replayed Diana's messages many times trying to gauge her state of mind from the tone of her voice and her choice of words.

'How do you *think* I sound?' he heard her ask him in the ongoing mental conversation he had with her.

'I would say you sound . . . defensive.'

'How about cautious?'

'Okay then, cautious.'

'Do you think I have a right to be cautious?' he heard Diana ask.

'I think you have a right to be defensive.'

'Look how magnanimous you've become!'

'Yes, look. Please . . . look. I'm feeling better about things now, about work, about myself and . . . Shit, that's you!'

Adam had arrived early so, although Diana came after him, she wasn't late. He saw her come inside and walk towards him. They smiled at each other, different smiles, but there wasn't time to analyse the aetiology of each smile. Her hair was longer. She wore clothes he didn't recognise. They hugged. She smelled the same as she always had in spite of the unfamiliar clothes. His mouth was dry. She sat opposite him in the booth he'd secured by coming early. He was terrified.

'You look great,' Adam said.

'So do you.'

'No, not really, I don't, but it's nice of you . . . Well, how are you?'

'I'm fine, I'm well. How are you?'

'Well, right now . . . Right now, frankly, I'm a bit nervous but I've been . . . I think I'm doing okay now. Work is –'

'You're nervous?'

'Sure. It's weird, don't you think? This . . .'

'Yeah, I guess it is a bit but you don't have anything to be . . . I mean . . . don't be nervous.'

'All right then, I won't be. You're not . . .'

'Nervous? No . . . I don't think I'm . . . I'm not nervous. Why, *should* I be nervous?'

'No.'

'I'm pleased to see you,' she said.

'Are you?'

'Of course.'

'Well, that's great 'cause I'm so pleased to see you. I really am.'

'Have you been seeing much of Michelle and Charles?'

'A little bit, not much really. Probably see more of Sonia.'

'Really?'

'Yeah, she's taken to dropping in on me.'

'She's looking after you. That's sweet!'

'Yeah, she doesn't always tell me she's coming but, yeah, it is sweet.'

'She doesn't tell you she's coming?'

'No, not all the time.'

'So, what, she just drops in unannounced?'

'Sometimes it's announced, sometimes it's sort of . . . impromptu.'

'That could be awkward.'

'Awkward?'

'Yeah, I mean –'

'It's never *awkward*.'

'No?'

'It's not always . . . It's not always convenient but it's never awkward.'

'Okay.'

The waitress came up to them and took their order. Adam ordered a double Scotch and soda. Diana ordered still water and Adam had to work on himself not to construe her order as meaning anything other than that she wanted some water.

'She misses you. Sonia misses you,' Adam offered.

'Really?'

'Absolutely.'

'How would you know that?'

'She's told me.'

'Really?'

'I've been a little worried about her . . . about all three of them actually,' he confided.

'Really, why?'

'I don't know but I think they may be having . . . trouble.'

'What do you mean?'

'I know you've seen Michelle. I have too. But have you seen them both?'

'You mean marital trouble?'

'He works too hard.'

'He always did.'

'Yeah, well, that might be the problem.'

'What, that he's too focused on his career for the health of the relationship?'

They looked each other in the eye. There was nothing he could say to that.

'William misses you too,' Adam started.

'Oh really? I miss *him*. Please send him my love. How is he?'

'Well, for the most part I think he's well. I mean I think he's in good health.'

'But?'

'Well, he gets upset. Things in the news upset him.'

'Him and everyone else.'

'Yeah, but he used to be active, professionally, socially, politically active . . . you know, working for change. Now he reads the news and it increases his sense of powerlessness and I think –'

'You're talking about issues of race?'

'Yeah, not only but . . . He's very sweet. In the course of trying to help me after we . . . He even suggested a topic for me.'

'A research topic?'

'Yeah.'

'Is it any good?'

'You know, it sort of is. It's actually led me on a really fascinating path that I think is going to bear fruit, maybe more fruit than I can . . .'

'Eat?'

'I was going to say handle.'

'That's great! Isn't it?'

'Yeah, it is. I'm feeling more hopeful about things now. In fact this topic, I'd love to talk to you about it, it's taking me to Melbourne. Can you believe it? By chance I have to go to –'

'To live?'

'No, no, just to interview someone. Not to live.'

Adam's perception of her concern that he might be moving to Melbourne to live emboldened him.

'Diana, I made a mistake.'

'Oh, don't –'

'In a long line of mistakes this is the biggest one I've ever made.'

'Adam –'

'I want you to come back. I want us to be together –'

'Adam –'

'I'm feeling better about my work now and –'

'Adam, you can't turn people on and off depending on how you're feeling about your work.'

'No, I know. That's not what I mean. I mean that . . . Everything you said was right. I can see that. Look, it . . . it might have taken me till now. It might've taken me finding something to sink my teeth into for me to realise I could make a go of it professionally, but much more importantly than that, to feel confident that I could . . .'

'That you could what?'

'That I could provide for . . . take care of . . . a family. To feel that I would not be a husband to you and a father to our children like . . . like my father was to my mother and me.'

'And what if you don't get tenure?'

'I'm not going to get tenure, not at Columbia. I don't care. I mean of course I care but not as far as it affecting our plans to start a family. You were right. We should be together and have children irrespective of what's happening to us professionally. I see that now.'

He reached across the table and took her hand but after a few seconds she withdrew it. The waitress walked past just as this was happening. It didn't look like either of these two was going to leave much of a tip, but other people's turning points were often instructive and always entertaining, especially to the up-and-coming actress this young waitress thought of herself as. They looked like nice people. How old were they? she wondered.

'Would you care to order something else?' she asked just as Diana withdrew her hand.

'No,' Diana answered, seemingly for both of them. 'No, thank you.' Adam looked up at the waitress. She liked his eyes, mistaking the pain in them for something else. He wanted her to go away and having run out of questions, she went back in the direction of the barman.

'Adam, you can't turn people on and off. Do you know what I've been through?'

'I can imagine. I went through it too.'

'Yeah but you *did* it. It was all your fault.'

'I agree . . . completely. Like I said, it was a mistake . . . a terrible, terrible mistake.'

'You can't turn people on and off.'

'I know. You said that and I agree but I don't think that's something I generally do and –'

'I mean, who the hell do you think you are?'

'I think I'm someone who did something really, really stupid, but who before that loved you as much if not more than anyone has ever loved you or ever will, someone who made you laugh, someone who tried to take care of you, someone who shared your interests and your concerns, someone you thought you wanted to marry and have a child with.'

'Who *before* that?'

'What?'

'You said, "someone who *before* that loved you" –'

'I didn't mean "before that". I didn't mean *only* "before that". I still love you. I talk to you. I've continued talking to you, having conversations with you, even though you're not there.'

Tears welled in her eyes. Such was the sadness, frustration and regret that fuelled them that she was beyond pretending that she wasn't crying. Adam took her hand and again she let it rest in his for a few seconds before withdrawing it, this time, seemingly, in anger. That's the way the waitress interpreted the gesture.

'You're such an asshole, you know that?'

'No, I'm an arsehole but not *such* an arsehole. I am *such* an idiot though. Can we settle on that?'

'I can't do this.'

'Can't do what?'

'I can't get back with you.'

'Diana, you've got to trust me. I'm not playing games with your feelings. I mean it. Irrespective of what happens to me professionally, and I think things might be looking up, but . . . Sweetheart, you were right, I don't want to wake up without you any more. I'm tired of waking up in the middle of the night and going into the bathroom and –'

'I'm seeing someone.'

'What?'

'I met . . . someone.'

'When?'

'Adam, does it matter?'

'I don't . . . I don't know. I guess . . . Yeah, I guess it doesn't matter.'

He had not imagined this so it wasn't possible for him to have prepared himself for it although, as the Number One train took him back uptown from Times Square towards Columbia, it occurred to him that, perhaps like a parent's death, this was not something one could prepare for anyway. Now he really was alone. It wasn't a dress rehearsal for some possible eventuality. This was permanent. He was going to have to live with the consequences of his fear of being a failed academic and a failed father and husband. Back home he sat on the couch staring into space. It was the couch they had chosen together, had lain on together, the couch they had watched television on as they held on to each other.

'Now I can't even talk to *you*. I can't even imagine a private ongoing conversation with you . . . in my head.'

'Sweetheart, you can, of course you can.'

'How?'

'Like this, just like you're doing now.'

'But it was all . . . It's always been predicated on us eventually having these conversations for real.'

'No, it wasn't.'

'Yes, it was. Who are you to say? Who am I talking to? Who are you, anyway?'

'I'm still Diana. I'm your imagining of her.'

'Yeah but now that I know –'

'I can still live in your mind.'

'But who is it that's living in my mind? You won't marry me. You won't have children with me. You've met someone else . . . which I don't even want to think about.'

'*She* has but *I* haven't.'

'What's the difference between you and her?'

'*I'm* how you remember her. As long as you remember how she was when you two were together, you can keep talking to me.'

'But she's gone. She's met someone.'

'Yes, that's right. She has. She really has.'

'So I just keep talking in my mind to a version of her –'

'Yes, but it's based on all those years of knowing her and loving her –'

'Before I . . .'

'Before you fucked everything up.'

'So I'm talking to myself?'

'Sort of.'

'And it's all my fault?'

'Yes.'

'How sad is that?'

'You know very well how sad that is.'

'Is there anything sadder than living like this in some sort of permanent state of . . . knowing it's all . . . knowing this is all my fault?'

'You're a historian.'

'So?'

'Use your imagination.'

'I'm talking to myself and I don't even know what that means. What does that mean?'

'It means, if you think *this* feels bad, imagine being Henry Border.'

*

It was on 6 January 1945. The *Appel*, the roll call, in the women's camp in Auschwitz began at four o'clock in the afternoon and was all over unusually quickly, not out of consideration for the prisoners but because there was something the SS wanted them all to see. A group of prisoners, men, had been brought to the women's barracks in the camp and ordered to warm the rock-hard frozen ground. A small fire had been built with kindling in what would otherwise have been only snow. It was still light when the women who had returned from the day shift at the *Weichsel Union Metallwerke* factory and many others returning from other labour details arrived back inside the gates of the camp to see a structure that had been hastily erected on the warmed ground while they had been at work. It had not taken long to construct the scaffolding and gallows once the ground had been prepared. The Russians were coming. The rumours had reached fever pitch among the prisoners. They were coming, always coming, any day now. But then a new day came and on this day they still hadn't come. But they were coming, any day now. So you tried to survive just one more day. In the late afternoon of 6 January the rows and rows of women were made to form a semi-circle between Block 2 and Block 3 in Auschwitz I. They stood motionless in the cold fading winter light as the SS led two women from the direction of Block 11 to the gallows, Estusia Weiss and Rosa Rabinowicz.

An armed contingent of SS men surrounded the two frail young women who walked slowly towards the scaffolding, their arms unbound, their mouths ungagged; victims of beatings as vicious as any that had ever been meted out to prisoners whose death was to be kept from them a little longer. Four women had been arrested since the *Sonderkommando* uprising. All had been brutally beaten. They had not divulged the name of a single living person. This was widely known among the assembled women prisoners who stood in the snow watching in silence as the two tiny women were led to and then up the steps of the scaffolding.

A prisoner, a hulking man some knew simply as the 'Hangman' and whom others knew as the *Kapo* Jakub, was waiting there for them at the top of the stairs. They seemed calm, almost serene. All was silent until a prisoner from within the crowd noticed a tiny gesture from the *Kapo* Jakub. With the noose in one hand, he gently stroked the neck of the prisoner Estusia Weiss with his other hand before slipping the noose over her head and around her neck. Everyone saw this but only one prisoner was unable to contain herself despite the presence of the guards. A young twig of a woman, a girl of only fifteen, let out a piercing shriek. It was Hannah, the sister of Estusia Weiss. After her shriek she began to cry uncontrollably, offering hysterical moans to the heavens, heaving sobs that shook the cold ground beneath her feet. When Jakub kicked away the wooden stool from under the feet of Estusia Weiss, her sister Hannah fainted. She lay motionless in the snow. But by then the sobbing had spread throughout the ranks of the prisoners. They stood there in the snow watching the execution of two beaten, half-starved, wingless sparrows, each woman knowing that these two, the two on the scaffold, had fought back against the Nazis. Jakub made the same brief gesture, gently touching the neck of young Rosa Rabinowicz, once of Ciechanow. He had fed both Rosa and Estusia a drug half an hour earlier. He whispered something to Rosa as he slipped the noose around her neck and then, despite her tranquillised state, in the seconds before he kicked the wooden stool out from under her feet, she roused herself and called out to the assembled prisoners, to anyone who could hear her, 'Tell everyone what happened here! Tell everyone! Tell everyone!' Young Hannah Weiss had recovered in time to hear it.

Their bodies swung above the wooden planking as the *Kommandant* of the women's camp, *Kommandant* Hössler, made it a point to touch their bodies with his black leather-gloved hands. In a show for the prisoners he explained imperiously that the fate of these dangling women was the fate of anyone who conspired against the Reich. He made a similar speech at around 10 pm that night for the prisoners of the night shift when the other two women of the *Pulverraum*, Ala and Regina, were hanged. 'Sooner or later the Reich will find all those who conspire against it,' *Kommandant* Hössler bellowed in the floodlights beside the dangling, half-starved, badly beaten corpses of Ala and Regina. Eighteen days later he was nowhere to be found when Russian tanks entered Auschwitz.

*

It happened that in Chicago in the early 1950s a young postgraduate student of psychology, by the name of Wayne Rosenthal, was able to find an ideal thesis advisor and topic for his dissertation. But what could have been even harder, he was also able to convince his parents that this 'psychology business' was not some mumbo-jumbo waste of time. His parents were Eastern European Jews and, while they had no special need for their son to come to terms with anything called the 'Adjective–Verb Quotient', it made a lot of sense to them for their son to be working with the testimony of the survivors of the camps. It was their civilisation, it was their people. Whether or not their son could earn a living with this 'psychology business', for the time being it didn't matter to them. Moreover, the thesis advisor was a learned man, a cultured man who seemed to have a special fondness for their son. This fondness extended to inviting him to stay back late in his laboratory in the Main building at IIT where the young man took advantage of his first language, Yiddish, to translate wire recordings the professor had made in the summer of 1946. Quickly proficient in the use of the state-of-the-art wire recorder and fluent in Yiddish, the young man was a godsend to the Eastern European émigré.

It would save Border so much time if the student himself could directly translate some of the wire recordings. It was so much faster to edit the translations than to make them from scratch. Perhaps he might get all the wire recordings translated after all. His book of eight transla-tions had sold poorly but now there was the possibility, with the young man's help, of transcribing and then translating the full complement of wire recordings. Not wanting to be seen to be playing favourites from among his students, Border had hidden the gratitude he felt towards this young graduate student. And knowing the value his mentor placed on integrity, Wayne Rosenthal was content in public to play the role of just another one of the students fortunate to have Dr Border as his thesis advisor. But he knew the way his mentor really felt about him. He would have been grateful enough just to have found the topic, and more so to have found the man who was Border. But there was more.

The scholar had a daughter, a young woman who seemed to blossom a little more every day. At least, that was how Wayne Rosenthal saw her.

With dark eyes for falling into and jet-black hair, she could be both serious and funny, often at the same time. She was gentle, well read, interested in ideas and in the world around her, and all with a sense of humour. It was not easy to concentrate on those seminars at her father's home when you knew she was there listening in the back only a few feet behind you. When she served tea and coffee, when she cut up the cake while Callie Ford served sandwiches, more than anything else, the graduate student wanted to kiss her. But a seminar was neither the time nor the place. The time and the place, it turned out, was in the back of a movie theatre to which he had, with Dr Border's willing approval, taken her, where Wayne Rosenthal tentatively bestowed the first of many kisses on the young woman he thought he might one day want to marry. And she seemed to him to reciprocate his feelings. Certainly she never behaved in any way inconsistent with that hypothesis.

As was often the case, Wayne Rosenthal was alone in Dr Border's office late that afternoon. It was the night a party was to be held at the home of one of the other graduate students, Evie Harmon. Evie had invited Wayne along with all her classmates as well as Dr Border and his daughter Elly. Caught up in his work, Wayne was only peripherally aware of the time but he knew he was due to leave or risk being late for the party. It was in this hurried frame of mind that he came across a spool of wire that, although numbered, had become separated from the other spools of wire. Was this a mistake or did Dr Border have a reason for separating it from the others? He and Border had organised the spools into piles according to whether the recording had not yet been translated, translated but not yet transcribed, translated and partially transcribed, translated and completely transcribed, transcribed and fully edited. This particular spool was not in any of the piles. It sat under some papers on a shelf in the laboratory half of Border's two-roomed office.

Initially, Wayne thought that perhaps it was he who had been responsible for its being separated from the other spools. If he listened to just the beginning of it perhaps he would be able to identify which category this particular wire recording belonged to. He didn't really have time to listen to much of it but he knew he would be unsettled all night if he left the office with the wire recording uncategorised. So he threaded the wire into Marvin Cadden's machine and sat down to listen to just the first few minutes of the recording.

Immediately he knew that he hadn't heard this one at all. He wouldn't have forgotten it. While each wire recording contained stories that were capable of devastating the listener, none of them began the way this one began. A woman was abusing Henry Border in Yiddish.

'Now you will listen! No more of your stupid questions!'

What Wayne Rosenthal heard was the story of Estusia Weiss, Ala, Regina and of the *Sonderkommando* uprising. If all this did not astonish him enough, he heard his mentor interrupting the interviewee, a young woman called Hannah, to ask quite specific questions about one of the participants, the woman she called Rosa. He knew Border never interrupted his subjects. If something needed to be clarified he had always waited for his subject to finish a topic or at least to pause.

'What was her full name?' he heard Border ask in Yiddish that crackled through the wire in Marvin Cadden's machine.

'Rosa Rabinowicz.'

'Where did this Rosa Rabinowicz come from?'

'Originally she was from Ciechanow but she'd lived for a time before the war in Warsaw.'

'What did she look like?'

Wayne Rosenthal had never heard Border ask questions like this in the middle of an interview and he became convinced that Border must have known this Rosa Rabinowicz before the war. Was she a friend perhaps, or a relative?

He was running late for Evie Harmon's party. He was not going to have time to get changed beforehand and so he went directly to the Borders' home from where the three of them were to be driving. The Borders' housekeeper, Callie, and her son Russell, who had been engaged for the evening by the Harmons to help out, were also coming. It was on the way uptown to their place in Sheridan Road that he thought about the fact that the only wire recording to be uncategorised in Border's office was this one, the only one where the interviewee had been abusive to Dr Border, the only one where he had interrupted to ascertain the precise identity of someone in the interviewee's story. Wayne Rosenthal was standing at the Borders' front door when he heard Elly Border call out, 'It's okay, Callie. I'll get it. It's probably Wayne.'

He gave her a peck on the cheek to which, a little put out by the fact that he was running late and had not deemed the event worth changing for, she didn't respond but returned to the kitchen to collect Callie and Russell. This allowed Wayne Rosenthal just a minute or two to ask her father about this one uncategorised wire recording. When they all crammed into the Borders' car, Henry Border was already agitated. At the Harmons' party, after the various introductions, offers of drinks and social niceties had been exchanged, Dr Border took Wayne Rosenthal aside and, with uncharacteristic brusqueness, told him, 'That spool is not for you. Do you understand?'

But Border's anxiety and his tone had only succeeded in adding weight to what Wayne Rosenthal had already begun to suspect. Rosa Rabinowicz was not only familiar to Border, she had also been involved with him in some way. She could have been a girlfriend or maybe even his wife, Elly's mother. Could it be that Border, who wanted more than anything to tell the world what had happened to the Jews of Europe, had chanced upon the incredible story of his wife's fate and yet was not telling her daughter? But why wouldn't he want Elly to know? For all his respect for Dr Border, Wayne Rosenthal could not pretend that he didn't suspect what he now suspected.

*

When Adam Zignelik was a child growing up in the Melbourne bayside suburb of Elwood, his maternal grandfather liked to point out which of the bridges in Melbourne, the old man's adopted home town, were designed by Australia's most celebrated World War I general, Sir John Monash, who was in civilian life a distinguished engineer. He liked to tell Adam how Monash had overcome the obstacles of his German Jewish heritage to become a national hero in a predominantly Anglo-Celtic country. The little boy grew up asking his mother, his grandparents and sometimes his grandparents' closest friends, Mr and Mrs Leibowitz, 'Is this a Monash bridge?' whenever they went out for a drive. The answer was 'yes' more often than it was accurate.

What put him in mind of this now? He was sitting in the back of a Melbourne taxi going over the Elster Creek on his way from his hotel in St Kilda to a Jewish aged care facility to meet a woman there, a Holocaust survivor, who had been interviewed in a DP camp by Henry Border in 1946 and who had agreed to talk to him. Back in Melbourne after so many years he had directed the cab driver to take him on a tour of his old neighbourhood first.

The cab went over the bridge over the Elwood Canal and Adam smiled when he passed his old secondary school, Elwood High School, as it had then been called. He closed his eyes at the thought of his late mother. She had never remarried after Jake Zignelik. Nor had she ever complained when Adam returned to the US to go to college. Adam was going to be a big man in the history game. He never got to tell her. She had died far too young. When his cab got caught behind a crawling Number 64 tram on Hawthorn Road, he closed his eyes again for a moment in the back seat and hugged his day pack to his chest.

'Bloody trams!' the subcontinental cab driver, now a confirmed Melburnian, muttered under his breath.

His grandparents had predeceased his mother and there was nobody left, no family at all, none that he knew of. He could have started a family with Diana. She had begged him to but he hadn't shared her confidence in his ability to provide for one. There was nothing to stop a professor of history from being a fool. He saw that now but the realisation had come too late.

Looking to see where they were, Adam noticed the small Carlton Football Club logo on the windscreen of the cab.

'I used to be a Carlton supporter when I lived here a long time ago. How are they doing these days?' he asked.

'You don't want to know,' the cab driver grumbled. And continuing the grumble, 'They should get rid of the bloody "W" class trams.'

'I'm sorry?' Adam asked.

'The bloody "W" class trams, too slow. Get rid of them, I say.'

'Yep,' said Adam. 'Out with the old,' he added as they pulled up outside the Emmy Monash Jewish Aged Care facility in Dandenong Road.

A woman there, a manager of some sort, met him at reception. She wasn't the person Adam had spoken to the previous day, but she knew who he was and told him that she had been expecting him. She insisted on showing him around the facility as though it was the institution that was of professional interest to him, not one of its residents. But he was polite and just as Henry Border had thought it prudent to agree to being shown around any DP camp he was visiting before beginning his interviews, so would the man studying his work more than sixty years later take a short time to examine the surroundings that his work had led him to.

The administrator took him along several corridors to show him the residents' living quarters, at least from the outside. Occasionally someone had left their door ajar and Adam would catch a glimpse of an old person in his or her room. In one, a tiny man was peeling an orange. Outside each of the residents' rooms was a rectangular glass case, which each resident had filled with various mementos. There were small ceremonial silver *Kiddush* cups and *menorahs*, but mostly photographs of people of various ages, children, grandchildren. Some of the photos were of the resident many years earlier, smiling and seated beside a spouse, who, because each room was a single room, was likely no longer alive. The administrator noticed Adam's interest in the contents of the glass cases.

'These are our memory boxes. Many of our guests get lost after activities and aren't always sure which room is theirs. It can be embarrassing for them. They don't like to ask. The memory boxes allow them to manifest their pride in their families. That's the way we put it to them. But of course, their real purpose is to remind people which room is theirs. A lot of the residents on *this* floor are just at that stage where their memories about quite basic things are starting to go. The memory boxes give them tremendous comfort in a number of ways.'

The memory boxes of some of the residents contained black-and-white photos that they had recovered from their pre-war homes after the war. Unlike most old people, the tiny man peeling his orange had lost everyone in his one photo within a year of its being taken. Who knew that? Who but he ever looked inside his memory box and thought of that? Adam watched the little man slowly peeling his orange.

'You talked of residents on this floor. Is there a difference between this floor and other floors?' Adam asked the administrator.

'The floor below us, the basement, is where . . . It's for the residents who are no longer able to care for themselves at all. They've lost their memories maybe almost entirely. They can't wash or toilet themselves. They have trouble distinguishing between the present, the recent past and the distant past. If you look after they've had their lunch you'll find that they've put half of it in a bag.'

'In a bag?'

'They're saving it. They think they're still in the concentration camp they were in. You're not meant to go there without a pass or unaccompanied by one of the nursing staff but I could arrange it if you –'

'Thanks, but I should really begin the interview. Perhaps you could show me –'

Just then the administrator was approached by a dapper old man, a resident dressed in pleated trousers, shirt and tie, who interrupted them to greet her warmly. She knew the old man by name and it was only when she said the man's name that Adam, who was impatient to begin the interview, stopped silently cursing the timing of this exchange of pleasantries. With his notepad and recording equipment under one arm he looked quizzically at the old man who stood there stooped in his fawn cardigan and black trousers. So quizzically did he look at the old man that the smiling man looked back at him.

'Mr Leibowitz? I'm Adam.'

'Yes, Adam,' the old man said. The name meant nothing to him.

'I'm Adam Zignelik.' The man's eyes widened and he straightened as much as he could.

'Oh my God! Oh . . . my God! Little Adam!' The old man moved forward and, reaching the height of Adam's chest, he embraced Adam.

'You know Mr Leibowitz?' the administrator asked.

'Know him?' Mr Leibowitz interjected. 'I knew his grandfather and his grandmother from when they lived in Carlton. I knew his mother when she was just a little girl. Look at you, Adam. Little Adam!'

'Not so little any more,' the administrator said.

'We thought you lived in America,' Mr Leibowitz said. The old man was still using 'we' though his wife had died some years earlier. The administrator gave her version of the reason Adam was there.

'You want to interview *me*?' the old man asked hopefully.

'I certainly want to *talk* to you. When I've finished the interview with the woman I will come to see you so we can catch up. I'll come looking for you.'

'You won't forget?'

'Of course not! See you soon. Okay?'

'Yes. Okay, Little Adam!' the old man called as the administrator took Adam in the opposite direction. 'Adam, say hello to your mother for me.'

Adam set up his equipment. Out of his day pack he took a notepad, a couple of pens, headphones, which he attached to a digital audio recorder, and two tiny microphones, one to attach to his clothing and one to the dress of the woman he was about to interview.

'Yes, Dr Zignelik, I remember him very well.'

'Very well?'

'Yes, of course.'

'Can I ask you, why after everything you had been through, after all your war-time experiences, why should this man, Henry Border, stand out to you?'

'Well, because we argued.'

'You argued?'

'Yes. We didn't like each other. Well, I didn't like him.'

'Why not? Actually, before you answer that, can you tell me how you came to meet him?'

'How did I come to meet him? Well, I was at that time in Zeilsheim, the DP camp in Zeilsheim.'

'Yes.'

'Well, this is how I remember him so well. It was the day that the camp had a special visitor. We were all very excited to see her. Mrs Roosevelt was coming to visit the camp, the President's wife. He wasn't the President any more. It was Truman by then. Roosevelt had already died, but for us her visit to Zeilsheim was a very special thing and we . . . I mean everyone in the camp was looking forward to it very much. We wanted to meet her. I was hoping I would be able to talk to her.'

'Why did you want to talk to her?'

'Not only because she was famous. That wasn't really it. I wanted to tell her exactly what had happened to us. What an opportunity! You see we didn't know what people knew. We couldn't imagine that the Americans knew what had gone on. In the camp we believed, everybody did, that the Allies must be completely unaware of what was going on there every day, so loud was the silence. It was the only explanation for why nobody did anything . . . ever.

'Well, this funny-looking man, an older man . . . remember, I was still a teenager then, this man comes into the hall where we ate the food they gave us. And he has this wire recording device with which he could record what people said. He wanted people to tell him what they had gone through so he can record it and take it back to America. That's what he said, and people wanted to tell their stories. I did too; I wanted to tell what had happened to us. That's why I agreed to be interviewed. But he had this special way he wanted to do it.'

'What do you mean "he had this special way"? What was that way?'

'He wanted me to sit with my back to him . . . so that I couldn't see his face. What for? I didn't want to do it like this but he insisted. I insisted back. Then he insisted back. He had that strict manner, you know, like a teacher. Not like a teacher these days but the way they were in Europe, you know, before the war . . . He was very stern, very strict in the way he talked. This didn't help him, not with me. I didn't care what he wanted. What *I* wanted was to tell him the story of my sister . . .'

'And did you tell him?' Adam Zignelik asked the woman.

'Sure. I made a deal with him.'

'A deal?'

'If I would answer his questions . . . If I would do the interview his way, you know, in the order he wanted . . . well, then, he promised he would let me tell him what I wanted to tell him.'

'And did you tell him everything?'

'What do you think?' asked the woman, who had been the fifteen-year-old Hannah Weiss, the sister of the Estusia Weiss who was hanged for her role in the *Sonderkommando* uprising.

It was then that she told Adam Zignelik the entire story of the women in the *Weichsel Union Metallwerke* factory, of their role in smuggling the gun powder meant for munitions to the *Sonderkommando* resistance.

'I told him, I made him listen to everything.'

'About Estusia?'

'I told him about Estusia and also about the others. I told him about Rosa Rabinowicz and how she had approached us in our block. I told him about Ala and Regina, about the smuggling of the gunpowder from the *Pulverraum*. I told him how none of them ever betrayed me or a single other person from the resistance. I told him about –'

'Wait a minute. Did you say Rosa Rabinowicz?'

Recording every word just as Border had some sixty years earlier, Adam Zignelik sat in the temporarily empty dining room of the Emmy Monash Aged Care facility on the corner of Hawthorn and Dandenong roads in Melbourne and listened.

'You told him about a woman called Rosa Rabinowicz?'

'Yes.'

'Are you sure?'

'Yes, of course.'

'Do you remember how you identified her?'

'What do you mean "identified"?'

'How did you let him know who she was?'

'I used their names and, where I knew it, I also told him where they were from. I wanted to . . . I wanted the world to know how brave these girls were. Has there ever been anyone braver?' Now, for the first time since the interview had started, the old lady had tears in her eyes.

'Did you remember where Rosa Rabinowicz was from?'

'Yes, I remembered then and I remember now.'

'Where was she from?'

'Rosa? She was from Ciechanow, but she'd spent some time in Warsaw before the war. We knew this.'

'And you definitely told Border?'

'Yes.'

'How can you be so sure . . . all these years later?'

'Because that was the whole point of talking to him. I wanted to tell him, to tell the whole world what Estusia and Rosa and the other girls had done. I wasn't going to talk to him, not one word after he had made me miss out on seeing Mrs Roosevelt, but it was because I wanted to tell Estusia's story and also the story of Rosa and Ala and the others who had got the gunpowder to the *Sonderkommando* that I agreed to put up with his nonsense.'

'After this second interview, after you'd told him the story . . . about Rosa Rabinowicz and Estusia and the others . . . Do you remember how he reacted, what he said?'

'I don't know. Who remembers? It was what I wanted to tell him about. Why would I care what he thought?'

'Yes, of course.'

'Anyway, isn't it all on the recording?' she asked him.

'It probably is. I haven't got to your recording yet but I wondered if he said anything else . . . if you remembered anything that wasn't recorded for whatever reason.'

'I don't know. How could I know what was recorded? Maybe he thanked me. I couldn't have cared less. I just wanted Estusia's story to . . . to go out to the world. This is what I thought he was good for. I was saving the memory of my sister . . . and the other girls.'

'You wrote to me . . .' Adam pulled a letter from a file out of his day pack and began to read it. 'You wrote . . . He paid "particular attention to Rosa's story".'

'Okay, I believe you. If that's what I wrote then that's what I remembered.'

'Do you remember it now?'

'Look, I have to be honest, this Dr Border . . . he's not so important to me. He's just a man who interviewed me in the DP camp. Estusia was important to me . . . and Ala.'

'And Rosa?'

'Yes, but I didn't know Rosa so well. She was in *Kanada*. I wanted their story to become known. Why is it important to you? Why does it matter if he showed more interest in Rosa's story?'

'Because I think she might have been his wife.'

Adam Zignelik pictured the one photo he had seen of Henry Border and tried to imagine the man, the face on the inside sleeve of the barely read *I Did Not Interview the Dead*, when he quite unexpectedly learned what had happened to his young wife Rosa, the woman he had abandoned, the mother of his child. What Border had heard from Hannah Weiss all those years ago must have undammed a flood of feelings and thoughts and images, all of them heart-rendingly painful, and eclipsing all of them, unbearable guilt. It was there in his voice at the end of his very last interview when he asks the listener, 'Who is going to sit in judgement over all this? And who is going to judge . . . me?'

Who could ever begin to know how he had felt? Whenever Border had thought about it, and he must have often, other than learning she had survived, he must have hoped never to learn what had happened to the young woman Rosa Rabinowicz, the girl formerly of Ciechanow he had promised to protect, the woman he had married and had a daughter with, the daughter he had stolen from her when he abandoned her.

When Adam had finished interviewing Hannah he thanked her for all the valuable information she'd given him and praised her for her own heroism and contribution to the uprising, which she had made little of. They hugged each other and he wished her long life.

Seeing him packing up his equipment, Mr Leibowitz, who had been hovering, was unable to keep silent any longer.

'So now you have some time for me?'

'You bet. Can I take you out to lunch?'

'I hope so. Oh!' the old man said, suddenly remembering something else. 'But before we go, will you do me a favour?'

'Sure, if I can.'

'You can. Downstairs is where they put the ones who have no use any more for their memory boxes. These people are *famishte*. You understand? They have lost their sense of themselves, they can't control their minds and sometimes they can't control their bodies. You understand?'

'I understand.'

'There's a woman I know from when she used to live up here on this level. When they were moving her down there she was frightened of the change and I promised her that I would come visit her. She has no one.

No one ever comes to visit her so I try to go. Can we go down there for a few minutes? I'll introduce you. It will be the highlight of her day. It will be the only light.'

Adam agreed and the old man took him downstairs. After being granted entry through the glass security doors Mr Leibowitz introduced him to the woman he had talked about. Someone had brushed her hair but her eyes were wild as though blown about in a wind only she could feel, a gale inside her head. She could not be relied upon to know where she was.

'Can you go and get me glass of water?' she asked Mr Leibowitz.

'Yes, of course, darling,' he said, leaving Adam alone in a room full of broken old people moving around slowly, jerkily, in random directions. What private anarchy was it that made such frequent guerrilla raids on the minds of these people?

The friend of Mr Leibowitz suddenly entwined her arm in Adam Zignelik's and whispered to him, 'The camp guards won't give me any more water. He always does better with them.' Then taking his hand in hers for a moment she quickly turned it palm-up and stared at it.

'You know, all the boys liked me. You ask anyone. All the boys liked me. My father is away on business now so you don't need permission to visit me. I can read your palm. Do you want that?'

It took a little over thirty hours for Adam Zignelik to go from closing the door of his room at the Hotel Tolarno in Melbourne to opening the door to the apartment he rented from Columbia University. He put his luggage on the floor, closed the door, kicked off his shoes and flopped on the couch. Nobody knew he was home. Soon it wouldn't be his home. Next week he was going to have to empty his office. He had to figure out where he'd put the contents. What do you pay for storage now? he wondered.

He noticed the light on his answering machine blinking and on his way to the bathroom to take a shower he hit the button. There was only one person he wanted to hear from. Adam stood in the bathroom, the shower running, and held Diana's comb in his hand.

'Pathetic,' he said under his breath about himself. He'd been thinking about the comb, looking forward to it since some way across the Pacific.

From the other room came a woman's voice not entirely unfamiliar but not immediately welcome, not from its tone. It was the woman William McCray liked to call Charles' secretary. 'Personal Assistant, PA, Administrative Assistant, whatever you call her, she's his secretary,' he would say. 'Is there something offensive in the word?' Over the sound of the water Adam couldn't quite make out the message the woman had left but when he got out of the shower he heard it. There'd been a call for him while he was away that had come through to her. A man from Chicago had called. He left his number and asked Adam to call him back.

'His name . . .' she said, 'I'm sorry, Dr Zignelik, I seem to have misplaced it . . . oh here it is! Wayne Rosenthal. Dr Wayne Rosenthal. Said he's a psychologist. Something about your work . . . in Chicago?'

*

In the course of his research into the combat experiences of African American troops during World War II, Adam had found the 761st Tank Battalion of considerable interest. He had initially thought that this all-black battalion had been attached to the 79th Division of the US 7th Army in Lieutenant General Devers' 6th Army Group only to learn that it had been attached to that division for no more than a couple of weeks. For most of its active duty in Europe the 761st Tank Battalion was attached to the 87th Division of the US 3rd Army, becoming attached to the 71st Division of the 3rd Army only on 28 March 1945. The reason this stuck out to Adam was that from his research thus far he knew that the 71st Division had advanced through Bavaria in April of 1945. It was not disputed that the 761st had taken part in the liberation of a satellite camp of the Mauthausen concentration camp known as Gunskirchen on 5 May 1945.

'Did you know that the 761st had taken part in the liberation of Gunskirchen?' Adam Zignelik, with a hint of triumph in his voice, asked his friend William McCray over coffee.

'No, I have to admit, I did not. And this Gunskirchen, it was a satellite of Mauthausen, you say?'

'That's right.'

'And you just found this out?'

'*I* only just discovered it but it's known by people in the field.'

'It's not disputed?'

'No, it's widely accepted. As far as I know, no one disputes it.'

'And Dachau?' William asked, sipping on his coffee.

'Black troops at Dachau?'

'Yeah, anything?'

The disappointment on William McCray's face when Adam let him know that he hadn't uncovered anything to suggest black troops were involved in the liberation of Dachau made Adam feel as though he was letting William down. Perhaps this was how Charles sometimes felt.

'Is it your friend?'

'How do you mean?' William asked.

'Is it for your friend, the one in Boston, is that what makes it particularly important to you that someone definitively establishes African American troop involvement at the liberation of Dachau? I mean Gunskirchen was a satellite of Mauthausen. That's nothing to sneeze at. Frankly, it would help a lot if he'd reconsider and agree to talk to me because –'

'Adam, he's not talking to anyone –'

'I know, and I really do appreciate what he's been through but if you could explain that –'

'Adam, he's not talking to anyone. He died,' William explained, taking in a breath and trying to keep himself composed.

'William, I'm so sorry.'

'Yep, me too.' William paused for a moment, taking in the room around him before continuing.

'Look, Adam, I know Dachau wasn't a death camp but it was the first concentration camp Hitler set up when he came to power. I mean, this was as early as 1933. And it was one of the last to be liberated. So it would have particular significance if it could be shown that African Americans were involved in its liberation. And the vehemence of the campaign against recognising the role of black servicemen there – 'cause that's what it is, you know, a campaign – this makes me all the more keen for somebody to get to the bottom of it. And yes, truth be told, it's also for my friend.'

It was not for want of trying or for lack of regard for William McCray that Adam Zignelik had not managed to find any first-hand evidence, nothing from a primary source that placed a black unit at the liberation of Dachau. He tried to decide whether his time was best used further examining the combat experiences of the men of the all-black 761st Tank Battalion or whether he should bury himself in the transcripts and wire recordings of the Chicago psychologist, Henry Border. It was only when he turned his attention back to Border's interviews that he saw the beginnings of something that sooner or later he might be able to discuss with his old friend, the civil rights lawyer and World War II veteran. In a period of three weeks he came across the evidence of three survivors interviewed by Border who mentioned, just in passing, that the military force that had liberated the camp they found themselves in at the end of the war contained black soldiers. One of these three survivors didn't know the name of the camp he was liberated from or else Border hadn't elicited it from him but the other two seemed to think it was either Dachau or one of Dachau's Kaufering satellite camps. Of these two, one of them even mentioned his surprise at seeing a black officer, a captain, whose name he happened to have remembered with the help of a mnemonic.

From US Army records Adam found that although the 42nd and 45th Divisions of the US Seventh Army are credited with the liberation of Dachau on 29 April 1945, the 71st Infantry Division of the US Third Army, to which the black 761st Tank Battalion was at that time attached, was also not far from there at the relevant time. Eventually he was able to match the name remembered by Border's interviewee with the name of an African American captain in the 761st Tank Battalion. Border's interviewee was no longer alive but, by consulting US Army enlistment records, Adam was able to find the home address of the captain at the time of his enlistment in 1942. The address didn't yield the captain but it led Adam to a relative of his, a granddaughter who lived in New York.

For so long he hadn't made any progress with this but now, simply because one of the survivors Border had interviewed had spoken to the officer and had remembered his name and rank, Adam was able to track down the officer's granddaughter. The man on Border's wire recording had remembered the name because it was also the name of the country's capital and its first president.

This was how it happened that Adam found himself contacting the only living relative of Captain James Washington of the 761st Tank Battalion. Dr Ayesha Washington, it seemed, was a very busy woman but Adam was more than happy to meet her at her place of work at a time convenient for her. She worked as an oncologist at Memorial Sloan-Kettering Cancer Center.

*

Charles McCray felt it had been a compromise to bring work home that night rather than stay back late in his office in the Fayerweather building on the Columbia campus. His wife Michelle had been less sure. At least she and their daughter Sonia had to worry less about the volume of music or the radio they were playing or the movie they were watching when Charles worked late in his office. What was the point of him being there if he wasn't going to interact with anybody and, worse, was going to implicitly impose constraints on the way they spent the evening?

But he was trying. He wondered if she'd noticed. He wondered too about the point of what he'd been doing, looking through some recent journals only one of which had a paper in his area. Surely, he asked himself, a man in his position is expected to keep up with what was going on in his profession, even outside his specific area of expertise? Was he reading outside his area in order to be able to keep up with all his colleagues? With whom was he trying to keep up? Who was he trying to impress? Not his father. No amount of reading would impress him, not any more. Would it give him something to talk about? Maybe, but who was he going to talk to: colleagues, friends? His colleagues would talk to him at least until the chair was given to someone else in the department and if their need to engage him dropped off after that, what then? As for his friends . . . He wondered how Adam was faring with that Chicago research. He was going there often enough. Just because it was too late to save Adam's position at Columbia didn't mean Charles should ignore his friend's work. His father wasn't ignoring it.

Charles resolved to have lunch or at least coffee with Adam and to talk to him about his work, about his plans post Columbia. Was Adam still meeting up with William for coffee once every week or so? How was it, Charles wondered, that he didn't know? Adam was a good man. How was he coping after Diana? Maybe Michelle would know. And so again his questioning reached back to where it had started. How much point was there in reading all these journals, in even scanning them? Who was keeping up with the latest developments in his wife's life, in his daughter's mood swings? They had each come to him and kissed him goodnight. That was good.

Michelle had gone to bed an hour and a half before him and by the time he had brushed his teeth, put on his pyjamas and got into bed, she was long asleep. Was she dreaming? he wondered. When she was younger did she ever dream, did she ever even imagine the man she would end up being married to, a man like him, an intellectual, an academic? And if she had, how much of a disappointment had he, the man she'd actually married, turned out to be? He rolled over on his side in bed and looked at her. Was it her moisturiser or her shampoo that smelled like that? He closed his eyes and breathed in his wife deeply. It calmed him and soon he was asleep. It was almost 3 am and he had been asleep for just a little over two hours when the phone on his bedside table rang, waking both him and Michelle. Because it was next to him he was the one to answer it.

'Hello?' Charles said blearily.

'Is this the home of Mrs Michelle McCray?' a man asked.

'Who is this?'

'I'm sorry to bother you at this time of night, sir. I'm a police officer. Is this the home of Mrs Michelle McCray?'

'Yes, it is, I'm her husband. What's this all about?' Michelle stirred. Her first thought was of her clients. But she didn't give out her home number so that couldn't be it.

'May I speak with Mrs McCray please, sir? Again, apologies for –'

'It's for you,' Charles said, handing the phone over to Michelle.

'Who is it?'

'It's the police.'

'Police? Hello? Who is this?'

'I'm very sorry to trouble you at this hour, ma'am. Am I talking to a Mrs Michelle McCray?'

'Who is this?'

'This is Officer Brooks, NYPD. Am I talking to Mrs Michelle McCray?'

'This is Michelle McCray.'

'Sorry to bother you at this hour, ma'am. My partner and I were called to a disturbance in the north Bronx and we have a pretty severely distressed man here who has asked us to call you to confirm his story. The gentleman in question has no ID on his person and we have reason to believe that he might be under the influence of a prohibited substance . . . Ma'am, are you there?'

Sweating, unable to catch his breath and with a heart rate he felt was only a few beats away from flatlining, he had an urgent need to get himself outside no matter how late it was, no matter how cold it was, no matter how many floors down. As he leaned against the side of the downward moving elevator his only desire was to breathe the outside air. But when he reached the ground floor of his apartment block and went into the street he found that the cold air didn't help. Unsteady on his feet, he was terrified. He was losing control. Hot and cold and stumbling, under-dressed for the night and for the season, he mouthed something unintelligible to some passing kids coming home late from a night out. They thought he was tripping, possibly crazy, possibly dangerous. Not wanting to get involved, one of them called the police from a mobile phone and then at the end of the call used the phone to record scenes of the man as he spiralled out of all normal human ways of being. Now Officer Brooks was putting him on the phone to Michelle McCray.

''Chelle?'

'Hello?' The man was panting furiously. His mouth was dry, and his tongue, stuck to the roof of his mouth, made the sound of consonants as he tried, unsuccessfully, to speak. Painfully, he forced out a few words.

''Chelle, it's me . . . It's Lamont.'

'Lamont? What's –'

''Chelle, she's dead. Grandma's dead.'

part eleven

SONIA MCCRAY WAS FOURTEEN YEARS OLD when she stood a few feet from the grave, slightly behind but with one foot edged between both her father Charles and her grandfather, William. This was the first funeral she'd ever been to. Before this, death had been confined to stories in books, on television, in the movies and sometimes in songs in which the singer would suggest that without the person being sung to, the singer would die. It was a feeling she had never experienced. But here was a gaping gash in the cold earth containing someone Sonia had known, even loved in a way, someone she had never had enough time for, and yet someone who had loved *her* beyond reason. Standing there, almost hiding, behind her father and grandfather, she wanted to apologise for not visiting her more often, for not sharing more of her life with her great-grandmother, for rejecting the apple juice she always offered her. When had she last been to her apartment?

In front of both Sonia's father and her grandfather stood her mother Michelle, and next to her mother, also at the mouth of the grave, stood a man she had no memory of ever having met before. But apparently she had met him when she was very young. Her father and her grandfather were dressed in dark suits under their winter coats while her mother wore a black skirt with a black shirt and jacket under her coat but the man was dressed unlike all of them, completely informally. He was wearing jeans with a flannel shirt and a sweater under his coat but she understood that it did not reflect a lack of respect for Sonia's great-grandmother nor was it evidence that he felt any less grief at the loss. In fact, he was the most visibly moved. Sonia could not bear to look at the man any more than she could bear to look at the grave. As he rocked before the mouth of the grave, Sonia's mother, who was holding on to him, rocked with him. The man was her mother's cousin, her, Sonia's, great-grandmother's grandson, Lamont.

From the way they shared their grief Sonia pieced together that her mother had once been very close to him but that he'd been away and they hadn't been in touch again till now. He had been the one who had found Sonia's great-grandmother. She had died in her sleep. Sonia wondered whether she was meant to comfort her mother or whether she could leave that to her father and her grandfather. She looked at her grandfather standing bundled up in his coat. He was older than her great-grandmother had been. How would the funeral have made *him* feel? she wondered. Thank God he was still there. He hadn't changed. She vowed to see a lot more of him. Where was Lamont's family? she wondered. Then she realised that her mother and now Sonia herself were probably all he had. No wonder he rocked that way. How long before they could leave?

Were they going to have to go on comforting the rocking man? Things were worse for him than Sonia knew. He had lost the person who had brought him up, who had felt emotionally responsible for him for as long as he could remember. He owed her so much and now he would never be able to pay her back. His grandmother died just two weeks before he finished his six-month probation period as an employee at the hospital. He was going to get benefits. She wouldn't be there to see him leave every morning to go to a job with benefits. They send employees to college, he'd told her. First things first, he was going to find his daughter. Now his grandmother would never get to see his daughter, no longer a toddler any more but an eight-year-old, almost nine. He'd imagined showing the little girl his room, the room where he grew up, the room where you could still see the pencil marks his grandmother had made on the wall to chart his height. At ten he was already as tall as his grandmother. At thirty-eight he was back sleeping in the same room. He didn't know whether he would be able to go on living in the Co-op City apartment and, if he couldn't, he didn't know where he was going to live.

Sonia McCray watched her mother propping up the man who didn't wear a suit to his grandmother's funeral.

'Your grandma prob'ly outlive *you*, Lamont,' a man called Numbers had once said to him back in Mid-Orange Correctional Facility. 'Highly good chance, highly good! Nothin' as against you, just statistics, understand? No offence meant, I'm talkin' 'bout the science of statistics as it pertains to an African American man of your raw data and general . . . geneology.'

'Wouldn't bother me if she did,' Lamont had answered. Sonia watched this adult man trying to pull himself together as her grandfather, William McCray, stood tall and quietly thanked the minister. She was determined to spend more time with her grandfather but now she listened to her cousin Lamont clear his throat and try to speak.

'Mrs Martinez, thank you for coming. Really appreciate it. She was very fond of you. Always said what a good neighbour you were. Always there for us. You remember my cousin, Michelle . . . from the old days?' Sonia heard the man say. Lamont Williams was desperate for people to remember other people. If they didn't, what did anything mean, what had anything been for?

The fourteen-year-old girl stood with her gloved hands in her pockets and looked around the cemetery, so many tall Christs in the north Bronx, all of them under-dressed for early winter. You could see them from the overpass. Car horns let off steam in the distance. How few people had come.

*

Lamont Williams was sitting on a long bench in a corridor on the ground floor of Memorial Sloan-Kettering Cancer Center. He'd been asked to wait for a moment before his scheduled appointment. A message had been passed on to him from his supervisor that the Deputy Head of Human Resources wished to see him. In just under two weeks his six-month probation period was due to expire. His grandmother had been buried only days earlier. He'd told his supervisor and D'Sean, a colleague. Was that what this was about? No, probably not. It probably had something to do with the necessary paperwork that had to be completed when he transferred from probationary employee to the category of permanent employee.

People in suits walked past Lamont. Who were they – doctors, nurses, physicians' assistants? No, they couldn't be. These people looked more like business types, fundraisers and administrators. Lamont considered how much non-medical effort went into running a hospital like this. He read the titles on people's doors as well as on the strategically placed brochures. There were people who worked only in research, all different kinds of research. There were people who worked only in education; continuing medical education, continuing nursing education. There was someone in charge of PhD graduate education, someone in charge of post-doctoral training and even someone in charge of a high school outreach program. There was a library and there were administrators who had his name on file somewhere, probably on a computer somewhere; Lamont Williams, Building Services, on probation as part of a pilot program for ex-convicts. If the right people had known about his grandmother they might even have someone offer him grief counselling. That's what his cousin Michelle had said.

Michelle was a social worker, a senior one, and she knew about that sort of thing. What did it mean, 'grief counselling'? Do you tell a therapist what it's like to lose someone you love? Lamont wondered. Do you lie on a couch? Does the hospital pay the therapist money to hear about the grief of a man from Building Services who had lost his grandmother? She was like a mother to him, always had been, the only 'mother' he'd ever really known. He hadn't been able to sleep since finding her, not for more than a couple of hours at a time.

'Do you have any other family?'

'I have a daughter. She's eight. I'm going to find her.'

'Anyone else?'

'I have a cousin. We were close as kids . . . drifted for a while but now . . . We're in touch now . . . since my grandmother's passing. We were real close as kids and it's kind of funny that it's taken the passing of my grandma . . . I don't mean funny that way but –'

Lamont was woken from his daydream by an administrative assistant, a young woman who worked for the Deputy Head of Human Resources, Mr Juan Laviera.

'Mr Laviera will see you now,' she said without affect.

Mr Laviera had an office with a desk, a big chair for himself and two smaller chairs on the other side of the desk, one of which Lamont was invited to sit in. Lamont sneaked peeks at the photos of Mr Laviera and people in his life that had been placed around the office. From the other side of a door that seemed to lead to an adjoining office Lamont could hear the muffled sounds of a radio.

'Mr Williams,' said the Deputy Head of Human Resources, 'you might have some idea why you've been asked to come here today. One of our patients died recently, Mr . . .' Juan Laviera clicked the mouse on his desk and squinted at his computer terminal, 'Mr Henryk Mandelbrot. Did you know Mr Mandelbrot before he came to us?'

'Before he came to the hospital?'

'Yes.'

'No,' Lamont answered.

'It seems that after his passing his family members came to collect his possessions and they allege that something was missing. Do you know anything about that?'

All at once Lamont Williams understood why he had been asked to come down to see the Deputy Head of Human Resources. It had nothing to do with the preparation of the paperwork necessary upon his completion of his six months as a probationary employee and nothing to do with grief counselling.

'I think I know where you goin' with this,' Lamont said quietly.

'Where am I going with this?'

'This is about the candleholder, the Jewish candleholder.'

'Yes, the candelabrum. Do you know anything about this?'

'They call it a *menorah*. That's what he told me. Yeah, I know about it.'

'Did you . . . I'm sorry, I have to ask you this, Mr Williams. Did . . . You don't deny – ?'

'I have it but I didn't steal it.'

'What are you saying?'

'I'm saying he gave it to me.'

'The patient?'

'Right. Mr Mandelbrot gave me it.'

'He *gave* you it?'

'Yeah.'

'As . . . like a gift?'

'Right.'

'Would you excuse me a minute, Mr Williams?'

'Sure.'

'No, I mean, would you mind waiting outside for a moment?'

'Yeah, sure.'

It was early afternoon and, unusually for him at that time, Adam Zignelik was not teaching or in his office or anywhere else on campus but some two and a half miles uptown in his Morningside Heights apartment waiting for a van to come and deliver the contents of boxes he had packed. The boxes contained his career to date. He had emptied out his office of all but a few items. There was room on the bookshelves for much of its contents now that Diana wasn't there. Where the hell was the van driver?

On the ground floor of Memorial Sloan-Kettering Cancer Center Lamont Williams got up from Juan Laviera's office as requested and walked outside to where he had waited before. He had closed the door to Mr Laviera's office but it had not shut tight. From the hallway Lamont heard Mr Laviera knock on and then open the door to the adjacent office. From the tone of his interaction with its occupant, theirs was an easy relationship.

'Sorry to bother you, Dan.'

'No, what's up?'

'I got him waiting outside.'

Lamont could hear the radio playing louder now that the two doors were slightly ajar.

'He says he didn't do it, didn't steal it. Says the old man gave it to him.'

Lamont looked at the name on the outside door of the office next door to the Deputy Head of Human Resources. It belonged to the Head of Human Resources, the man Mr Laviera was now talking to. It read, 'Daniel Ehrlich, Head of Human Resources'. Where did Lamont know that name from? He used to go to school with a kid called Danny Ehrlich. It couldn't be the same one.

'The old man gave it to him . . . a *menorah*?'

'That's what he said.'

Lamont Williams sat out in the corridor. 'The trick is not to hate yourself.' That's what he'd been told inside. 'If you can manage not to hate yourself, then it won't hurt to remember almost anything: your childhood, your parents, what you've done or what's been done to you,' he was told. He thought of this as he heard the radio playing softly from inside the office of the Head of Human Resources, a Mr Danny Ehrlich.

Lamont was looking at his hands, the hands that once took a prized toy, a birthday present from an uncle to a new friend's home to show him the gift, hands that, when asked by an old friend, drove a van to a liquor store and waited outside while two other men spontaneously formed illegal intentions, hands that tried their hand at woodwork in Woodbourne Correctional Facility, hands that accepted a gift in the form of a silver candelabrum from an old white European man, hands that touched the cold forehead of his recently discovered dead grandmother, two hands fairly coordinated, appropriate in size for a man of his height and weight, hands unremarkable but for one characteristic never yet remarked upon – their innocence.

*

In the last gasps of the second half of the 1940s two men lay sleeping in different parts of a house on Sheridan Road, in Uptown Chicago. One of them, a father, was old enough to have been a grandfather; the other, a son, was still young enough to pass for a boy. There were areas of the country in which, no matter how old the young man got, he would only ever be seen as a boy. He had been to some of those places and he took what he'd seen into bed with him every night when he slept. It was unlikely that these two men, Henry Border and young Russell Ford, should be sleeping in the same house in mid-century Chicago but they were, and it was through their different connections to Russell's mother, Callie Pearson, that this came about.

Henry Border tended to retire for the evening long after everyone else. He would sit alone in his study reading and making notes or listening to foreigners talking about terrible events on strands of wire. The study door would be closed and he would rub his eyes, he would close his eyes and sometimes he would dab at his eyes with a handkerchief that Russell's mother, Callie, had laundered.

Then, quietly as he could, he would wash up in the bathroom and go to bed wearing only a nightshirt and a weight of lead on his chest that never shifted, even when he turned over. It had been this way since he'd visited the DP camps. The grandfather clock ticks downstairs. He takes off his watch and puts it on the dresser, turns out the bedside light and the familiar whispered question comes no sooner than his eyelids have closed. 'What kind of a man abandons his wife to be tortured and murdered?'

Henry Border had a professional interest in 'people in distress'. His 'Adjective–Verb Quotient' hypothesis asserted that people in 'distress' will use adjectives and verbs in a different ratio to each other than will people who are not in 'distress'. He had gone to Europe in search of distressed people to study. There were too many rooms in the house he shared for a time with his daughter, Russell Ford, Callie Pearson and her husband James Pearson, so the hallway was by necessity also too long. But it didn't stretch to Europe.

Close to Russell's bed in his room along the hall, so close that his hand could reach out from under the covers and touch it, was a worn leather satchel that had belonged to his father. Asleep in his bed Russell would suddenly grow cold from a sweat that announced the return of that hot Detroit Monday morning towards the end of the school year and he would see it all over again: his father being torn from the street car by strangers and being punched and hit and kicked and stomped on until he was bleeding, then unconscious, then dead, then no longer a dead man, no longer a deceased human but some wet and torn corpse lying on the roadside beside a leather satchel. And the scene visited him once

490

a night several nights a week and sometimes, often, it could be heard from the other side of the door. But Henry Border, the psychologist with the special interest in distressed people, never once went to the young boy to find out what was wrong, let alone to offer him any comfort. His own nightmares deafened him to the moans from the nightmares in the other room.

From the bedroom along the hall that she shared with her husband, Callie Pearson however would hear her son's distress. Her husband James Pearson, hearing it too, would put on a bathrobe and walk down the hall in the dark to his stepson's room often only to notice someone else already at the door.

'I got it, Mr Pearson,' Elly Border would whisper, a glass of water in one hand. She'd learned what it was that Russell had witnessed in Detroit and now, like his mother and his stepfather, she too heard him every time.

*

When Danny Ehrlich was a boy his laid-back and slightly indulgent parents, both teachers, encouraged discussion of social and political issues at the dinner table not just with each other but also with their children. Danny's relationship with them was close enough for him to want to inform them of anything of significance that happened to him as soon as he could. This was how it came about that when a new school friend visiting his place for the first time brought him what Danny thought was a gift, a quite outstanding gift, a Shogun Warrior action figure, he raced down the hallway of his family's apartment to his mother in the kitchen to show her what his new friend had given him. But after the new friend had left to go home the Shogun Warrior action figure was never to be seen again in that apartment. Everyone in the Ehrlich home just assumed that the visiting friend had grown overly fond of his own gift and had stolen it back.

It was only close friends, family and his wife who called Danny Ehrlich 'Danny' now that he was a grown man. Professionally he was known as Dan Ehrlich, Head of Human Resources at Memorial Sloan-Kettering

Cancer Center, and he had been hoping to avoid this now unavoidable meeting with the adult version of the little boy who had visited his apartment that day, the little boy who had given him and then taken back the Shogun Warrior action figure. On the door side of the desk sat Lamont Williams, an ex-convict who had been given a chance to start his life afresh with a six-month probationary stint in Building Services as a janitor. The decision to begin an outreach program for appropriate newly released ex-convicts had been made by a subcommittee chosen by the hospital's Board of Directors. Both Dan Ehrlich and Juan Laviera, the Deputy Head of Human Resources, had been on the subcommittee. Although the two men shared an easy working relationship that bordered on friendship, they had respectfully taken opposing sides on the question of whether the hospital should take on former convicts as probationary employees. Juan Laviera had been opposed to it. He had taken the view that the rehabilitation of former prisoners was not part of the hospital's core mission and that it would only lead to problems they didn't need.

'Dan, believe me, a lot of guys I grew up with went that way and . . . well, you knew even back then that they were headed for trouble. We might've been kids but people . . . they don't really change.'

Dan Ehrlich had taken the opposite view. He felt that people, *some* people at least, were capable of change and that they needed to be given a chance. And when they did change, it could be truly inspiring. It might be good for the morale of both the hospital staff and even some of the patients for the ex-cons working their six-month probations to feel part of a team effort, a community of carers of varying backgrounds all united in their attempts to help people with cancer. It would send out the right signals to the community about the hospital and, if they started off slowly, choosing one or two ex-prisoners at a time and very carefully, what was the worst that could happen? This was the worst that could happen.

Juan Laviera genuinely did not want to take an 'I-told-you-so' attitude but perhaps this theft of a dying man's *menorah* could put an end to the experiment. He liked working with Dan Ehrlich, he liked his easy-going manner, and was worried that the apparent failure of the program would redound to Dan's discredit. Surely now Dan should, and could without guilt, recommend that this, what he, Juan Laviera, had always regarded as a fraught program, be ended.

Opposite Lamont Williams, on the window side of the door with a desk that held photographs of his wife and twin daughters between them, sat Dan Ehrlich. This was the meeting his wife knew he had been dreading for days ever since the recently deceased patient's family had complained that one of their loved one's personal items, a silver *menorah*, had gone missing. The two men looked at each other and though both of them were equally close to certain that the man opposite him was the adult incarnation of a briefly adopted school friend, neither of them let on that they had a fair idea of the identity of the other. Instead they each waited for the other to bring it up and they each, for different reasons, wondered what good it would do them to bring it up now. After all, their association had ended as uncomfortably as their friendship had been brief.

Lamont's thoughts took him back for a moment to Danny Ehrlich's kitchen and Mrs Ehrlich's admiration of the toy before he shook himself and was suddenly re-deposited back in Dan Ehrlich's office, the office of the Head of Human Resources, some thirty years later. Under the terms of the pilot program for ex-prisoners the hospital was entitled to terminate its employment of and association with any given ex-prisoner without warning, written or otherwise, without explanation, indeed without just cause, up until the expiration of the six-month probation period. At the expiration of six months, the ex-prisoner was to be subject to the same rights and entitlements as any other employee of the hospital. Henryk Mandelbrot had died some two weeks shy of the expiration of six months from the day Lamont Williams had begun work in Building Services.

'The family of the deceased patient –'

'Mr Mandelbrot.'

'Ah . . . yeah, the Mandelbrots were particularly upset about the missing –'

'Mr Ehrlich, he gave it to me.'

'I told them that was your position but they –'

'Mr Ehrlich, it's not my position. It's my candleholder. He gave it to me as a gift. We were friends. I used to go there after my shift. I –'

'Mr Williams, they wanted to press charges.'

'What!'

'They wanted you charged.'

'With what?'

'I don't know. Theft, I suppose.'

'I can't be charged with –'

'Mr Williams, I didn't let on that you were ever in prison. I didn't even give them your name. They wanted the item back and I told them we didn't have it.'

'Where'd you say it was?'

'I told them the truth – that I didn't know where it was. They said that they'd seen a janitor hanging around the patient's room and –'

'They said I stole it?'

'They can't identify you but the hospital is liable for –'

'I have it.'

'Mr Williams, to avoid further unpleasantness and any possible negative press the hospital is going to reimburse the family for an agreed value of the item but –'

'I still have it.'

'It's too late to do –'

'He gave it to me and I still have it.'

'Mr Williams, the hospital has kept your identity from the Mandelbrot family and that wasn't easy but we're going to have to let you go. We won't be reporting the allegation of theft to the Department of Correctional Services. We'll just say that things didn't quite work out but there's no way we can continue to employ you. I'm sorry but it's just too –'

'This is bullshit, man!'

'Lamont, what the fuck do you want? It was the best I could do.'

The two men looked at each other with an intensity they'd not been able to muster since before the incident with the Shogun Warrior action figure some thirty years earlier.

'Lamont, I'm trying to help you make the best of a bad –'

'It's a *menorah*.'

'What?'

'The item . . . it's called a *menorah*, Danny. He told me 'bout it. Got to do with the Maccabees.'

Adam Zignelik wondered if it was his imagination or was he now regularly recognised by the bar staff at the Chi bar in the Chicago Sheraton? He had arrived in Chicago the previous day and had spent all of the day making copies of as many of Border's papers as time permitted to take back with him to New York. Certainly by then the staff of the Galvin Library at IIT knew well who he was. Today he was to be meeting Wayne Rosenthal, Henry Border's former student who had for so long refused to meet him. One day, Adam promised himself, he would visit Chicago and actually stay at the Sheraton where they were meeting but today was not that day and he took a cab there from the place he usually stayed and had nicknamed for himself 'the truck stop'.

'I hope you don't mind, Dr Zignelik, but I would prefer it if I wasn't recorded. I'm happy for you to take notes but –'

'No, that's fine. Absolutely. And it's Adam by the way.'

'Thank you . . . Adam. Well, feel free to call me Wayne.'

Dressed conservatively in a jacket and tie and carrying a leather satchel, Wayne Rosenthal was an intelligent-looking man of about eighty with perfectly trimmed silver hair. He immediately picked which of the people sitting on their own in the bar was Adam Zignelik, and they shook hands. The retired psychologist draped his overcoat over his chair, sat down at a table and volunteered that he was to call his granddaughter – it was she who had brought him there – when he wished to be picked up. Adam discerned that the man before him, Dr Wayne Rosenthal, possessed all his mental faculties but he suspected that the reference to being picked up at the end of their time together was more to calm himself than to answer a question Adam hadn't asked and whose answer he didn't really need to know. In order to relax him Adam, playing amateur psychologist, thought to begin by outlining what he already knew about Border's work and about his life and who he had already interviewed.

'Yes, well, Arch and the others – was it Amy you spoke to? She's a lovely person – they didn't quite have the kind of relationship with Dr Border that I had.' He paused to take a sip of tonic water.

'I've never really . . . I've never really discussed Dr Border with my family, not even with my late wife. It just . . . There wasn't any point. You see, it was personal with us and not just with us. He had a daughter.'

'Elly.'

'Yes, Elly. I don't know what the others told you.'

'Well, without meaning to embarrass you, they intimated that there might have been feelings between you and Elly.'

Wayne Rosenthal picked up his glass and held it in both hands and sat forward. 'There's nobody this can hurt now. I was deeply in love with her. I hadn't met my wife yet and yes, Elly and I . . . we had plans.'

Wayne Rosenthal took Adam to the day of Evie Harmon's party, when late in the afternoon, just by chance, he came across the uncategorised wire recording that contained Hannah Weiss' account of her sister Estusia and Ala and Rosa's smuggling of gunpowder to the men in the *Sonderkommando* resistance and of the uprising itself.

'He had to have been at least as angry with himself as he was with me,' Wayne Rosenthal said, sitting in the bar of the Chicago Sheraton and looking out ahead of him.

'Why do you say that?' Adam asked.

'Well, when you think about it, he almost got away with hiding the spool.'

'I don't get you.'

'I was the only person, other than him, who understood Yiddish, who knew how to work Marv Cadden's wire recorder and who had access to the spools. There was no one else. It was only me. And he had taken the trouble of removing it from the other piles. No one else would have had the chutzpah to go about his office the way I did. I mean . . . in my mind . . . I thought he was going to be my father-in-law. Hell, I thought I was helping him do really . . . incredibly important work.

'I mean, you have to imagine it. This was half a dozen or so years after the war. I was so in love with Elly. We were due to be going to a party and I'm in her father's office. I'm alone and I put on this wire recording. She'd met my parents. You know? And then . . . then I hear this woman's story. I hadn't intended to keep listening to the whole interview. I only wanted to know which pile to put it in.'

He took another sip of his drink before continuing.

'Every interview on those wires . . . they were all harrowing and people didn't know these things then, not in that kind of detail. And you were hearing from the mouths of those who'd lived it. But this one, this one was something else again. The woman was clearly trying to control herself.'

'How do you mean?'

'Well, he'd made her angry by getting her to stick to his regimen for what was to be the first of two interviews and by the time she got to the second one . . . she felt it was a chance to save, in some sense, her sister, to save her memory at least. She started to tell the whole thing; how they'd been approached by the woman . . . by Rosa . . . she wasn't much older than Elly was when I found the wire.'

'When did you suspect that Rosa might have been Border's wife?'

Completely thrown, Wayne Rosenthal sat back in his chair.

'How do you know about that?' he asked in astonishment before answering his own question. 'Amy . . . Amy Muirden told you, didn't she?'

'Yes.'

'I was putting it all together in my mind all the way from his office to the house where we were all supposed to leave together for the party.'

In spite of the more than fifty years that had passed, Adam could see that Wayne Rosenthal was still very deeply affected by what had happened. It was clear in the way he recounted the events. It was likely, Adam speculated, that he had never discussed them with anyone else.

The favourite student had pieced things together and when he had put his hypothesis to his mentor, Border had refused to comment directly. Instead he insisted that Wayne Rosenthal never touch the wire recording again and simply banned him from seeing Elly, effective immediately. In an impetuous act of will, Border tried to prevent Elly finding out that he had abandoned her mother by simply forbidding her from seeing the only other person who knew, and forbidding him from contacting her.

Border had taken Elly aside that night at the Harmons' party and, without offering any explanation, he had from that moment on forbidden her from having any contact with Wayne. She begged him to explain why but he wouldn't. To her the evening suddenly became a kind of nightmare. Her father was behaving irrationally, Wayne was refusing to talk to her for fear of Border making a scene in public and she, younger than all the other guests, was expected to behave with her usual grace. Unable to keep up the pretence for very long, she broke down crying and sought comfort in the company of Russell Ford and his mother, Callie Pearson, who were helping out with the serving of drinks and hors d'oeuvres. For all that Russell knew her well and wanted to be of comfort, it was not only that he had to work, but instinctively he knew to flee any place where he might be caught alone with a crying white girl. Even Callie whispered to her that whatever the matter was, it was going to have to wait till they got home.

'You don't be doin' no one no favours you be off cryin' with the "help".'

Elly stood shattered, bewildered, tear-stained and utterly alone among all the people she loved. Her father had brought her from Poland to the United States in just such a fit of will as had created this circumstance that evening at Evie Harmon's party.

'Why didn't you tell her? It must have been pretty traumatic for her,' Adam asked Wayne Rosenthal.

'As I understand it, it was incredibly traumatic for her.'

'As you understand it?'

'I think she suffered some kind of breakdown after this.'

'What, did you never speak to her again?'

'No, I did.'

'But you didn't tell her why all this had happened?'

'Dr Border intimated to her that he knew something about me and that it was best for her if he didn't tell her what it was, but that for her own sake, we shouldn't see each other any more.'

'Didn't she ask you what you'd done?'

'She did. I told her I hadn't done anything and that she should ask her father why he was forbidding us from seeing each other.'

'But didn't you tell her the truth, the real reason her father had broken you two up?'

The retired psychologist sat back in his chair for a moment. A cocktail waitress enquired as to whether either of them wanted another drink but neither of them did. Wayne Rosenthal stretched slightly and then he leaned back in.

'I've thought about this many times over the years. I don't think I can defend it but . . . perhaps I can explain it. Perhaps not. We were young, even I was still in my early twenties. I looked up to the man and I'd been shaken by what I'd learned about him and his wife. I think I hoped that he would think it over and sooner or later relent. I don't know. Maybe I'm just rationalising my moral cowardice. It was hard to be in contact in those days if you were young, lived at home and your parents were watching you.

'Like I said, she had some kind of breakdown in the immediate aftermath of the whole thing and within a year . . . everything had changed.'

'What had changed?'

'Well, she'd gone off to New York for college. The plan had been for us to be together while she was at college but by that time . . . I'd met the woman who was to be my wife.'

'So you never told her what you knew about her mother, about her role in the revolt in Auschwitz, her heroism?'

'Once she'd moved away and . . . and I'd met my wife, I don't actually remember which came first but . . . well, I thought . . . You see, the urgency had been taken out of it and I told myself that one day I'd track her down and tell her. I thought maybe she'd move back to Chicago.'

'And did she?'

'No, as far as I know she stayed in New York, had some job for a while in something to do with civil rights, something like the NAACP, and then eventually she became a teacher.'

'The NAACP?'

'I think so.'

'In New York?'

'Yeah, but it can't have been for long because I know for a fact that she was teaching at a school in Brooklyn around the time her father died and also for a while there afterwards. What was its name? I should remember it 'cause it was in the news in the late 1960s and she was still there then . . . as late as '68. She was involved in some kind of union business. That's how I tracked her down, through the United Federation of Teachers. What was the school? Oh yeah! Ocean Hill-Brownsville. I made a note of it 'cause I'd meant to track her down after Dr Border died.

'See, I'd decided that I would wait until after he'd died to tell her and that way, not rob her of her father . . . or him of his daughter. The only family they had was each other.'

'So you waited.'

'I waited. I read in an IIT newsletter that Dr Border had died and that's when I thought I'd track her down and tell her. Well, it wasn't that easy. I had a family, children and everything by then.'

'But you found her.'

'Yes, I found her, but by then I wasn't sure it was morally right to tell her. I mean she'd lost her father, the only parent she'd ever known, a man who loved her more than anything else, which is where the whole trouble started, and here I was with the capacity to take him away from her again. I wasn't sure that was the right thing to do. She had no one, she was an orphan.'

'An orphan?'

'Well, that's what I thought at the time. How old can you be and still be an orphan?'

'Sooner or later we're all orphans,' Adam said to himself.

'I guess that's right. She lived in Greenwich Village. Maybe she was bohemian or some kind of hippy or something, I don't know. However she lived, it seems she was dedicated to the things she believed in . . . from what I learned. I just hope she wasn't alone . . . when she died.'

'She died?'

'Some time not long after the Ocean Hill-Brownsville union thing.'

'How'd she die?'

'I asked a guy from the union when I was trying to track her down in the late '60s . . .'

'And?'

'I don't know.'

'The union guy didn't say?'

'He wouldn't say. I suspect he knew.'

'Why?'

'Well, he seemed to know a lot about her, at least professionally. Seems she'd been in the teachers' union a while, got quite involved, quite high up. Have you heard of the civil rights activist Bayard Rustin?'

'Sure. I knew him. I mean, I met him a few times when I was a kid. My father knew him well. Why?'

'Apparently, they were friends. The union guy said he'd been something of a mentor to her.'

'Really?'

'Yeah, that's what he said.'

Adam wondered if she'd ever met his father. How would he ever know? What did it matter? How tantalisingly small the world was, he thought, and then his thoughts returned to the man opposite him.

'But he didn't tell you how she died?'

'No, I asked him but he said he didn't know. It was the late '60s. She was still . . . so young.'

'And she never knew about her mother?'

'Not as far as I know,' said the elderly psychologist, now staring into space.

Adam explained that he'd tracked down the interviewee, Hannah Weiss, sister of Estusia.

'She's still alive?'

'Yes, still alive and living in an aged care facility not far from where I grew up in Melbourne.'

'Australia?'

'Yep.'

'Did you tell her the personal significance of her testimony to Dr Border?'

'Yes, I did, but I don't know that it counted for much with her and I had to admit that I had neither heard the recording of her interview nor read the transcript of it. No one's come across it yet.'

'Well, you couldn't have read it because he never got around to transcribing it. And you won't find the wire spool either.'

'Why not?'

'Because I never gave it back to him,' Wayne Rosenthal said, and then reaching into his leather satchel the retired psychologist pulled out a plastic bag and added, 'It's in here. You may as well have it. I didn't know who to leave it to anyway.'

'That's the interview with Hannah Weiss?'

'That's it.'

'That's where she tells the story of the women who smuggled the gunpowder from the munitions factory, the uprising and the execution of the women?'

'Everything she said is on there. He threatened to press charges.'

'But you held on to it anyway?'

'I knew he wouldn't.'

'Why not?'

'Because if he'd pressed charges it would have guaranteed, one way or another, that Elly would have found out about her mother, about the contents of the interview. That was the thing he was most afraid of. I knew it and he knew that I knew it.'

'I suppose hanging on to it also offered you some measure of protection.'

'How do you mean?'

'Well, not only could he prohibit his daughter from seeing you, he was still your thesis advisor. He held your academic prospects and therefore also your professional prospects in his hands.'

Wayne Rosenthal thought for a moment.

'Dr Zignelik . . . Adam, you may have trouble understanding this, you may not even believe me, but despite his stance . . . despite the whole business with the wire recording and my relationship with Elly, it never occurred to me that he might seek some sort of revenge or that he'd hold this over my head in that way. I never thought he'd even threaten to bring pressure to bear or to tamper in any way with my academic future.'

'Really?'

'Yeah, I know it sounds strange but this was a whole different . . . I don't know, maybe this is the key to understanding the man. This was where his honour kicked back in again. I never had the slightest doubt that he would treat me fairly. Honour, respect – that was the whole thing with him. I think he spent his whole life looking for it, trying to earn it. And who was the person he most needed it from?'

'His daughter.'

502

'That's right. I couldn't see that at the time. I was too enraged and then too bereft to realise what a sore spot I'd inadvertently pressed. And I was too embarrassed.'

'Embarrassed?'

'In front of my parents. I think they suspected that Dr Border had caught me in a compromising position with his daughter. We weren't like that,' he smiled, 'but how else could they explain that my mentor had cast me out of his house and suddenly everything, I mean *everything*, was off?'

'You didn't tell them either?'

'Looking back with the benefit of more than fifty years, I think I bought into it too, this question of honour. I had thought so much of him. In a way I had so much invested in him, in the idea of him, that I . . . I couldn't do it. I was always hoping that he would come 'round.'

'And tell her himself?'

'Yeah. How naïve was I?'

The two of them stood up. Wayne Rosenthal put on his scarf and his coat. They shook hands and Adam thanked him. The older man began walking towards the door of the hotel when Adam called out to him.

'Do you want to use my phone?' The old man turned around.

'What for?' Wayne Rosenthal asked.

'To call your granddaughter . . . get her to come and pick you up.' Adam saw the psychologist's eyes were moist.

'No, I have a phone. I think I'll walk for a bit.'

*

There was a man who had a job dispatching crosstown buses in the New York borough of Manhattan for the Metropolitan Transit Authority, the MTA. He'd worked for the MTA for around forty years and for over twenty of them this man had, in all seasons, exuded warmth and good humour on and around the corner of 67th Street and York Avenue. He gave directions, advice and friendly greetings, not merely to MTA employees and their passengers, but to people he recognised from the area and also to passing strangers, visitors who had come to this

Manhattan neighbourhood in varying states of anxiety, sometimes in grief, sometimes even in despair. This prematurely wizened man, a rough diamond of sorts, who could be relied upon to be there day after day, to greet you irrespective of the weather, a man whose family had generations earlier made its way to New York from southern Italy, this man had a capacity for lifting the spirits of an occasional passer-by as well as of the regulars who had grown to know him and gain confidence from the very reliability of his anodyne presence. Indeed, so well known was he, and so well liked by everyone who had ever had anything to do with him, that he came to be known as the unofficial 'Mayor' of East 67th and York.

This was not just any street corner. This corner was within a few blocks of the Helmsley Medical Tower, New York-Presbyterian Hospital and the Weill-Cornell Medical Center, and it included part of Memorial Sloan-Kettering Cancer Center. It was there, in what some people called 'hospital mile', that the 'Mayor' of East 67th and York would daily find himself in the position of dispensing advice and comfort to people who had appeared out of nowhere suddenly needing, suddenly looking for something much more than just advice with respect to the crosstown traffic and modes of transportation.

In addition to a gift for raising people's spirits with merely a smile from his eyes or a warm 'Hey, how *you* doin'?' the Mayor had the ability to detect even the smallest shift in someone's circumstances. There might be many regulars and even irregular visitors in his constituency, most of whose names he didn't know and would never know, but that didn't stop the Mayor from noticing, as if by instinct, when a change had come about in the circumstances of one of his constituents. From his unprotected roost on East 67th and York the Mayor noticed something out of context one winter's afternoon.

A grown man, still a couple of years shy of forty, Lamont Williams had never seen his father. He had only the vaguest memory of his mother; he wasn't even sure it really was her that he was remembering. An ankle in a sandal, and a perfumed scent, he'd smelled it once in a store. He'd returned to the store some time later but the scent had gone. The memory was almost entirely sensory. He was raised by his grandmother in an apartment cluttered by magazines and TV guides and random things earned with coupons cut out of the magazines and with photographs of people long disappeared whom you weren't really supposed to talk about. Briefly encouraged at school just long enough for a moment of attention to waft onto him like a breath of air in a stuffy room, he had otherwise been ignored by teachers and people in authority until the day his offer of a ride to a friend and the friend's new friend got him sentenced to six years in prison for a spur of the moment decision the other two had made after leaving his van. Kept going in prison and during his six-month probationary job as a janitor in a cancer hospital by the desire to find his young daughter, he'd helped an old man who alone had befriended him there and gifted him a *menorah* before he died, which was only just before his grandmother had gone to sleep and never woken up, leaving him barely able to speak out of grief and uncertain of where he was going to live.

Dragging himself back to work and finding himself falsely accused of the theft of the *menorah*, too many thoughts crowded out the space that might have been taken by the words he could have used to pursue his defence as he sat in the office of a man who'd thought him dishonest and a thief even when he was a child.

Standing alone in the bowels of the cancer hospital's administration wing, at this precise moment in his life it was all that this particular man could do to breathe and walk more or less upright without succumbing to the ever increasing build-up of defeat that had lived deep in his chest for longer than he could remember. It hadn't taken any time at all to clean out his tiny locker and he was already walking out of the building when he heard behind him the voice of D'Sean, another man from Building Services, speaking to a colleague. 'Yeah, dead meat 'cause of them candles, silver candles or some shit. Eight candles, stole 'em off of an old man, patient, died. Then the Jews got his ass fired.'

He stepped out onto the street feeling utterly alone. But he was not entirely alone. The death of his grandmother had led to the rekindling of his relationship with his cousin Michelle, a rekindling that his grandmother had always hoped for. In an effort to comfort him, the very fact of this was something Michelle was keen to point out when she visited him not long after his last day in Building Services.

When she walked into her grandmother's apartment that night the place was quiet but for the sounds of distant televisions and remote conversations coming in from nearby apartments. 'Zoloft is not for everyone. Talk to your doctor about Zoloft. Because no one should have to feel this way.' Lamont sat numb on the couch in the living room inside the Co-op City apartment surrounded by their grandmother's things left scattered or else in the piles in which their grandmother had left them; a magazine, a hair brush, a CVS catalogue and, in the kitchen, a can of Seneca frozen apple juice that she'd forgotten to put away, things left untouched as though she would be back any minute.

Alone in the kitchen Michelle opened the freezer and saw her grand-mother's cooking frozen in Tupperware and labelled and though Michelle had promised herself she'd be strong for Lamont, she found herself crying silently but unambiguously and quite soon without restraint. If this was how *she* felt, with a career, a husband and a daughter, she wondered to herself, how must Lamont be feeling? She stayed alone in the kitchen she had visited as a child, where she had had so many meals with her grand-mother and with Lamont. She missed this woman. She regretted not spending more time with her. Had she told her how brave she thought she was? Her grandmother would not have understood what she would have meant by that, at least she would have claimed not to have under-stood. Had she told her how much she loved her? Had she thanked her enough? Had she loved her enough?

Michelle wiped her eyes with the backs of her hands and attempted to compose herself before joining her silent cousin back in the living room. They were going to have to talk about their grandmother's possessions. It felt wrong to throw them out, wrong even to sell them for what little they would fetch. But Lamont would no doubt need any money they could get and, anyway, what would she or Lamont want with any of the time-worn things their grandmother had saved? What would anybody want with them, Michelle wondered, walking back into the living room? When she stood in front of Lamont he told her, quietly, "Chelle, I lost my job.'

'At the hospital?'

'Uh-huh.'

'How, what happened?' she asked and so Lamont explained the story behind Mr Mandelbrot's *menorah*. It was there on the mantel. With memories of her grandmother churning with guilt and concern for her cousin, it was only now that she noticed it for the first time.

'But if you just gave it back –'

'It was a gift,' he said quietly.

'*I* know you didn't take it but if it gets you your job back –'

'It wouldn't. It would confirm for them what they already think . . . that I stole it.'

'But that . . . that doesn't make any sense. You'd only still have it if the old man *had* given it to you, not if you'd stolen –'

''Chelle, you of all people . . . I mean, given what you do . . . for work, for a living . . .'

'What?'

'You ought to know by now. It doesn't have to make sense.' Neither of them spoke for a few minutes as she sat down beside him on the couch and rubbed his back with the flat of her hand.

''Chelle, where am I going to live?'

Michelle suddenly realised that she had no idea what kind of proprietary interest, if any, their grandmother had had in the apartment she'd lived in all Michelle's life. It was called Co-op City but what kind of Co-op was it? Neither she nor Lamont knew.

She had to help her cousin. A social worker with more than fifteen years' experience, she should have immediately known what to do but, at least for a few days, her emotions clouded the intellect and experience she needed to deploy to devise a plan for him.

One thing she knew immediately was that despair couldn't be allowed to colonise his mind beyond the period a functioning, active, socially integrated person would grieve for a lost mother-figure. She guaranteed him that she and her husband Charles would not let him go homeless. She would investigate the status of their grandmother's apartment with the relevant people at Co-op City. In the meantime, she promised, she would secure him at least temporary employment, explaining that it was vitally important for his mental health and general wellbeing to be gainfully employed as soon as possible. To this end she put him in contact with the John Doe Fund, a charitable organisation dedicated to assisting both the homeless and ex-prisoners.

No longer in the uniform of a Building Services employee of Memorial Sloan-Kettering Cancer Center, Lamont Williams wore instead the bright blue uniform of members of the Ready, Willing and Able street cleaning crew of the John Doe Fund. Armed with a broom and a plastic garbage pail on wheels, there was a stretch of York Avenue that was all for him. He had chosen it from a few options and explained that, although it wasn't so close to where he was currently located, he knew the area fairly well. He used to work around there. The stretch that most appealed to him and where he showed the greatest attention to detail, the blocks where he was most scrupulous in his sweeping, were those that included or were adjacent to Memorial Sloan-Kettering Cancer Center.

It was the Mayor of East 67th and York who first noticed Lamont Williams in the area in the period after he'd been let go from Building Services two weeks shy of the six months he needed to get beyond his probation period. Although they had only ever exchanged nods and the briefest of pleasantries, the Mayor felt sufficiently emboldened to approach the street sweeper.

'Hey, buddy, you doin' a hell of a job. Am *I* crazy or did you used to work at Sloan-Kettering? 'Cause I'm tellin' you there's a guy there who looks –'

'No, you're not crazy.'

Sensing that the explanation that would take this man from hospital employee to a Ready, Willing and Able street sweeper would involve a disclosure of information that even he wasn't ready to seek, the Mayor removed himself from the situation with, 'I tend to be over there, you know, if anyone needs me. You take care o' y'self.'

It wasn't very much but those few words gave Lamont Williams just enough sense of himself to take the chance that was presented less than an hour later when he saw Dr Washington, the woman who had been his friend's oncologist before Mr Mandelbrot had died, and acting on a feeling he wasn't sure he could generate again at will, he approached the oncologist.

'Excuse me, ma'am. Ma'am? You remember me?'

'No,' she said, doing her best to ignore him.

'Dr Washington, you're Dr Washington, right?'

'Well, that's what it says,' she said distractedly, briefly pointing at the name tag pinned to her coat.

'You don't remember me, do you?'

'No, should I?'

'I'm Lamont Williams. I used to –'

'Have a good day, Mr Williams,' she said, pulling her mobile phone out from her pocket.

'No, wait a minute. See, I used to work here at Sloan-Kettering. I was in Building Services –'

'Uh-huh.'

'No, see, I was in Building Services and I used to visit one of your patients, Mr Mandelbrot. Henryk Mandelbrot? He only just died a little ways back. You remember him?'

'Of course.'

'Well, I'm the one they fired and –'

'Pardon me?'

'I'm the guy from Building Services they fired.'

'I don't know what you're talking about.' The Mayor was watching on as the doctor and the street sweeper talked. Nobody else was taking it in.

'See, I used to visit him . . . and I . . . like . . . we became kind of like . . . friends. And he would tell me his life story at the end of my shift when I used to visit him. And see, just before he died . . . I don't mean his last day but . . . he gave me, told me he wanted me to have this candleholder. It's a Jewish candleholder. They call it a *menorah*. It was his. His family brought in his *menorah* and he told me that he wanted me to have it. And when he died I took it home. Now his family sayin' I stole it whereas it was a gift and now I'm out here 'cause I got fired from the hospital and . . . and, you know, like I need this job . . . the Building Services job.'

'Well, I'm sorry, I'm on the medical staff so I don't –'

'Yeah, I know, but Dr Washington, you was his oncologist and you seen me in his room or near his room talkin' to Mr Mandelbrot a million times and you could tell them –'

'I'm sorry you lost your job but there's nothing I –'

'Sure is cold, huh!' the Mayor interjected. 'Everything okay, folks?'

'Yeah, we're fine, thanks,' said Dr Washington. 'Like I said, I'm sorry, but there's nothing I can do. I'm on the medical staff and that's –'

'No, no there *is*, Dr Washington, you could tell them that you saw me with him . . . I mean, you used to see me a lot . . . with Mr Mandelbrot. You could tell 'em that over in the Human Resources. You could tell 'em that we 'came like friends. You could tell 'em in the Human Resources how you remember me and then –'

'But I'm sorry, I don't remember you.'

*

A few weeks after the funeral of Michelle's grandmother, her husband Charles McCray caught up with his father in the Hungarian Pastry Shop on Amsterdam Avenue instead of on campus as he usually did.

'Well, I just thought if you meet Adam here, why not me?' he asked his father as they sipped their coffee.

'Yeah, but I don't see him here every week. You see him lately?'

'No, not for a little while.'

'I don't mean to nag you, Charlie, but . . . I think you should.'

'I know but . . . Is he okay?'

'Actually he's pretty good. I don't get into the whole thing with Diana. I mean, I have but not for a while. But it's his work, it's going well. You should talk to him about it.'

'That's good. What did he say?'

William told him what he knew not only about Adam's enquiry into the presence of black troops at the liberation of Dachau but also about his unearthing of Henry Border's 1946 wire recordings from DP camps and his lead on a resistance movement in Auschwitz. The combination of Charles' guilt at not having paid enough attention to his friend's work plus his father's enthusiastic and fairly detailed recollection of all that Adam had told him led Charles to call Adam to arrange to meet for lunch. There Adam put him up to date with what had happened at his meeting with Diana. There was no way either of them could put a positive spin on what she had said but Adam was buoyed by his friend's genuine interest in his work. It was no small thing to earn Charles' professional interest and Charles felt a little ashamed when he noticed how much this interest meant to Adam.

'Listen, you got to know . . . I really wish I could have done more.'

'You talking about tenure?' Adam asked and his friend nodded. 'Charlie, I brought that on myself. We both know I did. Like a few things that haven't worked out that well for me, I brought it on myself.'

'Well, I wish I could have . . . I don't know, maybe if we'd talked before you . . .' Charles hesitated before finishing his own sentence. 'I know, sometimes you want to talk to a friend without having to make an appointment.' Adam smiled at his friend. It was a moment whose seed had been planted by William McCray a week or two earlier in the always crowded Hungarian Pastry Shop. It could have been planted at any time but somehow, despite its still being winter, the seed had taken that day the father and son had talked over coffee and a strawberry strudel.

'Dad,' Charles asked his father a little tentatively as he sipped the last of his coffee that afternoon, 'I've always meant to ask you . . . Never really got 'round to it. When Thurgood made the recommendation to the executive committee that they appoint Jake as LDF General Counsel, how did you feel?'

William McCray leaned back in his chair and thought for a moment before speaking.

'Well, by about as early as May of '61 or certainly by the summer of that year, Thurgood was pretty confident Kennedy was going to give him the call and he'd get a judicial appointment of some kind or another. Couldn't be sure of the level but he knew he'd better start thinking of a successor. And we knew that too.

'So it was a matter of looking for the right person, right qualities as a lawyer and as an administrator, right seniority so as not to put too many noses out of joint. So who were the best of the more senior lawyers? I'd like to think I was one of them along with Jake and Connie Motley. More than thirty years had to pass before they appointed a woman.'

'What about Carter?'

'Bob Carter? Bob Carter . . . I think Thurgood probably regarded Bob as about the best legal mind he'd ever come across . . . and *nobody* wrote a better brief.'

'So why not him?'

'Well, there were personal problems between them . . . had been for a while. Also, Bob was with the NAACP then. You have to remember that by then the NAACP and the LDF were quite separate entities, had been for many years so Bob *couldn't* be a candidate. They were separate institutions by then.'

William noticed Charles shifting uneasily in his seat.

'I haven't answered your question, have I?'

'Yes you have. Well, in part,' his son answered.

'You mean, how did I feel, because he was white, because he was a Jew?'

'Well, yeah, I guess.'

'That he was Jewish didn't enter into it, not for me. Of all the attorneys who signed the brief in *Brown*, only a few of them were white but of those that were, all but one were Jews. That stuff didn't become an issue till much later.'

'But you noticed that.'

'No, *I* didn't. Charles Black did. I'm remembering Charles Black pointing it out.'

'Who was Charles Black, again?'

'Charles Black was the white attorney who *wasn't* Jewish.'

'And that he was white, that Jake was white?' Charles asked. His father leaned back in his chair.

'No question there was a danger that it would open up the possibility for people to distort history and say that blacks had not been the intellectual force behind their own emancipation. That was certainly a danger, still is. But then there was the politics of the decision. It looked good to many of the people to whom we wanted it to look good.'

'But what about you?'

'What about me personally? Jake's appointment made good news. *He* made good news. He was good at it.' William saw that his son was still not completely satisfied so he went further.

'Look, Charlie, some men do their best work *away* from the camera, quietly, diligently, consistently, but *out* of the limelight.'

Charles leaned in across the table and took his father's hand in his and clasped it.

'I know, Dad. That's what I've been trying to tell you.'

*

Having already by chance once run into Dr Washington coming out of the York Avenue entrance of Memorial Sloan-Kettering Cancer Center at a particular time in the afternoon, Lamont Williams, the street sweeper, member of the John Doe Fund's Ready, Willing and Able team, made a point of being there at exactly the same time on another day. Over several nights in his late grandmother's Co-op City apartment since he had last seen the oncologist he went over his earlier conversation with her. It seemed impossible to him that she would not, with some effort, perhaps on both their parts, remember him as the Building Services worker who had so often visited Dr Washington's patient, Henryk Mandelbrot. He needed to approach her again and when he saw her at that same time exiting the York Avenue entrance he knew he had to ignore his nervousness and try again.

'Dr Washington, I'm Lamont Williams.'

'Yes?'

'Now I'm not crazy or dangerous or nothin' but I just need to talk to you about your patient who died, Henryk Mandelbrot.'

She remembered him from his previous approach to her on York Avenue and was not frightened of him. There were many people on the street, medical and non-medical staff from the hospital, people visiting the hospital and random passers-by. Although she did not notice, the Mayor of East 67th and York was also there. Lamont Williams was too intent on restating his case to Dr Washington to notice the Mayor but the Mayor had noticed both of them again. He was again perplexed by the interaction of the young doctor and the street sweeper.

'Just for a couple of minutes. Don't mean to take up too much of your time.' Standing near visitors and staff smoking on their break, she was perplexed more than anything else.

'Okay, Mr Williams, what do you want to tell me about Henryk Mandelbrot?'

'Well . . . well, now, he was in Auschwitz. It was a death camp in Poland. Did you know that?'

'I knew he was a Holocaust survivor.'

'Auschwitz. You remember the number tattoo . . . on his arm, on his left forearm? He got it in Auschwitz.'

'I didn't know that.'

'He was in the *Sonderkommando* there. They were the prisoners forced to deal with the bodies there in the crematoria, the gas chambers and the ovens. He was part of the resistance inside the camp, I mean resistance from inside, from *within* the *Sonderkommando*. There was a *Sonderkommando* uprising. Did you know that, Doctor?' In the chill of the winter air the words he spoke were accompanied by steam. People walked past them going uptown, some downtown and the Mayor looked on.

'No, I didn't know that. I have to admit, I didn't know that.'

'Yeah, he worked in the crematoria there,' Lamont said, rising to his theme.

'I still don't know why you want to tell me all this.'

''Cause we were friends.'

'You and Henryk Mandelbrot?'

'That's right and he told me all sorts of things.'

'But why does it matter to you . . . that I know you were . . . friends?'

'Look, Dr Washington, I know we're very different people, me and him, different background, race, age . . . everything. But I met him in the hospital, right there actually outside that door, in my first week. He was in the hospital two times. Right? First time he stayed a while but the second he was in just a few days and then he died. Remember? Over the two times he told me his life story and I told him some of mine and before he died he told me he wanted me to have that candleholder, the Jewish candleholder.'

'The *menorah*?'

'Right. The family brought in his *menorah* but he gave it to me and when he died I took it home.'

'I can see this is important to you but I still don't know why you're telling me all this.'

''Cause they said I stole the *menorah* and they fired me on account of this. Now, I need this job and you saw me with him. You saw me visit him. Don't you remember? He made jokes about us, like . . . like he was going to set us up or something. That was just once or twice but I was always there at the end of my shift. You got to remember.'

'Even if I do, what difference does it make?'

'Do you remember?' The question hung frozen in the air.

'I think I do,' she said, now looking him in the eye. 'But even if I do, what difference does it make?'

'You could tell 'em in the Human Resources that you saw me there all the time . . . that we were friends, Mr Mandelbrot and me.'

'But even if I told them that I'd seen you there, often even, what does it prove? Even if I vouched for your friendship, even if I could do that, what difference would it make? Friends sometimes steal from friends.'

'What use would I have for a *menorah*?'

'I don't know. I guess you could sell it.'

'I still have it.'

'I don't know, Mr Williams.'

'It's Lamont, Lamont Williams.'

The oncologist looked around for a moment and rubbed her hands together to warm them. 'I can see this is important to you, Lamont,' she said, her tone now changed, softened, 'but what difference would it make to Human Resources if I did say –'

Lamont interrupted her as the Mayor looked on. The M66 was arriving. It slowed, stopped, exhaled and opened its doors. Passengers began getting off. It was cold.

'He was born 15 December 1922 in the town of Olkusz,' Lamont Williams began. 'His father was a butcher. He escaped from the ghetto at Dabrowa Gornicza.' There was desperation now in his voice mixed with a resolve. People were getting off the bus. The Mayor needed to say something to the driver but felt compelled to keep watching them.

'What?' the oncologist asked. 'The ghetto *where*?'

'Dab-rov-a Gorn-itch-a,' Lamont Williams answered on the partially snow-covered sidewalk of York Avenue. She looked at him. Did he speak Polish? What kind of African American street sweeper was this?

'Dab-rov-a Gorn-itch-a,' he repeated. He was going to have to speak louder. The bus was idling, people were lined up to get on.

'Dab-rov-a Gorn-itch-a, it was one of the ghettoes. It was the one he was put in. Doctor, I have a daughter. I need this job.'

The 'Mayor' waved to the driver. He looked at the doctor and the street sweeper still talking. The M66 headed off to the west side on its crosstown journey. The end of the line was also the beginning.

*

It was early May of 1960 and President Eisenhower was both embarrassed and angry. He had denied publicly that the plane that had gone missing over the Soviet Union had been a spy plane only to have Premier Khrushchev announce that not only had the American U2 spy plane been shot down but that they had its pilot, Francis Gary Powers, and all of this only days before a scheduled East–West summit to be held in Paris. The papers were full of it and Elise Border carried the story under her arm as she raced home from work in time to greet her father who was due in from the airport. Where was she going to put everything? Her father was moving out from Chicago to be with her. She was the only family Henry Border had and his health had been poor. She felt she had no choice but to offer to share her apartment with him even though it was cramped enough as it was. What would she do if she met someone? Perhaps it would be only a temporary measure. But her father had been unwell and he had to come first.

Greenwich Village had meant nothing to him when she had said it over the phone, MacDougal Street even less. But a sixth-floor walk-up was immediately understood by everybody, Elise, her father and especially by the men who were paid to carry his possessions up to the two-bedroom apartment in the old brick tenement. Most of what they brought up in the cardboard boxes Arch Sanasarian had helped him pack was the remnant of his career. There were very few personal items he took with

516

him. But the work he brought over, which she subsequently arranged to have housed at IIT in Chicago after his death, was substantial and the movers took slight comfort from the fact that they could go in and out of the building as the rhythm of their work dictated without continually needing to ask to be let in. This was because the street door didn't lock and it was just as well because the doorbell was broken. At forty dollars a month it was all Elly Border could afford.

To walk up and down the six flights was a major achievement for a man in Henry Border's condition but he tried to make himself do it once a day, each day after his daughter had left for work. Maybe there was a café he could sit in. But Greenwich Village in 1960 was not for him with its stream of tourists desperate for a peek into the carnival that was the bohemian street world, the cafés and noisy coffee shops where it was said marijuana and heroin was sold by dubious types amid mention of Ginsburg, Kerouac and Baldwin. You didn't need to strain your ear to hear evidence of the folk revival and you could watch 'free love' for free if you knew where to look in Washington Square Park. But none of it meant anything to him as more and more of his life took place in his head. He would sit alone in his daughter's dingy apartment and remember. He thought of his parents and his siblings, all gone, and he thought of the slip of a girl he had married, Rosa Rabinowicz, whom he felt he had deserted twice over.

To make it down, out and back again was getting harder and harder for him and, anyway, his work was still the most important thing to him. Each day he would sit in the kitchen and continue to transcribe the wire recordings he had made in the DP camps of Europe in the summer of 1946. Barely anyone had been interested in them but it had now become something akin to a religious ritual with him.

Eventually he had to give up his daily attempts to go out altogether. His health would no longer permit it. Distracted by his work, he failed to realise that he would never again go for a walk. It was a restriction that was in part mitigated by the capture of another man around the time of the capture of Francis Gary Powers, the pilot of the U2 spy plane.

In May of 1960 *Obersturmbannführer* Adolf Eichmann of the SS, the administrator of what the Nazis had called 'The Final Solution of the

Jewish Problem', was captured by the *Mossad* on Garibaldi Street, Buenos Aires, kidnapped and taken to Jerusalem. Now it seemed to Border, fourteen years after his expedition to the DP camps, that the world might be interested in the voices of Eichmann's victims. The Eichmann trial began eleven months later but by then Henry Border was in such bad health he had difficulty making it to the bathroom and back on his own. He really needed a full-time nurse, someone to be in attendance at all times, but his daughter Elly did not earn anywhere near enough to provide this kind of attention. All she could do was to serve him as well as she could before and after teaching at school and on weekends.

During the working day she was forced to leave him on his own. She would leave food for him and something to drink. If he wanted his window open or closed in the morning she would open or close it before heading off to work and it would stay that way all day, irrespective of any change in the weather, until she came home. To try to block out some of the noise from MacDougal Street and to keep him company during the day, she bought him a brand new Admiral television set and installed it in his room where he could watch it from his bed.

There had not been many women in his life. Only one had he asked to marry and she had said 'yes'. She'd said it immediately and he thought of her more than ever now. He thought of her hair, of her eyes and of her smile. His daughter carried all of these features out into the world each day. He thought of how he had abandoned her and of what had happened to her subsequently. Why had it taken that ultimate demonstration of Rosa's unhappiness to propel him to leave Europe? If he had left sooner he would have taken her with him.

How much control do we have over what is remembered and when? He could never completely erase from his mind the image of that man on top of his wife on their couch when, having carried his migraine across the streets of Warsaw, he'd opened the door. It justified nothing. Alone now in his bed in Elly's apartment on the sixth floor, with his eyes closed, he saw them again. Why now? Why still? He opened his eyes slightly to see the jug of water that his daughter had left for him.

'What is your full name?' he heard a voice ask. 'Who is it?' Henry Border asked from his bed. Was there someone there with him in the room? He couldn't see them. Was that Elise? He hadn't heard anyone come in. Was someone there? There was no one there.

Again Henry Border heard a strange voice from his bed. 'Who is it?' he said but perhaps his own voice had not carried. However loud his question had been, the voice did not answer him but carried on speaking as though to someone else. Henry Border was irrelevant. The voice didn't care to answer Border but continued speaking regardless. It told a story but Border couldn't place it.

'She begged him to shoot her but he wouldn't. "*Jüdische Schlampe!*" he said. Then he kicked her hard in the mouth with his boot and she spat out her teeth in order not to choke on them.' Border shuddered when he heard this. Why was he hearing such voices? He screwed his eyes shut and tears came out, leaving a trail on the otherwise dry skin on his cheeks.

'I would have done anything for you, Rosa,' mumbled Henry Border feverishly. 'I would have done anything for you. So how did it happen that I let them beat you? How did it happen that I let them hang you?' Rosa Rabinowicz gave no answer, none that he could hear over the wheezing sounds he was making.

'What is your full name?' Henry Border heard a voice ask. 'Who is it?' he asked the voice. Still there was no answer. When was his daughter due home? What time was it now?

'I know what happened. Rosa, I know it all,' Border whispered. 'I can't say anything. You want to blame me? You can. I never remarried. I lived alone. I tried to tell . . . what happened but they didn't want to hear. No, not what happened to *you*. It's true. I never said a word about what they did to you, but Rosa . . . she's all I had. You were gone. It would have made no difference to you but for *me* . . . she was all I had. Rosa, it was wrong. Everything I did was wrong. But she lives and breathes. Do you know? That I took her away was wrong. But that's why she's alive. Tell me you agree.' His mouth was dry. She didn't answer but the voice did. He heard a man's voice answering someone else's question. Henry Border didn't know where he was any more. He found it hard to breathe.

'We were in the ghetto. There were four families sleeping in one room in makeshift beds or bunks one on top of the other. It was night.'

'And what happened that particular night?'

'They knocked on the door and then kicked it in and walked into the room where four couples were sleeping.'

'Who did this?'

'The SS. There were four of them, all of them armed. They . . .'

'What is your full name?'

'Rosa? Who's there? Who keeps asking these questions? And who is answering them?' Henry Border called out. No one answered. Perhaps no one could hear him over the sounds of MacDougal Street. Perhaps he only thought he was calling out. But the voice he heard, though slightly muffled like one of his wire recordings, was as real as anything he had ever heard. It was a man's voice and it spoke again.

'He used to wear a long coat and gloves. But he wore only one glove, the other glove he used to hold in his hand. He would come to see the pits, the new pits that were dug when the ovens couldn't cope. Yes, I saw Eichmann many times in Auschwitz-Birkenau,' said the voice from the new Admiral television set Henry Border's daughter had bought him. Adolf Eichmann was on trial and the world had tuned in. Finally, it was listening.

'Rosa?'

'Please tell the court where you were born.'

'I was born in Ciechanow, Poland.'

'Where exactly is Ciechanow?'

'It's a little over thirty kilometres from the Polish border with East Germany.'

'How many Jews were in Ciechanow at the start of the war?'

'About six thousand.'

'How many were transferred to Auschwitz-Birkenau?'

'From the ghetto, all of them.'

'So how many came from the ghetto to Auschwitz-Birkenau?'

'Six thousand minus those who died in the ghetto.'

'Do you know how many Ciechanow Jews are alive today?'

'As it happens, I am president of the Ciechanow *Landsmannschaft* so I do know this.'

'And how many Ciechanow Jews are alive today?'

'There are seventy-two men . . . and ten women.'

'What is your full name?' asked the presiding judge in Jerusalem.

'Rosa?' Henry Border tried to call out.

The breaths were loud, fast and shallow from the bed on the sixth floor walk-up. No one heard them, no one at all. Children squealed as they rode their bikes down on MacDougal Street. A baby cried in the apartment next door. Upstairs two people argued in three languages. From a parked car's radio out on the street came Hank Ballard and the Midnighters' 'Let's Go, Let's Go, Let's Go'. Elly Border had left the window open that morning before she went to work but her father was no longer warm.

'What is your full name?' asked the presiding judge in Jerusalem.

Hank Ballard sang from down on MacDougal Street, 'There's a thrill upon the hill. Let's go, let's go, let's go.' The wind teased the chiffon curtain. Longing to be out of there and free of the heaviness of this man, free of the illness that had confined him to bed, free of the guilt-sodden memories and hallucinations that churned with the real and ongoing lives of other people, it was tethered to the curtain rod and so it danced a prisoner's dance. It flapped helplessly a few times at the sixth-floor window and then gave up. By that time nothing in the room stirred, nothing but the vibrations in the air that were the voices coming from the television set where Adolf Eichmann was on trial. Henry Border, once Chaim Broder, no longer moved at all, as far away in Jerusalem the question was asked, 'What is your full name?'

'Noah Lewental,' the witness answered.

*

'Hello, is this Dr Ayesha Washington?' Adam Zignelik asked over the phone in his Morningside Heights apartment.

'Yes, who's this?'

'Dr Washington, I'm Dr Zignelik, Adam Zignelik. I'm a historian . . . from the History Department at Columbia University.' Adam told himself that there might be time later to clarify the true extent of his relationship with the History Department at Columbia, a relationship that was now itself history. Technically, within a minute of his first phone call, Adam had lied to her. But he'd called her at work, she sounded busy and since she might well become very important to him, he drew upon the name of the institution he'd worked at before it had found him wanting.

Adam had discovered that the 71st Infantry Division of the US Third Army, to which the black 761st Tank Battalion was at least at that time attached, had not been far from Dachau concentration camp in southern Germany around 29 April 1945, the time the camp had been liberated. Eventually he had been able to match the name remembered by one of Henry Border's interviewees with the name of an African American captain in the 761st Tank Battalion. The captain's name was James Washington. Adam Zignelik, now a freelance historian, was hoping that the woman on the other end of the phone speaking from Memorial Sloan-Kettering Cancer Center was the captain's relative.

'I'm sorry to be taking up your time, especially in the middle of a work day, but to cut a long story short my research has led me to a World War II veteran named James Washington and I wondered whether you are related to him at all.'

'James Washington?'

'Yes.'

'He's my grandfather.'

'Your grandfather?'

'Yes.'

'Are we talking about Captain James Washington of the 761st Tank Battalion?'

'Yes, that's right.'

It's rare that relief and excitement can co-exist. Usually one so overpowers the other that we are aware of experiencing only one of them at any one time. Excitement permits a nervousness, even if joyous, that might be said to be the very antithesis of relief. Nonetheless, for a very brief moment, Adam Zignelik experienced them both and was aware of it. Whatever it might or might not be worth, his instincts, skill and perseverance had led him to a relative of the captain mentioned by Henry Border's DP in the 1946 interview. But when he heard Dr Ayesha

Washington say that not only was Captain James Washington of the 761st Tank Battalion her grandfather, but that he was still alive, it was excitement alone that he experienced. At best, he'd thought, there might be some written record of the man's combat experiences, contemporaneous or otherwise. That the man might still be alive was more than he'd allowed himself to hope for. And he certainly hadn't expected the enthusiasm he encountered from his granddaughter, the oncologist Ayesha Washington.

'This will mean the world to him,' she said, 'Just your interest . . . He hasn't been well and I think this will really . . . You want to talk to him, right?'

'I do but . . . can I ask you about his cognitive capacity, his memory, his –'

'He's sharp as a tack. I have to watch what I say around him, he remembers everything.'

''Cause you said he's not been well and I just wondered –'

'It's his hip,' she shot back. 'He needs surgery. It's important, frankly it's serious, but his mind is as good as it ever was. And he has a fine mind, Dr Zignelik.'

She made no attempt to hide her enthusiasm in a way that Adam could not have known she reserved for situations she considered of tremendous personal importance. Her professional demeanour permitted no hint of this kind of near exuberance. It was as though she was selling her grandfather to the historian. Nor could she have known the professional importance of her grandfather, the captain, to the man on the other end of the line. They agreed to meet before she'd mention Adam's interest to her grandfather. She was concerned to avoid dashing the old man's undoubted elation at the prospect of talking about his war-time experiences to a historian should anything go amiss. To accommodate her as much as possible, Adam told her he would be happy to meet her at her workplace during her lunch hour.

She seldom took a whole hour off for lunch but agreed immediately and, some short time later, the two of them met in person at the tiny Fresh Food Kitchen on 68th Street. There, over the din made by the overworked staff and the busy lunch crowd, Adam explained the possible importance to his work of her grandfather. He told her that he had unearthed a 1946 interview with a Holocaust survivor, which referred to being liberated by black troops and to an officer named Washington. Ayesha Washington had been very close to her grandfather all her life. Not only was he immensely proud of her, but she was all he had now. She, on her part, personally oversaw any medical treatment he needed, his financial needs and his living circumstances.

'He talks about the war all the time. And he *has* talked about taking part in the liberation of a concentration camp.'

It was safe for her to tell her grandfather about the historian's interest. Adam wasn't going to go cold on this. He promised. Adam assured her that he would interview the captain after he had recovered from surgery, as soon as Ayesha Washington said he was ready.

'Just the prospect of being interviewed will be enough to guarantee he pulls through. You see, no one ever wants to talk to him . . . not about that stuff.'

*

Ayesha Washington thought again of the man who had confronted her more than once on York Avenue outside Sloan-Kettering. She had to admit that she now did remember seeing that man, the street sweeper, visiting her former patient Henryk Mandelbrot. And he did seem to know a lot about him, certainly more than she'd known about him. Was it a con? If it was, it was certainly an elaborate one, and a highly unusual one. But what if he was telling the truth?

This man, who now swept the streets, had once worked at the hospital. If he had befriended the old man, swapped stories with him, if he had visited him after hours he would have been comforting the patient in his own time, time he wasn't being paid for. Maybe the old man *had* given him the candelabrum. If their relationship had been as the former Building Services worker had described it, why couldn't that have happened? And if it had happened, what a tremendous injustice it was for him to be accused of theft and fired because of it. But she wasn't a lawyer, a private investigator, a police officer or an ethicist. She worked at the hospital but not in Human Resources. She had her own life. She had her own problems. Who had time for this kind of thing?

She asked herself this and then wondered what she meant by 'this kind of thing'. She concluded a few seconds later that what she had really meant was 'justice' of some kind. So what she had, in fact, asked herself was 'who had time for justice?' and the fact that she had articulated this question, even if only privately to herself, jolted her. She caught a vague, elongated momentary glimpse of herself walking past a reflecting surface and, not wanting to be the sort of person who asked herself that question, reached into her pocket and took out the diary with Adam Zignelik's name and number in it.

What did she owe the street sweeper? She happened to have in her pocket the name and number of a Columbia historian who it might be said owed her something. A call, a quick call made on a whim, who had time for these things?

Adam Zignelik had given her the number to his mobile phone because he didn't want either of them dwelling on the fact that in truth his association with the History Department at Columbia was ending. She dialled his number and instead of answering with his name he just said, not recognising the number, 'Hello.'

'Is this Dr Zignelik?' Ayesha Washington asked.

'Yes, who's this?'

'Hi, Dr Zignelik. I'm sorry to bother you. It's Ayesha Washington.'

'Ayesha, hi. Is everything okay with your grandfather?'

'Oh sure, he's fine. We're still going ahead with the surgery. Actually, he's really excited to meet with you.'

'Really?'

'Oh yeah, it's kind of distracting him from the surgery so it's . . . it's good for his morale.'

'Oh that's great.' A beat or two passed as he waited to find out why she was calling.

'Actually, Dr Zignelik.'

'Listen, if I can call you Ayesha, you have to call me Adam.'

'Sure. Adam, I'm calling . . . This is going to sound weird but I might have the sudden need for a historian. I mean . . . I don't even know if this is your area but there's something, I don't know if I could check this out myself but –'

'What's up?'

'Do you have a minute?'

'Sure.'

'There's a guy . . .' She let out a breath. 'God, where do I begin? Okay, I had a patient who died . . . an old man . . . And he was a Holocaust survivor.'

Over the phone she told him all she knew of the purported relationship between her late patient and the one-time Building Services employee, a man who now worked as part of the cleaning crew of the John Doe Fund's Ready, Willing and Able team. She told him that the man had been fired by the hospital for the alleged theft of the old man's *menorah* and that the man persists in saying that it had been a gift and that it wasn't theft. He claimed that he and the patient had become friends over a period of months and as proof of their friendship he offers quite astoundingly specific details of the old man's life story. If he's now working with the John Doe Fund it means he's either homeless or an ex-con, possibly both. She'd checked with the hospital and it had tried this man as a Building Services employee as part of a pilot program. If it was true that the *menorah* had been a gift and that this man in fairly desperate circumstances had been wrongly accused and in a sense convicted and punished, it would be a grave injustice. Adam had to agree.

'The credibility of the claim by the former employee that he and the patient had become friends,' Ayesha Washington went on, 'ultimately rests on the authenticity of his account of the conversations he insists they had. What I thought was that perhaps I could ask you for an expert opinion as to whether the detailed knowledge of the Holocaust he apparently gained from them is historically accurate.'

'I understand,' Adam replied. 'But this is the thing. Although my area is twentieth-century political history, I've tended to specialise in civil rights history. It's true that I have lately, without any conscious decision on my part, developed a professional interest in the Holocaust. It's connected with my interest in the armed services experiences of people like your grandfather. But I have to tell you, I'm not really an expert, not yet, anyway.'

'Sure, I'm sorry, Adam. It's pretty crazy and I don't want to waste your time –'

'No, you misunderstand me. I'll do it. I'll listen to him. I really owe you, of course I'll do it. I'm just offering the caveat that there are plenty of people you could find who are more expert in this area than me. But what I do have going for me is that I owe you. And historians still make house calls. Where do you want me to go to meet this guy? I'll tell you if I don't feel qualified to attest to the accuracy of the man's account of your patient's story. I can always recommend other people more expert in the field.'

'Adam, I already felt silly enough getting *you* involved in this, and *we've* already met.'

'I assure you, it's not a problem. You're right, if he has intimate knowledge of the old man's story then it does make it more likely they were friends, which makes it more likely he didn't steal the *menorah* and shouldn't have been fired.'

'Thanks for this. I felt silly but I thought I had to do something –'

'Ayesha, I owe you. So don't think twice.'

She explained that she often saw the man, the street sweeper, on York Avenue near the hospital. She would look out for him and try to make an arrangement with him or at least get some kind of contact details for him. A few days later the Mayor of East 67th and York saw the young oncologist for the first time *initiate* a conversation with the street sweeper.

Some two weeks later, in the late afternoon when the sun had almost disappeared, an oncologist, a historian and a street sweeper crammed around a tiny table in the Fresh Food Kitchen on 68th Street to talk in depth about the war-time experiences of Henryk Mandelbrot. No one can accurately describe the effect on Adam Zignelik of hearing this African American street sweeper, whose broom and cart rested against the window of the eatery, describe life in the *Sonderkommando*. Sensing the importance of the opportunity, Lamont Williams told Ayesha Washington and Adam Zignelik everything he could remember and he remembered a lot. The old man had written it all down in Yiddish in a notebook but all Lamont had was his memory of Mandelbrot's story. When he was finished Adam Zignelik was not immediately able to speak. 'Did you say the old man had made a written record of this?'

'That's what he said but . . . I mean . . . I never saw it. Anyway, it wouldn't be in English. Might be Yiddish, might be Polish. Mr Mandelbrot spoke a lot of languages but Yiddish was his first.'

'Did you see these notes?'

'No, he never brought them into the hospital. But his people would have found 'em. He said he'd put 'em where they'd find them after he died. So they should have found 'em by now.'

Adam rubbed his face with the palms of his hands. Then he spoke slowly and explained to both of them how it was only in the last six months that his work had taken him anywhere near this material but, from what he knew, it was almost impossible to account for Lamont's knowledge other than by the man who had lived it having told him. He said that although he did not consider himself a real expert he felt confident enough to say that relatively few people on earth knew the details Lamont knew about the *Sonderkommando*, the work they did and the uprising they carried off.

*

Adam Zignelik was sitting home alone in his Morningside Heights apartment on a Saturday in late winter surrounded by the boxes that contained his career and going through copies of the papers of the Chicago psychologist, Henry Border, when the thought occurred to him that the great advance of the second half of the twentieth century was storage. To a large extent he had packed the boxes from his office at Columbia in such a way that each box contained a topic, a category of his own work or of history more generally that was of professional interest to him. Often a box also acted as a kind of time capsule recording what he had been doing during a given span of his professional life. The boxes physically closest to where he was sitting at the time, the thought occurred to him, contained information pertaining to Border, the 1946 interviews, and Adam's own interview with the woman, Hannah, and the role she and her sister, Estusia Weiss, and Border's wife, Rosa Rabinowicz, played in the plot to smuggle gunpowder to the men of the *Sonderkommando* resistance. But of even greater significance, if the notes kept by the recently deceased cancer patient, the friend of the street sweeper, were anywhere near as detailed as the account given by the street sweeper himself, Adam would also have a first-hand written account of life in the *Sonderkommando* in Auschwitz and of the *Sonderkommando* uprising there. In addition to all that, there was the issue of the role of black troops in the liberation of Dachau to follow up. As soon as the grandfather of the oncologist, Ayesha Washington, had recovered from hip surgery, he would have a first-hand account of that too.

What is memory? It is the storage, the retention and the recall of the constituents, gross and nuanced, of information. How is it called upon? A certain protein in the brain, an enzyme, acts upon one neuron after another in rapid sequence as if to light them up in such a way as to paint a picture or spell a word, as if to cause an arpeggio of cellular stores of data to suddenly ring out some long-stored melody in your mind and you remember her face, her voice, her laugh, the way she moved, something she said, her views and tastes, until you remember the way her eyes widened with the pre-rational wonder of a child when watching a wildlife documentary or the way they move slowly downwards when her frustration with someone she loves starts to leak sympathy. When she is gone, that cascade of cellular data is all you have. Each neuron holds some pixel, some datum, and if even one is lost, the sequence is interrupted. Then you have started to forget.

How do we fight to preserve each tiny datum? Everyone tries different things, different strategies which we call on until we are distracted by events or overwhelmed by weakness or infirmity. Adam kept a comb in his bathroom mirror cabinet.

Again Adam was distracted, this time by noise coming from somewhere in the building. Before he could decide whether to search for the source of the noise or try to put up with it and return to his work, his intercom buzzed. He carefully put the copy of the page from Border's papers he was holding back on his desk and went over to answer it.

On the weekends it was as likely as not to be someone looking for a neighbour who had pressed his apartment's buzzer by mistake.

'Hello,' Adam said, expecting to be asked for someone else followed by an enquiry as to whether he was sure he wasn't speaking from the apartment the visitor had intended to call.

'Adam?' It was Sonia. He held the receiver to his chest so she wouldn't hear him exhale.

'Adam, it's me, Sonia.'

'Hi, sweetie, what's up?'

'Would it be a bad time for me to come up? I know I'm meant to call first but I was out and I left my cell at home.'

'Sure, come on up.'

'You're not entertaining?'

'I'm not even entertaining myself.'

'Okay, coming up! You can go in,' he heard her saying as he returned the receiver to its vertical cradle on the wall and he thought, Oh great! Not only is she still coming uninvited, now she's letting random passers-by into the building. Was he too soft on her? he wondered. The problem was that whenever he saw her, he could never be stern enough for long enough to show her he was serious about teaching her anything and instead would be consumed by an overwhelming urge to be the 'good cop' even though there was never any 'bad cop' around. By the time the knock at the door came he was already looking forward to the hug she was going to give him when he opened the door. But it wasn't Sonia. It was Diana.

'Hi, I'm sorry to –'

'Hey! Come in!'

She was embarrassed. 'It's not a bad time?'

'No, not at all. Where's Sonia?'

'She's gone.'

'What?'

'This was a ruse, her idea, to get me to come and visit you. I'd come uptown to have lunch with the McCrays and . . . sure it's not inconvenient? I don't think I've ever done anything like –'

'It's not a bad time. Please come in. It's so good to see you. Everything okay?'

'Yeah.'

'Really?'

'Yeah.'

Diana took just three steps inside the apartment she used to share with Adam before the proliferation of boxes left her unable to contain herself. 'Are you moving?'

'What? Oh, the boxes. No, that's my career all lined up against the wall. I had to vacate my office. See, I promised everyone I'd commit career suicide and I'm a man of my word.'

He closed the door and she came inside. He showed her to the gap between the boxes on the couch and that's where she sat down.

'Can I get you a drink, coffee, tea?'

'Maybe something stronger?'

'Sure, what do you have in mind?'

'Are you still drinking cheap Scotch?'

'Only when I'm alone or when I'm buying the round.'

'Scotch please.'

'Sure.'

He went to the kitchenette to pour the drinks and Diana called to him, 'You don't seem very unhappy.'

'I like that you're here drinking my Scotch.'

'No, I mean about your so-called career suicide.'

He returned with a drink for each of them and the bottle under his arm and perched on a box that was beside her on the couch.

'I don't seem very unhappy? I guess I'm not.'

'That's . . . good.'

'You seem to hesitate about that.'

'I'm nervous. I don't know if I should've come like this.'

'I'm so glad you did. Maybe that's why I don't seem unhappy about my career suicide. Actually, boxes notwithstanding – and they've withstood quite a lot – I have to admit to being pretty upbeat about my work, bordering on optimistic.'

'Bordering?'

'Yeah. I've just made a pun which you couldn't possibly have picked up and which I didn't even intend. But you would have liked it. I mustn't talk to you like you're not here when you really are here.'

'What?'

'Do you remember when we met at that place in Hell's Kitchen last time I was telling you –?'

'You said you had some leads that were going to take you to Melbourne and that William had something to do with it.'

'Well, in a way he did, but now it's gone much further than even he could have imagined. You're not in a hurry, are you?'

'No, I'm not.'

He poured them each another drink and began a truncated but none-too-brief version of the story of Henry Border, Elly Border, Rosa Rabinowicz, Estusia and Hannah Weiss and the women of the *Pulverraum* in Auschwitz's *Weichsel Union Metallwerke* factory, and the oncologist from Memorial Sloan-Kettering Cancer Center, her grandfather and her street sweeper.

'So you're going to be talking to the black veteran, Captain Washington, you hope to be getting the written testimony of the *Sonderkommando* guy from his family via a hospital janitor –'

'Mandelbrot – that's the plan, assuming the family hasn't thrown it out.'

'And the original wire recording of Border's interview with the woman you met in Melbourne?'

'It's in that box. His former student had kept it.'

'Is that the one that had been involved with the daughter?'

'Wayne Rosenthal, that's right.'

'Adam, that's incredible! It's an incredible story. No wonder you're hopeful. You've got so much to go on with. Does anybody know what you've got?'

Adam ignored her last question. He had refilled their glasses a few times by then. 'I'm really so happy to see you. I really am. Does he know . . . you're here, the guy . . . you're seeing? You didn't . . . I don't think you told me his name.'

'I'm not seeing him any more.'

'Really?'

'Really. Don't sound so happy.'

'How long did it last?'

'A few weeks.'

'A few weeks!' A few weeks, Adam thought, that wasn't very long.

'Well, he never made me laugh like you did. Are you seeing anyone?'

'No, not even for a few weeks. I never get the time. I'm too busy talking to you. I just keep –'

'Don't . . . Adam . . . you're making me –'

'Look, I made a mistake but I only made one. I haven't changed my mind.'

Now she was crying and she got up to get herself a tissue, which she remembered they used to keep in the bathroom. Adam watched her walk away and heard her turn on the light. He heard her grab some tissues out of the box and then for a moment he heard nothing at all. He wondered what she was doing. Then he heard small sobs that graduated quickly to a much louder cry than any he had heard since his own in the middle of many of the nights since she'd left. The catalyst had been the same for him then as it was for Diana now, her comb. She saw it there and picked it up. She looked at it and momentarily thought it to be another woman's comb before its origin dawned on her and then its significance. By the time Adam came to her in the bathroom they used to share she was crying uncontrollably.

*

There was to be a meeting. How long had it taken to arrange this meeting? The answer will vary depending on when the counting starts. By one measure it had taken almost forty years to arrange, by other measures even longer. But at last it was time. Some things will not be hurried. How should he start? He had lain in bed and asked himself this question in the dark in the middle of the night before the meeting. He had asked his grandmother who, in so many ways was still there as well. He woke that morning in the room of his childhood with the tart taste of uncertainty and anxiety born of the lucklessness that rarely left him. Orphaned twice before and so recently again, he poured his apple juice.

Young and old drink Seneca ...
Rich, delicious ...

It's funny what you remember. The tune stayed with him on the bus, holding his hand when he had a seat and also when he had to stand. She didn't care. She would hold his hand when this was over, no matter how it turned out, no matter how he started. How would he start? His grandma advised him to just start from the beginning and tell the truth. He couldn't do any more. She was right, he said to himself, taking a seat inside Danny Ehrlich's office on the ground floor of Memorial Sloan-Kettering Cancer Center. There wasn't any more that he could do than that. 'Don't be afraid, honey child, not any more.'

He had taken that *menorah* around the streets of the east side of Manhattan with him all morning and all afternoon until the meeting. What a sight he must have made, one of those 'only in New York' sights. How many street sweepers were there in all the world carrying a *menorah* with them under their arms? Not even Numbers would pretend there was one. But there was one, just one. Lamont had to make sure he had it with him when he went to the meeting. That was part of the deal. No music came from the radio or anywhere else inside the office of the Head of Human Resources at Memorial Sloan-Kettering Cancer Center that afternoon. But there were more people there than usual and extra chairs had to be brought in from the office of Juan Laviera, Deputy Head of Human Resources, and from other offices too. For in that office gathered for the meeting was Dan Ehrlich, Juan Laviera, Ayesha Washington, Lamont Williams, Adam Zignelik, a historian with an Australian accent, and the son and daughter-in-law of the late Henryk Mandelbrot, formerly of the *Sonderkommando* in Auschwitz-Birkenau. On Danny Ehrlich's desk, between the monitor for his computer and his visitors, sat the silver *menorah*.

Danny Ehrlich began the meeting by thanking everyone for coming, particularly Mr and Mrs Mandelbrot. He explained his position within the hospital and that of his deputy, Juan Laviera, and then he introduced the oncologist Ayesha Washington, whom they already knew, the historian Adam Zignelik and the man, Lamont Williams, who had been a probationary employee of the hospital's in Building Services and who had brought in the late Mr Mandelbrot's *menorah*. At first the Mandelbrots were unable to make eye contact with Lamont Williams but the way Dan Ehrlich had structured the meeting they were not immediately obliged to.

Mr Ehrlich explained the purpose of the meeting, which was slightly different from the way the Mandelbrots had previously had it described to them over the phone. Then they had been told that the *menorah* had been recovered and that if they were able to come in and verify that it was indeed the *menorah* they had brought in to the late patient, Mr Mandelbrot, they could take it with them. But now, surprised to see themselves as part of a meeting of seven people, another explanation was proffered. Danny Ehrlich had been approached by Mr Mandelbrot's oncologist, Dr Washington, because she felt that an injustice might have been perpetrated against the hospital's probationary employee. This man, Lamont Williams, had been dismissed from the hospital staff because of the missing *menorah*, which everyone had assumed he stole. But Dr Washington remembers a number of occasions when she had found the employee, Lamont Williams, visiting the patient for conversations of varying lengths, both during and after Mr Williams' working hours. This, in and of itself, proves nothing but it does go some of the way towards corroborating Mr Williams' story, namely that he had struck up a friendship with Henryk Mandelbrot and that in the days before his death Mr Mandelbrot had made a gift of the *menorah* to him.

Then Dr Ayesha Washington took over the story. She explained that in conversation with Lamont Williams Mr Williams had displayed a quite specific and even remarkable knowledge of what sounded like the life story of the Mandelbrots' father and father-in-law, particularly his war-time experiences. She said she happened to have been in contact with a historian from Columbia, she explained, at which point Dr Adam Zignelik introduced himself and gave the son of Henryk Mandelbrot a business card that carried both his name and that of Columbia University, his erstwhile employer.

Adam interjected, 'My area is twentieth-century political history, which recently has broadened to include the Holocaust. It's just by chance that my work has taken me to some of the events that your father lived through. Dr Washington contacted me and asked me to meet with her and Mr Williams to help ascertain the credibility of his account of your father's story. I've met him once before today and listened to his account of your father's experiences, particularly in Auschwitz and, in my opinion, it's almost inconceivable that he could be making up this stuff. I'm here to tell you that and also to ask for your assistance with respect to my own research. Mr Williams told me that your father told him that he'd made notes of his wartime experiences, particularly his time in the *Sonderkommando* in Auschwitz. I want to ask your permission to get a copy of the notes your father made.'

'Notes?' enquired the younger Mr Mandelbrot. 'We haven't seen any notes,' he said, looking at his wife.

'They're in Yiddish,' Lamont Williams interjected. 'I think they're in Yiddish.' Now for the first time the son and the daughter-in-law looked closely at the black man in the bright blue overalls.

'That must be what's in that exercise book,' the daughter-in-law said confidentially to her husband. 'In the drawer with his *tefellin*.'

'I understand a little Yiddish but I can't read it,' said the son by way of explanation and with some embarrassment as though now suddenly he was the one defending himself.

'What I propose, subject to what you say, is that you hear from Mr Williams. Hear what he has to say,' suggested Danny Ehrlich, 'and if, at the end of his account, you still think that he stole the *menorah*, Mr Williams has agreed to give it to you even though he says your father gave it to him as a gift. But if you think that it's likely, given the detailed knowledge Mr Williams has of your father's experiences, that a friendship developed between the two of them and that your father gave Mr Williams the *menorah* out of friendship, you might want to consider letting him keep it. Mr Williams has said he'll abide by your decision.'

The son and the daughter-in-law needed only to look at each other for the son to nod his assent. Then Dan Ehrlich, the Head of the hospital's Human Resources Department, who had been known in grade school as Danny Ehrlich, looked to his old school friend and said, 'You want to . . . say a few words, Lamont?'

Lamont Williams cleared his throat and prepared himself to speak. No one else in the room spoke or looked like speaking. He had not commanded a room like this since his trial for armed robbery. But even then he hadn't been required to speak. In fact his attorney had advised him not to speak. The last time any gathering of people had waited to hear what he had to say was in grade school when he addressed Mr Shapiro and his class on the topic of horseshoe crabs. The six other people in the room waited for him to begin speaking.

'So like you know,' he began, 'my name's Lamont Williams. I met Mr Mandelbrot . . . your father, on my fourth day in Building Services. I was sweeping up outside on York Avenue. Someone from PES brought him down but he was cold –'

'Patient Escort Services,' explained Danny Ehrlich.

'Right,' said Lamont Williams. 'See I'm not, we're not s'posed to move patients around. That's only for PES and Mr Mandelbrot . . . see, he was cold and he asked me if I could take him back up . . . you know . . . to his room? Well, I told him I couldn't, you know, 'cause I wasn't allowed but he kept at me, you know? He was cold and he . . . someone from PES had brought him down but now they were gone and Mr Mandel-brot, he didn't care, he just wanted to go back to his room. That was all he cared about.'

The son of the late patient had a smile on his face now.

'I mean, you know how he might be, right? He got me to bring him up to his room on the ninth floor . . . It was my first week here. And he was lookin' out the window, out at the East River and . . . and he thought he was lookin' at New Jersey. Maybe my third or fourth day here and I told him . . . Then he saw this . . . he saw . . . like a chimney, three of 'em. He saw three chimneys out the window 'cross the East River and I remember 'cause he looked at 'em and he said just, you know, suddenly . . . like out of the blue, that there were six death camps, and then later on he made me learn all their names and I did, you know: Belzec, Chelmno, Sobibor, Majdanek, Treblinka and Auschwitz, where he was. That's the six of 'em. You all know what a death camp is? I didn't know but he told me. It's not a concentration camp, not the same thing. People think it is. He wanted me to know all this. Was important to him. I don't know why he chose me. He said there were hundreds of concentration camps all over Germany and occupied Europe but there were only ever six death camps, extermination camps, and they were all in Poland and they were purpose-built with gas chambers or sealed gas vans and ovens and pits to exterminate every last Jew in Europe. That's the whole reason they were built: to kill people, Jews mainly. He said Majdanek and Auschwitz had slave labour factories too but the others didn't. But I'm maybe getting ahead o' myself . . . Should I . . . should I be standing up for this?'

Over the next almost ninety minutes Lamont Williams held the room with his recollection of what Mr Mandelbrot had told him had happened to him during the war.

'Leading out of the ghetto in Dabrowa Gornicza from the street where Mr Mandelbrot's family lived there was a street where an SA man and his wife lived in a house.

'You all know what the SA was?' Lamont Williams asked them before continuing with his late friend's story, how his friend was eventually captured, identified by a now adult version of a boy who'd been at school with him and from there, after a beating, he was sent to Auschwitz-Birkenau. They all sat in the office of the Head of Human Resources and listened without stirring. Before too long he had reached the *Sonderkommando*. Lamont took them to the undressing room. He told them how the Jews would come down the stairs in fives, the first to come down usually being women, exhausted, confused and very ashamed to have to undress until they were completely naked in front of strangers.

'"The showers . . ." Mr Mandelbrot was sometimes asked. "They're the same one for men *and* for women?" Or "You're a Jew?"

'Then five more would come down followed by another five, some bleeding, and all pushed by the five behind them. Then another five . . .

'"It's gas, isn't it?" some would guess.'

Lamont told everybody in the office of the Head of Human Resources how the Jews would walk naked to the door, the only door, marked 'To the Disinfection Room'.

'It was warmer there than in the undressing room. Adults would cry softly. Children separated from their parents would call out for them in terror as the room filled.'

He told them how, as the hydrogen cyanide gas, given off by the Zyklon B pellets released into perforated shafts through ports in the roof by the SS, rose upward from the bottoms of the shafts to fill higher and higher levels of the chamber, the climbing would start, the climbing to get air. He told them how quickly the pain would become extreme and how people would drool and how their eyes would bulge and how their bodies would jerk in wild spasms as the gas rendered completely useless whatever oxygen they could find. He told them how after three minutes they were bleeding, some from the scramble, the struggle to climb to the top of the heap, but all from the effect of the gas, bleeding from their noses, from their ears. He told them how people lost continence and how they were pushed down into a mess of blood, urine, vomit and excrement. He told how human beings with memories, affections, ambitions, relationships, opinions, values and accomplishments all sank into a tangled phalanx of human beings a metre deep covered in their own fluids, all of them gasping, their bodies jerking, their faces distorted by their agony till they were no more. Lamont Williams left nothing out.

He told them about *Oberscharführer* Moll, *Oberscharführer* Schillinger, about a man called Ochrenberg, about the two Zalmans, Gradowski and Lewental, who kept a record of the work of *Sonderkommando* and buried it so that after the war people would know what happened there.

He told them how women in *Kanada* and in the gunpowder section of the *Weichsel Union Metallwerke* factory smuggled gunpowder to the *Sonderkommando*.

'Know why they called it *Kanada*?' Lamont Williams asked his audience didactically.

He told them about the various resistance movements within the camp, about the joint Auschwitz Military Council and the *Sonderkommando* resistance. He told them how Chaim Neuhof and Mr Mandelbrot had been sent to plead with the joint Auschwitz Military Council without success and explained why.

'So now it's 7 October 1944.'

Then he told them about the *Sonderkommando* uprising. He told them about the *Kapo* Kalniak who had prepared for the uprising the night before and wouldn't save himself, about the destruction of Crematorium IV and how, when Mr Mandelbrot got up from the ground, of the 663 *Sonderkommando* men alive before the uprising only 212 were left and neither Zalman Gradowski nor Zalman Lewental were among them.

When Lamont Williams was finished he was taken back to the basement where he collected the broom and the cart that was legally the property of the John Doe Fund. The son and daughter-in-law of the late patient had not needed to hear the story in its entirety but no one wanted to stop him. He got to say everything he wanted. He walked out onto York Avenue with the oncologist Dr Ayesha Washington and the historian Dr Adam Zignelik. He hadn't realised the time. He was going to be late for dinner with his cousin Michelle and her family. He had to call them. Adam Zignelik proffered his mobile phone and, to give Lamont some privacy for the call, he and Dr Washington turned away.

Lamont's call from Adam Zignelik's mobile phone to his cousin Michelle was about to be connected when, seeing him trying to negotiate the phone, his broom and his cart, Dr Washington offered, 'Here, let me take that for you,' and she took hold of the broom and also of the silver *menorah*. The son and the daughter-in-law had been convinced from early in Lamont's testimony that the old man had given his unlikely friend the candelabrum. This was their conclusion and this was what Lamont was explaining to his cousin on the phone. He was going to get his job back. Later, Adam Zignelik would tell the whole story to Diana and later still to Charles and Michelle McCray, which was when he would become aware of the connection between Michelle and the street sweeper. Had Adam perchance looked, he would have found that the last number dialled came up as 'Michelle', although it had been called not by him but by the street sweeper. But he didn't look.

Dr Washington thanked Adam. He replied that, on the contrary, he was grateful to her because his involvement had led him to a memoir of the war-time experiences of a *Sonderkommando*, something that would be invaluable for his research. It was, he said, a godsend. When Lamont was finished with the phone he began thanking them both for their assistance. They couldn't imagine, he explained, what this meant to him. He was getting his job back. He would have two more weeks in Building Services as a probationary employee and then he would be full time and permanent. He couldn't remember when he last felt like this. In the course of congratulating him, Dr Washington gave him back his broom and the cart.

'I believe this is yours too,' she said.

'I believe so,' he said as she gave him back the *menorah*.

*

Most of the afternoon was spent but it was still light enough on York Avenue for oncoming strangers to see each other from a distance. People walking past the three of them, the oncologist, the historian and the street sweeper, paid them little if any attention. On the other side of the street, on the leafy campus of Rockefeller University, a Nobel laureate walked his dog leash-free. The university, it appeared, allowed the disregard of certain university laws by Nobel laureates (and their dogs) in recognition of the natural laws they might have discovered. Despite the strong wind that was blowing, the entirety of one particular tree seemed impervious to the ferocity of the various gusts that played mercilessly with the composure of all the other surrounding trees. Yet no part of this particular tree near Founders Hall on the campus of Rockefeller University on York Avenue opposite Memorial Sloan-Kettering moved in any way that was perceptible to the human eye, no part of it except the smallest branch at the very top. The tiniest twig-like apogee of this old, much-revered tree shuddered as though in spasm while the rest of the tree remained as impassive as a monolith.

Neither the Nobel laureate nor his dog noticed the strange behaviour of the tree but it was appreciated by a young graduate student. This young woman from a province in northern China noticed the phenomenon on her way out of Founders Hall where she had gone to collect her mail. On her way to First Avenue to buy groceries, she had been contemplating the gap between her expectations and her experience, both in the lab and out of it, when she caught sight of the convulsing twig at the end of the otherwise unmoving tree and, quite taken by what she saw, she wished she could share the sight with the sort of transient random group of people that sometimes forms to stare at something out of the ordinary. Then suddenly, this strange arborial behaviour stopped. As far as the Chinese student was aware, no one else had noticed it.

The Nobel laureate with his, dog now on a leash, was stopped at York Avenue waiting for the lights to change when she caught up to them. Other people waited too, some from the university, some not, none of them known personally to each other.

When the people who had congregated waiting for the lights to change reached the western side of York Avenue they became momentarily part of a disparate group of people who slowed, some even stopped, to see something that aroused their curiosity. On the western side of York Avenue between 67th and 68th streets a young African American oncologist and a white Jewish historian stood smiling and talking to a skinny black street sweeper in a bright blue uniform. The oncologist handed the street sweeper a silver *menorah*, which he took in his one bandaged hand while the other hand lightly held a large broom that rested against a cart with its own shovel of sorts attached to it.

It was the late afternoon rush hour and a light-skinned black girl with braided hair tied tight with red ribbons, aged somewhere between seven and ten, had been unable to find a free seat ever since she had got on the M66 bus way over on the west side. She was still standing when the wheels stopped at 68th Street and the bus suddenly jerked forward and then back before coming to rest completely. With the emission of a gasp the doors opened and the passengers began spilling out.

'Thank you,' she said as she filed past the driver slowly. But once the pavement was able to beckon the soles of her shoes, she hit the ground in an automatic skip that quickly became a trot and was already a full gallop by the time she reached the corner and turned into York Avenue. Despite the school bag strapped to her back full of books she sped up when she saw the group of three, the oncologist, the historian and the street sweeper. Perhaps it was the Mayor of East 67th and York who was the first to notice what happened next or perhaps he was just the one the others followed but the people on the corner seemed to want to see and then even people on the eastern side of York Avenue craned their necks to see what it was that seemed to suddenly have captured everyone's attention.

'Mom!' the little girl cried, interrupting the conversation of the three adults and lunging at her mother with arms that soon met each other around the waist of the oncologist.

'This your daughter?' the street sweeper asked and the oncologist nodded and smiled. Then the man in the bright blue uniform from Co-op City with a broom in one hand and a *menorah* in the other, the nobody, the skinny-assed black man cabs would pass by, this man squatted down on his haunches and raised the *menorah* in one hand as though expecting one of his new companions to take it for him, which the oncologist did.

'Hey, little girl. I got a little girl 'bout your age,' Lamont said. Kneeling down on the pavement to improve his balance he moved towards the little girl as if to hug her. She looked up at her mother for some kind of a signal for guidance on how to respond. Her mother looked down at her, smiled a smile of pride and nodded whereupon the little girl gently, politely permitted herself to be hugged by the street sweeper, just tentatively. Still looking up at her mother as the man on his knees rubbed her back with one hand, the girl saw her mother's polite smile transform into a broad grin that mixed approval with pride and the satisfaction of accomplishment. Unsure of the protocol for this situation and too young to know there was none, trustingly and as a matter of instinct that seemed only encouraged by her mother's smile, the little girl deliberately put more weight into the hug. Quite unambiguously she leaned in to him. And when this happened he felt the full weight of the little girl on his chest as she hugged him and he let out a cry. It was as involuntary as it was unexpected. Tears began to stream down this man's face as he held on to the little girl as she hugged him and the sound he made, coming from deep within him, was loud enough for all those around to hear. And when they heard it they looked to see.

Everybody in the random group of onlookers wondered what it was they were witnessing. Of all the strangers there on that corner and those approaching it, only the Mayor had ever seen the man before and though even he had no idea what was really going on, he found himself grinning and then beaming. But his was not a unique response. Others looking at the scene found themselves similarly uplifted.

Nobody, not the Nobel laureate, not the young graduate student, not the Mayor nor anyone else on the corner really understood what they were seeing or why they were so heartened by it. The onlookers had no idea what it was that had led to the strange convergence of these three diverse individuals and the little girl. But if they had known the people they were looking at, if they had known where they had come from, if they had known their histories, if they'd had even an inkling of the events the historian, the street sweeper with the *menorah*, and the oncologist had knowledge of, if they had known the whole story of everything that had got these three people to that block at that time, they might well have felt compelled to tell everyone what happened here. Tell everyone what happened here.

author's note

Nearly all the present-day characters in *The Street Sweeper*, and therefore their interactions, are fictional.

Apart from a few minor exceptions, the mid-twentieth-century events depicted here all occurred and are on the historical record.

Of the characters who inhabit the novel during that mid-twentieth-century period, some are real people (well known and less known), but most are fictional characters many of whom are based partly on real people.

Of the fictionalised characters based partly on real people, the ones who should be mentioned are: Henryk Mandelbrot, Henry Border, Rosa Rabinowicz, Estusia, Ala, Regina, Hannah, Zalman Gradowski, Zalman Lewental, Noah Lewental, Chaim Neuhof, Dorebus, Panusz, Handels-mann, Kalniak, 'Rot', Dürmayer, Kazuba, Nahum Grzywacz, Tommy Parks, James Pearson, Ralph Hellerstein, Herb Marks, Eileen Miller, Marvin Cadden, Cecilya Slepak, Rafal Gutman, Eliyahu Gutkowski, Jacob Grojanowski, Israel Lichtenstein, David Graber, Israel Gutman, Joshua Leifer, Jake Zignelik, SS Kommandant Hössler, SS *Oberscharführer* Moll, SS *Oberscharführer* Schillinger and SS *Scharführer* Busch.

In the writing of this book I was conscious of the possibility of causing offence by employing the idioms of cultures other than my own. It is my hope that no offence has been caused. On reflection, I think that possi-bility, in a general sense, is a risk more or less inherent in writing about anyone other than oneself.

sources consulted

Hirsz Abramowicz, *Profiles of a Lost World Memoirs of East European Jewish Life Before World War II*, YIVO Institute for Jewish Research and Wayne University Press, (1999).

R.H. Abzug, *Inside the Vicious Heart*, Oxford University Press, (1987).

Tanner Akcam, *A Shameful Act*, Metropolitan Books, (2006),

Antony Beevor, *Berlin*, Penguin, (2007).

Eberhard Bethge, *Dietrich Bonhoeffer: A Biography*, Fortress Press, (2000).

David P. Boder, *I Did Not Interview the Dead*, University of Illinois Press, (1949).

Robert Brazil, *Memoirs of Bronzeville*, Author House, (2004).

Michael Brenner, *After the Holocaust*, Princeton University Press, (1997).

Gwendolyn Brooks, *Blacks*, Third World Press, (1987).

Earl Brown, 'The Truth About the Detroit Riot'. *Harper's Magazine*, Vol. 187, No. 1122, November 1943, pp. 488–99.

Christopher R. Browning, *The Origins of the Final Solution*, Arrow Books, (2005).

Judge Robert Carter, *A Matter of Law*, The New Press, (2005).

Lizabeth Cohen, *Making a New Deal*, Cambridge University Press, (1990).

David P. Colley, *Decision at Strasbourg: Ike's Strategic Mistake to Halt the Sixth Army Group at the Rhine in 1944*, Naval Institute Press, (2008).

Vicki L. Crawford, Jacqueline Anne Rouse and Barbara Woods, *Women in the Civil Rights Movement*, Indiana University Press, (1990).

Irving Cutler, *Jewish Chicago*, Arcadia Publishing, (2000).

Floyd Dade Jr, *Interview*, 761st Tank Battalion web site.

Lucy Dawidowicz, *The War Against the Jews 1933–45*, Penguin, (1975).

Christopher C. De Santis (ed.), *Langston Hughes and the Chicago Defender*, University of Illinois Press, (1995).

Waclaw Dlugoborski, Franciszek Piper (eds), *Auschwitz 1940–1945, Vols 1–V*, Auschwitz-Birkenau State Museum, Oświęcim, (2000).

Martin Doblmeier (dir.), *Bonhoeffer* (a documentary film), (2003).

Deborah Dwork and Robert Jan Van Pelt, *Auschwitz 1270 to the Present*, W.W. Norton & Co., (1996).

Barbara Engelking, Jacek Leociak, *The Warsaw Ghetto A Guide to the Perished City*, Yale University Press, (2009).

Richard J. Evans, *In Defense of History*, Norton, (1999).

Eric Foner, *Who Owns History*, Hill & Wang, (2002).

M.K. Gandhi, *An Autobiography*, Penguin, (2001).

Jay Howard Geller, *Jews in Post-Holocaust Germany*, Cambridge University Press, (2005).

Doris Kearns Goodwin, *No Ordinary Time*, Simon & Schuster, (1994).

Paul M. Green and Melvin G. Holli, *World War II Chicago*, Arcadia Publishing, (2003).

Jack Greenberg, *Crusaders in the Courts*, Basic Books, (1994).

Gideon Greif, *We Wept Without Tears*, Yale University Press, (2005).

James R. Grossman, Anne Durkin Keating, Janice L. Reiff, *The Encyclopedia of Chicago*, University of Chicago Press, (2004).

Atina Grossmann, *Jews, Germans, and Allies*, Princeton University Press, (2007).

Brana Gurewitsch (ed.), *Mothers, Sisters and Resisters*, University of Alabama Press, (1998).

Yisrael Gutman and Michael Berenbaum, *Anatomy of the Auschwitz Death Camp*, Indiana University Press, (1998).

Yisrael Gutman, Michael Berenbaum, Ezra Mendelsohn, Jehuda Reinharz and Chone Shmeruk (eds), *The Jews of Poland Between Two World Wars*, Brandeis University Press by University Press of New England, (1989).

Rick Halpern, *Down on the Killing Floor*, University of Illinois Press (1997).

Rick Halpern and Roger Horowitz, *Meatpackers*, Monthly Review Press, (1999).

Henry Hampton (dir.), *Eyes on the Prize: America's Civil Rights Movement* (documentary film series) (1986).

Leslie M. Harris, *In the Shadow of Slavery: African Americans in New York City, 1626–1863*, University of Chicago Press, (2003).

Anna Heilman, *Never Far Away*, University of Calgary Press, (2001).

Celia S. Heller, *On the Edge of Destruction*, Columbia University Press, (1977).

Raul Hilberg, Stanislaw Staron and Josef Kermisz (eds.), *The Warsaw Diary of Adam Czerniakow*, Yad Vashem, (1979).

Roger Horowitz, *'Negro and White, Unite and Fight!'*, University of Illinois Press, (1997).

Alter Kacyzne, *Poyln. Jewish Life in the Old Country*, YIVO Institute for Jewish Research, Henry Holt & Company, (1999).

Samuel D. Kassow, *Who Will Write Our History? Rediscovering a Hidden Archive From the Warsaw Ghetto*, Indiana University Press, (2007).

David M. Kennedy, *Freedom From Fear*, Oxford University Press, (1999).

Joseph Kermish (ed.), *To Live and Die With Honour: Selected Documents from the Warsaw Ghetto Underground Archives 'O.S.' (Oneg Shabbath)*, Yad Vashem, (1986).

Ian Kershaw, *Fateful Choices*, Penguin, (2008).

Richard Kluger, *Simple Justice*, Vintage, (2004).

Angelika Konigseder and Juliane Wetzel, *Waiting for Hope*, Northwestern University Press, (2001).

Abba Kovner, *Sloan-Kettering*, Schocken Books, (2002).

Hermann Langbein, *Against All Hope*, Paragon House, (1999).

Hermann Langbein, *People in Auschwitz*, University of North Carolina Press, (2005).

Spike Lee (dir.), *4 Little Girls* (a documentary film), (1998).

Nicholas Lemann, *The Promised Land*, Vintage, (1991).

Marc Levin (dir.), *Protocols of Zion* (a documentary film), (2005).

Richard Lingeman, *Don't You Know There's a War On?* G.P. Putnam & Sons, (1970).

Mary Patillo-McCoy, *Black Picket Fences*, University of Chicago Press, (1999).

John Bartlow Martin, 'The Strangest Place in Chicago', *Harper's Magazine*, Vol. 201, No. 1207, December 1950, pp. 86–97.

Carl Marziali and Ira Glass, 'Mr Boder Vanishes' from the WBZ Chicago radio program, *This American Life*, produced by Chicago Public Radio and first broadcast on 26 October, 2001. (To hear the original Boder recordings or read Boder's transcripts go to the official Illinois Institute of Technology *Voices of the Holocaust* website at http://voices.iit.edu/).

G.P. Megargee (ed.), *Encyclopedia of Camps and Ghettos*, Vol. 1, Part B.

Ezra Mendelsohn, *The Jews of East Central Europe Between the World Wars*, Indiana University Press, (1983).

Donald E. Miller and Lorna Touryan Miller, *Survivors: An Oral History of the Armenian Genocide*, University of California Press, (1993).

Wayne F. Miller, *Chicago's South Side*, University California Press, (2000).

James Moll (dir.), *The Last Days* (a documentary film).

Simon Sebag Montefiore, *Young Stalin*, Phoenix, (2007).

Deborah Dash Moore (ed.), *East European Jews in Two Worlds*, Studies from the YIVO Annual, YIVO Institute for Jewish Research, Northwestern University Press, (1946).

Mary P. Motley (ed.), *The Invisible Soldier*, Wayne State University Press, (1975).

Filip Müller, *Eyewitness Auschwitz*, Ivan R. Dee/US Holocaust Memorial Museum, (1999).

Donald Niewyk, *Fresh Wounds: Early Narratives of Holocaust Survival*, University of North Carolina Press, (1998).

Miklos Nyiszli, *Auschwitz: A Doctor's Eyewitness Account*, Arcade Publishing, (1993).

Dalia Ofer and Lenore J. Weitzman (eds), *Women in the Holocaust*, Yale University Press, (1998).

Lynne Olson, *Freedom's Daughters*, Touchstone, (2001).

Phyllis Palmer, *Domesticity and Dirt*, Temple University Press, (1989).

John Paulett and Ron Gordon, *Forgotten Chicago*, Arcadia Publishing, (2004).

Christopher Robert Reed, *The Chicago NAACP*, Indiana University Press, (1997).

Irving Richter, *Labor's Struggles, 1945–1950*, Cambridge University Press, (1994).

Emmanuel Ringelblum, *Notes from the Warsaw Ghetto*, ibooks, (2006).

Beryl Sattler, *Family Properties*, Metropolitan Books, (2009).

Jeffrey Shandler (ed.), *Awakening Lives Autobiographies of Jewish Youth in Poland Before the Holocaust*, YIVO Institute for Jewish Research Yale University Press, (2002).

Lore Shelley (ed.), *The Union Kommando in Auschwitz*, University Press of America, (1996).

Upton Sinclair, *The Jungle*, Barnes & Noble Books, (2003).

Isaac Bashevis Singer, *Love and Exile: The Early Years – A Memoir*, Penguin, (1984).

Maren Stange, *Bronzeville*, The New Press, (2003).

Yuri Suhl (ed.), *They Fought Back*, Shocken Books, (1975).

Thomas J. Surgue, *Sweet Land of Liberty*, Random House, (2008).

Barbara W. Tuchman, *Practicing History*, Ballantine, (1981).

Barbara W. Tuchman, *The Guns of August*, Ballantine, (1994).

Shlomo Venezia, *Inside the Gas Chambers*, Polity, (2009).

Rudolf Vrba, *I Escaped from Auschwitz*, Barricade Books, (2002).

Deborah Gray White, *Too Heavy a Load*, W.W. Norton & Co., (1999).

Juan Williams, *Eyes on the Prize: America's Civil Rights Years 1954–1965*, Penguin, (1987).

Juan Williams, *Thurgood Marshall American Revolutionary*, Three Rivers Press, (1998).

Mark Wyman, *DPs*, Associated University Press, (1989).

H. Yeide and M. Stout, *First to the Rhine: The 6th Army Group in World War II*, Zenith Press, (2007).

interviews

Henryk Mandelbaum, Robert Nowak, M. Ellen Mitchell, Nina Kliger, Mira Unreich, Paul Bruce, Sarah T. Phillips, Evan Haefeli, Eric Foner, Tobie Meyer-Fong, Amy Harfeld, Pablo 'Paulie' Santos, Charles 'Arch' Pounian, Audrey Uhre Mivelaz, Allen Howard, Yale Reisner, Memorial Sloan-Kettering Cancer Center employees who chose to remain anonymous.

acknowledgements

For the friendship and support that have sustained me through the gestation of this novel I wish to thank Robert Chazan, Nikki Christer, Rick Goldberg, Carmen Gurner, Deborah Gurner, Diego Gurner, Fred Gurner, Jack Gurner, Deborah Gutman, George Halasz, Ken Jacobsen, Matthias Jendis, Jennifer Keyte, Hootan Khatami, Greg Levin, Sharon Lewin, Brendan Miller, Robert Milstein, Robert Nowak, Corrie Perkin, Suzie Sharp, Mira Unreich, Rachelle Unreich, Larissa Vetrova, Gabrielle Williams and Ted Woodward.

My thanks to those for whom this acknowledgement is superfluous and therefore all the more necessary, Lena Martin and Ross Martin, Harry Perlman and Dorothy Kovacs, and, not least, Janine Perlman, Toby Handfield and Liv Perlman Handfield.

For their role in bringing this book to publication, for their advice with respect to my writing career and for their friendship I wish to thank Jin Auh, Tracy Bohan, Angus Cargill, Sarah Chalfant, Nikki Christer, Britta Claus, Cathryn Game, Jo Jarrah, Geoff Kloske, Marion Kohler, Stephen Page, Brandon VanOver, Katja Scholtz, Stephanie Sorensen and Andrew Wylie.

I wish to acknowledge and to thank the following for their help with the gathering of the background material for this book: Henryk Mandelbaum, who was the inspiration for the character of Henryk Mandelbrot, Nina Kliger, Mira Unreich, Audrey Uhre Mivelaz, Charles 'Arch' Pounian,

Allen Howard, Robert Yufit, Pablo 'Paulie' Santos, Wanda Nogeura-Irizarry of New York–Presbyterian/Weill Cornell Medical Center, Ira Glass and Carl Marziali from the WBZ Chicago radio program, *This American Life* (whose segment 'Mr Boder Vanishes' alerted me to the work of David Boder, whose professional life inspired the character Henry Border), Sarah T. Phillips and Evan Haefeli and Eric Foner for the hospitality of the History Department at Columbia University, Barry Campbell and Amy Harfeld from the Fortune Society of New York, M. Ellen Mitchell (who discovered the transcripts of David Boder) and Olivia Anderson and Catherine Bruck and Christopher Stewart and Kristin Standaert and Sohair Elbaz for the hospitality of the Illinois Institute of Technology, Yale Reisner from the Jewish Historical Institute, Warsaw, Dena Everett from the United States Army Center of Military History, Rebecca Erbelding from the United States Holocaust Memorial Museum, Bethany Fleming from the Holocaust Memorial Foundation of Illinois and Tobie Meyer-Fong of the Department of History at Johns Hopkins University, and Rich Cohen.

Special mention should be made of Robert Nowak whom I met through his work as a guide at the Auschwitz-Birkenau State Museum. In the course of our work together over six visits he went from being a trusted guide and expert in the history of the camp to a dear friend and confidant. I doubt if I could have endured the hours there necessary to write the book without the benefit of his encouragement, linguistic skills, intellect, knowledge, grace, humour and his insistence that this story had to be told. A fine son of Poland, he is living proof that his home town of Oświęcim is not Auschwitz.

Harry Perlman deserves to be singled out for the critical attention he lavished on the many incarnations of this book over the many years of its creation. For not the first time, his close reading and thoughtful advice proved invaluable and cannot be repaid in words alone.